EAST LYNNE

E · A · S · T L · Y · N · N · E

by Mrs. Henry Wood

with an introduction by Sally Mitchell

Rutgers University Press

New Brunswick, New Jersey

Library of Congress Cataloging in Publication Data

Wood, Henry, Mrs., 1814–1887.
East Lynne.

Bibliography: p.
I. Title.
[PR5842.W8E3   1984]   823'.8   83–23041
ISBN 0–8135–1041–4
ISBN 0–8135–1042–2 (pbk.)

❦ CONTENTS ❦

Introduction vii
For Further Reading xix

EAST LYNNE

Part the First

I.	*The Lady Isabel* 3	XI.	*The New Peer, and the Bank-Note* 83
II.	*The Broken Cross* 10		
III.	*Barbara Hare* 15	XII.	*Life at Castle Marling* 93
IV.	*The Moonlight Interview* 26	XIII.	*Mr. Dill's Shaking* 102
V.	*Mr. Carlyle's Office* 30	XIV.	*The Earl's Astonishment* 113
VI.	*Richard Hare, the Younger* 39	XV.	*Coming Home* 118
VII.	*Miss Carlyle at Home* 49	XVI.	*Barbara Hare's Revelation* 129
VIII.	*Mr. Kane's Concert* 56	XVII.	*Death or Life* 140
IX.	*The Bats at the Window* 62	XVIII.	*Wilson's Tongue* 147
X.	*The Keepers of the Dead* 73	XIX.	*Captain Thorn at West Lynne* 154

Part the Second

I.	*Going from Home* 164	XII.	*Alone for Evermore* 251
II.	*Francis Levison* 169	XIII.	*Barbara's Misdoings* 260
III.	*Quitting the Danger* 178	XIV.	*An Accident* 268
IV.	*The Fractured Ankle* 184	XV.	*An Unexpected Visitor at East Lynne* 274
V.	*Mrs. Hare's Dream* 191		
VI.	*Captain Thorn in Trouble* 204	XVI.	*A Night Invasion of East Lynne* 284
VII.	*The Secret Scrap of Paper* 210		
VIII.	*Richard Hare at Mr. Dill's Window* 218	XVII.	*Barbara's Heart at Rest* 298
IX.	*Never to be Redeemed* 227	XVIII.	*Frozen to Death in the Snow* 309
X.	*Charming Results* 237	XIX.	*Mr. Dill in an Embroidered Shirt-Front* 318
XI.	*Mutual Compliments* 242		

Part the Third

I. *Stalkenberg* 323

II. *Change and Change* 335

III. *The Yearning of a Breaking Heart* 347

IV. *Then You'll Remember Me* 357

V. *An M.P. for West Lynne* 363

VI. *Sir Francis Levison at Home* 375

VII. *A Mishap to the Blue Spectacles* 383

VIII. *A Treat in a Green Pond* 390

IX. *Appearance of a Russian Bear at West Lynne* 398

X. *A Fading Child* 408

XI. *Mr. Carlyle Invited to Some Pâté de Foie Gras* 418

XII. *An Application to the Bench* 428

XIII. *The World Turned Upside Down* 432

XIV. *Miss Carlyle in Full Dress. Afy Also* 440

XV. *Mr. Jiffin* 445

XVI. *The Justice-Room* 451

XVII. *Fire* 463

XVIII. *Three Months Longer* 469

XIX. *The Trial* 475

XX. *The Death Chamber* 484

XXI. *Lord Vane Dating Forwards* 495

XXII. *It Won't Do, Afy* 505

XXIII. *Until Eternity* 511

XXIV. *I. M. V.* 520

East Lynne (first published in 1861) was one of the most astonishingly successful books of the nineteenth century. Its author, always referred to as Mrs. Henry Wood, was a forty-seven-year-old woman with no previous literary reputation. The book was rejected by two publishers; George Meredith, reader for one of them, called it "foul." By the end of the century it had sold almost half a million copies in England, was pirated by two dozen American publishers, and was so popular on stage that its title became a watchword: "Next Week—East Lynne!" the posters promised, whenever receipts were down and the stock company needed surefire revenue. Considering the number that were once in print, copies of *East Lynne* are surprisingly hard to find today, even in major libraries. They may simply have been read to pieces. Samuel Lucas, who wrote the review in the London *Times* on January 25, 1862, spoke for many another reader with a sense of literary standards: he loved the book but felt that he shouldn't. After criticizing the flaws of plot, motive and characterization, he concluded that "as regards its satisfaction of the indispensable requirement which is the rude test of the merits of any work of fiction . . . *East Lynne* is found by all its readers to be highly *entertaining.*"

More than a hundred years later, *East Lynne* remains a fine book for the beach or a rainy weekend. It offers some further rewards for those interested in literature, popular culture, and social history. It was one of the first blockbuster novels; its success depended on changes in the reading public and on Wood's skill in interweaving two forms which became mainstays of popular fiction—the sentimental woman's novel and the sensation novel (forerunner of the detective story). The book exemplifies middle-class values yet subverts the authoritarianism of a patriarchal father; it takes up issues of perfect ladyhood, feminine individuality, divorce, sexuality, repression, and revenge. Adeline Sergeant, a contemporary, remarked that *East Lynne* owed half its popularity to the reaction against "inane and impossible goodness" as the only suitable characteristic for a heroine. The layers of repression and frustration account for the tears, which release tensions, express sympathy and self-pity, yet reaffirm an essentially moral view of the world. Although the author, Ellen Price Wood (1814–1887) was unknown, she was not unpracticed (even at the time that *East Lynne* was published) and by the end of her career had produced more than thirty novels and perhaps three hundred short stories, edited a popular magazine, and handed it on to her son as an inheritance. She was an accomplished storyteller who shared the mass public's values and had no pretensions as a literary artist. She has been called the most truly representative woman novelist of the mid-Victorian era.

Ellen Price was born in Worcester on January 17, 1814. Her father, Thomas Price, was a prosperous glove manufacturer interested in music and classical scholarship; her mother, born Elizabeth Evans, was active in Worcester Cathedral's work parties and social life. When she was thirteen, Ellen Price suffered from spinal weakness and was bedridden for four years. Her son makes the Victorian suggestion that the "strength and activity of the brain overpowered the weaker body"—she had already been marked as a precocious reader—but the symptoms sound like typical adolescent scoliosis. By the time she was seventeen the disease had settled. She was able to walk but had a forward curvature of the spine; she appeared fragile, was under five feet tall and could not lift anything heavier than a book or small parcel.

In 1836, when she was twenty-two, Ellen Price married Henry Wood. He was apparently the head, or perhaps the overseas manager, of a family-owned banking and shipping firm. He may also have performed some consular services. Mr. and Mrs. Henry Wood lived for the next twenty years in France. Several children were born and at least one died of scarlet fever. There were also other difficulties. A great many Victorian women took up writing because the men who should have provided for them proved inadequate. Their biographies typically use financial necessity as an excuse for breaking into print but maintain decent and protective silence about the circumstances. *Memorials of Mrs. Henry Wood* (1894), written by her son Charles, is not even that open. The most that Charles Wood manages to say about his father is that Henry Wood "wanted . . . solidity of character and earnest steadfastness of purpose." Some undisclosed event in 1856 caused him to "retire young from business life." The family returned from France and took up inexpensive lodgings in a furnished house in Norwood.

Ellen Wood had already been publishing short stories anonymously for several years. The first that has been identified appeared in *New Monthly Magazine* in February 1851. Charles Wood says that these early stories were produced for her own amusement and without pay, but their quantity suggests something more than pleasant relaxation. Throughout the early 1850s she had ten or twelve stories each year in *New Monthly Magazine*. When the magazine's editor, William Harrison Ainsworth, took over *Bentley's Miscellany* in December 1854, her stories began to appear there as well. Given Ainsworth's reputation for generosity to his contributors, the sheer volume of the work—as many as twenty stories in a single year—suggests that Ellen Wood was learning how a semi-invalid with a house and children to care for could earn money. Moreover, this period of apprenticeship made possible the enormous success of her first commercial novel. Some of the early stories bore seeds of subsequent books. Mildred Arkell, for example, made her first appearance in a short tale in *New Monthly Magazine* in October 1854. After she returned to England in 1856 Ellen Wood looked for ways to earn a secure living. The Scottish Temperance League was offering one hundred pounds for a tale that it could publish. In twenty-eight days of work, Wood wrote *Danesbury House* (1860) and won the prize. The book was said to reveal remarkable familiarity with the drinking habits of people in good society.

Having proved that she could sustain a long tale, Wood began writing *East Lynne*. Ainsworth started running it in *New Monthly Magazine* in January 1861, before he had read the end, and he introduced Wood to his own publishers, Chapman and Hall. The book was rejected there—it was not up to the literary standards of George Meredith, who had recently become reader—and rejected also by Smith and Elder. Richard Bentley, however, accepted it. He paid her over six hundred pounds—far more than most beginners were offered—and ordered an initial print run of 2,750. (Five hundred was usual for a library novel.) He was rewarded with Wood's loyalty throughout her publishing career and with a book of which his firm had printed 400,000 copies by 1895.

Wood responded to success, as have so many popular writers, by doing far too much. Magazines clamored for her work. In 1862 and 1863 she had two serials in *The Quiver*, one in *Once a Week*, and one in *New Monthly Magazine*. Although her son and the others who wrote about her emphasized home duties and invalidism, we are more likely to be astonished by her incredible energy and professionalism. In the seven years after *East Lynne* she wrote fifteen novels, often working on two at a time and producing installments of both month by month under the pressures of serialization. Her health was, indeed, frail: she wrote in a reclining chair, with the manuscript on her knees. But the books were tightly plotted and carefully developed, with little of the space-filling digression that tempts serialists. She needed three weeks of absolute concentration while she worked out the plot and made a detailed outline; after that she could produce the monthly installment as time permitted without deviating from her plan or allowing interruptions to derail her story.

Henry Wood died in 1866. Shortly thereafter his widow moved to a substantial house in St. John's Wood and became editor and proprietor of *Argosy*, a monthly magazine of fiction, verse and miscellaneous prose. One of the many shilling monthlies launched in the 1860s, when paper prices dropped and publishers began to tap the broad mass of middle-class and lower-middle-class readers, *Argosy* had fallen on hard times when it printed Charles Reade's *Griffith Gaunt*, a novel that came perilously close to obscenity. Shilling monthly magazines needed the family audience to survive. Wood commanded the mixture of excitement and propriety that could rescue *Argosy*. Under her management the circulation reached approximately twenty thousand per month, somewhat less than *Cornhill* but more than *Belgravia*, which was run by Mary Elizabeth Braddon (the other best-selling sensation novelist), and three times as much as the more expensive and reputable magazines such as *Blackwood's*.

Between 1868 and 1873 the main feature of *Argosy* was a serial by Wood. She may have written up to half the remaining contents of the magazine. Among these unattributed works were a series of stories about Worcestershire scenes and characters narrated by young Johnny Ludlow. These stories are distinguished by striking portraits of individuals in all walks of life, by lively humor, and by an absence of direct moralizing. Some contemporaries remarked that they were much better than the work of sensationalists such as Mrs. Henry Wood, editor of the magazine where they appeared—which must have given her great glee when it became known that she had written them.

Anonymous publication and identification by an earlier work were customary among Victorian fictionists. *East Lynne* ran in *New Monthly Magazine* under "the author of 'Ashley'" (one of the short stories). It is probably not significant that she was usually referred to as "Mrs. Henry Wood." Unless a woman writer specifically chose to conceal her name and sex (like George Eliot or Currer Bell), reviewers and publishers simply tended to use her legal name.

Considering her health and the enormous amount of work she did, it is not surprising that Ellen Wood's private life was largely domestic and quite prosaic. She made her son Charles managing editor and then editor of *Argosy* and took little part in the social side of literary life. She was a generation older than the other writers who became popular at the same time; her few literary friends were earnest, provincial, hard-working women close to her own age, including Mary Howitt and Mrs. S. C. Hall. Young admirers who met her were disappointed that she had nothing to talk about except some servant, or how she had watched a man removing snow across the street.

The close observation of ordinary people does, however, lend interest to a few of her novels besides *East Lynne*. Although the highly sensational tales and the romantic adventures spiced with a touch of the supernatural have little to recommend them, Wood's stories of provincial life are concrete and vivid. Like Anthony Trollope, she could create a whole world, although her chosen scene was a degree or two lower on the social scale than his. An obituary article in the *Spectator* (19 February 1887) suggested that

> What she really knew was vulgarish country-town life, and the stories,
> ways, motives of the people engaged in it,—the bankers, professionals,

shopkeepers, and flirts . . . she could embody for us the ordinary middle-class, unintellectual, half-disagreeable folk of whom there are thousands round us, courting, fighting, stealing, giving, exactly as she has described them. . . . She was the novelist of the commonplace respectables, and they, like the masses and the classes, should have an interest.

Of her more than thirty novels, the others that might reward contemporary readers are *The Channings* (1862), its sequel *Roland Yorke* (1869), *Mildred Arkell* (1865), the *Johnny Ludlow Stories* (six series, 1874–1899), *Mrs. Halliburton's Troubles* (1862) and *A Life's Secret* (1867). The latter two novels have scenes of industrial disputes drawn from Wood's background as a manufacturer's daughter.

What makes it possible for a novelist who was once so popular to be now almost forgotten? For one thing, England's literary marketplace changed significantly in the latter half of the nineteenth century. In the early Victorian years, the novel was the dominant literary form and the vehicle for serious thought. There were, of course, also light and ephemeral fictions, but it was generally assumed that a book read by a great many people was probably worth reading. By 1880, however, "best seller" had become a pejorative term. The reading public was growing rapidly, as expanding business and government created thousands of openings for clerks, supervisors, technicians, accountants, teachers, middle managers—posts which required literacy and recruited the upwardly mobile. Middle-class readers were no longer people of traditional education and some leisure. They now included men and women who worked long hours, rode commuter trains, used gaslight to extend the evenings. A fall in paper prices made magazines cheaper and introduced the shilling "railway novel" to station newsstands.

Three novels in a very short space of time became what we would now call blockbusters: Wilkie Collins's *The Woman in White* (serialized in *All the Year Round* from November 26, 1859), Ellen Wood's *East Lynne* (serialized in *New Monthly Magazine* from January 1861), and Mary Elizabeth Braddon's *Lady Audley's Secret* (serialized in *Sixpenny Magazine* from March 1862). All of these novels went through many three-volume editions and a succession of cheap reprints; all became successful on stage; Collins's had commercial offshoots ("Woman in White" perfume, bonnets, etc.); Braddon and Wood edited magazines and earned the money to buy houses and educate their children. "Sensation novel" was the term applied to these books and their successors. Sensational qualities are certainly found in the literature of earlier decades, but the term, the fashion, and ultimately the formula originated with these three books.

The essential elements of sensationalism were secrets, surprises, suspense, and shocks to the nerves and emotions. The commerce of literature created the demand. A great many competing magazines were established when publishers realized the potential for mass sales. Mystery, frequent peaks of excitement, emotional involvement, and cliffhanging conclusions to each installment induced readers to buy issue after issue. The sensation novel was almost always specific and contemporary: It used real places, train schedules, telegraph messages, current events; it peered beneath the conventional surface of propriety for the secrets that might be hidden in the lives of people one knew. It also indulged the common reader's taste for peeping into wealthy homes and bedrooms. *East Lynne*, *Lady Audley's Secret*, and *The Woman in White* introduced most of the themes and situations that became the sensationalist's stock-in-trade: bigamy, adultery, illegitimacy, disguise, changed names, railway accidents, poison, fire, murder, concealed identity, false reports of death, the doubling of characters or incidents.

Sensation novels popularized the amateur detective in characters such as Walter Hartright, Robert Audley, or Archibald Carlyle and Barbara Hare who ask questions, add up evidence, and try to untangle the mystery. Although the hard-working middle-class sleuth is admired, and the idle aristocrat despised, the hero's virtue is sometimes rewarded by wealth and a title. Sensation novels provide enough clues so that we know what confrontations to expect and thus, with the characters, we, too, become anxious, annoyed, or even terrified as the expected events supply further surprises. In other words, sensation novels shaped many of the values and techniques that are common in twentieth-century popular novels, movies, and television.

In the Victorian mainstream novel, the trend was increasingly towards what Vineta Colby has termed domestic realism: the story deals almost exclusively with human relationships in a small social community, drawing its subjects from the home and family of ordinary people. A subspecies of this realistic social novel had come by midcentury to be described as the "woman's novel." The typical woman's novel is largely a novel of emotion rather than idea; it concentrates on those aspects of ordinary life that elicit strong feelings: home, motherhood, children, religion, jealousy, loneliness, misunderstandings, illness, pain, anxiety, death, love, undeserved suffering.

East Lynne is a consummate merging of these two popular forms. The sensational Richard Hare plot not only alternates with incidents from the woman's novel involving Isabel and Carlyle but also alters it; the same event can be fortunate in one plot and a terrible blow in the other, even though both Richard and Isabel are objects of our sympathetic interest. Thus the reader's emotional response at any given moment is complex and contradictory as well as strong.

The very presence of heightened emotion made sensation novels an object of condemnation in the 1860s. They existed, said the Archbishop of York, only for the purpose of "exciting in the mind some deep feeling of over-wrought interest." Most of the intellectual periodicals criticized sensationalism; moralists felt that a taste for scenes of crime and a craving for artificial excitements were symptoms of rot at the core of society. A writer in Ellen Wood's *Argosy*, however, suggested that it was "shallow to pick out the frivolities of the day as its regular characteristics." She believed that people sought relaxation in sensation fiction because of "the very thoughtfulness of the age."

A hundred years later it is easy to see that both sensationalism and the woman's novel did, indeed, provide escape. Probing beneath the surface, we can discover evidence of the pressures that made readers seek escape. It was the age of the angel in the house, repressive morality, and the Ruskin ideal of women's domestic kingdom—under a legal system that made women totally subordinate to their husbands. The woman's novel often showed the pain and anxiety of domestic situations. More surprisingly, sensation novels also generally had a woman at their center, whether as victim (the woman in white), villain (Lady Audley), or someone ambiguously neither, as in the case of *East Lynne*'s Lady Isabel. These women do not simply react, wait to be loved, and serve those around them; they move the tale and create its events. Their perfect ladyhood sometimes cloaks vicious anger or a totally inadequate personality. Furthermore, despite the "crime does not pay" moralizing, a reader's feelings may reveal secrets that an author could not write into the tale. Margaret Oliphant objected to *East Lynne* because she perceived that when Isabel returns home "there is not a reader who does not feel disposed to turn her virtuous successor to the door and reinstate the suffering heroine." In another example, the novels about bigamy gave readers a concealed opportunity to imagine divorce and to think about living with a person who was not one's lawful spouse. One of the pleasures of reading *East Lynne* with our psychologically-aware twentieth-century eyes comes from our apprehension of the subtext and the covert messages it supplies.

East Lynne's enormous success as a play also indicates its emotional appeal. In any given week for more than forty years, some version of the drama inspired by Ellen Wood's book was probably seen by an audience somewhere in England or North America. It was apparently first staged in Brooklyn on January 26, 1863. By March, three competing versions drew crowds to New York theaters. The most successful was written for Lucille Western by Clifton W. Tayleur. She paid him $100 and signed an agreement with the theater that gave her half the gross. During the New York engagement that began on March 23, 1863, she earned at least $350 every night. Western continued to bring *East Lynne* to New York annually for the next ten years and made the play a mainstay of her national tours.

Serious reviewers scoffed at the exaggerated emotions and at Lady Isabel's absurd disguise. (Beauty-conscious actresses tended simply to put on a pair of blue eyeglasses.) On February 12, 1866, Frank Drew did a burlesque version entitled *The Great Western:* he played Lady Isabel. But the part was a boon for many performers. It was permanent in the repertoire of Mrs. Conway, Ida Vernon, Sophie Miles. The great Modjeska played Lady Isabel for a week in 1879 at the Grand Opera House on Eighth Avenue. Several of the next generation's stars had their first prime role as Little Willie, including Lisle Leigh and a child named Gladys Smith, who, when she moved to Hollywood, changed her name to Mary Pickford. The range of the role—and the profits—made actresses choose Isabel for their benefit performances. They also fell back on it when things were not going well. The rather plump Josephine Cameron hastily substituted *East Lynne* when audiences were rude enough to laugh at her Camille.

In England, at the time of Ellen Wood's death, obituaries noted that the play based on her most famous book was "almost constantly acted" either in London or the provinces. Three London theaters had versions in 1879. At least nine different adaptations by unknown authors were presented between 1866 and 1899. There were also plays such as W. Archer's *The Marriage Bells* that used a different title for the sake of some copyright protection.

By the last decades of the century provincial audiences were the primary target. Ada Gray toured with the play almost constantly; in 1890 she said that she had performed it over four thousand times. She continued to make an annual visit to New York but, by the nineties, often played houses where she shared the stage with trained seals, the tattooed Captain Baum and his tattooed wife and tattooed dog, and a boxing match. Across the farmlands and prairies, however, the play held its appeal, especially for Wednesday ladies' matinees. It continued to be seen in tents, showboats and village schoolrooms past the turn of the century, until motion pictures penetrated to the most isolated spots and drove the last touring stock companies out of business.

Actresses loved the play because Lady Isabel was such a tremendous role—virtually two roles, considering the disguise—with opportunities to display love, flirtatiousness, anger, grief, and determination as well as the pathos that brought such a satisfactory response from the audience. Ellen Wood was responsible for many other features that worked well on stage. *East Lynne* was easy to cast from the standard players of a stock company: leading man and woman, black-haired villain, juvenile and ingenue (Richard and Barbara Hare), comic woman and man (Cornelia and Dill). Simplification eliminated most other characters—Afy Hallijohn, with her dubious reputation, was not usually included in the cast, and even Justice Hare was often missing. The play was Isabel's; the Richard Hare plot became only a device to affect the domestic story. (Leading players in the nineteenth century expected to dominate the script. Full development of the Hare plot would have not only lengthened the play but also given Barbara several more good scenes.)

The typical nineteenth-century melodrama was made up of about eight to twelve highly dramatic confrontations. The essential scenes were in Wood's novel, along with most of the dialogue required. Some adapters, in fact, supplied page references in their scripts and took the words wholesale from the book. Playbills labelled the scenes in large print: "The Fugitive's Return Home!"; "Fall of Isabel"; "Separation—Alone with Sorrow and Remorse"; "The Exile's Return"; "Farewell." Wood also supplied the song "Then You'll Remember Me," sung first by Isabel and then by Barbara while the disguised Isabel looks on—an enormously effective piece of business that might have been written for the stage. Most of the dramatic versions emphasized the comedy in Cornelia's role (the program often listed her as "Corney," and actresses made the most of the red flannel petticoat) but even these suggestions exist in the novel.

The book dramatized well because the concentrated scenes suitable for melodrama are also the basis of successful serialization: each installment had an intense interest of its own, in addition to suspense which led the readers on. Wood's ten years of practice as a writer of short stories may account for her ability to focus so fully on the development of one incident at a time. Furthermore, her instinct for mass audience response was so sure that it worked equally well in print or through the theater.

For theatergoers the moral may have been particularly important, considering the taint that still lingered around plays and players. One of the standard posters was headed "The Great Moral Lesson of the Age." At the midpoint of the play Isabel delivered the "Lady—wife—mother!" passage from chapter ten of the second volume as a soliloquy; from that point on no eye in the house was expected to be dry. The audience did not allow any tampering with their sympathetic identification with Isabel. When Edwin Forrest starred as Carlyle, he tried to shift the weight of the final scene by giving himself a long speech blaming Isabel for the suffering she had brought to him and to the children. The audience booed so much that he quickly returned to the ending they expected. The popular audience for *East Lynne* came to cry, and their release in tears required not only Isabel's suffering but also her virtual apotheosis. Some versions closed with a tableau of Willie and his mother enthroned on a golden cloud.

Popular fictions that deeply move great numbers of people generally do so because they rest on shared assumptions. The popular novel reflects values that are important to the mass of its readers. Furthermore, it touches feelings that might not otherwise be brought into the open; it provides codes to express emotional tensions that are formless (because no one has named them) or severely repressed by social constraints. The very force of Isabel's punishment and Wood's rhetoric suggest the enormous strength of the repression:

> Whatever trials may be the lot of your married life, though they may magnify themselves to your crushed spirit as beyond the endurance of woman to bear, *resolve* to bear them; fall down on your knees and pray to be enabled to bear them; pray for patience; pray for strength to resist the demon that would urge you to escape; bear unto death, rather than forfeit your fair name and your good conscience . . .

Marriage itself creates Isabel's misery. Even though Archibald Carlyle is the best of all possible husbands, utter dependence makes Isabel timid. She is afraid to ask questions. Her requests are ignored. She is protected, cherished, and prevented from taking adult responsibilities. She has nothing to do. Her jealousy of Barbara takes root because Carlyle does not confide in her; he has a business to attend to, but the business of a woman's life, so far as she can see, is to maintain a perfect relationship with her husband. At that business she believes she has failed. Since her husband and the marriage bond are the focus of her pain, she strikes at them by using the most effective weapon in the battle of the sexes. And her love of her children—a woman's most noble characteristic—is the source of Isabel's subsequent error and of her greatest punishment.

Behind the tears that flow so freely in the scenes of death and mother-love are unacceptable emotions that must be defused and sublimated. Barbara's love for Carlyle leads to an outburst of hysteria. Isabel knows that her attraction to Levison is irrational and unworthy. Cornelia is frustrated by the lack of a suitable role; she is "as good a lawyer as her father had been" but has no outlet for her intelligence and managerial ability. Her unwillingness to give up quasi-maternal control over her half brother reveals the dark side of the family ideal and woman's power in the home.

East Lynne's central emotion is the pain of exclusion. Barbara in the first half of the novel and Isabel in the second ache for the love that is not theirs. Richard as accused murderer and Isabel as runaway wife are both isolated, forced into lower social status, and rendered powerless. Richard, like Cornelia, is partly a victim of stereotyped sex roles: he is gentle, amiable, timid, and "unmanly." Like Isabel, he falls prey to his own feelings, fears, and unsuitable physical attractions. For both Richard and Isabel, the greatest pain is loss of family; once excluded from family life they are without power, social role, companionship, and love.

Stereotyped sex roles damage other characters as well. Justice Hare is a caricature patriarch, who puts his own will and his obsession with law and reputation above family feeling. Women have little real influence even in the "woman's kingdom" of the home: Mrs. Hare, agreeable, gentle, compliant, and motherly, is both futile and miserable. Even Carlyle makes decisions without listening seriously to Isabel.

East Lynne uses—for purely emotional effect—conditions that inspired more serious novelists to write with a purpose. Although the central figure is a helpless orphan at the mercy of her relatives, Wood says nothing about educating women to support themselves. The sensation plot revolves around a man in danger of hanging for a crime he did not commit, but Wood does not examine the criminal justice system. Because he needs a puppet to vote with him, a cabinet minister arranges to nominate a dishonest debtor to Parliament, but Wood avoids criticizing the political process. As Margaret Maison has pointed out, the divorce law that passed in 1857, three years before *East Lynne* was written, is essential to the story. Carlyle is morally free to marry again because he thinks Isabel is dead, but if he had not divorced her first, his marriage to Barbara would be invalid. In popular fiction, contemporary issues fuel strong emotions when they affect people we care about—but these issues are not objects of thought.

Mass values are also seen in the issues of class, the drama of unearned money versus earned respect, and the social placement of "good" and "bad" characters. The comforting belief that inherited wealth brings misery sets the tone of the opening passage. One reviewer found it amusing that a country lawyer—a man who "might have charged six-and-eightpence for the conversations with which he charms us"—is the romantic hero, but for Wood and the working middle class Carlyle is an admirable model: he continues to work hard even after he becomes a man of property, he serves as a justice, and he wins enough respect among neighboring gentry to be put up for Parliament against the candidate supported by the government and the House of Lords.

The society in *East Lynne* is fluid within limits. The lawyer can propose to the earl's daughter; the justice's son had honorable intentions towards the child of a lawyer's clerk. But the aristocrat could never have been an honest suitor for Afy. Although Wood insists that Isabel was totally unlike typical aristocratic women, part of her inadequacy may stem from her ladyhood— she is delicate, gentle, and ignorant about money and household duties. The work ethic is further revealed in the contrast between Joyce and Afy; the specifics of social evaluation in the exact placing of such characters as Otway Bethel, Ebenezer James, Jim Jiffin—and, of course, in the identity of the ultimate villain.

Popular fiction's effect depends in part on the connections that readers make with their own repressed desires. Dozens of women's novels in the later 1860s and 1870s imitated a piece of *East Lynne*'s central situation. An unhappy wife elopes but the elopement is aborted: she falls ill and her husband rushes to her bedside, or perhaps the husband engages the other man in a duel and gives the wife a chance to step between the weapons and save her husband's life. These books embody what must be the most common fantasy of unhappily married women: the husband has a change of heart.

Like most popular novelists, Wood worked from ideas that were in the air.

The estranged wife in disguise appeared in a melodrama by Augustus von Kotzebue which was performed in London in 1798 as *The Stranger* and continued to be seen from time to time throughout the nineteenth century. (The son in Kotzebue's play is also named William.) Dinah Mulock Craik's *A Life for a Life*, a success at the libraries in 1859, contained parallel stories of a man guilty of murder and a woman who bears a child out of wedlock, though the woman is not the center of the tale. Furthermore, Wood's book, like many of the serious novels written after the midcentury, was a story of woman's adulthood, with marriage as not the ending but the beginning of the tale. Reviewers sometimes criticized Wood for the pity and forgiveness surrounding Isabel, but the willingness to accept a heroine who was not perfect in every way would, in the next generation, have a profound effect on serious literature.

The mass values reflected in a book such as *East Lynne* help us to see the context in which major writers of the period worked. Wood uses feeling to evade idea. Blame rests in circumstances, misunderstandings, and gratuitous villainy. The actions that women take when driven by their own desires are generally unfortunate: Barbara's revelation of love, Cornelia's exercise of management, Isabel's response to her feelings. Wood maintains the reader's sympathy for Isabel in the second half of the novel by manipulating effects so that she comes to seem almost entirely a victim, rather than a woman who has made a choice. Family and children are the center of woman's life; the punishment for self-will is immediate and extreme. The real pains of woman's situation are transferred to the dramatic suffering that follows moral transgression, and the only conceivable solution is death.

Serious fiction is controlled by an individual vision and valued for uniqueness, for insight, and often for critical examination of the human condition. Most serious novels stimulate thought; they may force readers to face unpleasant truths about human nature. Popular fiction provides emotional indulgence; it avoids analysis and lets readers escape from the tensions that grow out of social conditions or their own nature. *East Lynne* remains a consummate popular fiction—a story of marriage, murder, adultery and suspense masterfully brought together at last on the public platform of a contested election. And, for many readers, the springs of emotion are also still there to be touched.

Sally Mitchell

✄ FOR FURTHER READING ✄

Auerbach, Nina. *Woman and the Demon: The Life of a Victorian Myth.*
Cambridge, Mass.: Harvard University Press, 1982.

Elliot, Jeanne B. "A Lady to the End: The Case of Isabel Vane." *Victorian
Studies* 19 (1976): 329–344.

Elwin, Malcolm. *Victorian Wallflowers: A Panoramic Survey of the Popular
Literary Periodicals.* 1934. Reprint. Port Washington, N. Y.: Kennikat,
1966.

Hughes, Winifred. *The Maniac in the Cellar: Sensation Novels of the
1860s.* Princeton: Princeton University Press, 1980.

Sergeant, Adeline. "Mrs. Henry Wood." In *Women Novelists of Queen
Victoria's Reign,* 174–192. London: Hurst and Blackett, 1897.

Showalter, Elaine. *A Literature of Their Own: British Women Novelists
from Brontë to Lessing.* Princeton: Princeton University Press, 1977.

Wood, Charles W. *Memorials of Mrs. Henry Wood.* London: Bentley,
1894.

A NOTE ON THE TEXT

The text has been reset, following the
one-volume 1890 edition of *East Lynne*
by the original publisher, Richard Bentley and Son (London).

EAST LYNNE

I

The Lady Isabel

In an easy chair of the spacious and handsome library of his townhouse sat William, Earl of Mount Severn. His hair was grey, the smoothness of his expansive brow was defaced by premature wrinkles, and his once attractive face bore the pale, unmistakable look of dissipation. One of his feet was cased in folds of linen, as it rested on a soft velvet ottoman, speaking of gout as plainly as any foot ever spoke yet. It would seem—to look at the man as he sat there—that he had grown old before his time. And so he had. His years were barely nine-and-forty; yet in all, save years, he was an aged man.

A noted character had been the Earl of Mount Severn. Not that he had been a renowned politician, or a great general, or an eminent statesman, or even an active member of the Upper House: not for any of these had the earl's name been in the mouths of men. But for the most reckless among the reckless, for the spendthrift among spendthrifts, for the gamester above all gamesters, and for a gay man outstripping the gay; by these characteristics did the world know Lord Mount Severn. It was said his faults were those of the head; that a better heart or more generous spirit never beat in human form; and there was much of truth in this. It had been well for him had he lived and died plain William Vane. Up to his five-and-twentieth year he had been industrious and steady, had kept his terms in the Temple, and studied late and early. The sober application of William Vane had been a byword with the embryo barristers around; Judge Vane, they ironically called him, and they strove ineffectually to allure him away to idleness and pleasure. But young Vane was ambitious, and he knew that on his own talents and exertions must depend his rising in the world. He was poor, of excellent family, but counting a relative in the old Earl of Mount Severn. The possibility of his succeeding to the earldom never occurred to him, for three healthy lives, two of them young, stood between him and the title. Yet those lives died off; one of apoplexy, one of fever in Africa, the third boating at Oxford; and the young Temple student, William Vane, suddenly found himself Earl of Mount Severn, and the lawful possessor of sixty thousand pounds a year.

His first idea was, that he should never know how to spend his money: that such a sum, year by year, could *not* be spent. It was a wonder his head was not turned by adulation at the onset; he was courted, flattered, and caressed by all classes. He became the most attractive man of his day; for, independent of his newly-acquired wealth and title, he was of distinguished appearance and fascinating manners. Unfortunately, the prudence which had sustained William Vane, the poor law student, in his solitary Temple chambers, entirely forsook William Vane, the young Earl of Mount Severn, and he commenced his career at a speed so great, that all staid people said he was going to ruin and the deuce headlong.

But a peer of the realm, and one whose rent-roll is sixty thousand per annum, does not go to ruin in a day. There sat the earl in his library now, in his nine-and-fortieth year, and ruin had not come yet—that is, it had not overwhelmed him. But the embarrassments which had clung to him, and been the destruction of his tranquillity, the bane of his existence, who shall describe them? The public knew them pretty well, his private friends better, his creditors best; but none, save himself, knew, or could ever know, the worrying torment that was his portion; well-nigh driving him to distraction. Years ago, by dint of looking things steadily in the face, and by economizing, he might have retrieved his position; but he had done what most people will do in such cases—put off the evil day *sine die*, and gone on increasing his enormous list of debts. The hour of exposure and ruin was now advancing fast.

Perhaps the earl himself was thinking so, as he sat there before an ominous mass of papers which strewed the library table. His thoughts were back in the past. That was a foolish marriage of his, that Gretna Green match for love, foolish so far as prudence went; but the countess had been an affectionate wife to him, had borne with his follies and his neglect, and been an admirable mother to their only child. One child alone had been theirs, and in her thirteenth year the countess had died. If they had but been blessed with a son—the earl groaned over the long-continued disappointment still—he might then have seen a way out of his difficulties. The boy, as soon as he was of age, would have joined with him in cutting off the entail, and—

'My lord,' said a servant, entering the room and interrupting the earl's castles in the air, 'a gentleman is asking to see you.'

'Who?' cried the earl, sharply, not perceiving the card the man was bringing. No unknown person, although wearing the externals of a foreign ambassador, was ever admitted unceremoniously to the presence of Lord Mount Severn. Years of duns had taught the servants caution.

'His card is here, my lord. It is Mr. Carlyle, of West Lynne.'

'Mr. Carlyle, of West Lynne,' groaned the earl, whose foot just then had an awful twinge; 'what does he want? Show him up.'

The servant did as he was bid, and introduced Mr. Carlyle. He was a very tall man of seven-and-twenty, of remarkably noble presence. He was somewhat given to stooping his head when he spoke to any one shorter than himself; it was a peculiar habit, almost to be called a bowing habit, and his father had possessed it before him; when told of it, he would laugh, and say he was unconscious of doing it. His features were good, his complexion was pale and clear, his hair dark, and his full eyelids drooped over his deep grey eyes. Altogether it was a countenance that both men and women liked to look upon, the index of an honourable, sincere nature; not that it would have been called a handsome face so much as a pleasing and distinguished one. Though but the son of a country lawyer, and destined to be a lawyer himself, he had received the training of a gentleman, had been educated at Rugby, and taken his degree at Oxford. He advanced at once to the earl in the straightforward way of a man who has come on business.

'Mr. Carlyle,' said the latter, holding out his hand—he was always deemed the most affiable peer of the age—'I am happy to see you. You perceive I cannot rise; at least without great pain and inconvenience: my enemy, the gout, has possession of me again. Take a seat. Are you staying in town?'

'I have just arrived from West Lynne. The chief object of my journey was to see your lordship.'

'What can I do for you?' asked the earl, uneasily, for a suspicion now crossed his mind that Mr. Carlyle might be acting for some one of his many toublesome creditors.

Mr. Carlyle drew his chair nearer to the earl and spoke in a low tone:

'A rumour came to my ears, my lord, that East Lynne was in the market.'

'A moment, sir,' exclaimed the earl, with reserve, not to say hauteur, in his tone, for his suspicions were gaining ground; 'are we to converse confidentially together, as men of honour, or is there something concealed behind?'

'I do not understand you,' said Mr. Carlyle.

'In a word—excuse my speaking plainly, but I must feel my ground—are you here on the part of some of my rascally creditors, to pump information out of me that overwise they would not get?'

'My lord,' said the visitor, 'I know that a lawyer gets credit for possessing but lax notions on the score of honour, but you can scarcely suspect I should be guilty of underhand work towards you. I never was guilty of a mean trick in my life, to my recollection, and I do not think I ever shall be.'

'Pardon me, Mr. Carlyle. If you knew half the tricks and *ruses* played upon me, you would not wonder at my suspecting all the world. Proceed with your business.'

'I heard that East Lynne was for private sale: your agent dropped half a word to me in confidence. If so, I should wish to be the purchaser.'

'For whom?' inquired the earl.

'Myself.'

'You!' laughed the earl. 'Egad! lawyering can't be such bad work, Carlyle.'

'Nor is it,' rejoined Mr. Carlyle, 'with an extensive first-class connexion, such as ours. But you must remember that a good fortune was left me by my uncle, and a large one by my father.'

'I know. The proceeds of lawyering also.'

'Not altogether. My mother brought a fortune on her marriage, and it enabled my father to speculate successfully. I have been looking out for an eligible property to invest my money upon, and East Lynne will suit me well, provided I can have the refusal of it, and we can agree about terms.'

Lord Mount Severn mused for a few moments before he spoke. 'Mr. Carlyle,' he began, 'my affairs are very bad, and ready money I must find somewhere. Now, East Lynne is not entailed; neither is it mortgaged to anything like its value, though the latter fact, as you may imagine, is not patent to the world. When I bought it a bargain, eighteen years ago, you were the lawyer on the other side, I remember.'

'My father,' smiled Mr. Carlyle. 'I was a child at the time.'

'Of course: I ought to have said your father. By selling East Lynne, a few thousands will come into my hands, after claims on it are settled; I have no other means of raising the wind, and that is why I have resolved to part with it. But now, understand: if it were known abroad that East Lynne is going from me, I should have a hornet's nest about my ears: so that it must be disposed of *privately*. Do you comprehend?'

'Perfectly,' replied Mr. Carlyle.

'I would as soon you bought it as anyone else, if, as you say, we can agree about terms.'

'What does your lordship expect for it—at a rough estimate?'

'For particulars I must refer you to my men of business, Warburton and Ware. Not less than seventy thousand pounds.'

'Too much, my lord,' cried Mr. Carlyle, decisively.

'And that's not its value,' returned the earl.

'These forced sales never do fetch their value,' answered the plain-speaking lawyer. 'I had thought, until this hint was given me by Beauchamp, that East Lynne was settled on your lordship's daughter.'

'There's nothing settled on her,' rejoined the earl, the contraction on his brow standing out more plainly. 'That comes of your thoughtless, runaway marriages. I fell in love with General Conway's daughter, and she ran away with me, like a fool: that is, we were both fools together for our pains. The general objected to me; and said I must sow my wild oats before he would give me Mary: so I took her to Gretna Green, and she became Countess of Mount Severn, without a settlement. It was an unfortunate affair, taking one thing with another. When her elopement was made known to the general, it killed him.'

'Killed him!' interrupted Mr. Carlyle.

'It did. He had disease of the heart, and the excitement brought on the crisis. My poor wife never was happy from that hour: she blamed herself for her father's death; and I believe it led to her own. She was ill for years: the doctors called it consumption; but it was more like a wasting insensibly away, and consumption never had been in her family. No luck ever attends runaway marriages: I have noticed it since, in many, many instances: something bad is sure to turn up from it.'

'There might have been a settlement executed after the marriage,' observed Mr. Carlyle, for the earl had stopped, and seemed lost in thought.

'I know there might: but there was not. My wife had possessed no fortune; I was already deep in my career of extravagance; and neither of us thought of making provision for our future children: or, if we thought of it, we did not do it. There is an old saying, Mr. Carlyle, that what may be done at any time, is never done.'

Mr. Carlyle bowed.

'So my child is portionless,' resumed the earl, with a suppressed sigh. 'The thought that it may be an embarrassing thing for her, were I to die before she is settled in life, crosses my mind when I am in a serious mood. That she will marry well there is little doubt, for she possesses beauty in a rare degree, and has been reared as an English girl should be, not to frivolity and foppery. She was trained by her mother, who (save for the mad act which she was persuaded into by me) was all goodness and refinement, for the first twelve years of her life, and, since then, by an admirable governess. No fear that she will be decamping to Gretna Green.'

'She was a very lovely child,' observed the lawyer. ' I remember that.'

'Ay; you have seen her at East Lynne, in her mother's lifetime. But, to return to business. If you become the purchaser of the East Lynne estate, Mr. Carlyle, it must be under the rose. The money that it brings, after paying off the mortgage, I must have, as I tell you, for my private use; and you know I should not be able to touch a farthing of it, if the confounded public got an inkling of the transfer. In the eyes of the world, the proprietor of East Lynne must still be Lord Mount Severn—at least for some little time afterwards. Perhaps you will not object to that?'

Mr. Carlyle considered before replying: and then the conversation was resumed, when it was decided that he should see Warburton and Ware the first thing in the morning, and confer with them. It was growing late when he rose to leave.

'Stay and dine with me,' said the earl.

Mr. Carlyle hesitated, and looked down at his dress: plain, gentlemanly morning attire, but certainly not dinner costume for a peer's table.

'Oh, that's nothing,' said the earl; 'we shall be quite alone, except my daughter. Mrs. Vane, of Castle Marling, is staying with us; she came up to present my child at the last Drawing-room, but I think I heard something about her dining out to-day. If not, we will have it by ourselves here. Oblige me by touching the bell, Mr. Carlyle, and set the trouble down to the score of my unfortunate foot.'

The servant entered.

'Inquire whether Mrs. Vane dines at home,' said the earl.

'Mrs. Vane dines out, my lord,' was the man's immediate reply. 'The carriage is at the door now, waiting to take her.'

'Very well. Mr. Carlyle remains.'

At seven o'clock the dinner was announced, and the earl was wheeled into the adjoining room. As he and Mr. Carlyle entered it at one door, some one else came in by the opposite one. Who—what—was it? Mr. Carlyle looked, not quite sure whether it was a human being: he almost thought it more like an angel.

A light, graceful, girlish form, a face of surpassing beauty, beauty that is rarely seen, save from the imagination of a painter, dark shining curls falling on her neck and shoulders smooth as a child's, fair delicate arms decorated with pearls, and a flowing dress of costly white lace. Altogether the vision did indeed look to the lawyer as one from a fairer world than this.

'My daughter, Mr. Carlyle; the Lady Isabel.'

They took their seats at the table. Lord Mount Severn at its head, in spite of his gout and his footstool, and the young lady and Mr. Carlyle opposite each other. Mr. Carlyle had not deemed himself a particular admirer of woman's beauty, but the extraordinary loveliness of the young girl before him nearly took away his senses and his self-possession. It was not so much the perfect contour of the exquisite features that struck him, or the rich damask of the delicate cheek, or the luxuriant falling hair; no, it was the sweet expression of the soft dark eyes. Never in his life had he seen eyes so pleasing. He could not keep his gaze from her, and he became conscious, as he grew more familiar with her face, that there was in its character a sad, sorrowful look; only at times was it to be noticed, when the features were in repose, and it lay chiefly in the very eyes he was admiring. Never does this unconsciously mournful expression exist, but it is a sure index of sorrow and suffering; but Mr. Carlyle understood it not. And who could connect sorrow with the anticipated brilliant future of Isabel Vane?

'Isabel,' observed the earl, 'you are dressed.'

'Yes, papa. Not to keep old Mrs. Levison waiting tea. She likes to take it early, and I know Mrs. Vane must have kept her waiting dinner. It was past six when she drove from here.'

'I hope you will not be late to-night, Isabel.'

'It depends upon Mrs. Vane.'

'Then I am sure you will be. When the young ladies, in this fashionable world of ours, turn night into day, it is a bad thing for their roses. What say you, Mr. Carlyle?'

Mr. Carlyle glanced at the roses on the cheeks opposite to him; they looked too fresh and bright to fade lightly.

At the conclusion of dinner, a maid entered the room with a white cashmere mantle, placing it over the shoulders of her young lady, as she said the carriage was waiting.

Lady Isabel advanced to the earl. 'Good-bye, papa.'

'Good night, my love,' he answered, drawing her towards him, and kissing her sweet face. 'Tell Mrs. Vane I will not have you kept out till morning hours: you are but a child yet. Mr. Carlyle, will you ring? I am debarred from seeing my daughter to the carriage.'

'If your lordship will allow me—if Lady Isabel will pardon the attendance of one little used to wait upon young ladies, I shall be proud to see her to her carriage,' was the somewhat confused answer of Mr. Carlyle, as he touched the bell.

The earl thanked him, the young lady smiled, and Mr. Carlyle conducted her down the broad lighted staircase, and stood bareheaded by the door of the luxurious chariot, and handed her in. She put out her hand in her frank, pleasant manner, as she wished him good night. The carriage rolled on its way, and Mr. Carlyle returned to the earl.

'Well, is she not a handsome girl?' he demanded.

'Handsome is not the word for beauty such as hers,' was Mr. Carlyle's reply, in a low warm tone. 'I never saw a face half so beautiful.'

'She caused quite a sensation at the Drawing-room last week—as I hear. This everlasting gout kept me in-doors all day. And she is as good as she is beautiful.'

The earl was not partial. Lady Isabel was wondrously gifted by nature, not only in mind and person, but in heart. She was as little like a fashionable young lady as it was well possible to be, partly because she had hitherto been secluded from the great world, partly from the care bestowed upon her training. During the lifetime of her mother, she had lived occasionally at East Lynne, but mostly at a larger seat of the earl's in Wales, Mount Severn: since her mother's death, she had remained entirely at Mount Severn, under the charge of a judicious governess, a very small establishment being kept up for them, and the earl paying them impromptu and flying visits. Generous and benevolent she was; timid and sensitive to a degree; gentle and considerate to all. Do not cavil at her being thus praised: admire and love her whilst you may, she is worthy of it now, in her innocent girlhood; the time will come when such praise would be misplaced. Could the fate, that was to overtake his child, have been foreseen by the earl, he would have struck her down to death, in his love, as she stood before him, rather than suffer her to enter upon it.

❧ II ☙

The Broken Cross

Lady Isabel's carriage continued its way, and deposited her at the residence of Mrs. Levison. Mrs. Levison was nearly eighty years of age, and very severe in speech and manner; or, as Mrs. Vane expressed it, 'crabbed.' She looked the image of impatience when Isabel entered, with her cap pushed all awry as she pulled at her black satin gown, for Mrs. Vane had kept her waiting dinner, and Isabel was keeping her from her tea: and that does not agree with the aged, with their health or their temper.

'I fear I am late,' exclaimed Lady Isabel, as she advanced to Mrs. Levison; 'but a gentleman dined with papa to-day, and it made us rather longer at table.'

'You are twenty-five minutes behind your time,' cried the old lady, sharply, 'and I want my tea. Emma, order it in.'

Mrs. Vane rang the bell, and did as she was bid. She was a little woman of six-and-twenty, very plain in face, but elegant in figure, vastly accomplished, and vain to her fingers' ends. Her mother, who was dead, had been Mrs. Levison's daughter, and her husband, Raymond Vane, was presumptive heir to the earldom of Mount Severn.

'Won't you take that tippet off, child?' asked Mrs. Levison, who knew nothing of the new-fashioned names for such articles; mantle, bernous, and all the string of them. Isabel threw it off, and sat down by her.

'The tea is not made, grandmamma!' exclaimed Mrs. Vane, in an accent of astonishment, as the servants appeared with the tray and the silver urn. 'You surely do not have it made in this room!'

'Where should I have it made?' inquired Mrs. Levison.

'It is much more convenient to have it brought in ready made,' said Mrs. Vane. 'I dislike the *embarras* of making it.'

'Indeed!' was the reply of the old lady; 'and get it slopped over in the saucers, and as cold as milk! You always were lazy, Emma—and given to use those French words. I'd rather stick a printed label on my forehead, for my part, "I speak French," and let the world know it that way.'

'Who makes tea for you in general?' asked Mrs. Vane, telegraphing a contemptuous grimace to Isabel behind her grandmother.

But the eyes of Lady Isabel fell timidly, and a blush rose to her cheeks. She did not like to appear to differ from Mrs. Vane, her senior, and her father's guest; but her mind revolted at the bare idea of ingratitude or ridicule cast to an aged parent.

'Harriet comes in and makes it for me,' replied Mrs. Levison: 'ay, and sits down and takes it with me when I am alone, which is pretty often. What do you say to that, Madame Emma; you, with your fine notions?'

'Just as you please, of course, grandmamma.'

'And there's the tea caddy at your elbow, and the urn's fizzing away, and if we are to have any tea to-night, it had better be made.'

'I don't know how much to put in,' grumbled Mrs. Vane, who had the greatest horror of soiling her hands or her gloves: who, in short, had a particular antipathy to doing anything useful.

'Shall I make it, dear Miss Levison?' said Isabel, rising with alacrity. 'I used to make it at Mount Severn, and I make it for papa.'

'Do, child,' replied the old lady. 'You are worth ten of her.'

Isabel laughed merrily, drew off her gloves, and sat down to the table: and at that moment a young and elegant man lounged into the room. He was deemed handsome, with his clearly-cut features, his dark eyes, his raven hair, and his white teeth; but, to a keen observer, those features had not an attractive expression, and the dark eyes had a great knack of looking away while he spoke to you. It was Francis, Captain Levison.

He was grandson to the old lady, and first cousin to Mrs. Vane. Few men were so fascinating in manners (at times and seasons), in face, and in form; few men won so completely upon their hearers' ears, and few were so heartless in their heart of hearts. The world courted him, and society humoured him: for, though he was a graceless spendthrift, and it was known that he was, he was the presumptive heir to the old and rich Sir Peter Levison.

The ancient lady spoke up. 'Captain Levison; Lady Isabel Vane.' They both acknowledged the introduction: and Isabel, a child yet in the ways of the world, blushed crimson at the admiring looks cast upon her by the young Guardsman. Strange—strange that she should make the acquaintance of those two men in the same day, almost in the same hour: the two, of all the human race, who were to exercise so powerful an influence over her future life!

'That's a pretty cross, child,' cried Mrs. Levison, as Isabel stood by her when tea was over, and she and Mrs. Vane were about to depart on their evening visit.

She alluded to a golden cross, set with seven emeralds, which Isabel wore around her neck. It was of light, delicate texture, and was suspended from a thin, short gold chain.

'Is it not pretty?' answered Isabel. 'It was given me by my dear mamma just before she died. Stay, I will take it off for you. I only wear it upon great occasions.'

This, her first grand party at a duke's, seemed a very great occasion to the simply reared and inexperienced girl. She unclasped the chain, and placed it with the cross in the hands of Mrs. Levison.

'Why, I declare you have nothing on, but that cross and some rubbishing pearl bracelets!' uttered Mrs. Vane to Isabel. 'I did not look at you before.'

'Mamma gave me both. The bracelets are those she used frequently to wear.'

'You old-fashioned child! Because your mamma wore those bracelets years ago, is that a reason for your doing so?' retorted Mrs. Vane. 'Why did you not put on your diamonds?'

'I—did—put on my diamonds; but I—took them off again,' stammered Isabel.

'What on earth for?'

'I did not like to be too fine,' answered Isabel, with a laugh and a blush. 'They glittered so! I feared it might be thought I had put them on to *look* fine.'

'Ah! I see you mean to set up in that class of people who pretend to despise ornaments,' scornfully remarked Mrs. Vane. 'It is the refinement of affectation, Lady Isabel.'

The sneer fell harmlessly on Isabel's ear. She only believed something had put Mrs. Vane out of temper. It certainly had: and that something, though Isabel little suspected it, was the evident admiration Captain Levison evinced for her fresh young beauty. It quite absorbed him, and rendered him neglectful even of Mrs. Vane.

'Here, child, take your cross,' said the old lady. 'It is very pretty; prettier on your neck than diamonds would be. You don't want embellishing: never mind what Emma says.'

Francis Levison took the cross and chain from her hand to pass them to Lady Isabel. Whether he was awkward, or whether her hands were full, for she held her gloves, her handkerchief, and had just taken up her mantle, certain it is that it fell; and the gentleman, in his too quick effort to regain it, managed to set his foot upon it, and the cross was broken in two.

'There! Now whose fault was that?' cried Mrs. Levison.

Isabel did not answer: her heart was very full. She took the broken cross, and the tears dropped from her eyes: she could not help it.

'Why! you are never crying over a stupid bauble of a cross!' uttered Mrs. Vane, interrupting Captain Levison's expressions of regret at his awkwardness.

'You can have it mended, dear,' interposed Mrs. Levison.

Lady Isabel chased away the tears, and turned to Captain Levison with a cheerful look. 'Pray do not blame yourself,' she good-naturedly said; 'the fault was as much mine as yours: and, as Mrs. Levison says, I can get it mended.'

She disengaged the upper part of the cross from the chain as she spoke, and clasped the latter round her neck.

'You will not go with that thin string of gold on, and nothing else!' uttered Mrs. Vane.

'Why not?' returned Isabel. 'If people say anything, I can tell them an accident happened to the cross.'

Mrs. Vane burst into a laugh of mocking ridicule. '"If people say anything!"' she repeated, in a tone according with the laugh. 'They are not likely to "say anything," but they will deem Lord Mount Severn's daughter unfortunately short of jewellery.'

Isabel smiled and shook her head. 'They saw my diamonds at the Drawing-room.'

'If you had done such an awkward thing for me, Francis Levison,' burst forth the old lady, 'my doors should have been closed against you for a month. There! if you are to go, Emma, you had better go: dancing off to begin an evening at ten o'clock at night! In my time we used to go at seven: but it's the custom now to turn night into day.'

'When George the Third dined at one o'clock upon boiled mutton and turnips,' put in the graceless captain, who certainly held his grandmother in no greater reverence than did Mrs. Vane.

He turned to Isabel as he spoke, to hand her downstairs. Thus she was conducted to her carriage the second time that night by a stranger. Mrs. Vane got down by herself, as she best could, and her temper was not improved by the process.

'Good-night,' said she to the captain.

'I shall not say good-night. You will find me there almost as soon as you.'

'You told me you were not coming. Some bachelors' party in the way.'

'Yes, but I have changed my mind. Farewell for the present, Lady Isabel.'

'What an object you will look, with nothing on your neck but a schoolgirl's chain!' began Mrs. Vane, returning to the grievance as the carriage drove on.

'Oh, Mrs. Vane, what does it signify? I can only think of my broken cross. I am sure it must be an evil omen.'

'An evil—what?'

'An evil omen. Mamma gave me that cross when she was dying. She told me to let it be to me as a talisman, always to keep it safely; and when I was in any distress, or in need of counsel, to look at it, and strive to recall what her advice would be, and to act accordingly. And now it is broken—broken!'

A glaring gaslight flashed into the carriage, right into the face of Isabel. 'I declare,' uttered Mrs. Vane, 'you are crying again! I tell you what, Isabel: I am not going to chaperone red eyes to the Duchess of Dartford's, so if you can't put a stop to this, I shall order the carriage home, and go on alone.'

Isabel meekly dried her eyes, sighing deeply as she did so. 'I can have the pieces joined, I dare say; but it will never be the same cross to me again.'

'What have you done with the pieces?' irascibly asked Mrs. Vane.

'I folded them in the thin paper Mrs. Levison gave me, and put it inside my frock. Here it is,' touching the body. 'I have no pocket on.'

Mrs. Vane gave vent to a groan. She never had been a girl herself, she had been a woman at ten; and she complimented Isabel upon being little better than an imbecile. '"Put it inside my frock!"' she uttered, in a tone of scorn. 'And you eighteen years of age! I fancied you left off "frocks" when you left the nursery.'

'I meant to say my dress,' corrected Isabel.

'Meant to say you are a baby idiot!' was the inward comment of Mrs. Vane.

A few minutes, and Isabel forgot her grievance. The brilliant rooms were to her as an enchanting scene of dreamland, for her heart was in its spring-tide of early freshness, and the satiety of experience had not come. How could she remember even the broken cross, as she bent to the homage offered her, and drank in the honeyed words poured forth into her ear?

'Halloa!' cried an Oxford student, with a long rent-roll in prospective, who was screwing himself against the wall, not to be in the way of the waltzers, 'I thought you had given up coming to these places.'

'So I had,' replied the fast nobleman addressed; 'but I am on the look-out, so am forced into them again. I think a ball-room the greatest bore in life.'

'On the look-out for what?'

'For a wife. My governor has stopped supplies; and has vowed, by his beard, not to advance another shilling, or pay a debt, till I reform. As a preliminary step towards it, he insists upon a wife, and I am trying to choose one, for I am deeper in than you can imagine.'

'Take the new beauty, then.'

'Who is she?'

'Lady Isabel Vane.'

'Much obliged for the suggestion,' replied the earl. 'But one likes a respectable father-in-law. Mount Severn and I are too much in the same line, and might clash in the long run.'

'One can't have everything: the girl's beauty is beyond common. I saw that rake, Levison, make up to her. He fancies he can carry all before him, where women are concerned.'

'So he does, often,' was the quiet reply.

'I hate the fellow! He thinks so much of himself, with his curled hair and his shining teeth and his white hands; he's as heartless as an owl. What was that hushed-up business about Miss Charteris?'

'Who's to know? Levison slipped out of the escapade like an eel, and the women protested that he was more sinned against than sinning. Three-fourths of the world believed them. Here he comes! And Mount Severn's daughter with him.'

They were approaching at that moment, Francis Levison and Lady Isabel.

He was expressing his regret at the untoward accident of the cross, for the tenth time that night. 'I feel that it can never be atoned for,' whispered he; 'that the heartfelt homage of my whole life would not be sufficient compensation.'

He spoke in a tone of thrilling gentleness, gratifying to the ear, but dangerous to the heart. Lady Isabel glanced up, and caught his eyes fixed upon her with the deepest tenderness, a language hers had never yet encountered. A vivid blush again rose to her cheek, her eyelids fell, and her timid words died away in silence.

'Take care, take care, my young Lady Isabel,' murmured the Oxonian under his breath as they passed him; 'that man is as false as he is high.'

'I think he's a rascal,' remarked the earl.

'I know he is: I know a thing or two about him. He would ruin her heart for the renown of the exploit, because she's a beauty, and then fling it away broken. He has none to give in return for the gift.'

'Just as much as my race-horse has,' concluded the earl. 'She is very beautiful.'

❧ I I I ❧

Barbara Hare

West Lynne was a town of some importance, particularly in its own eyes, though being neither a manufacturing town nor a cathedral town, nor even the chief town of the county, it was somewhat primitive in its manners and customs. It sent two members to parliament, and it boasted a good market-place, covered over, and a large room above that, which was called the 'town-hall,' where the justices met and transacted their business—for the county magistrates still retained there, that nearly obsolete name. Passing out at the town, towards the east, you came upon several detached gentlemen's houses, in the vicinity of which stood the church of St. Jude, which was more aristocratic (in the matter of its congregation) than the other churches of West Lynne. For about a mile these houses were scattered, the church being situated at their commencement close to the busy part of the place, and about a mile farther on you came upon the beautiful estate which was called East Lynne. As you drove along the road you might admire its green, undulating park; not as you walked, for an envious wall, mounting itself unconscionably high, obstructed your view. Large, beautiful trees, affording a shelter, alike for human beings and for the deer, on a day of summer's heat, rose in that park, and a great gate between two lodges on the right-hand side the road, gave you entrance to it, and conducted you to the house. It was not a very large house, compared with some country seats, but it was built in the villa style, was white and remarkably cheerful, altogether a desirable place to look upon.

Between the gentlemen's houses mentioned, and East Lynne, the mile of road was very solitary, much overshadowed by trees. One house alone stood there, and that was about three-quarters of a mile before you came to East Lynne, and full a quarter of a mile after you had passed the houses. It was on the left-hand side, a square ugly red brick house with a weathercock on the top, standing some little distance from the road. A flat lawn extended before it, and close to the palings, which divided it from the road, was a grove of trees, some yards in depth. The lawn was divided by a narrow middle gravel path, to which you gained access from the road by a narrow iron gate, which took you to the rustic portico of the house. You entered upon a large flagged hall with a reception room on either hand, and the staircase, a wide one, facing you; by the side of the staircase you passed on to the servants' apartments and offices. This place was called the Grove, and was the property and residence of Richard Hare, Esquire, commonly called Mr. Justice Hare.

The room to the left hand, as you went in, was the general sitting-room, the other was very much kept boxed up in lavender and brown holland, to be opened on state occasions. Justice and Mrs. Hare had three children, a son and two daughters. Anne was the elder of the girls, and had married young; Barbara, the younger was now nineteen; and Richard, the eldest—But we shall come to him hereafter.

In this sitting-room, on a chilly evening early in May, a few days subsequent to that which had witnessed the visit of Mr. Carlyle to the Earl of Mount Severn, sat Mrs. Hare, a pale, delicate woman, buried in shawls and cushions: her arm-chair was drawn to the hearth, though there was no fire: but the day had been warm. At the window sat a pretty girl, very fair, with blue eyes, light hair, a bright complexion, and small aquiline features. She was listlessly turning over the leaves of a book.

'Barbara, I am sure it must be tea-time, now.'

'Time seems to move slowly with you, mamma. It is scarcely a quarter of an hour since I told you it was but ten minutes past six.'

'I am so thirsty,' murmured the poor invalid. 'Do go and look at the clock again, Barbara.'

Barbara Hare rose with a gesture of impatience, opened the door, and glanced at the large clock in the hall. 'It wants nine-and-twenty minutes to seven, mamma. I wish you would put your watch on of a day: four times you have sent me to look at that clock since dinner.

'I am so thirsty,' repeated Mrs. Hare, with a sort of sob. 'If seven o'clock would but strike! I am dying for my tea.'

It may occur to the reader that a lady in her own house, 'dying for her tea,' might surely order it brought in, although the customary hour had not struck. Not so Mrs. Hare. Since her husband had first brought her home to that house, four-and-twenty years ago, she had never dared to express a will in it; scarcely, on her own responsibility, to give an order. Justice Hare was stern, imperative, obstinate, and self-conceited; she, timid, gentle, and submissive. She had loved him with all her heart, and her life had been one long yielding of her will to his: in fact, she had no will; his, was all in all. Far was she from feeling the servitude a yoke: some natures do not: and, to do Mr. Hare justice, his powerful will, that *must* bear down all before it, was in fault; not his kindness: he never meant to be unkind to his wife. Of his three children, Barbara alone had inherited this will, but in her it was softened down.

'Barbara,' began Mrs. Hare again, when she thought another quarter of an hour at least must have elapsed.

'Well, mamma.'

'Ring, and tell them to be getting it in readiness, so that when seven strikes there may be no delay.'

'Goodness, mamma! you know they always do have it ready. And there's no such hurry, for papa may not be home.' But she rose, and rang the bell with a petulant motion, and when the man answered it, told him to have tea in to its time.

'If you knew, dear, how dry my throat is, how parched my mouth, you would have more patience with me.'

Barbara closed her book, kissed her mamma with a repentant air, and turned listlessly to the window. She seemed tired, not with fatigue, but with what the French express by the word *ennui*. 'Here comes papa,' she presently said.

'Oh, I am so glad!' cried poor Mrs. Hare. 'Perhaps he will not mind having the tea in at once, if I tell him how thirsty I am.'

The justice came in. A middle-sized man, with pompous features, a pompous walk, and a flaxen wig. In his aquiline nose, compressed lips, and pointed chin, might be traced a resemblance to his daughter; though he never could have been half so good-looking as was pretty Barbara.

'Richard,' said Mrs. Hare from between her shawls, the instant he opened the door.

'Well?'

'Would you please let me have tea in now? Would you very much mind taking it a little earlier this evening? I am feverish again, and my tongue is so parched, I don't know how to speak.'

'Oh, it's near seven: you won't have long to wait.'

With this exceedingly gracious answer to an invalid's request, Mr. Hare quitted the room again, and banged the door. He had not spoken unkindly or roughly, simply with indifference. But, ere Mrs. Hare's meek sigh of disappointment was over, the door was re-opened, and the flaxen wig thrust in again.

'I don't mind if I do have it now. It will be a fine moonlight night, and I am going with Pinner as far as Beauchamp's, to smoke a pipe. Order it in, Barbara.'

The tea was made, and partaken of, and the justice departed for Mr. Beauchamp's, Squire Pinner calling for him at the gate. Mr. Beauchamp was a gentleman who farmed a great deal of land, and was also Lord Mount Severn's agent, or steward, for East Lynne. He lived higher up the road, some little distance beyond East Lynne.

'I am so cold, Barbara,' shivered Mrs. Hare, as she watched the justice down the gravel path. 'I wonder if your papa would say it was foolish of me, if I told them to light a bit of fire?'

'Have it lighted, if you like,' responded Barbara, ringing the bell. 'Papa will know nothing about it, one way or the other, for he won't be home till after bed-time. Jasper, mamma is cold, and would like a fire lighted.'

'Plenty of sticks, Jasper, that it may burn up quickly,' said Mrs. Hare, in a pleading voice; as if the sticks were Jasper's, and not hers.

Mrs. Hare got her fire, and she drew her chair in front, and put her feet on the fender, to catch its warmth. Barbara, listless still, went into the hall, took a woollen shawl from the stand there, threw it over her shoulders, and went out. She strolled down the straight, formal path, and stood at the iron gate, looking over it into the public road. Not very public in that spot, and at that hour, but as lonely as one could wish. The night was calm and pleasant, though somewhat chilly for the beginning of May, and the moon was getting high in the sky.

'When will he come home?' she murmured, as she leaned her head upon the gate. 'Oh, what would life be without him? How miserable these few days have been! I wonder what took him there! I wonder what is detaining him! Cornelia said he was only gone for a day.'

The faint echo of footsteps in the distance stole upon her ear, and Barbara drew a little back, and hid herself under the shelter of the trees, not choosing to be seen by any stray passer-by. But, as they drew near, a sudden change came over her; her eyes lighted up, her cheeks were dyed with crimson, and her veins tingled with excess of rapture—for she knew those footsteps, and loved them, only too well.

Cautiously peeping over the gate again, she looked down the road. A tall form, whose very height and strength bore a grace of which its owner was unconscious, was advancing rapidly towards her from the direction of West Lynne. Again she shrank away: true love is ever timid: and whatever may have been Barbara Hare's other qualities, her love at least was true and deep. But, instead of the gate opening, with the firm, quick motion peculiar to the hand which guided it, the footsteps seemed to pass, and not to have turned at all towards it. Barbara's heart sank, and she stole to the gate again, and looked out with a yearning look.

Yes, sure enough, he was striding on, not thinking of her, not coming to her; and she, in the disappointment and impulse of the moment, called to him.

'Archibald!'

Mr. Carlyle—it was no other—turned on his heel, and approached the gate.

'Is it you, Barbara? Watching for thieves and poachers? How are you?'

'How are you?' she returned, holding the gate open for him to enter, as he shook hands, and striving to calm down her agitation. 'When did you return?'

'Only now: by the eight o'clock train, which got in beyond its time, having dawdled unpardonably at the stations. They little thought they had me in it, as their looks betrayed, when I got out. I have not been home yet.'

'No! What will Cornelia say?'

'I went into the office for five minutes. But I have a few words to say to Beauchamp, and am going up at once. Thank you, I cannot come in now: I intend to do so on my return.'

'Papa has gone up to Mr. Beauchamp's.'

'Mr. Hare! Has he?'

'He and Squire Pinner,' continued Barbara. 'They are gone to have a smoking bout. And if you wait there with papa, it will be too late to come in, for he is sure not to be home before eleven or twelve.'

Mr. Carlyle bent his head in deliberation. 'Then I think it is of little use my going on,' said he, 'for my business with Beauchamp is private. I must defer it until to-morrow.'

He took the gate out of her hand, closed it, and placed the hand within his own arm, to walk with her to the house. It was done in a matter-of-fact, real sort of a way, with nothing of romance or sentiment: but Barbara Hare felt that she was in Eden.

'And how have you all been, Barbara, these few days?'

'Oh, very well. What made you start off so suddenly? You never said you were going, or came to wish us good-bye.'

'You have just expressed it, Barbara—"suddenly." A matter of business suddenly arose, and I suddenly went up upon it.'

'Cornelia said you were only gone for a day.'

'Did she? When in London I find many things to do. Is Mrs. Hare better?'

'Just the same. I think mamma's ailments are fancies, half of them: if she would but rouse herself, she would be better. What is in that parcel?'

'You are not to inquire, Miss Barbara. It does not concern you. It only concerns Mrs. Hare.'

'It is something you have brought for mamma, Archibald!'

'Of course. A countryman's visit to London entails buying presents for his friends: at least, it used to do so in the old-fashioned days.'

'When people made their wills before starting, and were a fortnight doing the journey in the waggon,' laughed Barbara. 'Grandpapa used to tell us tales of that, when we were children. But is it really something for mamma?'

'Don't I tell you so? I have brought something for you.'

'Oh! What is it?' she uttered, her colour rising, and wondering whether he was in jest or earnest.

'There's an impatient girl! "What is it?" Wait a moment, and you shall see what it is.'

He put the parcel, or roll, he was carrying upon a garden chair, and proceeded to search his pockets. Every pocket was visited, apparently in vain.

'Barbara, I think it is gone. I must have lost it somehow.'

Her heart beat as she stood there silently, looking up at him in the moonlight. *Was* it lost? *What* had it been?

But, upon a second search, he came upon something in the pocket of his coat-tail. 'Here it is, I believe: what brought it in there?' He opened a small box, and taking out a long gold chain, threw it round her neck. A locket was attached to it.

Her cheeks' crimson went and came, her heart beat more rapidly. She could not speak a word of thanks; and Mr. Carlyle took up the roll, and walked on into the presence of Mrs. Hare.

Barbara followed in a few minutes. Her mother was standing up, watching with pleased expectation the movements of Mr. Carlyle. No candles were in the room, but it was bright with firelight.

'Now don't you laugh at me,' quoth he, untying the string of the parcel. 'It is not a roll of velvet for a dress, and it is not a roll of parchment, conferring twenty thousand pounds a year. But it is—an air-cushion.'

It was what poor Mrs. Hare, so worn with sitting and lying, had often longed for; she had heard such a luxury was to be bought in London, but never remembered to have seen one. She took it almost with a greedy hand, casting a grateful look at Mr. Carlyle.

'How am I to thank you for it?' she murmured through her tears.

'If you thank me at all, I will never bring you anything again,' cried he, gaily, pleased to see her so pleased; for, whatever the justice and Barbara may have done, *he* felt lively pity for Mrs. Hare, sympathising with her sufferings. 'I have heard you wish for the comfort of an air-cushion, and happening to see some displayed in a window in the Strand, it put me in mind to bring you one.'

'How thin it is!' exclaimed Mrs. Hare.

'Thin! Oh yes, thin at present, because it is not "fixed," as our friends over the Atlantic say. See: this is the way to fill it with air. There; it is thick now.'

'It was so truly kind of you to think of me, Archibald.'

'I have been telling Barbara that a visit to London entails bringing gifts for friends,' returned Mr. Carlyle. 'Do you see how smart I have made Barbara?'

Barbara hastily took off the chain, and laid it before her mother.

'What a beautiful chain!' uttered Mrs. Hare, in surprise. 'Archibald, you are too good, too generous! This must have cost a great deal; this is beyond a trifle.'

'Nonsense!' laughed Mr. Carlyle. 'I'll tell you both how I came to buy it. I went into a jeweller's about my watch, which has taken to lose lately in a most unceremonious fashion, and there I saw a whole display of chains, hanging up; some ponderous enough for a sheriff, some light and elegant enough for Barbara; I dislike to see a thick chain on a lady's neck. They put me in mind of the chain she lost the day she and Cornelia went with me to Lynneborough; which loss Barbara persisted in declaring was my fault, for dragging her through the town, sight-seeing, while Cornelia did her shopping.'

'But I was only joking when I said so,' was the interruption of Barbara. 'Of course it would have happened had you not been with me; the links were always snapping.'

'Well; these chains in the shop in London put me in mind of Barbara's misfortune, and I chose one. Then the shopman brought forth some lockets, and enlarged upon their convenience for holding deceased relatives' hair, not to speak of sweethearts', until I told him he might attach one. I thought it might hold that piece of hair you prize, Barbara,' he concluded, dropping his voice.

'What piece?' asked Mrs. Hare.

Mr. Carlyle glanced round the room, as if fearful the very walls might hear his whisper. 'Richard's. Barbara showed it to me one day when she was turning out her desk, and said it was a curl cut off in that illness.'

Mrs. Hare sank back in her chair, and hid her face in her hands, shivering visibly. The words evidently awoke some poignant source of deep sorrow. 'Oh, my boy! my boy!' she wailed: 'my boy! my unhappy boy! Mr. Hare wonders at my ill-health, Archibald; Barbara ridicules it; but there lies the source of all my misery, mental and bodily. Oh, Richard! Richard!'

There was a distressing pause: for the topic admitted of neither hope nor consolation. 'Put your chain on again, Barbara,' Mr. Carlyle said, after a while, 'and I wish you health to wear it out. Health and reformation, young-lady.'

Barbara smiled, and glanced at him with her pretty blue eyes, so full of love. 'What have you brought for Cornelia?' she resumed.

'Something splendid,' he answered, with a mock serious face; 'only, I hope I have not been taken in. I bought her a shawl. The vendors vowed it was true Parisian cashmere: I hope it won't turn out to be common Manchester.'

'If it does, Cornelia will not know the difference.'

'I can't answer for that. But, for my part, I don't see why foreign goods should bear the palm over British,' observed Mr. Carlyle, becoming national. 'If I wore shawls, I would discard the best French one ever made, for a good honest one from our own manufactories, Norwich or Paisley.'

'Wait till you do wear them, you would soon tell a different tale,' said Barbara, significantly.

Mrs. Hare took her hands from her pale face. 'What was the price?' she inquired.

'If I tell you, you must promise not to betray it to Cornelia. She would rail at me for extravagance, and lay it up between folds of tissue paper, and never bring it out again. I gave eighteen guineas.'

'That is a great deal,' observed Mrs. Hare. 'It ought to be a very good one. I never gave more than six guineas for a shawl in all my life.'

'And Cornelia, I dare say, never more than half six,' laughed Mr. Carlyle. 'Well, I shall wish you good evening and go to her; for if she knows I am back, all this while, I shall be lectured.'

He shook hands with them both. Barbara, however, accompanied him to the front door, and stepped outside with him.

'You will catch cold, Barbara. You have left your shawl in-doors.'

'Oh no, I shall not. How very soon you are leaving; you have scarcely stayed ten minutes.'

'But you forget I have not been home.'

'You were on your road to Beauchamp's, and would not have been home for an hour or two in that case,' spoke Barbara in a tone that savoured of resentment.

'That was different; that was upon business; and nobody allows for business more readily than Cornelia. But I shall not hear the last of it, if I suffer anything but business to keep me away from her; she has five hundred inquiries, touching London, at her tongue's end, this instant, be you very sure. Barbara, I think your mamma looks unusually ill.'

'You know how she suffers a little thing to upset her, and last night she had what she calls one of her dreams,' answered Barbara. 'She says it is a warning that something bad is going to happen, and she has been in the most unhappy, feverish state possible all day. Papa has been quite angry about her being so weak and nervous, declaring that she ought to rouse herself out of "nerves." Of course we dare not tell him about the dream.'

'It relates to—the—'

Mr. Carlyle stopped, and Barbara glanced round with a shudder, and drew closer to him as she whispered. He had not given her his arm this time.

'Yes; to the murder. You know mamma has always declared that Bethel had something to do with it; she says her dreams would have convinced her of it, if nothing else did, and she dreamt she saw him with—with—you know.'

'Hallijohn?' whispered Mr. Carlyle.

'With Hallijohn,' assented Barbara with a shiver. 'He appeared to be standing over him, as he lay on the floor; just as he *did* lie on it. And that wretched Afy was standing at the end of the kitchen, looking on.'

'But Mrs. Hare ought not to suffer dreams to disturb her peace by day,' remonstrated Mr. Carlyle. 'It is not to be surprised at, that she dreams of the murder, because she is always dwelling upon it, but she should strive and throw the feeling from her with the night.'

'You know what mamma is. Of course she ought to do so, but she cannot. Papa wonders what makes her get up so ill and trembling of a morning, and mamma has to make all sorts of excuses, for not a hint, as you are aware, must be breathed to him about the murder.'

Mr. Carlyle gravely nodded.

'Mamma does so harp upon Bethel. And I know that this dream arose from nothing in the world but because she saw him pass the gate yesterday. Not that she thinks it was he who did it; unfortunately, there is no room for that; but she will persist that he had a hand in it some way; and he haunts her dreams.'

Mr. Carlyle walked on in silence: indeed, there was no reply that he could make. A cloud had fallen upon the house of Mr. Hare, and it was an unhappy subject. Barbara continued:

'But, for mamma to have taken it into her head that "some evil is going to happen" because she has had this dream, and to make herself miserable over it, is so very absurd, that I have felt quite cross with her all day. Such nonsense, you know, Archibald, to believe that dreams give signs of what is going to happen? so far behind these enlightened days!'

'Your mamma's trouble is great, Barbara; and she is not strong.'

'I think all our troubles have been great since—since that dark evening,'
responded Barbara.

'Have you heard from Anne?' inquired Mr. Carlyle, willing to change the
subject.

'Yes, she is very well. What do you think they are going to name the baby?
Anne: after her and mamma. So very ugly a name! Anne!'

'I do not think so,' said Mr. Carlyle. 'It is simple and unpretending; I like it
much. Look at the long, pretentious names in our family—Archibald! Cornelia! And yours, too—Barbara! What a mouthful they all are!'

Barbara contracted her eyebrows. It was equivalent to saying that he did
not like her name.

'Had the magistrates a busy day yesterday, do you know?' he resumed.

'Very much so, I believe. But you have not remained long enough for me to
tell you any news.'

They reached the gate, and Mr. Carlyle was about to pass out of it, when
Barbara laid her hand on his arm to detain him, and spoke in a timid voice.
'Archibald.'

'What is it?'

'I have not said a word of thanks to you for this,' she said, touching the
chain and locket: 'my tongue seemed tied. Do not deem me ungrateful.'

'You foolish girl!—it is not worth thanks. There! now I am paid. Good
night, Barbara.'

He had bent down and kissed her cheek; swung through the gate, laughing, and strode away. 'Don't say I never give you anything,' he turned his
head round to say. 'Good night.'

All her veins were tingling, all her pulses beating; her heart was throbbing
with its sense of bliss. He had never kissed her, that she could remember,
since she was a child. And when she returned in-doors, her spirits were so
extravagantly high, that Mrs. Hare wondered.

'Ring for the lamp, Barbara, and you can get to your work. But don't have
the shutters closed: I like to look out on these light nights.'

Barbara, however, did not get to her work; she also perhaps liked 'looking
out on a light night,' for she sat down at the window. She was living the last
half hour over again. '"Don't say I never give you anything,"' she murmured: 'did he allude to the chain, or to the—the kiss? Oh, Archibald! why
don't you say that you love me?'

Mr. Carlyle had been all his life upon intimate terms with the Hares. His
father's first wife—for the late lawyer Carlyle had been twice married—had
been a cousin of justice Hare's, and this had caused the families to be much
together. Archibald, the child of the second Mrs. Carlyle, had alternately
teased and petted Anne and Barbara Hare, boy fashion. Sometimes he quarrelled with the pretty little girls, sometimes he caressed them, as he would
have done had they been his sisters; and he made no scruple of declaring

publicly to the pair, that Anne was his favourite. A gentle, yielding girl she was, like her mother; whereas Barbara displayed her own will, and it sometimes clashed with young Carlyle's.

The clock struck ten. Mrs. Hare took her customary sup of brandy-and-water, a small tumbler three parts full. Without it, she believed she could never get to sleep; it deadened unhappy thought, she said. Barbara, after making it, had turned again to the window, but she did not resume her seat. She stood right in front of it, her forehead bent forward against the middle pane. The lamp, casting a bright light, was behind her, so that her figure might be distinctly observable from the lawn, had any one been there to look upon it.

She stood there in the midst of dreamland, giving way to all its enchanting and most delusive fascinations. She saw herself, in anticipation, the wife of Mr. Carlyle, the envied, thrice envied of all West Lynne; for, like as he was the dearest on earth to her heart, so was he the greatest match in the neighbourhood around. Not a mother but coveted him for her child; not a daughter but would have said 'Yes, and thank you' to an offer from the attractive Archibald Carlyle. 'I never was sure, quite sure, of it till to-night,' murmured Barbara, caressing the locket, and holding it to her cheek: 'I always thought he might mean something, or he might mean nothing; but to give me this—to kiss me—oh, Archibald!'

A pause. Barbara's eyes were fixed upon the moonlight.

'If he would but say he loved me! if he would but ease my aching heart! But it must come; I know it will; and if that cantankerous cross old Corny—'

Barbara Hare stopped. What was that, at the far end of the lawn, just in advance of the shade of the thick trees? Their leaves were not causing the movement, for it was a still night. It had been there some minutes; it was evidently a human form. What *was* it? Surely it was making signs to her!

Or else it looked as though it was. That was certainly its arm moving, and now it advanced a pace nearer, and raised something which it wore on its head—a battered hat with a broad brim, a 'wide-awake,' encircled with a wisp of straw.

Barbara Hare's heart leaped, as the saying runs, into her mouth, and her face became deadly white in the moonlight. Her first thought was to alarm the servants; her second, to be still; for she remembered the fear and mystery that attached to the house. She went into the hall, shutting her mamma in the parlour, and stood in the shade of the portico, gazing still. But the figure evidently followed her movements with its sight, and the hat was again taken off, and waved violently.

Barbara Hare turned sick with utter terror; *she* must fathom it; she must see who and what it was; for the servants she dared not call, and those movements were imperative, and might not be disregarded; but she possessed more innate courage than falls to the lot of some young ladies.

'Mamma,' she said, returning to the parlour and catching up her shawl, while striving to speak without emotion, 'I shall just walk down the path, and see if papa is coming.'

Mrs. Hare did not reply. She was musing upon other things, in that quiescent, happy mood, which a small portion of spirits will impart to one weak in body; and Barbara softly closed the door, and stole out again to the portico. She stood a moment to rally her courage, and again the hat was waved impatiently.

Barbara Hare commenced her walk towards it; an undefined sense of evil filling her sinking heart; mingling with which came, with a rush of terror, a fear of that other undefined evil—the evil Mrs. Hare had declared was foreboded in her dream.

⚓ IV ⚓

The Moonlight Interview

Cold and still looked the old house in the moonbeams. Never was the moon brighter: it lighted the far-stretching garden, it illumined even the weathercock aloft, it shone upon the portico, and upon Barbara as she had appeared in it. Stealing from the portico, walked Barbara, her eyes strained in dread affright on that grove of trees, at the foot of the garden. What was it that had stepped out of the trees, and mysteriously beckoned to her as she stood at the window, turning her heart to sickness as she gazed? Was it a human being, one to bring more evil on the house, where so much evil had already fallen; was it a supernatural visitant; or was it but a delusion of her own eyesight? Not the latter, certainly, for the figure was now emerging again, motioning to her as before; and, with a white face and shaking limbs, Barbara clutched her shawl round her and went down the path in the moonlight. The beckoning form retreated within the dark trees as she neared it, and Barbara halted.

'Who and what are you?' she asked under her breath. 'What do you want?'

'Barbara,' was the whispered, eager answer, 'don't you recognize me?'

Too surely she did, the voice at any rate, and a cry escaped her, telling more of terror than of joy, though betraying both. She penetrated the trees, and burst into tears as one, in the dress of a farm labourer, caught her in his arms. In spite of his smock-frock and his straw-wisped hat, and his false whiskers, black as Erebus, she knew him for her brother.

'Oh, Richard! where have you come from? What brings you here?'

'Did you know me, Barbara?' was his rejoinder.

'How was it likely—in this disguise? A thought crossed my mind that it might be some one from you, and even that made me sick with terror. How could you be so hazardous as to come here?' she added, wringing her hands. 'If you are discovered, it is certain death; death—upon—you know!'

'Upon the gallows,' returned Richard Hare. 'I do know it, Barbara.'

'Then why risk it? Should mamma see you, it will kill her outright.'

'I can't live on as I am living,' he answered, gloomily. 'I have been working in London ever since—'

'In London!' interrupted Barbara.

'In London; and have never stirred out of it. But it is hard work for me, and now I have an opportunity of doing better, if I can get a little money. Perhaps my mother can let me have it; it is what I have come to ask for.'

'How are you working? What at?'

'In a stable-yard.'

'A stable-yard!' she uttered, in a deeply-shocked tone. 'Richard!'

'Did you expect it would be as a merchant; or a banker; or perhaps as secretary to one of her Majesty's ministers—or that I was a gentleman at large, living on my fortune?' retorted Richard Hare, in a tone of chafed anguish, painful to hear. 'I get twelve shillings a week, Barbara, and that has to find me in everything.'

'Poor Richard! poor Richard!' she wailed, caressing his hand, and weeping over it. 'Oh, what a miserable night's work that was! Our only comfort is, Richard, that you must have committed the deed in madness.'

'I did not commit it at all,' he replied.

'What!' she exclaimed.

'Barbara, I swear that I am innocent; I swear I was not present when the man was murdered; I swear that, from my own positive knowledge, my eyesight, I know no more who did it than you. The guessing at it is enough for me; and my guess is as sure and true a one as that that moon is in the heavens.'

Barbara shivered as she drew closer to him. It was a shivering subject, 'You surely do not mean to throw the guilt on Bethel?'

'Bethel?' slightly returned Richard Hare. 'He had nothing to do with it. He was after his gins and his snares that night, though, poacher that he is!'

'Bethel is no poacher, Richard.'

'Is he not?' rejoined Richard Hare, significantly. 'The truth, as to what he is, may come out some time. Not that I wish it to come out; the man has done no harm to me, and he may go on poaching with impunity till doomsday, for all I care. He and Locksley—'

'Richard,' interrupted his sister, in a hushed voice, 'mamma entertains one fixed idea, which she cannot put from her. She says she is certain Bethel had something to do with the murder.'

'Then she is wrong. Why should she think so?'

'How the conviction arose at first, I cannot tell you; I do not think she knows herself. But you remember how weak and fanciful she is, and since that dreadful night she is always having what she calls "dreams," meaning that she dreams of the murder. In all these dreams Bethel is prominent; and she says she feels an absolute certainty that he was, in some way, mixed up in it.'

'Barbara, he was no more mixed up in it than you.'

'And—you say that you were not?'

'I was not even at the cottage at the time; I swear it to you. The man who did the deed was Thorn.'

'Thorn!' echoed Barbara, lifting her head. 'Who is Thorn?'

'I don't know who. I wish I did: I wish I could unearth him. He was a friend of Afy's.'

Barbara threw back her neck with a haughty gesture. 'Richard!'

'What?'

'You forget yourself, when you mention that name to me.'

'Well,' returned Richard, 'it was not to discuss these things that I put myself in jeopardy. And to assert my innocence can do no good: it cannot set aside the coroner's verdict of "Wilful Murder against Richard Hare, the younger." Is my father as bitter against me as ever?'

'Quite. He never mentions your name, or suffers it to be mentioned; he gave his orders to the servants that it never was to be spoken in the house again. Eliza could not, or would not, remember, and she persisted in still calling your room "Mr. Richard's." I think the woman did it heedlessly; not mischievously, to provoke papa: she was a good servant, and had been with us three years, you know. The first time she transgressed, papa warned her; the second, he thundered at her, as I believe nobody else in the world can thunder; and the third time he turned her from the doors, never allowing her to get her bonnet: one of the others carried her bonnet and shawl out to the gate, and her boxes were sent away the same day. Papa took an oath that—Did you hear of it?'

'What oath? He takes many.'

'This was a solemn one, Richard. After the delivery of the verdict, he took an oath in the justice-room, in the presence of his brother magistrates, that if he could find you he would deliver you up to justice, and that he *would* do it, though you might not turn up for ten years to come. You know his disposition, Richard, and therefore may be sure that he will keep it. Indeed, it is most dangerous for you to be here.'

'I know that he never treated me as he ought,' cried Richard, bitterly. 'If my health was delicate, causing my poor mother to indulge me, ought that to have been a reason for his ridiculing me on every possible occasion, public and private? Had my home been made happier, I should not have sought the society I did elsewhere. Barbara, I must be allowed an interview with my mother.'

Barbara Hare reflected before she spoke. 'I do not see how it could be managed.'

'Why can't she come out to me, as you have done? Is she up or in bed?'

'It is impossible to think of it to-night,' returned Barbara, in an alarmed tone. 'Papa may be in at any moment; he is spending the evening at Beauchamp's.'

'It is hard to have been separated from her for eighteen months, and to go back without seeing her,' returned Richard. 'And about the money? It is a hundred pounds that I want.'

'You must be here again to-morrow night, Richard; the money, no doubt, can be yours, but I am not so sure about your seeing mamma. I am terrified for your safety. But if it is as you say, that you are innocent,' she added, after a pause, 'could it not be proved?'

'Who is to prove it? The evidence is strong against me; and Thorn, did I mention him, would be as a myth to other people: nobody knew anything of him.'

'Is he a myth?' asked Barbara, in a low tone.

'Are you and I myths?' retorted Richard. 'So! even *you* doubt me.'

'Richard,' she suddenly exclaimed, 'why not tell the whole circumstances to Archibald Carlyle? If any one can help you, or take means to establish your innocence, he can. And you know that he is true as steel.'

'There's no other man living should be trusted with the secret that I am here, except Carlyle. Where is it supposed that I am, Barbara?'

'Some think you are dead, some that you are in Australia: the very uncertainty has nearly killed mamma. A report arose that you had been seen at Liverpool, in an Australian-bound ship, but we could not trace it to any foundation.'

'It had none. I dodged my way to London, and there I have been.'

'Working in a stableyard!'

'I could not do better. I was not brought up to anything; and I did understand horses. Besides, a man that the police-runners were after could be more safe in obscurity, considering he was a gentleman, than—'

Barbara turned suddenly and placed her hand upon her brother's mouth. 'Be silent for your life,' she whispered; 'here's papa.'

Voices were heard approaching the gate, that of Justice Hare and of Squire Pinner. The latter walked on, the former came in. The brother and sister cowered together, scarcely daring to breathe: you might have heard Barbara's heart beating. Mr. Hare closed the gate, and walked on up the path.

'I must go, Richard,' she hastily said; 'I dare not stay another minute. Be here again to-morrow night, and meanwhile I will see what can be done.'

She was speeding away, but Richard held her back.

'You did not seem to believe my assertion of innocence. Barbara, we are here alone in the still night, with God above us: as truly as that you and I must some time meet Him face to face, I told you truth. It was Thorn murdered Hallijohn, and I had nothing whatever to do with it.'

Barbara broke out of the trees and flew along, but Mr. Hare was already in, locking and barring the door. 'Let me in, papa,' she called out.

The justice opened the door again, and his flaxen wig, his aquiline nose, and his amazed eyes gazed at Barbara. 'Halloa! what brings you out at this time of night, young lady?'

'I went down to the gate to look for you,' she panted, 'and had—had—strolled over to the side path. Did you not see me?'

Barbara was truthful by nature and habit; but, in such a cause, how could she avoid dissimulation? 'Thank you, papa,' she said, as she went in.

'You ought to have been in bed an hour ago,' angrily responded Mr. Justice Hare.

♣ V ♣

Mr. Carlyle's Office

In the centre of West Lynne stood two houses adjoining each other, one large, the other much smaller. The large one was the Carlyle residence, and the small one was devoted to the Carlyle offices. The name of Carlyle bore a lofty standing in the county; Carlyle and Davidson were known as first-class practitioners; no pettifogging lawyers were they. It was Carlyle and Davidson in the days gone by; now it was Archibald Carlyle. The old firm were brothers-in-law, the first Mrs. Carlyle having been Mr. Davidson's sister. She had died and left one child, Cornelia, who was grown up when her father married again. The second Mrs. Carlyle died when her son, Archibald, was born, and his half-sister reared him, loved him, and ruled him. She bore for him all the authority of a mother; the body had known no other, and when a little child, he had called her Mamma Corny. Mamma Corny had done her duty by him, that was undoubted; but Mamma Corny had never relaxed her rule; with an iron hand she liked to rule him now, in great things as in small, just as she had done in the days of his babyhood. And Archibald generally submitted, for the force of habit is strong. She was a woman of strong sense, but, in some things, weak of judgment: and the ruling passions of her life were love of Archibald, and love of saving money. Mr. Davidson had died earlier than Mr. Carlyle, and his fortune—he had never married—was left equally divided between Cornelia and Archibald. Archibald was no blood relation to him, but he loved the open-hearted boy better than he did his niece Cornelia. Of Mr. Carlyle's property, a small portion only was bequeathed to his daughter, the rest to his son: and in this perhaps there was justice, since the 20,000£. brought to Mr. Carlyle by his second wife had been chiefly instrumental in the accumulation of his large fortune.

Miss Carlyle, or, as she was called in the town, Miss Corny, had never married; it was pretty certain she never would; people thought that her intense love of her young brother kept her single, for it was not likely that the daughter of the rich Mr. Carlyle had wanted for offers. Other maidens confess to soft and tender impressions; to a hope of being, some time or another, solicited to abandon their father's name, and become somebody's better half. Not so, Miss Carlyle: all who had approached her with the love-lorn tale, she sent quickly to the right-about. The last venture was from the new curate, and occurred when she was in her fortieth year. He made his appearance at her house one morning betimes, in his white Sunday necktie, and a pair of new gloves drawn on for the occasion, colour lavender. Miss Corny, who was an exceedingly active housekeeper in her own house, a great deal more so than the servants liked, had just been giving her orders for dinner. They comprised, amongst other things, a treacle-pudding for the kitchen, and she went herself to the store-closet with a basin to ladle out the necessary treacle. The closet opened from the dining-room, and it was while she was in it that the curate was ushered in. Miss Carlyle, who completely ignored ceremony, and had never stood upon it in her life, came out, basin of treacle in hand, which she deposited on the table while she disposed herself to listen to the reverend gentleman, who was twelve years her junior, and very diffident, so that he was some time getting his business out. Miss Corny wished him and his stammering somewhere, for she knew the pudding was waiting for the treacle, and helped him out as much as she could, putting in words when he seemed at fault for them. She supposed he wanted her name to some subscription, and she stood looking down at him with impatience, he being at least a foot shorter than she. When the startling truth at length disclosed itself, that he had come begging for *her*, and not for money, Miss Carlyle for once lost her temper. She screamed out that he ought to be ashamed of himself for a raw boy as he was, and she flung the contents of the basin over his spotless shirt-front. How the crest-fallen divine got out of the house and down West Lynne to his lodgings, he never cared to recall. Sundry juveniles of both sexes, nursing babies or carrying out parcels, collected at his heels and escorted him, openly surmising, with various degrees of envy, that he had been caught dipping his head for a sly lick into the grocer's treacle-barrel, and the indignant owner had soused him in. The story got wind, and Miss Corny was not troubled with any more offers.

Mr. Carlyle was seated in his own private room in his office the morning after his return from town; his confidential clerk and manager stood near him, one who had far more to do with the management than Mr. Carlyle himself. It was Mr. Dill, a little, meek-looking man, with a bald head. He was on the rolls, had been admitted years and years ago, but had never set up for himself: perhaps he deemed the post of head manager in the office of Carlyle and Davidson, with its substantial salary, sufficient for his ambition; and manager he had been to them when the present Mr. Carlyle was in long petticoats; he was a single man, and occupied handsome apartments near. A shrewd surmise obtained weight in West Lynne that he was a devoted admirer of Miss Carlyle, humbly worshipping her at a distance. Whether this was so or not, certain it is that he was very fond of his present master, Mr. Archibald, as he generally styled him. He was now giving an account of what had transpired during the few days of absence.

'Jones and Rushworth have come to an outbreak at last,' cried he, when he had pretty nearly arrived at the end of his catalogue, 'and the upshot will be an action at the summer assizes. They were both here yesterday, one after the other, each wanting you to act for him, and will be here to-day for an answer.'

'I will not act for either,' said Mr. Carlyle; 'I will have nothing to do with them. They are a bad lot, and it was an iniquitous piece of business their obtaining the money in the first instance. When rogues fall out, honest men get their own. I decline it altogether; let them carry themselves to somebody else.'

'Very good,' replied Mr. Dill.

'Colonel Bethel's here, sir,' said a clerk, opening the door, and addressing Mr. Carlyle. 'Can you see him?'

Mr. Dill turned round to the clerk. 'Ask the colonel to wait. I think that's about all,' he added to his master, as the man withdrew.

'Very well. Dill, certain papers will be down in a few days, relating to mortgages and claims on the East Lynne estate; they are coming with the title deeds. I want them carefully looked over *by you*, and nothing said.'

Mr. Dill gave a quiet nod.

'East Lynne is about to change hands. And, in purchasing property from an embarrassed man like Mount Severn, it is necessary to be keen and cautious,' continued Mr. Carlyle.

'It is. Has he come to the end of his tether?'

'Not far short of it, I fancy; but East Lynne will be disposed of *sub rosa*. Not a syllable abroad, you understand.'

'All right, Mr. Archibald. Who is the purchaser? It is a fine property.'

Mr. Carlyle smiled. 'You will know who, long before the world does. Examine the deeds with a Jew's eye. And now send in Bethel.'

Between the room of Mr. Carlyle and that of the clerks' was a small square space, or hall, having ingress also from the house passage; another room opened from it, a narrow one which was Mr. Dill's own peculiar sanctum; here he saw clients when Mr. Carlyle was out or engaged, and here he issued private orders. A little window, not larger than a pane of glass, looked out from it on the clerks' office; they called it Old Dill's peep-hole, and wished it anywhere else, for his spectacles might be discerned at it more often than was agreeable. The old gentleman had a desk also in their office, and there he frequently sat; he was sitting there in state, this same morning, keeping a sharp look out around him, when the door timidly opened, and the pretty face of Barbara Hare appeared at it, rosy with blushes.

'Can I see Mr. Carlyle?'

Mr. Dill rose from his seat and shook hands with her. She drew him into the passage, and he closed the door. Perhaps he felt surprised, for it was *not* the custom for ladies, young and single, to come there after Mr. Carlyle.

'Presently, Miss Barbara; he is engaged just now. The justices are with him.'

'The justices!' uttered Barbara, in alarm, 'and papa one? Whatever shall I do? He must not see me; I would not have him see me here for the world.'

An ominous sound of talking: the justices were evidently coming forth. Mr. Dill laid hold of Barbara, whisked her through the clerk's room, not daring to take her the other way lest he should encounter them, and shut her in his own. 'What brought papa here at this moment?' thought Barbara, whose face was crimson.

A few minutes and Mr. Dill opened the door again. 'They are gone now, and the coast's clear, Miss Barbara.'

'I don't know what opinion you must form of me, Mr. Dill,' she whispered, 'but I will tell you in confidence that I am here on some business for mamma, who was not well enough to come herself. It is a little private matter that she does not wish papa to know of.'

'Child,' answered the manger, 'a lawyer receives visits from many people; and it is not the place of those about him to "think."'

He opened the door as he spoke, ushered her into the presence of Mr. Carlyle, and left her. The latter rose in astonishment.

'You must regard me as a client, and pardon the intrusion,' said Barbara, with a forced laugh to hide her agitation. 'I am here on the part of mamma: and I nearly met papa in your passage, which terrified me out of my senses. Mr. Dill shut me into his room.'

Mr. Carlyle motioned to Barbara to seat herself, and then resumed his own seat, beside his table. Barbara could not avoid noticing how different his manners were in his office, from his evening manners when he was 'off duty.' Here he was the staid, calm man of business.

'I have a strange thing to tell you,' she began, in a whisper, 'but—is it possible that any one can hear us?' she broke off with a look of dread. 'It would be—it might be—death.'

'It is quite impossible,' calmly replied Mr. Carlyle. 'The doors are double doors: did you not notice that they were?'

Nevertheless, she left her chair, and stood close to Mr. Carlyle, resting her hand upon the table. He rose, of course.

'Richard is here.'

'Richard!' repeated Mr. Carlyle. 'At West Lynne!'

'He appeared at the house last night in disguise, and made signs to me from the grove of trees. You may imagine my alarm. He has been in London all this while, half starving, working—I feel ashamed to mention it to you— in a stable-yard. And oh, Archibald! he says he is innocent.'

Mr. Carlyle made no reply to this: he probably had no faith in the assertion. 'Sit down, Barbara,' he said, drawing her chair closer.

Barbara sat down again, but her manner was hurried and nervous. 'Is it quite sure that no stranger will be coming in? It would look so peculiar to see me here. But mamma was too unwell to come herself—or rather, she feared papa's questioning, if he found out that she came.'

'Be at ease,' replied Mr. Carlyle: 'this room is sacred from the intrusion of strangers. What of Richard?'

'He says that he was not in the cottage at the time the murder was committed. That the person who really did it was a man of the name of Thorn.'

'What Thorn?' asked Mr. Carlyle, suppressing all sign of incredulity.

'I don't know: a friend of Afy's, he said. Archibald, he swore to it in the most solemn manner: and I believe, as truly as that I am now repeating it to you, that he was speaking truth. I want you to see Richard, if possible: he is coming to the same place to-night. If he can tell his own tale to you, perhaps you might find out a way by which his innocence may be made manifest. You are so clever; you can do anything.'

Mr. Carlyle smiled. 'Not quite anything, Barbara. Was this the purport of Richard's visit—to say this?'

'Oh no: he thinks it is of no use to say it, for nobody would believe him against the evidence. He came to ask for a hundred pounds; he says he has an opportunity of doing better if he can have that sum. Mamma has sent me to you: she has not the money by her, and she dare not ask papa for it, as it is for Richard. She bade me say that if you will kindly oblige her with the money to-day, she will arrange with you about the repayment.'

'Do you want it now?' asked Mr. Carlyle. 'If so I must send to the bank. Dill never keeps much money in the house when I am away.'

'Not until evening. Can you manage to see Richard?'

'It is hazardous,' mused Mr. Carlyle: 'for him, I mean. Still, if he is to be in the grove to-night, I may as well be there also. What disguise is he in?'

'A farm labourer's—the best he could adopt about here—with large black whiskers. He is stopping about three miles off, he said, in some obscure hiding-place. And now,' continued Barbara, 'I want you to advise me: had I better inform mamma that Richard is here or not?'

Mr. Carlyle did not understand: and said so.

'I declare I am bewildered,' she exclaimed. 'I should have premised that I have not yet told mamma it is Richard himself that is here: but that he had sent a messenger to beg for this money. Would it be advisable to acquaint her?'

'Why should you not? I think you ought to do so.'

'Then I will. I was fearing the hazard, for she is sure to insist upon seeing him. Richard also wishes for an interview.'

'It is only natural. Mrs. Hare must be thankful to hear, so far, that he is safe.'

'I never saw anything like it,' returned Barbara; 'the change is akin to magic: she says it has put life into her anew. And now for the last thing: how can we secure papa's absence from home to-night? It must be accomplished in some way. You know his temper: were I or mamma to suggest to him to go and see any friend, or to go to the club, he would immediately stop at home. Can you devise any plan? You see I appeal to you in all my troubles,' she added, 'as I and Anne used to do, when we were children.'

It may be questioned if Mr. Carlyle heard the last remark. He drooped his eyelids in thought. 'Have you told me all?' he asked presently, lifting them.

'I think so.'

'Then I will consider it over, and—'

'I shall not like to come here again,' interrupted Barbara. 'It—it—might excite suspicion; some one might see me, too, and mention it to papa. Neither ought you to send to our house.'

'Well—contrive to be in the street at four this afternoon. Stay, that's your dinner-hour; be walking up the street at three, three precisely; I will meet you.'

He rose, shook hands, and escorted Barbara through the small hall, along the passage to the house door: a courtesy probably not yet shown to any client by Mr. Carlyle. The door closed upon her, and Barbara had taken one step from it when something large loomed down upon her, like a ship in full sail.

She must have been the tallest lady in the world—out of a caravan. A fine woman in her day, but angular and bony now. Still, in spite of the angles and the bones, there was majesty in the appearance of Miss Carlyle.

'Why—what on earth!" began she—'have *you* been with Archibald?'

Barbara Hare stammered out the excuse she had given Mr. Dill.

'Your mamma sent you on business! I never heard of such a thing. Twice have I been in to see Archibald, and twice did Dill answer that he was engaged and must not be interrupted. I shall make old Dill explain his meaning for observing a mystery to me.'

'There is no mystery,' answered Barbara, feeling quite sick lest Miss Carlyle should proclaim there was, before the clerks, or to her father. 'Mamma wanted Mr. Carlyle's opinion upon a little private business, and, not feeling well enough to come herself, she sent me.'

Miss Carlyle did not believe a word. 'What business?' asked she, unceremoniously.

'It is nothing that could interest you. A trifling matter, relating to a little money. It's nothing, indeed.'

'Then, if it's nothing, why were you closeted so long with Archibald?'

'He was asking the particulars,' replied Barbara, recovering her equanimity.

Miss Carlyle sniffed: as she invariably did when dissenting from a problem. She was sure there was some mystery astir. She turned, and walked down the street with Barbara, but she was none the more likely to get anything out of her.

Mr. Carlyle returned to his room, deliberated a few moments, and then rang his bell. A clerk answered it.

'Go to the Buck's Head. If Mr. Hare and the other magistrates are there, ask them to step over to me.'

The young man did as he was bid, and came back with the noted justices at his heels. They obeyed the summons with alacrity: for they believed they had got themselves into a judicial scrape, and that Mr. Carlyle alone could get them out of it.

'I will not request you to sit down,' began Mr. Carlyle, 'for it is barely a moment I shall detain you. The more I think about this man's having been put in prison, the less I like it; and I have been considering that you had better, all five, come and smoke your pipes at my house this evening, when we shall have time to discuss what must be done. Come at seven, not later; and you will find my father's old jar replenished with the best broadcut, and half a dozen churchwarden pipes. Shall it be so?'

The whole five accepted the invitation eagerly. And they were filing out, when Mr. Carlyle laid his finger on the arm of Justice Hare.

'*You* will be sure to come, Mr. Hare,' he whispered. 'We could not get on without you: all heads,' with a slight inclination towards those going out, 'are not gifted with the clear good sense of yours.'

'Sure and certain,' responded the gratified justice: 'fire and water shouldn't keep me away.'

Soon after Mr. Carlyle was left alone, another clerk entered. 'Miss Carlyle is asking to see you, sir, and Colonel Bethel's come again.'

'Send in Miss Carlyle first,' was the answer. 'What is it, Cornelia?'

'Ah! You may well ask me what! Saying this morning that you could not dine at six, as usual, and then marching off, and never fixing the hour. How can I give my orders?'

'I thought business would have called me out, but I am not going now. We will dine a little earlier, Cornelia: say a quarter before six. I have invit—'

'What's up, Archibald?' interrupted Miss Carlyle.

'Up! Nothing, that I know of. I am very busy, Cornelia, and Colonel Bethel is waiting; I will talk to you at dinner-time.'

In reply to this plain hint, Miss Carlyle deliberately seated herself in the client's chair, and crossed her legs, her shoes and her white stockings in full view: for Miss Corny disdained long dresses as much as she disdained crinoline; or, as the inflated machines were called then, corded petticoats, crinoline not having come in. 'I mean, what's up at the Hares, that Barbara should come here and be closeted with you? Business for her mother, she said.'

'Why, you know the mess that Hare and the other justices have got into; committing that poor fellow to prison, because he was seen to pull up a weed in his garden on the Sunday,' returned Mr. Carlyle, after an almost imperceptible pause. 'Mrs. Hare—'

'A set of bumber-headed old donkeys!' was the complimentary interruption of Miss Carlyle. 'The whole bench have not an ounce of sense between them.'

'Mrs. Hare is naturally anxious for my opinion, for there may be some trouble over it, the man having appealed to the Secretary of State. She was too ill, Barbara said, to come to me herself. Cornelia, I have invited a party for to-night.'

'A party!' echoed Miss Carlyle.

'Four or five of the justices; they are coming in to smoke their pipes. You must put out my father's leaden tobacco box, and—'

'They shan't come,' screamed Miss Carlyle. 'Do you think I'll be poisoned with tobacco-smoke from a dozen pipes?'

'You need not sit in the room.'

'Nor they either. Clean curtains are just put up throughout the house, and I'll have no horrid pipes to blacken them.'

'Cornelia,' returned Mr. Carlyle, in a grave, firm tone, which, opinionated as she was, never failed in its effect upon her, 'my having them is a matter of business; of business, you understand; and come they must. If you object to their being in the sitting-rooms, they must be in my bedroom.'

The word 'business' always bore for Miss Carlyle one meaning, that of money-making. Mr. Carlyle knew her weak point, and sometimes played upon it, when he could gain his end by no other means. Her love for money amounted almost to a passion; to acquire it, or to hear that he was acquiring it, was very dear to her. The same could not be said of him; many and many a dispute, that would have brought him in pounds and pounds, had it gone on to an action, did he labour to soothe down; and had reconciled his litigants by his plain sincere advice.

'I'll buy you some new curtains, Cornelia, if their pipes spoil these,' he quietly resumed. 'And I really must beg you to leave me.'

'When I have come to the bottom of this affair with Barbara Hare,' resolutely returned Miss Corny, dropping the point of contest as to the pipes. 'You are very clever, Archie, but you can't deceive me. I asked Barbara what she came here for: business for her mamma, touching money matters, was her reply. I ask you: to hear your opinion about the scrape the bench have got into, is yours. Now, its neither one nor the other, and I tell you, Archibald, I'll hear what it is. I should like to know what you and Barbara do with a secret between you.'

She sat bolt upright in her chair and stared at him, her lofty figure drawn to its full height. Not in features were they alike; some resemblance, perhaps, there might be in the expanse of the forehead and the way in which the hair grew, arched from the temples: Miss Carlyle's hair was going grey now, and she wore it in curls which were rarely smooth, fastened back by combs which were rarely in their places. Her face was pale, well-shaped, and remarkable for nothing but a hard, decisive expression; her eyes, wide open and penetrating, were of a shade called 'green.' But though she could not boast her brother's good looks, there were many plainer women in West Lynne than Cornelia Carlyle.

Mr. Carlyle knew her and her resolute expression well, and he took his course, to tell her the truth. She was, to borrow the words Barbara had used to her brother with regard to him, true as steel. Confide to Miss Carlyle a secret, and she was trustworthy and impervious as he could be: but, let her once suspect that there was a secret which was being kept from her, and she would set to work like a ferret, and never stop till it was unearthed.

Mr. Carlyle bent forward and spoke in a whisper. 'I will tell you if you wish, Cornelia, but it is not a pleasant thing to hear. Richard Hare has returned.'

Miss Carlyle looked perfectly aghast. 'Richard Hare! Is he mad?'

'It is not a very sane proceeding. He wants money from his mother, and Mrs. Hare sent Barbara to ask me to manage it for her. No wonder poor Barbara was flurried and nervous, for there's danger on all sides.'

'Is he at their house?'

'How could he be there, and his father in it? He is in hiding two or three miles off, disguised as a labourer, and will be at the Grove to-night to receive this money. I have invited the justices, to get Mr. Hare safe away from his own house: if he saw Richard, he would undoubtedly give him up to justice, and—putting graver considerations aside—that would be pleasant neither for you nor for me. To have a connection hanged for wilful murder would be an ugly blot on the Carlyle escutcheon, Cornelia.'

Miss Carlyle sat in silence, revolving the news, a contraction on her ample brow.

'And now you know all, Cornelia, and I do beg you to leave me, for I am overwhelmed with work to-day.'

She rose without a word, passed out, and left her brother in peace. He snatched up a note, the first apparently that lay to hand, put it in an envelope, sealed and addressed it to himself. Then he called in Mr. Dill, and gave it to him. The latter looked in surprise at the superscription.

'At eight o'clock to-night, Dill, bring this to my house. Don't send it in, ask for me. You understand.'

The old gentleman replied by a nod, and put the note in his pocket.

Mr. Carlyle was walking down the street at three o'clock that afternoon, when he met Barbara Hare. 'It is all arranged,' he said to her in passing. 'I entertain the bench of justices to-night, Barbara, to pipes and ale, Mr. Hare being one.'

She looked up in doubt. 'Then—if you entertain them, you will not be able to come and meet Richard.'

'Trust to me,' was all his answer, as he hurried on.

✿ V I ✿

Richard Hare, the Younger

The bench of justices did not fail to keep their appointment: at seven o'clock they arrived at Miss Carlyle's, one following closely upon the heels of another. The reader may dissent from the expression 'Miss Carlyle's,' but it is the correct one, for the house was hers, not her brother's. Though it remained his home, as it had been in his father's time, the house was amongst the property bequeathed to Miss Carlyle.

Miss Carlyle chose to be present, in spite of the pipes and the smoke, and she was soon as deep in the discussion as the justices were. It was said in the town that she was as good a lawyer as her father had been: she undoubtedly possessed sound judgment in legal matters, and quick penetration. At eight oclock a servant entered the room and addressed his master.

'Mr. Dill is asking to see you, sir.'

Mr. Carlyle rose, and came back with an open note in his hand.

'I am sorry to find that I must leave you for half an hour. Some important business has arisen, but I will be back as soon as I can.'

'Who has sent for you?' immediately demanded Miss Corny.

He gave her a quiet look, which she interpreted into a warning not to question. 'Mr. Dill is here, and will join you to talk the affair over,' he said to his guests. 'He knows the law better than I do: but I shall not be long.'

He quitted his house, and walked with a rapid step towards the Grove. The moon was bright, as on the previous evening. After he had left the town behind him, and was passing the scattered villas already mentioned, he cast an involuntary glance at the Wood, which rose behind them on his left hand. It was called Abbey Wood, from the circumstance that in old days an abbey had stood in its vicinity, all trace of which, save tradition, had long passed away. There was one small house, or cottage, just within the wood, and in that cottage had occurred the murder for which Richard Hare's life was in jeopardy. It was no longer occupied, for nobody would rent it or live in it.

Mr. Carlyle opened the gate of the Grove, and glanced at the trees on either side him, but he neither saw nor heard any signs of Richard's being concealed there. Barbara was at the window, looking out, and she came herself and opened the door to Mr. Carlyle.

'Mamma is in a most excited state,' she whispered to him as he entered. 'I knew how it would be.'

'Has he come yet?'

'I have no doubt of it, but he has made no signal.'

Mrs. Hare, feverish and agitated, with a burning spot on her delicate cheeks, stood by her chair, not occupying it. Mr. Carlyle placed a pocketbook in her hands. 'I have brought it chiefly in notes,' he said; 'they will be easier for him to carry than gold.'

Mrs. Hare answered only by a look of gratitude, and clasped Mr. Carlyle's hand in both of hers. 'Archibald, I *must* see my boy; how can it be managed? Must I go into the garden to him, or may he come in here?'

'I think he might come in; you know how very bad the night air is for you. Are the servants astir much this evening?'

'Things seem to have turned out quite kindly,' said Barbara. 'It happens to be Anne's birthday, so mamma sent me just now into the kitchen with a cake and a bottle of wine, desiring them to drink her health. I shut the door, and told them to make themselves comfortable; that if we wanted anything, we would ring.'

'Then they are safe,' observed Mr. Carlyle, 'and Richard may come in.'

'I will go and ascertain whether he is come,' said Barbara.

'Stay where you are, Barbara, I will go myself,' interposed Mr. Carlyle. 'Have the door open when you see us coming up the path.'

Barbara gave a faint cry, and, trembling, clutched the arm of Mr. Carlyle. 'There he is! See: standing out from the trees, just opposite this window.'

Mr. Carlyle turned to Mrs. Hare. 'I shall not bring him in immediately. For, if I am to have an interview with him, it must be got over first, that I may go back home to the justices, and keep Mr. Hare all safe.'

He proceeded on his way, gained the trees, and plunged into them; and, leaning against one, stood Richard Hare. Apart from his disguise, and the false and fierce black whiskers, he was a blue-eyed, fair, pleasant-looking young man, slight, and of middle height, and quite as yielding and gentle as his mother. In her, this mild yieldingness of disposition was rather a graceful quality; in Richard it was regarded as a contemptible misfortune. In his boyhood he had been nicknamed Leafy Dick, and when a stranger inquired why, the answer was, that as a leaf is swayed by the wind, so he was swayed by everybody about him, never possessing a will of his own. In short, Richard Hare, though of an amiable, loving nature, was not overburdened with what the world call brains. Brains he certainly had, but they were not sharp ones.

'Is my mother coming out to me?' asked Richard, after a few interchanged sentences with Mr. Carlyle.

'No. You are to go in-doors. Your father is away, and the servants are shut up in the kitchen and will not see you. Though if they did, they could never recognize you in that trim. A fine pair of whiskers, Richard.'

'Let us go in, then. I am all in a twitter till I get away. Am I to have the money?'

'Yes, yes. But, Richard, your sister says you wish to disclose to me the true history of that lamentable night. You had better speak while we are here.'

'It was Barbara who wanted you to hear it; I think it of little moment. If the whole place heard the truth from me, it would do no good, for I should get no belief: not even from you.'

'Try me, Richard: in as few words as possible.'

'Well—there was a row at home about my going so much to Hallijohn's. The governor and my mother thought I went after Afy; perhaps I did, perhaps I didn't. Hallijohn had asked me to lend him my gun, and that evening, when I went to see Af—when I went to see some one—never mind——'

'Richard,' interrupted Mr. Carlyle, 'there's an old saying, and it is sound advice, "Tell the whole truth to your lawyer and your doctor." If I am to judge whether anything can be attempted for you, you must tell it to me; otherwise I would rather hear nothing. It shall be sacred trust.'

'Then, if I must, I must,' returned the yielding Richard. 'I did love the girl; I would have waited till I was my own master to make her my wife, though it had been for years and years. I could not do it, you know, in the face of my father's opposition.'

'Your wife?' rejoined Mr. Carlyle, with some emphasis.

Richard looked surprised. 'Why, you don't suppose I meant anything else! I wouldn't have been such a blackguard.'

'Well, go on, Richard. Did she return your love?'

'I can't be certain. Sometimes I thought she did, sometimes not; she used to play and shuffle, and she liked too much to be with—him. I thought her capricious—telling me I must not come this evening, and I must not come the other; but I found out they were the evenings she expected him. We were never there together.'

'You forget that you have not indicated "him" by any name, Richard. I am at fault.'

Richard Hare bent forward till his black whiskers brushed Mr. Carlyle's shoulder. 'It was that cursed Thorn.'

Mr. Carlyle remembered the name Barbara had mentioned. 'Who was Thorn? I never heard of him.'

'Neither did anybody else, I expect, in West Lynne. He took precious good care of that. He lived some miles away, and used to come over in secret.'

'Courting Afy?'

'Yes, he did come courting her,' returned Richard, in a savage tone. 'Distance was no barrier. He would come galloping over at dusk, tie his horse to a tree in the wood, and pass an hour or two with Afy, in the house, when her father was not at home; roaming about the wood with her, when he was.'

'Come to the point, Richard: to the evening.'

'Hallijohn's gun was out of order, and he requested the loan of mine. I had made an appointment with Afy to be at her house that evening, and I went down after dinner, carrying the gun with me. My father called after me to know where I was going: I said, out with young Beauchamp, not caring to meet with his opposition; and the lie told against me at the inquest. When I reached Hallijohn's, going the back way along the fields and through the wood path as I generally did go, Afy came out all reserve, as she could be at times, and said she was unable to receive me then, that I must go back home. We had a few words about it, and as we were speaking, Locksley passed, and saw me with the gun in my hand; I gave way to her, she could do just what she liked with me, for I loved the very ground she trod on. I gave her the gun, telling her it was loaded, and she took it in-doors, shutting me out. I did not go away, I had a suspicion that she had got Thorn there, though she denied it to me; and I hid myself in some trees near the house. Again Locksley came in view and saw me there, and called out to know why I was hiding. I went farther off, and did not answer him—what were my private movements to him?—and that also told against me at the inquest. Not long afterwards, twenty minutes, perhaps, I heard a shot, which seemed to be in the direction of the cottage. "Somebody having a late pop at the partridges," thought I: for the sun was then setting, and at the moment I saw Bethel emerge from the trees and run in the direction of the cottage. That was the shot that killed Hallijohn.'

There was a pause. Mr. Carlyle looked keenly at Richard Hare in the moonlight.

'Very soon, almost in the same minute, as it seemed, one came panting and tearing along the path leading from the cottage. It was Thorn. His appearance startled me: I had never seen a man show more utter terror. His face was livid, his eyes seemed starting, and his lips were drawn back from his teeth. Had I been a strong man, I should surely have attacked him; I was mad with jealousy; for I then saw that Afy had sent me away that she might entertain him.'

'I thought you said this Thorn never came but at dusk?' observed Mr. Carlyle.

'I never knew him to do so until that evening. All I can say is, he was there then. He flew along swiftly, and I afterwards heard the sound of his horse's hoofs, galloping away. I wondered what was up, that he should look so scared; I wondered whether he had quarrelled with Afy. I ran to the house, leaped up the two steps, and—Carlyle—I fell over the prostrate body of Hallijohn! He was lying just within, on the kitchen floor, dead. Blood was round about him, and my gun, just discharged, was thrown near: he had been shot in the side.'

Richard stopped for breath. Mr. Carlyle did not speak.

'I called to Afy. No one answered. No one was in the lower rooms; and it seemed that no one was in the upper. A sort of panic came over me, a fear: you know they always said at home I was a coward: I could not have remained another minute with that dead man, had it been to save my own life. I caught up the gun, and was making off, when—'

'Why did you catch up the gun?' interrupted Mr. Carlyle.

'Ideas pass through our minds quicker than we can speak them, especially in these sort of moments,' was the reply of Richard Hare. 'Some vague notion flashed on my brain that *my gun* ought not to be found near the murdered body of Hallijohn. I was flying from the door, I say, when Locksley emerged from the wood, full in view, and what possessed me I can't tell, but I did the worst thing I could do—flung the gun in-doors again, and got away, although Locksley called after me to stop.'

'Nothing told so much against you as that,' observed Mr. Carlyle. 'Locksley deposed that he had seen you leave the cottage, gun in hand, apparently in great commotion; that the moment you saw him, you hesitated, as from fear, flung back the gun, and escaped.'

Richard stamped his foot. 'Ay; and all owing to my cursed cowardice. They had better have made a woman of me, and brought me up in petticoats. But let me go on. I came upon Bethel: he was standing in that half-circle where the trees have been cut. Now I knew that Bethel, if he had gone straight in the direction of the cottage, must have met Thorn quitting it. "Did you encounter that hound?" I asked him. "What hound?" returned Bethel. "That fine fellow, that Thorn, who comes after Afy," I answered, for I did not mind mentioning her name in my passion. "I don't know any Thorn," returned Bethel, "and I did not know anybody was after Afy, but yourself." "Did you hear a shot?" I went on. "Yes, I did," he replied; "I suppose it was Locksley, for he's about this evening." "And I saw you," I continued, "just in the moment the shot was fired, turn round the corner in the direction of Hal-lijohn's." "So I did," he said, "but only to strike into the wood, a few paces up. What's your drift?" "Did you not encounter Thorn, running from the cottage?" I persisted. "I have encountered no one," he said, "and I don't be-lieve anybody is about but ourselves and Locksley." 'I quitted him and came off,' concluded Richard Hare; 'he evidently had not seen Thorn, and knew nothing.'

'And you decamped the same night, Richard? It was a fatal step.'

'Yes, I was a fool. I thought I'd wait quiet, and see how things turned out; but you don't know all. Three or four hours later, I went to the cottage again, and I managed to get a minute's speech with Afy. I never shall forget it; be-fore I could say a syllable she flew out at me, accusing me of being the mur-derer of her father, and she fell into hysterics out there on the grass. The noise brought people from the house—plenty were in it then—and I re-treated. "If *she* can think me guilty, the world will think me guilty," was my argument, and that night I went right off, to stop in hiding for a day or two, till I saw my way clear. It never came clear: the coroner's inquest sat, and the verdict floored me for ever. And Afy—but I won't curse her—fanned the flame against me, by denying that any one had been there that night. She had been at home alone, she said, and had strolled out at the back door, to the path that led from West Lynne, and was lingering there when she heard a shot. Five minutes afterwards she returned to the house, and found Locksley standing over her dead father.'

Mr. Carlyle remained silent, rapidly running over in his mind the chief points of Richard Hare's communication. 'Four of you, as I understand it, were in the vicinity of the cottage that night, and from one or other the shot no doubt proceeded. You were at a distance, you say, Richard; Bethel also could not have been—'

'It was not Bethel who did it,' interrupted Richard; 'it is an impossibility. I saw him, as I tell you, in the same moment that the gun was fired.'

'But now, where was Locksley?'

'It is equally impossible that it could have been Locksley. He was within my view at the time, at right angles from me, deep in the wood, away from the paths altogether. It was Thorn did the deed, beyond all doubt, and the verdict ought to have been wilful murder against him. Carlyle, I see you don't believe my story.'

'What you say has startled me, and I must take time to consider whether I believe it or not,' replied Mr. Carlyle, in his straightforward manner. 'The most singular thing, if you witnessed Thorn's running away from the cottage in the manner you describe, is, that you did not come forward, and denounce him.'

'I didn't do it because I was a fool, a weak coward, as I have been all my life,' rejoined Richard. 'I can't help it: it was born with me, and will go with me to my grave. What would have been my word, that it was Thorn, when there was nobody to corroborate it? and the discharged gun, mine, was a damnatory proof against me.'

'Another thing strikes me as curious,' cried Mr. Carlyle. 'If this man, Thorn, was in the habit of coming to West Lynne, evening after evening, how was it that he was never observed? This is the first time I have heard any stranger's name mentioned in connection with the affair, or with Afy.'

'Thorn chose by-roads, and he never came, save that once, but at dusk or dark. It was evident to me at the time that he was courting her in secret. I told Afy so; and that it argued no good for her. You are not attaching credit to what I say, and it is only what I expected; nevertheless, I swear that I have related facts. As surely as that we—I, Thorn, Afy, and Hallijohn—must one day meet together before our Maker, I have told you the truth.'

The words were solemn, their tone earnest, and Mr. Carlyle remained silent, his thoughts full.

'To what end, else, should I say this?' went on Richard. 'It can do me no service: all the assertions I could put forth would not go a jot towards clearing me.'

'No, it would not,' assented Mr. Carlyle. 'If ever you are cleared, it must be by proofs. But—I will keep my thoughts on the matter, and should anything arise—What sort of a man was this Thorn?'

'In age he might have been three or four and twenty, tall and slender; an out-and-out aristocrat.'

'And his connections? Where did he live?'

'I never knew. Afy, in her boasting way, would say he had to come from Swainson! a ten-mile ride!'

'From Swainson!' quickly interrupted Mr. Carlyle. 'Could it be one of the Thorns of Swainson?'

'None of the Thorns there that I know. He was a totally different man, with his perfumed hands, and his rings, and his dainty gloves. That he was an aristocrat I believe, but of bad taste and style, displaying a profusion of jewellery.'

A half smile flitted over Mr. Carlyle's face. 'Was it real, Richard?'

'It was. He would wear diamond shirt-studs, diamond rings, diamond pins; brilliants, all of the first water. My impression was, that he put them on to dazzle Afy. She told me once that she could be a grander lady, if she chose, than I could ever make her. A lady on the cross, I answered her, but never on the square. Thorn was not a man to entertain honest intentions to one in the station of Afy Hallijohn; but girls are as simple as geese.'

'By your description it could not have been one of the Thorns of Swainson. Wealthy tradesmen, fathers of young families, short, stout, and heavy as Dutchmen, staid and most respectable. Very unlikely men, are they, to run into an expedition of the sort.'

'What expedition?' questioned Richard. 'The murder?'

'The riding after Afy. Richard, where is Afy?'

Richard Hare lifted his face in surprise. 'How should I know? I was just going to ask you.'

Mr. Carlyle paused. He thought Richard's answer an evasive one. 'She disappeared immediately after the funeral; and it was thought—in short, Richard, the neighbourhood gave her credit for having gone after and joined you.'

'No! did they? what a pack of idiots! I have never seen or heard of her, Carlyle, since that unfortunate night. If she went after anybody, it was after Thorn.'

'Was the man good-looking?'

'I suppose the world would call him so. Afy thought such an Adonis had never been coined, out of fable. He had shiny black hair and whiskers, dark eyes and handsome features. But his vain dandyism spoilt him.'

Mr. Carlyle could ascertain no more particulars, and it was time Richard went in-doors. They proceeded up the path. 'What a blessing it is the servants' windows don't look this way,' shivered Richard, treading on Mr. Carlyle's heels. 'If they should be looking out up-stairs!'

His apprehensions were groundless, and he entered unseen. Mr. Carlyle's part was over; he left the banned exile to his short interview with his hysterical and tearful mother, Richard nearly as hysterical as she, and made the best of his way home again, pondering over what he had heard.

Not a shadow of doubt had hitherto existed in his mind that George Hallijohn had met his death at the hands of Richard Hare. But, in defiance of the coroner's jury, and the universal opinion, he had never believed it to be *wilful* murder. Richard was mild, kind, inoffensive, the last man to be guilty of cruelty, or to commit a deliberate crime; and Mr. Carlyle had always thought that, could the truth be brought to light, the fatal shot would be found to have been the result of an accident, or, at worst, a scuffle, in which the gun might have gone off. It was rumoured that Hallijohn had objected to Richard's visits to his daughter, and it might have come, that night, to an outbreak.

Who was this Thorn? He certainly could not be a creation of Richard's inventive faculties; still, it was strange that his name had never been mentioned; that himself and his visits were unknown to the neighbourhood. Was the fellow an aristocrat, as Richard had called him, shallow-pated and contemptible, with his shiny hair and his bejewelled fingers, or was he a member of the swell mob? And was he in truth the real author of the murder? Be it as it would, sufficient food had been supplied to call forth all Mr. Carlyle's acumen—and he possessed no slight share.

The magistrates made a good evening of it, Mr. Carlyle entertaining them to supper, mutton-chops and bread-and-cheese. They took up their pipes for another whiff when the meal was over, but Miss Carlyle retired to bed: the smoke, to which she had not been accustomed since her father's death, had made her head ache and her eyes smart. About eleven they wished Mr. Carlyle good night, and departed, but Mr. Dill, in obedience to a nod from his superior, remained.

'Sit down again a moment, Dill; I want to ask you a question. You are intimate with the Thorns of Swainson: do they happen to have any relative, a nephew, or cousin perhaps, a dandy young fellow?'

'I went over last Sunday fortnight to spend the day with young Jacob,' was the answer of Mr. Dill, one wider from the point than he generally gave. Mr. Carlyle smiled.

'*Young* Jacob! He must be forty, I suppose.'

'About that. But you and I estimate age differently, Mr. Archibald. They have no nephew: the old man never had but those two children, Jacob and Edward. Neither have they any cousin. Rich men they are growing now: Jacob has set up his carriage.'

Mr. Carlyle mused, but he expected the answer, for neither had he heard of the brothers Thorn, tanners, curriers, and leather-dressers, possessing a relative of the name. 'Dill,' he said, 'something has arisen which, in my mind, casts a doubt upon Richard Hare's guilt. I question whether he had anything to do with the murder.'

Mr. Dill opened his eyes. 'But his flight, Mr. Archibald? And his stopping away?'

'Suspicious circumstances, I grant: still, I have good cause to doubt. At the time it happened, some dandy fellow used to come courting Afy Hallijohn in secret: a tall, slender man, as he is described to me, bearing the name of Thorn, and living at Swainson. Could it have been one of the Thorn family?'

'Mr. Archibald!' remonstrated the old clerk: 'as if those two respected gentlemen, with wives and babies, would come sneaking after that fly-away Afy?'

'No reflection on them,' returned Mr. Carlyle. 'This was a young man, three or four and twenty, a head taller than either. I thought it might be a relative.'

'I have repeatedly heard them say that they are alone in the world; that they are the two last of the name. Depend upon it, it was nobody connected with them. Who says anybody came over after Afy, Mr. Archibald? I never knew but of one doing so, and that was Richard Hare.'

Mr. Carlyle could not say, 'Richard himself told me,' so he left the question unanswered. 'Sufficient grounds have been furnished me to cast a doubt upon Richard Hare's guilt, and to lay it upon this Thorn,' he observed. 'And I intend to institute a little private investigation, under the rose, and see if any fact can be brought to light. You must help me.'

'With all my heart,' responded Mr. Dil. 'Not that I believe it could have been any one but Richard.'

'The next time you go to Swainson, try and discover whether a young fellow named Thorn (whether connected with the Thorns or not) was living there at the time. Good-looking, black hair, whiskers, and eyes, and given to deck himself out in diamond pins, studs, and rings. He has been called an aristocrat to me, but I think it equally likely that he was a member of the swell mob, doing the fine gentleman—which they always overdo. See if you can ferret out anything.'

'I will,' said Mr. Dill. And he wished Mr. Carlyle good night.

The servant came in to remove the glasses and the obnoxious pipes, which later Miss Carlyle had ordered to be consigned to the open air the instant they were done with. Mr. Carlyle sat in a brown study: presently he looked round at the man.

'Is Joyce gone to bed?'

'No, sir. She's just going.'

'Send her here when you have taken away those things.'

Joyce came in, the upper servant at Miss Carlyle's. She was of middle height, and would never see five-and-thirty again; her forehead was broad, her grey eyes were deeply set, and her face was pale. Altogether she was plain, but sensible-looking. She was the half-sister to Afy Hallijohn.

'Shut the door, Joyce.'

Joyce did as she was bid, came forward and stood by the table.

'Have you ever heard from your sister, Joyce?' began Mr. Carlyle, somewhat abruptly.

'No, sir,' was the reply. 'I think it would be a wonder if I did hear.'

'Why so?'

'If she could go off after Richard Hare, who had sent her father into his grave, she would be more likely to hide herself and her doings, than to proclaim them to me, sir.'

'Who was that other, that fine gentleman, who came after her?'

The colour mantled in Joyce's cheeks, and she dropped her voice. 'Sir! did you hear of him?'

'Not at the time. Since. He came from Swainson, did he not?'

'I believe so, sir. Afy never would say much about him. We did not agree upon the point; I said a person of his rank would do her no good; and Afy flew out when I spoke against him.'

Mr. Carlyle caught her up. 'His rank! what was his rank?'

'Afy bragged of his being next door to a lord; and he looked like it. I only saw him once; I had gone home early, and there he sat with Afy. His white hands were all glittering with rings, and his shirt was finished off with shining stones, where the buttons ought to be.'

'Have you seen him since?'

'Never since, never but that once, and I don't think I should know him if I did see him. He got up, sir, as soon as I went into the parlour, shook hands with Afy, and left. A fine upright man he was, nearly as tall as you, sir, but very thin; those soldiers always do carry themselves well.'

'How do you know he was a soldier?' quickly rejoined Mr. Carlyle.

'Afy told me so. "The captain," she had used to call him; but she said he was not a captain yet a while—the next grade below it. A—a—

'Lieutenant?' suggested Mr. Carlyle.

'Yes, sir, that was it; Lieutenant Thorn. As he was going through the kitchen that evening he dropped his handkerchief, such a beauty, it was. I picked it up, but Afy snatched it from me, and running to the door, called after him, "Captain Thorn, you have dropped your handkerchief," and he turned, and took it from her. And when he was fairly off she began upon me for coming home and spoiling sport, and we had a quarrel. I had seen young Hare also the same evening in the wood, dodging about as if he waited for the other to go. "She'll come to no good between the two," was my thought, and I said it to her, and a fine passion it put her in. It was but a week afterwards that—the evil happened to poor father.'

'Joyce,' said Mr. Carlyle, 'has it never struck you that Afy is more likely to have followed this Lieutenant Thorn than Richard Hare?'

'No, sir,' answered Joyce; 'I have felt certain always that she is with Richard Hare, and nothing can turn me from the belief. All West Lynne is convinced of it.'

Mr. Carlyle did not attempt to 'turn her from the belief.' He dismissed her, and sat on still revolving the case in all its bearings.

Richard Hare's short interview with his mother had soon terminated. It lasted but a quarter of an hour, both dreading interruption from the servants. And, with the hundred pounds in his pocket and desolation at his heart, the ill-fated young man once more quitted his childhood's home. Mrs. Hare and Barbara watched him steal down the path in the tell-tale moonlight, and gain the road, both feeling that those farewell kisses they had pressed upon his lips would not be renewed for years, and might be never.

⚜ VII ⚜

Miss Carlyle at Home

The church clocks of West Lynne struck eight one lovely morning in July, and then the bells chimed out, giving token that it was Sunday. Simultaneously with the bells, Miss Carlyle burst out of her bedroom in one of her ordinary morning costumes, but not the one in which she was wont to be seen on a Sunday. She wore a buff gingham gown, reaching nearly to her ankles, and a lavender print 'bedgown, which was tied round the waist with a cord and tassels, and ornamented off below with a frill. It had been the morning costume of her mother in the old-fashioned days, and Miss Carlyle despised new fashions too much to discard it. Modern ladies might cavil at the style, but they could not at the quality and freshness of the materials, for in that Miss Carlyle was scrupulously particular. On Sunday mornings it was her custom to appear attired for the day, and her not doing so now proved that she must have some domestic work in prospect. Her head-dress cannot be described; it was like nothing in the mode-book or out of it: some might have called it a turban, some a night-cap, and some might have thought it was taken from a model of the dunce's cap and bells in the parish school; at any rate, it was something very high, and expansive, and white, and stern and imposing.

Miss Carlyle stepped across the corridor to a door opposite her own, and gave a thump at it, sufficiently loud to awaken the seven sleepers. 'Get up, Archibald.'

'Up!' cried a drowsy voice within. 'What for? It's only eight o'clock.'

'If it's only six, you must get up,' repeated Miss Carlyle, in her authoritative manner. 'The breakfast is waiting, and I must have it over, for we are all at sixes and sevens.'

Miss Carlyle descended the stairs, and entered the breakfast-room, where all appeared in readiness for the meal. She had a sharp tongue on occasions, and a sharp eye always, which saw everything. The room looked on to the street, and the windows were up, their handsome white curtains, spotless as Miss Carlyle's head-dress, waving gently in the summer breeze. Miss Carlyle's eyes peered round the room, and they caught sight of some dust. She strode into the kitchen to salute Joyce with the information. Joyce stood at the kitchen fire superintending the toasting of some bacon.

'How dare you be so negligent, Joyce? You have never dusted the breakfast-parlour.'

'Never dusted it!' returned Joyce; 'where could your eyes have been, ma'am, to see that?'

'On the dust,' replied Miss Carlyle. 'Go and put yours on it, and take the duster with you. I cannot sit down in an untidy room. Just because you have a little extra work to do this morning, you are turning lazy.'

'No, ma'am,' retorted Joyce with spirit, for she felt the charge was perfectly unfounded, 'I have exerted myself to the utmost this morning. I was up at five o'clock to get the double work comfortably over, that you might have no occasion to find fault, and I was as particular over the breakfast-parlour as I always am. You insist upon having the windows thrown up, and of course the dust will fly in.'

Joyce retreated with her duster just as a bell was heard to ring, and a most respectable-looking serving-man, of middle height, portly form, fair complexion, and a scant portion of hair that was turning grey, entered the kitchen.

'Do you want anything, Peter?' inquired Miss Carlyle.

'Master's shaving water, ma'am. He has rung for it.'

'Master can't have it, then,' was the retort of Miss Carlyle. 'Go and say so. Tell him that the breakfast is waiting, and he must shave afterwards.'

Peter retired with the message, most probably softening it in the delivery, and Miss Carlyle presently returned to the breakfast-parlour and seated herself at the table to wait for her brother.

Miss Carlyle the previous evening had embroiled herself in a dispute with her cook. The latter, who was of a fiery temper, retorted insolently, and her mistress gave her warning, for insolence from a servant she never put up with, and rarely indeed was it offered her. The girl, in her heat of passion, said she did not want to wait for warning, she'd go at once: and off she went. Miss Carlyle pronounced the house well rid of her. Miss Carlyle was rigid upon one point—that of having as little work done upon a Sunday as possible, and when the Sunday's dinner was of a nature that could be put forward upon the Saturday, it was required to be done: upon this rock had Miss Carlyle and the cook split. To add to the inconvenience, the housemaid was from home enjoying a holiday.

Mr. Carlyle came into the breakfast-room completely dressed: he had an invincible dislike to appear like a sloven, and he had shaved in cold water. 'Why are we breakfasting at eight this morning?' he inquired.

'Because I have so much to do. And if I cannot get breakfast over early I shall never finish it in time for church,' was the reply of Miss Carlyle. 'The cook's gone.'

'The cook gone!' repeated Mr. Carlyle.

'It all happened after you went out to spend the evening, and I did not sit up to tell you. We are to have ducks for dinner to-day, and she knew they were to be stuffed and prepared yesterday, the gravy made, and the giblet-pie made and baked: in short, everything done, except just the roasting. I asked her last night if it was done. "Oh yes, it was all done," she said; and I told her to bring me the giblet-pie to look at, knowing she has a knack of burning the crust of her pies. Well, she could not; she had told me a falsehood, Archibald, and had got no pie to bring, for the ducks were untouched, just as they came into the house; she had idly put it all off till to-day, thinking I should never find her out, but my asking for the pie floored her. She was insolent, and what with that and the lie, I gave her warning, but she chose to leave last night. I have got it all to do myself this morning.'

'Can't Joyce do it?' returned Mr. Carlyle.

'Joyce! Much she knows about cooking; Joyce's cooking won't do for my table. Barbara Hare is going to spend the day here.'

'Indeed.'

'Barbara called last evening, full of trouble. She and the justice had been having a dispute, and she said she wished I would invite her for to-day. Barbara has been laying in a stock of finery; the justice caught sight of it as it came home, and Barbara suffered. Serve her right, vain little minx. Just hark at the bells clattering out!'

Mr. Carlyle lifted his head. The bells of St. Jude's Church were ringing out a merry peal as for a wedding, or for any other festivity. 'What can that be for?' he exclaimed.

'Archibald, you are not half as sharp as I was at your age. What should they be ringing for, but out of compliment to the arrival of Lord Mount Severn?'

'Ay; no doubt. The East Lynne pew is in St. Jude's Church.'

East Lynne had changed owners, and was now the property of Mr. Carlyle. He had bought it as it stood, furniture and all; but the transfer had been conducted with secrecy, and was suspected by none. Whether Lord Mount Severn thought it might prevent one getting on the scent, or whether he wished to take farewell of a place he had formerly been fond of, certain it is that he desired to visit it for a week or two. Mr. Carlyle most readily and graciously acquiesced; and the earl, his daughter, and retinue had arrived the previous day.

West Lynne was in ecstasies. It called itself an aristocratic place, and it indulged hopes that the earl might be intending to confer upon it permanently the light of his presence, by taking up his residence again at East Lynne. The toilets prepared to greet his admiring eyes were prodigious, and pretty Barbara Hare was not the only young lady who had thereby to encounter the paternal storm.

Miss Carlyle completed her dinner preparations, all she did not choose to trust to Joyce, and was ready for church at the usual time, plainly but well dressed. As she and Archibald were leaving their house, they saw something looming up the street, flashing and gleaming in the sun. A pink parasol came first, a pink bonnet and feather came behind it, a grey brocaded dress, and white gloves.

'The little vain idiot!' ejaculated Miss Carlyle. But Barbara sailed up the street towards them, unconscious of the apostrophe.

'Well done, Barbara!' was the salutation of Miss Carlyle. 'The justice might well call out! you are finer than a sunbeam.'

'Not half so fine as many another in the church will be to-day,' responded Barbara, as she lifted her shy blue eyes and blushing face to answer the greeting of Mr. Carlyle. 'West Lynne seems bent on out-dressing the Lady Isabel. You should have been in at the milliner's yesterday morning, Miss Carlyle.'

'Is all the finery coming out to-day?' gravely inquired Mr. Carlyle, as Barbara turned with them towards the church and he walked by her side and his sister's, for he had an objection, almost as invincible as a Frenchman's, to give his arm to two ladies.

'Of course,' replied Barbara. 'The earl and his daughter will be coming to church.'

'Suppose she should not be in peacock's plumes,' cried Miss Carlyle, with an imperturbable face.

'Oh, but she's sure to be—if you mean richly dressed,' cried Barbara, hastily.

'Or, suppose they should not come to church?' laughed Mr. Carlyle. 'What a disappointment to the bonnets and feathers!'

'After all, Barbara, what are they to us, or we to them?' resumed Miss Carlyle. 'We may never meet. We insignificant West Lynne gentry shall not intrude ourselves into East Lynne. It would scarcely be fitting: or be deemed so by the earl and Lady Isabel.'

'That's just what papa said,' grumbled Barbara. 'He caught sight of this bonnet yesterday, and, when by way of excuse, I said I had it to call on them, he asked whether I thought the obscure West Lynne families would venture to thrust their calls on Lord Mount Severn, as though they were of the county aristocracy. It was the feather put him out.'

'It is a very long one,' remarked Miss Carlyle, grimly surveying it.

Barbara was to sit in the Carlyle pew that day, for she thought the farther she was off the justice the better: there was no knowing but he might take a sly revengeful cut at the feather in the middle of the service, and so dock its beauty. Scarcely were they seated, when some strangers came quietly up the aisle; a gentleman who limped as he walked, with a furrowed brow and grey hair; and a young lady. Barbara looked round with eagerness, but looked away again; they could not be the expected strangers, the young lady's dress was too plain. A clear muslin dress with small lilac sprigs upon it, and a straw bonnet: Miss Corny might have worn it herself on a week day, and not have found herself too smart; but it was a pleasant dress for a hot summer's day. But the old beadle, in his many caped coat, was walking before them sideways with his marshalling baton, and he marshalled them into the East Lynne pew, unoccupied for so many years.

'Who in the world can they be?' whispered Barbara to Miss Carlyle.

'The earl and Lady Isabel.'

The colour flushed into Barbara's face, and she stared at Miss Corny. 'Why—she has no silks, and no feathers, and no anything!' cried Barbara. 'She's plainer than anybody in the church!'

'Plainer than any of the fine ones—than you, for instance. The earl is much altered, but I should have known them both anywhere. I should have known her from her likeness to her poor mother; just the same eyes, and sweet expression.'

Ay, those brown eyes, so full of sweetness and melancholy: few, who had once seen, could mistake or forget them, and Barbara Hare, forgetting where she was, looked at them much that day. 'She is very lovely,' thought Barbara, 'and her dress is certainly that of a lady. I wish I had not had this streaming pink feather. What fine jackdaws she must deem us all!'

The earl's carriage, an open barouche, was waiting at the gate at the conclusion of the service. He handed his daughter in, and was putting his gouty foot upon the step to follow her, when he observed Mr. Carlyle. The earl turned and held out his hand. A man who could purchase East Lynne was worthy of being received as an equal, though he was but a country lawyer.

Mr. Carlyle shook hands with the earl, approached the carriage, and raised his hat to Lady Isabel. She bent forward with her pleasant smile, and put her hand into his.

'I have many things to say to you,' said the earl. 'I wish you would go home with us. If you have nothing better to do, be East Lynne's guest for the remainder of the day.'

He smiled peculiarly as he spoke, and Mr. Carlyle echoed it. East Lynne's guest! that is what the earl was, at present. Mr. Carlyle turned aside to tell his sister.

'Cornelia, I shall not be home to dinner, I am going with Lord Mount Severn. Good day, Barbara.'

Mr. Carlyle stepped into the carriage, was followed by the earl, and it drove away. The sun shone still, but the day's brightness had gone out for Barbara Hare.

'How does he know the earl so well? how does he know Lady Isabel?' she reiterated in her astonishment.

'Archibald knows something of most people,' replied Miss Corny. 'He saw the earl frequently when he was in town in the spring, and Lady Isabel once or twice. What a lovely face she has!'

Barbara made no reply. She returned with Miss Carlyle to the attraction of the ducks and the giblet-pie, but her manner was as absent as her heart, and that had run away to East Lynne.

'Oh, the refinement of courtly life, the unnecessary profusion of splendour!' thought Mr. Carlyle, as he sat down to the earl's dinner-table that day. The display of shining silver, of glittering glass, of costly china; the various wines and the rich viands, too varied and rich for the earl's gout; the many servants in their handsome livery; the table's pleasant master, and its refined young mistress! In spite of the earl's terrible embarrassments, he had never yet curtailed the pomp of home expenditure: how he had maintained it was a marvel; how long he would succeed in maintaining it was another. Very unnecessary and unjustifiable was the splendour under the circumstances, but it had its attractions. Exceedingly great were the attractions that day, all things combined. Take care of your senses, Mr. Carlyle.

Isabel left them after dinner, and sat alone, her thoughts running on many things. On her dear mother, with whom she was last at East Lynne, on the troublesome gout that would not quite leave her father, and on the scenes she had lately mixed in in London. She had met one there so constantly that he had almost become dangerous to her peace, or would have done so, had she remained much longer; even now, as she thought of him, a thrill quickened her veins; it was Francis Levison. Mrs. Vane had been guilty of worse than thoughtlessness, to throw them so frequently together. Mrs. Vane was a cold, selfish, and a bad woman; bad, inasmuch as, save her own heartless self, she cared for no human being on the face of the wide earth.

With a sigh, Isabel rose, and scattered her reflections to the winds. Her father and his guest did not appear to be in a haste to come into tea, and she sat down to the piano.

The earl was certainly not in a haste; he never was in a haste to quit his wine; every glass was little less than poison to him in his state of health, but he would not forego it. They were deep in conversation, when Mr. Carlyle, who was speaking, broke off in the middle of a sentence and listened.

A strain of the sweetest music had arisen; it seemed almost close to his ear, but he knew not whence it came; a voice, low and clear and sweet, was accompanying it, and Mr. Carlyle held his breath. It was the Benedictus, sung to Mornington's chant.

'Blessed be the Lord God of Israel: for he hath visited and redeemed his people. And hath raised up a mighty salvation for us: in the house of his servant David.'

The conversation of the earl and Mr. Carlyle had been of the eager bustling world, of money getting and money spending, money owing and money paying, and that sacred chant broke in upon them with strange contrast, soothing to the ear, but reproving to the heart.

'It is Isabel,' explained the earl. 'Her singing carries a singular charm with it; and I think that charm lies in her subdued, quiet style: I hate squalling display. Her playing is the same. Are you fond of music?'

'I have been reproached by scientific performers with having neither ear nor taste for what they style good music,' smiled Mr. Carlyle; 'but I like *that*.'

'The instrument is placed against the wall, and the partition is thin,' remarked the earl. 'Isabel little thinks she is entertaining us, as well as herself.'

Indeed she did not. She sang chant after chant, now one psalm to them, now another. Then she sang the collect for the seventh Sunday after Trinity, and then she went back again to the chants. And Mr. Carlyle sat on, drinking in that delightful music, and never heeding how the evening was running on into night.

⚜ VIII ⚜

Mr. Kane's Concert

Before Lord Mount Severn had completed the fortnight of his proposed stay, the gout came back seriously. It was impossible for him to move away from East Lynne. Mr. Carlyle assured him he was only too pleased that he should remain as long as might be convenient, and the earl expressed his acknowledgments; he hoped soon to be re-established on his legs.

But he was not. The gout came and the gout went; not positively laying him up in bed, but rendering him unable to leave his rooms: and this continued till October, when he grew much better. The county families had been neighbourly, calling on the invalid earl, and occasionally carrying off Lady Isabel, but his chief and constant visitor had been Mr. Carlyle. The earl had grown to like him in no common degree, and was disappointed if Mr. Carlyle spent an evening away from him, so that he had become, as it were, quite domesticated with the earl and Isabel. 'I am not equal to general society,' he observed to his daughter, 'and it is considerate and kind of Carlyle to come here and cheer my loneliness.'

'Extremely kind,' said Isabel. 'I like him very much, papa.'

'I don't know anybody whom I like half as well,' was the rejoinder of the earl.

Mr. Carlyle went up as usual the same evening, and in the course of it the earl asked Isabel to sing.

'I will if you wish, papa,' was the reply, 'but the piano is so much out of tune that it is not pleasant to sing to it. Is there nobody in West Lynne who could come here and tune my piano, Mr. Carlyle?' she added, turning to him.

'Certainly there is. Kane would do it. Shall I send him to-morrow?'

'I should be glad; if it would not be giving you too much trouble. Not that tuning will benefit it greatly, old thing that it is. Were we to be much at East Lynne, I should get papa to exchange it for a good one.'

Little thought Lady Isabel that very piano was Mr. Carlyle's, and not hers. The earl coughed, and exchanged a smile and a glance with his guest.

Mr. Kane was the organist of St. Jude's Church, a man of embarrassment and sorrow, who had long had a sore fight with the world. When he arrived at East Lynne the following day, Lady Isabel happened to be playing, and she stood by and watched him begin his work. She was courteous and affable; she was so to every one; and the poor music-master took courage to speak of his own affairs, and to prefer an humble request—that she and Lord Mount

Severn would patronize and personally attend a concert he was about to give the following week. A scarlet blush came into his thin cheeks as he confessed that he was very poor, could scarcely live, and that he was getting up this concert in his desperate need. If it succeeded—well: he could then go on again; if not, he should be turned out of his home, and his furniture sold for the two years' rent he owed—and he had seven children.

Isabel, all her sympathies awakened, sought the earl. 'Oh, papa! I have to ask you the greatest favour! Will you grant it?'

'Ay, child, you don't ask them often. What is it?'

'I want you to take me to a concert at West Lynne.'

The earl fell back in surprise and stared at Isabel.

'A concert at West Lynne!' he laughed. 'To hear rustics scraping the fiddle! My dear Isabel!'

She poured out what she had just heard, with her own comments and additions. 'Seven children, papa! and if the concert does not succeed he must give up his home, and turn out into the streets with them—it is, you see, almost as a matter of life or death to him. He is very poor.'

'I am poor myself,' said the earl.

'I was so sorry for him when he was speaking. He kept turning red and white, and catching up his breath in agitation; it was painful to him to tell of his embarrassments. I am sure he is a gentleman.'

'Well, you may take a pound's worth of tickets, Isabel, and give them to the upper servants. A village concert!'

'Oh, papa, it is not that; can't you see it is not? If you and I promise to be present, all the families round West Lynne will attend, and he will have the room full. They will go because we do; he said so; if they thought it was our servants who were going, they would keep away. Just think, papa, how you would like for this furniture to be taken away from you! and his having a full concert would stop it. Make a sacrifice for once, dearest papa, and go, if it be only for an hour: *I* shall enjoy it, if there's nothing but a fiddle and a tambourine.'

'You gipsy! you are as bad as a professional beggar. There, go and tell the fellow we will look in for half an hour.'

She flew back to Mr. Kane, her eyes dancing. She spoke quietly, as she always did, but her own satisfaction gladdened her voice.

'I am happy to tell you that papa has consented. He will take four tickets, and we will attend the concert.'

The tears rushed into Mr. Kane's eyes: Isabel was not sure but they were in her own. He was a tall, thin, delicate-looking man, with long white fingers and a long neck. He faltered forth his thanks, and an inquiry whether he might be allowed to state openly that they would be present.

'Tell everybody,' said she, eagerly—'everybody you meet, if you think it will be the means of inducing people to attend. I shall tell all friends who call upon me, and ask them to go.'

When Mr. Carlyle came up in the evening, the earl was temporarily absent from the room. Isabel began to speak of the concert.

'It is a hazardous venture for Kane,' observed Mr. Carlyle. 'I fear he will only lose money, and add to his embarrassments.'

'Why do you fear that?' she asked.

'Because, Lady Isabel, nothing gets patronized at West Lynne; nothing native; and people have heard so long of poor Kane's necessities, that they think little of them. If some foreign artist, with an unpronounceable name, came flashing down to give a concert, West Lynne would flock to it.'

'Is he so poor, very poor?'

'Very. He is half starved.'

'Starved!' repeated Isabel, an expression of perplexity arising to her face, as she looked at Mr. Carlyle, for she scarcely understood him. 'Do you mean that he does not have enough to eat?'

'Of bread he may, but not much better nourishment. His salary, as organist, is thirty pounds, and he gets a little stray teaching. But he has his wife and children to keep, and no doubt serves them before himself. I dare say he scarcely knows what it is to taste meat.'

The words brought a bitter pang to Lady Isabel. Not enough to eat! Never to taste meat! And she, in her carelessness, her ignorance, her indifference— she scarcely knew what term to give it—had not thought to order him a meal in their house of plenty! He had walked from West Lynne, occupied himself an hour with her piano, and set off to walk back again, battling with his hunger. A word from her, and a repast had been set before him, out of their superfluities, such as he never now sat down to: and that word she had not spoken.

'You are looking grave, Lady Isabel.'

'I am taking contrition to myself. Never mind; it cannot now be helped; but it will always be a dark spot on my memory.'

'What is it?'

She lifted her repentant face to his, and smiled. 'Never mind, I say, Mr. Carlyle; what is past cannot be recalled. He looks like a gentleman.'

'Who? Kane? A gentleman bred: his father was a clergyman. Kane's ruin was his love of music; it prevented his settling to any better-paid profession; his early marriage also was a drawback, and kept him down. He is young still.'

'Mr. Carlyle, I would not be one of your West Lynne people for the world. Here is a poor gentleman struggling with adversity, and you won't put your hands out to help him!'

He smiled at her warmth. 'Some of us will take tickets, I for one, but I don't know about attending the concert. I fear few will do that.'

'Because that's just the thing that would serve him! if one went, another would. Well, I shall try and show West Lynne that I don't take a lesson from their book; I shall be there before it begins, and never come out till the last song is over. I am not too grand to go, if West Lynne is.'

'You surely do not think of going!'

'I surely do think of it. And papa goes with me; I persuaded him. And I have given Mr. Kane the promise.'

Mr. Carlyle paused. 'I am glad to hear it; it will be a perfect boon to Kane. If it once gets abroad that Lord Mount Severn and Lady Isabel intend to honour the concert, there won't be standing room.'

She danced round with a little gleeful step. 'What high and mighty personages Lord Mount Severn and Lady Isabel seem to be! If you had any goodness of heart, Mr. Carlyle, you would enlist yourself in the cause also.'

'I think I will,' he smiled.

'Papa says you hold sway at West Lynne. If you proclaim that you mean to go, you will induce others.'

'I will proclaim that you do,' he answered. 'That will be sufficient. But, Lady Isabel, you must not expect much gratification from the performances.'

'A tambourine will be quite enough for me; I told papa so. I shan't think of the music, I shall think of poor Mr. Kane. Mr. Carlyle, I know you can be kind if you like; I know you would rather be kind than otherwise, it is to be read in your face; try and do what you can do for him.'

'Yes, I will,' he warmly answered.

Mr. Carlyle sold many tickets the following day; or, rather, caused them to be sold. He praised the concert far and wide, and proclaimed that Lord Mount Severn and his daughter would not think of missing it. Mr. Kane's house was besieged for tickets, faster than he could write his signature in their corner, and when Mr. Carlyle went home to luncheon at midday, which he did not often do, he laid down two at Miss Corny's elbow.

'What's this? Concert tickets! Archibald, you have never gone and bought these!'

What would she have said had she known that the two were not the extent of his investment?

'Ten shillings to throw away upon two paltry bits of cardboard!' chafed Miss Carlyle. 'You always were a noodle in money matters, Archibald, and always will be. I wish I had the keeping of your purse!'

'What I have given will not hurt me, Cornelia, and Kane is badly off. Think of his troop of children.'

'Oh dear,' said Miss Corny, 'I imagine he should think of them; I suppose it was his own fault they came. That's always it: poor folks get a heap of children about them, and then ask for pity. I should say it would be more just if they asked for blame.'

'Well, there the tickets are, bought and paid for, so they may as well be used. You will go with me, Cornelia.'

'And stick ourselves there upon empty benches, like two geese, and set staring and counting the candles! A pleasant evening!'

'You need not fear empty benches. The Mount Severns are going, and West Lynne is in a fever, racing after tickets. I suppose you have got a—a—cap,' looking at the nondescript article decorating his sister's head, 'that will be suitable to go in, Cornelia: if not, you had better order one.'

This suggestion put up Miss Carlyle. 'Hadn't you better have your hair curled, and your coat-tails lined with white satin, and buy a gold opera-glass, and a cocked hat?' retorted she. 'My gracious me! a fine new cap to go to their mess of a concert in, after paying ten shillings for the tickets! The world's coming to something.'

Mr. Carlyle left her and her grumbling to return to the office. Lord Mount Severn's carriage was passing at the moment, and Isabel Vane was within it. She caused it to stop when she saw Mr. Carlyle, and he advanced to her.

'I have been to Mr. Kane's myself for the tickets,' she said, with a beaming look; 'I came into West Lynne on purpose. I told the coachman to find out where he lived, and he did. I thought if the people saw me and the carriage there, they would guess what I wanted. I do hope he will have a full concert.'

'I am sure he will,' replied Mr. Carlyle , as he released her hand. And Lady Isabel signed the carriage to drive on.

As Mr. Carlyle turned away, he met Otway Bethel, a nephew of Colonel Bethel's, who was tolerated in the colonel's house because he had no other home, and appeared incapable of making himself one. Some persons persisted in calling him a gentleman—as he was by birth—others called him a *mauvais sujet*. The two are united sometimes. He was dressed in a velveteen suit, and had a gun in his hand; indeed, he was rarely seen without a gun, being inordinately fond of sport; but, if all tales whispered were true, he supplied himself with game in other ways than by shooting, which had the credit of going up to London dealers. For the last six months, or near upon it, he had been away from West Lynne.

'Why, where have you been hiding yourself?' exclaimed Mr. Carlyle. 'The colonel has been inconsolable.'

'Come, no gammon, Carlyle. I have been on the tramp through France and Germany. Man likes a change sometimes. As to the revered colonel, he would not be inconsolable if he saw me nailed up in a six-foot box, and carried out feet foremost.'

'Bethel, I have a question to ask you,' continued Mr. Carlyle, dropping his light manner and his voice together. 'Take your thoughts back to the night of Hallijohn's murder.'

'I wish you may get it!' cried Mr. Bethel. 'The reminiscence is not attractive.'

'You'll do it,' quietly said Mr. Carlyle. 'It has been told to me, though it did not appear at the inquest, that Richard Hare held a conversation with you in the wood, a few minutes after the deed was done. Now—'

'Who told you that?' interrupted Bethel.

'That is not the question. My authority is indisputable.'

'It is true that he did. I said nothing about it, for I did not want to make the case worse against Dick Hare than it already was. He certainly did accost me, like a man flurried out of his life.'

'Asking if you had seen a certain lover of Afy's fly from the cottage. One Thorn.'

'That was the purport. Thorn? Thorn?—I think Thorn was the name he mentioned. My opinion was, that Dick was either wild, or acting a part.'

'Now, Bethel, I want you to answer me truly. The question cannot affect your either way, but I must know whether you did see this Thorn leave the cottage.'

Bethel shook his head. 'I know nothing whatever about any Thorn, and I saw nobody but Dick Hare. Not but what a dozen Thorns might have run from the cottage without my seeing them.'

'You heard this shot fired?'

'Yes; but I never gave a thought to mischief. I knew Locksley was in the wood, and supposed it came from him. I ran across the path, bearing towards the cottage, and struck into the wood on the other side. By-and-by, Dick Hare pitched upon me, like one startled out of his senses, and asked if I had seen Thorn leave the cottage. Thorn—that *was* the name.'

'And you had not?'

'I had seen nobody but Dick, excepting Locksley. My impression was that nobody was about; I think so still.'

'But Richard—'

'Now look you here, Carlyle, I won't do Dick Hare an injury, even by a single word, if I can help it. And it is of no use setting me on to it.'

'I should be the last to set you on to injure any one, especially Richard Hare,' rejoined Mr. Carlyle, 'and my motive is to do Richard good, not harm. I hold a suspicion, no matter whence gathered, that it was not Richard Hare who committed the murder, but another. Can you throw any light upon the subject?'

'No, I can't. I have always thought poor wavering Dick was nobody's enemy but his own: but as to throwing any light upon that night's work, I can't do it. Cords should not have dragged me to the inquest to give evidence against Dick, and for that reason I was glad Locksley never let out that I was on the spot. How the deuce it got about afterwards that I was, I can't tell; but that was no matter; *my* evidence did not help on the verdict. And, talking of that, Carlyle, how has it come to your knowledge that Richard Hare accosted me? I have not opened my lips upon it to mortal man.'

'It is of no consequence how,' repeated Mr. Carlyle; 'I do know it, and that is sufficient. I was in hopes you had really seen this Thorn leave the cottage.'

Otway Bethel shook his head. 'I should not lay too much stress upon any "Thorn's" having been there, were I you, Carlyle. Dick Hare was as one crazy that night, and might see shapes and forms where there were none.'

✄ I X ✄

The Bats at the Window

The concert was to take place on a Thursday, and on the following Saturday Lord Mount Severn intended finally to quit East Lynne. The necessary preparations for departure were in progress, but when Thursday morning dawned, it appeared a question whether they would not once more be rendered nugatory. The house was roused betimes, and Mr. Wainwright, the surgeon from West Lynne, summoned to the earl's bedside: he had experienced another and a violent attack. The peer was exceedingly annoyed and vexed, and very irritable.

'I may be kept here a week—a fortnight—a month longer now!' he uttered fretfully to Isabel.

'I am very sorry, papa. I dare say you do find East Lynne dull.'

'Dull! that's not it: I have other reasons for wishing East Lynne to be quit of us. And now you can't go to this fine concert.'

Isabel's face flushed. 'Not go, papa?'

'Why, who is to take you? I can't get out of bed.'

'Oh, papa, I must be there. Otherwise it would look almost as though—as though we had announced what we did not mean to perform. You know it was arranged that we should join the Ducies: the carriage can still take me to the concert-room, and I can go in with them.'

'Just as you please. I thought you would have jumped at any plea for staying away.'

'Not at all,' laughed Isabel. 'I should like West Lynne to see that I don't despise Mr. Kane and his concert.'

Later in the day, the earl grew alarmingly worse: his paroxysms of pain were awful. Isabel, who was kept from the room, knew nothing of the danger, and the earl's groans did not penetrate to her ears. She dressed herself in a gleeful mood, full of laughing wilfulness, Marvel, her maid, superintending in stiff displeasure, for the attire chosen did not meet her approbation. When ready, she went into the earl's room.

'Shall I do, papa?'

Lord Mount Severn raised his swollen eyelids and drew the clothes from his flushed face. A shining vision was standing before him, a beauteous queen, a gleaming fairy; he hardly knew what she looked like. She had put on a white lace dress and her diamonds; the dress was rich, and the jewels gleamed from her hair, from her pretty neck, from her delicate arms; and her cheeks were flushed and her curls were flowing.

The earl stared at her in amazement. 'How could you dress yourself like that for a concert? You are out of your senses, Isabel.'

'Marvel thinks so too,' was the gay answer; 'she has had a cross face since I told her what to put out. But I did it on purpose, papa; I thought I would show those West Lynne people that *I* think the poor man's concert worth going to, and worth dressing for.'

'You will have the whole room gaping at you.'

'I don't mind. I'll bring you word all about it. Let them gape.'

'You vain child! You have dressed yourself to please your vanity. But, Isabel, you—oooooooh!'

Isabel started as she stood: the earl's groan of pain was dreadful.

'An awful twinge, child. There, go along: talking makes me worse.'

'Papa, shall I stay at home with you?' she gravely asked. 'Every consideration should give way to illness. If you would like me to remain, or if I can do any good, pray let me.'

'Quite the contrary; I had rather you were away. You can do no earthly good, for I could not have you in the room. Good-bye, darling. If you see Carlyle, tell him I hope to see him to-morrow.'

Marvel threw a mantle over her shoulders, and she went down to the carriage, which waited.

The concert was held in the noted justice-room, over the marketplace, called by courtesy the town-hall. It was large, commodius, and good for sound; many a town of far greater importance cannot boast so good a music-room. In the way of performers, Mr. Kane had done his poor best; a lady, quite fourth rate, was engaged from London, and the rest were local artistes.

Barbara Hare would not have missed the concert for the world, but Mrs. Hare had neither health nor spirits for it. It was arranged that the justice and Barbara should accompany the Carlyles, and they proceeded to Miss Carlyle's in time for coffee. Something was said about a fly, but

Miss Carlyle negatived it, asking what had come to their legs: it was a fine night, and the distance very short. Barbara had no objection to the walk with Mr. Carlyle.

'How is it that we see so little of you now?' she began, as they went along, Mr. Justice Hare and Miss Carlyle preceding them.

'I have been so much engaged at East Lynne: the earl finds his evenings dull. They go on Saturday, and my time will be my own again.'

'You were expected at the parsonage last night; we were looking for you all the evening.'

'Not expected by Mr. and Mrs. Little, I think. I told them I was engaged to dine at East Lynne.'

'They were saying—some of them—that you might as well take up your abode at East Lynne, and wondered what your attraction could be. They said'—Barbara compelled her voice to calmness—'that if Isabel Vane were not the Lady Isabel, they should think you went there courting.'

'I am much obliged at their interesting themselves so much about me,' equably returned Mr. Carlyle. 'More so than Lady Isabel Vane would probably be. I am surprised that you should retail such nonsense, Barbara.'

'They said it; I did not,' answered Barbara, with a swelling heart. 'Is it true that Lady Isabel sings so well? They were making out that her singing is divine.'

'You had better not let Cornelia hear you say that, or you will get a reproof,' laughed Mr. Carlyle, 'like I did, when I said she had an angel's face.'

Barbara turned her own face full upon him: it looked pale in the gaslight. 'Did you say she had an angel's face? Do you think it one?'

'I really believe I did say so, but I can't be quite sure; Cornelia snapped me up so quickly,' he answered, laughing. 'Barbara,' he added, dropping his voice, 'we have still not heard from Richard.'

'No. You and mamma both think we shall hear; I say not, for I feel sure he will be afraid to write. I know he promised, but I have never thought he would perform.'

'There would be no risk, sending the letters under cover to me, and it would be a relief and a comfort to Mrs. Hare.'

'You know how timorous Richard is. Otway Bethel is home again,' she continued. 'You said you should question him when he returned, Archibald.'

'I have done so, but he appears to know nothng. He seems well disposed to Richard, but casts doubt on the assertion that Thorn, or any stranger, was in the wood that night.'

'It is very strange what Thorn it could have been.'

'Very,' assented Mr. Carlyle. 'I can make out nothing from Swainson. No person whatever, answering the description and named Thorn, was living there at the time, so far as I am able to ascertain. All we can do is to wait, and hope that time may bring elucidation with it.'

They reached the town-hall as he spoke. A busy crowd was gathered round the entrance; people going in to attend the concert, and the mob watching them. Drawn up at a short distance, so as not to obstruct other vehicles, was the aristocratic carriage of Lord Mount Severn; the coachman sat on his hammercloth, and two powdered footmen waited with it.

'Lady Isabel Vane is sitting there,' exclaimed Barbara as she passed.

Mr. Carlyle felt surprised. What could she be waiting there for? where could the earl be? A doubt came over him, he could not define why, that something was wrong.

'Will you pardon me if I quit you for one moment, Barbara, whilst I speak to Lady Isabel?'

He waited for neither acquiescence nor dissent, but left Barbara standing where she was, and accosted Isabel. The diamonds gleamed in her shining curls, as she bent towards him.

'I am waiting for Mrs. Ducie, Mr. Carlyle. I did not like to remain all alone in the ante-room, so I stayed here. When Mrs. Ducie's carriage comes up, I shall get out. I am going in with her, you know.'

'And the earl?'

'Oh, have you not heard? Papa is ill again.'

'Ill again?' repeated Mr. Carlyle.

'Very ill indeed. Mr. Wainwright was sent for at five o'clock this morning, and has been with him a good deal of the day. Papa bade me say that he hoped to see you to-morrow.'

Mr. Carlyle rejoined Barbara: they entered the hall and began to ascend the stairs, just as another aristocratic equipage dashed up, to scatter and gratify the mob. Barbara turned her head to look: it was that of the Honourable Mrs. Ducie.

The room was pretty full then, and Mrs. Ducie, her two daughters, and Isabel were conducted to seats by Mr. Kane—seats he had reserved for them at the upper end, near the orchestra. The same dazzling vision which had burst on the sight of Lord Mount Severn fell on that of the audience, in Isabel, with her rich white dress, her glittering diamonds, her flowing curls, and her wondrous beauty. The Miss Ducies, plain girls, in brown silks, turned up their noses worse than ever nature had done it for them, and Mrs. Ducie heaved an audible sigh. 'The poor motherless girl is to be pitied, my dears,' she whispered; 'she has nobody to point out to her suitable attire: this ridiculous decking out must have been Marvel's idea.'

But she looked like a lily amidst poppies and sun-flowers, whether the 'decking out' was ridiculous or not. Was Lord Mount Severn right, when he accused her of so dressing in self-gratification? Very likely: for, has not the great preacher said, that childhood and youth are vanity?

Miss Carlyle, the justice, and Barbara also had seats near the orchestra, for Miss Carlyle in West Lynne was a person to be considered, and not hidden behind others. Mr. Carlyle, however, preferred to join the gentlemen who congregated and stood round about the door, inside and out. There was scarcely standing room in the place: Mr. Kane had, as was anticipated, a bumper, and the poor man could have worshipped Lady Isabel, for he knew he owed it to her.

It was very long: country concerts generally are: and was about three parts over when a powdered head, larger than any cauliflower ever grown, was discerned ascending the stairs behind the group of gentlemen: which head, when it brought its body in full view, was discovered to belong to one of the footmen of Lord Mount Severn. The calves alone, cased in their silk stockings, were a sight to be seen; and these calves betook themselves inside the concert-room, with a depreciatory bow for permission to the gentlemen they had to steer through, and there they came to a stand-still, the cauliflower extending forward, and turning itself about from right to left.

'Well, I'll be jiffied!' cried an astonished old foxhunter, who had been elbowed by the footman. 'The cheek these fellows have!'

The fellow in question did not appear, however, to be enjoying any great amount of cheek just then, for he looked perplexed, humbled, and uneasy. Suddenly his eye fell on Mr. Carlyle, and it lighted up.

'Beg pardon, sir: could you happen to inform me whereabouts my young lady is sitting?'

'At the other end of the room, near the orchestra.'

'I am sure I don't know how ever I am to get to her, then,' returned the man, more in self-soliloquy, than to Mr. Carlyle. 'The room's choke full, and I don't like crushing by. My Lord is taken alarmingly worse, sir,' he explained, in an awe-struck tone; 'it is feared he is dying.'

Mr. Carlyle was painfully startled.

'His screams of pain are awful, sir. Mr. Wainwright and another doctor from West Lynne are with him, and an express has gone to Lynneborough for physicians. Mrs. Mason said we were to fetch my young lady home, and not lose a moment; and we brought the carriage, sir, Wells galloping his horses all the way.'

'I will bring Lady Isabel,' said Mr. Carlyle.

'I'm sure, sir, I should be under everlasting obligation if you would,' returned the man.

Mr. Carlyle worked his way through the crowded room. He was tall and slender, many looking daggers at him, for a pathetic song was just then being given by the London lady. He disregarded all, and stood before Isabel.

'I thought you were not coming to speak to me to-night. Is it not a famous room? I am so pleased.'

'More than famous, Lady Isabel. But,' continued he gravely, 'Lord Mount Severn does not find himself so well, and he has sent the carriage for you.'

'Papa not so well!' she quickly exclaimed.

'Not quite. At any rate, he wishes you to go home. Will you allow me to pilot you through the room?'

'Oh, my dear, considerate papa!' she laughed. 'He fears I shall be weary, and would emancipate me before the time. Thank you, Mr. Carlyle, but I will wait till the conclusion.'

'No, no, Lady Isabel, it is not that. Lord Mount Severn is indeed worse.'

Her countenance changed to seriousness; but she was not alarmed. 'Very well. When this song is over: not to disturb the room.'

'I think you had better lose no time,' he urged. 'Never mind the song and the room.'

She rose instantly, and put her arm within Mr. Carlyle's. A hasty word of explanation to Mrs. Ducie, and he led her away, the room, in its surprise, making for them what space it might. Many an eye followed them, but none more curiously and eagerly than Barbara Hare's. 'Where is he going to take her?' involuntarily uttered Barbara.

'How should I know?' retorted Miss Corny. 'Barbara, you have done nothing but fidget all the night: what's the matter with you? Folks come to a concert to listen, not to talk and fidget.'

Isabel's mantle was procured from the ante-room, where it had been left, and she descended the stairs with Mr. Carlyle. The carriage was drawn up close to the entrance, and the coachman had his reins gathered ready to start. The footman, not the one who had gone upstairs, threw open the chariot door as soon as he saw her. He was new in the service; a simple country native, just engaged. She withdrew her arm from Mr. Carlyle's, and stood a moment before stepping in, looking at the man.

'Is papa much worse?'

'Oh yes, my lady: he was screaming shocking. But they think he'll live till morning.'

With a sharp cry, she seized the arm of Mr. Carlyle, seized it for support in her shock of agony. Mr. Carlyle rudely thrust the man away: he could willingly have flung him at full length on the pavement.

'Oh, Mr. Carlyle, why did you not tell me?' she shivered.

'My dear Lady Isabel, I am grieved that you are told now. But, take comfort: you know how ill he frequently is, and this may be but an ordinary attack. Step in. I trust we shall find it nothing more.'

'Are you going home with me?'

'Certainly. I shall not leave you to go alone.'

She moved to the other side of the chariot, making room for him.

'Thank you: I will sit outside.'

'But the night is cold.'

'Oh no.' He closed the door, and took his seat by the coachman: the footmen got up behind, and the carriage sped away. Isabel gathered herself into her corner, and moaned aloud in her suspense and helplessness.

'Do not spare your horses,' said Mr. Carlyle to Wells. 'Lady Isabel will be ill with anxiety.'

'She'll be worse before morning, poor child,' returned the coachman. 'I have lived in the service fifteen year, sir, and have watched her grow up from a little thing,' he hastened to add, as if in apology for his familiarity.

'Is the earl really in danger?'

'Ay, sir, that he is. I have seen two cases in my life of gout in the stomach, and a few hours closed both. I heard a word dropped, as I came out, that Mr. Wainwright thought it was going on to the heart.'

'The earl's former attacks have been alarming and painful,' remarked Mr. Carlyle, clinging to hope.

'Yes, sir, I know; but this bout is different. Besides,' resumed Wells, in a confidential tone, 'them bats didn't come for nothing.'

'Bats!' uttered Mr. Carlyle.

'And it's a sure sign, sir, that death is on its road to the house, safe and speedy.'

'Wells, what are you talking about?'

'The bats have been round the house this evening, sir. Nasty things! I hate 'em at all times.'

'Bats are fond of flying about at night-time,' remarked Mr. Carlyle, glancing aside at the steady old coachman, with a half suspicion that he might not have been keeping himself quite so steady as usual. 'It is their nature.'

'But they don't come in shoals, sir, round about you, and in at the windows. To-night, when we got back, after leaving my young lady at the concert, I told Joe just to take out the horses and leave the carriage outside, as it would be required again. I went in-doors, and there they told me that Mrs. Mason wanted me, and I was to go up to the library to her. She was sitting there, sir, you see, to be close at hand, if anything was needed in my lord's room. So I wiped my shoes, and up to the library I went, and knocked at the door. "Come in," she called out, and in I walked, and there she was by herself, standing at the open window. "You are airy to-night, ma'am," says I; "it's hardly weather for open windows:" for, as you see, sir, it's quite a frost.'

Mr. Carlyle glanced down at the road and at the hedges.

' "Come in, Wells," Mrs. Mason called out, sharply, "come and look here." I went and stood by her side, sir, and I never saw such a sight in my life. The bats were flying about in scores, in hundreds, a cloud of them, diving down at the window, and flapping their wings. Right inside they came, and would have touched our faces, only we drew back. Where on earth they had come from I can't think, for I had not been in-doors a minute, and there was not one about outside, that I had seen. "What does all this mean, Wells?" cried Mrs. Mason, "the bats must have turned wild to-night. I opened the window to look at them, for they quite startled me. Did you ever see them so thick?" "No, ma'am, nor so near," I answered her. "And I don't like to see them, for

it betokens no good: it's a sign." Well, sir, with that she burst out laughing,'
continued Wells, 'for she's one of those who ridicule signs and dreams, and
the like. She is an educated woman, perhaps you know, sir, and, years ago,
was nursery governess to Lady Isabel; and those educated people are mighty
hard of belief.'

Mr. Carlyle nodded.

'"What is it a sign of, Wells?" Mrs. Mason went on to me, in a jesting sort
of way. "Mrs. Mason, ma'am," said I, "I can't say that I ever saw the bats
clanned together and making their visit, like this; but I have heard, times out
of number, that they have been known to do it, and that it is a sure sign death
is at the very door of the house." "I hope death is not at the door of this
house," sighed Mrs. Mason, thinking, no doubt, of my lord, and she closed
the window as she spoke, and the nasty things beat against it with their
wings. Mrs. Mason then spoke to me of the business she had wanted me
upon; she was talking to me three minutes, perhaps, and when she had
finished, I turned to look at the window again. But there was not a single bat
there; they had all gone, all disappeared in that little space of time. "What
has become of them?" cried Mrs. Mason; and I opened the window, and
looked up and down, but they were clean gone, and the air and the sky were
as clear as they are at this moment.'

'Gone to flap at somebody else's window, perhaps,' remarked Mr. Carlyle,
with a very disbelieving smile.

'Not long after that, sir, the house was in commotion. My lord was in mortal agony, and Mr. Wainwright said (so the word ran in the servants'-hall)
that the gout had reached the stomach, and might be rushing on to the heart.
Denis went galloping off to Lynneborough for physicians, and we put to the
horses and came tearing off for my young lady.'

'Well,' observed Mr. Carlyle, 'I hope he will recover the attack, Wells, in
spite of the gout and the bats.'

The coachman shook his head, and turning his horses sharply round,
whipped them up through the lodge gates.

The housekeeper, Mrs. Mason, waited at the hall door to receive Lady Isabel. Mr. Carlyle helped her out of the carriage, and gave her his arm up the
steps. She scarcely dared to inquire.

'Is he better? May I go to his room?' she panted.

Yes, the earl was better; better, in so far that he was quiet and senseless.
She moved hastily towards the chamber. Mr. Carlyle drew the housekeeper
aside.

'Is there any hope?'

'Not the slightest, sir. He is dying.'

The earl knew no one: pain was gone for the present, and he lay on his
bed, calm; but his face, which had death in it all too plainly, startled Isabel.
She did not scream or cry; she was perfectly quiet, save that she had a fit of

shivering. 'Will he soon be better?' she whispered to Mr. Wainwright, who stood there.

The surgeon coughed. 'Well, he—he—we must hope it, my lady.'

'But why does his face look like that? It is pale—grey: I never saw anybody else look so.'

'He has been in great pain, my lady; and pain leaves its traces on the countenance.'

Mr. Carlyle, who had come in, and was standing by the surgeon, touched his arm to draw him from the room. He noticed the look on the earl's face, and did not like it; he wished to question the surgeon. Lady Isabel saw that Mr. Carlyle was about to quit the room, and beckoned to him.

'Do not leave the house, Mr. Carlyle. When he wakes up, it may cheer him to see you here; he liked you very much.'

'I will not leave it, Lady Isabel. I did not think of doing so.'

In time—it seemed an age—the medical men arrived from Lynneborough; three of them; the groom had thought he could not summon too many. It was a strange scene they entered upon: the ghastly peer, growing restless again now, battling with his departing spirit; and the gala robes, the sparkling gems adorning the young girl, watching at his side. They comprehended the case without difficulty: that she had been suddenly called from some scene of gaiety.

They stooped to look at the earl, and felt his pulse, and touched his heart, and exchanged a few murmured words with Mr. Wainwright. Isabel had stood back to give them place, but her anxious eyes followed their every movement. They did not seem to notice her, and she stepped forward.

'Can you do anything for him? Will he recover?'

They all turned at the address, and looked at her. One spoke: it was an evasive answer.

'Tell me the truth,' she implored, with feverish impatience; 'you must not trifle with me. Do you now know me? I am his only child, and I am here alone.'

The first thing was to get her away from the room, for the great change was approaching, and the parting struggle between the body and the spirit might be one of warfare; no sight for her. But, in answer to their suggestions that she should go, she only leaned her head upon the pillow by her father, and moaned in despair.

'She must be got out of the room,' cried one of the physicians, almost angrily. 'Ma'am'—turning suddenly upon Mrs. Mason—'are there no relatives in the house, no one who can exert influence over the young lady?'

'She has scarcely any relatives in the world,' replied the housekeeper; 'no near ones. And we happen to be, just now, quite alone.'

But Mr. Carlyle, seeing the urgency of the case, for the earl with every minute grew more excited, approached and whispered her. 'You are as anxious as we can be for your father's recovery.'

'*As* anxious!' she uttered reproachfully.

'You know what I would imply. Of course our anxiety can be as nothing to yours.'

'As nothing; as *nothing*. I think my heart will break.'

'Then—forgive me—you should not oppose the wishes of his medical attendants. They wish to be alone with him; and time is being lost.'

She rose up; she placed her hands on her brow as if to collect the sense of the words; and then she addressed the doctors.

'Is it really necessary that I should leave the room; necessary *for him*?'

'It is necessary, my lady; absolutely essential.'

She quitted the room without another word, and turned into the library, an apartment in the same wing, where the bats had paid their visits earlier in the evening. A large fire burnt in the grate, and she walked up to it, and leaned her hand and forehead on the mantlepiece.

'Mr. Carlyle,' she said, without raising it.

'I am here,' he answered, for he had followed her in. 'What can I do for you?'

'I have come away, you see. Until I may go in again will you bring me word how he is—continually?'

'Indeed I will.'

As he quitted the room, Marvel sailed into it, a very fine lady's maid. 'Would my lady change her dress?'

No, my lady would not. 'They might be calling me to papa at the moment the dress was off.'

'But so very unsuitable, my lady—that rich dress for a night-scene, such as this.'

'Unsuitable! What does it signify? Who thinks of my dress?'

But, by-and-by, Mrs. Mason quietly took off the diamonds, and threw a warm shawl over her neck and arms, for she was shivering still.

Some of the medical men left; Mr. Wainwright remained. Nothing more could be done for Lord Mount Severn in this world, and the death scene was prolonged and terrible. He was awake to pain again of some sort; whether of mind or body they could not say. Pain! mortal, shrieking, writhing agony. Is it, or is it not the case, that a badly-spent life entails one of these awful death-beds?

Very rebellious, very excited grew Isabel towards morning. Mr. Carlyle had brought her perpetual tidings from the sick-room, softening down the actual facts. She could not understand that she need be kept away from it, and she nearly had a battle with Mr. Carlyle.

'It is cruel so to treat me,' she exclaimed, pride alone enabling her to suppress her sobs. 'Pent up here, the night has seemed to me as long as ten. When your father was dying, were you kept away from him?'

'My dear young lady—a hardy, callous man may go where you may not.'

'You are not hardy and callous.'

'I spoke of man's general nature.'

'I shall act upon my responsibility. I am obliged by all your kindness, Mr. Carlyle,' she hastily added, 'but you really have no right to keep me from my father. And I shall go to him.'

Mr. Carlyle placed himself before her, his back against the door. His grave, kind face looked into hers with the deepest sympathy and tenderness. 'Forgive me, dear Lady Isabel; I cannot let you go.'

She broke into a passion of tears and sobs as he led her back to the fire, and stood there with her.

'He is my dear father, I have but him in the wide world.'

'I know; I know: I feel for you all that you are feeling. Twenty times this night I have wished, forgive me the thought, that you were my sister, so that I might express my sympathy more freely, and comfort you.'

'Tell me the truth, then, why I am kept away. If you can show me a sufficient cause, I will be reasonable and obey, but do not say again I should be disturbing him, for it is not true.'

'He is too ill for you to see him, his symptoms are too painful; were you to go in, in defiance of advice, you would regret it all your after life.'

'Is he dying?'

Mr. Carlyle hesitated. Ought he to dissemble with her as the doctors had done? A strong feeling was upon him that he ought not.

'I trust to you not to deceive me,' she simply said.

'I fear he is. I believe he is.'

She rose up; she grapsed his arm in the sudden fear that flashed over her. 'You are deceiving me, and he is dead!'

'I am not deceiving you, Lady Isabel. He is not dead: but—it may be very near.'

She laid her face down upon the sofa pillow. 'Going for ever from me! going for ever. Oh, Mr. Carlyle, let me see him for a minute! just one farewell! will you not try for me?'

He knew how hopeless it was, but he turned to leave the room. 'I will go and see. But you will remain here quietly: you will not come.'

She bowed her head in acquiescence, and he closed the door. Had she indeed been his sister, he would probably have turned the key upon her. He entered the earl's chamber, but not many seconds did he remain in it.

'It is over,' he whispered to Mrs. Mason, whom he met in the corridor. 'And Mr. Wainwright is asking for you.'

'You are soon back,' cried Isabel, lifting her head. 'May I go?'

He sat down and took her hand, shrinking from his task. 'I wish I could comfort you,' he exclaimed in a tone of deep emotion.

Her face turned a ghastly whiteness, as white as another's not far away. 'Tell me the worst,' she breathed.

'I have nothing to tell you, but the worst. May God support you, dear Lady Isabel.'

She turned to hide her face and its misery from him, and a low wail of anguish broke from her, betraying its own tale of despair.

The grey dawn of morning was breaking over the world, advent of another bustling day in life's history: but the spirit of William Vane, Earl of Mount Severn, had soared away from it for ever.

❧ X ❧

The Keepers of the Dead

Events, between the death of Lord Mount Severn and his interment, occurred quickly; to one of them the reader may feel inclined to demur, as believing that it could have no foundation in fact, in the actions of real life. He would be wrong. The circumstance really occurred.

The earl died on Friday morning, at daylight. The news spread rapidly; it generally does on the death of a peer, if he have been of note (whether good or bad) in the world. It was known in London before the day was over; the consequence of which was, that by Saturday morning early, a shoal of what the late earl would have called harpies had arrived to surround East Lynne. There were creditors for small sums and for great, for five or ten pounds, up to five or ten thousand. Some were civil; some impatient; some loud and rough and angry; some came in to put executions on the effects, and some— *to arrest the body!*

This last act was accomplished cleverly. Two men, each with a remarkably hooked nose, stole away from the hubbub of the clamourers, and peering cunningly about, made their way to the side, or tradesman's entrance. A kitchen maid answered their general appeal at the bell.

'Is the coffin come yet?' said they.

'Coffin? no!' was the girl's reply. 'The shell ain't here yet. Mr. Jones didn't promise that till nine o'clock, and it haven't gone eight.'

'It won't be long,' quoth they, 'it's on its road. We'll go up to his lordship's room, and be getting ready for it.'

The girl called the butler. 'Two men from Jones's, the undertaker's, sir,' announced she. 'The shell's a coming on, and they want to go up and make ready for it.'

The butler marshalled them up-stairs himself, and introduced them to the room. 'That will do,' said they, as he was about to enter with them, 'we won't trouble you to wait.' And, closing the door upon the unsuspicious butler, they took up their station on either side the dead, like a couple of ill-omened mutes. They had placed an arrest upon the corpse; it was theirs, until their claim was satisfied, and they sat down to thus watch and secure it. Pleasant occupation!

It may have been an hour later that Lady Isabel, leaving her own chamber, opened noiselessly that of the dead. She had been in it several times the previous day; at first with the housekeeper; afterwards, when the nameless dread was somewhat effaced, alone. But she felt nervous again this morning, and had gained the bed before she ventured to lift her eyes from the carpet and encounter the sight. Then she started, for there sat two strange-looking men—and not attractive men, either.

It darted through her mind that they must be people from the neighbourhood, come to gratify an idle and unpardonable curiosity: her first impulse was to summon the butler: her second, to speak to them herself.

'Do you want anything here?' she quietly said.

'Much obleeged for the inquiry, miss. We are all right.'

The words and the tone struck her as being singular in the extreme: and they kept their seats, too, as though they had a right to be there.

'Why are you here?' she repeated. 'What are you doing?'

'Well, miss, I don't mind telling you, for I suppose you are his daughter'—pointing his left thumb over his shoulder at the late peer—'and we hear he have got no other relative anigh him. We have been obleeged, miss, to perform a unpleasant dooty, and secure him.'

The words were like Greek to her: and the men saw that they were.

'He unfort'nately owed a sight of money, miss—as you perhaps be aware on, and our employers is in, deep. So, as soon as they heard what had happened, they sent us down to arrest the dead corpse: and we have done it.'

Amazement, horror, fear, struggled together in the shocked mind of Lady Isabel. Arrest the dead! She had never heard of a like calamity: nor could she have believed in such. Arrest it for what purpose? What to do? To disfigure it?—to sell it? With a panting heart and ashy lips she turned from the room. Mrs. Mason happened to be passing near the stairs, and Isabel flew to her, laying hold of her with both hands in her terror, as she burst into a fit of nervous tears.

'Those men—in there!' she gasped.

'What men, my lady?' returned Mrs. Mason in surprise.

'I don't know; I don't know. I think they are going to stop there: they say they have taken papa.'

After a pause of bewildered astonishment, the housekeeper left her standing where she was, and went to the earl's chamber, to see if she could fathom the mystery of the words. Isabel leaned against the balustrades; partly for support, partly that she seemed afraid to stir from them; and the ominous disturbance, down-stairs, reached her ears. Strangers, interlopers, appeared to be in the hall, talking vehemently, and complaining in bitter tones. More and more terrified, she held her breath to listen.

'Where's the good of your seeing the young lady?' cried the butler, in a tone of remonstrance. 'She knows nothing about the earl's affairs; she is in grief enough, just now, without any other worry.'

'I will see her,' retorted a dogged voice. 'If she's too upstart and mighty to come down and answer a question or two, why, I'll find my way on to her. Here we are, a shameful crowd of us, swindled out of our own, told there's nobody we can speak to; nobody here but the young lady, and she must not be troubled! She didn't find it trouble to help to spend our money! She has got no honour and no feelings of a lady, if she don't come and speak to us.'

Repressing her rebellious emotion, Lady Isabel glided partly down the staircase, and softly called to the butler.

'What is all this?' she asked. 'I must know.'

'Oh, my lady, don't go amongst those rough men! You cannot do any good; pray go back before they see you. I have sent for Mr. Carlyle, and expect him here every moment.'

'Did papa owe them *all* money?' she shivered.

'I am afraid he did, my lady.'

She went swiftly on; and, passing through the few stragglers in the hall, entered the dining-room, where the chief mass had congregated, and the hubbub was loudest. All anger, at least all external anger, was hushed at her sight. She looked so young, so innocent, so childlike in her pretty morning dress of peach-coloured muslin, her fair face shaded by its falling curls, so little fit to combat with, or understand *their* business, that instead of pouring forth complaints, they hushed them into silence.

'I heard some one calling out that I ought to see you,' she began, her agitation causing the words to come forth in a jerking manner. 'What did you want with me?'

Then they poured out their complaints, but not angrily, and she listened till she grew sick. There were many and formidable claims; promissory notes and IOU's, overdue bills and underdue bills: heavy outstanding debts of all sorts, and trifles (comparatively speaking) for housekeeping, servants' liveries, out-door servants' wages, bread and meat.

What was Isabel Vane to answer? what excuse to offer? what hope or promise to give? She stood in bewilderment, unable to speak, turning from one to the other, her sweet eyes full of pity and contrition.

'The fact is, young lady,' said one who bore the exterior of a gentleman, 'we should not have come down to trouble you—at least, I can answer for myself—but his lordship's men of business, Warburton and Ware, to whom many of us hastened last evening, told us there would not be a shilling for anybody, unless it could be got from the furniture. When it comes to that, it is, "first come, first served," and I got down by morning light, and levied an execution.'

'Which was levied before you came,' put in a man, who might be brother to the two up-stairs, to judge by his nose. 'But what's such furniture as this, to our claims—if you come to combine 'em? no more than a bucket of water is to the Thames.'

'What can I do?' shivered Lady Isabel. 'What is it you wish me to do? I have no money to give you. I—'

'No, miss,' broke in a quiet, pale man; 'if report tells true, you are worse wronged than we are, for you won't have a roof to put your head under, or a guinea to call your own.'

'He has been a scoundrel to everybody,' interrupted an intemperate voice; 'he has ruined thousands.'

The speech was hissed down: even they were not men gratuitously to insult a delicate young lady.

'Perhaps you'll just answer us a question, miss,' persisted the voice, in spite of the hisses. 'Is there any ready money that can—'

But another person had entered the room—Mr. Carlyle. He caught sight of the white face and trembling hands of Isabel, and interrupted the last speaker with scant ceremony.

'What is the meaning of this?' he demanded, in a tone of authority. 'What do you want?'

'If you are a friend of the late peer's, you ought to know what we want,' was the response. 'We want our debts paid.'

'But this is not the place to come to,' returned Mr. Carlyle: 'your flocking here, in this extraordinary manner, will do no good. You must go to Warburton and Ware.'

'We have been to them—and received their answer. A cool assurance that there'll be nothing for anybody.'

'At any rate, you will get nothing here,' observed Mr. Carlyle, to the assembly collectively. 'Allow me to request you to leave the house at once.'

It was little likely that they would go for his bidding. And they said it.

'Then I warn you of the consequences of a refusal,' quietly said Mr. Carlyle: 'you are trespassing upon a stranger's property. This house was not Lord Mount Severn's: he sold it some time back.'

They knew better. Some laughed, and said these tricks were stale.

'Listen, gentlemen,' rejoined Mr. Carlyle, in the plain, straightforward manner that carried its own truth. 'To make an assertion that could be disproved when the earl's affairs came to be investigated, would be simply foolish. I give you my word of honour as a man—that this estate, with the house and all that it contains, passed legally, months ago, from the hands of Lord Mount Severn: and, during his recent sojourn here, he was but a visitor in it. Go and ask his men of business.'

'Who purchased it?' was the inquiry.

'Mr. Carlyle, of West Lynne. Some of you may possibly know him by reputation.'

Some of them did. 'A cute young lawyer,' observed a voice; 'as his father was before him.'

'I am he,' proceeded Mr. Carlyle. 'And being a "cute lawyer," as you do me the honour to decide, you cannot suppose I should risk my money upon any sale, not perfectly safe and legal. I was not an agent in the affair; I employed agents: for it was my own money that I invested, and East Lynne is mine.'

'Is the purchase-money paid over?' inquired more than one.

'It was paid over at the time: last June.'

'What did Lord Mount Severn do with the money?'

'I do not know,' replied Mr. Carlyle. 'I am not cognisant of Lord Mount Severn's private affairs.'

Significant murmurs arose: 'Strange that the earl should stop two or three months at a place that wasn't his!'

'It may appear to you, but allow me to explain,' returned Mr. Carlyle. 'The earl expressed a wish to pay East Lynne a few days' visit, by way of farewell, and I acceded. Before the few days were over, he was taken ill, and remained, from that time, too ill to quit it. This very day, this day, gentlemen, was at length fixed for his departure.'

'And you tell us you bought the furniture!'

'Everything as it stands. You need not doubt my word, for the proofs will be forthcoming. East Lynne was in the market for sale: I heard of it, and became the purchaser—just as I might have bought an estate from any of you. And now, as this is my house, and you have no claim upon me, I should be obliged to you to withdraw.'

'Perhaps you will claim the horses and carriages next, sir,' cried the man with the hooked nose.

Mr. Carlyle lifted his head haughtily. 'What is mine, is mine; legally purchased and paid for; a fair, just price. The carriages and horses I have nothing to do with: Lord Mount Severn brought them down with him.'

'And I have got a safe watcher over them in the out premises, to see as they don't run away,' nodded the man, complacently: 'and, if I don't mistake, there's a safe watcher over something else up-stairs.'

'What a cursed scoundrel Mount Severn was!'

'Whatever he may have been, it does not give you the right to outrage the feelings of his daughter,' warmly interrupted Mr. Carlyle: 'and I should have thought that men, calling themselves Englishmen, would have disdained the shame. Allow me, Lady Isabel,' he added, imperatively taking her hand to lead her from the room. 'I will remain and deal with this business.'

But she hesitated and stopped. The injury her father had done these men was telling painfully on her sense of right, and she essayed to speak a word of apology, of sorrow: she thought she ought to do so; she did not like them to deem her quite heartless. But it was a painful task, and the colour went and came in her pale face, and her breath was laboured with the excess of her tribulation.

'I am very sorry,' she stammered; and, with the effort of speaking, emotion quite got the better of her, and she burst into tears. 'I did not know anything of all this: my father's affairs were not spoken of before me. I believe I have not anything: if I had, I would divide it amongst you as equally as I could. But should the means ever be in my power, should money ever be mine, I will thankfully pay all your claims.'

All your claims! Lady Isabel little thought what that 'all' would comprise. However, such promises, made at such a moment, fall heedlessly on the ear. Scarcely one present but felt sympathy and sorrow for her, and Mr. Carlyle drew her from the room. He closed the door upon the noisy crew, and then her sobs came forth hysterically.

'I am so grieved, Lady Isabel! Had I foreseen this annoyance, you should have been spared it. Can you go up-stairs alone?—or shall I call Mrs. Mason?'

'Oh yes, I can go alone: I am not ill, only frightened and sick. This is not the worst,' she shivered 'There are two men up—up—with—with papa.'

Up with papa! Mr. Carlyle was puzzled. He saw that she was shaking from head to foot as she stood before him.

'I cannot understand it, and it terrifies me,' she continued, attempting an explanation. 'They are sitting in the room close to him; they have taken him, they say.'

A blank, thunderstruck pause. Mr. Carlyle looked at her, he did not speak; and then he turned and looked at the butler, who was standing near. But the man only responded by giving his head a half shake, and Mr. Carlyle saw that it was an ominous one.

'I will clear the house of these,' he said to Lady Isabel, pointing back to the dining-room, 'and then join you up-stairs.'

'Two ruffians, sir, and they have got possession of the body,' whispered the butler into Mr. Carlyle's ear, as Lady Isabel departed. 'They obtained entrance to the chamber by a sly, deceitful trick, saying they were the undertaker's men, and that he can't be buried, unless their claims are paid, if it's for a month to come. It has upset all our stomachs, sir; Mrs. Mason, while telling me—for she was the first to know it—was as sick as she could be.'

At present Mr. Carlyle returned to the dining-room, and bore the brunt of the anger of those savage, and—it may be said—ill-used men. Not that it was vented upon him; quite the contrary; but on the memory of the unhappy peer, who lay overhead. A few had taken the precaution to insure the earl's life, and they were the best off. They left the house after a short space of time, for Mr. Carlyle's statement was indisputable, and they knew the law better than to remain trespassers on his property.

But the custodians of the dead could not be so got rid of. Mr. Carlyle proceeded to the death-chamber, and examined their authority. A similar case had never occurred under his own observation: though it had under his father's, and Mr. Carlyle remembered hearing of it. The body of a church dignitary, who had died deeply in debt, was arrested as it was being carried through the cloisters to its grave in the cathedral. These men, sitting over Lord Mount Severn, enforced heavy claims, and there they must sit, until the arrival of Mr. Vane from Castle Marling—now the Earl of Mount Severn.

On the following morning, Sunday, Mr. Carlyle proceeded again to East Lynne, and found, to his surprise, that there was no arrival. Isabel was in the breakfast-room alone, the meal on the table untouched, and she shivering— on a low ottoman before the fire. She looked so ill, that Mr. Carlyle could not forbear remarking upon it.

'I have not slept, and I am very cold,' she answered. 'I did not close my eyes all night; I was too terrified.'

'Terrified at what?' he asked.

'At those men,' she whispered. 'It is strange that Mr. Vane is not come.'

'Is the post in?'

'I don't know,' she apathetically replied. 'I have received nothing.'

She had scarcely spoken when the butler entered with his salver full of letters, most of them bearing condolence to Lady Isabel. She singled out one and hastened to open it, for it bore the Castle Marling postmark. 'It is Mrs. Vane's handwriting,' she remarked to Mr. Carlyle.

'Castle Marling, Saturday.

'My dear Isabel,—I am dreadfully grieved and shocked at the news conveyed in Mr. Carlyle's letter to my husband, for he is gone cruising in his yacht, and I opened it. Goodness knows where he may be, round the coast somewhere; but he said he should be home by Sunday, and as he is pretty punctual generally in keeping his word, I expect him. Be assured he will not lose a moment in hastening to East Lynne.

'I cannot express what I feel for you, and am too bouleversée to write more. Try and keep up your spirits, and believe me, dear Isabel, with sincere sympathy and regret, faithfully yours,

'EMMA MOUNT SEVERN.'

The colour came into Isabel's pale cheek when she read the signature. She thought, had she been the writer, she should, in that first, early letter, have still signed herself Emma Vane. Isabel handed the note to Mr. Carlyle. 'It is very unfortunate,' she sighed.

Mr. Carlyle glanced over it, as quickly as Mrs. Vane's illegible writing allowed him, and drew in his lips in a peculiar manner when he came to the signature. Perhaps at the same thought which had struck Isabel.

'Had Mrs. Vane been worth a rush, she would have come herself, knowing your lonely situation,' he uttered impulsively.

Isabel leaned her head upon her hand. All the difficulties and embarrassments of her position came crowding upon her mind. No orders had been given in preparation for the funeral, and she felt that she had no right to give any. The Earls of Mount Severn were buried at Mount Severn, but to take her father thither would involve great expense: would the present earl sanction that? Since the previous morning, she seemed to have grown old in the world's experiences; her ideas were changed, the bent of her thoughts had been violently turned from its course. Instead of being a young lady of high position, of wealth and rank, she appeared to herself more in the light of an unfortunate pauper; an interloper in the house she was inhabiting. It has been the custom in romance to represent young ladies, especially if they be handsome and interesting, as being entirely oblivious of matter-of-fact cares and necessities, supremely indifferent to future prospects of poverty—poverty that brings hunger and thirst and cold and nakedness; but, be assured, this apathy never exists in real life. Isabel Vane's grief for her father—whom, whatever may have been the aspect he wore for others, *she* had deeply loved and reverenced—was sharply poignant: but in the midst of that grief, and of the singular troubles his death had brought forth, she could not shut her eyes to her own future. Its uncertainty, its shadowed-forth embarrassments did obtrude themselves, and the words of that plain-speaking creditor kept ringing in her ears—'You won't have a roof to put your head under, or a guinea to call your own.' Where was she to go?—with whom to live? she was in Mr. Carlyle's house, now. And how was she to pay the servants? Money was owing to them all.

'Mr. Carlyle, how long has this house been yours?' she asked, breaking the silence.

'It was in June that the purchase was completed. Did Lord Mount Severn never tell you he had sold it to me?'

'No; never. All these things are yours?' glancing round the room.

'The furniture was sold with the house. Not these sort of things,' he added, his eye falling on the silver on the breakfast-table, 'not the plate and linen.'

'Not the plate and linen! Then those poor men, who were here yesterday, have a right to them,' she quickly cried.

'I scarcely know. I believe the plate goes with the entail—and the jewels go also. The linen cannot be of much consequence, either way.'

'Are my clothes my own?'

He smiled at her simplicity; and assured her that they were nobody else's.

'I did not know,' she sighed; 'I did not understand. So many strange things have happened in the last day or two, that I seem to understand nothing.'

Indeed she could not understand. She had no definite ideas on the subject of this transfer of East Lynne to Mr. Carlyle: plenty of indefinite ones, and they were haunting her. Fears of debt to him, and of the house and its contents being handed over to him in liquidation, perhaps only partial, were working in her brain.

'Does my father owe you any money?' she breathed in a timid tone.

'Not any,' he replied. 'Lord Mount Severn was never indebted to me in his life.'

'Yet you purchased East Lynne!'

'As any one else might have done,' he answered, discerning the drift of her thoughts. 'I was in search of an eligible estate to invest money in, and East Lynne suited me.'

'I feel my position, Mr. Carlyle,' she resumed, the rebellious tears forcing themselves to her eyes, 'thus to be intruding upon you for a shelter. And I cannot help myself.'

'You can help grieving me,' he gently answered, 'which you do when you talk of obligation. The obligation is on my side, Lady Isabel; and when I express a hope that you will continue at East Lynne while it can be of service, however prolonged that period may be, I assure you I say it in all sincerity.'

'You are truly kind,' she faltered, 'and for a few days; until I can think, until———Oh, Mr. Carlyle, are papa's affairs really so bad as they said yesterday?' she broke off, her perplexities recurring to her with vehement force. 'Is there nothing left?'

Now, Mr. Carlyle might have given the evasive assurance that there would be plenty left, just to tranquillize her. But to use deceit with her would have pricked against every feeling of his nature; and he saw how implicitly she relied upon his truth.

'I fear things are not very bright,' he answered. 'That is, so far as we can see at present. But there may be some settlement effected for you that you do not know of. Warburton and Ware—'

'No,' she interrupted; 'I never heard of a settlement, and I am sure there is none. I see the worst plainly: I have no home; no home, and no money. This house is yours; the town-house and Mount Severn go to Mr. Vane. And I have nothing.'

'But surely Mr. Vane will be delighted to welcome you to your old home. The houses pass to him—it almost seems as though you had the greater right in them, than he or Mrs. Vane.'

'My home with them!' she retorted, as if the words had stung her. 'What are you saying, Mr. Carlyle?'

'I beg your pardon, Laby Isabel. I should not have presumed to touch upon these points myself, but—'

'Nay, I think I ought to beg yours,' she interrupted, more calmly. 'I am only grateful for the interest you take in them; the kindness you have shown. But I could never make my home with Mrs. Vane.'

Mr. Carlyle rose. He could do no good by remaining, and did not think well to intrude longer. He suggested that it might be more pleasant if Isabel had a friend with her: Mrs. Ducie would, no doubt, be willing to come, and she was a kind and motherly woman.

Isabel shook her head with a passing shudder. 'Have strangers here, with—all—that—in papa's chamber!' she uttered. 'Mrs. Ducie drove over yesterday; perhaps to remain; I don't know; but I was afraid of questions, and would not see her. When I think of—that—I feel thankful that I am alone.'

The housekeeper stopped Mr. Carlyle as he was going out. 'Sir, what is the news from Castle Marling? Pounds said there was a letter. Is Mr. Vane coming?'

'He was out yachting. Mrs. Vane expected him home yesterday, so it is to be hoped he will be here to-day.'

'Whatever will be done if he does not come?' she breathed. 'The leaden coffin ought to be soldered down—for you know, sir, the state he was in when he died.'

'It can be soldered down without Mr. Vane.'

'Of course—without Mr. Vane. It's not that, sir. Will those men allow it to be done? The undertakers were here this morning at daybreak, and those men intimated that they were not going to *lose sight* of the dead. The words sounded significant to us, but we asked them no questions. Have they a right to prevent it, sir?'

'Upon my word I cannot tell,' replied Mr. Carlyle. 'The proceeding is so rare a one that I know little what right of law they have, or have not. Do not mention this fear to Lady Isabel. And when Mr. Va—— when Lord Mount Severn arrives, send down to apprise me of it.'

❧ XI ☙

The New Peer, and the Bank-Note

A post-chaise was driven furiously up the avenue that Sunday afternoon. It contained the new peer, Lord Mount Severn. The more direct line of rail from Castle Marling brought him within five miles of West Lynne, and thence he had travelled in a hired chaise. Mr. Carlyle soon joined him, and almost at the same time Mr. Warburton arrived from London. Absence from town at the period of the earl's death had prevented Mr. Warburton's earlier attendance. Business was entered upon immediately.

The present earl knew that his predecessor had been an embarrassed man, but he had no conception of the extent of the evil: they had not been intimate, and rarely came in contact. As the various items of news were now detailed to him—the wasteful expenditure, the disastrous ruin, the total absence of provision for Isabel, he stood petrified and aghast. He was a tall, stout man of three-and forty years, his nature honourable, his manners cold, and his countenance severe.

'It is the most iniquitous piece of business I ever heard of,' he exclaimed to the two lawyers. 'Of all reckless fools, Mount Severn must have been the worst!'

'Unpardonably improvident, as regards his daughter,' was the assenting remark.

'Improvident! it must have been rank madness,' retorted the earl. 'No man in his senses could leave a child to the mercy of the world, as he has left her. She has not a shilling; literally not a shilling in her possession. I put the question to her—what money there was in the house when the earl died. Twenty or twenty-five pounds, she answered, which she had since given to Mason, who required it for housekeeping purposes. If the girl wants a yard of ribbon for herself, she has not the pence to pay for it! Can you realize such a case to the mind?' continued the excited peer. 'I will stake my veracity that such a one never occurred yet.'

'No money for her own personal wants!' exclaimed Mr. Carlyle.

'Not a halfpenny in the world. And there are no funds, and will be none, that I can see, for her to draw upon.'

'Quite correct, my lord,' nodded Mr. Warburton. 'The entailed estates go to you, and what trifling matters of personal property may be left, the creditors will take care of.'

'I understand East Lynne is yours,' cried the earl, turning sharply upon Mr. Carlyle. 'Isabel has just said so.'

'It is,' was the reply. 'It became mine last June. I believe his lordship kept the fact a close secret.'

'He was obliged to keep it secret,' interposed Mr. Warburton, addressing Lord Mount Severn, 'for not a stiver of the purchase-money could he have fingered, had it got wind. Except ourselves and Mr. Carlyle's agents, the fact was made known to none.'

'It is strange, sir, that you could not urge the claims of his child upon the earl,' rejoined the new peer to Mr. Warburton, his tone one of harsh reproof. 'You were in his confidence, you knew the state of his affairs; it was in your line of duty to do it.'

'And, knowing the state of his affairs, my lord, we knew how useless the urging it would be,' returned Mr. Warburton. 'He had let the time slip by, when he could have made a provision for her: the power to do so was past, years ago. Once or twice I have called it to his notice, but it was a sore point with him, and he would not pursue it. I do not think he was uneasy about her: he depended upon her making a good marriage during his lifetime; not expecting to die so young.'

'Out of his power!' repeated the earl, stopping in his impatient pacings of the room and facing Mr. Warburton. 'Don't tell me, sir! he should have done something. He might have insured his life for a few thousands, if nothing else. The child is without anything; without even pocket-money! Do you understand?'

'Unfortunately I understand only too well,' returned the lawyer. 'But your lordship has but a faint idea of the burdens Lord Mount Severn had upon him. The interest alone on his debts was frightful—and the deuce's own work there used to be to get it. Not to speak of the kites he let loose: he would fly them, and nothing could stop him; and they had to be provided for.'

'Oh, I know,' replied the earl, with a gesture of contempt. 'Drawing one bill to cover another: that was his system.'

'Draw!' echoed Mr. Warburton, 'he would have drawn a bill upon Aldgate pump. It was a downright mania with him.'

'Urged to it by his necessities, I conclude,' put in Mr. Carlyle.

'He had no business to have such necessities, sir,' cried the earl, wrathfully. 'But let us proceed to business. What money is there, lying at his bankers, Mr. Warburton? Do you know?'

'None,' was the blank reply. 'We overdrew the account ourselves, a fortnight ago, to meet one of his pressing liabilities. We hold a little; and, had he lived a week or two longer, the autumn rents would have been paid in—though they must have been as quickly paid out again.'

'I'm glad there's something. What is the amount?'

'My lord,' answered Mr. Warburton, shaking his head in a self-condoling manner, 'I am sorry to tell you that what we hold will not half satisfy our own claims: money actually paid out of our pockets.'

'Then where on earth is the money to come from, sir? For the funeral; for the servants' wages; for everything, in short?'

'There is none to come from anywhere,' was the reply of Mr. Warburton.

Lord Mount Severn strode the carpet more fiercely. 'Wicked improvidence! shameful profligacy! callous-hearted man! To live a rogue, and die a beggar, leaving his daughter to the charity of strangers!'

'Her case presents the worst feature of the whole,' remarked Mr. Carlyle. 'What will she do for a home?'

'She must, of course, find it with me,' replied his lordship. 'And, I should hope, a better one than this. With all these debts and duns at his elbow, Mount Severn's house could not have been a bower of roses.'

'I fancy she knew nothing of the state of affairs; had seen little, if anything, of the embarrassments,' returned Mr. Carlyle.

'Nonsense!' said the peer.

'Mr. Carlyle is right, my lord,' observed Mr. Warburton, looking over his spectacles. 'Lady Isabel was in safety at Mount Severn till the spring, and the purchase-money from East Lynne was a stop-gap for many things, and made matters easy for the moment. However, his imprudences are at an end now.'

'No, they are not at an end,' returned Lord Mount Severn: 'they leave their effects behind them. I hear there was a fine scene yesterday morning: some of the unfortunate wretches he has taken in made there appearance here, all the way from town.'

'Oh, they are Jews, half of them,' slightingly spoke Mr. Warburton. 'If they do lose a little, it will be an agreeable novelty to them.'

'Jews have as much right to their own as we have, Mr. Warburton,' was the peer's angry reprimand. 'And if they were Turks and infidels, it would not excuse Mount Severn's practices. Isabel says it was you, Mr. Carlyle, who contrived to get rid of them.'

'By convincing them that East Lynne and its furniture belonged to me. But there are those two men up-stairs, in possession of—of him: I could not get rid of them.'

The earl looked at him. 'I do not understand you.'

'Did you not know that they have seized the corpse?' asked Mr. Carlyle, dropping his voice. 'Two men have been posted over it, like sentinels, since yesterday morning. And there's a third in the house, I hear, who relieves each by turn, that they may go down in the hall and take their meals.'

The earl had halted in his walk and drawn near to Mr. Carlyle, his mouth open, his face a marvel of consternation. 'By George!' was all Mr. Warburton uttered, and snatched off his glasses.

'Mr. Carlyle, do I understand you aright—that the body of the late earl has been seized for debt?' demanded the peer solemnly. 'Seize a dead body! Am I awake or dreaming?'

'It is what they have done. They got into the room by stratagem.'

'Is it possible that transactions so infamous are permitted by our law?' ejaculated the earl. 'Arrest a dead man! I never heard of such a thing: I am shocked beyond expression. Isabel said something about two men, I remember: but she was so full of grief and agitation altogether, that I but half comprehended what she said upon any subject. Why, what will be done? Cannot we bury him?'

'I fancy not. The housekeeper told me this morning she feared they would not even suffer the coffins to be closed down. And that ought to be done with all convenient speed.'

'It is perfectly horrible,' uttered the earl.

'Who has done it? do you know?' inquired Mr. Warburton.

'Somebody of the name of Anstey,' replied Mr. Carlyle. 'In the absence of any member of the family, I took upon myself to pay the chamber a visit, and examine into the men's authority. The claim is about three thousand pounds.'

'If it's Anstey who has done it, it is a personal debt of the earl's, really owing, every pound of it,' observed Mr. Warburton. 'A sharp man, though, that Anstey, to hit upon such a scheme.'

'And a shameless, and a scandalous man,' added Lord Mount Severn. 'Well, this is a pretty thing! What's to be done?'

While they consult let us look for a moment at Lady Isabel. She sat alone, in great perplexity, indulging the deepest grief. Lord Mount Severn had intimated to her, kindly and affectionately, that henceforth she must find her home with him and his wife. Isabel returned a faint 'thank you,' and as soon as he left her burst into a paroxysm of rebellious tears. 'Have her home with Mrs. Vane!' she uttered to her own heart. 'No, never: rather would she die, rather would she work for her living, rather would she eat a crust and drink water!' And so on, and so on. Young demoiselles are somewhat prone to indulge in these flights of fancy: but they are in most cases impracticable and foolish; exceedingly so were they in that of Lady Isabel Vane. Work for their living! It may appear very feasible in theory; but theory and practice are as opposite as light and dark. The plain fact was, that Isabel had no alternative whatever: she must accept a home with Lady Mount Severn: and the conviction that it must be so stole over her spirit, even while her hasty lips were protesting that she would not. Lord Mount Severn wished to despatch her to Castle Marling at once, but this she successfully resisted, and it was decided that she should travel the day subsequent to the funeral.

Mr. Warburton, authorized by the earl, relieved the death-chamber of its two intruders: though—very much to the surprise of the household—the obnoxious men still remained in the house. Mr. Warburton no doubt had his reasons; he was a cautious practitioner: and the men continued, ostensibly, in charge, until the earl was buried. Some said that if the lawyer released them, another arrest might be expected.

On Friday morning the interment took place—in St. Jude's church-yard, at West Lynne. Isabel's heart again rebelled bitterly: she thought it would have been at Mount Severn. The earl remarked, but not in her hearing, that he should have too much expense upon him, to go to unnecessary outlay over the funeral. Certainly he performed honourably all that could be required from him. He paid all tradesmen's debts, and those owing to the servants, gave them each a month's wages and a month's board wages, in lieu of the customary warning of dismissal, and paid for their mourning. Pound, the butler, he retained in his own service. With regard to Isabel's mourning, he had desired her to have everything suited to her degree. The carriages and horses, on which a detainer had been placed, he bought in for his own use: they were in excellent condition.

Two mourners only attended the funeral, the earl and Mr. Carlyle: the latter was no relative of the deceased, and but a recent friend: but the earl had invited him, probably not liking to parade alone his trappings of woe. Some of the county aristocracy were pall-bearers, and many private carriages followed.

All was bustle on the following morning. The earl was to depart, and Isabel was to depart; but not together. In the course of the day the domestics would disperse. The earl was speeding to London, and the chaise to convey him to the railway station at West Lynne was already at the door when Mr. Carlyle arrived.

'I was beginning to fear you would not be here, I have barely five minutes to spare,' observed the earl, as he shook hands. 'You are sure you fully understood about the tombstone?'

'Perfectly,' replied Mr. Carlyle. 'How is Lady Isabel?'

'Very down-hearted, I fear, poor child, for she did not breakfast with me,' returned the earl. 'Mason told me that she was in a convulsion of grief. A bad man, a *bad* man was Mount Severn,' he emphatically added, as he rose and rang the bell.

'Let Lady Isabel be informed that I am ready to depart, and that I wait to see her,' he said to the servant who answered it. 'And while she is coming, Mr. Carlyle,' he added, 'allow me to express my obligation to you. How I should have got through this worrying business without you, I cannot divine. You have promised, mind, to pay me a visit, and I shall expect it speedily.'

'Promised conditionally—that I find myself in your neighbourhood,' smiled Mr. Carlyle. 'Should—'

Isabel entered, dressed also, and ready, for she was to depart immediately after the earl. Her crape veil was over her face, but she threw it back.

'My time is up, Isabel, and I must go. Is there anything you wish to say to me?'

She opened her lips to speak, but glanced at Mr. Carlyle, and hesitated. He was standing at the window, with his back towards them.

'I suppose not,' said the earl, answering himself, for he was in a hurry to be off, like many others are when starting on a journey. 'You will have no trouble whatever, my dear; Pound will see to everything, only mind you get some refreshment in the middle of the day, for you won't be at Castle Marling before dinner-time. Tell Mrs. Va—— tell Lady Mount Severn that I had no time to write, but will do so from town.'

But Isabel stood before him in an attitude of uncertainty—of expectancy, it may be said, her colour varying.

'What is it? You wish to say something.'

She certainly did wish to say something, but she did not know how. It was a moment of embarrassment to her, intensely painful; and the presence of Mr. Carlyle did not tend to lessen it. The latter had no idea his absence was wished for.

'I—I—do not like to ask you, but I—have—no money,' she stammered, her delicate features flushing crimson.

'Bless me, Isabel! I declare I forgot all about it,' cried the earl, in a tone of vexation. 'Not being accustomed to—this aspect of affairs is so new—' He broke off his disjointed sentences, and unbuttoned his coat, drew out his purse, and paused over its contents.

'Isabel, I have run myself very short, and have but little beyond what will take me to town. You must make three pounds do for the present, my dear. Pound has the funds for the journey. Once at Castle Marling, Lady Mount Severn will supply you: but you must tell her, or she will not know.'

He shot some gold out of his purse as he spoke, and left two sovereigns, and two half-sovereigns on the table. 'Farewell, my dear; make yourself happy at Castle Marling; I shall be home soon.'

Passing from the room with Mr. Carlyle, he stood talking with that gentleman a minute, his foot on the step of the chaise; and, the next, was being whirled away. Mr. Carlyle returned to the breakfast-room, where Isabel, an ashy whiteness having replaced the crimson on her cheeks, was picking up the gold.

'Will you do me a favour, Mr. Carlyle?'

'I will do anything I can for you.'

She pushed a sovereign and a half towards him. 'It is for Mr. Kane. I told Marvel to send and pay him, but it seems she forgot it, or put it off, and he is not paid. The tickets were a sovereign: the rest is for tuning the piano. Will you kindly give it to him? If I trust one of the servants, it may be forgotten again in the hurry of their departure.'

'Kane's charge for tuning a piano is five shillings,' remarked Mr. Carlyle.

'But he was a long time occupied with it, and he did something to the leathers. It is not too much: besides, I never ordered him anything to eat. He wants money even worse than I do,' she added with a poor attempt at a smile. 'But for thinking of him, I should not have mustered the courage to beg of Lord Mount Severn—as you have just heard me do. In that case, do you know what I should have done?'

'What should you have done?' he smiled.

'I should have asked you to pay him for me, and I would have repaid you as soon as I had any money. I had a great mind to ask you, do you know; it would have seemed less painful than the being obliged to beg of Lord Mount Severn.'

'I hope it would,' he answered, in a low, earnest tone. 'What else can I do for you?'

She was about to answer 'Nothing; that he had done enough:' but at that moment their attention was attracted by a bustle outside, and they moved to the window.

It was the carriage coming round for Lady Isabel. The late earl's chariot, which was to convey her to the railway station six or seven miles off. It had four post-horses to it, the number having been designated by Lord Mount Severn, who appeared to wish Isabel to leave the neighbourhood in as much state as she had entered it. The carriage was packed, and Marvel was perched outside.

'All is ready,' she said, 'and the time is come for me to go. Mr. Carlyle, I am going to leave you a legacy—those pretty gold and silver fish, that I bought a few weeks back.'

'But why do you not take them?'

'Take them to Lady Mount Severn's! No, I would rather leave them with you. Throw a few crumbs into the globe now and then.'

Her face was wet with tears, and he knew she was talking hurriedly to cover her emotion.

'Sit down a few minutes,' he said.

'No—no. I had better go at once.'

He took her hand to conduct her to the carriage. The servants were gathered in the hall, waiting for her; some had grown grey in her father's service. She put out her hand, she strove to say a word of thanks and of fare-well, and she thought she should choke at the effort of keeping down the sobs. At length it was over; a kind look around, a yearning wave of the hand, and she passed on with Mr. Carlyle.

Pound had ascended to his place by Marvel, and the post-boys were waiting the signal to start, but Mr. Carlyle had the carriage-door open again, and was bending in, holding her hand.

'I have not said a word of thanks to you for all your kindness, Mr. Carlyle,' she cried, her breath very laboured. 'I am sure you have seen that I could not.'

'I wish I could have done more; I wish I could have shielded you from the annoyances you have been obliged to endure!' he answered. 'Should we never meet again—'

'Oh, but we shall meet again,' she interrupted. 'You promised Lord Mount Severn.'

'True: we may so meet; casually; once in a way: but our ordinary paths in life lie far and wide apart. God for ever bless you, dear lady Isabel!'

The post-boys touched their horses, and the carriage sped on. She drew down the blinds, and leaned back in an agony of tears: tears for the home she was leaving, for the father she had lost. Her last thoughts had been of gratitude to Mr. Carlyle; but she had more cause to be grateful to him than she yet knew of. Emotion soon spends itself, and as her eyes cleared, she saw a bit of crumpled paper lying on her lap, which appeared to have fallen from her hand. Mechanically she took it up and opened it: it was a bank-note for one hundred pounds.

Ah! reader, you will say this is a romance of fiction, and a far-fetched one, but it is verily and indeed true. Mr. Carlyle had taken it with him to East Lynne, that morning, with its destined purpose.

Lady Isabel strained her eyes and gazed at the note: gazed, and gazed again. Where could it come from? What brought it there? Suddenly the undoubted truth flashed upon her: Mr. Carlyle had left it in her hand.

Her checks burnt, her fingers trembled, her angry spirit was up in arms. In that first moment of discovery, she was ready to resent it as an insult; but when she came to remember the sober facts of the last few days, her anger subsided into admiration of his wondrous kindness. Did he not know that she was without a home to call her own, without money—absolutely without money, save what would be given her in charity?

Well now, what should she do? Of course she could not use the note, that was out of the question; and to re-enclose it to him would pain him; she felt that a nature, capable of generosity so delicate, would be deeply wounded at having its generosity thrown back upon itself. Should she so pain him? Did he deserve it at her hands? No. She would keep the note until she had an opportunity of personally returning it to him.

Leaning over the entrance-gate of their house, between the grove of dark trees, was Barbara Hare. She had heard the hour of Lady Isabel's departure named; and, woman-like, *rival*-like—for in that light had Barbara's fanciful and jealous heart grown to regard Lady Isabel—posted herself there, to watch for it. Little saw she. Nothing but the carriage, the horses, and the attendants; for the blinds were down.

She stood there long, long after the carriage had passed; and presently her father came up from the direction of West Lynne.

'Barbara, have you seen Carlyle?'

'No, papa.'

'I have been to his office, but they thought he had gone up to East Lynne. Perhaps he will be coming by. I want to catch him if I can.'

Mr. Hare stood outside, and rested his elbow on the gate: Barbara stood inside. It is probable the one was quite as anxious as the other to meet Mr. Carlyle.

'What do you think the report is?' suddenly exclaimed the justice. 'The place is full of it. That Carlyle—'

Justice Hare took a step into the road, to obtain a better view of the way from East Lynne. Barbara's face flushed in the suspense created by his unfinished words.

'That Mr. Carlyle, what, papa?' she asked, as he stepped back again.

'It is Carlyle coming,' observed the justice; 'I thought they were his long legs. That he has bought East Lynne, Barbara!'

'Oh, papa! Can it be true? Mr. Carlyle bought East Lynne!'

'As likely as not. He and Miss Corny have got a pretty nest of golden eggs laid by between them. I put the question to Dill just now; but he was as close as he always is, and said neither one way nor the other. Good morning!' called out the justice, as Mr. Carlyle approached. 'We are impatient on the bench to know if you have news from the Ipsley Union, because our Union vows the paupers shan't stop over to-day.'

'Yes,' answered Mr. Carlyle; 'they admit the claim, so you may despatch them at once. How are you, Barbara?'

'That's all right, then,' returned Mr. Hare. 'Carlyle, people are saying that you have purchased East Lynne.'

'Are they? Well, they are not far wrong. East Lynne is mine, I believe.'

'Let you lawyers alone for speed, when you have yourselves for clients. Here is the earl, dead scarcely a week, and East Lynne already transferred to you.'

'Not so, justice. East Lynne was mine months before the earl died.'

'What, when he was stopping there? To think of that! A pretty rent you charged him, I'll be bound.'

'No rent at all,' responded Mr. Carlyle, with a smile. 'He was an honorary tenant for the time being.'

'Then you were a great fool,' observed the justice. 'Beg pardon, Carlyle— you are a young man, and I am an old one; or soon shall be. The earl was another fool to get himself so awfully embarrassed.'

'Sadly embarrassed,' chimed in Barbara. 'I heard last night that there was nothing left for Lady Isabel; that she had actually no money to pay for her mourning. The Smiths told the Herberts, and the Herberts told me. Do you fancy it is true, Archibald?'

Mr. Carlyle appeared much amused. 'I wonder they did not say Lady Isabel had no mourning, as well as no money: it would have been but a little stretch further. What would East Lynne do without its marvels?'

'Ah, what indeed?' cried Justice Hare. 'I met her carriage, spanking along with four horses, her maid and man outside. A young lady, travelling in that state, would not be at a loss for mourning and money, Miss Barbara.'

'People must gossip, you know, sir,' said Mr. Carlyle. 'My East Lynne purchase will be magnified into the purchase of West Lynne also, before the day is over. Good morning; good morning, Barbara.'

When Lord Mount Severn reached London, and the hotel which the Vanes were in the habit of using, the first object his eyes lighted on was his own wife, whom he believed to be safe at Castle Marling. He inquired the cause.

Lady Mount Severn gave herself little trouble to explain. She had been up a day or two—could order her mourning so much better in person—and William did not seem well, so she brought him up for a change.

'I am sorry you came to town, Emma,' remarked the earl, after listening. 'Isabel is gone to-day to Castle Marling.'

Lady Mount Severn quickly lifted her head. 'What's she gone there for?'

'It is the most disgraceful piece of business altogether,' returned the earl, without replying to the immediate question. 'Mount Severn has died worse than a beggar, and there's not a shilling for Isabel.'

'It was not expected there would be much.'

'But there's nothing; not a penny; nothing for her own personal expenses. I gave her a pound or two to-day, for she was completely without.'

The countess opened her eyes. 'Where will she live? What will become of her?'

'She must live with us. She—'

'With us!' interrupted Lady Mount Severn, her voice almost reaching a scream. 'That she never shall.'

'She must, Emma. There is nowhere else for her to live. I have been obliged to decide it so; and she is gone, as I tell you, to Castle Marling to-day.'

Lady Mount Severn grew pale with anger. She rose from her seat, and confronted her husband, the table being between them. 'Listen, Raymond, I *will not* have Isabel Vane under my roof. I hate her. How could you be cajoled into sanctioning such a thing?'

'I was not cajoled, and my sanction was not asked,' he coldly replied: 'I proposed it. Where else is she to be?'

'I don't care where,' was the obstinate retort. 'Never with us.'

'Consider the thing dispassionately,' returned his lordship. 'She has no other relatives, no claim on any one. I, the succeeding peer (who might not have come into the estates for twenty years hence had Mount Severn's been a good life), am bound in courtesy, in good feeling, to afford her a home. Do you not see it?'

'No, I do not,' returned the countess. 'And I will not have her.'

'She is at Castle Marling now, gone to it as her home,' resumed the earl; and even you, when you return, will scarcely venture to turn her out again, into the road, or send her to the workhouse, or solicit her Majesty's ministers for a grant for her from the pension fund, and draw down upon yourself the censure of the world. I think you might show better feeling, Emma.'

Lady Mount Severn did not retort openly. She possessed her share of common sense, and the argument of the earl was certainly difficult to answer—'Where was Isabel to go if not to them?' But she muttered angry words, and her face looked ready to spit fire.

'She will not trouble you long,' carelessly remarked the earl. 'One so lovely as Isabel will be sure to marry early; and she appears as gentle and sweet-tempered a girl as I ever saw, so whence can arise your dislike to her, I don't pretend to guess. Many a man will be too ready to forget her want of fortune for the sake of her face.'

'She shall marry the first who asks her,' snapped the angry lady. 'I'll take care of that.'

✛ X I I ✛

Life at Castle Marling

Isabel had been in her new home about ten days when Lord and Lady Mount Severn arrived at Castle Marling, which was not a castle, you may as well be told, but only the name of a town, nearly contiguous to which was their residence, a small estate. Lord Mount Severn welcomed Isabel; Lady Mount Severn, also, after a fashion; but her manner was so repellant, so insolently patronizing, that it brought the indignant crimson to the cheeks of Isabel. And, if this was the case at the first meeting, what do you suppose it must have been as time went on? Galling slights, petty vexations, chilling annoyances were put upon her, trying her powers of endurance to the very length of their tether: she would wring her hands when alone, and passionately wish that she could find another refuge.

Lady Mount Severn lived but in admiration, and she gathered around her those who would offer its incense. She carried her flirtations to the very verge of propriety; no further: there existed not a woman less likely to forget herself, or peril her fair fame, than Emma, Countess of Mount Severn; and no woman was more scornfully unforgiving to those who did forget themselves. She was the very essence of envy, of selfishness: she had never been known to invite a young and attractive woman to her house; she would as soon have invited a leper: and now you can understand her wrath, when she heard that Isabel Vane was to be her permanent inmate; Isabel, with her many charms, her youth, and her unusual beauty. At Christmas some visitors were down; mostly young men, and they were not wary enough to dissemble the fact that the young beauty was a far greater attraction than the exacting countess. Then broke forth, beyond bounds, her passion; and in a certain private scene, when she forgot all about passion, and lost sight of the proprieties of life, Isabel was *told* that she was a hated intruder, her presence only suffered because there was no help for it.

The earl and countess had two children, both boys, and in February the younger one, always a delicate child, died. This somewhat altered their plans. Instead of proceeding to London after Easter, as had been decided upon, they would not go until May. The earl had passed part of the winter at Mount Severn, looking after the repairs and renovations that were being made there. In March he went to Paris, full of grief for the loss of his boy; far greater grief than was experienced by Lady Mount Severn.

April approached; and, with it, Easter. To the unconcealed dismay of Lady Mount Severn, her grandmother, Mrs. Levison, wrote her word that she required change, and should pass Easter with her at Castle Marling. Lady Mount Severn would have given her diamonds to have got out of it, but there was no escape: diamonds that were once Isabel's; at least, what Isabel had worn. On the Monday in Passion Week the old lady arrived: and, with her, Francis Levison. They had no other guests.

Things went on pretty smoothly till Good Friday, but it was a deceitful calm: my lady's jealousy was kindling, for Captain Levison's attentions to Isabel were driving her wild. At Christmas his admiration had been open enough, but it was more so now. Better from any one else could Lady Mount Severn have borne this than from Francis Levison: she had suffered the young Guardsman, cousin though he was, to grow rather dear; dangerously dear it might have become had she been a less cautious woman. More welcome to her that all the world, rather than he, had given admiration to Isabel. Why did she have him there, throwing him into Isabel's companionship, as she had done the previous year in London? asks the reader. It is more than I can tell; why do people do foolish things?

On Good Friday afternoon, Isabel strolled out with little William Vane: Captain Levison joined them, and they never came in till nearly dinner-time, when the three entered together, Lady Mount Severn doing penance all the time, and nursing her rage against Isabel, for Mrs. Levison kept her indoors.

There was barely time to dress for dinner, and Isabel went straight to her room. Her dress was off, her dressing-gown on, Marvel was busy with her hair, and William chattering at her knee, when the door was flung open, and my lady entered.

'Where have you been?' demanded she, shaking with passion. Isabel knew the signs.

'Strolling about in the shrubberies and grounds,' answered Isabel.

'How dare you disgrace yourself?'

'I do not understand you,' said Isabel, her heart beginning to beat unpleasantly. 'Marvel, you are pulling my hair.'

When women, liable to intemperate fits of passion, give the reins to them, they neither know nor care what they say. Lady Mount Severn broke into a torrent of reproach and abuse, most degrading and unjustifiable.

'Is it not sufficient that you are allowed an asylum in my house, but you must also disgrace it? Three hours have you been hiding yourself with Francis Levison! You have done nothing but flirt with him from the moment he came; you did nothing else at Christmas.'

The attack was longer and broader, but that was the substance of it, and Isabel was goaded to resistance, to anger little less great than that of the countess. This!—and before her attendant! She, an earl's daughter, so much better born than Emma Mount Severn, to be thus insultingly accused in the other's mad jealousy. Isabel tossed her hair from the hands of Marvel, rose up, and confronted the countess, constraining her voice to calmness.

'I do not flirt,' she said; 'I have never flirted. I leave that'—and she could not wholly suppress in tone the scorn she felt—'to married women: though it seems to me that it is a fault less venial in them than in single ones. There is but one inmate of this house who flirts, so far as I have seen since I have lived in it: it is you, not I, Lady Mount Severn.'

The home truth told on her ladyship. She turned white with rage, forgot her manners, and, raising her right hand, struck Isabel a stinging blow upon the left cheek. Confused and terrified, Isabel stood in pain, and before she could speak or act, my lady's left hand was raised to the other cheek, and a blow left on that. Lady Isabel shivered as with a sudden chill, and cried out, a sharp, quick cry; covered her outraged face and sank down upon the dressing-chair. Marvel threw up her hands in dismay, and William Vane could not have burst into a louder roar had he been beaten himself. The boy was of a sensitive nature—and he was frightened.

Lady Mount Severn finished up the scene by boxing William for his noise, jerked him out of the room, and told him he was a monkey.

Isabel Vane lay through the livelong night, weeping tears of anguish and indignation. She could not remain at Castle Marling: who would, after so great an outrage?—Yet, where was she to go? Fifty times in the course of the night did she wish that she was laid beside her father; for her feelings obtained the mastery of her reason: in her calm moments she would have shrunk from the idea of death, as the young and healthy must do. Various schemes crossed her brain: that she would take flight to France, and lay her case before Mount Severn; that she would beg an asylum with old Mrs. Levison; that she would find out Mason, and live with her. Daylight rejected them all. She had not flirted with Captain Levison, but she had received his attention, and suffered his admiration: a woman never flirts where she loves; and it had come to love, or something very near it, in Isabel's heart.

She rose on the Saturday morning, weak and languid, the effects of the night of grief, and Marvel brought her breakfast up. William Vane stole into her room afterwards: he was attached to her in a remarkable degree.

'Mamma's going out,' he exclaimed in the course of the morning. 'Look, Isabel.'

Isabel went to the window. Lady Mount Severn was in the pony carriage, Francis Levison driving.

'We can go down now, Isabel. Nobody will be there.'

She assented, and went down with William. But scarcely were they in the drawing-room when a servant entered with a card on a salver.

'A gentleman, my lady, wishes to see you.'

'To see me?' returned Isabel, in surprise. 'Or Lady Mount Severn?'

'He asked for you, my lady.'

She took up the card. 'Mr. Carlyle.' 'Oh!' she uttered, in a tone of joyful surprise, 'show him in.'

It is curious, nay, appalling, to trace the thread in a human life; how the most trivial occurrences lead to the great events of existence, bringing forth happiness or misery, weal or woe. A client of Mr. Carlyle's, travelling from one part of England to the other, was arrested by illness at Castle Marling: grave illness it appeared to be, inducing fears of death. He had not, as the phrase goes, settled his affairs, and Mr. Carlyle was telegraphed for in haste, to make his will, and for other private matters. This journey appeared to Mr. Carlyle a very simple occurrence, and yet it was destined to lead to events that would end only with his own life.

Mr. Carlyle entered, unaffected and gentlemanly as ever, with his noble form, his attractive face, and his drooping eyelids. She advanced to meet him, holding out her hand, her countenance betraying her pleasure. 'This is indeed unexpected,' she exclaimed. 'How very glad I am to see you!'

'Business brought me yesterday to Castle Marling. I could not leave it again without calling on you. I hear that Lord Mount Severn is absent.'

'He is in France,' she rejoined. 'I said we should be sure to meet again: do you remember, Mr. Carlyle? You—'

Isabel suddenly stopped, for with the word 'remember,' she also remembered something—the hundred-pound note; and what she was saying faltered on her tongue. She grew confused, indeed, for alas! she had changed and partly spent it. *How* was it possible to ask Lady Mount Severn for money? and the earl was nearly always away. Mr. Carlyle saw her embarrassment, though he did not detect its cause.

'What a fine boy!' exclaimed he, looking at the child.

'It is Lord Vane,' said Isabel.

'A truthful, earnest spirit, I am sure,' he continued, gazing at his open countenance. 'How old are you, my little man?'

'I am six, sir; and my brother was four.'

Isabel bent over the child; an excuse to cover her embarrassment. 'You do not know this gentleman, William. It is Mr. Carlyle, and he has been very kind to me.'

The little lord turned his thoughtful eyes on Mr. Carlyle, apparently studying his countenance. 'I shall like you, sir, if you are kind to Isabel. Are you kind to her?'

'Very, very kind,' murmured Isabel, leaving William and turning to Mr. Carlyle, but not looking at him. 'I don't know what to say; I ought to thank you: I did not intend to use the—to use it—but I—I—'

'Hush!' he interrupted, laughing at her confusion; 'I do not know what you are talking of. I have a great misfortune to break to you, Lady Isabel.'

She lifted her eyes and her glowing cheeks, somewhat aroused from her own thoughts.

'Two of your fish are dead. The gold ones.'

'Are they?'

'I believe it was the frost killed them: I don't know what else it could have been. You may remember those bitter days we had in January: they died then.'

'You are very good to take care of them, all this while. How is East Lynne looking? Dear East Lynne! Is it occupied?'

'Not yet. I have spent some money upon it, and it repays the outlay.'

The excitement of his arrival had worn off, and she was looking herself again, pale and sad: he could not help observing that she was changed.

'I cannot expect to look so well at Castle Marling as I did at East Lynne,' she answered.

'I trust it is a happy home to you?' said Mr. Carlyle, speaking upon impulse.

She glanced up at him, a look that he would never forget: it certainly told of despair. 'No,' she said, shaking her head, 'it is a miserable home, and I cannot remain in it. I have been awake all night, thinking where I can go, but I cannot tell. I have not a friend in the wide world.'

Never let people talk secrets before children, for be assured that they comprehend a vast deal more than is expedient: the saying that 'Little pitch-ers have great ears' is wonderfully true. Lord Vane held up his head to Mr. Carlyle:

'Isabel told me this morning that she should go away from us. Shall I tell you why? Mamma beat her yesterday when she was angry.'

'Be quiet, William!' interrupted Lady Isabel, her face in a flame.

'Two great slaps upon her cheeks,' continued the young viscount; 'and Isabel cried so, and I screamed, and then mamma hit me. But boys are made to be hit; nurse says they are. Marvel came into the nursery when we were at tea, and told nurse about it. She says Isabel's too good-looking, and that's why mamma—'

Isabel stopped the child's tongue, rang a peal on the bell, and marshalled him to the door; despatching him to the nursery by the servant who answered it.

Mr. Carlyle's eyes were full of indignant sympathy. 'Can this be true?' he asked, in a low tone, when she returned to him. 'You do, indeed, want a friend.'

'I must bear my lot,' she replied, obeying the impulse which prompted her to confide in Mr. Carlyle. 'At least till Lord Mount Severn returns.'

'And then?'

'I really do not know,' she said, the rebellious tears rising faster than she could choke them down. 'He has no other home to offer me; but with Lady Mount Severn I cannot and will not remain. She would break my heart, as she has already well-nigh broken my spirit. I have not deserved it of her, Mr. Carlyle.'

'No, I am sure you have not,' he warmly answered. 'I wish I could help you! What can I do?'

'You can do nothing,' she said. 'What can any one do?'

'I wish, I wish I could help you!' he repeated. 'East Lynne was not, take it for all in all, a pleasant home to you, but it seems you changed for the worse when you left it.'

'Not a pleasant home!' she echoed, its reminiscences appearing delightful in that moment, for it must be remembered that all things are estimated by comparison. 'Indeed it was; I may never have so pleasant a one again. Oh, Mr. Carlyle, do not disparage East Lynne to me! Would I could awake, and find the last few months but a hideous dream!—that I would find my dear father alive again!—that we were still living peacefully at East Lynne! It would be a very Eden to me now.'

What was Mr. Carlyle about to say? What emotion was it that agitated his countenance, impeded his breath, and dyed his face blood-red? His better genius was surely not watching over him, or those words had never been spoken.

'There is but one way,' he began, taking her hand and nervously playing with it, probably unconscious that he did so; 'only one way in which you could return to East Lynne. And that way—I may not presume, perhaps, to point it out.'

She looked at him, and waited for an explanation.

'If my words offend you, Lady Isabel, check them, as their presumption deserves, and pardon me. May I—dare I—offer you to return to East Lynne as its mistress?'

She did not comprehend him in the slightest degree; the drift of his meaning never dawned upon her. 'Return to East Lynne as its mistress?' she repeated, in bewilderment.

'And as my wife.'

No possibility of misunderstanding him now, and the shock and surprise were great. She had stood there by Mr. Carlyle's side, conversing confidentially with him, esteeming him greatly, feeling as if he were her truest friend on earth, clinging to him in her heart, as to a powerful haven of refuge, loving him almost as she would love a brother, suffering her hand to remain in his. *But to be his wife!*—the idea had never presented itself to her in any shape until this moment, and her first emotion was one of entire opposition, her first movement to express it, as she essayed to withdraw herself and her hand away from him.

But Mr. Carlyle did not suffer it. He not only retained that hand, but took the other also, and spoke, now the ice was broken, eloquent words of love. Not unmeaning phrases of rhapsody, about hearts and darts and dying for her, like somebody else might have spoken, but earnest-hearted words of deep tenderness, calculated to win upon the mind's good sense, as well as upon the ear and heart: and, it may be, that had her imagination not been filled up with that 'somebody else,' she would have said Yes there and then.

They were suddenly interrupted. Lady Mount Severn entered, and took in the scene at a glance: Mr. Carlyle's bent attitude of devotion, his imprisonment of the hands, and Isabel's perplexed and blushing countenance. She threw up her head and her little inquisitive nose, and stopped short on the carpet; her freezing looks demanding an explanation, as plainly as looks can do it. Mr. Carlyle turned to her, and, by way of sparing Isabel, proceeded to introduce himself. Isabel had just presence of mind left to name her: 'Lady Mount Severn.'

'I am sorry that Lord Mount Severn should be absent, to whom I have the honour of being known,' he said. 'I am Mr. Carlyle.'

'I have heard of you,' replied her ladyship, scanning his good looks, and feeling cross that his homage should be given where she saw it was given, 'but I had *not* heard that you and Lady Isabel Vane were on the extraordinary terms of intimacy that—that—'

'Madam,' he interrupted, as he handed a chair to her ladyship and took another himself, 'we have never yet been on terms of extraordinary intimacy. I was begging the Lady Isabel to grant that we might be: I was asking her to become my wife.'

The avowal was as a shower of incense to the countess, and her ill-humour melted into sunshine. It was a solution to her great difficulty, a loophole by which she might get rid of her *bête noire*, the hated Isabel. A flush of gratification lighted her face, and she became full of graciousness to Mr. Carlyle.

'How very grateful Isabel must feel to you,' quoth she. 'I speak openly, Mr. Carlyle, because I know that you were cognizant of the unprotected state in which she was left by the earl's improvidence, putting marriage for her, at any rate, a high marriage, nearly out of the question. East Lynne is a beautiful place, I have heard.'

'For its size, it is not large,' replied Mr. Carlyle, as he rose; for Isabel had also risen and was coming forward.

'And pray what is Lady Isabel's answer?' quickly asked the countess, turning to her.

Not to her did Isabel condescend to give an answer, but she approached Mr. Carlyle, and spoke in a low tone.

'Will you give me a few hours for consideration?'

'I am only too happy that you should accord it consideration, for it speaks to me of hope,' was his reply, as he opened the door for her to pass out. 'I will be here again this afternoon.'

It was a perplexing debate that Lady Isabel held with herself in the solitude of her chamber, whilst Mr. Carlyle touched upon ways and means to Lady Mount Severn. Isabel was little more than a child, and as a child she reasoned, looking neither far nor deep: the shallow, palpable aspect of affairs alone presenting itself to her view. That Mr. Carlyle was not of rank equal to her own, she scarcely remembered: East Lynne seemed a very fair settlement in life, and in point of size, beauty, and importance, it was superior to the home she was now in. She forgot that her position at East Lynne as Mr. Carlyle's wife would not be what it had been as Lord Mount Severn's daughter; she forgot that she would be tied to a quiet home, shut out from the great world, from the pomps and vanities to which she was born. She liked Mr. Carlyle much, she liked to be with him, she experienced pleasure in conversing with him; in short, but for that other ill-omened fancy which had crept over her, there would have been a danger of her falling in love with Mr. Carlyle. And oh! to be removed for ever from the bitter dependence on Lady Mount Severn—East Lynne would, after that, seem what she had called it, Eden.

'So far it looks favourable,' mentally exclaimed poor Isabel, 'but there is the other side of the question. It is not only that I do not love Mr. Carlyle, but I fear I do love, or very nearly love, Francis Levison. I wish *he* would ask me to be his wife!—or that I had never seen him.'

Isabel's soliloquy was interrupted by the entrance of Mrs. Levison and the countess. What the latter had said to the old lady to win her to the cause, was best known to herself, but she was eloquent in it. They both used every possible argument to induce her to accept Mr. Carlyle: the old lady declaring that he was worth a dozen empty-headed men of the great world.

Isabel listened, now swayed one way, now the other, and when the afternoon came, her head was aching with perplexity. The stumbling-block that she could not get over was Francis Levison. She saw Mr. Carlyle's approach from her window, and went down to the drawing-room, not in the least knowing what her answer was to be—a shadowy idea was presenting itself that she would ask him for longer time, and write her answer.

In the drawing-room was Francis Levison, and her heart beat wildly: which said beating might have convinced her that she ought not to marry another.

'Where have you been hiding yourself?' cried he. 'Did you hear of our mishap with the pony carriage?'

'No,' was her answer.

'I was driving Emma into town. The pony took fright, kicked, plunged, and went down upon his knees; she took fright in her turn, got out, and walked back. I gave the brute some chastisement and a race, and brought him to the stables, getting home in time to be introduced to Mr. Carlyle. He seems an out-and-out good fellow, Isabel, and I congratulate you.'

She looked up at him.

'Don't start. We are all in the family, and my lady told me; I won't betray it abroad. She says East Lynne is a place to be coveted. I wish you happiness, Isabel.'

'Thank you,' she returned, in a sarcastic tone, though her throat beat and her lips quivered. 'You are premature in your congratulations, Captain Levison.'

'Am I? Keep my good wishes, then, till the right man comes. I am beyond the pale myself, and dare not think of entering the happy state,' he added, in a pointed tone. 'I have indulged dreams of it, like others, but I cannot afford to indulge them seriously: a poor man, with uncertain prospects, can only play the butterfly, perhaps to his life's end.'

He quitted the room as he spoke. It was impossible for Isabel to misunderstand him, but a feeling shot across her mind, for the first time, that he was false and heartless. One of the servants appeared, showing in Mr. Carlyle: nothing false or heartless about *him*. He closed the door, and approached her. She did not speak, and her lips were white and trembling. Mr. Carlyle waited.

'Well?' he said, at length, in a gentle tone. 'Have you decided to grant my prayer?'

'Yes. But—' She could not go on. What with one agitation and another, she had difficulty in conquering her emotion. 'But—I was going to tell you—'

'Presently,' he whispered, leading her to a sofa; 'we can both afford to wait now. Isabel, you have made me very happy!'

'I ought to tell you, I must tell you,' she began again, in the midst of hysterical tears. 'Though I have said Yes to your proposal, I do not—yet—It has come upon me by surprise,' she stammered. 'I like you very much; I esteem and respect you: but I do not yet love you.'

'I should wonder if you did. But you will let me earn your love, Isabel?'

'Oh yes,' she earnestly answered. 'I hope so.'

He drew her closer to him, bent his face, and took from her lips his first kiss. Isabel was passive; she supposed he had gained the right. 'My dearest! it is all I ask!'

Mr. Carlyle stayed over the following day, and before he departed, in the evening, arrangements had been discussed. The marriage was to take place immediately: all concerned had a motive for hurrying it on. Mr. Carlyle was anxious that the fair flower should be his; Isabel was sick of Castle Marling, sick of some of the people in it; my lady was sick of Isabel. In less than a month it was to be, and Francis Levison sneered over the 'indecent haste.' Mr. Carlyle wrote to the earl. Lady Mount Severn announced that she should present Isabel with the trousseau, and wrote to London to order it. It is a positive fact that when he was taking leave of Isabel she clung to him.

'I wish I could take you now, my darling,' he uttered. 'I cannot bear to leave you here.'

'I wish you could!' she sighed. 'You have seen only the sunny side of Lady Mount Severn.'

⚔ XIII ⚔

Mr. Dill's Shaking

The sensations of Mr. Carlyle when he returned to West Lynne were very much like those of an Eton boy, who knows he has been in mischief, and dreads detection. Always open as to his own affairs, for he had nothing to conceal, he yet deemed it expedient to dissemble now. He felt that his sister would be bitter at the prospect of his marrying; instinct had taught him that, years past; and he believed that, of all women, the most objectionable to her would be Lady Isabel, for Miss Carlyle looked to the useful, and had neither sympathy nor admiration for the beautiful. He was not sure but she might be capable of endeavouring to frustrate the marriage, should news of it reach her ears, and her indomitable will had carried many strange things in her life: therefore you will not blame Mr. Carlyle for observing entire reticence as to his future plans.

A family of the name of Carew had been about taking East Lynne: they wished to rent it, furnished for three years. Upon some of the minor arrangements they and Mr. Carlyle were opposed, but the latter declined to give way. During his absence at Castle Marling, news had arrived from them— that they acceded to all his terms, and would enter upon East Lynne as soon as was convenient. Miss Carlyle was full of congratulation; it was off their hands, she said: but the first letter Mr. Carlyle wrote was—to decline them. He did not tell this to Miss Carlyle. The final touches of the house were given, preparatory to the reception of its inhabitants, three maid and two men-servants hired and sent there, upon board wages, until the family should arrive.

One evening, three weeks subsequent to Mr. Carlyle's visit to Castle Marling, Barbara Hare called at Miss Carlyle's, and found them going to tea, much earlier than usual.

'We dined earlier,' said Miss Corny, 'and I ordered tea in as soon as dinner went away. Otherwise Archibald would have taken none.'

'I am as well without tea,' said he. 'I have a mass of business to get through yet.'

'You are not so well without it,' cried Miss Corny, 'and I don't choose that you should go without it. Take off your bonnet, Barbara. He does things like nobody else: he is off to Castle Marling to-morrow, and never could open his lips till just now that he was going.'

'Is that invalid—Brewster, or whatever his name is—laid up at Castle Marling still?' asked Barbara.

'He is there still,' said Mr. Carlyle.

Barbara sat down to the tea-table, though protesting that she ought not to remain, for she had told her mamma she should be home to make tea. Miss Carlyle interrupted what she was saying, by telling her brother that she should go presently and pack his things.

'Oh no,' returned he, with alarming quickness, 'I will pack them myself, thank you. Peter, you can put the portmanteau in my room. The large one.'

'The large one!' echoed Miss Corny, who never could let anything pass without her interference, 'why, it's as big as a house. What in the world can you want dragging that with you?'

'I have papers and things to take, besides clothes.'

'I am sure I could pack all your things in the small one,' persisted Miss Corny. 'I'll try. You only tell me what you want put in. Take the small portmanteau to your master's room, Peter.'

Mr. Carlyle glanced at Peter, and Peter glanced back again with an imperceptible nod. 'I prefer to pack my things myself, Cornelia. What have you done now?'

'A stupid trick,' she answered—for, in fidgeting with a knife, Miss Corny had cut her finger. 'Have you any sticking-plaster, Archibald?'

He opened his pocket-book, and laid it out on the table while he took from it some black plaster. Miss Carlyle's inquisitive eyes caught sight of a letter lying there; *sans cérémonie*, she stretched out her hand, caught it up, and opened it.

'Who is this from? It is a lady's writing.'

Mr. Carlyle laid his hand flat upon it, as if to hide it from her view. 'Excuse me, Cornelia; that is a private letter.'

'Private nonsense!' retorted Miss Corny. 'I am sure you get no letters that I may not read. It bears yesterday's postmark.'

'Oblige me with the letter,' he returned; and Miss Carlyle, in her astonishment at the calmly authoritative tone, yielded it to him.

'Archibald, what is the matter with you?'

'Nothing,' answered he, shutting the letter in the pocket-book, and returning it to his pocket, leaving out the sticking-plaster for Miss Corny's benefit. 'It's not fair to look into a man's private letters, is it, Barbara?'

He laughed good-humouredly as he looked at Barbara. But she had seen with surprise that a deep flush of emotion had risen to his face—he, so calm a man! Miss Carlyle was not one to be put down easily, and she returned to the charge.

'Archibald, if ever I saw the Vane crest, it is on the seal of that letter.'

'Whether the Vane crest is on the letter, or not, the contents of it were written for my eye alone,' he rejoined. And, somehow, Miss Carlyle did not like the firm tone. Barbara broke the silence.

'Shall you call on the Mount Severns this time?'

'Yes,' he answered.

'Do they talk yet of Lady Isabel's marrying?' pursued Barbara. 'Did you hear anything of it?'

'I cannot charge my memory with all I heard or did not hear, Barbara. Your tea wants more sugar, does it not?'

'A little,' she answered, and Mr. Carlyle drew the sugar-basin towards her cup, and dropped four or five large lumps in, before anybody could stop him.

'What's that for?' asked Miss Corny.

He burst out laughing. 'I forgot what I was doing. Really, Barbara, I beg your tea's pardon. Cornelia will give you another cup.'

'But it's a cup of tea and so much good sugar wasted,' tartly responded Miss Corny.

Barbara sprang up the moment tea was over. 'I don't know what mamma will say to me. And it is beginning to grow dusk! She will think it is late for me to be out alone.'

'Archibald can walk with you,' said Miss Carlyle.

'I don't know that,' cried he, in his plain, open way. 'Dill is waiting for me in the office, and I have some hours' work before me. However—I suppose you won't care to put up with Peter's attendance; so make haste with your bonnet, Barbara.'

No need to tell Barbara that, when the choice between him and Peter depended on the speed she could make. She wished good evening to Miss Carlyle, and went out with him, he taking her parasol from her hand. It was a calm, lovely night, very light yet, and they took the field way.

Barbara could not forget Isabel Vane. She never had forgotten her, or the jealous feeling that arose in her heart at Mr. Carlyle's constant visits to East Lynne when she inhabited it. She returned to the subject now.

'I asked you, Archibald, whether you had heard that Lady Isabel was likely to marry.'

'And I answered you, Barbara: that my memory could not carry all I may have heard.'

'But did you?' persisted Barbara.

'You are persevering,' he smiled. 'I believe Lady Isabel is likely to marry.'

Barbara drew a relieved sigh. 'To whom?'

The same amused smile played on his lips. 'Do you suppose I could put premature questions? I may be able to tell you more about it after my next return from Castle Marling.'

'Do try and find out,' said she. 'Perhaps it is to Lord Vane. Who is it says that more marriages arise from habitual association than—'

She stopped, for Mr. Carlyle had turned his eyes upon her, and was laughing.

'You are a clever guesser, Barbara. Lord Vane is a little fellow, five or six years old.'

'Oh,' returned Barbara, considerably discomfited.

'And the nicest child,' he warmly continued: 'open tempered, generous hearted, earnest spirited. Should I have children of my own,' he added, switching the hedge with the parasol, and speaking in an abstracted manner as if forgetful of his companion, 'I could wish them to be like William Vane.'

'A very important confession,' gaily returned Barbara, 'after contriving to impress West Lynne with the conviction that you would be an old bachelor.'

'I don't know that I ever promised West Lynne anything of the sort,' cried Mr. Carlyle.

Barbara laughed now. 'I suppose West Lynne judges by appearances. When a man owns to thirty years—'

'Which I don't do,' interrupted Mr. Carlyle, considerably damaging the hedge and the parasol. 'I may be an old married man before I count thirty: the chances are, that I shall be.'

'Then you must have fixed upon your wife,' she quickly cried.

'I do not say I have not, Barbara. All in good time to proclaim it, though.'

Barbara withdrew her arm from Mr. Carlyle's, under pretence of repinning her shawl. Her heart was beating, her whole frame trembling, and she feared he might detect her emotion. She never thought he could allude to any one but herself. Poor Barbara!

'How flushed you look, Barbara!' he exclaimed. 'Have I walked too fast?'

She seemed not to hear, intent upon her shawl. Then she took his arm again, and they walked on, Mr. Carlyle striking the hedge and the grass more industriously than ever. Another minute, and—the handle was in two.

'I thought you would do it,' said Barbara, while he was regarding the parasol with ludicrous dismay. 'Never mind; it is an old one.'

'I will bring you another to replace it. What is the colour? Brown. I won't forget. Hold the relics a minute, Barbara.'

He put the pieces in her hand, and taking out a note-case, made a note in pencil.

'What's that for?' she inquired.

He held it close to her eyes that she might discern what he had written; 'Brown parasol. B. H.' 'A reminder for me, Barbara, in case I forget.'

Barbara's eye detected another item or two, already entered in the note-case. 'Piano.' 'Plate.' 'I jot down the things, as they occur to me, that I must get in London,' he explained. 'Otherwise I should forget half.'

'In London! I thought you were going in an opposite direction: to Castle Marling.'

It was a slip of the tongue, but Mr. Carlyle repaired it. 'I may probably have to visit London as well as Castle Marling. How bright the moon looks rising there, Barbara!'

'So bright—that, or the sky—that I saw your secrets,' answered she. 'Piano! Plate! What can you want with either, Archibald?'

'They are for East Lynne,' he quietly replied.

'Oh, for the Carews.' And Barbara's interest in the items was gone.

They turned into the road just below the Grove, and reached it. Mr. Carlyle held the gate open for Barbara.

'You will come in and say good night to mamma. She was saying to-day what a stranger you have made of yourself lately.'

'I have been busy. And I really have not the time to-night. You must remember me to her instead.'

He closed the gate again. But Barbara leaned over it, unwilling to let him go.

'Shall you be away a week?'

'I dare say I may. Here, take the wreck of the parasol, Barbara: I was about to carry it off with me. I can buy you a new one without stealing the old one.'

'Archibald, I have long wished to ask you something,' said she in a tone of suppressed agitation, as she took the pieces and flung them on the path by the thick trees. 'You will not deem me foolish?'

'What is it?'

'When you gave me the gold chain and locket a year ago—you remember?'

'Yes. Well?'

'I put some of that hair of Richard's in it, and a bit of Anne's, and of mamma's: a tiny little bit of each. And there is room for more, you see.'

She held it to him as she spoke, for she always wore it round her neck, attached to the chain.

'I cannot see well by this light, Barbara. If there is room for more, what of that?'

'I like to think that I possess a memento of my best friends, or of those who were dear to me. I wish you to give me a bit of your hair to put with the rest—as it was you who gave me the locket.'

'My hair!' replied Mr. Carlyle, in a tone of as much astonishment as if she had asked for his head. 'What good would that do you, Barbara, or the locket either?'

Her face flushed painfully: her heart beat. 'I like to have a remembrance of the friends I—I care for,' she stammered. 'Nothing more, Archibald.'

He detected neither the emotion nor the depth of feeling, the *sort* of feeling that had prompted the request, and he met it with good-natured ridicule.

'What a pity you did not tell me yesterday, Barbara! I had my hair cut, and might have sent you the snippings. Don't be a goose, child, and exalt me into a Wellington, to bestow hair and autographs. I can't stop a minute longer. Good night.'

He hastened away with quick strides, and Barbara covered her face with her hands. 'What have I done? what have I done?' she reiterated aloud. 'Is it in his nature to be thus indifferent—matter of fact? Has he no sentiment? But it will come. Oh, the bliss this night has brought forth! There was truth in his tone beneath its vein of mockery, when he spoke of his chosen wife. I need not go far to guess who it is—he has told no one else, and he pays attention to none but me. Archibald, when once I am your wife you shall know how fondly I love you; you cannot know till then.'

She lifted her fair young face, beautiful in its radiance, and gazed at the deepening moonlight; then turned away and pursued her path up the garden walk, unconscious that something, wearing a bonnet, pushed its head beyond the trees to steal a look after her. Barbara would have said less, had she divined there was a third party to the interview.

It was three mornings after the departure of Mr. Carlyle that Mr. Dill appeared before Miss Carlyle, bearing a letter. She was busy regarding the effect of some new muslin curtains, just put up, and did not pay attention to him.

'Will you please take the letter, Miss Cornelia. The postman left it in the office with ours. It is from Mr. Archibald.'

'Why, what has he got to write to me about?' retorted Miss Corny. 'Does he say when he is coming home?'

'You had better see, Miss Cornelia. He does not say anything about his return in mine.'

She opened the letter, glanced at it, and sank down in a chair: more overcome, more stupified than she had felt in her whole life.

> Castle Marling, May 1st
> 'MY DEAR CORNELIA,—I was married this morning to Lady Isabel
> Vane, and hasten briefly to acquaint you with the fact. I will write you
> more fully to-morrow or the next day, and explain all things.
> 'Ever your affectionate brother,
> 'ARCHIBALD CARLYLE.'

'It is a hoax,' were the first guttural sounds that escaped from Miss Carlyle's throat, when speech came to her.

Mr. Dill only stood like a stone image.

'It is a hoax, I say,' raved Miss Carlyle. 'What are you standing there for, like a gander, on one leg?' she reiterated, venting her anger upon the unoffending man. '*Is* it a hoax, or not?'

'I am overdone with amazement, Miss Corny. It is not a hoax: I have had a letter, too.'

'It can't be true; it *can't* be true. He had no more thought of being married when he left here, three days ago, than I have.'

'How can we tell that, Miss Corny? How are we to know he did not go to be married? I fancy he did.'

'Go to be married!' shrieked Miss Corny, in a passion, 'he would not be such a fool. And to that fine lady-child! No, no.'

'He has sent this to be put in the county journals,' said Mr. Dill, holding forth a scrap of paper. 'They are married, sure enough.'

Miss Carlyle took it and held it before her; her hand was cold as ice, and shook as if with palsy.

'Married.—On the 1st inst., at Castle Marling, by the chaplain to the Earl of Mount Severn, Archibald Carlyle, Esquire, of East Lynne, to the Lady Isabel Mary Vane, only child of William, late Earl of Mount Severn.'

Miss Carlyle tore the paper to atoms and scattered it. Mr. Dill afterwards made copies from memory, and sent them to the journal offices. But let that pass.

'I will never forgive him,' she deliberately uttered, 'and I will never forgive or tolerate her. The senseless idiot! to go and marry Mount Severn's expensive daughter! a thing who goes to court in feathers and a train—streaming out three yards behind her!'

'He is not an idiot, Miss Cornelia.'

'He is worse; he is a wicked madman,' she retorted, in a midway state between rage and tears. 'He must have been stark staring mad to go and do it; and had I gathered an inkling of the project I would have taken out a commission of lunacy against him. Ay, you may stare, old Dill, but I would, as truly as I hope to have my sins forgiven. Where are they to live?'

'I expect they will live at East Lynne.'

'What?' screamed Miss Corny. 'Live at East Lynne with the Carews! You are going mad too, I think.'

'The negotiation with the Carews is off, Miss Cornelia. When Mr. Archibald returned from Castle Marling at Easter, he wrote to decline them. I saw the copy of the letter in the copying-book. I expect he had settled matters then with Lady Isabel, and had decided to keep East Lynne for himself.'

Miss Carlyle's mouth had opened with consternation. Recovering partially, she rose from her seat, and drawing herself to her full and majestic height, she advanced behind the astounded gentleman, seized the collar of his coat with both hands, and shook him for several minutes. Poor old Dill, short and slight, was as a puppet in her hands, and thought his breath had gone for ever.

'I would have had out a lunacy commission for you also, you sly villain! You are in the plot: you have been aiding and abetting him: you knew as much of it as he did.'

'I declare solemnly, to the Goodness that made me, I did not,' gasped the ill-treated man, when he could gather speech. 'I am as innocent as a baby, Miss Corny. When I got the letter just now in the office, you might have knocked me down with a feather.'

'What has he gone and done it for? an expensive girl without a shilling! And how dared you be privy to the refusing of East Lynne to the Carews?

You *have* abetted him. But he never can be fool enough to think of living there!'

'I was not privy to it, Miss Corny, before it was done. And, had I been—I am only Mr. Archibald's servant. Had he not intended to take East Lynne for his residence, he would not announce himself as Archibald Carlyle, *of East Lynne*. And he can well afford it, Miss Corny; you know he can; and he only takes up his suitable position in going to it,' added the faithful clerk, soothingly, 'and she is a sweet, pretty, loveable creature, though she is a noble lady.'

'I hope his folly will come home to him!' was the wrathful rejoinder.

'Heaven forbid!' cried old Dill.

'Idiot! idiot! WHAT possessed him?' cried the exasperated Miss Corny.

'Well, Miss Corny, I must hasten back to the office,' concluded Mr. Dill, by way of terminating the conference. 'And I am truly vexed, ma'am, that you should have fancied there was cause to fall out upon me.'

'I shall do it again before the day's over, if you come in my way,' hotly responded Miss Corny.

She sat down as soon as she was alone, and her face assumed a stony, rigid look. Her hands fell upon her knees, and Mr. Carlyle's letter dropped to the ground. After a while her features began to work, and she nodded her head, and lifted, now one hand, now the other, apparently debating various points in her own mind. By-and-by she rose, attired herself in her bonnet and shawl, and took the way to Justice Hare's. She felt that the news which would be poured out to West Lynne before the day was over, did reflect a slight upon herself: her much loved brother had forsaken her, to take to himself one nearer and dearer, and had done it in dissimulation: therefore she herself would be the first to proclaim it, far and wide.

Barbara was at the window in the usual sitting-room, as Miss Corny entered the Grove. A grim smile, in spite of her outraged feelings, crossed that lady's lips, when she thought of the blow about to be dealt out to Barbara. Very clearly had she penetrated to the love of that young lady for Archibald; to her hopes of becoming his wife.

'What brings Cornelia here?' thought Barbara, who was looking very pretty in her summer attire, for the weather was unusually warm, and she had assumed it. 'How are you?' she said, leaning from the window. 'Would you believe it? the warm day has actually tempted mamma forth; papa is driving her to Lynneborough. Come in; the hall door is open.'

Miss Carlyle came in, without answering; and seating herself upon a chair, emitted a few dismal groans, by way of preliminary.

Barbara turned to her quickly. 'Are you ill? Has anything upset you?'

'Upset me! you may say that,' ejaculated Miss Corny, in wrath. 'It has turned my heart and my feelings inside out. What do you say? A glass of wine? Nonsense! don't talk of wine to me. A heavy misfortune has fallen us, Barbara. Archibald—'

'Upon Archibald!' interrupted Barbara, in her quick alarm. 'Oh! some accident has happened to him—to the railway train! Perhaps he—he—has got his legs broken!'

'I wish to my heart he had!' warmly returned Miss Corny. 'He and his legs are all right, more's the pity! It is worse than that, Barbara.'

Barbara ran over various disasters in her mind; and, knowing the bent of Miss Carlyle's disposition, began to refer to some pecuniary loss. 'Perhaps it is about East Lynne,' hazarded she. 'The Carews may not be coming to it.'

'No, they are not coming to it,' was the tart retort. 'Somebody else is, though; my wise brother. Archibald has gone and made a fool of himself, Barbara, and now he is coming home to live at East Lynne.'

Though there was much that was unintelligible to Barbara in this, she could not suppress the flush of gratification that rose to her cheek and dyed it with blushes. 'You are going to be taken down a notch or two, my lady,' thought the clear-sighted Miss Carlyle. 'The news fell upon me this morning like a thunderbolt,' she said aloud. 'Old Dill brought it to me. I shook him for his pains.'

'Shook old Dill!' reiterated the wondering Barbara.

'I shook him till my arms ached: he won't forget it in a hurry. He has been abetting Archibald in his wickedness; concealing things from me that he ought to have come and declared; and I am not sure that I can't have the two indicted for conspiracy.'

Barbara sat, all amazement; without the faintest idea of what Miss Corny could be driving at.

'You remember that child, Mount Severn's daughter? I think I see her now, coming into the concert-room, in her white robes, and her jewels, and her flowing hair, looking like a young princess in a fairytale—all very well for her, for what she is, but not for us.'

'What of her?' uttered Barbara.

'Archibald has married her.'

In spite of Barbara's full consciousness that she was before the penetrating eyes of Miss Corny, and in spite of her own efforts for calmness, every feature in her face turned of a ghastly whiteness. But, like Miss Carlyle, she at first took refuge in disbelief.

'It is not true, Cornelia.'

'It is quite true. They were married yesterday at Castle Marling, by Lord Mount Severn's chaplain. Had I known it then, and could I have got there, I might have contrived to part them, though the Church ceremony had passed: I should have tried. But,' added the plain-speaking Miss Corny, 'yesterday was one thing, and to-day's another; and of course nothing can be done now.'

'Excuse me an instant,' gasped Barbara, in a low tone, 'I forgot to give an order mamma left for the servants.'

An order for the servants! She swiftly passed up-stairs to her own room, and flung herself down on its floor in utter anguish. The past had cleared itself of its mists; the scales that were before Barbara's eyes had fallen from them. She saw now that while she had cherished false and delusive hopes in her almost idolatrous passion for Archibald Carlyle, she had never been cared for by him. Even the previous night she had lain awake some of its hours, indulging dreams of the sweetest phantasy—and that was the night of his wedding-day! With a sharp wail of despair, Barbara flung her arms up and closed her aching eyes: she knew that from that hour her life's sunshine had departed.

The cry had been louder than she heeded, and one of the maids, who was outside the door, opened it gently and looked in. There lay Barbara, and there was no mistaking that she lay in dire anguish; not of body, but of mind. The servant judged it an inopportune moment to intrude, and quickly re-closed the door.

Barbara heard the click of the latch, and it recalled her to herself; recalled her to reality; to the necessity of outwardly surmounting the distress at the present moment. She rose up, drank a glass of water, mechanically smoothed her hair and her brow, so contracted with pain, and forced her manner to calmness.

'Married to another! married to another!' she moaned, as she went down the stairs, 'and, that other, *her!* Oh, fortitude! oh, dissimulation! at least come to my aid before his sister!'

There was actually a smile on her face as she entered the room. Miss Carlyle broke open her grievance again without delay, as if to compensate for the few minutes' imposed silence.

'As sure as we are living here, I would have tried for a commission of lunacy against him, had I known this, and so I told Dill. Better have confined him as a harmless lunatic for a couple of years, than suffer him to go free and obtain his fling in this mad manner. I never thought he would marry: I have warned him against it ever since he was in leading-strings.'

'It is an unsuitable match,' said Barbara.

'It is just as suitable as Beauty and the Beast in the children's story. She, a high-born beauty, brought up to revel in expense, in jewels, in feasts, in show; and he, a—a—a—dull bear of a lawyer, like the beast in the tale.'

Had Barbara been less miserable she would have laughed outright. Miss Carlyle continued:

'I have taken my resolution. I go to East Lynne to-morrow, and discharge those five dandies of servants. I was up there on Saturday, and there were all three of my damsels cocketed up in fine mousseline-de-laine gowns, with peach bows in their caps, and the men in striped jackets, playing at footmen. Had I known then that they were Archibald's servants and not hired for the Carews!'

Barbara said nothing.

'I shall go up and dismiss the lot, and remove myself and servants to East Lynne, and let my own house furnished. Expenses will be high enough with *her* extravagant habits, too high to keep on two households. And a fine sort of household Archibald would have of it at East Lynne, with that ignorant baby, befrilled, and bejewelled, and becurled, to direct it.'

'But will she like that?'

'If she does not like it, she can lump it,' replied Miss Carlyle. 'And now that I have told you the news, Barbara, I am going back: and I had almost as soon have had to tell you that he was put into his coffin.'

'Are you sure you are not jealous?' asked Barbara, some uncontrollable impulse prompting her to say it.

'Perhaps I am,' returned Miss Carlyle, with asperity. 'Perhaps, had you brought up a lad as I have brought up Archibald, and loved nothing else in the world, far or near, you would be jealous, when you found him discarding you with contemptuous indifference, and taking a young wife to his bosom, to be more to him than you had been.'

ᚬ XIV ᚬ

The Earl's Astonishment

The announcement of the marriage in the newspapers was the first intimation of it Lord Mount Severn received. He was little less thunderstruck than Miss Corny, and came steaming to England the same day, thereby missing his wife's letter, which gave *her* version of the affair. He met Mr. Carlyle and Lady Isabel in London, where they were staying, at one of the West-end hotels, for a day or two: they were going farther. Isabel was alone when the earl was announced.

'What is the meaning of this, Isabel?' began he, without circumlocution of greeting. 'You are married!'

'Yes,' she answered, with her pretty, innocent blush. 'Some days ago.'

'And to Carlyle the lawyer! How did it come about?'

Isabel began to think how it had come about, sufficiently to give a clear answer. 'He asked me,' she said, 'and I accepted him. He came to Castle Marling at Easter, and asked me then. I was very much surprised.'

The earl looked at her attentively. 'Why was I kept in ignorance of this, Isabel?'

'I did not know you were kept in ignorance of it. Mr. Carlyle wrote to you, as did Lady Mount Severn.'

Lord Mount Severn was as a man in the dark, and looked like it. 'I suppose this comes,' soliloquized he aloud, 'of your father's having allowed the gentleman to dance daily attendance at East Lynne. And so you fell in love with him.'

'Indeed no,' answered she, in an amused tone. 'I never thought of such a thing as falling in love with Mr. Carlyle.'

'Then don't you love him?' abruptly asked the earl.

'No!' she whispered, timidly. 'But I like him much—oh, very much. And he is so good to me!'

The earl stroked his chin, and mused. Isabel had destroyed the only conclusion he had been able to come to, as to the motives for the hasty marriage. 'If you do not love Mr. Carlyle, how comes it that you are so wise in the distinction between "liking" and "love?" It cannot be that you love anybody else!'

The question told home, and Isabel turned crimson. 'I shall love my husband in time,' was all she answered, as she bent her head, and played nervously with her watch-chain.

'My poor child!' involuntarily exclaimed the earl. But he was one who liked to fathom the depth of everything. 'Who has been staying at Castle Marling since I left?' he asked sharply.

'Mrs. Levison came down.'

'I alluded to gentlemen—young men.'

'Only Francis Levison,' she replied.

'Francis Levison! You have never been so foolish as to fall in love with *him!*'

The question was so pointed, so abrupt, and Isabel's self-consciousness moreover so great, that she betrayed lamentable confusion; and the earl had no further need to ask. Pity stole into his hard eyes as they fixed themselves on her downcast glowing face.

'Isabel,' he gravely began, 'Captain Levison is not a good man: if ever you were inclined to think him one, dispossess your mind of the idea, and hold him at arm's distance. Drop his acquaintance; encourage no intimacy with him.'

'I have already dropped it,' said Isabel, 'and I shall not take it up again. But

Lady Mount Severn must think well of him, or she would not have him there.'

'She thinks none too well of him; none can, of Francis Levison,' returned the earl, significantly. 'He is her cousin, and is one of those idle, vain, empty-headed flatterers whom it is her pleasure to group about her. Do you be wiser, Isabel. But this does not solve the enigma of your marriage with Carlyle; on the contrary, it renders it the more unaccountable. He must have cajoled you into it.'

Before Isabel would reply, Mr. Carlyle entered. He held out his hand to the earl: the earl did not appear to see it.

'Isabel,' said he, 'I am sorry to turn you out, I suppose you have only this one sitting-room. I wish to say a few words to Mr. Carlyle.'

She quitted them, and the earl wheeled round and faced Mr. Carlyle, speaking in a stern, haughty tone.

'How came this marriage about, sir? Do you possess so little honour, that, taking advantage of my absence, you must intrude yourself into my family, and clandestinely espouse Lady Isabel Vane?'

Mr. Carlyle stood confounded, *not* confused. He drew himself up to his full height, looking every whit as fearless, and far more noble than the peer. 'My lord, I do not understand you.'

'Yet I speak plainly. What is it but a clandestine procedure, to take advantage of a guardian's absence, and beguile a young girl into a marriage beneath her?'

'There has been nothing clandestine in my conduct towards Lady Isabel Vane; there shall be nothing but honour in my conduct towards Lady Isabel Carlyle. Your lordship has been misinformed.'

'I have not been informed at all,' retorted the earl. 'I was allowed to learn this from the public papers; I, the only relative of Lady Isabel.'

'When I proposed for Lady Isabel—'

'But a month ago,' sarcastically interrupted the earl.

'But a month ago,' calmly repeated Mr. Carlyle, 'my first action, after Isabel accepted me, was to write to you. But, that I imagine you may not have received the letter, by stating you first heard of our marriage through the papers, I should say the want of courtesy lay on your lordship's side, for having vouchsafed me no reply to it.'

'What were the contents of the letter.'

'I stated what had occurred, mentioning what I was able to do in the way of settlements, also that both Isabel and myself wished that the ceremony might take place as soon as might be.'

'And pray where did you address the letter?'

'Lady Mount Severn could not give me the address. She said, if I would intrust the letter to her she would forward it, for she expected daily to hear from you. I did give her the letter, and I heard no more of the matter, except that her ladyship sent me a message, when Isabel was writing to me, that as you had returned no reply, you of course approved.'

'Is this the fact?' cried the earl.

'My lord!' coldly replied Mr. Carlyle. 'Whatever may be my defects in your eyes, I am at least a man of truth. Until this moment, the suspicion that you were in ignorance of the contemplated marriage never occurred to me.'

'So far, then, I beg your pardon, Mr. Carlyle. But how came the marriage about at all?—how came it to be hurried over in this unseemly fashion? You made the offer at Easter, Isabel tells me, and you married her three weeks after it.'

'And I would have married her and brought her away the day I did make it, had it been practicable,' returned Mr. Carlyle. 'I have acted throughout for her comfort and happiness.'

'Oh, indeed!' returned the earl, returning to his disagreeable tone. 'Perhaps you will put me in possession of the facts, and of your motives.'

'I warn you that the facts, to you, will not bear a pleasant sound, Lord Mount Severn.'

'Allow me to be the judge of that,' said the earl.

'Business took me to Castle Marling on Good Friday. On the following day I called at your house: after your own and Isabel's invitation, it was natural I should call: in fact, it would have been a breach of good feeling not to do so. I found Isabel ill-treated and miserable: far from enjoying a happy home in your house—'

'What, sir?' interrupted the earl. 'Ill-treated and miserable!'

'Ill-treated even to blows, my lord.'

The earl stood as one petrified, staring at Mr. Carlyle.

'I learnt it, I must premise, through the chattering revelations of your little son: Isabel of course would not have mentioned it to me; but when the child had spoken, she did not deny it. In short, she was too broken-hearted, too completely bowed in spirit, to deny it. It aroused all my feelings of indignation: it excited in me an irresistible desire to emancipate her from this cruel life, and take her where she would find affection and—I hope—happiness. There was only one way in which I could do this, and I risked it. I asked her to become my wife, and to return to her home at East Lynne.'

The earl was slowly recovering from his petrifaction. 'Then—am I to understand that, when you called that day at my house, you carried no intention with you of proposing to Isabel?'

'Not any. It was a sudden step, the circumstances under which I found her calling it forth.'

The earl paced the room, perplexed still, and evidently disturbed. 'May I inquire if you love her?' he abruptly said.

Mr. Carlyle paused ere he spoke, and a red flush dyed his face. 'Those are feelings man rarely acknowledges to man, Lord Mount Severn, but I will answer you. I do love her passionately and sincerely. I learnt to love her at East Lynne; but I could have carried my love silently within me to the end of my life, and never betrayed it, but for that unexpected visit to Castle Marling. If the idea of making her my wife had not previously occurred to me as practicable, it was that I deemed her rank incompatible wity my own.'

'As it was,' said the earl.

'Country solicitors have married peers' daughters before now,' remarked Mr. Carlyle. 'I only add another to the list.'

'But you cannot keep her as a peer's daughter, I presume?'

'East Lynne will be her home. Our establishment will be small and quiet, as compared with her father's. I explained to Isabel how quiet at the first, and she might have retracted, had she wished: I explained also in full to Lady Mount Severn. East Lynne will descend to our eldest son, should we have children. My profession is most lucrative, my income good: were I to die tomorrow, Isabel would enjoy East Lynne, and about three thousand pounds per annum. I gave these details in the letter which appears to have miscarried.'

The earl made no immediate reply: he was absorbed in thought.

'Your lordship perceives, I hope, that there has been nothing "clandestine" in my conduct to Lady Isabel.'

Lord Mount Severn held out his hand. 'I refused your hand when I came in, Mr. Carlyle, as you may have observed: perhaps you will refuse yours now, though I should be proud to shake it. When I find myself in the wrong, I am not above acknowledging the fact: and I must state my opinion that you have behaved most kindly and honourably.'

Mr. Carlyle smiled and put his hand into the earl's. The latter retained it, while he spoke in a whisper.

'Of course I cannot be ignorant that, in speaking of Isabel's ill-treatment, you alluded to my wife. Has it transpired beyond yourselves?'

'You may be sure that neither Isabel nor myself would mention it: we shall dismiss it from amongst our reminiscences. Let it be as though you had never heard it: it is past and done with.'

'Isabel,' said the earl, as he was departing that evening, for he remained to spend the day with them, 'I came here this morning almost prepared to strike your husband, and I go away honouring him. Be a good and faithful wife to him, for he deserves it.'

'Of course I shall,' she answered, in surprise.

Lord Mount Severn went on to Castle Marling, and there he had a stormy interview with his wife: so stormy that the sounds penetrated to the ears of the domestics. He left again the same day, in anger, and proceeded to Mount Severn.

'He will have time to cool down before we meet in London,' was the comment of my lady.

❧ X V ☙

Coming Home

Miss Carlyle was as good as her word. She quitted her own house, and removed to East Lynne with Peter and two of her handmaidens. In spite of Mr. Dill's grieved remonstrances, she discharged the servants whom Mr. Carlyle had engaged, all save one man: she might have retained one of the maids also, but for the episode of the mousseline-de-laine dresses and the caps with peach bows: for she had the sense to remember in spite of her prejudices, that East Lynne would require more hands in its service than her own home.

On a Friday night, about a month after the wedding, Mr. Carlyle and his wife came home. They were expected, and Miss Carlyle went through the hall to receive them, and stood on the upper steps, between the pillars of the portico. An elegant chariot with four post horses was drawing up: Miss Carlyle compressed her lips as she scanned it. She was attired in a handsome dark silk dress and a new cap: her anger had had time to cool down in the last month, and her strong common sense told her that the wiser plan would be to make the best of it. Mr. Carlyle came up the steps with Isabel.

'You here, Cornelia! that was kind. How are you? Isabel, this is my sister.'

Lady Isabel put forth her hand, and Miss Carlyle condescended to touch the tips of her fingers. 'I hope you are well, ma'am,' she jerked out.

Mr. Carlyle left them together, and went back to search for some trifles which had been left in the carriage. Miss Carlyle led the way to a sitting-room, where the supper-tray was laid. 'You would like to go up-stairs and take your things off before supper, ma'am?' she said, in the same jerking tone, to Lady Isabel.

'Thank you. I will go to my rooms, but I do not require supper. We have dined.'

'Then what would you like to take?' asked Miss Corny.

'Some tea, if you please. I am very thirsty.'

'Tea!' ejaculated Miss Corny. 'So late as this! I don't know that they have boiling water. You'd never sleep a wink all night, ma'am, if you took tea at eleven o'clock.'

'Oh—then never mind,' replied Lady Isabel. 'It is of no consequence. Do not let me give trouble.'

Miss Carlyle whisked out of the room; upon what errand was best known to herself: and in the hall she and Marvel came to an encounter. No words passed, but each eyed the other grimly. Marvel was very stylish, with five flounces to her dress, a veil and a parasol. Meanwhile, Lady Isabel sat down and burst into tears and sobs. A chill had come over her: it did not seem like coming home to East Lynne. Mr. Carlyle entered and witnessed the grief.

'Isabel!' he uttered in amazement, as he hastened up to her. 'My darling, what ails you?'

'I am tired, I think,' she gently answered; 'and coming into the house again made me think of papa. I should like to go to my rooms, Archibald, but I don't know which they are.'

Neither did Mr. Carlyle know, but Miss Carlyle came whisking in again, and said, 'The best rooms; those next the library. Should she go up with my lady?'

Mr. Carlyle preferred to go himself, and he held out his arm to Isabel. She drew her veil over her face as she passed Miss Carlyle.

The branches were not lighted, and the room looked cold and comfortless. 'Things seem all at sixes and sevens in the house,' remarked Mr. Carlyle. 'I fancy the servants must have misunderstood my letter, and not have expected us until to-morrow night.'

'Archibald,' she said, taking off her bonnet, 'I do feel very tired, and—and—low-spirited: may I undress at once, and not go down again to-night?'

He looked at her and smiled. '*May* you not go down again! Have you forgotten that you are at last in your own home? A happy home, I trust, it will be to you, my darling: I will strive to render it so.'

She leaned upon him and sobbed aloud. He tenderly bore with her mood, soothing her to composure, gently kissing the face she held to him, now and then. Oh, his was a true heart; he fervently intended to cherish this fair flower he had won: but, alas! it was just possible he might miss the way, unless he could emancipate himself from his sister's thraldom. Isabel did not love him: of that she was conscious; but her deep and earnest hope by night and by day was, that she might learn to love him, for she knew that he deserved it.

They heard Marvel's voice, and Isabel turned, poured out some water, and began dashing it over her face and eyes. She did not care that Marvel, who was haughtily giving orders about some particular trunk, should see her grief.

'What will you take, Isabel?' asked Mr. Carlyle. 'Some tea?'

'No, thank you,' replied she, remembering Miss Carlyle's answer.

'But you must take something. You complained of thirst in the carriage.'

'Water will do—will be the best for me, I mean. Marvel can get it for me.'

Mr. Carlyle quitted the room, and the lady's-maid undressed her mistress in swelling silence, her tongue quivering with its own rage and wrongs. Marvel deemed herself worse used than any lady's-maid ever had been yet. From the very hour of the wedding her anger had been gathering, for there had been no gentleman-valet to take care of *her* during the wedding-journey. Bad enough! but she had come home to find that there was no staff of upper servants at all: no housekeeper; no steward; no, as she expressed it, nobody. Moreover, she and Miss Carlyle had just come to a clash. Marvel was loftily calling about her in the hall for somebody to carry up a small parcel, which contained, in fact, her lady's dressing-case, and Miss Carlyle had desired her to carry it up herself. But that she had learnt who the lady was, Marvel in her indignation might have felt inclined to throw the dressing-case at her head.

'Anything else, my lady?'

'No,' replied Lady Isabel. 'You may go.'

Isabel, wrapped in her dressing-gown, her warm slippers on, sat with a book; and Marvel, wishing her good night, retired. Mr. Carlyle, meanwhile, had sought his sister, who, finding she was to be the only one to take supper, was then helping herself to the wing of a fowl. She had chosen that day to dine early.

'Cornelia,' he began, 'I do not understand all this. I don't see my servants, and I see yours. Where are mine?'

'Gone away,' said Miss Carlyle, in her decisive, off-hand manner.

'Gone away!' responded Mr. Carlyle. 'What for? I believe they were excellent servants.'

'Very excellent! Decking themselves out in buff mousseline-de-laine dresses on a Saturday morning, and fine caps garnished with peach. Never attempt to dabble in domestic matters again, Archibald, for you only get taken in. Cut me a slice of that tongue.'

'But in what did they do wrong?' he repeated, as he obeyed her.

'Archibald Carlyle, how could you go and make a fool of yourself? If you must have married, were there not plenty of young ladies in your own sphere of society—'

'Stay,' he interrupted. 'I wrote you a full statement of my motives and actions, Cornelia: I concealed nothing that it was necessary you should know: I am not disposed to enter upon a further discussion of the subject, and you must pardon my saying so. Let us return to the topic of the servants. Where are they?'

'I sent them away. Because they were superfluous encumbrances,' she hastily added, as he would have interrupted her. 'We have four in the house, and my lady has brought a fine maid, I see, making five. I have come up here to live.'

Mr. Carlyle felt checkmated. He had always bowed to the will of Miss

Corny, but he had an idea that he and his wife would be better without her. 'And your own house?' he exclaimed.

'I have let it furnished: the people entered to-day. You cannot turn me out of East Lynne, into the road, or to furnished lodgings, Archibald. There will be enough expense, without our keeping on two houses: and most people, in your place, would jump at the prospect of my living here. Your wife will be mistress; I do not intend to take her honours from her; but I shall save her a world of trouble in management, and be as useful to her as a housekeeper. She will be glad of that, inexperienced as she is: I dare say she never gave a domestic order in her life.'

This was a view of the case to Mr. Carlyle, so plausibly put, that he began to think it might be all for the best. He had great reverence for his sister's judgment: force of habit is strong upon all of us. Still—he did not know.

'There is certainly room for you at East Lynne, Cornelia, but—'

'A little too much,' put in Miss Corny. 'I think a house half its size might content us all, and still have been grand enough for Lady Isabel.'

'East Lynne is mine,' said Mr. Carlyle.

'So is your folly,' rejoined Miss Cornelia.

'And with regard to servants,' proceeded Mr. Carlyle, passing over the remark, 'I shall certainly keep as many as I deem necessary. I cannot give my wife splendour, but I will give her comfort. The horses and carriages will take one man's—'

Miss Corny turned faint all over. 'What on earth are you talking of?'

'I bought a pretty open carriage in town, and a pair of ponies for it. The carriage we came home in was Lord Mount Severn's present. Post-horses will do for that at present, but—'

'Oh, Archibald! the sins that you are committing!'

'Sins!' echoed Mr. Carlyle.

'Wilful waste makes woful want. I taught that to you as a child. To be thrifty is a virtue; to squander is a sin.'

'It may be a sin where you cannot afford it. To spend wisely is neither a squander nor a sin. Never you fear, Cornelia, that I shall run beyond my income.'

'Say at once an empty pocket is better than a full one,' angrily returned Miss Carlyle. 'Did you buy that fine piano which has arrived?'

'It was my present to Isabel.'

Miss Corny groaned. 'What did it cost?'

'The cost is of no consequence. The old piano here was a bad one, and I bought a better.'

'What did it cost?' repeated Miss Carlyle.

'A hundred and twenty guineas,' he answered. Obedience to her will was yet powerful within him.

Miss Corny threw up her hands and eyes. At that moment Peter entered with some hot water which his master had rung for. Mr. Carlyle rose, and looked on the sideboard.

'Where's the wine, Peter?'

The servant put it out, port and sherry. Mr. Carlyle drank a glass, and then proceeded to mix some wine and water. 'Shall I mix some for you, Cornelia?' he asked.

'I'll mix for myself if I want any. Who is that for?'

'Isabel.'

He quitted the room, carrying the wine-and-water, and entered his wife's. She was sitting half buried it seemed in the arm-chair, her face muffled up. As she raised it he saw that it was flushed and agitated, that her eyes were bright and her frame was trembling.

'What is the matter?' he hastily asked.

'I got nervous after Marvel went,' she whispered, laying hold of him, as if for protection from terror. 'I could not find the bell, and that made me worse; so I came back to the chair and covered my head over, hoping somebody would come up.'

'I have been talking to Cornelia. But what made you nervous?'

'Oh! I was very foolish. I kept thinking of frightful things; they would come into my mind. Do not blame me, Archibald. This is the room papa died in.'

'Blame you, my darling!' he uttered with deep feeling.

'I thought of a dreadful story about the bats, that the servants told—I dare say you never heard it; and I kept thinking, "Suppose they were at the windows now, behind the blinds." And then I was afraid to look at the bed: I fancied I might see—You are laughing!'

Yes, he was smiling; for he knew that these moments of nervous fear are best met jestingly. He made her drink the wine-and-water, and then he showed her where the bell was, ringing it as he did so. Its position had been moved in some late alterations to the house.

'Your rooms shall be changed to-morrow, Isabel.'

'No, let us remain in these. I shall like to feel that papa was once their occupant. I won't get nervous again.'

But, even as she spoke, her actions belied her words. Mr. Carlyle had gone to the door and opened it, and she flew close up to him, cowering behind him.

'Shall you be very long, Archibald?' she whispered.

'Not more than an hour,' he answered. But he hastily put back one of his hands, and held her tightly in his protecting grasp. Marvel was coming along the corridor in answer to the bell.

'Have the goodness to let Miss Carlyle know that I am not coming down again to-night,' he said.

'Yes, sir.'

Mr. Carlyle shut the door, and then looked at his wife and laughed. 'He is very kind to me,' thought Isabel.

With the morning began the perplexities of Lady Isabel Carlyle. But first of all, just fancy the group at breakfast. Miss Carlyle descended in the starling costume the reader has seen; took her seat at the breakfast-table, and there sat bolt upright. Mr. Carlyle came down next; and then Lady Isabel entered in an elegant half-mourning dress with flowing black ribbons.

'Good morning, ma'am. I hope you slept well?' was Miss Carlyle's salutation.

'Quite well, thank you,' she answered, as she took her seat opposite Miss Carlyle. Miss Carlyle pointed to the top of the table.

'That is your place, ma'am. But I will pour out the coffee, and save you the trouble, if you wish it.'

'I should be glad if you would,' answered Lady Isabel.

So Miss Carlyle proceeded to her duties, very stern and grim. The meal was nearly over, when Peter came in, and said the butcher had come up for orders. Miss Carlyle looked at Lady Isabel, waiting, of course, for her to give them. Isabel was silent with perplexity: she had never given such an order in her life. Totally ignorant was she of the requirements of a household; and did not know whether to suggest a few pounds of meat or a whole cow. It was the presence of that grim Miss Corny which put her out: alone with her husband, she would have said, 'What ought I to order, Archibald? Tell me.' Peter waited.

'A—Something to roast and boil, if you please,' stammered Lady Isabel.

She spoke in a low tone; embarrassment makes cowards of the best of us; and Mr. Carlyle repeated it after her. He knew no more about housekeeping than she did.'

'Something to roast and boil, tell the man, Peter.'

Up started Miss Corny; she could not stand that. 'Are you aware, Lady Isabel, that an order, such as that, would only puzzle the butcher? Shall I give the necessary orders for to-day. The fish-monger will be up presently.'

'Oh! I wish you would!' cried the relieved Lady Isabel. 'I have not been accustomed to it; but I must learn. I don't think I know anything about housekeeping.'

Miss Corny's answer was to stalk from the room. Isabel rose from her chair, like a bird released from its cage, and stood by her husband's side. 'Have you finished, Archibald?'

'I think I have, dear. Oh! here's my coffee. There; I have finished now.'

'Let us go round the grounds.'

He rose, laid his hands playfully on her slender waist, and looked at her. 'You may as well ask me to take a journey to the moon. It is past nine, and I have not been to the office for a month.'

The tears rose in her eyes. 'I wish you could stay with me! I wish you could be always with me. East Lynne will not be East Lynne without you.'

'I will be with you as much as ever I can, my dearest,' he whispered. 'Come and walk with me through the park.'

She ran for her bonnet, gloves, and parasol. Mr. Carlyle waited for her in the hall, and they went out together.

He thought it a good opportunity to speak about his sister. 'She wishes to remain with us,' he said. 'I do not know what to decide. On the one hand, I think she might save you the worry of household management: on the other, I fancy we shall be happier by ourselves.'

Isabel's heart sank within her at the idea of that stern Miss Corny, mounted over her as resident guard; but, refined and sensitive, almost painfully considerate of the feelings of others, she raised no word of objection. As he and Miss Carlyle pleased, she answered.

'Isabel,' he said, with grave earnestness, 'I wish it to be as you please: that is, I wish matters to be arranged as may best please you; and I will have them so arranged. My chief object in life now is your happiness.'

He spoke in all the sincerity of truth, and Isabel knew it; and the thought came across her that with him by her side, her loving protector, Miss Carlyle could not mar her life's peace. 'Let her stay, Archibald: she will not incommode us.'

'At any rate, it can be tried for a month or two, and we shall see how it works,' he musingly observed.

They reached the park gates. 'I wish I could go with you and be your clerk,' she cried, unwilling to release his hand. 'I should not have all that long way to go back by myself.'

He laughed and shook his head, telling her that she wanted to bribe him into taking her back, but it could not be. And away he went, after saying farewell.

Isabel wandered back, and then wandered through the rooms: they looked lonely, not as they had seemed to look in her father's time. In her dressing-room knelt Marvel, unpacking. She rose when Lady Isabel entered.

'Can I speak to you a moment, if you please, my lady?'

'What is it?'

Then Marvel poured forth her tale. That she feared so small an establishment would not suit her, and if my lady pleased she would like to leave at once: that day. Anticipating it, she had not unpacked her things.

'There has been some mistake about the servants, Marvel, but it will be remedied as soon as possible. And I told you, before I married, that Mr. Carlyle's establishment would be a limited one.'

'My lady, perhaps I could put up with that; but I never could stop in the house with'—that female Guy, had been on the tip of Marvel's tongue; but she remembered in time of whom she was speaking— 'with Miss Carlyle. I

fear, my lady, we have both got tempers that would clash, and might be flying at each other: I could not stop, my lady, for untold gold. And if you
please to make me forfeit my running quarter's salary, why, I must do it. So
when I have set your ladyship's things to rights, I hope you'll allow me
to go.'

Lady Isabel would not condescend to ask her to remain, but she wondered
how she should manage without a maid. She drew her desk towards her.
'What is the amount due to you?' she inquired, as she unlocked it.

'Up to the end of the quarter, my lady?' cried Marvel, in a brisk tone.

'No,' coldly replied Lady Isabel. 'Up to to-day.'

'I have not had time to reckon, my lady.'

Lady Isabel took a pencil and paper, made out the account, and laid it
down in gold and silver on the table. 'It is more than you deserve, Marvel,'
she remarked, 'and more than you would get in most places. You ought to
have given me proper notice.'

Marvel melted into tears, and began a string of excuses. 'She should never
have wished to leave so kind a lady, but for attendant ill-conveniences, and
she hoped my lady would not object to testify to her character.' Lady Isabel
quitted the room in the midst of it: and in the course of the day Marvel took
her departure, Joyce telling her that she ought to be ashamed of herself.

'I couldn't help myself,' retorted Marvel, 'and I'm sorry to leave her, for
she's a pleasant young lady to serve.'

'Well, I know I'd have helped myself,' was Joyce's remark. 'I would not go
off in this unhandsome way from a good mistress.'

'Perhaps you wouldn't,' loftily returned Marvel, 'but my inside feelings are
delicate, and can't bear to be trampled upon. The same house is not going to
hold me and that tall female image, who's more fit to be carried about at a
foreign carnival than some that they do carry.'

So Marvel left. And when Lady Isabel went to her room to dress for dinner, Joyce entered it.

'I am not much accustomed to a lady's-maid's duties,' said she, 'but
Miss Carlyle has sent me, my lady, to do what I can for you, if you will
allow me.'

Isabel thought it was kind of Miss Carlyle.

'And if you please to trust me with the keys of your things, I will take
charge of them for you, my lady, until you are suited with a maid,' Joyce
resumed.

'I don't know anything about the keys,' answered Isabel. 'I never keep
them.'

Joyce did her best, and Lady Isabel went down. It was nearly six o'clock,
the dinner hour, and she strolled to the park gates, hoping to meet Mr. Carlyle. Taking a few steps out, she looked down the road, but could not see him

coming; so she turned in again, and sat down under a shady tree and out of view of the road. It was remarkably warm weather for the closing days of May.

Half an hour, and then Mr. Carlyle came pelting up, passed the gates, and turned on to the grass. There was his wife. She had fallen asleep, her head leaning against the trunk of the tree. Her bonnet and parasol lay at her feet, her scarf had dropped, and she looked like a lovely child, her lips partly open, her cheeks flushed, and her beautiful hair falling around. It was an exquisite picture, and his heart beat quicker within him as he felt it was his own. A smile stole over his lips as he stood looking at her. She opened her eyes, and for a moment could not remember where she was. Then she started up.

'Oh, Archibald! have I been asleep?'

'Ay; and might have been stolen and carried off. I could not afford that, Isabel.'

'I don't know how I came to fall asleep. I was listening for you.'

'What have you been doing all day?' he asked, as he drew her arm within his, and they walked on.

'Oh, I hardly know,' she sighed. 'Trying the new piano, and looking at my watch, wishing the time would go quicker, that you might come home. The ponies and carriage have arrived, Archibald.'

'I know they have, my dear. Have you been out-of-doors much?'

'No, I waited for you.' And then she told him about Marvel. He felt vexed, saying she must replace her with all speed. Isabel said she knew of one, a young woman who had left Lady Mount Severn while she, Isabel, was at Castle Marling: her health was delicate, and Lady Mount Severn's place was too hard for her.

'Write to her,' said Mr. Carlyle.

'You have kept dinner waiting more than half an hour,' began Miss Corny, in a loud tone of complaint, to her brother, meeting them in the hall. 'And I thought you must be lost, ma'am,' she added, to Isabel.

Why in the world did she tack on that objectionable 'ma'am' to every sentence? It was out of place in all respects to Isabel: more especially considering her own age and Isabel's youth. Mr. Carlyle knitted his brow whenever it came out, and Joyce felt sure that Miss Corny did it 'in her temper.' He hastily answered her that he could not get away from the office earlier, and went up to his dressing-room. Isabel hurried after him, probably dreading some outbreak of Miss Carlyle's displeasure, but the door was shut, and, scarcely at home yet as a wife, she did not like to open it. When he appeared, there she was, leaning against the door-post.

'Isabel! Are you there?'

'I am waiting for you. Are you ready?'

'Nearly.' He drew her inside, caught her to him, and held her against his heart.

There was an explosion on the following morning. Mr. Carlyle ordered the pony-carriage for church, but his sister interrupted him.

'Archibald! what are you thinking of? I will not permit it.'

'Permit what?' asked Mr. Carlyle.

'The cattle to be taken out on a Sunday. I am a religious woman, ma'am,' she added, turning sharply to Isabel, 'and I cannot countenance Sunday travelling. I was taught my catechism, Lady Isabel.'

Isabel did not feel comfortable. She knew that a walk to St. Jude's Church and back in the present heat would knock her up for the day, but she shrank from offending Miss Carlyle's prejudices. She was standing at the window with her husband, Miss Carlyle being seated at a distant table, with the Bible before her.

'Archibald, perhaps if we walk very slowly, it will not hurt me,' she softly whispered.

He smiled and nodded, and whispered in return: 'Be quite ready by half-past ten.'

'Well—is she going to walk?' snapped Miss Corny, as Isabel left the room.

'No. She could not bear the walk in this heat, and I shall certainly not allow her to attempt it. We shall go early. John will put up the ponies and be at church before the service begins.'

'Is she made of glass, that she'd melt?' retorted Miss Corny.

'She is a gentle, tender plant; one that I have taken to my bosom and vowed before my Maker to love and to cherish: and, by His help, I will do so.'

He spoke in a firm tone, almost as sharp as Miss Corny's, and quitted the room. Miss Carlyle raised her hand and pressed it upon her temples: as if something pained her there.

The carriage came round, a beautiful little equipage, and Isabel was ready. As Mr. Carlyle drove slowly down the dusty road they came upon Miss Corny striding along in the sun, with a great umbrella over her head. She would not turn to look at them.

Once more, as in the year gone by, St. Jude's Church was in a flutter of expectation. It expected to see a whole paraphernalia of bridal finery, and again it was doomed to disappointment, for Isabel had not put off the mourning of her father. She was in black, a thin gauze dress, and her white bonnet had small black flowers inside and out. For the first time in his life Mr. Carlyle took possession of the pew belonging to East Lynne, filling the place where the poor earl used to sit. Not so Miss Corny: she sat in her own.

Barbara was there with the justice and Mrs. Hare. Her face wore a grey, dusky hue, of which she was only too conscious, but could not subdue. Her covetous eyes would wander to that other face with its singular loveliness, and its sweetly earnest eyes, sheltered under the protection of him, for whose sheltering protection she had so long yearned. Poor Barbara did not benefit much by the services that day.

Afterwards, they went across the churchyard to the west corner, where stood the tomb of Lord Mount Severn. Isabel looked at the inscription, her veil shading her face.

'Not here, and now, my darling,' he whispered, pressing her arm to his side, for he felt her silent sobs. 'Strive for calmness.'

'It seems but the other day he was at church with me, and now—here!'

Mr. Carlyle suddenly changed their places, so that they stood with their backs to the hedge and to any staring stragglers who might be lingering in the road.

'There ought to be railings round the tomb,' she presently said, after a successful battle with her emotion.

'I thought so, and I suggested it to Lord Mount Severn, but he appeared to think differently. I will have it done.'

'I put you to great expense,' she said.

Mr. Carlyle glanced quickly at her, a dim fear penetrating his mind that his sister might have been *talking* in her hearing. 'An expense I would not be without for the whole world. You know it, Isabel.'

'And I have nothing to repay you with,' she sighed.

He looked excessively amused; and, gazing into her face, the expression of his eyes made her smile. 'Here is John with the carriage,' she exclaimed. 'Let us go, Archibald.'

Standing outside the gates, talking to the rector's family, were several ladies, one of them Barbara Hare. She watched Mr. Carlyle place his wife in the carriage, she watched him drive away. Barbara's very lips were white as she bowed in return to his greeting.

'The heat is so great,' murmured Barbara, when those around noticed her paleness.

'Ah! you ought to have gone home in the phaeton with Mr. and Mrs. Hare—as they desired you.'

'I wished to walk,' returned the unhappy Barbara.

'What a pretty girl!' said Lady Isabel to her husband. 'What is her name?'

'Barbara Hare.'

❧ X V I ❧

Barbara Hare's Revelation

The county carriages began to arrive at East Lynne, to pay the wedding visit
to Mr. and Lady Isabel Carlyle. Some appeared with all the pomp of coro-
nets and hammercloths, and bedizened footmen with calves and wigs and
gold-headed canes; some came with four horses, and some even with outriders. It is the custom still in certain localities to be preceded by outriders
when paying visits of ceremony, and there are people who like the dash.
Mr. Carlyle might have taken up his abode at East Lynne without any such
honours being paid him, but his marriage with Lady Isabel had sent him up
in county estimation. Amongst the rest went Justice and Mrs. Hare and Barbara. The old-fashioned, large yellow chariot was brought out, and the fat,
sleek, long-tailed coach-horses: only on state occasions was that chariot
awakened out of its repose.

Isabel happened to be in her dressing-room, talking to Joyce. She had
grown to like Joyce very much, and was asking her whether she would continue to wait upon her—as the maid, for whom she had written, was not
well enough to come.

Joyce's face lighted up with pleasure at the proposal. 'Oh, my lady, you are
very kind! I should so like it. I would serve you faithfully to the best of my
ability: and I know I could do your hair well, if you allowed me to try: I have
been practising upon my own, night and morning.'

Isabel laughed. 'But Miss Carlyle may not be inclined to transfer you.'

'I think she would be, my lady. She said, a day or two ago, that I appeared
to suit you, and you might have me altogether if you wished, provided I
could still make her gowns, which I could very well do, for yours is an easy
service. I make them to please her, you see, my lady.'

'Do you make her caps also?' demurely asked Lady Isabel.

Joyce smiled. 'Yes, my lady: but I am allowed to make them only according to her own pattern.'

'Joyce, if you become my maid, you must wear smarter caps yourself.'

'I know that, my lady—at least, different ones. But Miss Carlyle is very
particular, and only allows muslin caps to her servants. I would wear plain
white net ones, if you don't object, my lady: neat and close, with a little
quilled white ribbon.'

'They are the best that you can wear. I do not wish you to be fine, like
Marvel.'

'Oh, my lady! I shall never be fine,' shuddered Joyce. And Joyce believed
she had cause to shudder at finery. She was about to speak further, when a

knock came to the dressing-room door. Joyce went to open it, and saw one of the housemaids, a girl who had recently been engaged, a native of West Lynne. Isabel heard the colloquy.

'Is my lady there?'

'Yes.'

'Some visitors. Peter ordered me to come and tell you. I say, Joyce, it's the Hares. And *she's* with them. Her bonnet's got blue convolvulums inside, and a white feather on the out, as long as Martha's back'us hearth-broom. I watched her get out of the carriage.'

'Who?' sharply returned Joyce.

'Why, Miss Barbara. Only fancy her coming to pay the wedding visit *here*. My lady had better take care that she don't get a bowl of poison mixed for her. Master's out, or else I'd have given a shilling to see the interview between the three.'

Joyce sent the girl away, shut the door, and turned to her mistress, quite unconscious that the half-whispered conversation had been audible.

'Some visitors in the drawing-room, my lady, Susan says. Mr. Justice Hare and Mrs. Hare, and Miss Barbara.'

Isabel descended, her mind full of the mysterious words spoken by Susan. The justice was in a new flaxen wig, obstinate-looking and pompous; Mrs. Hare pale, delicate, and lady-like; Barbara, beautiful: such was the impression they made upon Isabel.

They paid rather a long visit. Isabel quite fell in love with the gentle and suffering Mrs. Hare, who had risen to leave when Miss Carlyle entered. Miss Carlyle wished them to remain longer, had something, she said, to show Barbara. The justice declined: he had a brother-justice coming to dine with him at five; it was then half-past four: Barbara might stay if she liked.

Barbara's face turned crimson: but nevertheless she accepted the invitation, proffered her by Miss Carlyle, to remain at East Lynne for the rest of the day.

Dinner-time approached, and Isabel went up to dress for it. Joyce was waiting, and entered upon the subject of the service.

'My lady, I have spoken to Miss Carlyle, and she is willing that I should be transferred to you, but she says I ought first of all to acquaint you with certain unpleasant facts in my history, and the same thought had occurred to me. Miss Carlyle is not over pleasant in manner, my lady, but she is very upright and just.'

'What facts?' asked Lady Isabel, sitting down to have her hair brushed.

'My lady, I'll tell you as shortly as I can. My father was a clerk in Mr. Carlyle's office—of course I mean the late Mr. Carlyle. My mother died when I was eight years old, and my father afterwards married again, a sister of Mr. Kane's wife—'

'Mr. Kane, the music-master?'

'Yes, my lady. She was a governess; she and Mrs. Kane had both been governesses, they were quite ladies, so far as education and manners went, and West Lynne said that in stooping to marry my father she lowered herself dreadfully. But he was a very handsome man, and a clever man also, though self-taught. Well, they married, and at the end of a year Afy was born—'

'Who?' interrupted Lady Isabel.

'My half-sister, Afy. In another year her mother died, and an aunt of her mother sent for the child, and said she should bring her up. I remained at home with my father, going to school by day, and when I grew up, I went by day to learn millinery and dressmaking. We lived in the prettiest cottage, my lady; it was in the wood, and it was my father's own. After I was out of my time, I used to go round to different ladies' houses to work, seeing to my father's comforts night and morning, for the woman who did the housework only came in for a few hours in the day. That went on for years, and then Afy came home. Her aunt had died, and her money died with her, so that though she had brought up Afy well, she could leave her nothing. Afy quite frightened us. Her notions were fine, and her dress was fine; she was gay and giddy and very pretty, and would do nothing all day but read books, which she used to get at the West Lynne library. My father did not like it: we were only plain working people, and she wanted to set up for a lady—the effect of bringing her up above her station. Many a breeze had she and I together, chiefly about her dress. The next thing, she got acquainted with young Richard Hare.'

Lady Isabel looked up quickly.

'Mr. Justice Hare's only son; own brother to Miss Barbara,' proceeded Joyce, dropping her voice, as though Barbara could hear her in the drawing-room. 'Oh, she was very flighty; she encouraged Mr. Richard, and he soon grew to love her with quite a wild sort of love; he was rather simple, and Afy used to laugh at him behind his back. She encouraged others too, and would have them there in an evening, when the house was free. My father was secretary to the literary institution, and had to be there two evenings in the week, after office hours at Mr. Carlyle's; he was fond of shooting, too, and, if home in time, would go out with his gun; and as I scarcely ever got home before nine o'clock, Afy was often alone, and she took the opportunity of having one or other of her admirers there.'

'Had she many admirers?' asked Lady Isabel, who seemed inclined to treat the tale in a joking spirit.

'The chief one, my lady, was Richard Hare. She got acquainted with somebody else, a stranger, who used to ride over from a distance to see her, but I fancy there was nothing in it; Mr. Richard was the one. And it went on, and on, till—till—he killed her father.'

'Who?' uttered the startled Lady Isabel.

'Richard Hare, my lady. My father had told Afy that Mr. Richard should not come there any longer, for when gentlemen go in secret after poor girls, it is well known they have not marriage in their thoughts: my father would have interfered more than he did, but that he judged well of Mr. Richard, and did not think he was one to do Afy real harm—but he did not know how flighty she was. However, one day he heard people talking about it in West Lynne, coupling her name and Mr. Richard's offensively together, and at night he told Afy, before me, that it should not go on any longer, and she must not encourage him. My lady, the next night Richard Hare shot my father.'

'How very dreadful!'

'Whether it was done on purpose, or whether the gun went off in a scuffle, I can't tell: people think it was wilful murder. I never shall forget the scene, my lady, when I got home that night: it was at Justice Hare's that I had been working. My father was lying on the floor, dead; and the house was full of people. Afy could give no particulars: she had gone out to the wood path at the back, and never heard or saw anything amiss; but when she went in again, there lay father. Mr. Locksley was leaning over him; he told Afy that he had heard the shot, and came up in time to see Richard Hare fling the gun away, and fly from the house with his shoes stained with blood.'

'Oh, Joyce! I do not like to hear this. What was done to Richard Hare?'

'He escaped, my lady. He went off that same night, and has never been heard of since. There's a judgment of murder out against him, and his own father would be the first to deliver him up to justice. It is a dreadful thing to have befallen the Hare family, who are most high and respectable people: it is killing Mrs. Hare by inches. Afy—'

'What is it, that name, Joyce?'

'My lady, she was christened by a very fine name—Aphrodite: so I and my father never called her anything but Afy. But I have got the worst to tell you yet, my lady—the worst as regards her. As soon as the inquest was over she went off, after Richard Hare.'

Lady Isabel uttered an exclamation.

'She did indeed, my lady,' returned Joyce, turning away her moist eye-lashes and her shamed cheeks from the gaze of her mistress. 'Nothing has been heard of either of them: and it is hardly likely but what they went out of England—perhaps to Australia; perhaps to America; nobody knows. What with the shame of that, and the shock of my poor father's murder, I had an attack of illness. It was a nervous fever, and it lasted long: Miss Carlyle had me at her house, and she and her servants nursed me through it. She's good at heart, my lady, is Miss Carlyle, only her manners are against her, and she will think herself better than other people. After that illness, I stayed with her as upper maid, and never went out to work again.'

'How long is it since this happened?'

'It will be four years next September, my lady. The cottage has stood empty ever since, for nobody will live in it; they say it smells of murder. And I can't sell it, because Afy has a right in it as well as I. I go to it sometimes, and open the windows, and air it. And this was what I had to tell you, my lady, before you decide to take me into your service: it is not every lady would like to engage one whose sister has turned out so badly.'

Lady Isabel did not see that it ought to make any difference. She said so: and then leaned back in her chair, and mused.

'Which dress, my lady?'

'Joyce, what was that I heard you and Susan gossiping over at the door?' Lady Isabel suddenly asked. 'About Miss Hare giving me a bowl of poison. You should tell Susan not to make her whispers so loud.'

Joyce smiled; though she was rather confused. 'It was only a bit of non-sense, of course, my lady. The fact is, that people think Miss Barbara was much attached to Mr. Carlyle, regularly in love with him, and many thought it would be a match. But I don't fancy she would have been the one to make him happy, with all her love.'

A hot flush passed over the brow of Lady Isabel; a sensation very like jeal-ousy flew to her heart. No woman likes to hear that another woman either is or has been attached to her husband: a doubt always arises whether the feel-ing may not have been reciprocated.

Lady Isabel descended. She wore a costly black lace dress, its low body and sleeves trimmed with white lace as costly: and ornaments of jet. She looked inexpressibly beautiful, and Barbara turned from her with a feeling of sick-ening jealousy; from her beauty, from her attire, even from the fine, soft handkerchief, which displayed the badge of her rank—the coronet of an earl's daughter. Barbara looked well too: she was in a light blue silk robe, and her pretty cheeks were damask with her mind's excitement. On her neck she wore the gold chain given to her by Mr. Carlyle—she had not discarded that.

They stood together at the window, looking at Mr. Carlyle as he came up the avenue. He saw them, and nodded. Lady Isabel watched the damask cheeks turn to crimson at sight of him.

'How do you do, Barbara?' he cried, as he shook hands. 'Come to pay us a visit at last? you have been tardy over it. And how are you, my darling?' he whispered, bending over his wife: but she missed his kiss of greeting. Well; would she have had him give it her in public? No; but she was in the mood to notice the omission.

Dinner over, Miss Carlyle beguiled Barbara out-of-doors. To exhibit the beauties of the East Lynne pleasure-grounds, the rarities of the conservatory, thinks the reader. Not at all: she was anxious to show off the stock of vegeta-bles, the asparagus and cucumber beds; worth a hundred acres of flowers in Miss Carlyle's estimation. Barbara went unwillingly: she would rather be in *his* presence than away from it; and she could not help feeling this, although he was the husband of another. Isabel remained in-doors: Barbara was Miss Carlyle's guest.

'How do you like her?' abruptly asked Barbara, alluding to Lady Isabel.

'Better than I thought I should,' acknowledged Miss Carlyle. 'I had expected airs and graces and pretence, and I must say she is free from them. She seems quite wrapped up in Archibald, and watches for his coming home like a cat watches for a mouse. She is dull without him.'

Barbara plucked a rose as they passed a bush, and began pulling it to pieces, leaf by leaf. 'Dull! how does she employ her time?'

'In doing nothing,' snappishly retorted Miss Carlyle. 'Sings a bit, and plays a bit, and reads a bit, and receives her visitors, and idles away her days in that manner. She coaxes Archibald out here after breakfast, and he ought not to let himself be coaxed, making him late at his office; and then she dances down to the park gates with him, hindering him still further, for he would go alone in half the time. One morning it poured with rain; she actually went all the same. I told her she would spoil her dress: oh, that was nothing, she said, and Archibald wrapped a shawl round her and took her. Of course the spoiling of dresses is nothing to her! And in an evening she goes down to meet him again; she would have gone to-day, if you had not been here. Oh, she is first with him now; business is second.'

Barbara compelled her manner to indifference. 'I suppose it is natural.'

'I suppose it is absurd,' was the retort of Miss Carlyle. 'I give them very little of my company, especially in an evening. They go strolling out together, or she sings to him, he hanging over her as if she were gold; to judge by appearances, she is more precious to him than any gold that ever was coined into money. I'll tell you what I saw last night. They had post-horses to the close carriage yesterday, and went to return some visits, never getting home till past seven, and keeping me and dinner waiting. Archibald had what he is not often subject to, a severe headache, and he went in the next room after dinner, and lay on the sofa. She carried a cup of tea to him, and never came back, leaving her own on the table till it was perfectly cold. I pushed open the door to tell her so. There was my lady's cambric handkerchief, soaked in eau-de-Cologne, lying on his forehead; and there was my lady herself, kneeling down and looking at him, he with his arm thrown round her to hold her there. Now I just ask you, Barbara, whether there's any sense in fadding with a man like that? If ever he had the headache before he was married, I used to mix him up a good dose of salts and senna, and tell him to go to bed early and sleep the pain off.'

Barbara made no reply: but she turned her face from Miss Carlyle.

They came upon the gardener, and Miss Carlyle got into a discussion with him, a somewhat warm one; she insisted upon having certain work done in a certain way; he standing to it that Mr. Carlyle had ordered it done another.

Barbara grew tired, and returned to the house.

Isabel and her husband were in the adjoining room, at the piano, and Barbara had an opportunity of hearing that sweet voice. She did as Miss Carlyle confessed to have done, pushed open the door between the two rooms, and looked in. It was the twilight hour, almost too dusk to see; but she could distinguish Isabel seated at the piano, and Mr. Carlyle standing behind her. She was singing one of the ballads from the opera of the 'Bohemian Girl,' 'When other lips.'

'Why do you like the song so much, Archibald?' she asked when she had finished it.

'I don't know. I never liked it so much until I heard it from you.'

'I wonder if they are come in. Shall we go into the next room?'

'Just this one first, this translation from the German. "'Twere vain to tell thee all I feel." There's real music in that song.'

'Yes, there is. Do you know, Archibald, your taste is just like papa's. He liked all these quiet, imaginative songs and so do you. And so do I,' she laughingly added, 'if I must speak the truth. Mrs. Vane used to stop her ears and make a face, when papa made me sing them. Papa returned the compliment; for he would walk out of the room if she began her loud Italian songs. I speak of the time when she was with us in London.'

She ceased, and began the song, singing it exquisitely, in a low, sweet, earnest tone, the chords of the accompaniment, at its conclusion, dying off gradually into silence.

'There, Archibald! I am sure I have sung you ten songs at least,' she said, leaning her head back against him, and looking at him from her upturned face. 'You ought to pay me.'

He did pay her; holding the dear face to him, and taking from it some impassioned kisses. Barbara turned to the window, a low moan of pain escaping her, as she pressed her forehead on one of its panes, and looked forth at the dusky night. Isabel came in on her husband's arm.

'Are you here alone, Miss Hare? I really beg your pardon. I supposed you were with Miss Carlyle?'

'Where is Cornelia, Barbara?'

'I have but just come in,' was Barbara's reply. 'I dare say she is following me.'

So she was, for she came upon them as they were speaking, her voice raised to tones of anger.

'Archibald, what have you been telling Blair about that geranium bed? He says you have been ordering him to make it oval. We decided that it should be square.'

'Isabel would prefer it oval,' was his reply.

'But it will be best square,' repeated Miss Carlyle.

'It is all right, Cornelia; Blair has his orders. I wish it to be oval.'

'He is a regular muff, is that Blair, and as obstinate as a mule,' cried Miss Carlyle.

'Indeed, then, Cornelia, I think him a very civil, good servant.'

'Oh, of course,' snapped Miss Carlyle. 'You never can see faults in anybody. You always were a simpleton in some things, Archibald.'

Mr. Carlyle laughed good-humouredly; he was of an even, calm temper: and he had, all his life, been subjected to the left-handed compliments of his sister. Isabel resented these speeches in her heart; she was growing more attached to her husband day by day.

'It is well everybody does not think so,' cried he, with a glance at his wife and Barbara, as they drew round the tea-table.

The evening went on to ten, and as the time-piece struck the hour, Barbara rose from her chair in amazement. 'I did not think it was so late. Surely some one must have come for me.'

'I will inquire,' was Lady Isabel's answer; and Mr. Carlyle rang the bell. No one had come for Miss Hare.

'Then I fear I must trouble Peter,' cried Barbara. 'Mamma may be gone to rest, tired, and papa must have forgotten me. It would never do for me to get locked out,' she gaily added.

'Like you were one night before,' said Mr. Carlyle, significantly.

He alluded to the night when Barbara was in the grove of trees with her unfortunate brother, and Mr. Hare was on the point, unconsciously, of locking her out. She had given Mr. Carlyle the history; but its recollection now called up a smart pain, and a change passed over her face.

'Oh! don't, Archibald!' she uttered, in the impulse of the moment; 'don't recall it.' Isabel wondered.

'Can Peter take me?' continued Barbara.

'I had better take you,' said Mr. Carlyle. 'It is late.'

Barbara's heart beat at the words; it beat as she put her things on; as she said good night to Lady Isabel and Miss Carlyle; it beat to throbbing as she went out with him and took his arm. All just as it used to be—only that he was now the husband of another. Only!

It was a warm lovely June night, not moonlight, but bright with its summer's twilight. They went down the park into the road, which they crossed, and soon came to a stile. From that stile led a path through the fields which would pass the back of Justice Hare's. Barbara stopped at it.

'Would you choose the field way to-night, Barbara? The grass will be damp. And this is the longest way.'

'But we shall escape the dust of the road.'

'Oh! very well, if you prefer it. It will not make three minutes' difference.'

'He is very anxious to get home to *her!*' mentally exclaimed Barbara. 'I shall fly out upon him presently, or my heart will burst.'

Mr. Carlyle crossed the stile, helped over Barbara, and then gave her his arm again. He had taken her parasol, he had taken it the last night they had walked together; an elegant little parasol, this was, of blue silk and white lace, and he did not switch the hedges with it. That night was present to Barbara now, with all its words and its delusive hopes; terribly present to her was their bitter ending.

There are moments in a woman's life when she is betrayed into forgetting the ordinary rules of conduct and propriety; when she is betrayed into making a scene. It may not often occur; perhaps never to a cold, secretive nature, where impulse, feeling, and above all, temper, are under strict control. Barbara Hare's temper was not under strict control. Her love, her jealousy, the never-dying pain always preying on her heart-strings since the marriage took place, her keen sense of the humiliation which had come home to her, were all rising fiercely, bubbling up with fiery heat. The evening she had just passed in their company, their evident happiness, the endearments she had seen him lavish upon his wife, were working her up to that state of nervous excitement when temper, tongue, and imagination fly off at a mad tangent. She felt like one isolated for ever, shut out from all that could make life dear; *they* were the world, she was out of it: what was her existence to him? A little self-control and Barbara would not have uttered words that must remain on her mind hereafter like an incubus, dyeing her cheeks red whenever she recalled them. It must be remembered too (if anything in the shape of excuse can be allowed) that she was upon terms of close intimacy with Mr. Carlyle. Independent of her own sentiments for him, they had been reared in free intercourse, the one with the other, almost as brother and sister. Mr. Carlyle walked on, utterly unconscious of the storm that was raging within her; more than that, he was unconscious of having given cause for one; and dashed into topics, indifferent and commonplace, in the most provoking manner.

'When does the justice begin haymaking, Barbara?'

There was no reply; Barbara was trying to keep down her emotion. Mr. Carlyle tried again:

'Barbara, I asked you which day your papa cuts his hay!'

Still no reply. Barbara was literally incapable of making one. Her throat was working, the muscles of her mouth began to twitch, and a convulsive sob, or what sounded like it, broke from her. Mr. Carlyle turned his head hastily.

'Barbara! are you ill? What is it?'

On it came, passion, temper, wrongs, and nervousness, all boiling over together. She was in strong hysterics. Mr. Carlyle half carried, half dragged her to the second stile, and placed her against it, his arm supporting her; and an old cow and two calves, wondering what the disturbance could mean at that sober time of night, walked up and stared at them.

Barbara struggled with her emotion, struggled bravely, and the sobs and the hysterical symptoms subsided; not the excitement or the passion. She put away his arm, and stood with her back to the stile, leaning against it. Mr. Carlyle felt inclined to fly to the pond for water, only he had nothing but his hat to get it in.

'Are you better, Barbara? What can have caused all this?'

'What can have caused it!' she burst forth in passionate uncontrol. '*You* can ask me that?'

Mr. Carlyle was struck dumb: but, by some inexplicable laws of sympathy, a dim and very unpleasant consciousness of the truth began to steal over him.

'I don't understand you, Barbara. If I have offended you in any way, I am truly sorry.'

'Truly sorry, no doubt! What do you care for me? If I go under the sod to-morrow,' stamping it with her foot, 'you have your wife to care for: what am I?'

'Hush!' he interposed, glancing round, more mindful for her than she was for herself.

'Hush, yes! what is my misery to you? I would rather be in my grave, Archibald Carlyle, than endure the life I lead. My pain is greater than I know how to bear.'

'I cannot affect to misunderstand you,' he said, feeling extremely annoyed and vexed. 'But, my dear Barbara, I never gave you cause to think that I—that I—cared for you more than I did care.'

'Never gave me cause!' she gasped. 'When you have been coming to our house constantly, almost like my shadow; when you gave me this'—dashing open her mantle, and holding up the locket to his view; 'when you have been more intimate with me than a brother!'

'Stay, Barbara. There it is—a brother. I have been nothing else: it never occurred to me to be anything else,' he added, in his straightforward truth.

'Ay, as a brother, nothing else!' and her voice rose once more with her excitement; it seemed that she would not long control it. 'What cared you for my feelings? what recked you that you gained my love?'

'Barbara, hush!' he implored; 'do be calm and reasonable. If I ever gave you cause to think I regarded you with deeper feeling, I can only express to you my deep regret, and assure you it was done unconsciously.'

She was growing calmer. The passion was fading, leaving her face still and white. She lifted it towards Mr. Carlyle.

'If *she* had not come between us, should you have loved me?'

'I don't know. How can I know? Do I not say to you, Barbara, that I only thought of you as a friend, as a sister? I cannot tell what might have been.'

'I could bear it better, but that it was known,' she murmured. 'All West Lynne had coupled us together in their prying gossip, and they have only pity to cast to me now. I would far rather you had killed me, Archibald.'

'I can but express to you my deep regret,' he repeated. 'I can only hope you will soon forget it all. Let the remembrance of this conversation pass away with to-night; let us still be to each other as friends—as brother and sister. Believe me,' he concluded, in a deeper tone, 'the confession has not lessened you in my estimation.'

He made a movement as though he would get over the stile, but Barbara did not stir: the tears were silently coursing down her pallid face. At that moment there was an interruption.

'Is that you, Miss Barbara?'

Barbara started as if she had been shot. On the other side of the stile stood Wilson, their upper maid. How long might she have been there! She began to explain that Mr. Hare had sent Jasper out, and Mrs. Hare had thought it better to wait no longer for the man's return, so had despatched her, Wilson, for Miss Barbara. Mr. Carlyle got over the stile, and handed over Barbara.

'You need not come any further now,' she said to him, in a low tone.

'I shall see you home,' was his reply: and he held out his arm. Barbara took it.

They walked on in silence. Arrived at the back gate of the Grove, which gave entrance to the kitchen-garden, Wilson went forward. Mr. Carlyle took both Barbara's hands in his.

'Good night, Barbara. God bless you.'

She had had time for reflection; and the excitement gone, she saw her outbreak in all its shame and folly. Mr. Carlyle noticed how subdued and white she looked.

'I think I have been mad,' she groaned. 'I must have been mad to say what I did. Forget that it was uttered.'

'I told you I would.'

'You will not betray me to—to—your wife?' she panted.

'Barbara!'

'Thank you. Good night.'

But he still retained her hands. 'In a short time, Barbara, I trust you will find one more worthy to receive your love than I have been.'

'Never,' she impulsively answered. 'I do not love and forget so lightly. In the years to come, in my old age, I shall still be nothing but Barbara Hare.'

Mr. Carlyle walked away in a fit of musing. The revelation had given him pain (and possibly a little flattery), for he was fond of pretty Barbara. Fond in his way; not in hers; not with the sort of fondness he felt for his wife. He asked his conscience whether his manner to her during past days had been a tinge warmer than we bestow upon a sister, and he decided that it might have been, but that he most certainly had never cast a suspicion to the mischief it was doing.

'I heartily hope she will soon find somebody to her liking, and forget me,' was his concluding thought. 'As to living and dying Barbara Hare, that is all moonshine; the sentimental rubbish that girls like to——'

'Archibald!'

He was passing the very last tree in the park, the nearest to his house, and the interruption came from a dark form standing under it.

'Is it you, my dearest?'

'I came out to meet you. Have you not been very long?'

'I think I have,' he answered, as he drew his wife to his side, and walked on with her. 'We met one of the servants at the second stile, but I went all the way.'

'You have been intimate with the Hares?'

'Quite so. Cornelia is related to them.'

'Do you think Barbara pretty?'

'Very.'

'Then—intimate as you were—I wonder you never fell in love with her.'

Mr. Carlyle laughed; a very conscious laugh, considering the recent interview.

'Did you, Archibald?'

The words were spoken in a low tone, almost, or he fancied it, a tone of emotion, and he looked at her in amazement. 'Did I what, Isabel?'

'You never loved Barbara Hare?'

'Loved *her!* What is your head running on, Isabel? I never loved but one woman: and that one I made my wife.'

✠ XVII ✠

Death or Life

Another year came in. Isabel would have been altogether happy but for Miss Carlyle: that lady still inflicted her presence upon East Lynne, and made the bane of its household. She deferred outwardly to Lady Isabel as the mistress;

but the real mistress was herself, Isabel little more than an automaton. Her impulses were checked, her wishes frustrated, her actions tacitly condemned by the imperiously willed Miss Carlyle: poor Isabel, with her refined manners and her timid and sensitive temperament, had no chance against the strong-minded woman, and she was in a state of galling subjection in her own house. Mr. Carlyle suspected it not. At home but morning and evening, and then generally alone with his wife, and becoming gradually more absorbed with the cares of his business, which increased upon him, he saw not that anything was wrong. Once, certain counter-orders of the two ladies had clashed, and caused a commotion in the household: Miss Carlyle immediately withdrew hers, but, in doing so, her peculiarly ungracious manner was more ungracious than ever. Isabel had then hinted to her husband that they might be happier if they lived alone, hinted it with a changing cheek and beating heart, as if she were committing a wrong upon Miss Carlyle. He proposed to his sister that she should return to her own home; she turned round and accused him of speaking for Isabel. In his truthful, open way, he acknowledged the fact, making no secret of it. Miss Carlyle bounced off and presented herself before Lady Isabel, demanding to know what offence she had committed, and why the house was not large enough for her to have a corner in it. Isabel, shrinkingly tenacious of hurting the feelings even of an enemy, absolutely made a sort of apology, and afterwards begged her husband to think no more of what she had said. He did not; he was easy and unsuspicious; but had he but gained the faintest inkling of the truth, he would not have lost a moment in emancipating his wife from the thraldom of Miss Corny.

Not a day passed but Miss Carlyle, by dint of hints and inuendoes, contrived to impress upon Lady Isabel the unfortunate blow to his own interests that Mr. Carlyle's marriage had been, the ruinous expense she had entailed upon the family. It struck a complete chill to Isabel's heart, and she became painfully imbued with the incubus she must be to Mr. Carlyle—so far as his pocket was concerned. Lord Mount Severn, with his little son, had paid them a short visit at Christmas, and Isabel had asked him, apparently with unconcern, whether Mr. Carlyle had put himself very much out of the way to marry her; whether it had entailed on him an expense and a style of living he would not otherwise have deemed himself justified in affording. Lord Mount Severn's reply was an unfortunate one: he said his opinion was that it had, and that Isabel ought to feel grateful to him for his generosity. She sighed as she listened, and from thenceforth determined to *put up* with Miss Carlyle. That lady contributed a liberal share to the maintenance of the household, and *would* do it, quite as much as she would have kept up her establishment at home. She was not at East Lynne to save her own pocket, and there lay a

greater difficulty in getting rid of her. Whether she spent her money at East
Lynne or not, it would come to the same in the end, for it was known that all
she had would go to Archibald.

More timid and sensitive by nature than many would believe or can imagine, reared in seclusion more simply and quietly than falls to the general lot
of peers' daughters, and completely inexperienced, Isabel was unfit to battle
with the world, totally unfit to battle with Miss Carlyle. The penniless state
in which she was left at her father's death: the want of a home, save that
accorded her at Castle Marling, even the hundred pound note left in her
hand by Mr. Carlyle, all had imbued her with a deep consciousness of humiliation; and, far from rebelling at or despising the small establishment (comparatively speaking) provided for her by Mr. Carlyle, she felt thankful to him
for it. But to be told continually that this was more than he could afford, that
she was in fact a blight upon his prospects, was enough to turn her heart to
bitterness. Oh, that she had had the courage to speak out openly to her husband! that he might, by a single word of earnest love and assurance, have
taken the weight from her heart, and rejoiced it with the truth—that all
these miserable complaints were but the phantoms of his narrow-minded sister. But Isabel never did: when Miss Corny lapsed into her grumbling mood,
she would hear in silence, or gently bend her aching forehead in her hands,
never retorting.

One day, it was in the month of February, after a tolerably long explosion
of wrath on Miss Corny's part, not directed against Isabel, but at something
which had gone wrong amongst the servants, silence supervened. Isabel, who
was sitting listless and dispirited, suddenly broke it, speaking more to herself
than to Miss Carlyle.

'I wish evening was come!'

'Why do you wish that?'

'Because Archibald would be at home.'

Miss Carlyle gave an unsatisfactory grunt. 'You seem tired, Lady Isabel.'

'I am very tired.'

'I don't wonder at it. I should be tired to death if I sat doing nothing all
day. Indeed, I think I should soon drop into my grave.'

'There's nothing to do,' returned Lady Isabel.

'There's always something to do when people like to look for it. You might
help me with these new table napkins, rather than do nothing.'

'I make table napkins!' exclaimed Lady Isabel.

'You might do a worse thing, ma'am,' snapped Miss Corny.

'I don't understand that sort of work,' said Isabel, gently.

'Neither does anybody else till they try. For my part, I'd rather sit on and
make and mend shoes, than I'd sit with my hands before me. It's a sinful
waste of time.'

'I never feel very well now,' answered poor Isabel, in an apologetic tone. 'I am not equal to exertion.'

'Then I'd go out for a drive, and take the air. Moping in-doors all day does invalids no good.'

'But, since the ponies started last week and alarmed me, Archibald will not allow me to go out, unless he drives me himself.'

'There's nothing the matter with John's driving,' returned Miss Corny, in her spirit of contradiction. 'And in the matter of experience, he has had quite as much as your husband, ma'am.'

'John was driving when the ponies took fright.'

'If ponies take fright once, it's no reason that they should a second time. Ring the bell, and order John to bring the carriage round: it is what I should advise.'

Isabel shook her head decisively. 'No: Archibald bade me not go out without him, unless it was in the close carriage. He is so careful of me just now; and he knows that I should not be alarmed with him, if the ponies did start, like I should with a servant.'

'It occurs to me that you have grown a little fanciful of late, Lady Isabel.'

'I suppose I have,' was the meek answer. 'I shall be better when the baby is born: and I shall never feel at a loss then, I shall have plenty to do.'

'So will most of us, I expect,' returned Miss Corny, with a groan. 'Why, what on earth—why, if I don't believe here's Archibald! What brings him home at this time of day?'

'Archibald!' Out she flew in her glad surprise, meeting him in the hall, and falling upon him in her delight. 'Oh, Archibald, my darling, it is as if the sun had shone! What have you come home for?'

'To drive you out, love,' he whispered, as he took her back with him and rang the bell.

'You never told me this morning.'

'Because I was not sure of being able to come. Peter, let the pony-carriage be brought round without delay. I am waiting for it.'

'Why, where are you going with the pony-carriage?' exclaimed Miss Carlyle, as Isabel left the room to dress herself.

'Only for a drive.'

'A drive!' repeated Miss Corny, looking at him in bewilderment.

'To take Isabel for one. I shall not trust her to John again, yet awhile.'

'*That's* the way to get on with your business!' retorted Miss Corny, when she could find temper to speak. 'Deserting the office in the middle of the day!'

'Isabel's health is of more consequence, just now, than business,' he returned, good-humouredly 'And you really speak, Cornelia, as if I had neither Dill to replace me, nor plenty of clerks under him.'

'John is a better driver than you are.'

'He is as good a one. But that is not the question.'

Isabel came down, looking radiant, all her listlessness gone. Mr. Carlyle placed her in the carriage, and drove away, Miss Corny gazing after them with an expression of face enough to turn a whole dairy of milk sour.

There were many such little episodes as these, so you need not wonder that Isabel was not altogether happy. But never, before Mr. Carlyle, was the lady's temper vented upon her; plenty fell to his own share when he and his sister were alone; and he had been so accustomed to the sort of thing all his life, had got so used to it, that it made no impression: he never dreamt that Isabel also received her portion.

It was a morning early in April. Joyce sat, in its grey dawn, over a large fire in the dressing-room of Lady Isabel Carlyle, her hands clasped to pain, and the tears coursing down her cheeks. Joyce was frightened; she had had some experience in illness; but illness of this nature she had never witnessed, and she was fervently hoping never to witness it again. In the adjoining room was Lady Isabel, lying between life and death.

The door from the corridor softly opened, and Miss Carlyle entered. She had probably never walked with so gentle a step in all her life, and she had a thick wadded mantle over her head and ears. She sat down in a chair quite meekly, and Joyce saw that her face looked grey as the early morning.

'Joyce,' whispered she, 'is there danger?'

'Oh, ma'am, I trust not! But it's hard to witness, and it must be awful to bear.'

'It is our common curse, Joyce. You and I may congratulate ourselves that we have not chosen to encounter it. Joyce,' she added, after a pause, 'I trust there's no danger: I should not like her to die.'

Miss Carlyle spoke in a low, dread tone. Was she fearing that if her poor young sister-in-law did die, a weight would rest on her conscience for all time?—a heavy, ever-present weight, whispering that she might have rendered her short year of marriage more happy, had she chosen; and that she had not so chosen, but had deliberately steeled every crevice of her heart against her? Very probably: she looked anxious and apprehensive in the dusky twilight.

'If there's danger, Joyce—'

'Why do you think there is danger, ma'am?' interrupted Joyce. 'Are other people not as ill as this?'

'It is to be hoped they are not,' rejoined Miss Carlyle. 'And why is the express gone to Lynneborough for Dr. Martin?'

Up started Joyce, awe-struck. 'An express for Dr. Martin! Oh, ma'am! Who sent it? When did it go?'

'All I know is that it's gone. Mr. Wainwright went to your master, and he came out of his room and sent John galloping to the telegraph-office at West

Lynne: where could your ears have been not to hear the horse tearing off? *I* heard it, I know that, and a nice fright it put me in. I went to Mr. Carlyle's room to ask what was amiss, and he said he did not know himself; nothing, he hoped. And then he shut his door again in my face, instead of stopping to speak to me as any other Christian would.'

Joyce did not answer: she was faint with apprehension; and there was a silence, broken only by the sounds from the next room. Miss Carlyle rose, and a fanciful person might have thought she was shivering.

'I can't stand this, Joyce; I shall go. If they want coffee, or anything, it can be sent in. Ask.'

'I will presently; in a few minutes,' answered Joyce, with a real shiver. 'You are not going in, are you, ma'am?' she uttered in apprehension, as Miss Carlyle began to steal on tiptoe to the inner door, and Joyce had a lively consciousness that her sight would not be an agreeable one to Lady Isabel. 'They want the room free: they sent me out.'

'No,' answered Miss Corny. 'I could do no good; and those, who cannot, are better away.'

'Just what Mr. Wainwright said, when he dismissed me,' murmured Joyce. And Miss Carlyle finally passed into the corridor and withdrew.

Joyce sat on: the time seemed to her interminable. And then she heard the arrival of Dr. Martin; heard him go into the next room. By-and-by Mr. Wainwright came out of it, into the room where Joyce was sitting. Her tongue clove to the roof of her mouth, and before she could bring out the ominous words, 'Is there danger?' he had passed through it.

Mr. Wainwright was on his way to the apartment where he expected to find Mr. Carlyle. The latter was pacing it: he had so paced it all the night. His pale face flushed as the surgeon entered.

'You have little mercy on my suspense, Wainwright. Dr. Martin has been here these twenty minutes. What does he say?'

'Well, he cannot say any more than I did. The symptoms are critical, but he hopes she will do well. There's nothing for it but patience.'

Mr. Carlyle resumed his weary walk.

'I come now to suggest that you should send for Little. In these protracted cases—'

The speech was interrupted by a cry from Mr. Carlyle, half horror, half despair. For the Reverend Mr. Little was the incumbent of St. Jude's, and his apprehensions had flown—he hardly knew to what they had not flown.

'Not for you wife!' hastily rejoined the surgeon. 'I spoke for the child. Should it not live, it may be satisfactory to you and Lady Isabel to know that it was baptized.'

'I thank you, I thank you,' said Mr. Carlyle, grasping his hand in his inexpressible relief. 'Little shall be sent for.'

'You jumped to the conclusion that your wife's soul was flitting. Please

God, she may yet live to bear you other children, if this one should die.'

'Please God!' was the inward aspiration of Mr. Carlyle.

'Carlyle,' added the surgeon, in a musing sort of tone, as he laid his hand on Mr. Carlyle's shoulder, which his own head scarcely reached, 'I am sometimes at death-beds where the clergyman is sent for, in this desperate need, to the fleeting spirit: and I am tempted to ask myself what good another man, priest though he be, can do at the twelfth hour, where the accounts have not been made up previously?'

It was hard upon midday. The Reverend Mr. Little, Mr. Carlyle, and Miss Carlyle were gathered in the dressing-room, round a table on which stood a rich china bowl, containing water for the baptism. Joyce, her pale face working with emotion, came into the room, carrying what looked like a bundle of flannel. Little cared Mr. Carlyle for that bundle, in comparison with his care for his wife.

'Joyce,' he whispered, 'is all well still?'

'I believe so, sir.'

The service commenced. The clergyman took the child. 'What name?' he asked.

Mr. Carlyle had never thought about the name. But he replied pretty promptly.

'William.' For he knew it was the name revered and loved by Lady Isabel.

The minister dipped his fingers in the water. Joyce interrupted, in much confusion, looking at her master.

'It is a little girl, sir. I beg your pardon, I'm sure I thought I had said so: but I am flurried as I never was before.'

There was a pause, and then the minister spoke again. 'Name this child.'

'Isabel Lucy,' said Mr. Carlyle. Upon which a strange sort of resentful sniff was heard from Miss Corny. She had probably thought to hear him mention her own; but he had named it after his wife and his mother.

Mr. Carlyle was not allowed to see his wife until the evening. His eyelashes glistened as he looked down at her. She detected his emotion, and a faint smile parted her lips.

'I fear I bore it badly, Archibald; but let us be thankful that it is over. How thankful, none can know, save those who have gone through it.'

'I think they can,' he murmured. 'I never knew what thankfulness was until this day.'

'That the baby is safe?'

'That *you* are safe, my darling; safe and spared to me. Isabel,' he whispered, hiding his face upon hers, 'I never until to-day knew what prayer was—the prayer of a heart in its sore need.'

'Have you written to Lord Mount Severn?' she asked, after a while.

'This afternoon,' he replied.

'Why did you give baby my name—Isabel?'

'Do you think I could have given it a prettier one? I don't.'

'Why do you not bring a chair and sit down by me?'

He smiled and shook his head. 'I wish I might. But they limited my stay with you to four minutes, and Wainwright has posted himself outside the door with his watch in his hand.'

Quite true. There stood the careful surgeon: and the short interview was over almost as soon as it had begun.

❧ XVIII ❧

Wilson's Tongue

The baby lived, and appeared likely to live, and of course the next thing was to look out for a maid for it. Isabel did not get strong very quickly; fever and weakness had a struggle with each other, and with her. One day when she was dressed and sitting in her easy chair Miss Carlyle entered.

'Of all the servants in the neighbourhood, who should you suppose is come up after the place of nurse?' she said to Lady Isabel.

'Indeed I cannot guess.'

'Why, Wilson, Mrs. Hare's maid. Three years and five months she has been with them, and now leaves in consequence of a quarrel with Barbara. Will you see her?'

'Is she likely to suit? Is she a good servant?'

'She's not a bad servant, as servants go,' responded Miss Carlyle. 'She's steady and respectable; but she has got a tongue as long as from here to Lynneborough.'

'That won't hurt the baby,' said Lady Isabel. 'But if she has lived as lady's-maid, she probably does not understand the care of infants.'

'Yes, she does. She was upper nurse at Squire Pinner's, before going to Mrs. Hare's. She lived there five years.'

'I will see her,' said Lady Isabel.

Miss Carlyle left the room to send the servant in, but came back first alone.

'Mind, Lady Isabel, don't you engage her. If she is likely to suit you, let her come again for the answer, and meanwhile I will go down to Mrs. Hare's and learn the ins and outs of her leaving. It is all very plausible for her to put it upon Barbara, but that is only one side of the question. Before engaging her, it may be as well to hear the other.'

Of course this was but right. Isabel acquiesced, and the servant was introduced: a tall, pleasant-looking woman, with black eyes. Lady Isabel inquired why she was leaving Mrs. Hare's.

'My lady, it was through Miss Barbara's temper. Latterly—oh, for this year past—nothing has pleased her; she has grown nearly as imperious as the justice himself. I have threatened many times to leave, and last evening we came to another outbreak, and I left this morning.'

'Left entirely?'

'Yes, my lady. Miss Barbara provoked me so, that I said last night I would leave as soon as breakfast was over. And I did so. I should be very glad to take your situation, my lady, if you would please to try me.'

'You have been the upper maid at Mrs. Hare's?'

'Oh yes, my lady.'

'Then possibly this situation might not suit you so well as you imagine. Joyce is the upper servant here, and you would, in a manner, be under her. I have great confidence in Joyce; and in case of my illness or absence, Joyce would superintend the nursery.'

'I should not mind that,' was the applicant's answer. 'We all like Joyce, my lady.'

A few more questions, and then the girl was told to come again in the evening for her answer. Miss Carlyle went to the Grove for the 'ins and outs' of the affair, when Mrs. Hare frankly stated that she had nothing to urge against Wilson, save her hasty manner of leaving, of which she believed the chief blame to be due to Barbara. Wilson was therefore engaged, and was to enter upon her new service the following morning.

In the afternoon succeeding to it, Isabel was lying on the sofa in her bed-room, asleep, as was supposed. In point of fact, she was in that state, half sleep, half wakeful delirium, which those who suffer from weakness and fever know only too well. Suddenly she was aroused from it by hearing her own name mentioned in the adjoining room, where sat Joyce and Wilson, the latter holding the sleeping infant on her knee, the former sewing, the door between the rooms being ajar.

'How ill she looks,' observed Wilson.

'Who?' asked Joyce.

'Her ladyship. She looks as if she'd never get over it.'

'She is getting over it quickly, now,' returned Joyce. 'If you had seen her a week ago, you would not say she was looking ill now—speaking in comparison.'

'My goodness! would not somebody's hopes be up again if anything should happen?'

'Nonsense!' crossly returned Joyce.

'You may cry out "nonsense" for ever, Joyce, but they would,' went on Wilson. 'And she would snap him up, to a dead certainty: she'd never let him escape her a second time. She is as much in love with him as she ever was.'

'It was all talk and fancy,' said Joyce. 'West Lynne must be busy. Mr. Carlyle never cared for her.'

'That's more than you know. I have seen a little, Joyce; I have seen him kiss her.'

'A pack of rubbish!' remarked Joyce. 'That tells nothing.'

'I don't say it does: he gave her that locket and chain she wears.'

'Who wears?' retorted Joyce, determined not graciously to countenance the subject. 'I don't want to hear anything about it?'

'"Who," now! Why, Miss Barbara. She has hardly had it off her neck since: my belief is, she wears it in her sleep.'

'More simpleton she!' echoed Joyce.

'The night before he left West Lynne to marry Lady Isabel—and didn't the news come upon us like a thunderclap!—Miss Barbara had been at Miss Carlyle's, and he brought her home. A lovely night it was, the moon rising, and nearly as light as day. He somehow broke her parasol in coming home, and when they got to our gate there was a love scene.'

'Were you a third in it?' sarcastically demanded Joyce.

'Yes—without meaning to be. That skinflint old justice won't allow followers in-doors, and there's no seeing anybody on the sly in that conspicuous back kitchen-garden, when there's nothing higher than a cauliflower, so the only chance we have is to get half an hour's chat amidst the grove trees in the front, if a friend comes up. I was expecting somebody that evening—a horrid faithless fellow he turned out, and went, three months after, and married the barmaid at the Buck's Head—and I was in the trees waiting for him. Up came Mr. Carlyle and Miss Barbara. She wanted him to go in, but he would not, and they stood there. Something was said about the locket, and about his giving her a piece of his hair to put it in: I could not catch the words distinctly, and I did not dare to stir nearer, for fear of their hearing me. It was a regular love scene; I could hear enough for that. If ever anybody thought to be Mrs. Carlyle, Barbara Hare did that night.'

'Why, you great gaby! You have just said it was the night before he went to be married!'

'I don't care; she did. After he was gone, I saw her lift up her hands and her face in ecstasy, and say he could never know how much she loved him until she was his wife. Be you very sure, Joyce, many a love passage had passed between them two; but I suppose when my lady was thrown in his way he couldn't resist her rank and her beauty, and the old love was cast over. It is in the nature of man to be fickle, especially those that can boast of their own good looks, like Mr. Carlyle.'

'Mr. Carlyle's not fickle.'

'I can tell you some more yet. Two or three days after that, Miss Corny came up to our house with the news of his marriage. I was in mistress's bedroom, and they were in the room underneath, the windows open, and I heard Miss Corny tell the tale, for I was leaning out. Up came Miss Barbara upon an excuse and flew into her room, and I went into the corridor. A few moments, and I heard a noise; it was a sort of wail, or groan, and I opened the door softly, fearing she might be fainting. Joyce, if my heart never ached for anybody before, it ached then. She was lying on the floor, her hands writhed together, and her poor face all white, like one in mortal agony. I'd have given a quarter's wages to be able to say a word of comfort to her; but I didn't dare interfere with such sorrow as that. I came out again and shut the door without her seeing me.'

'How thoroughly stupid she must have been,' uttered Joyce, 'to go caring for one who did not care for her!'

'I tell you, Joyce, you don't know that he did not care. You are as obstinate as the justice! And I wish to goodness you wouldn't interrupt me. They came up here to pay the wedding visit, master, mistress, and she; came in state in the grand chariot, with the coachman and Jasper; if you have got any memory at all, you can't fail to recollect it. Miss Barbara remained behind at East Lynne to spend the rest of the day.'

'I remember it.'

'I was sent to attend her home in the evening, Jasper being out. I came the field way; for the dust by the road was enough to smother one, and at the last stile but one, what do you think I came upon?'

Joyce lifted her eyes. 'A snake, perhaps.'

'I came upon Miss Barbara and Mr. Carlyle. What had passed, nobody knows but themselves. She was leaning her back against the stile, crying; sobs breaking from her, like one might expect to hear from a breaking heart. It seemed as if she had been reproaching him, as if some explanation had passed, and I heard him say that from henceforth they could only be brother and sister. I spoke soon, for fear they should see me, and Mr. Carlyle got over the stile. Miss Barbara said to him that he need not come any farther, but he just held out his arm and came with her to our back gate. I went on then to open the door, and I saw him with his head bent down to her, and her two hands held in his. We don't know how it was between them, I tell you.'

'At any rate she is a downright fool, to suffer herself to love him still!' uttered Joyce indignantly.

'So she is, but she does do it. She'll often steal out of the gate about the time she knows he'll be passing, and watch him by, not letting him see her. It is nothing but her unhappiness, her jealousy of Lady Isabel, that makes her cross: I assure you, Joyce, in this past year she has so changed that she's not like the same person. If Mr. Carlyle should ever get tired of my lady, and——'

'Wilson!' harshly interrupted Joyce. 'Have the goodness to recollect yourself.'

'What have I said now? Nothing but truth. Men are shamefully fickle; husbands worse than sweethearts, and I'm sure I'm not thinking of anything wrong. But to go back to the argument that we began with—I say that if anything happened to my lady, Miss Barbara, as sure as fate, would step into her shoes.'

'Nothing is going to happen to her,' returned Joyce with composure.

'I hope it is not, now or later—for the sake of this dear little innocent thing upon my lap,' went on the undaunted Wilson. 'She would not make a very kind stepmother, for it is certain that where the first wife has been hated, her children won't be loved. She would turn Mr. Carlyle against them——'

'I tell you what it is, Wilson,' interrupted Joyce, in a firm unmistakeable tone, 'if you think to pursue these sort of topics at East Lynne, I shall inform my lady that you are unsuitable for the situation.'

'I dare say!'

'And you know that when I make up my mind to a thing, I do it,' continued Joyce. 'Miss Carlyle may well say you have the longest tongue in West Lynne; but you might have the grace to know that this subject is one more unsuitable to it than another, whether you are eating Mr. Hare's bread, or whether you are eating Mr. Carlyle's. Another word, Wilson; it appears to me that you have carried on a prying system in Mrs. Hare's house; do not attempt such a thing in this.'

'You were always one of the straightlaced sort, Joyce,' cried Wilson, laughing good-humouredly. 'But now that I have had my say out, I shall stop; and you need not fear I should be such a simpleton as to go prattling of this kind of thing to the servants.'

Now just fancy this conversation penetrating to Lady Isabel. She heard it, every word. It is all very well to oppose the argument, 'Who attends to the gossip of servants?' Let me tell you it depends upon what the subject may be, whether the gossip is attended to or not. It might not, and indeed would not, have made so great an impression upon her had she been in strong health, but she was weak, feverish, in a state of partial delirium: and she hastily took up the idea that Archibald Carlyle had never loved her, that he had admired her and made her his wife in his ambition, but that his heart had been given to Barbara Hare.

A pretty state of excitement she worked herself into as she lay there; jealousy and fever, ay, and love too, playing pranks with her brain. It was near the dinner hour, and when Mr. Carlyle entered, he was startled to see her: her pallid cheeks were burning with a red hectic, and her eyes glistened with fever.

'Isabel, you are worse!' he uttered, approaching her with a quick step.

She partially rose from the sofa, and clasped hold of him in her emotion. 'Oh, Archibald! Archibald!' she uttered, 'don't marry her! I could not rest in my grave.'

Mr. Carlyle, in his puzzled astonishment, believed her to be labouring under some temporary hallucination, the result of weakness. He set himself to soothe her, but it seemed that she could not be soothed. She burst into a storm of tears, and began again: wild words.

'She would ill-treat my child; she would draw your love from it, and from my memory. Archibald, you must not marry her.'

'You must be speaking from the influence of a dream, Isabel,' he soothingly said; 'you have been asleep, and are not yet awake. Be still, and recollection will return to you. There, love; rest upon me.'

'To think of her as your wife brings pain enough to kill me,' she continued to reiterate. 'Promise me that you will not marry her: Archibald promise it!'

'I will promise you anything in reason,' he replied, bewildered with her words, 'but I do not know what you mean. There is no possibility of my marrying any one, Isabel: you are my wife.'

'But if I die? I may; you know I may; and many think I shall—do not let her usurp my place.'

'Indeed she shall not—whoever you may be talking of. What have you been dreaming? Who is it that is troubling your mind?'

'Archibald, do you need to ask? Did you love no one before you married me? Perhaps you have loved her since—perhaps you love her still?'

Mr. Carlyle began to discern 'method in her madness.' He changed his cheering tone to one of grave earnestness. 'Of whom do you speak, Isabel?'

'Of Barbara Hare.'

He knitted his brow; he was both annoyed and vexed. Whatever had put this bygone nonsense into his wife's head? He quitted the sofa where he had been supporting her, and stood upright before her, calm, dignified, almost solemn in his seriousness.

'Isabel, what notion can you possibly have picked up about myself and Barbara Hare, I am unable to conceive. I never loved Barbara Hare; I never entertained the faintest shadow of love for her; either before my marriage or since. You must tell me what has given rise to this idea in your mind.'

'But she loved you.'

A moment's hesitation; for of course Mr. Carlyle was conscious she had; but, taking all the circumstances into consideration, more especially how he learnt the fact, he could not in honour acknowledge it even to his wife. 'If it was so, Isabel, she was more reprehensibly foolish than I should have given Barbara's good sense credit for: a woman may almost as well lose herself, as suffer herself to love unsought. If she did give her love to me, I can only say I was entirely unconscious of it. Believe me, you have as much cause to be jealous of Cornelia, as you have of Barbara Hare.'

Isabel sighed, it was a sigh of relief, and her breath grew calmer. She felt inexpressibly reassured. Mr. Carlyle bent his head, and spoke in a tender, though a pained tone.

'I had not thought that the past year was quite thrown away. What proof can a man give of true and earnest love, that I have not given to you?'

She looked up, her eyelashes wet with contrition, took his hand and held it between hers. 'Don't be angry with me, Archibald: the trouble and the doubt would not have arisen had I cared for you less.'

He smiled again, his own fond smile, and bent lower. 'And now tell me what put this into your brain?'

An impulse arose within her that she would tell him all, the few words dropped by Susan and Joyce twelve months before, the conversation she had just overheard; but in that moment of renewed confidence it appeared to her that she must have been very foolish to attach importance to it—that a sort of humiliation, in listening to the converse of servants, was reflected on her; and she remained silent.

'Has any one been striving to bias your mind against me?' he resumed.

'Archibald! no. Would any one dare to do it?'

'Then did you dream?—and could not forget it on awaking?'

'I do sometimes dream strange things, especially in my feverish afternoon sleeps. I think I am a little delirious at times, Archibald, and do not know what is real, and what fancy.'

The answer, while expressing correctly her physical state, was an evasive one, but not evasively did it fall upon the ear of Mr. Carlyle. It presented to him the only probable solution of the enigma, and he never questioned it.

'Don't have any more of these dreams if you can help it,' he said. 'Regard them for what they are—illusions, neither pleasant for you, nor fair to me. I am bound to you by fond ties as well as by legal ones, remember, Isabel; and it is out of Barbara Hare's power to step between us.'

There never was a passion in this world, there never will be one, so fantastic, so delusive, so powerful as jealousy. Mr. Carlyle dismissed the episode from his thoughts; he believed his wife's emotion to have arisen simply from a feverish dream, and never supposed but that, with the dream, its recollection would pass away from her. Not so. Implicitly relying upon her husband's words at the moment, feeling quite ashamed at her own suspicion, Lady Isabel afterwards suffered the unhappy fear to regain its influence; the ill-starred revelations of Wilson reasserted their power, over-mastering the denial of Mr. Carlyle. Shakespeare calls jealousy yellow and green: I think it may be called black and white, for it most assuredly views white as black, and black as white. The most fanciful surmises wear the aspect of truth, the greatest improbabilities appear as consistent realities. Isabel said not another word to her husband; and the feeling—you will understand this if you have ever been foolish enough to sun yourself in its delights—only caused her to grow more attached to him, to be more eager for his love. But certain it is that Barbara Hare dwelt on her heart like an incubus.

XIX

Captain Thorn at West Lynne

'Barbara, how fine the day seems!'

'It is a beautiful day, mamma.'

'I think I should be all the better for going out.'

'I am sure you would, mamma,' was Barbara's answer. 'If you went out more, you would find the benefit: every fine day you ought to do so.'

'But I have not spirits for it, dear,' sighed Mrs. Hare. 'The first bright days of spring, the first warm days of summer, always have an exhilarating effect upon me. I think I must go out to-day. There's your papa in the garden: ask him if it will be convenient.'

Barbara was darting off, but arrested her steps for a moment. 'Mamma, you have been talking these three weeks of buying the new dresses and other things that we require: why not do so to-day?'

'Well—I don't know,' hesitated Mrs. Hare, in the irresolution natural to her.

'Yes, yes, you will not find a better opportunity.' And away went Barbara.

Justice Hare was in his front garden, imperiously pointing out to his servant, Benjamin, something which had not been done according to his directions. Benjamin fulfilled the duties of coachman and groom at the Grove, filling up his spare time with gardening. He was a married man, and slept at home, though he took his meals in the house; coming to it early, and going away late. The justice was in his dressing-gown and wig, and was working himself into a passion when Barbara approached. She was the only one of the three children not afraid of her father: Barbara stood in awe of him, but not so utterly as the others.

'Papa.'

'What do you want?' said the justice, turning round his portly person.

'Mamma thinks that it would do her good to go out this fine day. Can we have the carriage?'

The justice paused before he answered, and looked up at the sky. 'Where does she want to be off to?'

'We wish to do some shopping, please, papa. Only in West Lynne,' hastily added Barbara, seeing a cloud rise on the paternal countenance. 'Not at Lynneborough.'

'And your mamma thinks I am going to drive her!' cried Justice Hare. 'I'd see the shops further first. The last time you and she went into one, you kept me waiting an hour and a half.'

'Benjamin can drive us, papa.'

Mr. Hare strode pompously across the grass to the dining-room window, threw it up, and addressed his wife. Barbara drew close, and stood timidly at his side.

'Do you say you want to go shopping to-day, Anne?'

'Not particularly to-day,' was the meek answer, meekly delivered; 'any day will do for it. Did you think of using the carriage yourself?'

'I don't know,' replied the justice. The fact is, he had not thought about it at all; but he liked every scheme, every movement to be proposed by himself, to be regulated by his own will.

'The day is so fine that I think I should like to take advantage of it,' said Mrs. Hare. 'And Barbara must have her summer dresses bought.'

'She's always having dresses bought,' growled the justice.

'Oh, papa! I—'

'Silence, young lady, you have twice as many as you need.'

'Perhaps, Richard, I might manage to walk in and back, without being much fatigued, if you cannot spare me the carriage,' said Mrs. Hare, gently.

'And have you laid up for a week! What next! The idea of your walking into West Lynne and back! that would be a piece of folly.'

The justice shut down the window, and strode back to Benjamin, leaving Mrs. Hare and Barbara at an uncertainty: were they to go, or were they not? Barbara went indoors to her mother.

'Barbara, dear, I wonder where your papa was thinking of going in the carriage?'

'I don't believe he was going anywhere," replied independent Miss Barbara.

'Oh, child!'

'Well, I don't. Only he always must oppose everybody. Mamma I do think you might walk in, and we could come back in one of Coke's flys.'

Mrs. Hare shook her head. 'I have no doubt I could walk quite well one way, Barbara: but I should not think of doing so, unless your papa approved.'

Barbara was looking from the window. She saw Benjamin gather up his garden tools and put them away. He then crossed to the narrow side-path which led down by the house to the back, where the stables were situated. Barbara ran through the hall and intercepted him.

'Has papa given any orders about the carriage, Benjamin?'

'Yes, miss. I am to drive you and mistress into West Lynne. I was to get ready directly, he said.'

Back waltzed Barbara. 'Mamma, it is all right: Benjamin is gone to get the carriage ready. You would like luncheon before you go? I will order in the tray.'

'Anything you please, my dear,' said the sweet-tempered, gentle woman. 'I don't know why, but I feel glad to go out to-day: perhaps, because it is lovely.'

Benjamin made ready his carriage and himself, drove out of the yard at the back, and brought the carriage round to the front gate. As Mrs. Hare and Barbara went down the path, Mr. Hare was in the garden still.

'Thank you, Richard,' she said, as she passed him, a loving smile lighting her delicate face.

'Mind you are home by the dinner hour, and don't let Barbara spend too much money,' cried the justice, in return. But he was not polite enough to go and hand them in.

The carriage—or phaeton, as it was often called—was a somewhat old-fashioned concern, as many country things are apt to be. A small box in front for the driver, and a wide seat with a head behind, accommodating Barbara well between them when Mr. and Mrs. Hare both sat in it. Mr. Hare, however, generally drove himself, taking no servant. The head was down to-day, but it was found convenient in rainy weather; and there were a double set of poles so that one horse or a pair might be driven in it. Very rarely, never unless they were going a distance, was a pair used; the long-tailed, black coach horses were taken out in turn, for the justice kept but that pair, and a saddle-horse for himself.

Benjamin drew the rug carefully over his mistress's knees—the servants did not like Mr. Hare, but would have laid down their lives for her—ascended to his box, and drove them to their destination, the linendraper's. It was an excellent shop, situated a little beyond the office of Mr. Carlyle, and Mrs. Hare and Barbara were soon engaged in that occupation, said to possess for all women a fascination. They had been deep in it about an hour, when Mrs. Hare discovered that her bag was missing.

'I must have left it in the carriage, Barbara. Go and bring it, will you, my dear? the pattern of that silk is in it.'

Barbara went out. The carriage and Benjamin, and the sleek old horse were all waiting drowsily together. Barbara could not see the bag, and she appealed to the servant.

'Find mamma's bag, Benjamin. It must be somewhere in the carriage.'

Benjamin got off his box, and began to search. Barbara waited, gazing listlessly down the street. The sun was shining brilliantly, and its rays fell upon the large cable chain of a gentleman, who was sauntering idly up the pavement, making its gold links and its drooping seal and key glitter, as they crossed his waistcoat. It shone also upon the enamelled gold studs of his shirt front, making *them* glitter; and as he suddenly raised his ungloved hand, a white hand, to stroke his moustache—by which action you may know a vain man—a diamond ring gleamed with a light that was positively dazzling. Involuntarily Barbara thought of the description her brother Richard had given of certain dazzling jewels worn by another.

She watched him advance. He was a handsome man of, perhaps, seven or eight-and-twenty, tall, slender, and well made, his eyes and hair black. A very pleasant expression sat upon his countenance, and on the left hand he wore a light buff kid glove, and was swinging its fellow by the fingers, apparently in deep thought, as he softly whistled to himself. But for the great light cast at that moment by the sun, Barbara might not have noticed the jewellery, or connected it in her mind with the other jewellery in that unhappy secret.

'Halloa! Thorn, is that you? Just step over here!'

The speaker was Otway Bethel, who was on the opposite side of the street! the spoken-to, the gentleman with the jewellery. But the latter was in a brown study, and did not hear. Bethel called out again, louder.

'Captain Thorn!'

That was heard. Captain Thorn nodded, and turned short off across the street. Barbara stood like one in a dream, her brain, her mind, her fancy all a confused mass together.

'Here's the bag, Miss Barbara. It had got among the folds of the rug.'

Benjamin held it out to her, but she took no notice: she was unconscious of all external things, save one. That she beheld the real murderer of Hallijohn she entertained no manner of doubt. In every particular he tallied with the description given by Richard: tall, dark, vain, handsome, delicate hands, jewellery, and—Captain Thorn! Barbara's cheeks grew white, and her heart turned sick.

'The bag, Miss Barbara.'

But Barbara was gone, leaving Benjamin and the bag. She had caught sight of Mr. Wainwright, the surgeon, at a little distance, and sped towards him.

'Mr. Wainwright,' began she, forgetting ceremony in her agitation, 'you see that gentleman talking to Otway Bethel. Who is he?'

Mr. Wainwright had to put his glasses across the bridge of his nose before he could answer, for he was short-sighted. 'That? Oh, it is a Captain Thorn. He is visiting the Herberts, I believe.'

'Where does he come from? Where does he live?' reiterated Barbara, in her eagerness.

'I don't know anything about him. I saw him this morning with young Smith, and he told me he was a friend of the Herberts. You are not looking well, Miss Barbara.'

She made no answer. Captain Thorn and Mr. Bethel came walking down the street, and the latter saluted her, but she was too much confused to re-spond to it. Mr. Wainwright then wished her good day, and Barbara walked slowly back. Mrs. Hare was appearing at the shop door.

'My dear, how long you are! Cannot the bag be found?'

'I went to speak to Mr. Wainwright,' answered Barbara, mechanically tak-ing the bag from Benjamin and giving it to her mother, her whole heart and eyes still absorbed with that one subject moving away in the distance.

'You look pale, child. Are you well?'

'Oh yes, quite. Let us get our shopping over, mamma.'

She moved on to their places at the counter as she spoke, eager to 'get it

over' and be at home, that she might have time for thought. Mrs. Hare wondered what had come to her; the pleasant interest, displayed in their pur-
chases previously, was now gone, and she sat inattentive and absorbed.

'Now, my dear, it is only waiting for you to choose. Which of the two silks
will you have?'

'Either. Any. Take which you like, mamma.'

'Barbara, what *has* come to you?'

'I believe I am tired,' said Barbara, with a forced laugh, as she compelled
herself to pay some sort of attention. 'I don't like the green: I will take the
other.'

They arrived at home. Barbara was five minutes alone in her chamber, before the dinner was on the table. All the conclusion she could come to, was
that *she* could do nothing, save tell the facts to Archibald Carlyle.

How could she contrive to see him? The business might admit of no delay.
She supposed she must go to East Lynne that evening; but where would be
her excuse for it at home? Puzzling over it, she went down to dinner. During
the meal, Mrs. Hare began talking of some silk she had purchased for a mantle. She should have it made like Miss Carlyle's new one: when Miss Carlyle
was at the Grove the other day, about Wilson's character, she had offered her
the pattern, and she, Mrs. Hare, would send one of the servants up for it,
after dinner.

'Oh, mamma, let me go!' burst forth Barbara. She spoke so vehemently,
that the justice paused in his carving, and demanded what ailed her. Barbara
made some timid excuse.

'Her eagerness is natural, Richard,' smiled Mrs. Hare. 'Barbara thinks she
shall get a peep at the baby, I expect. All young folks are fond of babies.'

Barbara's face flushed crimson: but she did not contradict the opinion. She
could not eat her dinner; she was too full of poor Richard: she played with it
and then sent away her plate, nearly untouched.

'That's through the finery she has been buying,' pronounced Justice Hare.
'Her head is stuffed up with it.'

No opposition was offered to Barbara's going to East Lynne. She reached
it just as their dinner was over. It was for Miss Carlyle she asked.

'Miss Carlyle is not at home, miss. She is spending the day out; and my
lady does not receive visitors yet.'

It was a sort of checkmate. Barbara was compelled to say she would see
Mr. Carlyle. Peter ushered her into the drawing-room, and Mr. Carlyle came
to her.

'I am so very sorry to disturb you; to have asked for you,' began Barbara,
with a burning face, for a certain evening interview of hers with him, twelve
months before, was disagreeably present to her. Never, since that evening of
agitation, had Barbara suffered herself to betray emotion to Mr. Carlyle: her

manners to him had been calm, courteous, and indifferent. And she now more frequently called him 'Mr. Carlyle' than 'Archibald.'

'Take a seat, take a seat, Barbara.'

'I asked for Miss Carlyle,' she continued, 'for mamma is in want of a pattern that she promised to lend her; but, in point of fact, it was you I wished to see. You remember the Lieutenant Thorn, whom Richard spoke of as being the real criminal?'

'Yes.'

'I think he is at West Lynne.'

Mr Carlyle was aroused to eager interest. 'He! That same Thorn?'

'It can be no other. Mamma and I were shopping to-day, and I went out for her bag which she had left in the carriage. While Benjamin was getting it, I saw a stranger coming up the street; a tall, good-looking, dark-haired man, with a conspicuous gold chain and studs. The sun was full upon him, causing the ornaments to shine, especially a diamond ring which he wore, for he had one hand raised to his face. The thought flashed over me, "That is like the description Richard gave of the man Thorn." Why the idea should have occurred to me in that strange manner I do not know, but it most assuredly did occur, though I did not really suppose him to be the same. Just then I heard him spoken to by some one on the other side of the street; it was Otway Bethel, and he called him *Captain Thorn*.'

'That is curious indeed, Barbara. I did not know any stranger was at West Lynne.'

'I saw Mr. Wainwright, and asked him who it was. He said a Captain Thorn, a friend of the Herberts. A Lieutenant Thorn four or five years ago would probably be Captain Thorn now.'

Mr. Carlyle nodded, and there was a pause.

'What can be done?' asked Barbara.

Mr. Carlyle was passing one hand over his brow; it was a habit of his when deep in thought. 'It is hard to say what is to be done, Barbara. The description you give of this man certainly tallies with that given by Richard. Did he look like a gentleman?'

'Very much so. A remarkably aristocratic-looking man, as it struck me.'

Mr. Carlyle again nodded assentingly. He remembered Richard's words, when describing the other; 'an out-and-out aristocrat.' 'Of course, Barbara, the first thing must be to try and ascertain whether it is the same,' he observed. 'If we find that it is, then we must deliberate upon future measures. I will see what I can ascertain, and let you know.'

Barbara rose. Mr. Carlyle escorted her across the hall, and then strolled down the park by her side, deep in the subject; and quite unconscious that Lady Isabel's jealous eyes were watching them from her dressing-room window.

'You say he seemed intimate with Otway Bethel?'

'As to being intimate, I do not know. Otway Bethel spoke as though he knew him.'

'This must have caused excitement to Mrs. Hare.'

'You forgot that mamma was not told anything about Thorn,' was the answer of Barbara. 'The uncertainty would have worried her to death. All Richard said to her was, that he was innocent, that it was a stranger who did the deed, and she asked for no particulars: she has implicit faith in Richard's truth.'

'True; I did forget,' replied Mr. Carlyle. 'I wish we could find out some one who knew the other Thorn: to ascertain that they were the same would be a great point gained.'

He went as far as the park gates with Barbara, shook hands, and wished her good evening. Scarcely had she departed, when Mr. Carlyle saw two gentlemen advancing from the opposite direction, in one of whom he recognized Tom Herbert, and the other—instinct told him—was Captain Thorn. He waited till they came up.

'If this isn't lucky, seeing you,' cried Mr. Tom Herbert, who was a free-and-easy sort of gentleman, the second son of a brother-justice of Mr. Hare's. 'I wish to goodness you'd give us a draught of your cider, Carlyle. We went up to Beauchamp's for a stroll, but found them all out; and I'm awfully thirsty. Captain Thorn, Carlyle.'

Mr. Carlyle invited them to his house, and ordered in refreshments. Young Herbert coolly threw himself into an arm-chair and lit a cigar. 'Come, Thorn,' cried he, 'here's a weed for you.'

Captain Thorn glanced towards Mr. Carlyle: he appeared of a far more gentlemanly nature than Tom Herbert.

'You'll have one too, Carlyle,' said Herbert, holding out his cigar case. 'Oh, I forgot; you are a muff; don't smoke one twice in a year. I say, how's Lady Isabel?'

'Very ill still.'

'By Jove! is she, though? Tell her I am sorry to hear it, will you, Carlyle? But—I say! will she smell the smoke?' asked he, with a mixture of alarm and concern in his face.

Mr. Carlyle reassured him upon that point, and turned to Captain Thorn. 'Are you acquainted with this neighbourhood?'

Captain Thorn smiled. 'I only reached West Lynne yesterday.'

'You were never here before, then?' continued Mr. Carlyle, setting down the last as a probably evasive answer.

'No.'

'He and my brother Jack, you know, are in the same regiment,' put in Tom Herbert, with scant ceremony. 'Jack had invited him down for some fishing, and Thorn arrives. But he never sent word he was coming. Jack had given him up, and is off on some Irish expedition, the deuce knows where. Precious unlucky that it should have happened so. Thorn says he shall cut short his stay, and go again.'

The conversation turned upon fishing, and in the heat of argument the stranger mentioned a certain pond, and its famous eels—'the Low Pond.' Mr. Carlyle looked at him, speaking, however, in a careless manner.

'Which do you mean? We have two ponds not far apart, each called the "Low Pond."'

'I mean the one on an estate about three miles from here: Squire Thorpe's, unless I am mistaken.'

Mr. Carlyle smiled. 'I think you must have been in the neighbourhood before, Captain Thorn. Squire Thorpe is dead, and the property has passed to his daughter's husband, and that Low Pond was filled up three years ago.'

'I have heard a friend mention it,' was Captain Thorn's reply, spoken in an indifferent tone, though he evidently wished not to pursue the subject.

Mr. Carlyle, by easy degrees, turned the conversation upon Swainson, the place whence Richard Hare's Captain Thorn was suspected to have come. The present Captain Thorn said he knew it 'a little,' he had once been 'staying there a short time.' Mr. Carlyle became nearly convinced that Barbara's suspicions were correct. The descriptions certainly agreed, as far as he could judge, in the most minute particulars. The man before him wore two rings, a diamond—and a very beautiful diamond, too—on the one hand, a seal ring on the other; his hands were delicate to a degree, and his handkerchief, a cambric one of unusually fine texture, was not entirely guiltless of scent: a mark of dandyism, which, in the other Captain Thorn, used considerably to annoy Richard. Mr. Carlyle quitted the room for a moment, and summoned Joyce to him.

'My lady has been asking for you, sir.' said Joyce.

'Tell her I will be up the moment these gentlemen leave. Joyce,' he added, 'find an excuse to come into the room presently; you can bring something or other in; I want you to look at this stranger who is with young Mr. Herbert. Notice him well; I fancy you may have seen him before.'

Mr. Carlyle returned to the room, leaving Joyce surprised. However, she presently followed, taking in some water, and lingered a few minutes, apparently placing the things on the table in better order.

When the two departed, Mr. Carlyle called Joyce, before proceeding to his wife's room. 'Well?' he questioned, 'did you recognize him?'

'Not at all, sir. He seemed quite strange to me.'

'Cast your thoughts back, Joyce. Did you never see him in years gone by?' Joyce looked puzzled, but she replied in the negative.

'Is he the man, think you, who used to ride over from Swainson to see Afy?'

Joyce's face flushed crimson. 'Oh, sir!' was all she uttered.

'The name is the same, Thorn: I thought it possible the man might be,' observed Mr. Carlyle.

'Sir, I cannot say. I never saw that Captain Thorn but once, and I don't know—I don't know'—Joyce spoke slowly and with consideration—'that I should at all know him again. I did not think of him when I looked at this gentleman; but, at any rate, no appearance in this one struck upon my memory as being familiar.'

So, from Joyce Mr. Carlyle obtained no clue, one way or the other. The following day he sought out Otway Bethel.

'Are you intimate with that Captain Thorn who is staying with the Herberts?' asked he.

'Yes,' answered Bethel, derisively, 'if passing a couple of hours in his company can constitute intimacy. That's all I have seen of Thorn.'

'Are you sure?' pursued Mr. Carlyle.

'Sure!' returned Bethel; 'why, what are you driving at now? I called in at Herbert's the night before last, and Tom asked me to stay the evening. Thorn had just come. A jolly bout we had: cigars and cold punch.'

'Bethel,' said Mr. Carlyle, dashing to the point, 'is it the Thorn who used to go after Afy Hallijohn? Come, you can tell if you like.'

Bethel remained dumb for a moment, apparently with amazement. 'What a confounded lie!' uttered he, at length. 'Why it's no more that Thorn than— What Thorn?' he broke off, abruptly.

'You are equivocating, Bethel. The Thorn who was mixed up—or said to be—in the Hallijohn affair. Is this the same man?'

'You are a fool, Carlyle: which is what I never took you to be yet,' was Mr. Bethel's rejoinder, spoken in a savage tone. 'I have told you that I never knew there was any Thorn mixed up with Afy , and I should like to know why my word is not to be believed? I never saw Thorn in my life till I saw him the other night at the Herbert's, and that I would take an oath to, if put to it.'

Bethel quitted Mr. Carlyle with the last word, and the latter gazed after him, revolving points in his brain. The mention of Thorn's name (the one spoken of by Richard Hare) appeared to excite some sore feeling in Bethel's mind, arousing it to irritation. Mr. Carlyle remembered that it had done so previously, and now it had done so again: and yet, Bethel was an easy-natured man in general, far better tempered than principled. That there was something hidden, some mystery connected with the affair, Mr. Carlyle felt sure, but he could not attempt so much as a guess at what it might be; and his interview with Bethel brought him no nearer the point he wished to find out—whether this Thorn was the same man. In walking back to his office, he met Mr. Tom Herbert.

'Does Captain Thorn purpose making a long stay with you?' he stopped him to inquire.

'He's gone: I have just seen him off by the train,' was the reply of Tom

Herbert. 'It seemed rather slow work for him without Jack, so he shortened his visit, and says he will pay us one when Jack's to the fore.'

As Mr. Carlyle went home to dinner that evening, he entered the Grove, ostensibly to make a short call on Mrs. Hare. Barbara, on the tenterhooks of impatience, accompanied him outside when he departed, and walked down the path.

'What have you learnt?' she eagerly asked.

'Nothing satisfactory,' was the reply of Mr. Carlyle. 'The man is gone.'

'Gone!' said Barbara.

Mr. Carlyle explained. He told her how they had come to his house the previous evening after Barbara's departure, and his encounter with Tom Herbert that day: he mentioned, also, his interview with Bethel.

'Can he have gone on purpose, fearing consequences?' wondered Barbara.

'Scarcely: or why should he have come?'

'You did not suffer any word to escape you last night, causing him to suspect that he was doubted?'

'Not any. You would make a bad lawyer, Barbara.'

'Who or what is he?'

'An officer in her Majesty's service, in John Herbert's regiment. I ascertained no more. Tom said he was of good family. But I cannot help suspecting it is the same man.'

'Can nothing more be done?'

'Nothing, in the present stage of the affair,' concluded Mr. Carlyle, as he passed through the gate to continue his way. 'We can only wait on again with what patience we may, hoping that time will bring about its own elucidation.'

Barbara pressed her forehead down on the cold iron of the gate as his footsteps died away. 'Ay, to wait on,' she murmured, 'to wait on in dreary pain; to wait on, perhaps for years, perhaps for ever! And poor Richard—wearing out his days in poverty and exile!'

Lady Isabel recovered, and grew strong; and a few years passed smoothly on, no particular event occurring to note them.

PART THE SECOND

❧ I ❧

Going from Home

A few years had passed.

'I should recommend a complete change of scene altogether, Mr. Carlyle. Say, some place on the French or Belgian coast. Sea-bathing might do wonders.'

'Should you think it well for her to go so far from home?'

'I should. Where there is any chronic or confirmed disorder, one we can grapple with, I don't care a straw for change of scene or air, a patient is as well at his own home as away, a certain treatment must be gone through, surgical or physical, and it is of little moment whether it is pursued on a mountain in Switzerland or in a vale in Devonshire. But in these cases of protracted weakness, where you can do nothing but try to coax the strength back again, change of air and scene are of immense benefit.'

'I will propose it to her,' said Mr. Carlyle.

'I have just done so,' replied Dr. Martin, who was the other speaker. 'She met it with objection; which I expected, for invalids naturally feel a disinclination to move from home. But it is necessary that she should go.'

The object of their conversation was Lady Isabel. There were three children now at East Lynne; Isabel, William, and Archibald; the latter twelve months old. Lady Isabel had, a month or two back, been attacked with illness: she recovered from it; that is, she recovered from the disorder; but it had left her in an alarming state of weakness. Mr. Wainwright tried in vain to grapple with the weakness; she seemed to get worse, rather than better, and Dr. Martin was summoned from Lynneborough. The best thing he could recommend—as you have seen—was change of scene and air.

Lady Isabel was unwilling to take the advice; more especially to go so far as the 'French coast,' and, but for a circumstance that seemed to have happened purposely to induce her to decide, would probably never have gone. Mrs. Ducie—the reader may not have forgotten her name—had, in conjunction with her husband, the Honourable Augustus, somewhat run herself out at elbows, and found it convenient to enter for a time on the less expensive life of the Continent. For eighteen months she had been staying at Paris, the education of her younger daughters being the plea put forth for the sojourn, and a very convenient plea it is, and serves hundreds. Isabel had had two or three letters from her during her absence, and she now received another, saying they were going to spend a month or two at Boulogne-sur-Mer. Dr. Martin and Mr. Wainwright declared that this must remove all Lady Isabel's unwillingness to go from home, for Mrs. Ducie's society would do away with the loneliness she had anticipated, which had been the ostensible score of her objection.

'Boulogne-sur-Mer, of all places in the world!' remonstrated Lady Isabel. 'It is spoken of as being crowded and vulgar.'

Mr. Carlyle also demurred at Boulogne-sur-Mer. It did not stand high in his estimation. It was not a place he cared to send his wife to: the more especially as he could not remain with her. Trouville, a pleasant, retired watering place, situated near Harfleur, and little known in those days, had been the one fixed upon. Lady Isabel probably would have found it dull.

Dr. Martin strongly urged its being changed for Boulogne. 'What did it matter if Boulogne was crowded and vulgar?' he asked: 'there would be the more amusement for Lady Isabel. He had had his doubts of Trouville before, in regard to its dullness: by all means let her go to Boulogne to join Mrs. Ducie.'

Mr. Carlyle yielded the point, and finished by approving it; and Lady Isabel finding she had no chance against them all, consented to go, and plans were hastily decided upon.

She certainly was looking very ill: her features were white and attenuated, her sweet, sad eyes had grown larger and darker; her hands were hot and sickly. Though warm weather, she had generally a shawl folded round her, and would sit for hours without rousing herself, as those suffering from great weakness like to do; would sit gazing out on the calm landscape, or watching her children at play. She went out once a day in the close carriage, and that was all: no other exertion could she be aroused to make.

In this illness the old trouble had come back again—the sore feeling touching her husband and Barbara Hare. It had lain pretty dormant in the last few years, nothing having occurred to excite it; but Lady Isabel was in that state of weakness, where grievances, let them be old or new, grow upon the mind. Her thoughts would wander to the unsatisfactory question of whether Mr. Carlyle had ever truly loved her; or whether, lured by her rank and her beauty, he had married her, loving Barbara. Mr. Carlyle's demonstrative affection, shown so greatly for her in the first twelve months or so of their married life, had subsided into calmness. Is not a similar result arrived at by every husband that the Church ever made one with woman? It was not that his love had faded, but that time and custom had wrought their natural effects. Look at children with their toys; a boy with a new drum, a girl with a new doll. Are not the playthings kissed, and hugged, and clasped in arms, and never put down? Did ever playthings seem like them? Are not all other things neglected, or submitted to unwillingly—the reading lessons, the sports, the daily works, even the pudding at dinner, while the new toy is all in all? But, wait a little time, and the drum (if it has escaped breakage) is consigned to some dark closet; the doll to its cradle; and neither of them is visited or looked at. Tell the children to go and get their lately cherished playthings, to make them their evening's amusement; and they will go unwillingly (if they don't openly rebel), for they are tired of them. It is of no use scolding the children for being fickle: it is in their nature to be fickle, for they are human. Are grown children otherwise? Do we not all, men and women, become indifferent to our toys when we hold them securely in possession? Young lady, when he, who is soon to be your lord and master, protests to you that he shall always be as ardent a lover as he is now, believe him if you like, but don't reproach him when the disappointment comes. He does not wilfully deceive you; he only forgets that it is in the constitution of man to change, the very essence of his nature. The time will arrive when his manner must settle down into a calmness, which to you, if you be of an exacting temperament, may look like indifference or coldness; but you will do well to put up with it, for it will never now be otherwise. Never: the heyday of early love, of youth, and of novelty is past.

Lady Isabel did not understand the even manner, the quiet calmness into which her husband's once passionate love had subsided, and in her fanciful jealousy she attributed it to the influence Barbara held upon his memory. She looked for the little tender episodes of daily life: she would fain have had him hang over her chair as she sang, and draw her face to his, and feel his kisses on her lips, as when she first came, a wife, to East Lynne. It has been seen that Lady Isabel did not love Mr. Carlyle; but his tenderness, his anxious care for her in their early married days, caused her to lift up her heart to him with gratitude, and to try earnestly to love him. But—to try to love! Vain effort: Love never yet came for the *trying*: it is a capricious passion, and generally comes without the knowledge and against the will. It is possible she thought she had succeeded, for her whole esteem, her respect, and her admiration were his. When she compared him with other men, and saw how far he surpassed them, how noble and how good he was, how little the rest looked beside him, her heart rose up with pride at the consciousness of being his wife: a princess might have deemed it an honour to be the chosen of such a man as Archibald Carlyle. Spare one single corner of *his* heart to Barbara Hare! No indeed; Isabel could not afford that.

On the day that the journey was finally decided, Lady Isabel was in the drawing-room with her three children; even the little fellow was sitting on the carpet. Isabel was a delicate, pretty child in her fifth year, William was the very image of his mother, Archibald was like Mr. Carlyle.

'Come hither, my darlings,' she cried.

Isabel and William ran to her, and she placed an arm round each. Master Archie was kicking his heels on the carpet at a distance. They looked up at their mother.

'Would my little dears like to go a great way with mamma? Over the sea in a boat?'

Isabel—she had inherited the refined, sensitive feelings of her mother—replied only by a smile and a vivid blush. William clapped his hands. 'Oh yes, in a boat! Arty too, mamma?'

'Archie and all,' answered Lady Isabel. 'And Joyce, and Wilson, and—'

Miss Carlyle, who was seated near one of the windows, sewing, turned sharply round to interrupt the gladness. Miss Carlyle, though not openly dissenting, did not inwardly approve of the proposed emigration. What did people want with change of air? thought she. *She* had never wanted any. A pack of new-fangled notions that doctors had got into, recommending change of air for everything! they'd order it, next, for a cut finger. If Lady Isabel would make an effort, she'd get strong fast enough at home.

'The children are not going to the seaside,' said she. 'They are not ordered there.'

'But they must go with me,' replied Lady Isabel. 'Of course they are not expressly ordered to it. Why should they not go?'

'Why should they not?' retorted Miss Corny. 'Why, on account of the expense, to be sure. I can tell you what it is, Lady Isabel, what with one expense and another, your husband will soon be on the road to ruin. Your journey with Joyce and Peter will cost enough, ma'am, without taking a van-load of nurses and children.'

Lady Isabel's heart sank within her.

'Besides, your object in going is to pick up health, and how can you do that, if you are to be worried with the children?' pursued Miss Corny. 'People who go abroad for pleasure, or invalids in search of health, won't find much of either if they carry their cares with them.'

Lady Isabel rose, and, with difficulty, lifted Archibald from the carpet; sat down with him on her knee, and pressed his little face to hers.

'Would my baby like mamma to go away and leave him?' she asked, the tears falling fast on his fair curls. 'Oh! I could not leave them behind me!' she added, looking imploringly at Miss Carlyle. 'I should get no better if you send me there alone; I should ever be yearning for the children.'

'Alone, Lady Isabel! is your husband nothing?'

'But he will only take me; he will not remain.'

'Well, you can't expect his business to go to rack and ruin,' snapped Miss Corny. 'How can he stay away from it? With all these heavy expenses upon him, there's more need than ever for his sticking to it closely. And, before the children are gallavanted over the water, it might be as well to sit down and calculate the cost. Of course, Lady Isabel, I only offer my opinion; you are Archibald's wife, and sole mistress, and will do as you please.'

Do as she pleased! Poor Lady Isabel laid her head meekly down upon her children, effectually silenced, and her heart breaking with pain. Joyce, who was then in the room, heard a little, and conjectured much of what had passed.

In the evening Mr. Carlyle carried little Isabel up to the nursery on his shoulder. Joyce happened to be there, and thought it a good opportunity to speak.

'My lady wishes to take the children with her to France, sir.'

'Does she?' replied Mr. Carlyle.

'And I fear she will make herself very unhappy if they do not go, sir.'

'Why should they not go?' asked Mr. Carlyle.

He went back to the drawing-room, where his wife was alone. 'Isabel, do you wish to take the children with you?'

'Oh, I did so wish it!' she replied, the hectic of hope lighting her pale cheeks. 'If they might but go, Archibald?'

'Of course they may go. It will be a nice change for them, as well as for you. Why should you hesitate?'

'The expense,' she timidly whispered, the hectic growing deeper.

He looked right into her eyes with his pleasant smile. 'Expense is no concern of yours, Isabel: it is mine. Never let the word expense trouble you, until I tell you that it must.'

'It will not increase the cost so very much,' she returned, her eyes smiling with happiness. 'And I shall get well all the sooner for having them with me.'

'And, to further that, you should take them, if it were to the end of the world. Why should you study aught but your own wishes and comfort?'

She took his hand in her love and gratitude—for every tone of his voice spoke of care and tenderness for her; all jealous fancies were forgotten, all recollection, in that moment, that his manner was calmer than of old. 'Archibald! I do believe you care for me as much as you used to?'

He did not understand the words, but he held her to him as in days gone by, and kissed her tenderly. 'More precious, far more precious to me than of yore, Isabel!'

Miss Carlyle flew out when she heard the decision, and frightened her brother to repentance, assuring him that his sending the children was the certain way to preclude all chance of his wife's recovery. Mr. Carlyle was sorely puzzled between Isabel's wishes and Isabel's welfare: he would promote both if he could, but if they clashed—? He feared his own judgment, he feared his wife's; and he appealed to the medical men. But Miss Corny had forestalled him there: she had contrived so to impress those gentlemen of the incessant worry the children would prove to Lady Isabel, that they pronounced their veto, and forbade the children's going. So, after all, Lady Isabel had to resign herself to the disappointment.

'Joyce,' said she to her waiting-maid, 'I shall leave you at home; I must take Wilson instead.'

'Oh, my lady! what have I done?'

'You have done all that you ought, Joyce, but you must stay with the children. If I may not take them, the next best thing will be to leave them with you. I shall give them into your charge, not into Miss Carlyle's,' she said, sinking her voice: 'if it were Wilson who remained, I could not do that.'

'My lady, I must do whatever you think best. I wish I could attend you and stay with them, but of course I cannot do both.'

'I am sent away to get health and strength, but it may be I shall die, Joyce. If I never come back, will you promise to remain with my children?'

Joyce felt a creeping sensation in her veins: the sobs rose in her throat, but she swallowed them down, and constrained her voice to calmness. 'My lady, I hope you will come back to us as well as you used to be. I trust you will hope so too, my lady, and not give way to low spirits.'

'I sincerely hope and trust I shall,' answered Lady Isabel, fervently. 'Still, there is no telling, for I am very ill. Joyce, give me your promise in case of the worst, that you will remain with the children.'

'I will, my lady—as long as I am permitted.'

'And be kind to them, and love them, and shield them from—from—any unkindness that may be put upon them,' she added, her head full of Miss Carlyle. 'And talk to them sometimes of their poor mother who is gone.'

'I will, I will: oh, my lady, I will!' And Joyce sat down in the rocking-chair as Lady Isabel quitted her, and burst into tears.

⚜ 11 ⚜

Francis Levison

Mr. Carlyle and Lady Isabel, with Wilson and Peter in attendance, arrived at Boulogne, and proceeded to the Hôtel des Bains. It may be as well to mention that Peter had been transferred from Miss Carlyle's service to theirs, when the establishment was first formed at East Lynne. Upon entering the hotel, they inquired for Mrs. Ducie, and then a disappointment awaited them: a letter was handed them, which had arrived that morning from Mrs.

Ducie, expressing her regret that certain family arrangements prevented her visiting Boulogne; she was proceeding to some of the baths in Germany instead.

'I might almost have known it,' remarked Isabel. 'She was always the most changeable of women.'

Mr. Carlyle proposed that they should, after all, go on to Trouville, but Isabel said she would stay, now she had come. He went out in search of lodgings, Isabel objecting to remain in the bustling hotel. He succeeded in finding some very desirable ones, situated in the Rue de l'Ecu, near the port, and they moved into them. He thought the journey had done her good, for she looked better, and said she already felt stronger. Mr. Carlyle remained with her three days; he had promised only one, but he was pleased with Isabel's returning glimpses of health, and amused with the scenes of the busy town.

'I shall make no acquaintance here,' Isabel observed to him, as they sat together at the end of the first division of the pier, which she had reached without much fatigue, and watched the gay idlers flocking past them.

'It would not be advisable to do so indiscriminately,' he replied, 'but you may chance to find some whom you know. All sorts of people come over here: some respectable, and from respectable motives; others the contrary. Some of these men, going by now, are here because they have kites flying in England.'

'Kites!' echoed Lady Isabel.

'Kites, and bills, and ghosts of renewed acceptances,' returned Mr. Carlyle. 'And well for them if they are over here for nothing else. The worse a man's conduct has been at home, the more assurance he puts on abroad, and is the first to rush and proclaim his arrival at the consulate. To hear these men boast, we might deem they were millionaires in England, and had led the lives of saints.'

'You have never stayed in these continental towns, Archibald: how do you know this?'

'I have had plenty to do with those who have stayed in them. There goes Buxton!' he suddenly exclaimed; 'he sees me, too. Look at him, Isabel. He does not know whether to come on, or to turn and make a run for it.'

'Who? Which?' inquired Isabel, confused by the many passers-by.

'That stout, well-dressed man, with the light hair, and bunch of seals hanging to his watch-chain. He thinks better of it, and comes on. All safe, my good sir, on Boulogne pier, but if they catch you on the other side of the water— Here comes his wife, following with some ladies. Look at her satins, and her chains, and her hanging bracelets—all swindled out of credulous tradespeople. There's not a doubt they are playing at being grand people in the English society here. It must be as good as a comedy to be behind the scenes in this Anglo-French town, and watch the airs and graces of some of its sojourners. Are you tired, Isabel?'

'A little. I should like to return.'

Mr. Carlyle rose, and giving his arm to his wife, they walked slowly down the pier. Many an eye was turned to look at them; at his tall, noble form; at her young beauty; at the unmistakable air of distinction which enshrined both: they were not like the ordinary visitors of Boulogne-sur-Mer.

The tide served at eight o'clock the following morning, and Mr. Carlyle left by the Folkestone boat. Wilson made his breakfast, and after swallowing it in haste, he returned to his wife's room to say farewell.

'Good-bye, my love,' he said, stooping to kiss her. 'Take care of yourself.'

'Give my dear love to the darlings, Archibald. And—and—'

'And what?' he asked. 'I have not a moment to lose.'

'Do not get making love to Barbara Hare while I am away.'

She spoke in a tone half jest, half serious—could he but have seen how her heart was beating! Mr. Carlyle took it wholly as a jest, and went away laughing. Had he believed she was serious, he could have been little more surprised had she charged him not to go about the country on a dromedary.

Isabel rose later, and lingered over her breakfast, listless enough. She was wondering how she could make the next few weeks pass: what she could do with her time. She had taken two sea-baths since her arrival, but they had appeared not to agree with her, leaving her low and shivering afterwards, so it was not deemed advisable that she should attempt more. It was a lovely morning, and she determined to venture on to the pier, where they had been the previous evening. She had not Mr. Carlyle's arm, but it was not far, and she could take a good rest at the end of it.

She went, attended by Peter, took her seat, and told him to come for her in an hour. She watched the strollers on the pier; not in crowds now, but stragglers, coming on at intervals. There came a gouty man, in a list shoe, there came three young ladies and their governess, there came two fast puppies in shooting-jackets and eyeglasses, which they turned with a broad stare on Lady Isabel; but there was something about her which caused them to drop their glasses and their ill manners together. After an interval, there appeared another, a tall, handsome, gentlemanly man. Her eyes fell upon him; and—what was it that caused every nerve in her frame to vibrate, every pulse to quicken? *Whose* form was it that was thus advancing, and changing the monotony of her mind into a tumult? It was that of one who, she was soon to find, had never been entirely forgotten.

Captain Levison came slowly on, approaching the part of the pier where she sat. He glanced at her, not with the hardihood displayed by the two young men, but with quite sufficiently evident admiration.

'What a lovely girl!' thought he to himself. 'Who can she be, sitting there alone?' All at once a recollection flashed into his mind: he raised his hat and extended his hand, his fascinating smile in full play.

'I certainly cannot be mistaken. Have I not the honour of once more meeting Lady Isabel Vane?'

She allowed him to take her hand, answering a few words at random, for her wits seemed to have gone wool-gathering.

'I beg your pardon—I should have said Lady Isabel Carlyle. Time has elapsed since we parted, and in the pleasure of seeing you again so unexpectedly, I thought of you as you were then.'

She sat down again, the brilliant flush of emotion dying away on her cheeks. It was the loveliest face Francis Levison had seen since he had last seen hers, and he thought so as he gazed at it.

'What can have brought you to this place?' he inquired, taking a seat by her.

'I have been ill,' she explained, 'and am ordered to the sea-side. We should not have come here but for Mrs. Ducie; we expected to meet her. Mr. Carlyle only left me this morning.'

'Mrs. Ducie is off to Ems. I see them occasionally. They have been fixtures in Paris for some time. You do indeed look ill!' he abruptly added, in a tone of sympathy. 'alarmingly ill. Is there anything I can do for you?'

She was aware that she looked unusually ill at that moment, for the agitation and surprise of meeting him were fading away, leaving her face of an ashy whiteness. She was exceedingly vexed and angry with herself, that the meeting him should have had power to call forth emotion. Until that moment she was unconscious that she retained any sort of feeling for Captain Levison.

'Perhaps I have ventured out too early,' she said, in a tone that would seem to apologize for her looks; 'I think I will return. I shall meet my servant, no doubt. Good morning, Captain Levison.'

'But indeed you do not appear fit to walk alone,' he remonstrated. 'You must allow me to see you safely home.'

Drawing her hand within his arm quite as a matter of course, as he had done many a time in the days gone by, he proceeded to assist her down the pier. Lady Isabel, conscious of her own feelings, felt that it was not quite the thing to walk thus familiarly with him, but he was a sort of relation of the family—a connection at any rate, and she could find no ready excuse for declining.

'Have you seen Lady Mount Severn lately?' he inquired.

"I saw her when I was in London this spring with Mr. Carlyle. The first time we have met since my marriage: we do not correspond. Lord Mount Severn has paid us some visits at East Lynne. They are in town yet, I believe.'

'For all I know. I have not seen them, or England either, for ten months. I have been staying in Paris, and got here yesterday.'

'A long leave of absence,' she observed.

'Oh, I have left the army. I sold out. The truth is, Lady Isabel—for I don't mind telling you—things are rather down with me at present. My old uncle has behaved shamefully: he has married again.'

'I heard that Sir Peter had married.'

'He is seventy-three—the old simpleton! Of course this materially alters my prospects, for it is just possible he may have a son of his own now; and my creditors all came down upon me. They allowed me to run into debt with complacency when I was heir to the title and estates, but as soon as Sir Peter's marriage appeared in the papers, myself and my consequence dropped a hundred per cent; credit was stopped, and I was dunned for payment. So I sold out and came abroad.'

'Leaving your creditors?'

'What else could I do? My uncle would not pay them, or increase my allowance.'

'What are your prospects, then?' resumed Lady Isabel.

'Prospects? Do you see that little ragged boy, throwing stones into the harbour?—it is well if the police don't drop upon him. Ask him what his prospects are, and he would stare in your face, and say, "None." Mine are on a par.'

'You may succeed Sir Peter yet.'

'I may: but I may not. When these old idiots get a young wife—'

'Have you quarrelled with Sir Peter?' interrupted Lady Isabel.

'I should quarrel with him, as he deserves, if it would do any good: but I might get my allowance stopped. Self-interest, you see, Lady Isabel, is the order of the day with most of us.'

'Do you purpose staying in Boulogne long?'

'I don't know. As I may find amusement. Paris is a fast capital, with its heated rooms and its late hours, and I came down for the refreshment of a few sea-dips. Am I walking too fast for you?'

'You increased your pace alarmingly when you spoke of Sir Peter's marriage. And I am not sorry for it,' she added, good-naturedly, 'for it has proved to me how strong I am getting. A week ago I could not have walked so fast.'

He interrupted with eager apologies, and soon they reached her home. Captain Levison entered with her—uninvited. He probably deemed that between connections great ceremony might be dispensed with, and he sat a quarter of an hour, chatting to amuse her. When he rose, he inquired what she meant to do with herself in the afternoon.

'To lie down,' replied Lady Isabel. 'I am not strong enough to sit up all day.'

'Should you be going out again afterwards, you must allow me to take care of you,' he observed. 'I am glad that I happen to be here, for I am sure you are not fit to wander out only followed by a servant. When Mr. Carlyle comes, he will thank me for my pains.'

What was she to urge in objection? Simply nothing. He spoke, let us not doubt, from a genuine wish to serve her in a plain, easy tone, as any acquaintance might speak. Lady Isabel schooled herself severely; if those old feelings were not quite dead within her, why, she must smother them down again as effectually as if they were: the very fact of recognizing such to her own heart, brought its glow of shame to her brow. She would meet Captain Levison and suffer his companionship as she would that of the most indifferent stranger.

It was just the wrong way for her to go to work.

As the days passed on, Lady Isabel improved wonderfully. She was soon able to go to the sands in a morning and sit there to enjoy the sea-air, watching the waves come up or recede with the tide. She made no acquaintance whatever in the place, and when she had a companion it was Captain Levison. He would frequently join her there, sometimes take her, almost always give her his arm home. She disliked to having to take his arm: her conscience whispered it might be better if she did not. One day she said, in a joking sort of manner—she would not say it in any other—that now she was strong she had no need of his arm and his escort. He demanded, in evident astonishment, what had arisen that he might not still afford it, as her husband was not with her to give her his. She had no answer to reply to this, no excuse to urge, and, in default, took his arm as usual. In the evening, he was always ready to take her to the pier, but they sat apart, mixing not with the bustling crowd, he lending to his manner, as he conversed with her, all that it could call up of fascination—and fascination, such as Francis Levison's, might be dangerous to any ear in the sweet evening twilight. The walk over, he left her at her own door; in the evening she never asked him in, and he did not intrude without, as he sometimes would of a morning.

Now, where was the help for this? You may say that she should have remained in-doors, and not have subjected herself to his companionship. But the remaining in-doors would not have brought her health, and it was health that she was staying in Boulogne to acquire, and the sooner it came the better pleased she would be, for she wanted to be at home with her husband and children.

In a fortnight from the period of his departure, Mr. Carlyle was expected in Boulogne. But what a marvellous change had this fortnight wrought in Lady Isabel! She did not dare to analyze her feelings, but she was conscious that all the fresh emotions of her youth had come again. The blue sky seemed as of the sweetest sapphire, the green fields and the waving trees were of an emerald brightness, the perfume of the flowers was more fragrant than any perfume had yet seemed. She knew that the sky, that the grassy plains, the leafy trees, the brilliant flowers were but as they ever had been; she knew that the sunny atmosphere possessed no more of loveliness or power of imparting delight than of old: and she knew that the change, the sensation of ecstasy, was in her own heart. No wonder that she shrank from self-examination.

The change from listless langour to her present feelings brought the hue and contour of health to her face far sooner than anything else could have done. She went down with Captain Levison to meet Mr. Carlyle the evening he came in, and when Mr. Carlyle saw her behind the cords, as he was going to the custom-house, he scarcely knew her. Her features had lost their sharpness, her cheeks wore a rosy flush, and the light of pleasure at meeting him again shone in her eyes.

'What can you have been doing to yourself, my darling?' he uttered in delight, as he emerged from the custom-house and took her hand in his. 'You look almost well.'

'Yes, I am much better, Archibald, but I am warm now and flushed. We have waited here some time; and the setting sun was full upon us. How long the boat was coming in.'

'The wind was dead against us,' replied Mr. Carlyle, wondering who the exquisite was, at his wife's side. He thought he remembered his face.

'Captain Levison,' said Lady Isabel. 'I wrote you word in one of my letters that he was here. Have you forgotten it?' Yes, it had slipped from his memory.

'And I am pleased that it happened to be so,' said that gentleman, interposing, 'for it has enabled me to attend Lady Isabel in some of her walks. She is stronger now, but at first she was unfit to venture alone.'

'I feel much indebted to you,' said Mr. Carlyle, warmly.

Lady Isabel had taken her husband's arm, and Francis Levison walked by the side of Mr. Carlyle. 'To tell you the truth,' he said, dropping his voice so that it reached only Mr. Carlyle's ear, 'when I met Lady Isabel, I was shocked to see her. I thought her days were numbered; that a very short period must close them. I therefore considered it a bounden duty to render her any slight service that might be in my power.'

'I am sure she has been obliged for your attention,' responded Mr. Carlyle. 'And as to her visible improvement, it seems little short of a miracle. I expected, from Lady Isabel's letters to me, to find her better, but she is more than better; she looks well. Do you hear, Isabel? I say a miracle must have been wrought, to bring back your bloom, for a fortnight's space of time could scarcely have done it. This must be a famous air for invalids.'

The bloom that Mr. Carlyle spoke of deepened to a glowing crimson as she listened. She knew—and she could not stifle the knowledge, however she might wish to do so—that it was not the place or the sea-air which had renovated her heart and her countenance. But she clasped her husband's arm the closer, and inwardly prayed for strength and power to thrust away from her this dangerous foe, that was creeping on in guise so insidious.

'You have not said a word to me about the children,' exclaimed Lady Isabel, as she and her husband entered their rooms, Francis Levison not having been invited to enter. 'Did they all send me some kisses? Did Archie send me any?'

Mr. Carlyle laughed: he was not a mother, he was only a father. Archie, with his year of age, send kisses?

'Had you been away, as I am, he should have sent some to you,' murmured Lady Isabel. 'I would have taken a thousand from him, and told him they were for papa.'

'I will take a thousand back to him,' answered Mr. Carlyle, folding his wife to his heart. 'My dearest, the sight of you has made me glad.'

The following day was Sunday, and Francis Levison was asked to dine with them: the first meal he had been invited to in the house. After dinner, when Lady Isabel left them, he grew confidential with Mr. Carlyle; laying open all his intricate affairs and his cargo of troubles.

'This compulsory exile abroad is becoming intolerable,' he concluded; 'and a Paris life plays the very deuce with one. Do you see any chance of my getting back to England?'

'Not the least,' was the candid answer; 'unless you can manage to satisfy, or partially satisfy, these claims you have been telling me of. Will not Sir Peter assist you?'

'I believe he would were the case fairly represented to him; but how am I to get over to do it? I have written several letters to him lately, and for some time I got no reply. Then came an epistle from Lady Levison; not short and sweet, but short and sour. It was to the effect that Sir Peter was ill, and could not at present be troubled with business matters.'

'He cannot be very ill,' remarked Mr. Carlyle; 'he passed through West Lynne in his open carriage a week ago.'

'He ought to help me,' grumbled Captain Levison. 'I am his heir, so long as Lady Levison does not give him one. I do not hear that she has expectations.'

'You should contrive to see him.'

'I know I should: but it is not possible, under present circumstances. With these thunder-clouds hanging over me, I dare not set foot in England, and run the risk of being dropped upon. I can stand a few things, but I shudder at the bare idea of a prison. Something peculiar to my idiosyncrasy I take it, for those who have tried it say that it's nothing when you're used to it.'

'Some one might see him for you.'

'Some one!—who? I have quarrelled with my lawyers, Sharp and Steel, of Lincoln's Inn.'

'Keen practitioners,' put in Mr. Carlyle.

'Too keen for me. I'd send them over the herring-pond if I could. They have used me shamefully since my uncle's marriage. If ever I do come into the Levison estates, they'll be ready to eat their ears off: they would like a finger in the pie with such a property as that.'

'Shall I see Sir Peter Levison for you?'

'*Will* you?' returned Captain Levison, his dark eyes lighting up.

'If you like; as your friend, you understand, not as your solicitor: that I should decline. I have a slight knowledge of Sir Peter; my father was well acquainted with him: and if I can render you any little service, I shall be happy, in return for your kind attention to my wife. I cannot promise to see him for these two or three weeks,' resumed Mr. Carlyle, 'for we are terribly busy. Otherwise I should be staying here with my wife.'

Francis Levison expressed his gratitude, and the prospect, however remote, of being enabled to return to England, increased his spirits to exultation. Whilst they continued to converse, Lady Isabel sat at the window in the adjoining room, listlessly looking out on the crowds of French, who were crowding to and from the port in their Sunday holiday attire: looking at them with her eyes, not with her senses; her senses were holding commune with herself, and it was not altogether satisfactory. She was aware that a sensation all too warm, a feeling of attraction towards Francis Levison, was working within her; not a voluntary one; she could no more repress it than she could repress her own sense of being; and, mixed with it was the stern voice of conscience, overwhelming her with the most lively terror. She would have given all she possessed to be able to overcome it; she would have given half the years of her future life to separate herself at once and for ever from the man.

But, do not mistake the word terror; or suppose that Lady Isabel Carlyle applied it here in the vulgar acceptation of the term. She did not fear for herself; none could be more securely conscious of their own rectitude of principle and conduct: and she would have believed it as impossible for her ever to forsake her duty as a wife, a gentlewoman, and a Christian, as for the sun to turn round from the west to the east. That was not the fear which possessed her; it had never presented itself to her mind: what she did fear was, that further companionship, especially lonely companionship, with Francis Levison might augment the sentiments she entertained for him to a height, that her life, for perhaps years to come, would be one of unhappiness and concealment: more than all, she shrank from the consciousness of the bitter wrong that these sentiments cast upon her husband.

'Archibald, I have a favour to ask you,' she timidly began, as they sat together after Captain Levison's departure. 'You must promise to grant it me.'

'What is it?'

'But that is not promising.'

'I will grant it, Isabel; if it be in my power.'

'I want you to remain with me for the rest of the time that I must stay here.'

Mr. Carlyle looked at her in surprise. 'My dear, how could you think of wishing anything so unlikely? It is circuit time.'

'Oh, Archibald, you must remain.'

'I wish I could; but it is impossible; you must know it to be so, Isabel. A few weeks later in the year, and I could have stayed the whole of the time with you. As it is I did not know how to get away for these two or three days.'

'And you go back to-morrow?'

'Necessity has no law, my darling.'

'Then take me with you.'

Mr. Carlyle smiled. 'No, Isabel: not while I find the change is doing you so much good. I took these rooms for six weeks; you must remain certainly until the end of the term, if not longer.'

The colour came flowing painfully into her cheek. 'I cannot stay without you, Archibald.'

'Tell me why,' smiled Mr. Carlyle.

Tell him why! 'I am so dull without you,' was the best argument she could offer, but her voice faltered, for she felt that it would not be listened to.

Neither was it. Mr. Carlyle left the following day, and when he was departing, commended his wife to the further attention of Captain Levison. Not the faintest suspicion that it might be unwise to do so ever crossed his mind. How should it? Perfectly correct and honourable himself, it never occurred to him that Captain Levison might be less so; and as to his wife—he would fearlessly have left her alone with him, or with any one else, on a desert island, so entire was his confidence in her.

⚡ III ⚡

Quitting the Danger

Lady Isabel was seated on one of the benches of the Petit Camp, as it is called, underneath the ramparts of the upper town. A week or ten days had passed away since the departure of Mr. Carlyle, and in her health there was a further visible improvement. In her strength, the change was almost beyond belief. She had walked from her home to the cemetery, had lingered there, reading the inscriptions on the English graves, and now on her departure sat down to rest; tired, it must be owned, but not much more so than many a lady would be, rejoicing in rude health. Captain Levison was her companion,

as he mostly was in her walks; shake him off she could not. She had tried
a few stratagems; going out at unusual hours, or choosing unfrequented
routes; but he was sure to trace her steps and come upon her. Isabel thought
he must watch: probably he did. She would not take more decided steps, or
say to him, you shall not join me; he might have asked for an explanation,
and Isabel, in her conscious state of feeling, avoided that above all things. It
will be but for a little time, she reflected; I shall soon be gone, and leave him,
I hope, for ever. But meanwhile, she felt that this prolonged intercourse with
him was bringing its fruits; that her cheek blushed at his approach, her heart
beat with something too like rapture. She tried to put it down: why did she
not try to stop the breeze as it filled the sails of the passing vessels? It would
not have been a more hopeless task.

It was a still evening, cool for July, no sound was heard save the hum of the
summer insects, and Lady Isabel sat in silence with her companion, her rebellious heart beating with a sense of his own happiness. But for the voice of
conscience, strong within her; but for the sense of right and wrong; but for
existing things; in short, but that she was a wife, she might have been content
so to sit by his side for ever, never to wish to move, or to break the silence.
Did he read her feelings? He told her, months afterward, that he did: but it
might have been only a vain boast.

'Do you remember the evening, Lady Isabel, just such a one as this, that
we all passed at Richmond?' he suddenly asked. 'Your father, Mrs. Vane,
you, I, and others?'

'Yes, I remember it. We had spent a pleasant day: the two Miss Challoners
were with us. You drove Mrs. Vane home, and I went with papa. You drove
recklessly, I recollect; and Mrs. Vane said when we got home that you should
never drive her again.'

'Which meant, not till the next time. Of all capricious, vain, exacting
women, Emma Vane was the worst; and Emma Mount Severn is no improvement upon it: she's a systematic flirt, and nothing better; I drove recklessly
on purpose to put her in a fright, and pay her off.'

'What had she done to you?'

'Put me in a rage. She had saddled herself upon me when I wanted—I
wished for—another to be my companion.'

'Blanche Challoner.'

'Blanche Challoner!' echoed Captain Levison, in a mocking tone: 'what
did I care for Blanche Challoner?'

Isabel remembered that he had been supposed in those days to care a great
deal for Miss Blanche Challoner—a most lovely girl of seventeen. 'Mrs. Vane
used to accuse you of caring too much for her,' she said aloud.

'She accused me of caring for some one else more than for Blanche Challoner,' he significantly returned, 'and for once her jealous surmises were not

misplaced. No, Lady Isabel, it was not Blanche Challoner I wished to drive home. Could you not have given a better guess than that at the time?' he added, turning to her.

There was no mistaking the tone of his voice or the glance of his eye. Lady Isabel felt a crimson flush rising, and she turned her face away.

'The past is gone, and cannot be recalled,' he continued, 'but we both played our cards like simpletons. If ever two beings were formed to love each other, you and I were. I sometimes thought you read my feelings—'

Surprise had kept her silent, but she interrupted him now, haughtily enough.

'I must speak, Lady Isabel: a few words, and then I am silent for ever. I would have declared myself had I dared, but my uncertain position, my debts, my inability to keep a wife, weighed me down; and instead of appealing to Sir Peter, as I hoped to have done, for the means to assume a position that would justify me in asking for Lord Mount Severn's daughter, I crushed my hopes within me, and suffered you to escape—'

'I will not hear this, Captain Levison,' she cried, rising from her seat in anger.

He touched her arm to place her on it again. 'One single moment yet, I pray you. I have for years wished that you should know why I lost you, a loss that tells upon me yet. I have bitterly worked out my own folly since. I knew not how passionately I loved you, until you became the wife of another. Isabel, I love you passionately still.'

'How dare you to presume so to address me?'

She spoke in a cold dignified tone of hauteur, as it was her bounden duty to speak. But nevertheless she was conscious of an undercurrent of feeling, whispering that under other auspices the avowal would have brought to her heart the most intense bliss.

'What I have said can do no harm now,' resumed Captain Levison: 'the time has gone by for it; for neither you nor I are likely to forget that you are a wife. We have each chosen our path in life, and must abide by it; the gulf between us is impassable; but the fault was mine. I ought to have avowed my affection, and not have suffered you to throw yourself away upon Mr. Carlyle.'

'Throw myself away!' she indignantly uttered, roused to the retort. 'Mr. Carlyle is my dear husband; esteemed, respected, beloved. I married him of my own free choice, and I have never repented it; I have grown more attached to him day by day. Look at his noble nature, his noble form: what are *you* by his side? You forget yourself, Francis Levison.'

He bit his lips. 'No, I do not.'

'You are talking to me as you have no right to talk,' she exclaimed in her agitation. 'Who, but you, would so insult me, or take advantage of my momentarily unprotected condition? Would you dare to do it, were Mr. Carlyle within reach? I wish you good evening, sir.'

She walked away as quickly as her tired frame would permit. Captain

Levison strode after her. He took forcible possession of her hand, and placed it within his arm.

'I pray you forgive and forget what has escaped me, Lady Isabel. Suffer me to be as before, the kind friend, the anxious brother, endeavouring to be of service to you in the absence of Mr. Carlyle.'

'It is what I have suffered you to be, looking upon you as—I may say—a relative,' she coldly rejoined, withdrawing her hand from his contact. 'Not else should I have permitted your incessant companionship: and this is how you have repaid it! My husband thanked you for your attention to me; could he have read what was in your false heart, he had offered you a different sort of thanks, I fancy.'

'I ask you for pardon, Lady Isabel; I have acknowledged my fault; and I can do no more. I will not so offend again: but there are moments when our dearest feelings break through the rules of life, and betray themselves, in spite of our sober judgment. Suffer me to support you down this steep hill,' he added, for they were then going over the sharp stones of the Grande Rue; 'you are not strong enough to proceed alone, after this evening's long walk.'

'You should have thought of that before,' she said, some sarcasm in her tone. 'No. I have declined.'

So he had to put his arm back, which he was holding out, and she walked on unsupported, with what strength she had, he continuing to walk by her side. Arrived at her own door, she wished him a cold good evening, and he turned away in the direction of his hotel.

Lady Isabel brushed past Peter, and flew upstairs, startling Wilson, who had taken possession of the drawing-room to air her smart cap at its windows in the absence of her lady.

'My desk, Wilson, immediately,' cried she, tearing off her gloves, her bonnet, and her shawl. 'Tell Peter to be in readiness to take a letter to the post; and he must walk fast, or he will not catch it before the English mail is closed.'

The symptoms of sinful happiness throbbing at her heart, while Francis Levison told her of his love, spoke plainly to Lady Isabel of the expediency of withdrawing entirely from his society and his dangerous sophistries; she would be away from the very place that contained him; put the sea between them. So she dashed off a letter to her husband; an urgent summons that he should come for her without delay, for, remain away longer, she *would not*. It is probable she would have started alone, not waiting for Mr. Carlyle, but for fear of not having sufficient funds for the journey, after the rent and other things were paid.

Mr. Carlyle, when he received the letter and marked its earnest tone, wondered much. In reply, he stated he would be with her on the following Saturday, and then her returning, or not, with him could be settled. Fully determined not to meet Captain Levison, Isabel, in the intervening days, only went out in a carriage. He called once, and was shown into the drawing-room: but Lady Isabel, who happened to be in her own chamber, sent out a message, which was delivered by Peter. 'My lady's compliments, but she must decline receiving visitors.'

Sunday morning—it had been impossible for him to get away before—brought Mr. Carlyle. He strongly combated her wish to return home until the six weeks should have expired, he nearly said he would not take her, and she grew earnest over it, almost to agitation.

'Isabel,' he said, 'let me know your motive, for it appears to me that you have one. The sojourn here is evidently doing you a vast deal of good, and what you urge about "being dull" sounds very like nonsense. Tell me what it is.'

A sudden impulse flashed over her that she *would* tell him the truth. Not tell him that she loved Francis Levison, or that he had spoken to her as he did: she valued her husband too greatly to draw him into any unpleasantness whose end could not be seen; but own to him that she had once felt a passing fancy for Francis Levison, and preferred not to be subjected to his companionship now. Oh, that she had done so! her kind, her noble, her judicious husband! Why did she not? The whole truth, as to her present feelings, it was not expedient that she should tell, but she might have confided to him quite sufficient. He would only have cherished her the more deeply, and sheltered her under his fostering care, safe from harm.

Why did she not? In the impulse of the moment she was about to do so, when Mr. Carlyle, who had been taking a letter from his pocket-book, put it into her hand. Upon what slight threads do the events of life turn! Her thoughts diverted, she remained silent while she opened the letter. It was from Miss Carlyle, who had handed it to her brother in the moment of his departure, to carry to Lady Isabel and save postage. Mr. Carlyle had nearly dropped it into the Folkestone post-office.

A letter as stiff as Miss Corny herself. The children were well, and the house was going on well, and she hoped Lady Isabel was better. It filled three sides of note-paper, but that was all the news it contained, and it wound up with the following sentence: 'I would continue my epistle, but Barbara Hare, who is to spend the day with us, has just arrived.'

Barbara Hare spending the day at East Lynne! That item was quite enough for Lady Isabel; and her heart and her confidence closed to her husband. 'She must go home to her children,' she urged; she could not remain longer away from them; and she urged it at length with tears.

'Nay, Isabel,' said Mr. Carlyle, 'if you are so much in earnest as this, you shall certainly go back with me.'

Then she was like a child let loose from school. She laughed; she danced in her excess of content; she showered kisses on her husband, thanking him in her gleeful gratitude. Mr. Carlyle set it down to her love for him; he arrived at the conclusion that, in reiterating that she could not bear to be away from him, she spoke the fond truth.

'Isabel,' he said, smiling tenderly upon her, 'do you remember, in the first days of our marriage, you told me you did not love me, but that the love would come. I think this is it.'

Her face flushed nearly to tears at the word; a bright, glowing, all too conscious flush. Mr. Carlyle mistook its source, and caught her to his heart.

One day more, and then they—she and that man—should be separated by the broad sea. The thought caused her to lift up her heart in thankfulness. She knew that to leave him would be as though she left the sun behind her, that the other side might for a time be somewhat dreary; nevertheless, she fervently thanked Heaven. Oh, reader! never doubt the principles of poor Lady Isabel, her rectitude of mind, her wish and endeavour to do right, her abhorrence of wrong; her spirit was earnest and true, her intentions were pure.

Captain Levison paid a visit to Mr. Carlyle, and inquired if he had had time to see Sir Peter. Not yet; Mr. Carlyle had been too busy to think of it; but he should soon have more leisure on his hands, and would not fail him. Such was the reply; the reply of an honourable man to a man of dishonour: but, of the dishonour, Mr. Carlyle suspected nothing. It is a pity but what bad men could be turned inside out sometimes: to put others on their guard.

It was high water in the afternoon, and the Folkestone boat was announced to start at one. The Carlyles and their servants went on board in good time, and Captain Levison greeted them and said farewell as they stepped on the steamer. Lady Isabel took her seat on the deck, her husband standing by her; the cords were unloosened, and the boat moved slowly down the harbour. On the shore stood Francis Levison, watching its progress, watching *her*. He was a bold, unscrupulous man; and there was little doubt that the more refined feelings, both of the past and the present, he had thought fit to avow for Lady Isabel, were all put on, meant to serve a purpose. However, he had received his checkmate.

As he receded from Isabel's view, a sensation of relief thrilled through her whole frame, causing it to shudder, and involuntarily she clasped the hand of Mr. Carlyle.

'You are not cold, Isabel?' he said, bending over her.

'Oh no: I am very comfortable; very happy.'

'But you were surely shivering?'

'At the thought of what I could have done with myself, had you come away, and left me there still, all alone. Archibald,' she continued in an impassioned whisper, 'never let me go away from you again; keep me by you always.'

He smiled as he looked down into her pleading eyes, and a whole world of tender response and love might be detected in his earnest tone. 'Always

and always, Isabel. It is greater pain to me than to you, to have you away
from me.'

How could she ever doubt him?

✻ IV ✻

The Fractured Ankle

Lady Isabel had returned home to bodily health, to the delight of meeting her
children, to the glad sensation of security. But, as the days went on, a miserable feeling of apathy stole over her: a feeling as if all whom she had loved in
the world had died, leaving her living and alone. It was a painful depression,
the vacuum in her heart which was making itself felt in its keen intensity. She
strove to drive that bad man away from her thoughts; but even while she so
strove, he was again in them. Too frequently she caught herself thinking that
if she could but see him once again, for ever so short a period, one hour, one
day, she could compose her spirit afterwards to rest. She did not encourage
these reflections: from what you know of her, you may be sure of that: but
they thrust themselves continually forward. The form of Francis Levison was
ever present to her; not a minute of the day but it gave the colouring to her
thoughts, and at night it made the subject of her dreams. Oh, those dreams!
they were painful to awake from; painful from the contrast they presented to
reality; and equally painful to her conscience, in its strife after what was
right. She would have given much not to have these dreams; never to see or
think of him in her sleep. But, how prevent it? There was no prevention; for
when the mind (or the imagination, if you like the word better) is thoroughly
imbued with a subject of this nature, especially if unhappiness mingles with
it, then the dreams follow necessarily the bent of the waking thoughts. Poor
Lady Isabel would awake to self-reproach, restless and feverish; wishing that
this terrible disease could be driven away, root and branch: but Time, the
great healer, must, she knew, pass over her, before that could be.

Mr. Carlyle mounted his horse one morning and rode over to Levison
Park. He asked for Sir Peter, but was shown into the presence of Lady Levison: a young and pretty woman, dressed showily. She inquired his business.

'My business, madam, is with Sir Peter.'

'But Sir Peter is not well enough to attend to business. It upsets him; wor-
ries him.'

'Nevertheless, I am here by his own appointment. Twelve o'clock he mentioned; and the hour has barely struck.'

Lady Levison bit her lip and bowed coldly; and at that moment a servant appeared to conduct Mr. Carlyle to Sir Peter. The matter which had taken Mr. Carlyle thither was entered upon immediately—Francis Levison, his debts, and his gracelessness. Sir Peter, an old gentleman in a velvet skull-cap, particularly enlarged upon the latter.

'I would pay his debts to-day and set him upon his legs again, but that I know I should have to do the same thing over, and over again to the end of the chapter—as I have done before,' cried Sir Peter. 'His grandfather was my only brother, his father my dutiful and beloved nephew; but he is just as bad as they were estimable. He is a worthless fellow, and nothing else, Mr. Carlyle.'

'His tale drew forth my compassion, and I promised I would see you and speak for him,' returned Mr. Carlyle. 'Of Captain Levison's personal virtues or vices I know nothing.'

'And the less you know the better,' growled Sir Peter. 'I suppose he wants me to clear him and start him afresh?'

'Something of the sort, I conclude.'

'But how is it to be done? I am at home, and he is over there. His affairs are in a state of confusion, and nobody can come to the bottom of them without an explanation from him. Some liabilities, for which I have furnished the money, the creditors swear have not yet been liquidated. He must come over if he wants anything done.'

'Where is he to come to? He must be in England *sub rosâ*.'

'He can't be here,' hastily rejoined Sir Peter. 'Lady Levison would not have him for a day.'

'He might be at East Lynne,' good-naturedly observed Mr. Carlyle. 'Nobody would think of looking for him there. I think it is a pity that you should not meet, if you do feel inclined to help him.'

'You are a great deal more considerate to him than he deserves, Mr. Carlyle. May I ask if you intend to act for him in a professional capacity?'

'I do not.'

A few more words, and it was decided that Captain Levison should be immediately sent for. As Mr. Carlyle left Sir Peter's presence, he encountered Lady Levison.

'I can scarcely be ignorant that your conference with my husband has reference to his grand-nephew,' she observed.

'It has,' replied Mr. Carlyle.

'I have a very bad opinion of him, Mr. Carlyle: at the same time I do not wish you to carry away a wrong impression of me. Francis Levison is my husband's nephew, his presumptive heir; it may therefore appear strange that I set my face so determinately against him. Two or three years ago, previous to my marriage with Sir Peter, in fact before I knew Sir Peter, I was brought into contact with Francis Levison. He was acquainted with some friends of mine, and at their house I met him. He behaved shamefully ill; he repaid their hospitality with gross ingratitude: other details and facts, regarding his conduct, also became known to me. Altogether, I believe him to be a base and despicable man, both by nature and by inclination, and that he will remain such to the end of time.'

'I know very little indeed of him,' observed Mr. Carlyle. 'May I inquire the nature of his ill conduct in the instance you mention?'

'He ruined them. He ruined them, Mr. Carlyle. They were simple, unsuspicious country people, understanding neither fraud nor vice, nor the ways of an evil world. Francis Levison got them to put their names to bills, "as a simple matter of form, to accommodate him for a month or so," he stated, and so they believed. They were not wealthy: they lived upon their own small estate in comfort, but with no superfluous money to spare, and when the time came for them to pay—as come it did—it brought ruin, and they had to leave their home. He deliberately did it: I am certain that Francis Levison deliberately did it, knowing what would be the end. And I could tell you of other things. Sir Peter may have informed you that I object to receive him here. I do. My objection is to the man, to his character; not owing, as I hear it has been said, to any jealous, paltry feeling touching his being the heir. I must lose my own self-respect before I admit Francis Levison to my house, an inmate. Sir Peter may assist him and welcome, may pay his debts and get him out of his scrapes as often as he pleases; but I will not have him here.'

'Sir Peter said you declined to receive him. But it is necessary he should come to England—if his affairs are to be set straight—and also that he should see Sir Peter.'

'Come to England?' interrupted Lady Levison. 'How can he come to England under present circumstances? Unless, indeed, he comes *en cachette*.'

'*En cachette*, of course,' replied Mr. Carlyle. 'There is no other way. I have offered to let him stay at East Lynne: he is, you may be aware, a connection of Lady Isabel's.'

'Take care that he does not repay *your* hospitality with ingratitude,' warmly returned Lady Levison. 'It would only be in accordance with his practice.'

Mr. Carlyle laughed. 'I do not well see what harm he could do me, allowing that he had the inclination. He would not scare my clients from me; nor beat my children; and I can take care of my pocket. A few days, no doubt, will be the extent of his sojourn.'

Lady Levison smiled too, and shook hands with Mr. Carlyle. 'In your house perhaps there may be no field for his vagaries; but rely upon it, where there is one, he is sure to be at some mischief or other.'

This visit of Mr. Carlyle's to Levison Park took place on a Friday morning, and on his return to his office he despatched an account of it to Captain Levison at Boulogne, telling him to come over. But Mr. Carlyle, like many an-other man whose brain has its share of work, was sometimes forgetful of trifles, and it entirely slipped his memory to mention the expected arrival at home. The following evening, Saturday, he and Lady Isabel were dining in the neighbourhood, when the conversation at table turned upon the Ducies and their embarrassments. The association of ideas led Mr. Carlyle's thoughts to Boulogne, to Captain Levison and *his* embarrassments, and it imme-diately occurred to him that he had not told his wife of the anticipated visit. He kept it in his mind, and spoke as soon as they were in the chariot return-ing home.

'Isabel,' he began, 'I suppose we have always rooms ready for visitors. Be-cause I am expecting one.'

'Oh yes. Or, if not, they are soon made ready.'

'Ay, but to-morrow is Sunday, and I have no doubt that it is the day he will take advantage of to come. I am sorry I forgot to mention it yesterday.'

'Who is coming?'

'Captain Levison.'

'Who?' repeated Lady Isabel in a sharp tone of consternation.

'Captain Levison. Sir Peter consents to see him, with a view to the settle-ment of his liabilities, but Lady Levison declines to receive him at the park. So I offered to give him house room at East Lynne for a few days.'

There is an old saying—the heart leaping into the mouth; and Lady Isa-bel's heart leaped into hers. She grew dizzy at the words; her senses seemed for the moment to desert her: her first sensation was as if the dull earth had opened and shown her a way into paradise; her second was a lively con-sciousness that Francis Levison ought not to be suffered to come again into companionship with her. Mr. Carlyle continued to converse of the man's em-barrassments, of his own interview with Sir Peter, of Lady Levison; but Isa-bel was as one who heard not. She was debating the question, how could she prevent his coming?

'Archibald,' she presently said, 'I do not wish Francis Levison to stay at East Lynne.'

'It will only be for a few days; perhaps but a day or two. Sir Peter is in the humour to discharge the claims; and, the moment his resolve is known, the ex-captain can walk on her Majesty's dominions, an unmolested man; free to go where he will.'

'That may be,' interrupted Lady Isabel, in an accent of impatience, 'but why should he come to our house?'

'I proposed it myself. I had no idea you would dislike his coming. Why should you?'

'I don't like Francis Levison,' she murmured. 'That is, I don't care to have him at East Lynne.'

'My dear, I fear there is no help for it now: he is most likely on his road, and will arrive to-morrow: I cannot turn him out again, after my own voluntary invitation. Had I known it would be disagreeable to you, I should not have proposed it.'

'To-morrow!' she exclaimed, all of the words that caught her ear; 'is he coming to-morrow?'

'Being Sunday, a free day, he will be sure to take advantage of it. What has he done, that you should object to his coming? You did not say in Boulogne that you disliked him.'

'He has done nothing,' was her faltering answer, feeling that her grounds of opposition must melt under her, one by one.

'Lady Levison appears to possess a very ill opinion of him,' resumed Mr. Carlyle. 'She says she knew him in years gone by. She mentioned one or two things which, if true, were bad enough: but possibly she may be prejudiced.'

'She is prejudiced,' said Isabel. 'At least, so Francis Levison told me in Boulogne. There appeared to be no love lost between them.'

'At any rate, his ill doings or well doings cannot affect us for the short period he is likely to remain. You have taken a prejudice against him also, I suppose, Isabel?'

She suffered Mr. Carlyle to remain in the belief, and sat with clasped hands and a despairing spirit, feeling that Fate was against her. How could she accomplish her task of forgetting this man, if he was thus to be thrown into her home and her companionship? Suddenly she turned to her husband, and laid her cheek upon his shoulder.

He thought she was tired. He passed his arm round her waist, drew her face to a more comfortable position, and bent his own lovingly upon it. It came into her mind as she lay there, to tell him a portion of the truth, like it had done once before. It was a strong arm of shelter round her; a powerful pillar of protection, he upon whom she leaned; why did she not confide herself to him as trustingly as a little child? Simply because her courage failed. Once, twice, the opening words were upon her lips, but come forth they did not; and then the carriage stopped at East Lynne, and the opportunity was over. Oh, how many a time, in her after years, did Lady Isabel recall that midnight drive with her husband, and wish, in her vain repentance, that she had opened his eyes to that dangerous man!

The following morning proved a wet one, but it cleared up in the middle of the day. In the afternoon, however, whilst they were at church, the rain came on again.

'Cornelia,' whispered Mr. Carlyle, getting near to his sister when service was over, 'it is raining heavily: you had better return with us in the pony carriage. John can walk.'

Not she. Had it poured cats and dogs Miss Carlyle would not have gone to or from church otherwise than on her two legs, and off she started with her large umbrella. Mr. Carlyle and Isabel soon passed her, striding along the footpath, and some of the servants behind her. *Not* in attendance upon Miss Carlyle: she would have scorned such attendance worse than she scorned the pony carriage. No matter what might be the weather, this adventurous lady would be seen pushing through it; through the summer's heat, and the winter's snow; through the soft shower and the impetuous storm; the great umbrella (it might have covered any moderate sized haystack) her nearly constant companion, for Miss Corny was one of those prudent spirits who liked to be prepared for contingencies and be on the safe side; those who act up to the maxim "When it's fine take an umbrella; when it rains, do as you like.' In fine weather she chose the pathway through the fields, but not in wet, the damp grass not agreeing with her petticoats.

Mr. Carlyle had driven in at the gates and was winding up the avenue, when sounds of distress were heard, and they saw little Isabel flying towards them from the slopes, crying and sobbing in the greatest agitation. Mr. Carlyle jumped out and met the child.

'Oh, papa, papa! oh come, pray come! I think she is dead.'

He took the child in his arms to soothe her. 'Hush, my little darling, you will alarm mamma. Don't tremble so. Tell me what it is.'

Isabel told her tale. She had been a naughty child, she freely confessed, and had run out in the rain for fun because Joyce told her not, she had run amidst the wet grass of the park, down the slopes, Joyce after her. And Joyce had slipped and was lying at the foot of the slopes with a white face, never moving.

'Take care of her, Isabel,' said Mr. Carlyle, placing the agitated and repentant child by his wife's side. 'She says Joyce has fallen by the slopes. No, do not come: I will go first and see what is amiss.'

Joyce was lying just as she fell, at the foot of the slopes. But her eyes were open now, and if she had fainted—as might be inferred from the little girl's words—she had recovered consciousness.

'Oh, master, don't try to move me! I fear my leg is broken.'

He did, however, essay gently to raise her, but she screamed with the pain, and he found he must wait for assistance. 'I trust you are not much hurt,' he kindly said. 'How did it happen?'

'Miss Isabel ran out, sir, in all the rain and wet, and I went after her to bring her back again. But the slopes are slippery, and down I went, and just at first I remembered nothing more.'

Mr. Carlyle despatched John and the pony carriage back for Mr. Wainwright, and with the aid of the servants, who were soon up from church, Joyce was carried in, and laid on a bed, dressed as she was. Mr. Carlyle and Lady Isabel remained with her. Miss Carlyle also was there, fidgeting and banging about, getting things ready that she fancied might be wanted, and pressing cordials upon Joyce which the latter could not take. Miss Carlyle's frame of mind, between sympathy and anger, was rather an explosive one: altogether, she did more harm than good. Little Isabel stole in and drew her mother away from the bed.

'Mamma,' she whispered, 'there is a strange gentleman downstairs. He came in a chaise. He has got a portmanteau, and he is asking for you and papa.'

Lady Isabel turned sick with apprehension: was he really come?

'Who is it, Isabel?' she said, by way of making some answer: she guessed but too well.

'I don't know. I don't like him, mamma. He laid hold of me and held me tight, and there was an ugly look in his eyes.'

'Go round the bed and tell your papa that a stranger is downstairs,' said Lady Isabel.

'Mamma,' shivered the child, before she stirred to obey, 'will Joyce die?'

'No, dear; I hope not.'

'Because you know it will be my fault. Oh, mamma, I am so sorry! what can I do?'

'Hush! If you sob, it will make Joyce worse. Go and whisper to papa about the gentleman.'

'But will Joyce ever forgive me?'

'She has forgiven you already, I am sure, Isabel, but you must be all the more obedient to her for the future. Go to papa, my dear, as I tell you.'

The stranger was of course Captain Levison. Mr. Carlyle went down to receive and entertain him. Lady Isabel did not, the accident to her maid being put forth as an excuse.

Mr. Wainwright pronounced the injury to be a simple fracture of the ankle-bone. It might have been much worse, he observed, but Joyce would be confined to her bed for three or four weeks.

'Joyce,' whispered Isabel, 'I'll come and read my Bible-stories to you always; always and always; I know mamma will let me, and then you won't be dull. And there's that beautiful new book of fairy tales with the pictures; you'll like to hear them; there's about a princess who was locked up in a castle with nothing to eat.'

Joyce faintly smiled, and took the child's eager little hand in hers.

Later in the evening, Isabel and William were in the room with Mr. Carlyle. 'These are fine children,' observed Francis Levison. 'Beautiful faces!'

'They resemble their mother much, I think,' was the reply of Mr. Carlyle. 'She was a very lovely child.'

'Did you know Lady Isabel as a child?' inquired Francis Levison, some surprise in his tone.

'I frequently saw her. She used to stay here with Lady Mount Severn.'

'Ah, by the way, this place was Mount Severn's property then. What a reckless man he was! Young lady, I must take possession of you,' continued

Captain Levison, extending his hand and pulling Isabel towards him. 'You ran away from me when I first came, and would not tell me what your name was.'

'I ran away to tell mamma that you were come. She was with Joyce.'

'Joyce! Who is Joyce!'

'Lady Isabel's maid,' interposed Mr. Carlyle. 'The one to whom, as I told you, the accident has just happened. A particularly valued servant in our family, is Joyce.'

'It is a curious name,' remarked Captain Levison. 'Joyce—Joyce! I never heard such a name. Is it a Christian or surname?'

'She was baptized Joyce. It is not so very uncommon. Her name is Joyce Hallijohn. She has been with us several years.'

At this moment, Isabel, having been trying in vain to escape from Captain Levison, burst into tears. Mr. Carlyle inquired what was amiss.

'I don't like him to hold me,' was the response of Miss Isabel, ignoring ceremony.

Captain Levison laughed, and held her tighter. But Mr. Carlyle rose, and with quiet authority drew away the child, and placed her on his own knee. She hid her face upon him, and put up her little hand round his neck.

'Papa, I don't like him,' she whispered softly; 'I am afraid of him. Don't let him take me again.'

Mr. Carlyle's only answer was to press her to him. 'You are not accustomed to children, Captain Levison,' he observed. 'They are curious little plants to deal with, capricious and sensitive.'

'They must be a great worry,' was the rejoinder. 'This accident to your servant must be a serious one. It will confine her to her bed for some time, I presume?'

'For weeks, the doctor says. And no possibility of her getting up from it.'

Captain Levison rose, and caught hold of William in apparent glee, and swung him round. The boy laughed, unlike his sister, and seemed to enjoy the fun.

❧ V ❧

Mrs. Hare's Dream

The next day rose bright, warm, and cloudless, and the morning sun streamed into the bedroom of Mrs. Hare. That lady lay in bed, a flush on her delicate cheeks, and her soft eyes rather glistening, as if with a touch of fever. The justice, in a cotton nightcap with a little perky tassel, sat on a chair tying his drawers at the knee, preparatory to inducing his legs into his pantaloons—if any single damsel in years, who may read this, will forgive this slight revelation as to the mysteries of a gentleman's toilette. The pantaloons assumed, and the braces fastened, the justice threw his nightcap on to the bed and went up to the washhand-stand, where he splashed away for a few minutes at his face and hands: he never shaved till after breakfast. Mr. and Mrs. Hare were of the old-fashioned class who knew nothing about dressing-rooms; their bedroom was very large, and they had never used a dressing-room in their lives, or found the want of one. The justice rubbed his face to a shiny brilliancy, settled on his morning wig and his dressing-gown, and then turned to the bed.

'What will you have for breakfast?'

'Thank you, Richard, I do not think that I can eat anything. I shall be glad of my tea; I am very thirsty.'

'All nonsense,' responded the justice, alluding to the intimation of not eating. 'Have a poached egg.'

Mrs. Hare smiled at him and gently shook her head. 'You are very kind, Richard, but I could not eat it this morning. Barbara may send up the smallest bit of dry toast.'

'My belief is, that you just *give way* to this notion of feeling ill, Anne,' cried the justice. 'It's half fancy, I know. If you'd get up and shake it off, and come down, you would relish your breakfast and be set up for the day. Whereas you lie here, taking nothing but some trashy tea, and get up afterwards weak, shaky, and fit for nothing.'

'It is ever so many weeks, Richard, since I lay in bed to breakfast,' remonstrated poor Mrs. Hare. 'I really don't think I have once, since—since the spring.'

'And have been all the better for it.'

'But indeed I am not equal to getting up this morning. Would you please to throw this window open before you go down. I should like to feel the air.'

'You will get the air too near from this window,' replied Mr. Justice Hare, opening the further one. Had his wife requested that further one to be opened, he would have opened the other; his own will and opinions were ever paramount. Then he descended.

A minute or two, and up ran Barbara, looking bright and fair as the morning, her pink muslin dress with its ribbons and its open white lace sleeves as pretty as she was. She leaned over to kiss her mother.

Barbara had grown more gentle and tender of late years, the bitterness of her pain had passed away, leaving all that had been good in her love to mellow and fertilize her nature. Her character had been greatly improved by sorrow.

'Mamma, are you ill? And you have been so well lately; you went to bed so well last night! Papa says—'

'Barbara dear,' interrupted Mrs. Hare, glancing round the room with dread, and speaking in a deep whisper, 'I have had one of those dreadful dreams again.'

'Oh, mamma, how *can* you!' exclaimed Barbara, starting up in vexation. 'How can you suffer a foolish dream so to overcome you as to make you ill? You have good sense in other matters; but, in this, you seem to put all sense away from you.'

'Child, will you tell me how I am to help it?' returned Mrs. Hare, taking Barbara's hand and drawing her to her again. 'I do not give myself the dreams; I cannot prevent their making me sick, prostrate, feverish. I was as well yesterday as I could be; I went to bed quite comfortable, in excellent spirits; I do not know that I had even once thought of poor Richard during the day. And yet the dream came. There were no circumstances to lead to or induce it, either in my thoughts or in outward facts; but, come it did. How can I help these things, I ask?'

'And it is so long since you had one of these disagreeable dreams! Why, how long is it, mamma?'

'So long, Barbara, that the dread of them had nearly left me. I scarcely think I have had one since that stolen visit of Richard's, years ago.'

'Was it a very bad dream, mamma?'

'Oh, child, yes. I dreamt that the real murderer came to West Lynne: that he was with us here, and we—'

At this moment the bedroom door was flung open, and the face of the justice, especially stern and cross then, was pushed in. So startled was Mrs. Hare, that she shook till she shook the pillow, and Barbara sprang away from the bed. Surely he had not distinguished their topic of conversation!

'Are you coming to make breakfast to-day, or not, Barbara? Do you expect me to make it?'

'She is coming this instant, Richard,' said Mrs. Hare, her voice more faint than usual. And the justice turned and stamped down again.

'Barbara, could your papa have heard me mention Richard?'

'No, no, mamma, impossible; the door was shut. I will bring up your breakfast myself, and then you can tell me about the dream.'

Barbara flew after Mr. Hare, poured out his coffee, saw him settle at his breakfast, with a plateful of grouse-pie before him, and then returned upstairs with her mamma's tea and dry toast.

'Go on with the dream, mamma,' she said.

'But your own breakfast will be cold, child.'

'Oh, I don't mind that. Did you dream of Richard?'

'Not very much of Richard; except that the old and continuous trouble, of his being away and unable to return, seemed to pervade it all through. You remember, Barbara, Richard asserted to us, in that short, hidden night visit, that he did not commit the murder; that it was another who did?'

'Yes, I remember it,' replied Barbara.

'Barbara, I am convinced he spoke the truth: I trust him implicitly.'

'I feel sure of it also, mamma.'

'I asked him, you may remember, whether it was Otway Bethel who committed it; for I have always doubted Bethel in an indefinite, vague manner: Richard replied it was not Bethel, but a stranger. Well, Barbara, in my dream I thought that stranger came to West Lynne, that he came to this house, here, and we were talking to him of it, conversing as we might with any other visitor. Mind you, we seemed to *know* that he was the one who actually did it; but he denied it; he wanted to put it upon Richard: and I saw him—yes, I did, Barbara—whisper to Otway Bethel. But oh, I cannot tell you the sickening horror that was upon me throughout, and seemed to be upon you also, lest he should make good his own apparent innocence, and crush Richard, his victim. I think the dread and horror awoke me.'

'What was this stranger like?' asked Barbara, in a low tone.

'Well, I cannot quite tell you: the recollection of his appearance seemed to pass away from me with the dream. He was dressed as a gentleman, and we conversed with him as an equal.'

Barbara's mind was full of Captain Thorn; but his name had not been mentioned to Mrs. Hare, neither would she mention it now. She fell into deep thought, and Mrs. Hare had to speak twice before she could be aroused.

'Barbara, I say, don't you think that this dream, coming uncalled-for, uninduced, must forbode some ill? Rely upon it, something connected with that wretched murder is going to be stirred up again.'

'You know, mamma, I do not believe in dreams,' was Barbara's answer. 'I think when people say "this dream is a sign of such and such a thing," it is the greatest absurdity in the world. I wish you could remember what the man was like in your dream.'

'I wish I could,' answered Mrs. Hare, breaking off a particle of her dry toast. 'All I remember is, that he appeared to be a gentleman.'

'Was he tall? Had he black hair?'

Mrs. Hare shook her head. 'I tell you, my dear, the remembrance has passed from me; so whether his hair was black or light, I cannot say. I think he was tall: but he was sitting down, and Otway Bethel stood behind his chair. I seemed to feel that Richard was outside the door, in hiding, trembling lest the man should go out and see him there; and I trembled too. Oh, Barbara, it was a distressing dream!'

'I wish you could avoid having them, mamma, for they seem to upset you very much.'

'Why did you ask whether the man was tall, and had black hair?'

Barbara returned an evasive answer. It would not do to tell Mrs. Hare that her suspicions pointed to one particular quarter: it would have agitated her too greatly.

'So vivid was the dream, so matter-of-fact, and like reality, that even when I awoke I could not for some minutes believe but the murderer was actually at West Lynne,' resumed Mrs. Hare. 'The impression that he is here, or is coming here, is upon me yet; a sort of under-current of impression, you understand, Barbara: of course my own good sense tells me that there is no real foundation for supposing such to be the case. Oh, Barbara, Barbara!' she added, in a tone of wailing, as she let her head droop forward, in its pain, till it rested on her daughter's arm, 'when will this unhappy state of things end? One year glides away and another comes; year after year, year after year they drag on, and Richard remains a banned exile!'

Barbara spoke not: what sympathy or comfort could she offer in words? the case admitted of none: but she pressed her lips upon her mother's pale forehead.

'Child, I am getting sick, sick to hear of Richard. My heart aches for the sight of him,' went on the poor lady. 'Seven years next spring, it will be, since he stole here to see us. Seven years, and not a look at his beloved face, not a word of news from him to say that he is yet in life! Was any mother ever tried as I am tried?'

'Dear mamma, don't! You will make yourself ill.'

'I am ill already, Barbara.'

'Yes; but this grief and emotion will render you worse. People say that the seventh year always brings a change: it may bring one as regards Richard. It may bring him clearance, mamma, for all we know. Do not despair.'

'Child! I do not despair. Despondency I cannot help at times feeling, but it has not reached despair. I believe, I truly believe that God will some time bring the right to light; how can I despair, then, while I trust in Him?'

There was a pause, which Barbara broke. 'Shall I bring you up some more tea, mamma?'

'No, my dear. *Send* me some up, for I am thirsty still; but you must remain below and get your own breakfast. What may your papa not be suspecting, if you do not? Guard your very countenance. I always dread lest, if we appear sad, he should suppose we are thinking of Richard.'

'And what if he did, mamma? Surely thoughts are free.'

'Hush, Barbara! hush!' repeated Mrs. Hare, in a whispered tone of warning. 'You know the oath he has taken to bring Richard to justice; you know how determined he is; and you know that he fully believes Richard to be guilty. If he found we dwelt upon his innocence, he might be capable of scouring the whole land from one end of it to the other in search of him, to deliver him up for trial. Your papa is so very—'

'Pig-headed,' put in Barbara, saucily, though it was not precisely a young lady's word, and her cherry lips pouted after uttering it.

'Barbara!' remonstrated Mrs. Hare. 'I was going to say so very just.'

'Then I say he would be cruel and unnatural, rather than just, if he were to search the country that he might deliver up his own son to death,' returned Barbara, with a bold tongue, but wet eyelashes. Very carefully did she wipe them dry, before entering the breakfast-room.

The dinner-hour of the Hares, when they were alone, was four o'clock, and it arrived that day as usual, and they sat down to table. Mrs. Hare was better then; the sunshine and the business of stirring life had in some measure effaced the visions of the night, and restored her to her wonted frame of mind. The justice mentioned the accident to Joyce: they had not heard of it; but they had not been out during the day, and had received no visitors. Mrs. Hare was full of concern: Joyce was a universal favourite.

The cloth was removed, the justice sat but a little while over his port wine, for he was engaged to smoke an after-dinner pipe with a brother magistrate, Mr. Justice Herbert.

'Shall you be home to tea, papa?' inquired Barbara.

'Is it any business of yours, young lady?'

'Oh, not in the least,' answered Miss Barbara. 'Only, if you had been coming home to tea, I suppose we must have waited for you.'

'I thought you said, Richard, that you were going to stay the evening with Mr. Herbert,' observed Mrs. Hare.

'So I am,' responded the justice. 'But Barbara has a great liking for the sound of her own tongue.'

The justice departed, striding pompously down the gravel-walk. Barbara waltzed round the large room to a gleeful song, as if she felt his absence a relief. Perhaps she did. 'You can have tea now, mamma, at any time you please, if you are thirsty, without waiting till seven,' said she.

'Yes, dear. Barbara.'

'What, mamma?'

'I am sorry to hear of this calamity which has fallen upon Joyce. I should like to walk to East Lynne this evening and inquire after her; and see her, if I may. It would be but neighbourly.'

Barbara's heart beat quicker. Hers was indeed a true and lasting love, one that defied time and change. The having to bury it wholly within her, had perhaps but added to its force and depth. Who could suspect, under Barbara's sometimes cold, sometimes playful exterior, that *one* was hidden in her heart, filling up its every crevice? one who had no right there. The intimation that she might soon possibly be in his presence, sent every pulse throbbing.

'Walk, did you say, mamma? Should you do right to walk?'

'I feel quite equal to it. Since I have accustomed myself to take more exercise I feel better for it, and we have not been out to-day. Poor Joyce! What time shall we go, Barbara?'

'If we were to get up there by—by seven, I should think their dinner will be over then.'

'Yes,' answered Mrs. Hare with alacrity, who was always pleased when somebody else decided for her. 'But I should like some tea before we start, Barbara.'

Barbara took care that her mamma should have some tea, and then they proceeded towards East Lynne. It was a lovely evening. The air was warm, and the humming gnats sported in it, as if anxious to make the most of the waning summer. Mrs. Hare enjoyed it at first, but ere she reached East Lynne she became aware that the walk was too much for her. She did not usually venture upon so long a one; and probably the fever and agitation of the morning had somewhat impaired her day's strength. She laid her hand upon the iron gate as they were turning into the park, and stood still.

'I did wrong to come, Barbara.'

'Lean on me, mamma. When you reach those benches, you can rest before proceeding to the house. It is very warm, and that may have fatigued you.'

They gained the benches, which were placed under some of the dark trees, in view of the gates and the road, but not of the house, and Mrs. Hare sat down. Another minute, and they were surrounded. Mr. Carlyle, his wife and sister, who were taking an after-dinner stroll amidst the flowers with their guest, Francis Levison, discerned them and came up. The children, except the youngest, were of the party. Lady Isabel warmly welcomed Mrs. Hare: she had become quite attached to the delicate and suffering woman.

'I am a pretty one, am I not, Archibald, to come inquiring after an invalid, when I am so much of an invalid myself that I have to stop half way!' exclaimed Mrs. Hare, as Mr. Carlyle took her hand. 'I am greatly concerned to hear of poor Joyce.'

'You must stay the evening now you are here,' cried Lady Isabel. 'It will afford you a rest, and tea will refresh you.'

'Oh, thank you, but we have taken tea,' said Mrs. Hare.

'That is no reason why you should not take some more,' she laughed. 'Indeed, you seem too fatigued to be anything but a prisoner with us for this next hour or two.'

'I fear I am,' answered Mrs. Hare.

'Who are they?' Captain Levison was muttering to himself, as he contemplated the guests from a distance. 'It's a deuced lovely girl, whoever she may be. I think I'll approach; they don't look formidable.'

He did approach, and the introduction was made. 'Captain Levison, Mrs. Hare and Miss Hare.' A few formal words, and Captain Levison disappeared again, challenging little William Carlyle to a foot-race.

'How very poorly your mamma looks!' Mr. Carlyle exclaimed to Barbara, when they were beyond the hearing of Mrs. Hare, who was busy talking with Lady Isabel and Miss Carlyle. 'She has appeared so much stronger lately; altogether better.'

'The walk here has fatigued her; I feared it would be too long; so that she looks unusually pale,' replied Barbara. 'But what do you think it is that has upset her again, Mr. Carlyle?'

He turned his inquiring eyes on Barbara.

'Papa came downstairs this morning saying mamma was ill; that she had one of her old attacks of fever and restlessness. As papa spoke, I thought to myself, could mamma have been dreaming some foolish dream again— for you remember how ill she used to be after them. I ran upstairs, and the first thing mamma said to me was, that she had had one of those dreadful dreams.'

'I fancied she must have outlived her fear of them; that her own plain sense had come to her aid long ago, showing her how futile dreams are, meaning nothing, even if hers do occasionally touch upon that—that unhappy mystery.'

'You may just as well reason with a post as reason with mamma, when she is suffering from the influence of one of those dreams,' returned Barbara. 'I tried it this morning; I asked her to call up—as you observe—good sense to her aid. All her answer was, "How could she help her feelings? She did not induce the dream by thinking of Richard, or in any other way, and yet it came and shattered her." Of course, so far, mamma is right, for she cannot help the dreams coming.'

Mr. Carlyle made no immediate reply. He picked up a ball belonging to one of the children, which lay in his path, and began tossing it gently in his hand. 'It is a singular thing,' he observed, presently, 'that we do not hear from Richard.'

'Oh, very; very. And I know mamma distresses herself over it. A few words, which she let fall this morning, betrayed it plainly. I am no believer in dreams,' continued Barbara, 'but I cannot deny that these, which take such hold upon mamma, bear upon the case in a curious manner. The one she had last night especially.'

'What was it?' asked Mr. Carlyle.

'She dreamt that the real murderer was at West Lynne. She thought he was at our house—as a visitor, she said, or like one making a morning call—and that she and I were conversing with him about the murder. He wanted to deny it; to put it upon Richard; and he turned and whispered to Otway Bethel, who stood behind his chair. That is another strange thing,' added Barbara, lifting her blue eyes in their deep earnestness to the face of Mr. Carlyle.

'What is strange? You speak in enigmas, Barbara.'

'I mean, that Otway Bethel should invariably appear in her dreams. Until that stolen visit of Richard's we had no idea Bethel was near the spot at the time, and yet he had always made a prominent feature in these dreams. Richard assured mamma that Bethel had nothing to do with the murder, could have had nothing to do with it; but I do not think he shook mamma's belief that he *had*; that he was in some way connected with the mystery, though perhaps not the actual perpetrator. Well, Archibald, mamma has not dreamt of it, as she believes, since that visit of Richard's until last night; when again there was Bethel prominent in the dream. It certainly is singular.'

Barbara, in the heat of her subject, in forgetfulness of the past, had called him by the old familiar name 'Archibald:' it was only when she was on the stilts of propriety, of coldness, that she said 'Mr. Carlyle.'

'And who was the murderer—in your mamma's dream?' continued Mr. Carlyle, speaking as gravely as though he were upon a subject that men ridicule not.

'She cannot remember; except that he seemed a gentleman, and that we held intercourse with him as such. Now, that again is remarkable. We never told her, you know, our suspicions of Captain Thorn: Richard said 'another' had done it, but he did not give mamma the faintest indication of who that other might be, or what sphere of life he moved in. It seems to me that it would be more natural for mamma to have taken up the idea in her mind that he was a low, obscure man; we do not generally associate the notion of gentlemen with murderers: and yet, in her dream, she saw he was a gentleman.'

'I think you must be becoming a convert to the theory of dreams yourself, Barbara; you are so very earnest,' smiled Mr. Carlyle.

'No, not to dreams; but I am earnest for my dear brother Richard's sake. Were it in *my* power to do any anything to elucidate the mystery, I would spare no pains, no toil; I would walk barefoot to the end of the earth to bring the truth to light. If ever that Thorn should come to West Lynne again, I will hope, and pray, and strive, to be able to bring it home to him.'

'That Thorn does not appear in a hurry, again to favour West Lynne with his—'

Mr. Carlyle paused, for Barbara had hurriedly laid her hand upon his arm with a warning gesture. In talking, they had wandered across the park to its ornamental grounds, and were now in a quiet path, over-shaded on either side by a chain of imitation rocks. Seated astride on the summit of these rocks, right above where Mr. Carlyle and Barbara were standing, was Francis Levison. His face was turned from them, and he appeared intent upon a child's whip, winding leather round its handle. Whether he heard their footsteps or not, he did not turn. They quickened their pace, and quitted the walk, bending their steps backwards towards the group of ladies.

'Could he have heard what we were saying?' ejaculated Barbara, below her breath.

Mr. Carlyle looked down on the concerned, flushed cheeks, with a smile. Barbara was evidently perturbed. But for a certain episode of their lives, some years ago, he might have soothed her.

'I think he must have heard a little, Barbara: unless his own wits were wool-gathering: he might not be attending. What if he did hear? it is of no consequence.'

'I was speaking, you know, of Captain Thorn—of his being the murderer.'

'You were not speaking of Richard or his movements, so never mind. Levison is a stranger to the whole; it is nothing to him: if he heard the name of Thorn mentioned, or could even have distinguished the subject, it would bear for him no interest; would go, as the saying runs, in at one ear and out at the other. Be at rest, Barbara.'

He really did look somewhat tenderly upon her as he spoke—and they were near enough to Lady Isabel for her to note the glance. She need not have been jealous: it bore no treachery to her. But she did note it: she had noted also their wandering away together, and she jumped to the conclusion that it was premeditated—that they had gone beyond her sight to enjoy each other's society for a few stolen moments. Wonderfully attractive looked Barbara that evening for Mr. Carlyle or any one else to steal away with. Her elegant, airy summer attire, her bright blue eyes, her charming features, and her lovely complexion. She had untied the strings of her pretty white bonnet, and was restlessly playing with them, more in thought than nervousness.

'Barbara, love, how are we to get home?' asked Mrs. Hare. 'I fear I shall never be able to walk. I wish I had told Benjamin to bring the phaeton.'

'I can send to him,' said Mr. Carlyle.

'But it is too bad of me, Archibald, to take you and Lady Isabel by storm in this unceremonious manner, and to give your servants trouble besides.'

'A great deal too bad, I think,' returned Mr. Carlyle, with mock gravity. 'As to the servants, the one who has to go will never recover from the trouble, depend upon it. You always were more concerned for others than for yourself, dear Mrs. Hare.'

'And you were always kind, Archibald, smoothing difficulties for all, and making a trouble of nothing. Ah, Lady Isabel, were I a young woman, I should be envying you your good husband: there are not many like him.'

Possibly the sentence reminded Lady Isabel that another, who was young, might be envying her. Isabel's cheeks flushed crimson. Mr. Carlyle held out his strong arm of help to Mrs. Hare.

'If sufficiently rested, I fancy you would be more comfortable on a sofa indoors. Allow me to support you thither.'

'And you can take my arm on the other side,' cried Miss Carlyle, placing her tall form by Mrs. Hare. 'Between us both we will pull you bravely along: your feet need scarcely touch the ground.'

Mrs. Hare laughed, but said she thought Mr. Carlyle's arm would be sufficient. She took it, and they were turning towards the house, when her eye caught the form of a gentleman passing along the road by the park gates.

'Barbara, run!' she hurriedly exclaimed. 'There's Tom Herbert going towards our house: he will call in and tell them to send the phaeton, if you ask him, which will save the trouble to Mr. Carlyle's servants of going expressly. Haste, child; you will be up with him in half a minute.'

Barbara, thus urged, set off, on the spur of the moment, towards the gates, before the rest of the party well knew what was being done. It was too late for Mr. Carlyle to stop her and repeat that a servant should go, for Barbara was already up with Mr. Tom Herbert. The latter had seen her running towards him, and waited at the gate.

'Are you going past our house?' inquired Barbara, perceiving then that Otway Bethel also stood there, but just beyond view of the avenue.

'Yes. Why?' replied Tom Herbert, who was not famed for his politeness, being blunt by nature and 'fast' by habit.

'Mamma would be so much obliged to you if you would just call in and leave word that Benjamin is to bring up the phaeton. Mamma walked here, intending to walk home, but she finds herself so fatigued as to be unequal to it.'

'All right; I'll call and send him. What time?'

Nothing had been said to Barbara about the time, so she was at liberty to name her own. 'Ten o'clock. We shall be home then before papa.'

'That you will,' responded Tom Herbert. 'He and the governor and two or three more old codgers are blowing clouds till you can't see across the room: and they are sure to get at it again after supper. I say, Miss Barbara, are you good for a few picnics?'

'Good for a great many,' returned Barbara.

'Our girls want to get up some in the next week or two. Jack is at home, you know.'

'Is he?' said Barbara, in surprise.

'We had the letter yesterday, and he came to-day, a brother-officer with him. Jack vows if the girls don't cater well for them in the way of amusement, he'll never honour them by spending his leave at home again: so mind you keep yourself in readiness for any fun that may turn up. Good evening.'

'Good evening, Miss Hare,' added Otway Bethel. As Barbara was returning their salutation, she became conscious of other footsteps, advancing from the same direction that they had come, and moved her head hastily round. Two gentlemen, walking arm-in-arm, were close upon her, in one of whom she recognized 'Jack,' otherwise Major Herbert. He stopped and held out his hand.

'It is some years since we met, but I have not forgotten the pretty face of Miss Barbara,' he cried. 'A young girl's face it was then, but it is a stately young lady's now.'

Barbara laughed. 'Your brother told me you had arrived at West Lynne; but I did not know you were so close to me. He has been asking me if I am ready for some pic—'

Barbara's voice faltered, and the rushing crimson of emotion dyed her face. Whose face was *that*, who was he, standing opposite to her, side by side with John Herbert? She had seen the face but once, yet it had planted itself upon her memory in characters of fire. Major Herbert continued to talk, but Barbara for once lost her self-possession: she could not listen; she could not answer; she could only stare at that face as if fascinated to the gaze, looking herself something like a simpleton, her shy blue eyes anxious and restless, and her lips turning to an ashy whiteness. A strange feeling of wonder, of superstition, was creeping over Barbara. Was that man before her in sober veritable reality?—or was it but a phantom, called up in her mind by the associations arising from her mamma's dream; or by the conversation held not many moments ago with Mr. Carlyle?

Major Herbert may have deemed that Barbara, who was not attending to him, but to his companion, wished for an introduction, and he accordingly made it. '*Captain Thorn*; Miss Hare.'

Then Barbara roused herself; her senses were partially coming to her, and she became alive to the fact that they must deem her behaviour unorthodox for a young lady.

'I—I—looked at Captain Thorn, for I thought I remembered his face,' she stammered.

'I was in West Lynne for a day or two some five years ago,' he observed.

'Ah—yes,' returned Barbara. 'Are you going to make a long stay now?'

'We have several weeks' leave of absence. Whether we shall remain here all the time I cannot say.'

Barbara parted from them. Thought upon thought crowded upon her brain as she flew back to East Lynne. She ran up the steps to the hall, gliding towards a group which stood near its further end—her mother, Miss Carlyle, Mr. Carlyle, and little Isabel; Lady Isabel she did not see. Mrs. Hare was then going up to see Joyce. In the agitation of the moment she stealthily touched Mr. Carlyle, and he stepped away from the rest to speak to her, she drawing back towards the door of one of the reception rooms, and motioning him to approach.

'Oh, Archibald, I must speak to you alone. Could you not come out again for a little while?'

He nodded, and walked out openly by her side. Why should he not? What had he to conceal? But, unfortunately, Lady Isabel, who had but gone into that same room for a minute and was coming out again to join Miss Hare, both saw Barbara's touch upon her husband's arm, marked her agitation, and heard her words. She went to one of the hall windows and watched them saunter towards the more private parts of the grounds: she saw her husband send back Isabel. Never, since her marriage, had Lady Isabel's jealousy been excited as it was excited that evening.

'I—I feel—I scarcely know whether I am awake or dreaming,' began Barbara, putting up her hand to her brow, and speaking in a dreamy tone. 'Pardon me for bringing you out in this unceremonious fashion.'

'What state secrets have you to disclose?' asked Mr. Carlyle, in a jesting manner.

'We were speaking of mamma's dream. She said the impression it left upon her mind—that the murderer was at West Lynne—was so vivid that, in spite of common sense, she could not persuade herself that he was not. Well—just now—'

'Barbara, what *can* be the matter?' said Mr. Carlyle, perceiving that her agitation was so great as to impede her words.

'*I have just seen him,*' she rejoined.

'Seen him?' echoed Mr. Carlyle, looking at her fixedly, a doubt crossing his mind whether Barbara's mind might be as uncollected as her manner.

'What were nearly my last words to you? That if ever that Thorn did come to West Lynne again, I would leave no stone unturned to bring it home to him. He is here, Archibald. When I went to the gates to speak to Tom Herbert, his brother Major Herbert was also there, and with him Captain Thorn, Bethel also. Do you wonder, I say, that I know not whether I am awake or dreaming? They have some week's holiday, and are here to spend it.'

'It is a singular coincidence,' exclaimed Mr. Carlyle.

'Had anything been wanting to convince me that Thorn is the guilty man, this would have done it,' went on Barbara in her excitement. 'Mamma's dream, with the steadfast impression it left upon her that Hallijohn's murderer was now at West Lynne—'

In turning the sharp corner of the walk, they came in contact with Captain Levison, who appeared to be either standing or sauntering there, his hands underneath his coat-tails. Again Barbara felt vexed, wondering how much he had heard, and beginning in her heart to dislike the man. He accosted them familiarly, and appeared as if he would have turned with them; but none could put down presumption more effectually than Mr. Carlyle, calm and gentlemanly though he always was.

'I will join you presently, Captain Levison,' he said, with a wave of the hand. And he turned back with Barbara towards the open parts of the park.

'Do you like that Captain Levison?' she abruptly inquired, when they were beyond hearing.

'I cannot say that I do,' was Mr. Carlyle's reply. 'He is one who does not improve upon acquaintance.'

'To me, it looks as though he had placed himself in our way to hear what we were saying.'

'No, no, Barbara. What interest could it bear for him?'

Barbara did not contest the point: she turned to the one nearer at heart. 'What must be our course with regard to Thorn?'

'It is more than I can tell you,' replied Mr. Carlyle. 'I cannot go up to the man and unceremoniously accuse him of being Hallijohn's murderer. In the first place, Barbara, we are not positively sure that he is the same man spoken of by Richard.'

'Oh, Archibald, how can you doubt? The extraordinary fact of his appearing here at this moment, coupled with mamma's dream, might assure us of it.'

'Not quite,' smiled Mr. Carlyle. 'All we can do is to go cautiously to work, and endeavour to ascertain whether he is the same.'

'And there is no one but you to do it!' wailed Barbara. 'How vain and foolish are our boastings! I said I would not cease striving to bring it home to him, did he come again to West Lynne; and now he is here, even as the words were in my mouth, and what can I do? Nothing.'

They took their way to the house, for there was nothing further to discuss. Captain Levison had entered it before them, and saw Lady Isabel standing at the hall window. Yes, she was standing and looking; brooding over her fancied wrongs.

'Who is that Miss Hare?' he demanded in a cynical tone. 'They appear to have a pretty good understanding together: twice this evening I have met them in secret conversation.'

'Did you speak to me, sir?' sharply and haughtily returned Lady Isabel.

'I did not mean to offend you: I spoke of Mr. Carlyle and Miss Hare,' he replied in a gentle voice. He knew she had distinctly heard his first speech in spite of her question.

❦ VI ❦

Captain Thorn in Trouble about a 'Bill'

In talking over a bygone misfortune, we sometimes make the remark, or hear it made, 'Circumstances worked against it.' Such and such a thing might have turned out differently, we say, had the surrounding circumstances been more favourable, but they were in opposition: they were dead against it. Now, if ever attendant circumstances can be said to have borne a baneful influence upon any person in this world, they most assuredly did at the present time upon Lady Isabel Carlyle.

Coeval, you see, with the arrival of the ex-captain, Levison, at East Lynne, all the jealous feeling touching her husband and Barbara Hare, was renewed, and with greater force than ever. Barbara, painfully anxious that something should be brought to light by which her brother should be exonerated from the terrible charge under which he lay, fully believing that Frederick Thorn, Captain in her Majesty's service, was the man who had committed the crime, as asserted by Richard, was in a state of excitement bordering on frenzy. Too keenly she felt the truth of her own words, that she was powerless, that she could, herself, do nothing. When she rose in the morning, after a night passed in troubled reflection more than in sleep, her thoughts were, 'Oh, that I could this day find out something certain!' She was often at the Herberts; frequently invited there, sometimes going uninvited: she and the Miss Herberts were intimate, and they pressed Barbara into all the impromptu fêtes got up for their brother now he was at home. There she of course saw Captain Thorn, and now and then she was enabled to pick up scraps of his past history. Eagerly were these scraps carried to Mr. Carlyle. Not to his office; Barbara would not appear there. It may be, that she feared, if seen haunting Mr. Carlyle's office, Captain Thorn might come to hear of it and suspect the agitation that was afloat—for who could know better than he the guilt that was falsely attaching to Richard? Therefore she chose rather to go to East Lynne, or to waylay Mr. Carlyle as he passed to and from business. It was but little she gathered to tell him: one evening she met him with the news that Thorn *had* been in former years at West Lynne, though she could not fix the date: another time she went boldly to East Lynne in eager anxiety; ostensibly to make a call on Lady Isabel—and a very restless one it was—contriving to make Mr. Carlyle to understand that she wanted to see him alone. He went out with her when she departed, and accompanied her as far as the park gates, the two evidently absorbed in earnest converse: Lady Isabel's jealous eyes saw that. The communication Barbara had to make was, that Captain Thorn had let fall the avowal that he had once been 'in trouble,' though of its nature there was no indication given. Another journey of hers took the scrap of news, that she had discovered he knew Swainson well. Part of all this, nay, perhaps the whole of it, Mr. Carlyle had found out for himself; nevertheless he always received Barbara with vivid interest. Richard Hare was related to Miss Carlyle, and if his innocence could be made clear in the sight of men, it would be little less gratifying to them than to the Hares. Of Richard's innocence, Mr. Carlyle now entertained little, if any, doubt, and he was becoming impressed with the guilt of Captain Thorn. The latter spoke mysteriously of a portion of his past life—when he could be brought to speak of it at all—and he bore evidently some secret that he did not care to have alluded to.

But now, look at the mean treachery of that man, Francis Levison! The few meetings that Lady Isabel witnessed between her husband and Barbara would have been quite enough to excite her anger and jealousy, and to trou-

ble her peace; but, in addition, Francis Levison took care to tell her of those
she did not see. It pleased him—he could best tell his own motive—to watch
the movements of Mr. Carlyle and Barbara. There was a hedge pathway
through the fields on the opposite side of the road to the residence of Justice
Hare, and as Mr. Carlyle walked down the road to business, in his unsuspicion (not one time in fifty did he choose to ride: he said the walk to and fro
kept him in health), Captain Levison would be strolling down like a serpent
behind the hedge, watching all his movements, watching his interviews with
Barbara, if any took place, watching Mr. Carlyle turn into the Grove, as he
sometimes did, and perhaps watch Barbara run out of the house to meet him.
It was all retailed, with miserable exaggeration, to Lady Isabel, whose jealousy, as a natural sequence, grew feverish in its extent.

It is scarcely necessary to explain that of Lady Isabel's jealousy Barbara
knew nothing: not a shadow of suspicion had ever penetrated to her mind
that Lady Isabel was jealous of her. Had she been told that such was the fact
she would have laughed in derision at her informant. Mr. Carlyle's happy
wife, proudly secure in her position and in his affection, jealous of *her*; of
her, to whom he never gave an admiring look or a loving word! It would
have taken a good deal to make Barbara believe that.

How different were the facts in reality. These meetings of Mr. Carlyle's and
Barbara's, instead of being episodes of love-making and tender speeches, were
positively painful to Barbara, from the unhappy nature of the subject to be
discussed. Far from feeling a reprehensible pleasure in seeking the meetings
with Mr. Carlyle, Barbara shrank from them: but that she was urged by dire
necessity, in the interests of Richard, she would wholly have avoided them.
Poor Barbara, in spite of that explosion of feelings years back, was a lady,
possessed of lady's ideas and feelings, and—remembering that explosion—it
did not at all accord with her pride to be pushing herself into what might be
called secret meetings with Archibald Carlyle. But Barbara, in her love for
her brother, pressed down all thoughts of self, and went perseveringly forward for Richard's sake.

Mr. Carlyle was seated one morning in his private room at his office, when
his head clerk, Mr. Dill, came in. 'A gentleman is asking to see you, Mr.
Archibald.'

'I am too busy to see anybody for this hour to come. You know that, Dill.'

'So I told him, sir, and he says he will wait. It is that Captain Thorn who is
staying here with John Herbert.'

Mr. Carlyle raised his eyes, and they encountered those of the old man: a
peculiar expression was in the face of both. Mr. Carlyle glanced down at the
parchments he was perusing, as if calculating his time. Then he looked up
again and spoke.

'I will see *him*, Dill. Send him in.'

The business, leading to the visit, was quite simple. Captain Frederick

Thorn had got himself into some trouble and vexation about a 'bill'—like too many other captains do on occasions, and he had come to crave advice of Mr. Carlyle.

Mr. Carlyle felt dubious as to giving it. This Captain Thorn was a pleasant, attractive man, who won much on acquaintance; one whom Mr. Carlyle would have been pleased, in a friendly point of view, and setting professional interests apart, to help out of his difficulties; but if he were the villain they suspected him to be, the man with crime upon his hand, then Mr. Carlyle would have ordered his office door held wide for him to slink out of it.

'Cannot you advise me what my course ought to be?' he inquired, detecting Mr. Carlyle's hesitation.

'I could advise you, certainly. But—you must excuse my being plain, Captain Thorn—I like to know who my clients are, before I take up their cause or accept them as clients.'

'I am able to pay you,' was Captain Thorn's reply. 'I am not short of ready money; only this bill—'

Mr. Carlyle laughed out, after having bit his lip with annoyance. 'It was a natural inference of yours,' he said, 'but I assure you I was not thinking of your purse. My father held it right never to undertake business for a stranger: unless a man was good, and his cause good, he did not entertain it; and I have acted on the same principle. By these means, the position and character of our business is such as is rarely attained by a solicitor. Now, in saying that you are a stranger to me, I am not casting any doubt upon you, Captain Thorn; I am merely upholding my common practice.'

'My family is well connected,' was Captain Thorn's next venture.

'Excuse me; family has nothing to do with it. If the poorest day labourer, if a pauper out of the workhouse came to me for advice, he should be heartily welcome to it, provided he were an honest man in the face of day. Again I repeat, you must take no offence at what I say, for I cast no reflection on you: I only urge that you and your character are unknown to me.'

Curious words from a lawyer to a client-aspirant, and Captain Thorn found them so. But Mr. Carlyle's tone was so courteous, his manner so affable, in fact, he was so thoroughly the gentleman, that it was impossible to feel hurt.

'Well—how can I convince you that I am respectable? I have served my country ever since I was sixteen, and my brother officers have found no cause of complaint. My position as an officer and a gentleman would be generally deemed a sufficient guarantee. Inquire of John Herbert. The Herberts, too, are friends of yours, and they have not disdained to give me house room amidst their family.'

'True,' returned Mr. Carlyle, feeling that he could not well object further; and also that all men should be deemed innocent until proved guilty. 'At any rate, I will advise you what must be done at present,' he added, 'though if the affair must go on, do not promise that I can continue to act for you. I am very busy just now.'

Captain Thorn explained his dilemma, and Mr. Carlyle told him what to do in it. 'Were you not at West Lynne some ten years ago?' he suddenly inquired at the close of the conversation. 'You denied it to me once at my house, but I concluded, from an observation you let fall, that you had been here.'

'Yes, I was,' replied Captain Thorn, in a confidential tone. 'I don't mind owning it to you in confidence, but I do not wish it to get abroad. I was not at West Lynne, but in its neighbourhood. The fact is, when I was a careless young fellow, I was stopping a few miles from here, and got into a scrape, through a—a—in short, it was an affair of gallantry. I did not show out very well at the time, and I don't care that it should be known that I am in the county again.'

Mr. Carlyle's pulses—for Richard Hare's sake—beat a shade quicker. The avowal 'an affair of gallantry' was almost a confirmation of his suspicions.

'Yes,' he pointedly said. 'The girl was Afy Hallijohn.'

'Afy—who?' repeated Captain Thorn, opening his eyes, and fixing them on Mr. Carlyle's.

'Afy Hallijohn.'

Captain Thorn continued to look at Mr. Carlyle, an amused expression, rather than any other, predominant on his features. 'You are mistaken,' he observed. 'Afy Hallijohn? I never heard the name before in my life.'

'Did you never hear, or know, that a dreadful tragedy was enacted in this place about that period?' returned Mr. Carlyle, in a low, meaning tone. 'That Afy Hallijohn's father—'

'Oh, stay, stay, stay,' hastily interrupted Captain Thorn. 'I am telling a story in saying I never heard the name. Afy Hallijohn? Why, that's the girl Tom Herbert was telling me about: who—what was it?—disappeared, after her father was murdered.'

'Murdered in his own cottage; almost in Afy's presence; murdered by—by—' Mr. Carlyle recollected himself: he had spoken more impulsively than was his custom. 'Hallijohn was my father's faithful clerk for many years,' he more calmly concluded.

'And he who committed the murder, was young Hare, son of Justice Hare, and brother to that attractive girl, Barbara. Your speaking of this has recalled what they told me to my recollection. The first evening I was at the Herberts, Justice Hare and others were there, smoking—half a dozen pipes were going at once; I also saw Miss Barbara that evening at your park gates; and Tom told me of the murder. An awful calamity for the Hares. I suppose that is the reason the young lady is Miss Hare still: one, with her good fortune and good looks, ought to have changed her name ere this.'

'No, it is not the reason,' resumed Mr. Carlyle.

'What is the reason, then?'

A faint flush tinged the brow of Mr. Carlyle. 'I know more than one who would be glad to get Barbara, in spite of the murder. Do not depreciate Miss Hare.'

'Not I, indeed; I like the young lady too well,' replied Captain Thorn. 'The girl Afy has never been heard of since, has she?'

'Never,' said Mr. Carlyle. 'Did you know her well?' he deliberately added.

'I never knew her at all, if you mean Afy Hallijohn. Why should you think I did? I never heard of her till Tom Herbert amused me with the history.'

Mr. Carlyle devoutly wished he could tell whether the man before him was speaking the truth or falsehood. He continued.

'Afy's favours—I mean her smiles and her chatter—were pretty freely dispersed, for she was heedless and vain. Amidst others who got the credit for occasionally basking in her rays, was a gentleman of the name of Thorn. Was it not yourself?'

Captain Thorn stroked his moustache with an air that seemed to say he *could* boast of his share of such baskings; in short, as if he felt half inclined to do it. 'Upon my word,' he simpered, 'you do me too much honour: I cannot confess to having been favoured by Miss Afy.'

'Then she was not the—the damsel you speak of, who drove you—if I understood aright—from the locality?' resumed Mr. Carlyle, fixing his eyes upon him, so as to take in every tone of the answer, and shade of the countenance, as he gave it.

'I should think not, indeed. It was a married lady, more's the pity; young, pretty, vain, and heedless, as you represent this Afy. Things went smoother after a time, and she and her husband—a stupid country yeoman—became reconciled: but I have been ashamed of the affair ever since; doubly ashamed of it since I have grown wiser, and I do not care ever to be recognized as the actor in it, or to have it raked up against me.'

Captain Thorn rose and took a somewhat hasty leave. Was he, or was he not the man? Mr. Carlyle could not solve the doubt.

Mr. Dill came in as he disappeared, closed the door and advanced to his master, speaking in an undertone.

'Mr. Archibald, has it struck you that the gentleman just gone out may be the Lieutenant Thorn you once spoke to me about?—he who had used to gallop over from Swainson to court Afy Hallijohn?'

'It has struck me so most forcibly,' replied Mr. Carlyle. 'Dill, I would give five hundred pounds out of my pocket this moment, to be assured of the fact—if he is the same.'

'I have seen him several times since he has been staying with the Herberts,' pursued the old gentleman, 'and my doubts have naturally been excited, as to whether it could be the man in question. Curious enough, Bezant, the doctor, was over here yesterday from Swainson; and, as I was walking with him arm-in-arm, we met Captain Thorn. The two recognized each other and bowed, but merely as distant acquaintances. "Do you know that gentleman?" said I to Bezant. "Yes," he answered, "it is Mr. Frederick." "Mr. Frederick with something added to it," said I: "his name is Thorn." "I know that," returned Bezant, "but when he was in Swainson some years ago, he chose to drop the Thorn, and the town in general knew him only as Mr. Frederick." "What was he doing there, Bezant?" I asked. "Amusing himself and getting into mischief," was the answer: "nothing very bad, only the random scrapes of young men." "Was he often on horseback, riding to a distance?" was my next question. "Yes, that he was," replied Bezant; "none more fond of galloping across the country than he: I used to tell him he'd ride his horse's tail off." Now, Mr. Archibald, what do you think?' concluded the old clerk: 'and so far as I could make out, this was about the very time of the tragedy at Hallijohn's.'

'Think?' replied Mr. Carlyle, 'what can I think but that it is the same man? I am convinced of it now.'

And, leaning back in his chair, he fell into a deep reverie, regardless of the parchments that lay before him.

❧ V I I ☙

The Secret Scrap of Paper

The weeks went on; two or three: and things seemed to be progressing backwards rather than forwards—if that's not Irish. Francis Levison's affairs—that is, the adjustment of them—did not advance at all: creditors were obstinate. He had been three times over to Levison Park, securely boxed up in Mr. Carlyle's close carriage from the prying eyes of beholders; but Sir Peter seemed to be turning as obdurate as the creditors. Captain Levison had deceived him, he found out: inasmuch as certain sums of money, handed over by Sir Peter some time back to settle certain claims, had been by the gentleman appropriated to his own purposes. Sir Peter did not appear inclined to forgive the deceit, and vowed he would do nothing further yet awhile. There was nothing for him but to return to the Continent, Captain Levison observed. And the best place for him; plenty of scamps congregated there, was the retort of Sir Peter. He apparently meant what he said, for when Francis Levison rose to leave, Sir Peter took out of his pocket-book notes to the value of 100*l.*, told him that would pay for the expense he had been put to in coming, and that his allowance would be continued as usual.

'How did you get on to-day with Sir Peter?' inquired Mr. Carlyle, that evening at dinner, when his guest was back at East Lynne.

'Middling,' replied Francis Levison. 'I did not do much with him. These old stagers like to take their own time over things.'

An answer false as he was. It did not suit his plans to quit East Lynne yet; and, had he told the truth, he would have had no plea for remaining.

Another thing that was going on fast to bad, instead of to good, was the jealousy of Lady Isabel. How could it be otherwise, kept up, as it was by Barbara's frequent meetings with Mr. Carlyle, and by Captain Levison's comments and false insinuations regarding them? Discontented with herself and with everybody about her, Isabel was living now in a state of excitement; a dangerous resentment against her husband working in her heart. That very day, the one of Captain Levison's visit to Levison Park, in driving through West Lynne in the pony carriage, she had come upon her husband in close converse with Barbara Hare. So absorbed were they that they never saw her, though her carriage passed close to the pavement where they stood.

On the morning following, as the Hare family were seated at breakfast, the postman was seen coming towards the house. Barbara sprang from her seat to the open window, and the man advanced to her.

'Only one, miss. It is for yourself.'

'Who is it from?' began the justice, as Barbara returned to her chair. In letters, as in other things, he was curious to know their contents, whether they might be addressed to himself or not.

'It is from Anne, papa,' replied Barbara, as she laid the letter by her side on the table.

'Why don't you open it and see what she says?'

'I will, directly. I am just going to pour out some more tea for mamma.'

Barbara, handed her mamma the tea, and then took up her letter. As she opened it, a small bit of paper, folded, fell upon her lap. Fortunately, most fortunately, Justice Hare, who at the moment had his nose in his coffee-cup, did not see it, but Mrs. Hare did.

'Barbara you have dropped something.'

Barbara had seen it also, and was clutching stealthily at the 'something' with almost a guilty movement. She had no ready answer at hand, but bent her eyes upon the letter, and Mrs. Hare spoke again.

'My love, something dropped on your lap.'

'Don't you hear your mamma, young lady?' pursued the justice. 'What is it you have dropped?'

Barbara, with a crimson face of heat, rose from her chair and shook out her pretty muslin dress—somehow, Barbara's dresses were always pretty. 'There's nothing at all, papa, nothing that I can see.' And, in sitting down, she contrived to give her mother a warning look, which silenced Mrs. Hare. Then Barbara read her sister's letter, and laid it open on the table for the benefit of anybody else, who might like to do the same.

The justice snatched it up, taking first benefit to himself—as he was sure to do. He threw it down, grumbling.

'Not much in it. There never is in Anne's letters: she won't set the Thames on fire as a correspondent. As if anybody cared to hear about the baby's being "short-coated!" I think I'll have a cup more coffee, Barbara.'

Finally the justice finished his breakfast and strolled out into the garden. Mrs. Hare turned to Barbara.

'My dear, why did you give me that mysterious look? And what was it that dropped upon your lap? It seemed to fall from Anne's letter.'

'Well, mamma, it did fall from Anne's letter. You know how exacting papa is—always will see and inquire into everything—so, when Anne wants to tell me any bit of news that she does not care the whole world to know, she writes it on a separate bit of paper and puts it inside her letter. I suppose it was one of those bits that fell out.'

'Child, I cannot let you insinuate that your papa has no right to look into your letters.'

'Of course not, mamma,' was Miss Barbara's rejoinder. 'But if he had a grain of common sense, he might judge that I and Anne may sometimes have little private matters to say to each other, not necessary or expedient for him to pry into.'

Barbara had produced the scrap of paper as she spoke, and was opening it. Mrs. Hare watched her movements, and her countenance. She saw the latter flush suddenly and vividly, and then become deadly pale: she saw Barbara crush the note in her hand when read.

'Oh, mamma!' she uttered.

The flush of emotion came also into Mrs. Hare's delicate cheeks. 'Barbara! is it bad news?'

'Mamma,—it—it—is about Richard!' she whispered, glancing at the door and window, to see that none might be within sight or hearing. 'I never thought of him: I only fancied Anne might be sending me some bit of news concerning her own affairs. Good Heavens! how fortunate—how providential that papa did not see the paper fall; and that you did not persist in your inquiries! If he—'

'Barbara, you are keeping me in suspense,' interrupted Mrs. Hare, who had also grown white. 'What should Anne know about Richard?'

Barbara smoothed out the writing and held it before her mother. It was as follows:

'I have had a curious note from R. It was without date or signature, but I knew his handwriting. He tells me to let you know, in the most sure and private manner that I can, that he will soon be paying you another night visit. You are to watch the grove every evening when the present moon gets bright.'

Mrs. Hare covered her face for some minutes. 'Thank God for all His mercies!' she murmured.

'Oh, mamma, but it is an awful risk for him to run!'

'But to know that he is in life—to know that he is in life! And for the risk—Barbara, I dread it not. The same good God who protected him through the last visit, will protect him through this. He will not forsake the oppressed, the innocent. Destroy that paper, child.'

'Archibald Carlyle must first see it, mamma. I will destroy it afterwards.'

'Then seek him out to-day and show it him. I shall not be easy until it is destroyed, Barbara.'

Braving the comments of the gossips, hoping the visit would not reach the ears or eyes of the justice, Barbara went that day to the office of Mr. Carlyle. He was not there: he was not at West Lynne: he was gone to Lynneborough on business, and Mr. Dill thought it a question if he would be at the office again that day. If so, it would be late in the afternoon. Barbara, as soon as their own dinner was over, took up her patient station at the gate, hoping to see him pass; but the time went by, and he did not. She had little doubt that he had returned home without going again to West Lynne.

What should she do? Go up to East Lynne and see him, said her conscience. Barbara's mind was in a strangely excited state. It appeared to her that this visit of Richard's must have been especially designed by Providence, that he might be confronted with Thorn. That they must be confronted the one with the other, or rather, that Richard must have the opportunity given him of seeing Thorn, was a matter of course; though how it was to be brought about, Barbara could not guess. For all action, all plans, she must depend upon Mr. Carlyle; he ought to be put in immediate possession of the news, for the moon was already three or four days old, and there was no knowing when Richard might appear.

'Mamma,' she said, returning indoors, after seeing the justice depart upon an evening visit to the Buck's Head, where he and certain other justices and gentlemen sometimes congregated to smoke and chat, 'I shall go up to East Lynne if you have no objection. I must see Mr. Carlyle.'

'What objection can I have, my dear? I am all anxiety for you to see him. It was so unfortunate that he was out to-day when you ventured to his office. Mind you tell him all: and ask him what is best to be done.'

Away went Barbara. It had struck seven when she arrived at East Lynne. 'Is Mr. Carlyle disengaged?'

'Mr. Carlyle is not yet home, Miss. My lady and Miss Carlyle are waiting dinner for him.'

A check for Barbara. The servant asked her to walk in, but she declined, and turned from the door. She was in no mood for visit paying.

Lady Isabel had been standing at the window watching for her husband, wondering what made him so late: she observed Barbara approach the house, and saw her walk away again. Presently the servant who had answered the door entered the drawing-room.

'Was not that Miss Hare?'

'Yes, my lady,' was the man's reply. 'She wanted master. I said your lady-ship was at home, but she would not enter.'

Isabel said no more. She caught the eyes of Francis Levison fixed on her with as much compassionate meaning as they dared express. She clasped her hands in pain, and turned again to the window.

Barbara was slowly walking down the avenue, Mr. Carlyle was then in sight, coming on quickly. Lady Isabel saw their hands meet in greeting.

'Oh, I am so thankful to have met you!' exclaimed Barbara, impulsively. 'I actually went to your office to-day, and I have been now to your house. We have great news!'

'Ay! What? About Thorn?'

'No, about Richard,' replied Barbara, taking the scrap of paper from the folds of her dress. 'This came to me this morning, from Anne.'

Mr. Carlyle took the document, and Barbara looked over him whilst he read it: neither of them thinking that Lady Isabel's jealous eyes, and Captain Levison's evil ones, were strained on them from the distant windows. Miss Carlyle's also were for the matter of that.

'Archibald, it seems to me that Providence must be directing him hither at this moment. Our suspicions, with regard to Thorn, can now be set at rest. You must contrive that Richard shall see him. What can he be coming again for?'

More money, was the supposition of Mr. Carlyle. 'Does Mrs. Hare know of this?'

'She does, unfortunately. I opened the paper before her, never dreaming it was connected with Richard. I wish I could have spared mamma the news, until he was actually here: the expectation and suspense I fear will make her ill. It terrifies me to that extent that I don't know what I am about,' she continued. 'Not a moment's rest or peace shall I have until he has been and is gone again. Poor, wandering, unhappy Richard! and not to be guilty!'

'He acted as though he were guilty, Barbara. And that line of conduct often entails as much trouble as real guilt.'

'You do not believe him guilty?' she almost passionately uttered.

'I do not. I have little doubt of the guilt of Thorn.'

'Oh, if it could but be brought home to him!' reiterated Barbara; 'so that Richard might be cleared in the sight of day. How can you contrive that he shall see Thorn?'

'I cannot tell; I must think it over. Let me know the instant he arrives, Barbara.'

'Of course I shall. It may be, that he does not want money; that his errand is only to see mamma. He was always so fond of her.'

'I must leave you,' said Mr. Carlyle, taking her hand in token of farewell. Then, as the thought occurred to him, he turned and walked a few steps with her, without releasing it. He was probably quite unconscious that he retained it: she was not.

'You know, Barbara, if he should want money, and it should not be convenient to Mrs. Hare to supply it at so short a notice, I can give it him, as I did before.'

'Thank you, thank you, Archibald. Mamma felt sure you would.'

She lifted her eyes to his with an expression of gratitude: but for the habitual control to which she had schooled herself, a warmer feeling might have mingled with it. Mr. Carlyle nodded pleasantly, and then set off towards the house at the pace of a steam-engine.

Two minutes in his dressing-chamber, and he entered the drawing-room, apologizing for having kept them waiting dinner, and explaining that he had been compelled to go to his office to give some orders, subsequent to his return from Lynneborough. Lady Isabel's lips were pressed together, and she preserved an obstinate silence. Mr. Carlyle, in his unsuspicion, did not notice it.

'What did Barbara Hare want?' demanded Miss Carlyle, during dinner.

'She wanted to see me on business,' was his reply, given in a tone that certainly did not invite his sister to pursue the subject. 'Will you take some more fish, Isabel?'

'What was that you were reading over with her?' pursued the indefatigable Miss Corny. 'It looked like a note.'

'Ah, that would be telling,' returned Mr. Carlyle, willing to turn it off with gaiety. 'If young ladies choose to make me privy to their love-letters, I cannot betray confidence, you know.'

'What rubbish, Archibald!' quoth she. 'As if you could not say outright what Barbara wants, without making a mystery of it. And she seems to be always wanting you now.'

Mr. Carlyle glanced at his sister, a quick, peculiar look: it seemed, to her, to speak both of seriousness and warning. Involuntarily her thoughts—and her fears—flew back to the past.

'Archibald! Archibald!' she uttered, repeating the name as if she could not get any further words out, in her dread. 'It—it—is never—that old affair is never being reaped up again?'

Now, Miss Carlyle's 'old affair' referred to one sole and sore point— Richard Hare: and so Mr. Carlyle understood it. Lady Isabel unhappily believed that any 'old affair' could but have reference to the byegone loves of her husband and Barbara.

'You will oblige me by going on with your dinner, Cornelia,' gravely responded Mr. Carlyle. Then—assuming a more laughing tone—'I tell you it is unreasonable to expect me to betray a young lady's secrets, although she may choose to confide them professionally to me. What say you, Captain Levison?'

Captain Levison bowed; a smile of mockery, all too perceptible to Lady Isabel, on his lip. And Miss Carlyle bent her head over her plate, and went on with her dinner as meek as any lamb.

That same evening, Lady Isabel's indignant and rebellious heart condescended to speak of it when alone with her husband.

'What is it that she wants with you so much, that Barbara Hare?'

'It is private business, Isabel. She has to bring me messages from her mother.'

'Must the business be kept from me?'

He was silent for a moment, considering whether he might tell her. But it was impossible he could speak, even to his wife, of the suspicion they were attaching to Captain Thorn, it would have been unfair and wrong: neither could he betray that a secret visit was expected from Richard. To no one would he betray that: unless Miss Corny, with her questioning, got it out of him: and she was safe and true.

'It would not make you the happier to know it, Isabel. There is a dark secret, you are aware, touching the Hare family: it is connected with that.'

She did not put faith in a word of the reply. She believed he could not tell her because her feelings, as his wife, would be outraged by the confession: and it goaded her anger into recklessness. Mr. Carlyle on his part, never gave a thought to the supposition that she might be jealous: he had believed that nonsense at an end years ago. He was perfectly honourable and true, giving her no shadow of cause or reason to be jealous of him: and, being a practical, matter-of-fact man, it did not occur to him that she could be so.

Lady Isabel was sitting the following morning, moody and out of sorts. Captain Levison had accompanied Mr. Carlyle in the most friendly manner possible to the park gates on his departure, and then stolen along the hedge-walk. He returned to Lady Isabel with the news of an 'ardent' interview with Barbara, who had been watching for Mr. Carlyle at the gate of the Grove. She sat, sullenly digesting the tidings, when a note was brought in. It proved to be an invitation to dinner for the following Tuesday, at a Mrs. Jeafferson's—for Mr. and Lady Isabel Carlyle and Miss Carlyle.

She drew her desk towards her petulantly, to answer it on the spur of the moment, first of all passing the note across the table to Miss Carlyle.

'Do you go?' asked Miss Carlyle.

'Yes,' replied Lady Isabel. 'Mr. Carlyle and I both want a change of some sort,' she added, in a mocking sort of spirit; 'it may be as well to have it, if only for an evening.' In truth, this unhappy jealousy, this distrust of her husband, appeared to have altered Lady Isabel's very nature.

'And leave Captain Levison alone?' returned Miss Carlyle.

Lady Isabel bent over her desk, making no reply.

'What will you do with him, I ask?' persisted Miss Carlyle.

'He can remain here; he can dine by himself. Shall I accept the invitation for you?'

'No; I shall not go,' said Miss Carlyle.

'Then, in that case, there can be no difficulty with regard to Captain Levison,' coldly spoke Lady Isabel.

'I don't want his company: I am not fond of it,' cried Miss Carlyle. 'I would go to Mrs. Jeafferson's, but that I should require a new dress.'

'That's easily had,' said Lady Isabel. 'I shall want one myself.'

'*You* want a new dress!' uttered Miss Carlyle. 'Why, you have dozens!'

'I don't know that I could count a dozen in all,' returned Isabel, chafing at the remark and the continual thwarting put upon her by Miss Carlyle, which had latterly seemed to be more than usually hard to endure. Petty ills try the temper worse than great ones.

Lady Isabel concluded her note, folded, sealed it, and then rang the bell. As the man left the room with it, she desired that Wilson might be sent to her.

'Is it this morning, Wilson, that the dressmaker comes to try on Miss Isabel's dress?' she inquired.

Wilson hesitated and stammered, and glanced from her mistress to Miss Carlyle. The latter looked up from her work.

'The dressmaker's not coming,' spoke she, sharply. 'I countermanded the order for the frock, for Isabel does not require it.'

'She does require it,' answered Lady Isabel, in perhaps the most displeased tone she had ever used to Miss Carlyle. 'I am a competent judge of what is necessary for my own children.'

'She no more requires a new frock than that table requires one, or that you require the one you are longing for,' stoically persisted Miss Carlyle. 'She has got ever so many lying by: and her striped silk, turned, will make up as handsome as ever.'

Wilson backed out of the room and closed the door softly, but her mistress caught a compassionate look directed towards her. Her heart felt bursting with indignation and despair: there seemed to be no side on which she could turn for refuge. Pitied by her own servants!

She re-opened her desk, and dashed off a haughty, peremptory note for the attendance of the dressmaker at East Lynne, commanding its immediate despatch.

Miss Corny groaned in her wrath. 'You will be sorry for not listening to me, ma'am, when your husband shall be brought to poverty. He works like a horse now; and, with all his slaving, can scarcely, I fear, keep expenses down.'

Poor Lady Isabel, ever sensitive, began to think they might, what with one thing and another, be spending more than Mr. Carlyle's means would justify; she knew their expenses were heavy. The same tale had been dinned into her ear ever since she married him. She gave up in that moment all thought of the new dress for herself and for Isabel: but her spirit, in her deep unhappiness, felt sick and faint within her.

Wilson meanwhile had flown to Joyce's room, and was exercising her dearly-beloved tongue in an exaggerated account of the matter: how Miss Carlyle put upon my lady, and had forbidden a new dress to her, as well as the frock to Miss Isabel.

Joyce, sitting up that day for the first time, was gazing from the window at Captain Levison as Wilson spoke.

'He's a handsome man—to look at him from this,' she observed.

And yet a few more days passed on.

⚜ V I I I ⚜

Richard Hare at Mr. Dill's Window

Bright was the moon on that genial Monday night, bright were the evening stars as they shone upon a solitary wayfarer who walked on the shady side of the road, with his head down, as though he did not care to court observation. A labourer apparently, for he wore a smock frock and had hobnails in his shoes; but his whiskers were large and black, quite hiding the lower part of his face, and his broad-brimmed 'wide-awake' came far over his brows. He drew near the dwelling of Richard Hare, Esquire, plunged rapidly over some palings (after looking well to the right and left) into a field, and thence over the side wall in Mr. Hare's garden, where he remained amidst the thick trees.

Now, by some mischievous spirit of intuition or contrariety, Justice Hare was spending this evening at home, a thing which did not happen once in six months, unless he had friends with him. Things, in real life, mostly go by the rules of contrary—as the children say in their play, holding the corners of the handkerchief. 'Here we go round and round by the rules of conterrary: if I tell you to hold fast, you must loose: and if I tell you to loose, you must hold fast.' Just so, in the play of life. When we want people to 'hold fast,' they 'loose;' and when we want them to loose they hold fast.

Barbara, anxious, troubled, worn out with the suspense of watching for her brother, would have given her head for her father to go out. But no: things were going by the rules of contrary: there sat the stern justice in full view of the garden and the grove, his chair drawn precisely in front of the window, his wig awry, and a long pipe in his mouth.

'Are you not going out, Richard?' Mrs. Hare ventured to say.

'No.'

'Mamma, shall I ring for the shutters to be closed?' asked Barbara by-and-by.

'Shutters closed!' said the justice. 'Who'd shut out this bright moon? You have got the lamp at the far end of the room, young lady, and can go to it.'

Barbara ejaculated an inward prayer for patience—for safety for Richard, if he did come, and waited on, watching the grove in the distance. It came, the signal; her quick eye caught it; a movement as if some person or thing had stepped out beyond the trees and stepped back again. Barbara's face turned white and her lips dry.

'I am so hot!' she ejaculated, in her confused eagerness for an excuse; 'I must take a turn in the garden.'

She stole out, throwing a dark shawl over her shoulders, that it might render her less conspicuous to the justice, and her dress that evening was a dark silk. She did not dare to stand still when she reached the trees, or to penetrate them, but she caught glimpses of Richard's face, and her heart ached at the change in it. It was white, thin, and full of care; and his hair, he told her, was turning grey.

'Oh, Richard, darling, I may not stop and talk to you!' she wailed, in a deep whisper. 'Papa is at home, you see, of all nights in the world.'

'Can't I see my mother?'

'How can you? You must wait till to-morrow night.'

'I don't like waiting a second night, Barbara. There's danger in every inch of ground that this neighbourhood contains.'

'But you must wait, Richard; for reasons. That man who caused all the mischief, Thorn—'

'Hang him!' gloomily interrupted Richard.

'He is at West Lynne. At least, there is a Thorn here whom we, I and Mr. Carlyle, believe to be the same, and we want you to see him.'

'Let me see him,' panted Richard, whom the news appeared to agitate. 'Let me see him! Barbara—I say—'

Barbara had passed on again, returning presently. 'You know, Richard, I must keep moving, with papa's eyes there. He is a tall man, very good-looking, very fond of dress and ornaments, especially of diamonds.'

'That's he,' cried Richard, eagerly.

'Mr. Carlyle will contrive that you shall see him,' she continued, stooping down as if to tie her shoe. 'Should it prove to be the same, perhaps nothing can be immediately done towards clearing you, but it will be a great point ascertained. Are you sure you should know him again?'

'Sure! that I should know *him!*' uttered Richard Hare. 'Should I know my own father? should I know you? And you are not engraven on my heart in letters of blood, as he is. How and when am I to see him, Barbara?'

'I can tell you nothing till I have consulted Mr. Carlyle. Be here to-morrow as soon as ever the dusk will permit you: perhaps Mr. Carlyle will contrive to bring him here. If—'

The window was thrown open, and the stentorian voice of Justice Hare was heard from it.

'Barbara, are you wandering about there to take cold? Come in. Come in, I say.'

'Oh, Richard, I am so sorry!' she lingered to whisper. 'But papa is sure to be out to-morrow evening: he would not stay in two evenings running. Good night, dear.'

There must be no delay now, and the next day Barbara, braving comments, appeared once more at the office of Mr. Carlyle. Terribly did the rules of contrary seem in action just then: Mr. Carlyle was not in, and the clerks did not know when to expect him: he was gone out for some hours, they believed.

'Mr. Dill,' urged Barbara, as the old gentleman came to the door to greet her, 'I *must* see him.'

'He will not be in till late in the afternoon, Miss Barbara. I expect him then. Is it anything I can do?'

'No, no,' sighed Barbara.

At that moment Lady Isabel and her little girl passed in the chariot. She saw Barbara at her husband's door; what should she be doing there, unless paying him a visit? A slight, haughty bow to Barbara, a pleasant nod and smile to Mr. Dill, and the carriage bowled on.

It was four o'clock before Barbara could see Mr. Carlyle. She communicated her tidings, that Richard had arrived.

Mr. Carlyle held deceit and all underhanded doings in especial abhorrence: yet he deemed that he was acting right, under the circumstances, in allowing Captain Thorn to be secretly seen by Richard Hare. In haste he arranged his plans. It was the evening of his own dinner engagement at Mrs. Jeafferson's; but that he must give up. Telling Barbara to despatch Richard to his office as soon as he should make his appearance in the grove, and to urge him to come boldly, for that none would know him in his disguise, he wrote a hurried note to Thorn, requesting him also to be at his office at eight o'clock that evening, as he had something to communicate to him. The latter plea was no fiction, for he had received an important communication that morning relative to the business on which Captain Thorn had consulted him, and his own absence from the office had alone prevented his sending for him earlier.

Other matters were calling the attention of Mr. Carlyle, and it was five o'clock ere he departed for East Lynne: he would not have gone so early, but that he must inform his wife of his inability to keep the dinner engagement. Mr. Carlyle was one who never hesitated to sacrifice personal gratification to friendship or to business.

The chariot was at the door, and Lady Isabel was dressed and waiting for him in her dressing-room. 'Did you forget that the Jeaffersons dine at six?' was her greeting.

'No, Isabel; but it was impossible for me to get here before. And I should not have come so soon, but to tell you that I cannot accompany you. You must make my excuses to Mrs. Jeafferson.'

A pause. Strange thoughts were running through Lady Isabel's mind. 'Why so?' she inquired.

'Some business has arisen which I am compelled to attend to this evening. As soon as I have snatched my dinner at home, I must hasten back to the office.'

Was he making this excuse to spend the hours of her absence with Barbara Hare? The idea that it was so took firm possession of her mind, and remained there. Her face expressed a variety of feelings, the most prominent that of resentment. Mr. Carlyle saw it.

'You must not be vexed, Isabel. I assure you it is no fault of mine. It is important private business which cannot be put off, and which I cannot delegate to Dill. I am sorry it should so have happened.'

'You never return to the office in an evening,' she remarked, with pale lips.

'No: because, if anything arises to take us there after hours, Dill officiates. But the business to-night must be done by myself.'

Another pause. Lady Isabel suddenly broke it. 'Shall you join us later in the evening?'

'I believe I shall not be able to do so.'

She drew her light shawl round her shoulders, and swept down the staircase. Mr. Carlyle followed, to place her in the carriage. When he said farewell she never answered, but looked straight out before her with a stony look.

'What time, my lady?' inquired the footman, as she alighted at Mrs. Jeafferson's.

'Early. Half-past nine.'

A little before eight o'clock, Richard Hare, in his smock frock, his slouching hat, and his false whiskers, rang dubiously at the outer door of Mr. Carlyle's office. That gentleman instantly opened it. He was quite alone.

'Come in, Richard,' said he, grasping his hand. 'Did you meet many whom you knew?'

'I never looked whom I met, sir,' was the reply. 'I thought if I looked at people, they might look at me, so I came straight ahead with my eyes before me. How the place is altered! There's a new brick house at the corner where old Morgan's shop used to be.'

'That's the new police station: West Lynne, I assure you, is becoming grand in public buildings. And how have you been, Richard?'

'Ailing and wretched,' answered Richard Hare. 'How can I be otherwise, Mr. Carlyle, with so false an accusation attaching to me; and working like a slave, as I have to do.'

'You may take off that disfiguring hat, Richard. No one is here.'

Richard slowly heaved it from his brows, and his fair face, so like his mother's, was disclosed. But the moment he was uncovered, he turned shrinkingly towards the entrance door. 'If any one should come in, sir!'

'Impossible,' replied Mr. Carlyle. 'The front door is fast, and the office is supposed to be empty at this hour.'

'For, if I should be seen and recognized, it might come to hanging, you know, sir. You are expecting that accursed Thorn here, Barbara told me.'

'Directly,' replied Mr. Carlyle, observing the mode of addressing him 'sir.' It spoke plainly of the scale of society in which Richard must be mixing: that he was with those who said it habitually; that he used it habitually himself. "From your description of the Lieutenant Thorn who destroyed Hallijohn, we believe this Captain Thorn to be the same man,' pursued Mr. Carlyle. 'In person he appears to tally exactly; and I have ascertained that some years ago he was a great deal at Swainson, and got into some sort of scrape. He is in John Herbert's regiment, and he is here with him on a visit.'

'But what an idiot he must be to venture here!' uttered Richard. 'Here, of all places in the world.'

'He counts, no doubt, upon not being known. So far as I can find out, Richard, nobody here knew him, save you and Afy. I shall put you in Mr. Dill's room—you may remember the little window in it—and from thence you can take full view of Thorn, whom I shall keep in the front office. You are sure you would recognize him, at this distance of time?'

'I should know him if it were fifty years to come; I should know him if he were disguised as I am disguised. We cannot,' Richard sank his voice, 'forget a man who has been the object of our frenzied jealousy.'

'What has brought you to West Lynne again, Richard? Any particular object?'

'Chiefly a hankering within me that I could not get rid of,' replied Richard. 'It was not so much to see my mother and Barbara—though I have longed to see them since my illness—but a feeling was within me that I could not rest away from it. So I said I'd risk it again, just for a day.'

'I thought you might possibly want some assistance, as before.'

'I do want that, also,' said Richard. 'Not much. My illness has run me into debt, and if my mother can let me have a little I shall be thankful.'

'I am sure she will,' answered Mr. Carlyle. 'You shall have it from me to-night. What has been the matter with you?'

'The beginning of it was a kick from a horse, sir. That was last winter, and it laid me up for six weeks. Then, in the spring, after I had got well and was at work again, I caught some sort of fever, and down again I was for six weeks. I have not been to stay well since.'

'How is it you have never written, or sent me your address?'

'Because I dare not,' answered Richard, timorously. 'I should always be in fear; not of you, Mr. Carlyle, but of its becoming known in some way or other. The time is getting on, sir: is that Thorn sure to come?'

'He sent me word that he would, in reply to my note. And—there he is!' said Mr. Carlyle, as a ring was heard at the bell. 'Now, Richard, come this way. Bring your hat.'

Richard complied by putting the hat on his head, pulling it so low down that it touched his nose. He felt himself safer in it. Mr. Carlyle showed him into Mr. Dill's room, and then turned the key upon him, and put it in his pocket. Whether this precautionary measure was intended to prevent any possibility of Captain Thorn's finding his way in, or of Richard finding his way out, was best known to himself.

Mr. Carlyle went to the front door, opened it, and admitted Captain Thorn. He brought him into the clerk's office, which was bright with gas, keeping him in conversation for a few minutes standing, and then asking him to be seated: all in full view of the little window.

'I must beg your pardon for being late,' Captain Thorn observed. 'I am half an hour beyond the time you mentioned, but the Herberts had two or three friends at dinner, and I could not get away. I hope, Mr. Carlyle, you have not come to your office to-night purposely for me.'

'Business must be attended to,' somewhat evasively answered Mr. Carlyle: 'I have been out myself nearly all day. We received a communication from London this morning relative to your affair, and I am sorry to say it is anything but satisfactory. They will not wait.'

'But I am not liable, Mr. Carlyle. Not liable in justice.'

'No—if what you tell me be correct. But justice and law are sometimes in opposition, Captain Thorn.'

Captain Thorn sat in perplexity. 'They will not get me arrested here, will they?'

'They would have done it, beyond doubt; but I have caused a letter to be written and despatched to them, which must bring forth an answer before

any violent proceedings are taken. That answer will be here the morning
after to-morrow.'

'And what am I to do then?'

'I think it probable there may be a way then of checkmating them. But I
am not sure, Captain Thorn, that I can give my attention further to this
affair.'

'I hope and trust you will,' was the reply.

'You have not forgotten that I told you, at first, I could not promise to do
so,' rejoined Mr. Carlyle. 'You shall hear from me to-morrow. If I carry it on
for you, I will then appoint an hour for you to be here the following day: if
not—why, I dare say you will find a solicitor as capable of assisting you as I
am.'

'But why will you not? What is the reason?'

'I cannot always give reasons for what I do,' was the response. 'You shall
hear from me to-morrow.'

He rose as he spoke; Captain Thorn also rose. Mr. Carlyle detained him
yet a few moments, and then saw him out of the front door and fastened it.

He returned and released Richard. The latter took off his hat as he advanced into the blaze of light.

'Well, Richard, is it the same man?'

'No, sir. Nor in the least like him.'

Mr. Carlyle felt a strange relief; relief for Captain Thorn's sake. He had
rarely seen one whom he could so little associate with the notion of a murderer as Captain Thorn, and he was a man who exceedingly won his regard.
He could heartily help him out of his dilemma now.

'Excepting that they are both tall, with nearly the same coloured hair,
there is no resemblance whatever between them,' proceeded Richard. 'Their
faces, their figures are as opposite as light is from dark. That other, in spite of
his handsome features, has the expression at times of a demon; but the expression of this one is the best part of his face. Hallijohn's murderer had a
curious look here, sir.'

'Where?' questioned Mr. Carlyle, for Richard had only pointed to his face
generally.

'Well—I cannot say precisely where it lay, whether in the eyebrows or the
eyes: I could not tell when I used to have him before me: but it was in one of
them. Ah, Mr. Carlyle, I thought when Barbara told me Thorn was here, it
was too good news to be true; depend on't he won't venture to West Lynne
again. This man is no more like that other villain than you are like him.'

'Then—as that is set at rest—we had better be going, Richard. You have
to see your mother, and she must be waiting in anxiety. How much money do
you want?'

'Twenty-five pounds would do, but—' Richard stopped in hesitation.

'But what?' asked Mr. Carlyle. 'Speak out Richard.'

'Thirty would be more welcome. Thirty would put me at ease.'

'You shall have thirty,' said Mr. Carlyle, counting over the notes to him. 'Now—will you walk with me to the Grove, or will you walk alone? I mean to see you there in safety.'

Richard thought he would prefer to walk alone; everybody they met might be speaking to Mr. Carlyle. The latter inquired why he chose moonlight nights for his visits.

'It is pleasanter for night travelling. And, had I chosen dark nights, Barbara could not have seen my signal from the trees,' was the answer of Richard.

They went out, and proceeded unmolested to the house of Justice Hare. It was past nine then. 'I am so much obliged to you, Mr. Carlyle,' whispered Richard, as they walked up the path.

'I wish I could help you more effectually, Richrad, and clear up the mystery. Is Barbara on the watch? Yes; the door is slowly opening.'

Richard stole across the hall and into the parlour to his mother. Barbara approached and softly whispered to Mr. Carlyle, standing just outside the portico: her voice trembled with the suspense of what the answer might be.

'Is it the same man? The same Thorn?'

'No. Richard says this man bears no resemblance to the real one.'

'Oh!' uttered Barbara, in her surprise and disappointment. 'Not the same! and for the best part of poor Richard's evening to have been taken up for nothing.'

'Not quite for nothing,' said Mr. Carlyle. 'The question is now set at rest.'

'Set at rest!' repeated Barbara. 'It is left in more uncertainty than ever.'

'Set at rest as regards Captain Thorn. And whilst our suspicions were concentrated upon him, we did not look to other quarters.'

When they entered the sitting-room, Mrs. Hare was crying over Richard, and Richard was crying over her: but she seized the hand of Mr. Carlyle.

'You have been very kind: I don't know whatever we should do without you. And I want to tax your kindness yet further. Has Barbara mentioned it?'

'I could not talk in the hall, mamma: the servants might have overheard.'

'Mr. Hare is not well, and we terribly fear he will be home early in consequence: otherwise we should have been quite safe until ten, for he is gone to the Buck's Head, and they never leave, you know, till that hour has struck. Should he come in and see Richard—the very thought sends me into a shiver—Barbara and I have been discussing it all the evening, and we can only think of one plan. It is, that you will kindly stay in the garden near the gate; and, should he come in, stop him and keep him in conversation. Barbara will be with you, and will run in with the warning, and Richard can go inside the closet in the hall, till Mr. Hare has entered and is safe in this room, and then he can make his escape. Will you do this, Archibald?'

'Certainly I will.'

'I cannot part with him before ten o'clock, unless I am obliged,' she whispered, pressing Mr. Carlyle's hands in her earnest gratitude. 'You don't know what it is, Archibald, to have a lost son home for an hour but once in seven years. At ten o'clock we will part.'

Mr. Carlyle and Barbara began to pace the path, in compliance with the wishes of Mrs. Hare, keeping near the entrance gate. When they were turning the second time, Mr. Carlyle offered her his arm: it was an act of mere politeness. Barbara took it: and there they waited and waited, but the justice did not come.

Punctually to the minute, half after nine, Lady Isabel's carriage arrived at Mrs. Jeafferson's, and she came out immediately, a headache being the plea for her early departure. She had not far to go to reach East Lynne, about two miles: it was a by-road nearly all the way. They could emerge into the open road if they pleased, but it was a trifle further. Suddenly a gentleman approached the carriage as it was bowling along, and waved his hand to the coachman to pull up. In spite of the glowing moonlight, Lady Isabel did not at first recognize him, for he wore a disfiguring fur cap, the ears of which were tied over his ears and cheeks. It was Francis Levison. She put down the window.

'I thought it must be your carriage. How early you are returning! Were you tired of your entertainers?'

'Why, he knew what time my lady was returning,' thought John to himself; 'he asked me. A false sort of chap, that, I've a notion.'

'I came out for a stroll, and have tired myself,' he proceeded. 'Will you take compassion on me and give me a seat home?'

She acquiesced; she could not well do otherwise. The footman sprang from behind, to open the door, and Francis Levison took his place beside Lady Isabel. 'Take the high road,' he put out his head to say to the coachman, and the man touched his hat. Which high road would cause them to pass Mr. Hare's.

'I did not know you,' she began, gathering herself into her own corner. 'What ugly thing is that you have on? It is like a disguise.'

He was taking off the 'ugly thing' as she spoke, and began to twirl it round on his hand. 'Disguise? Oh no: I have no creditors in the immediate neighbourhood of East Lynne.'

False as ever. It *was* worn as a disguise, and he knew it.

'Is Mr. Carlyle at home?' she inquired.

'No.' Then after a pause—'I expect he is more agreeably engaged.'

The tone brought the tingling blood to the cheeks of Lady Isabel. She wished to preserve a dignified silence; and did so for a few moments: but the jealous question broke out.

'Engaged in what manner?'

'As I came by Hare's house just now, I saw two people, a gentleman and a young lady, coupled lovingly together, enjoying a *tête-à-tête* by moonlight. They were your husband and Miss Hare.'

Lady Isabel almost gnashed her teeth: the jealous doubts which had been tormenting her all evening were confirmed. That the man whom she hated— yes, in her blind anger, she hated him then—should so impose upon her, should excuse himself by lies, lies base and false, from accompanying her, on purpose to pass the hours with Barbara Hare! Had she been alone in the carriage, a torrent of passion had probably escaped her.

She leaned back, panting in her emotion, but concealed it from Captain Levison. As they came opposite to Justice Hare's, she deliberately bent forward, and scanned the garden with eager eyes.

There, in the bright moonlight, all too bright and clear, slowly paced, arm in arm, and drawn close to each other, her husband and Barbara. With a choking sob that could no longer be controlled or hidden, Lady Isabel sank back again.

He, that bold bad man, dared to put his arm round her; to draw her to his side; to whisper that *his* love was left her, if another's was withdrawn.

She was most assuredly out of her senses that night, or she never would have listened.

A jealous woman is mad; an outraged woman is doubly mad; and the ill-fated Lady Isabel truly believed that every sacred feeling which ought to exist between man and wife, was betrayed by Mr. Carlyle.

'Be avenged on that false hound, Isabel. He was never worthy of you. Leave your life of misery, and come to happiness.'

In her bitter distress and wrath, she broke into a storm of sobs. Were they caused by passion against her husband, or by these bold and shameless words? Alas! alas! Francis Levison applied himself to soothe her with all the sweet and dangerous sophistry of his crafty nature.

❧ I X ❧

Never to be Redeemed

The minutes flew on. A quarter to ten; ten; a quarter past ten; and still Richard Hare lingered on with his mother, and still Mr. Carlyle and Barbara paced patiently the garden path. At half-past ten Richard came forth, having taken his last farewell. Then came Barbara's tearful farewell, which Mr. Carlyle witnessed; then a hard grasp of that gentleman's hand, and Richard plunged amidst the trees, to depart the way he came.

'Good night, Barbara,' said Mr. Carlyle.

'Will you not come in, and say good night to mamma?'

'Not now; it is late. Tell her how glad I am things have gone off so well.'

He set off at a rapid pace towards his home, and Barbara leaned on the gate to indulge her tears. Not a soul passed to interrupt her, and the justice did not come. What could have become of him? What could the Buck's Head be thinking of, to detain respectable elderly justices from their beds, who ought to go home early and set a good example to the parish? Barbara knew, the next day, that Justice Hare, with a few more gentlemen, had been seduced from the staid old inn to a friend's house, to an entertainment of supper, pipes, and whist, two tables, sixpenny points, and it was between twelve and one ere the party rose from the fascination. So far, well—as it happened.

Barbara knew not how long she lingered at that gate; ten minutes it may have been. Nobody summoned her; Mrs. Hare was indulging her grief indoors, giving no thought to Barbara, and the justice did not make his appearance. Exceedingly surprised was Barbara to hear fast footsteps, and to find that they were Mr. Carlyle's.

'The more haste, the less speed, Barbara,' he called out as he came up. 'I had got half way home, and have had to come back again. When I went into your sitting-room, I left a small parcel, containing a parchment, on the sideboard. Will you get it for me?'

Barbara ran indoors and brought forth the parcel; and Mr. Carlyle, with a brief word of thanks, sped away with it.

She leaned on the gate as before, the ready tears flowing again: her heart was aching for Richard: it was aching for the disappointment the night had brought forth respecting Captain Thorn. Still nobody passed; still the steps of her father were not heard, and Barbara stayed on. But—what was that figure cowering under shade of the hedge at a distance, and seemingly watching her? Barbara strained her eyes, while her heart beat as if it would burst its bounds. Surely, surely, it was her brother! What had he ventured back for?

Richard Hare it was. When fully assured that Barbara was standing there, he knew the justice was still absent, and ventured to advance. He appeared to be in a strange state of emotion, his breath laboured, his whole frame trembling.

'Barbara! Barbara!' he ejaculated, 'I have seen Thorn.'

Barbara thought him demented. 'I know you saw him,' she slowly said; 'but it was not the right Thorn.'

'Not he,' breathed Richard; 'not the gentleman I saw to-night in Carlyle's office. I have seen the fellow himself. Why do you stare so at me, Barbara?'

Barbara was in truth scanning his face keenly. It appeared to her a strange tale that he was telling.

'When I left here, I cut across into Bean-lane, which is more private for me than this road,' proceeded Richard. 'Just as I got to that clump of trees—you know it, Barbara—I saw somebody coming towards me, from a distance. I stepped back behind the trunks of the trees, into the shade of the hedge, for I don't care to be met, though I am disguised. He came along the middle of the lane, going towards West Lynne, and I looked out upon him. I knew him long before he was abreast of me: it was Thorn.'

Barbara made no comment: she was digesting the news.

'Every drop of blood within me began to tingle, and an impulse came upon me to spring upon him and accuse him of the murder of Hallijohn,' went on Richard, in the same excited manner. 'But I restrained it: or, perhaps, my courage failed. One of the reproaches against me, had used to be that I was a physical coward, you know, Barbara,' he added, his tone changing to bitterness. 'In a struggle, Thorn would have had the best of it: he is taller and more powerful than I, and might have battered me to death. A man who can commit one murder, won't hesitate at a second.'

'Richard, do you think you could have been deceived?' she urged. 'You have been talking of Thorn, and your thoughts were, naturally, bearing upon him. Imagination——'

'Be still, Barbara!' he interrupted, in a tone of pain. 'Imagination, indeed! did I not tell you he was stamped here?' touching his breast. 'Do you take me for a child, or an imbecile, that I should fancy I see Thorn in every shadow, or meet people where I do not? He had his hat off as if he had been walking fast and had got hot—he was walking fast, and he carried the hat in one hand, and what looked like a small parcel. With the other hand he was pushing his hair from his brow—in this way, a peculiar way,' added Richard, slightly lifting his own hat, and pushing back his hair. 'By that action alone I should have known him, for he was always doing it in the old days. And there was his white hand, adorned with his diamond ring! Barbara, the diamond glittered in the moonlight.'

Richard's voice and manner were singularly earnest, and a conviction of the truth of his assertion flashed over his sister.

'I saw his face as plainly as I ever saw it, every feature: he is scarcely altered, save for a haggardness in his cheeks now. Barbara, you need not doubt me: I swear it was Thorn.'

She grew excited as he was; now that she believed the news, it was telling upon her: reason left its place, and impulse succeeded: Barbara did not wait to weigh her actions.

'Richard, Mr. Carlyle ought to know this. He has but just gone; we may overtake him if we try.'

Forgetting the strange appearance it would have, at that hour of the night, should she meet any one who knew her, forgetting what the consequences might be, did Justice Hare return and find her absent, Barbara set off with a fleet foot, Richard more stealthily following her, his eyes cast in all directions. Fortunately Barbara wore a bonnet and mantle, which she had put on to pace the garden with Mr. Carlyle; fortunately also, they met no one. She succeeded in reaching Mr. Carlyle before he turned into East Lynne gates.

'Barbara!' he exclaimed, in the extreme of astonishment. 'Barbara!'

'Archibald! Archibald!' she panted, gasping for breath. 'I am not out of my mind; but do come and speak to Richard! He has just seen the real Thorn.'

Mr. Carlyle, amazed and wondering, turned back. They got over the field stile nearly opposite to the gates, drew behind the hedge, and there Richard told his tale. Mr. Carlyle did not appear to doubt it, as Barbara had done: perhaps he could not, in the face of Richard's agitated and intense earnestness.

'I am sure there is no one named Thorn in the neighbourhood, save the gentleman you saw in my office to-night, Richard,' observed Mr. Carlyle, after some deliberation. 'It is very strange.'

'He may be staying here under a feigned name,' replied Richard. 'There can be no mistake that it is Thorn whom I have just met.'

'How was he dressed? As a gentleman?'

'Catch him dressing as anything else,' returned Richard. 'He was in an evening suit of black, with a sort of thin over-coat thrown on, but it was flung back at the shoulders, and I distinctly saw his clothes. A grey alpaca, it looked like. As I have told Barbara, I should have known him by this action of the hand,' imitating it, 'as he pushed his hair off his forehead: it was the delicate white hand of the days gone by, Mr. Carlyle; it was the flashing diamond ring.'

Mr. Carlyle was silent; Barbara also; but the thoughts of both were busy. 'Richard,' observed the former, 'I should advise you to remain a day or two in the neighbourhood, and look out for this man. You may see him again, and may track him home; it is very desirable to find out who he really is, if practicable.'

'But the danger?' urged Richard.

'Your fears magnify that. I am quite certain that nobody would know you in broad daylight, disguised as you are now. So many years have flown since, that people have forgotten to think about you, Richard.'

But Richard could not be persuaded; he was full of fears. He described the man as accurately as he could to Mr. Carlyle and Barbara, and told them *they* must look out. With some trouble Mr. Carlyle got from him an address in London to which he might write, in case anything turned up, and Richard's presence should be necessary. He then once more said farewell, and quitted them, his way lying past East Lynne.

'And now to see you back, Barbara,' said Mr. Carlyle.

'Indeed you shall not do it, late as it is, and tired as you must be. I came here alone: Richard did not keep near me.'

'I cannot help your having come here alone, but you may rely upon it I do not suffer you to go back so. Nonsense, Barbara! Allow you to go along the high road by yourself at eleven o'clock at night! What are you thinking of?'

He gave Barbara his arm, and they pursued their way. 'How late Lady Isabel will think you!' observed Barbara.

'I do not know that Lady Isabel has returned home yet. My being late once in a way is of no consequence.'

Not another word was spoken, save by Barbara. 'Whatever excuse can I make, should papa be come home?' Both were buried in their own reflections. 'Thank you very greatly,' she said as they reached the gate, and Mr. Carlyle finally turned away. Barbara stole in, and found the coast clear: her papa had not arrived.

Lady Isabel was in her dressing-room when Mr. Carlyle entered; she was seated at a table, writing. A few questions as to her evening's visit, which she answered in the briefest manner possible, and then he asked her if she was not going to bed.

'By-and-by. I am not sleepy.'

'I must go at once, Isabel, for I am dead tired.'

'You can go,' was her answer.

He bent down to kiss her, but she dexterously turned her face away. He supposed she felt hurt that he had not gone with her to the party, and placed his hand on her shoulder with a pleasant smile.

'You foolish child to be aggrieved at that! It was no fault of mine, Isabel: I could not help myself. I will talk to you in the morning: I am too tired to-night. I suppose you will not be long.'

Her head was bent over her writing again, and she made no reply. Mr. Carlyle went into the bedroom and shut the door. Some time after, Lady Isabel went softly upstairs to Joyce's room. Joyce, in her first sleep, was suddenly aroused from it. There stood her mistress, a waxlight in her hand. Joyce rubbed her eyes and collected her senses, and finally sat up in bed.

'My lady! Are you ill?'

'Ill? Yes; and wretched,' answered Lady Isabel: and ill she looked, for she was perfectly white. 'Joyce, I want a promise from you. If anything should happen to me, stay at East Lynne with my children.'

Joyce stared in amazement, too astonished to make any reply.

'Joyce, you promised it once before: promise it again. Whatever betide, you will stay with my children when I am gone.'

'I will stay with them. But, oh, my lady, what can be the matter with you? Are you taken suddenly ill?'

'Good-bye, Joyce,' murmured Lady Isabel, gliding from the chamber as softly as she had entered it. And Joyce, after an hour of perplexity, dropped asleep again.

Joyce was not the only one whose rest was disturbed that eventful night. Mr. Carlyle himself awoke, and to his surprise found that his wife had not come to bed. He wondered what the time was, and struck his repeater, a quarter-past three!

Rising, he made his way to the door of his wife's dressing-room. It was in darkness; and so far as he could judge by absence of sound, unoccupied.

'Isabel.'

No reply. Nothing but the echo of his own voice in the silence of the night.

He struck a match and lighted a taper, partially dressed himself, and went out to look for her. He feared she might have been taken ill: or else that she had fallen asleep in one of the rooms. But nowhere could he find her, and, feeling perplexed, he proceeded to his sister's chamber door and knocked.

Miss Carlyle was a light sleeper, and rose up in bed at once. 'Who's that?' called out she.

'It is only I, Cornelia,' said Mr. Carlyle.

'You!' ejaculated Miss Corny, 'what in the name of fortune do you want? You can come in.'

Mr. Carlyle opened the door, and met the keen eyes of his sister, bent on him from the bed. Her head was surmounted by a remarkable nightcap, at least a foot high.

'Is anybody ill?' she demanded.

'I think Isabel must be. I cannot find her.'

'Not find her!' echoed Miss Corny. 'Why, what's the time? Is she not in bed?'

'It is three o'clock. She has not been to bed. I cannot find her in the sitting-rooms; neither is she in the children's room.'

'Then I'll tell you what it is, Archibald; she's gone worrying after Joyce. Perhaps the girl may be in pain to-night.'

Mr. Carlyle was in full retreat towards Joyce's room, at this suggestion, when his sister called to him.

'If anything is amiss with Joyce, you come and tell me, Archibald, for I shall get up and see after her. The girl was my servant before she was your wife's.'

He reached Joyce's room and softly unlatched the door, fully expecting to find a light there, and his wife sitting by the bedside. There was no light, however, save that which came from the taper he held, and he saw no signs of his wife. *Where* was she? Was it probable that Joyce could tell him? He stepped inside the room and called to her.

Joyce started up in a fright, which changed to astonishment when she recognized her master. He inquired whether Lady Isabel had been there, and for a few moments Joyce did not answer. She had been dreaming of Lady Isabel, and could not at first detach the dream from the visit which had probably given rise to it.

'What did you say, sir? Is my lady worse?'

'I ask if she has been here. I cannot find her.'

'Why, yes,' said Joyce, now fully aroused. 'She came here and woke me. That was just before twelve, for I heard the clock strike. She did not stay here a minute, sir.'

'Woke you!' repeated Mr. Carlyle. 'What did she want? what did she come here for?'

Thoughts are quick; imagination is quicker; and Joyce was giving the reins to both. Her mistress's gloomy and ambiguous words were crowding on her brain. Three o'clock! and she had not been in bed, and was not to be found in the house! A nameless horror struggled to Joyce's face, her eyes were dilating with it: she seized and threw on a large flannel gown which lay on a chair by the bed, and forgetful of her ailing foot, forgetful of her master who stood there, out she sprang to the floor. All minor considerations faded to insiginificance beside the terrible dread which had taken possession of her. Clasping the flannel gown tight round her with one hand, she laid the other on the arm of Mr. Carlyle.

'Oh, master! oh, master! she has destroyed herself! I see it all now.'

'Joyce!' sternly interrupted Mr. Carlyle.

'She has destroyed herself, master, as true as that we two are living here!' persisted Joyce, her own face livid with emotion. 'I can understand her words now; I could not before. She came here—and her face was like a corpse as the light fell upon it—saying she had come to get a promise from me to stay with her children when she was gone. I asked whether she was ill, and she answered, "Yes, ill and wretched." Oh, sir, may heaven support you under this dreadful trial!'

Mr. Carlyle felt bewildered; perplexed. Not a syllable did he believe. He was not angry with Joyce, for he thought she had lost her reason.

'It is so, sir, incredible as you may deem my words,' pursued Joyce, wringing her hands. 'My lady has been miserably unhappy: and that has driven her to it.'

'Joyce, are you in your senses or out of them?' demanded Mr. Carlyle, a certain sternness in his tone. 'Your lady miserably unhappy! what do you mean by such an assertion?'

Before Joyce could answer, an addition was received to the company in the person of Miss Carlyle, who appeared in black stockings and a shawl, and the lofty nightcap. Hearing voices in Joyce's room, which was above her own, and full of curiosity, she ascended, not choosing to be shut out from the conference.

'Whatever's up?' cried she. 'Is Lady Isabel found?'

'She is not found, and she never will be found but in her winding-sheet,' returned Joyce, whose lamentable and unusual state of excitement completely overpowered her customary quiet respect and plain good sense. 'And, ma'am, I am glad that you have come up; for what I was about to say to my master I would prefer to say in your presence. When my lady is brought into this house, and laid down before us, dead, what will your feelings be? My master has done his duty by her in love; but you—you have made her life a misery. Yes, ma'am, you have.'

'Highty tighty!' uttered Miss Carlyle, staring at Joyce in consternation. 'What is all this? Where's my lady?'

'She has gone and taken the life that was not hers to take,' sobbed Joyce, 'and I say she has been driven to it. She has not been allowed to indulge a will of her own, poor thing, since she came to East Lynne: in her own house she has been less free than any one of her servants. You have curbed her, ma'am, and snapped at her, and made her feel that she was but a slave to your caprices and temper. All these years she has been crossed and put upon; everything, in short, but beaten—ma'am, you know she has!—and she has borne it all in silence, like a patient angel, never, as I believe, complaining to master: he can say whether she has or not. We all loved her, we all felt for her, and my master's heart would have bled, had he suspected what she had to put up with day after day, and year after year.'

Miss Carlyle's tongue was glued to her mouth. Her brother, confounded at the rapid words, could scarcely gather in their sense.

'What is it that you are saying, Joyce?' he asked, in a low tone. 'I do not understand.'

'I have longed to say it to you many a hundred times, sir: but it is right that you should hear it, now things have come to this dreadful ending. Since the very night Lady Isabel came home here, your wife, she has been taunted with the cost she has brought to East Lynne and to you. If she wanted but the simplest thing, she was forbidden to have it, and told that she was bringing her husband to poverty. For this very dinner party that she went to to-night, she wished for a new dress, and your cruel words, ma'am, forbade her having it. She ordered a new frock for Miss Isabel, and you countermanded it. You have told her that master worked like a dog to support her extravagances: when you know that she never was extravagant: that none were less inclined to go beyond proper limits than she. I have seen her, ma'am, come away from your reproaches with the tears in her eyes, and her hands meekly clasped upon her bosom, as though life was heavy to bear. A gentle-spirited, high-born lady, as she was, could not fail to be driven to desperation; and I know that she has been.'

Mr. Carlyle turned to his sister. 'Can this be true?' he inquired, in a tone of deep agitation.

She did not answer. Whether it was the shade cast by the nightcap or the reflection of the wax taper, her face looked of a green cast: and for the first time probably in Miss Carlyle's life, her words failed.

'May God forgive you, Cornelia!' he murmured, as he went out of the chamber.

He descended to his own. That his wife had laid violent hands upon herself, his reason utterly repudiated: she was one of the least likely to commit so great a sin. He believed that, in her unhappiness, she might have wandered out in the grounds, and was lingering there. By this time the house was aroused, and the servants were astir. Joyce—surely a supernatural strength was given her, for though she had been able to put her foot to the ground, she had not yet walked upon it—crept downstairs, and went into Lady Isabel's dressing-room. Mr. Carlyle was hastily assuming the articles of attire he had not yet put on, to go out and search the grounds, when Joyce limped in, holding out a note. Joyce did not stand on ceremony that night.

'I found this in the dressing-glass drawer, sir. It is my lady's writing.'

He took it in his hand and looked at the address. 'Archibald Carlyle.' Though a calm man, one who had his emotions under his own control, he was no stoic, and his fingers shook as he broke the seal.

'When years go on, and my children ask where their mother is, and why she left them, tell them that you, their father, goaded her to it. If they inquire *what* she is, tell them also, if so you will; but tell them at the same time that you outraged and betrayed her, driving her to the very depth of desperation, ere she quitted them in her despair.'

The handwriting, his wife's, swam before the eyes of Mr. Carlyle. All, save the disgraceful fact that she had *flown*—and a horrible suspicion began to dawn upon him with whom—was totally incomprehensible. How had he outraged her? in what manner had he goaded her to it? The discomforts alluded to by Joyce, as the work of his sister, had evidently no part in this; yet, what had *he* done? He read the letter again, more slowly. No, he could not comprehend it: he had not the clue.

At that moment the voices of the servants in the corridor outside penetrated to his ears: of course they were peering about, and making their own comments, Wilson, with her long tongue, the busiest. They were saying that Captain Levison was not in his room; that his bed had not been slept in.

Joyce sat on the edge of a chair—she could not stand—watching her master with the blanched face: never had she seen him betray agitation so powerful. Not the faintest suspicion of the dreadful truth had yet dawned upon her. He walked to the door, the open note in his hand, then turned, wavered, and stood still—as if he did not know what he was doing. Probably he did not. Then he took out his pocket-book, put the note inside it, and returned it to his pocket, his hands trembling equally with his livid lips.

'You need not mention this,' he said to Joyce, indicating the note. 'It concerns myself alone.'

'Sir, does it say she's dead?'

'She is not dead,' he answered. 'Worse than that,' he added in his heart.

'Why—who is this?' uttered Joyce.

It was little Isabel, stealing in with a frightened face, in her white night-gown. The commotion had aroused her.

'What is the matter?' she asked. 'Where's mamma?'

'Child, you'll catch your death of cold,' said Joyce. 'Go back to bed.'

'But I want mamma.'

'In the morning, dear,' evasively returned Joyce. 'Sir, please, must not Miss Isabel go back to bed?'

Mr. Carlyle had no reply to the question; most likely he never heard its import. But he touched Isabel's shoulder to draw Joyce's attention to the child.

'Joyce—*Miss Lucy*, in future.'

He left the room, and Joyce remained silent from amazement. She heard him go out at the hall door and bang it after him. Isabel—nay, we must say 'Lucy' also—went and stood outside the chamber door: the servants, gathered in a group near, did not observe her. Presently she came running back, and disturbed Joyce from her reverie.

'Joyce, is it true?'

'Is what true, my dear?'

'They are saying that Captain Levison has taken away mamma.'

Joyce fell back in her chair, with a scream. It changed to a long, low moan of anguish.

'What has he taken her for?—to kill her? I thought it was only kidnappers who took people.'

'Child, child, go to bed!'

'Oh, Joyce, I want mamma! When will she come back?'

Joyce hid her face in her hands to conceal its emotion from the motherless child. And just then Miss Carlyle entered on tiptoe and humbly sat down on a low chair, her green face—green that night—in its grief, its remorse, and its horror, looking nearly as dark as her stockings.

She broke out into a subdued wail.

'God be merciful to this dishonoured house!'

Mr. Justice Hare turned into his gate between twelve and one; turned in with a jaunty air: for the justice was in spirits, he having won nine sixpences, and his friend's tap of ale having been unusually good. When he reached his bedroom, he told Mrs. Hare of a chaise and four which had gone tearing past at a furious pace as he was closing the gate, coming from the direction of East Lynne. He wondered where it could be going at that midnight hour, and whom it contained.

☙ X ❧

Charming Results

Nearly a year went by.

Lady Isabel Carlyle had spent it on the Continent—that refuge for such fugitives—now removing about from place to place with her companion, now stationary and alone. Half the time—taking one absence with another—he had been away from her, chiefly in Paris, pursuing his own course and his own pleasure.

How fared it with Lady Isabel? Just as it must be expected to fare, and does fare, when a high-principled gentlewoman falls from her pedestal. Never had she experienced a moment's calm, or peace, or happiness, since the fatal night of quitting her home. She had taken a blind leap in a moment of wild passion; when, instead of the garden of roses it had been her persuader's pleasure to promise her (but which, in truth, she had barely glanced at, for that had not been her moving motive), she had found herself plunged into an abyss of horror, from which there was never more any escape; never more, never more. The very hour of her departure she awoke to what she had done: the guilt, whose aspect had been shunned in the prospective, assumed at once its true, frightful colour, the blackness of darkness; and a lively remorse, a never dying anguish, took possession of her soul for ever. Oh, reader, believe me! Lady—wife—mother! should you ever be tempted to abandon your home, so will you awake! Whatever trials may be the lot of your married life, though they may magnify themselves to your crushed spirit as beyond the endurance of woman to bear, *resolve* to bear them; fall down upon your knees and pray to be enabled to bear them: pray for patience; pray for strength to resist the demon that would urge you so to escape; bear unto death, rather than forfeit your fair name and your good conscience; for be assured that the alternative, if you rush on to it, will be found far worse than death!

Poor thing! poor Lady Isabel! She had sacrificed husband, children, reputation, home, all that makes life of value to woman; she had forfeited her duty to God, had deliberately broken His commandments, for the one poor miserable sake of flying with Francis Levison. But, the instant the step was irrevocable, the instant she had left the barrier behind, repentance set in. Even in the first days of her departure, in the fleeting moments of abandonment, when it may be supposed she might momentarily forget conscience, it was sharply wounding her with its adder stings: and she knew that her whole future existence, whether spent with that man or without him, would be one dark course of gnawing retribution.

It is possible remorse does not come to all erring wives so immediately as it came to Lady Isabel Carlyle—you need not be reminded that we speak of women in the better positions of life. Lady Isabel was endowed with sensitively refined delicacy, with an innate, lively consciousness of right and wrong: a nature, such as hers, is one of the last that may be expected to err; and, but for that most fatal misapprehension regarding her husband, the jealous belief, fanned by Captain Levison, that his love was given to Barbara Hare, and that the two were uniting to deceive her, she would never have forgotten herself. The haunting skeleton of remorse had taken up his lodging within her; a skeleton of living fire, that must prey upon her heartstrings for ever. Every taunt to be cast upon her by the world, every slight that would henceforth be her portion, for she had earned it, must tell but too surely upon her crushed spirit.

Nearly a year went by, save some six or eight weeks; when one morning in July, Lady Isabel made her appearance in the breakfast-room. They were staying now at Grenoble. Taking that town on their way from Switzerland, through Savoy, it had been Captain Levison's pleasure to halt in it. He engaged apartments, furnished, in the vicinity of the Place Grenette; it was a windy old house, full of doors and windows, chimneys and cupboards; and he said he should remain there. Lady Isabel remonstrated; she wished to go farther on, where they might get quicker news from England; but her will now was as nothing. She was looking like the ghost of her former self—talk of her having looked ill when she took that voyage over the water with Mr. Carlyle, you should have seen her now: misery marks the countenance worse than sickness. Her face was white and worn, her hands were thin, her eyes were sunken and surrounded by a black circle; care was digging caves for them. A stranger might have attributed these signs to her state of health: *she* knew better; knew that they were the effects of her wretched mind and heart.

It was very late for breakfast: but why should she rise early, only to drag through another endless day? Languidly she took her seat at the table, just as Captain Levison's servant, a Frenchman, whom he had engaged in Paris, entered the room with two letters.

'Point de gazette, Pierre?' she asked.

'Non, miladi.'

And all the while the sly fox had got the *Times* in his coat pocket! But he was only obeying the orders of his master. It had been Captain Levison's recent pleasure that the newspapers should not be seen by Lady Isabel until he had overlooked them. You will speedily gather his motive.

Pierre departed towards Captain Levison's room, and Lady Isabel took up the letters and examined their superscription with interest. It was known to her that Mr. Carlyle had not lost a moment in seeking a divorce, and the announcement, that it was granted, was now daily expected. She was anxious for it; anxious that Captain Levison should render her the only reparation in his power, before the birth of her child: she little knew that there was not the least intention on his part to make her reparation—any more than he had made it to others who had gone before her. She had become painfully aware of the fact that the man for whom she had sacrificed herself, was bad; but she had not learned all his badness yet.

Captain Levison, unwashed, unshaven, with a dressing-gown loosely flung on, lounged in to breakfast; the decked-out dandies before the world are frequently the greatest slovens in domestic privacy. He wished her good morning in a careless tone of apathy, and she as apathetically answered to it.

'Pierre says there are some letters,' he began. 'What a precious hot day it is!'

'Two,' was her short reply, her tone sullen as his. For, if you think, my good reader, that the flattering words, the ardent expressions which usually attend the beginning of these promising unions, last out a whole ten months, you are in egregious error. Compliments, the very opposite to honey and sweetness, have generally supervened long before. Try it, if you don't believe me.

'Two letters,' she continued, 'and they are both in the same handwriting: your solicitor's, I believe.'

Up went his head at the last word, and he made a snatch at the letters; stalked to the farthest window, opened one, and glanced over its contents.

> 'Sir,—We beg to inform you that the suit, Carlyle *v.* Carlyle, is at an end: the divorce was pronounced without opposition. According to your request, we hasten to forward you the earliest intimation of the fact. 'We are, sir, faithfully yours,
> 'Moss & Grab.
> 'F. Levison, Esq.'

It was over, then. And all claim to the name of Carlyle was declared to have been forfeited by the Lady Isabel for ever. Captain Levison folded up the letter, and placed it securely in an inner pocket.

'Is there any news?' she asked.

'News!'

'Of the divorce, I mean.'

'Tush!' was the response of Captain Levison, as if wishing to imply that the divorce was yet a far-off affair: and he proceeded to open the other letter.

> 'Sir,—After sending off our last, dated to-day, we received tidings of the demise of Sir Peter Levison, your great-uncle. He expired this afternoon in town, where he had come for the benefit of medical advice. We have much pleasure in congratulating you upon your accession to the title and estates: and beg to state that should it not be convenient

to you to visit England at present, we will be happy to transact all
necessary matters for you, on your favouring us with instructions.

                'And we remain, sir, most faithfully yours,

                                        'MOSS & GRAB.

    'Sir Francis Levison, Bart.'

    The outside of this letter was superscribed as the other, 'F. Levison, Es-
quire;' no doubt with a view to its more certain delivery.

    'At last! thank the pigs!' was the gentleman's euphonious expression, as he
tossed the letter open upon the breakfast-table.

    'The divorce is granted!' feverishly uttered Lady Isabel.

    He made no reply, but seated himself to breakfast.

    'May I read the letter? Is it for me to read?'

    'For what else should I have thrown it there?' he said.

    'A few days ago, you put a letter, open, on the table, I thought for me: but
when I took it up you swore at me. Do you remember it, Captain Levison?'

    'You may drop that odious title, Isabel, which has stuck to me all too long.
I own a better now.'

    'What is it, pray?'

    'You can look, and see.'

    Lady Isabel took up the letter and read it. Sir Francis swallowed his coffee,
and rang the table hand-bell—the only bell you generally meet with in
France. Pierre answered it.

    'Put me up a change of things,' said he, in French. 'I start for England in an
hour.'

    'It was very well,' Pierre responded: and departed to do it. Lady Isabel
waited till the man was gone, and then spoke, a faint flush of emotion appearing in her cheeks.

    'You do not mean what you say? You will not leave me yet?'

    'I cannot do otherwise,' he answered. 'There's a mountain of business to
be attended to, now that I am come into power.'

    'Moss and Grab say they will act for you. Had there been a necessity for
your going they would not have offered that.'

    'Ay, they say so—with a nice eye to the feathering of their pockets! Go to
England I must: it is absolutely essential. Besides, I should not choose the old
man's funeral to take place without me.'

    'Then I must accompany you,' she urged.

    'I wish you would not talk nonsense, Isabel. Are you in a state to travel
night and day? Neither would England be agreeable to you at present.'

    She felt the force of the objections: resuming, after a moment's pause.
'Were you to go to England, you might not be back in time.'

    'In time for what?'

'Oh, how can you ask?' she rejoined in a sharp tone of reproach; 'you know too well. In time to make me your wife when the divorce shall appear.'

'I must chance it,' coolly observed Sir Francis.

'Chance it! *chance* the legitimacy of the child? You must assure that, before all things. More terrible to me than all the rest would it be, if—'

'Now, don't put yourself in a fever, Isabel. How many times am I to be compelled to beg that of you? It does no good. Is it my fault if I am called suddenly to England?'

'Have you no pity for your child?' she urged, in agitation. 'Nothing can repair the injury, if you once suffer it to come upon him. He will be a byword amidst men throughout his life.'

'You had better have written to the law lords to urge on the divorce,' he retorted. 'I cannot help the delay.'

'There has been no delay: quite the contrary. But it may be expected hourly now.'

'You are worrying yourself for nothing, Isabel. I shall be back in time.'

He quitted the room as he spoke, and Lady Isabel remained in it the image of despair. Nearly an hour passed, when she remembered the breakfast things, and rang for them to be removed. A maid servant entered to do it, and she thought how ill miladi looked.

'Where was Pierre?' miladi asked.

'Pierre was making himself ready to attend monsieur to England.'

Scarcely had she closed the door upon herself and her tray when Sir Francis Levison appeared, equipped for travelling. 'Good-bye, Isabel,' said he, without further circumlocution or ceremony.

Lady Isabel, excited beyond all self control, slipped the bolt of the door; and, half leaning against it, half kneeling at his feet, held up her hands in supplication.

'Francis, have you any consideration left for me—any in the world?'

'How can you be so absurd, Isabel? Of course I have,' he continued, in a peevish though kind tone, as he took hold of her hands to raise her.

'No, not yet. I will remain here until you say you will wait another day or two. You know that the French Protestant minister is prepared to marry us, the instant news of the divorce shall arrive: if you do care still for me, you will wait.'

'I cannot wait,' he replied, his tone changing to one of determination. 'It is useless to urge it.'

'Say that you will not.'

'Well, then, I will not; if you would prefer to have it: anything to please you. Isabel, you are like a child. I shall be back in time.'

'Do not think I am urging it for my sake,' she panted, growing more agitated with every fleeting moment. 'You know that I am not. I do not care

what becomes of me. No; you shall not go till you hear me! Oh, Francis, by
all I have forfeited for your sake—'

'Get up, Isabel,' he interrupted.

'For the child's sake! for the child's sake. A whole long life before it; never
to hold up its head, of right; the reproach everlastingly upon it that it was
born in sin! Francis! Francis! if you have no pity for me, have pity upon it!'

'I think you are losing your senses, Isabel. There's a month yet, and I
promise you to be back ere it shall have elapsed. Nay, ere half of it shall have
elapsed: a week will accomplish all I want to do in London. Let me pass, you
have my promise, and I will keep it.'

She never moved; only stood where she was, raising her supplicating
hands. He grew impatient, and by some dexterous sleight of hand got the
door open. She seized his arm.

'Not for my sake,' she panted still, her dry lips drawn and livid.

'Nonsense about "not for your sake." It is for your sake that I will keep my
promise. I *must* go. There: good-bye, Isabel, and take care of yourself.'

He broke from her and left the room, and in another minute had left the
house, Pierre attending him. A feeling, amounting to a conviction, rushed
over the unhappy lady, that she had seen him for the last time until it should
be too late.

She was right. It was too late by weeks and months.

✤ X I ✤

Mutual Compliments

December came in. The Alps were covered with snow; Grenoble borrowed
the shade, and looked cold, and white, and sleety, and sloppy; the wide gut-
ters which run through the middle of certain of the streets, were unusually
black, and the people crept along, looking very dismal. Close to the fire, in
the barn of a French bedroom, full of windows, and doors, and draughts,
with its wide hearth, and its wide chimney, into which we could put four or
five of our English ones, shivered Lady Isabel Vane. She wore an invalid cap,
and a thick woollen invalid shawl, and she shook and shivered perpetually;
though she had drawn so close to the wood fire that there was a danger of
her petticoats igniting, and the attendant had frequently to spring up and
interpose between them and the crackling logs. Little did it seem to matter to
Lady Isabel: she sat in one position, her countenance the picture of stony
despair.

So had she sat, so looked, since she began to get better. She had had a long illness, terminating in low fever; but the attendants whispered amongst themselves that miladi would soon get about if she would only rouse herself. She had so far got about as to sit up in the windy chamber; and it seemed to be to her a matter of perfect indifference whether she ever got out of it.

This day she had partaken of her early dinner—such as it was, for appetite failed—and had dozed asleep in the arm-chair, when a noise arose from below, like a carriage driving into the court-yard through the porte-cochère. It instantly aroused her. Had *he* come?

'Who is it?' she asked of the nurse.

'Miladi, it is monsieur: and Pierre is with him. I have begged miladi often and often not to fret, for that monsieur would surely come: and miladi sees I am right.'

A strangely firm expression, speaking of severe resolution, overspread the face of Lady Isabel. It would appear to say that she had not 'fretted' much after him who had now arrived; or, at any rate, that she was not fretting after him now. 'Patience and calmness!' she murmured to herself. 'Oh, may they not desert me, now the time has come!'

'Monsieur looks so well!' proclaimed the maid, who had taken up her station at a window that overlooked the court-yard. 'He has got out of the carriage: he is shaking himself and stamping his feet.'

'You may leave the room, Susanne,' said Lady Isabel.

'But if the baby wakes, miladi?'

'I will ring.'

The girl departed, closing the door, and Lady Isabel sat looking at it, schooling herself into patience. Another moment and it was flung open.

Sir Francis Levison approached to greet her as he came in. She waved him off, begging him, in a subdued, quiet tone, not to draw too near, as any little excitement made her faint now. He took a seat opposite to her, and began pushing the logs together with his boot, as he explained that he really could not get away from town before.

'Why did you come now?' she quietly rejoined.

'Why did I come?' repeated he. 'Are these all the thanks a fellow gets for travelling in this inclement weather? I thought you would at least have been glad to welcome me, Isabel.'

'Sir Francis,' she rejoined, speaking still with almost unnatural calmness, as she continued to do throughout the interview—though the frequent changes in her countenance, and the movement of her hands, when she laid them from time to time on her chest to keep down its beating, told what an effort the struggle cost her—'Sir Francis, I am glad, for one reason, to welcome you: we must come to an understanding one with the other; and, so far, I am pleased that you are here. It was my intention to have communicated with you by letter as soon as I found myself capable of the necessary exertion, but your visit has removed the necessity. I wish to deal with you quite unreservedly, without concealment or deceit: I must request you so to deal with me.'

'What do you mean by "deal"?' he asked, settling the logs to his apparent satisfaction.

'To speak and act. Let there be plain truth between us at this interview, if there never has been before.'

'I don't understand you.'

'Naked truth, unglossed over,' she pursued, bending her eyes determinately upon him. 'It *must* be.'

'With all my heart,' returned Sir Francis. 'It is you who have thrown out the challenge, mind.'

'When you left in July you gave me a sacred promise to come back in time for our marriage: you know what I mean when I say "in time": but—'

'Of course I meant to do so when I gave the promise,' he interrupted. 'But no sooner had I set foot in London than I found myself overwhelmed with business, and away from it I could not get. Even now I can only remain with you a couple of days, for I must hasten back to town.'

'You are breaking faith already,' she said, after hearing him calmly to the end. 'Your words are not words of truth, but of deceit. You did not intend to be back in time for the marriage; or, otherwise, you would have caused it to take place ere you went at all.'

'What fancies you take up!' uttered Francis Levison.

'Some time subsequent to your departure,' she quietly went on, 'one of the maids was setting to rights the clothes in your dressing-closet, and she brought me a letter she found in one of the pockets. I saw, by the date, that it was one of those two which you received on the morning of your departure. It contained the information that the divorce was pronounced.'

She spoke so quietly, so apparently without feeling or passion, that Sir Francis was agreeably astonished. He should have less trouble in throwing off the mask. But he was an ill-tempered man; and, to hear that the letter had been found, to have the falseness of his fine protestations and promises so effectually laid bare, did not improve his temper now. Lady Isabel continued:

'It had been better to have undeceived me then; to have told me that the hopes I was cherishing for the sake of the unborn child, were worse than vain.'

'I did not judge so,' he replied. 'The excited state you then appeared to be in, would have precluded your listening to any sort of reason.'

Her heart beat a little quicker: but she stilled it.

'You deem that it was not in reason I should aspire to be made the wife of Sir Francis Levison?'

He rose and began kicking at the logs; with the heel of his boot this time.

'Well, Isabel—you must be aware that it is an awful sacrifice for a man in my position to marry a divorced woman.'

The hectic flushed into her thin cheeks, but her voice sounded calm as before.

'When I expected, or wished, for the "sacrifice," it was not for my own sake: I told you so then. But it was not made: and the child's inheritance is that of sin and shame. There he lies.'

Sir Francis half turned to where she pointed, and saw an infant's cradle by the side of the bed. He did not take the trouble to go to look at it.

'I am the representative now of an ancient and respected baronetcy,' he resumed, in a tone as of apology for his previously heartless words, 'and to make you my wife would so offend all my family, that—'

'Stay,' interrupted Lady Isabel; 'you need not trouble yourself to find needless excuses. Had you taken this journey for the purpose of making me your wife, were you to propose to do so this day, and bring a clergyman into the room to perform the ceremony, it would be futile. The injury to the child can never be repaired: and, for myself, I cannot imagine any fate in life worse than the being compelled to pass it with you.'

'If you have taken this aversion to me it cannot be helped,' he coolly said; inwardly congratulating himself at being spared the trouble he had anticipated. 'You made commotion enough once, about my making you "reparation."'

She shook her head. 'All the reparation in your power to make, all the reparation that the whole world can invent, could not undo my sin. It, and its effects, must lie upon me for ever.'

'Oh—sin!' was the derisive exclamation. 'You ladies should think of that beforehand.'

'Yes,' she sadly answered. 'May Heaven help all to do so, who may be tempted as I was.'

'If you mean that as a reproach to me, it's rather out of place,' chafed Sir Francis, whose fits of ill temper were under no control, and who never, when in them, cared what he said to outrage the feelings of another. 'The temptation to sin, as you call it, lay not in my persuasions, half so much as in your jealous anger towards your husband.'

'Quite true,' was her reply.

'And I believe you were on the wrong scent, Isabel—if it will be any satisfaction to you to hear it. Since we are mutually on this complimentary discourse, it is of no consequence to smooth over facts.'

'I do not understand what you would imply,' she said, drawing her shawl round her with a fresh shiver. 'How "on the wrong scent"?'

'With regard to your husband and that Hare girl. You were blindly, outrageously jealous of him.'

'Go on.'

'And I say I think you were on the wrong scent. I do not believe Carlyle ever thought of the girl—in that way.'

'What do you mean?' she gasped.

'They had a secret between them. Not of love. A secret of business: and those interviews they had together, her dancing attendance upon him perpetually, related to that; and to that alone.'

Her face was more flushed than it had been throughout the interview. He spoke quietly now, quite in an equable tone of reasoning: it was his way when his ill temper was upon him; and the calmer he spoke, the more cutting were his words. He *need* not have told her this.

'What was the secret?' she inquired in a low tone.

'Nay, I can't explain all; they did not take me into their confidence. They did not even take you: better, perhaps, that they had, though, as things have turned out—or seem to be turning. There's some disreputable secret attaching to the Hare family, and Carlyle was acting in it for Mrs. Hare. She could not seek out Carlyle herself, so she sent the young lady. That's all I knew.'

'How did you know it?'

'I had reason to think so.'

'What reason? I must request you to tell me.'

'I overheard scraps of their conversation now and then in those meetings, and so gathered my conclusions.'

'You told a different tale to me, Sir Francis,' was her remark, as she lifted her indignant eyes towards him.

Sir Francis laughed. 'All stratagems are fair in love and war.'

She dared not immediately trust herself to reply, and a silence ensued. Sir Francis broke it, pointing his left thumb over his shoulder in the direction of the cradle.

'What have you named that young article there?'

'The name which ought to have been his by inheritance: "Francis Levison,"' was her icy answer.

'Let's see—how old is he now?'

'He was born the last day of August.'

Sir Francis threw up his arms and stretched himself, as if a fit of idleness had overtaken him; then advanced to the cradle and pulled down the clothes.

'Who is he like, Isabel? My handsome self?'

'Were he like you—in spirit—I would pray that he might die, ere he could speak or think,' she burst forth; and then, remembering the resolution she had marked out for herself, subsided outwardly into calmness again.

'What else?' retorted Sir Francis. 'You know my disposition pretty well by this time, Isabel, and may be sure that if you deal out small change to me, you will get it back again with interest.'

She made no reply. Sir Francis put the clothes back over the sleeping child, returned to the fire and stood a few moments with his back to it.

'Is my room prepared for me, do you know?' he presently asked.

'No, it is not,' she quietly rejoined. 'These apartments are mine now: they have been transferred into my name, and they can never again afford you accommodation. Will you be so obliging—I am not strong—as to hand me that writing-case?'

Sir Francis walked to the table she indicated, which was at the far end of the great barn of a room; and, taking the writing-case from it, gave it to her.

She reached her keys from the stand at her elbow, unlocked the case, and took from it some bank-notes.

'I received these from you a month ago,' she said. 'They came by post.'

'And you never had the grace to acknowledge them,' he returned, in a sort of mock-reproachful tone.

'Forty pounds. That was the amount, was it?'

'I believe so.'

'Allow me to return them to you. Count them.'

'Return them to me, why?' inquired Sir Francis in amazement.

'I have no longer anything whatever to do with you, in any way. Do not make my arm ache, holding out the notes to you so long! Take them!'

Sir Francis took the notes from her hand and placed them on the stand near to her.

'If it be your wish that all relations should end between us, why, let it be so,' he said. 'I must confess I think it may be the wisest course, as things have come to this pass, for the cat-and-dog life, which would seemingly be ours, is not agreeable. Remember, that it is your doing; not mine. But you cannot think I am going to see you starve, Isabel. A sum—we will fix upon its amount amicably—shall be placed to your credit half yearly, and—'

'I beg of you to cease!' she passionately interrupted. 'What do you take me for?'

'Take you for! Why, and how can you live? You have no fortune; you must receive assistance from some one.'

'I will not receive it from you. If the whole world denied me, and I could find no help from strangers, or means of earning my own bread, and it was necessary that I should still exist, I would apply to my husband for means, rather than to you. This ought to convince you that the topic may cease.'

'Your husband?' sarcastically rejoined Sir Francis. 'Generous man!'

A flush, deep and painful, dyed her cheeks. 'I should have said my late husband. You need not have reminded me of the mistake.'

'If you will accept nothing for yourself, you must for the child. He, at any rate, falls to my share. I shall give you a few hundreds a year with him.'

She beat her hands before her, as if beating off the man and his words.

'Not a farthing, now or ever: were you to attempt to send money for him, I would throw it into the nearest river. *Whom* do you take me for?—*what* do you take me for?' she repeated, rising in her bitter mortification; 'if you have put me beyond the pale of the world, I am still Lord Mount Severn's daughter.'

'You did as much towards putting yourself beyond its pale, as—'

'Don't I know it? Have I not said so?' she sharply interrupted. And then she sat, striving to calm herself, clasping together her shaking hands.

'Well, if you will persist in this perverse resolution, I cannot mend it,' resumed Sir Francis. 'In a little time you may probably wish to recall it: in which case, a line, addressed to me at my bankers, will—'

Lady Isabel drew herself up. 'Put away these notes, if you please,' she interrupted, not allowing him to finish his sentence.

He took out his pocket-book, and placed the bank-notes within it.

'Your clothes—those you left here when you went to England—you will have the goodness to order Pierre to take away this afternoon. And now, Sir Francis, I believe that is all: we will part.'

'To remain mortal enemies from henceforth?' he rejoined. 'Is that to be it?'

'To be strangers,' she replied, correcting him.

'I wish you a good day.'

'So! you will not even shake hands with me, Isabel!'

'I would prefer not.'

And thus they parted. Sir Francis left the room, but not immediately the house. He went into a distant apartment, and, calling the servants before him—there were but two—gave them each a year's wages in advance. 'That they might not have to trouble miladi for money,' he said to them. Then he paid a visit to the landlord, and handed him likewise a year's rent in advance, making the same remark. After that, he ordered dinner at an hotel, and the same night he and Pierre departed on their journey home again, Sir Francis thanking his lucky star that he had so easily got rid of a vexatious annoyance.

And Lady Isabel? She passed her evening alone, sitting in the same place, close to the fire and the sparks. The attendant remonstrated that miladi was remaining up too late for her strength; but miladi ordered her and her remonstrance into an adjoining room.

Never had her remorseful repentance been more keenly vivid to her than it was that evening; never had her position, present and future, loomed out in blacker colours. The facts of her hideous case stood before her, naked and bare. She had wilfully abandoned her husband, her children, her home; she had cast away her good name and her position; and she had deliberately offended God. What had she gained in return? What was she? A poor outcast; one of those whom men pity, and whom women shrink from; a miserable, friendless creature, who had henceforth to earn the bread she, and the other life dependent on her, must eat, the clothes they must wear, the roof that must cover them, the fuel they must burn. She had a few valuable jewels, her mother's or her father's gifts, which she had brought away from East Lynne: she had brought no others, nothing given to her by Mr. Carlyle: and these she now intended to dispose of, and live upon until they were gone. The proceeds, with strict economy, might last her some twelve or eighteen months she calculated: after that she must find out some means of supply for the future. Put the child out to nurse, conceal her name, and go out as governess in a French or German family, was one of her visions in prospective.

A confused idea of revenge had been in her mind, urging her on to desperation, the night she quitted her home; of revenge on Mr. Carlyle for his supposed conduct to her. But what revenge had the step really brought to her heart? As her eyes opened to her folly and to the true character of Francis Levison, so in proportion did they close to the fault by which her husband had offended her. She saw it in fainter colours; she began to suspect—nay, she knew—that her own excited feelings had magnified it in length, and breadth, and height—had made a molehill into a mountain; and, long before the scandal of her act had died away in the mouths of men, and Mr. Carlyle had legally put her from him, she had repented of the false step for her husband's sake, and longed—though it could never be—to be back again, his wife. She remembered his noble qualities; doubly noble did they appear to her, now that her interest in them must cease; she remembered how happy they had been together, save for her own self-torment touching Barbara Hare; and, worse than all, her esteem, her admiration, her affection for him, had returned to her fourfold. We never know the full value of a thing until we lose it. Health, prosperity, happiness, a peaceful conscience; what think we of these blessings while they are ours? But, when we lose them! why, we look back in surprise at our ungrateful apathy. A friend may be very dear; but we don't know how dear until he is gone: let him go for ever, and the sorrow is almost greater than we can bear. *She* had lost Mr. Carlyle, and by her own act she had thrown him from her; and now she must make the best of her work, spending her whole future life probably in one long yearning for him and for her children. The hint thrown out by Sir Francis that afternoon, that her suspicions had been mistaken, that her jealousy had had no foundation, did not tend to mitigate her repentance. Whether he was right or wrong in his opinion, she did not know; but she dwelt upon it much: it was possible Sir Francis had merely said it to provoke her, for she knew his temper, and that he would be capable of it; but, if right, what an utterly blind fool she had been!

Her recent and depressing illness, the conviction of Sir Francis Levison's complete worthlessness, the terrible position in which she found herself, had brought to Lady Isabel *reflection*. Not the reflection, so called, that may come to us who yet live in and for the world, but that which must, almost of necessity, attend one whose part in the world is over, who has no interest left between this and the next. A conviction of her sin ever oppressed her; not only of the one act of it, patent to the scandalmongers, but of the long sinful life she had led from childhood; sinful, insomuch as that it had been carelessly indifferent. When thoughts of the future life and the necessity of preparing for it, had occasionally come over her—there are odd moments when they come over even the worst of us—she had been content to leave it to an indefinite future; possibly to a deathbed repentance. But now the truth had begun to dawn upon her, and was growing more clear day by day.

She leaned her aching head this night and dwelt upon these thoughts. She stretched out her wasted hand for a book, which she had rarely used to look into, save at stated times and periods, and more as a forced duty than with any other feeling. Opening it at a certain chapter, she read some verses at its commencement; she had read them often lately; for she had begun to hope that the same merciful tidings might be vouchsafed to her troubled spirit: 'Neither do I condemn thee: go, and sin no more.'

There was much to be blotted out; a whole life of apathy and errors and sinfulness. Her future days, spent in repentance, could they atone for the past? She hunted out some other words, though she did not know in what part they might be: 'If any man will come after me, let him take up his cross daily, and follow me.' What a cross was hers to take up! But she must do it; she would do it, by God's blessing—ah! had she got so far as to ask *that*? She would take it up from henceforth daily and hourly, and bear it as she best might: she had fully earned all its weight and its sharp pain, and must not shrink from her burden. That night, for the first time, a momentary vision floated before her mind's eye, a far off, far off, indistinct vision of the shame and remorse and sorrow of her breaking heart giving place to something like peace.

Susanne was called at last. Susanne was sleepy and cross. Miladi surely could not know that the clock of Notre-Dame had gone midnight: and— well! if there wasn't miladi's arrowroot cold as ice and good for nothing! Miladi wanted to go into her grave, that was a fact.

Miladi replied that she only wanted at present to go into her bed, if Susanne would undress her. Susanne applied herself to the task, indulging in sundry scraps of gossip the while: Susanne and her fellow-servant having had their curiosity uncommonly whetted that day.

A very miserable affair it must be, that monsieur should have had to go back as soon as he came! All those many miles, over those cold wretched roads, behind a shrieking and dangerous steam-engine, and across that abominable sea! She, once upon a time, when she was living with a family in Paris, had had leave to go down by one of those Sunday pleasure excursions to Dieppe, and she was asked to go upon the sea when she got there, and the wicked Fates put it into her poor ignorant heart to say Yes. Ah, dame! she should never forget it! it spoiled still the best supper ever put before her, when she thought of it. Let it be fromage de cochon and a glass of vin de

Bordeaux, or any other choice luxuries miladi might please to picture, not a bit of appetite had she, if those dreadful three hours on the pitching sea rose up in her mind: and she could hear yet her own groans, and see the state of her lovely green robe when she got back to land; and, oh! the trimmings in her cap! And monsieur had undergone all that, with the travelling besides, only to stop an hour and to go again. Pauline said he must have had bad news, to call him home, at the last post town, and would no doubt soon be here again. When would miladi be expecting him?

Miladi replied by desiring her not to talk so fast, and Susanne shrugged her shoulders in an ecstasy of disappointment. She had boasted to Pauline that *she* should learn all, for certain: though Pauline, entombed in the lower regions amidst her casseroles and marmites, could not of course expect to be enlightened, unless at second hand.

When Lady Isabel lay down to rest, she sank into somewhat calmer sleep than she had known of late; also into a dream. She thought she was back at East Lynne—not *back*, in one sense, but that she seemed never to have gone away from it—walking in the flower garden with Mr. Carlyle, while the three children played on the lawn. Her arm was within her husband's, and he was relating something to her: what the news was she could not remember afterwards, excepting that it was connected with the office and old Mr. Dill, and that Mr. Carlyle laughed when he told it. They appeared to be interrupted by the crying of Archibald: and, in turning to the lawn to ask what was the matter, she awoke. Alas! it was the actual crying of her own child which awoke her; this last child; the ill-fated little being in the cradle beside her. But, for a single instant, she forgot recent events and doings; she believed she was indeed in her happy home at East Lynne, a proud mother, an honoured wife. As recollection flashed across her with its piercing strings, she gave vent to a sharp cry of agony, of unavailing despair.

✌ X I I ✌

Alone for Evermore

A surprise awaited Lady Isabel Vane. It was on a windy day in the following March that a traveller arrived at Grenoble, and inquired his way, of a porter, to the best hotel in the place, his French being such that only an Englishman can produce.

'Hotel? let's see,' returned the man, politely, but with native indifference, 'there are two good hotels nearly contiguous to each other, and monsieur will find himself comfortable at either. There is the Trois Dauphins; and there is the Ambassadeurs.'

'Monsieur' chose, haphazard, the Hôtel des Ambassadeurs, and was conducted to it. Shortly after his arrival there, he inquired his road to the Place Grenette; a guide was offered, but he preferred to go alone. The place was found, and he thence turned to the apartments of Lady Isabel Vane.

Lady Isabel was sitting where you saw her the previous December, in the precise spot, courting the warmth of the fire, and—it seemed—courting the sparks also, for they appeared as fond of her as formerly: the marvel was, how she had escaped combustion. You might think but a night had passed when you looked at the room; for it wore precisely the same aspect now as then; everything was the same, even to the child's cradle in the remote corner, partially hidden by the bed-curtains, and the sleeping child in it. Lady Isabel's progress towards recovery had been lingering: as if frequently the case when mind and body are both diseased. She was sitting when Susanne entered the room, and said that a 'Monsieur Anglais' had arrived in the town to see her, and was waiting below, in the salon.

Lady Isabel was startled. An English gentleman—to see *her!*

'English for certain,' was Susanne's answer, for she had difficulty to comprehend his French.

Who could be desirous to see her? one out of the world, and forgotten! 'Susanne,' she suddenly cried aloud, a thought striking her, 'it is never Sir Fran—it is not monsieur?'

'Not in the least like monsieur,' complacently answered Susanne. 'It was a tall, brave English gentleman, proud and noble, looking like a prince.'

Every pulse within Lady Isabel's body throbbed rebelliously: her heart bounded till it was like to burst her side, and she turned sick with excitement. 'Tall, brave, noble!' could that description apply to any but Mr. Carlyle? Strange that so unnatural an idea should have occurred to her: it could not have done so in a calmer moment. She rose, tottered across the chamber, and prepared to descend. Susanne's tongue was let loose at the proceeding.

'Was miladi out of her senses? To attempt going downstairs would be a pretty ending, for she'd surely fall by the way. Miladi knew that the bottom step was of lead, and that no head could pitch down upon that, without ever being a head any more, except in the hospitals. Let miladi sit still in her place and she'd bring the monsieur up. What did it signify? He was not a young petit-maître, he was fifty, if he was a day; his hair already turned to a fine grey.'

This set the question, touching Mr. Carlyle, at rest, and her heart stilled again. The next moment she was inwardly laughing in bitter mockery at her insensate folly. Mr.Carlyle come to see her. *Her!* Francis Levison might be sending over some man of business, regarding the money question, was her next thought; if so, she should certainly not see him.

'Go down to the gentleman and ask his name, Susanne. Ask also from whence he comes.'

Susanne disappeared, and returned, and the gentleman behind her. Whether she had invited him, or whether he had chosen to come uninvited, there he was. Lady Isabel caught a glimpse, and flung her hands over her burning cheeks of shame. It was Lord Mount Severn.

'How did you find out where I was?' she gasped, when some painful words had been uttered on both sides.

'I went to Sir Francis Levison and demanded your address. Certain recent events implied that he and you must have parted, and I therefore deemed it time to inquire what he had done with you.'

'Since last July,' she interrupted, lifting her wan face, now colourless again. 'Do not think worse of me than I am. He was here in December for an hour's recriminating interview, and we then parted for life.'

'What have you heard of him lately?'

'Not anything. I never know what is passing in the world at home; I have no newspaper, no correspondence; and he would scarcely be so bold as to write to me again.'

'I shall not shock you, then, by some tidings I bring you regarding him,' returned Lord Mount Severn.

'The greatest shock to me would be to hear that I should ever again be subjected to see him,' she answered.

'He is married.'

'Heaven have pity on his poor wife!' was all the comment of Lady Isabel.

'He has married Alice Challoner.'

She lifted her head then, in simple surprise. 'Alice? Not Blanche?'

'The story runs that he has played Blanche very false. That he had been with her much, leading on her expectations; and then he suddenly proposed for her young sister. I know nothing of the details myself: it is not likely: and I had heard nothing, until one evening at the club I saw the announcement of the marriage for the following day at Saint George's. I was at the church the next morning before he was.'

'Not to stop it! not to intercept the marriage!' breathlessly uttered Lady Isabel.

'Certainly not. I had no power to attempt anything of the sort. I went to demand an answer to my question—what he had done with you, and where you were? He gave me this address, but said he knew nothing of your movements since December.'

There was a long silence. The earl appeared to be alternately ruminating and taking a survey of the room. Isabel sat with her head hanging down.

'Why did you seek me out?' she presently broke forth. 'I am not worth it. I have brought enough disgrace upon your name.'

'And upon your husband's, and upon your children's,' he rejoined in his most severe manner, for it was not the nature of the Earl of Mount Severn to gloss over guilt. 'Nevertheless, it is incumbent upon me, as your nearest blood relative, to see after you, now that you are alone again, and to take care—so far as I can—that you do not lapse lower.'

He might have spared her that stab. But she scarcely understood him. She looked at him, wondering whether she did understand.

'You have not a shilling in the world,' he resumed. 'How do you purpose to live?'

'I have some money yet. When—'

'*His* money?' sharply and haughtily interposed the earl.

'No,' she indignantly replied. 'I am selling my trinkets. Before they are all gone, I shall try to earn a livelihood in some way: by teaching probably.'

'Trinkets!' repeated Lord Mount Severn. 'Mr. Carlyle told me that you carried nothing away with you from East Lynne.'

'Nothing that he had given me. These were mine before I married. You have seen Mr. Carlyle then?' she faltered.

'Seen him!' echoed the indignant earl. 'When such a blow was dealt him by a member of my family, could I do less than hasten to East Lynne to tender my sympathies? I went with another object, also—to try to discover what could have been the moving springs of your conduct: for I protest when the black tidings reached me, I believed that you must have gone mad. You were one of the last whom I should have feared to trust. But I learned nothing, and Carlyle was ignorant as I. How could you strike him such a blow?'

Lower and lower dropped her head, brighter shone the shame on her hectic cheek. An awful blow to Mr. Carlyle it must indeed have been: she was feeling it in all its bitter intensity. Lord Mount Severn read her repentant looks.

'Isabel,' he said, in a tone which had lost something of its harshness—and it was the first time he had called her by her Christian name, 'I see that you are reaping the fruits. Tell me how it happened. What demon prompted you to sell yourself to that bad man?'

'He is a bad man,' she exclaimed. 'A base, heartless, bad man.'

'I warned you at the commencement of your married life, to avoid him; to shun all association with him; not to admit him to your house.'

'His coming to East Lynne was not my doing,' she whispered. 'Mr. Carlyle invited him.'

'I know he did. Invited him in his unsuspicious confidence, believing his wife to *be* his wife, a trustworthy woman of honour,' was the severe remark.

She did not reply; she could not gainsay it: she only sat with her meek face of shame, and her eyelids drooping.

'If ever a woman had a good husband, in every sense of the word, you had, in Carlyle: if ever man loved his wife, he loved you. *How* could you so requite him?'

She rolled, in a confused manner, the corners of her shawl over her unconscious fingers.

'I read the note you left for your husband. He showed it me; the only one, I believe, to whom he did show it. It was to him entirely inexplicable; it was so to me. A notion had been suggested to him, after your departure, that his sister had somewhat marred your peace at East Lynne; and he blamed you much—if it were so—for not giving him your full confidence on the point, that he might have set matters on the right footing. But it was impossible (and there was the evidence in the note besides) that the presence of Miss Carlyle at East Lynne could be any excuse for your disgracing us all and ruining yourself.'

'Do not let us speak of these things,' said Lady Isabel, faintly. 'It cannot redeem the past.'

'But I must speak of them; I am come to speak of them,' persisted the earl: 'I could not do so whilst that man was here. When these inexplicable events take place in the career of a woman, it is a father's duty to look into motives and causes and actions; although the events in themselves may be, as in this case, irreparable. Your father is gone, but I stand in his place; there is no one else to stand in it.'

Her tears began to fall. And she let them fall—in silence. The earl resumed.

'But for that extraordinary letter, I should have supposed you had been solely actuated by a mad infatuation for the cur, Levison: its tenor gave the affair a different aspect. To what did you allude when you asserted that your husband had driven you to it?'

'He knew,' she answered, scarcely above her breath.

'He did not know,' sternly replied the earl. 'A more truthful, honourable man than Carlyle does not exist on the face of the earth. When he told me then, in his agony of grief, that he was unable to form even a suspicion of your meaning, I could have staked my earldom on his veracity. I would stake it still.'

'I believed,' she began, in a low, nervous voice, for she knew that there was no evading the questions of Lord Mount Severn, when he was resolved to have an answer, and, indeed, she was too weak, both in body and spirit, to resist—'I believed that his love was no longer mine; and that he had deserted me for another.'

The earl stared at her. 'What can you mean by "deserted"? He was with you.'

'There is a desertion of the heart,' was her murmured answer.

'Desertion of a fiddlestick!' retorted his lordship. 'The interpretation we gave to the note, I and Carlyle, was that you had been actuated by motives of jealousy; had penned it in a jealous mood. I put the question to Carlyle—as between man and man—do you listen, Isabel?—whether he had given you cause; and he answered me as with God over us. He had never given you cause: he had been faithful to you in thought, word, and deed: he had never, so far as he could call to mind, even looked upon another woman with covetous feelings, since the hour that he made you his wife: his whole thoughts had been of you, and of you alone. It is more than many a husband can say,' significantly coughed Lord Mount Severn.

Her pulses were beating wildly. A powerful conviction, that the words were true; that her own blind jealousy had been utterly mistaken and unfounded, was forcing its way to her brain.

'After that, I could only set your letter down as a subterfuge,' resumed the earl: 'a false, barefaced plea, put forth to conceal your real motive: and I told Carlyle so. I inquired how it was he had never detected any secret understanding between you and that—that beast; located, as the fellow was, in the house. He replied, that no such suspicion had ever occurred to him. He placed the most implicit confidence in you, and would have trusted you with the man round the world; or with any one else.'

She entwined her hands one within the other, pressing them to pain. It could not deaden the pain at her heart.

'Carlyle told me he had been unusually occupied during the stay of that man. Besides his customary office work, his time was taken up with some secret business for a family in the neighbourhood, and he had repeatedly to see them after office hours. Very old acquaintants of his, he said, relatives of the Carlyle family, and he was as anxious about the secret as they were. This, I observed to him, may have rendered him unobservant to what was passing at home. He told me, I remember, that on the evening of the—the catastrophe, he ought to have gone with you to a dinner-party, but most important circumstances arose, in connection with the affair, which obliged him to meet two gentlemen at his office, and to receive them in secret, unknown to his clerks.'

'Did he—mention the name of the family?' inquired Lady Isabel, with white lips.

'Yes, he did. I forget it, though. Rabbit? Rabbit? some such name as that.'

'Was it Hare?'

'That was it. Hare. He said you appeared vexed that he did not accompany you to the dinner; perceiving this he intended to go in afterwards, but was prevented. When the interview was over in his office, he was again detained in Mrs. Hare's house; and by business as impossible to avoid as the other.'

'Important business!' she echoed, giving way for a moment to the bitterness of former feelings. 'He was promenading in their garden by moonlight with Barbara—Miss Hare. I saw them as my carriage passed.'

'And you were jealous!' exclaimed Lord Mount Severn, with mocking reproach, as he detected her mood. 'Listen!' he whispered, bending his head towards her. 'Whilst you thought, as your present tone would seem to intimate, that they were pacing there to enjoy each other's society, know that they—Carlyle, at any rate—was pacing the walk to keep guard. There was one within that house—for a short interview with his poor mother—one who lives in danger of the scaffold; to which his own father would be the first to deliver him up. They were keeping the path against that father, Carlyle and the young lady. Of all the nights in the previous seven years, that one only saw the unhappy son at home, for a half-hour's meeting with his mother and sister. Carlyle, in the grief and excitement caused by your conduct, confided so much to me, when mentioning what kept him from the dinner-party.'

Her face had become crimson; crimson at her past lamentable folly. And there was no redemption!

'But he was always with Barbara Hare!' she murmured, by way of some faint excuse.

'She had to see him upon this affair: her mother could not, for it was obliged to be kept from the father. And so you construed business interviews into assignations!' continued Lord Mount Severn with cutting derision. 'I had given you credit for better sense. But was this enough to hurl you on to the step you took? Surely not! You must have yielded to the persuasions of that wicked man.'

'It is all over now,' she wailed.

'Carlyle was true and faithful to you, and to you alone. Few women have the chance of happiness in their married life, in the degree that you had. He is an upright and good man; one of nature's gentlemen: one that England may be proud of, as having grown upon her soil. The more I see of him the greater becomes my admiration of him, and of his thorough honour. Do you know what he did in the matter of the damages?'

She shook her head.

'He did not wish to proceed for damages; or, only for the trifling sum demanded by law; but the jury, feeling for his wrongs, gave unprecedently heavy ones. Since the fellow came into his baronetcy, they have been paid: Carlyle immediately handed them over to the county hospital. He holds the apparently obsolete opinion, that money cannot wipe out a wife's dishonour.'

'Let us close these topics,' implored the poor invalid. 'I acted wickedly and madly; and I have the consequence to bear for ever. More I cannot say.'

'Where do you intend to fix your future residence?' inquired the earl.

'I am unable to tell. I shall leave this town as soon as I am well enough.'

'Ay. It cannot be pleasant for you to remain under the eyes of its inhabitants. You were here with him, were you not?'

'They think I am his wife,' she murmured. 'The servants think it.'

'That's well; so far. How many servants have you?'

'Two. I am not strong enough yet to do much myself, so am obliged to keep two,' she continued as if in apology for the extravagance, under her reduced circumstances. 'As soon as ever the baby can walk, I shall manage to do with one.'

The earl looked confounded. 'The baby!' he uttered, in a tone of astonishment and grief painful to her to hear. 'Isabel! is there a child?'

Not less painful was her own emotion, as she hid her face. Lord Mount Severn rose, and paced the room with striding steps.

'I did not know it! I did not know it! Wicked, heartless villain! He ought to have married you before its birth. Was the divorce out previously?' he added, stopping short in his strides to ask it.

'Yes.'

'Coward! sneak! May good men shun him from henceforth! may his Queen refuse to receive him! You, an earl's daughter! Oh, Isabel! How utterly you have lost yourself!'

Lady Isabel started from her chair, in a burst of hysterical sobs, her hands extended beseechingly towards the earl. 'Spare me! spare me! You have been rending my heart ever since you came; indeed I am too weak to bear it.'

The earl, in truth, had been betrayed into showing more of his sentiments than he intended. He recalled his recollection.

'Well, well, sit down again, Isabel,' he said, putting her into her chair. 'We will go to the point I chiefly came here to settle. What sum will it take you to live upon? Quietly: as of course you would now wish to live; but comfortably.'

'I will not accept anything,' she replied. 'I will get my own living;' and the earl's irascibility again rose at the speech. He spoke in a sharp tone:

'Absurd, Isabel! do not add romantic folly to your other mistakes. Get your own living, indeed! As much as is necessary for you to live upon, I shall supply. No remonstrance: I tell you I am acting as for your father. Do you suppose he would have abandoned you, to starve or to work?'

The allusion touched every chord within her bosom, and the tears fell fast. 'I thought I could get my living by teaching,' she sobbed.

'And how much did you anticipate the teaching would bring you in?'

'Not very much,' she listlessly said. 'A hundred a year, perhaps: I am very clever at music and singing. That sum might keep us, I fancy, even if I only went out by day.'

'And a fine "keep" it would be! You shall have that sum every quarter!'

'No, no! oh no! I do not deserve it; I could not accept it. I have forfeited all claim to assistance.'

'Not to mine. Now, it is of no use to excite yourself, for my mind is made up. I never willingly forego a duty, and I look upon this not only as a duty, but an imperative one. Upon my return, I shall immediately settle four hundred a year upon you, and you can draw it quarterly.'

'Then half the sum,' she reiterated, knowing how useless it was to contend with Lord Mount Severn when he got upon the stilts of 'duty.' 'Indeed, two hundred a year will be ample; it will seem like riches to me.'

'I have named the sum, Isabel and I shall not make it less. A hundred pounds every three months shall be paid to you, dating from this day. This does not count,' he continued, laying down some notes upon the table.

'Indeed, I have some ready money by me,' she urged, her cheeks flushing at what she looked upon as unmerited kindness: for none could think worse of her than she did of herself. 'Pray take it back: you are too good to me.'

'I don't know what you call "ready money,"' returned the earl, 'but you have just informed me you were selling your trinkets to live upon. Put up the notes, Isabel: they are only a small amount, just to go on with. Are you in debt?'

'Oh no.'

'And mind you don't get into it,' advised the earl, as he rose to depart. 'You can let me hear of you from time to time, Isabel.'

'What does the world say of me?' she took courage to whisper. It was a question often in her own mind. Lord Mount Severn paused before he replied, marvelling, probably, that she could ask it.

'Just what you may have said in the days now over, at any who had gone the way that you have done. What did you expect that it would say?'

What indeed! She stood there with her humble face and her beating heart. The earl took her hand within his in token of farewell: turned, and was gone.

Lord Mount Severn, stern and uncompromising as he was, had yet a large share of kindness and conscientiousness. From the moment he heard of the false step taken by Lady Isabel, and that it was with Francis Levison she had flown, he cast more blame than he had ever done upon the conduct of his wife, in having forced her—so he regarded it—upon Mr. Carlyle. In short, he considered his wife as the primary, though remote, cause of the present ill: not that he in the slightest degree underrated Lady Isabel's own share in it; quite the contrary. From this motive, no less than that he was her blood relative, he deemed it his duty to see after her in her shame and sadness.

Susanne attended Lord Mount Severn to the door and watched him down the street, thinking what a 'brave Monsieur Anglais,' he was, and how delighted miladi must be at seeing a friend, to break the monotony of her sick and lonely existence. Susanne made no doubt that the visit must so far have aroused miladi as to set her thinking about getting out her smart dresses once more, and that the first words she should hear, on entering miladi's presence, would touch on that attractive point.

The Earl of Mount Severn returned to the Hôtel des Ambassadeurs, dined, and slept there, and the following morning quitted it on his return to the pleasures and bustle of civilized life. And Lady Isabel remained in her chamber, alone.

Alone: alone! *Alone* for evermore.

✠ XIII ✠

Barbara's Misdoings

A sunny afternoon in summer. More correctly speaking, it may be said a summer's evening, for the bright beams were already slanting athwart the substantial garden of Mr. Justice Hare, and the tea hour, seven, was passing. Mr. and Mrs. Hare and Barbara were seated at the meal: somehow, meals always did seem in process at Justice Hare's; if it was not breakfast, it was luncheon; if it was not luncheon, it was dinner; if it was not dinner, it was tea. Barbara sat in tears, for the justice was giving her a 'piece of his mind,' and poor Mrs. Hare, agreeing with her husband (as she would have done had he proposed to set the house on fire and burn her up in it) yet sympathizing with Barbara, moved uneasily in her chair.

Barbara had been giving mortal offence. Barbara had been giving the same offence occasionally for some years past: she had just refused an eligible offer of marriage, and the justice was storming over it. In the abstract, it was of no moment whatever to Mr. Justice Hare whether his daughters pined and withered out their days as fading maidens, or whether they raced through life bustling matrons. Neither, in the abstract, did the justice want Barbara away from the paternal home, or deem her an incumbrance within it: on the contrary, were Barbara absent, he might be at fault for a target at which to shoot the arrows of his hard words. Neither had money anything to do with it: whether Barbara married or whether she remained single, she had an ample fortune. No: the anger of Justice Hare at Barbara's refusing the offers made to her, had nothing to do with ordinary causes.

How the world would get on without gossip, I'll leave the world to judge. That West Lynne could not have got on without it, and without interfering in everybody's business but its own, is enough for me. West Lynne had chosen to make a wonder of the fact that Barbara Hare should remain Barbara Hare. Of all the damsels indigenous to the soil, she, with her beauty, her attractive manners, and her good fortune, had appeared the most likely one to be appropriated. And yet she was still Barbara Hare! The gossips set their heads together to discover why she was neglected. *Neglected* they considered her, for Barbara was not one to talk of opportunities refused. The conclusion they came to was, that the unhappy crime attaching to her brother was the sole cause; and, by some mishap, this nonsense reached the ears of Justice Hare. If the justice was sensitive upon one point, it was upon what related to that dark and dreadful deed; if he was bitter against any living being, it was against his miserable son. To have it said that Barbara remained single because no one would have her on account of her brother, was gall and wormwood to Justice Hare, for the disgrace seemed then to be reflecting home on *him* and his. The justice would have liked to lift his foot and toss West Lynne into the nearest, and greenest, and muddiest of ponds, there to struggle together and cool their tongues; he would have liked to pounce on Richard, and hand him over to the mercies of the county assize; and he would have liked to marry Barbara off hand, that *that* part of the scandal at any rate might be refuted. Therefore, when Barbara refused offer after offer (four she had refused now), it may readily be credited how greatly it aroused the ire of the justice.

'You do it for the purpose; you do it to anger me,' thundered the justice, bringing down his hand on the tea-table, and causing the cups to rattle.

'No, I don't, papa,' sobbed Barbara.

'Then why *do* you do it?'

Barbara was silent.

'No; you can't answer: you have nothing to urge. What is the matter, pray, with Major Thorn? Come, I will be answered.'

'I don't like him,' faltered Barbara.

'You do like him; you are telling me an untruth. You have liked him well enough whenever he has been here.'

'I like him as an acquaintance, papa. Not as a husband.'

'Not as a husband!' repeated the exasperated justice. 'Why, bless my heart and body, the girl's going mad! Not as a husband! Who asked you to like him as a husband before he became such? Did you ever hear that it was necessary, or expedient, or becoming for a young lady to set on and begin to "like" a gentleman as "her husband"?'

Barbara felt a little bewildered.

'Here's the whole parish saying that Barbara Hare can't be married, that nobody will have her on account of—of—of that cursed stain left by—I won't trust myself to name him, I should go too far. Now don't you think that's a pretty disgrace, a fine state of things?'

'But it is not true,' said Barbara; 'people do propose for me.'

'But what's the use of their proposing when you say No?' raved the justice. 'Is that the way to let the parish know that they propose? you are an ungrateful, rebellious, self-willed daughter, and you'll never be otherwise.'

Barbara's tears flowed freely. The justice gave a dash at the bell-handle, to order the tea-things to be carried away; and after their removal the subject was renewed, together with Barbara's grief. That was the worst of Justice Hare. Let him seize hold of a grievance (it was not often he got upon a real one) and he kept on at it, like a blacksmith hammering at his forge. In the midst of a stormy oration, tongue and hands going together, Mr. Carlyle came in.

Not much altered; not much. A year and three-quarters had gone by, and they had served to silver his hair upon the temples. His manner too would never again be careless and light as it once had been. He was the same keen man of business, the same pleasant, intelligent companion: the generality of people saw no change in him. Barbara rose to escape.

'No,' said Justice Hare, planting himself between her and the door; 'that's the way you like to get out of my reach when I am talking to you. You won't go; so sit down again. I'll tell you of all your ill-conduct before Mr. Carlyle, and see if that will shame you.'

Barbara resumed her seat, a rush of crimson dyeing her cheeks. And Mr. Carlyle looked inquiringly, seeming to ask an explanation of her distress. The justice gave it after his own fashion.

'You know, Carlyle, that horrible blow that fell upon us, that shameful disgrace. Well, because the parish can't clack enough about the fact itself, it must begin upon Barbara, saying that the disgrace and humiliation are reflected upon her, and that nobody will come near her to ask her to be his wife. One would think, rather than lie under the stigma and afford the parish room to talk, she'd marry the first man that came, if it was the parish beadle—anybody else would. But now, what are the facts? You'll stare when you know them. She has received a bushel of good offers, a bushel of them,' repeated the justice, dashing his hand down on his knee, 'and she says No to all. The last was to-day, from Major Thorn, and my young lady takes and puts the stopper upon it, as usual, without reference to me or her mother, without saying with your leave or by your leave. She wants to be kept in her room for a week upon bread-and-water, to bring her to her senses.'

Mr. Carlyle glanced at Barbara. She was sitting meekly under the infliction, her wet eyelashes falling on her flushed cheeks and shading her eyes. The justice was heated enough, and had pushed his flaxen wig wrong side before in the warmth of his argument.

'What do you say to her?' snapped the justice.

'Matrimony may not have charms for Barbara,' replied Mr. Carlyle half jokingly.

'Nothing has charms for her that ought to have,' growled Justice Hare. 'She's one of the contrary ones. By the way, though,' hastily resumed the justice, leaving the objectionable subject, as another flashed across his memory, 'they were coupling your name and matrimony together, Carlyle, last night at the Buck's Head.'

A very perceptible tinge of red rose to the face of Mr. Carlyle, telling of inward emotion, but his voice and manner betrayed none.

'Indeed,' he carelessly said.

'Ah, you are a sly one; you are, Carlyle: remember how sly you were with your first—' marriage, Justice Hare was going to bring out, but it suddenly occurred to him that, all circumstances considered, it was not precisely the topic to recall to Mr. Carlyle. So he stopped himself in the utterance, coughed and went on again. 'There you go, over to Sir John Dobede's, *not* to see Sir John, but paying court to Miss Dobede.'

'So the Buck's Head was amusing itself with that!' good-humouredly observed Mr. Carlyle. 'Well, Miss Dobede is going to be married, and I am drawing up the settlements.'

'It's not she; she marries young Somerset; everybody knows that. It's the other one, Louisa. A nice girl, Carlyle.'

'Very,' responded Mr. Carlyle, and it was all the answer he gave. The justice, tired of sitting indoors, tired, perhaps, of extracting nothing satisfactory from Mr. Carlyle, rose, set his wig aright before the chimney-glass, and quitted the house on his customary evening visit to the Buck's Head. Barbara, who watched him down the path, saw that he encountered some one who happened to be passing the gate. She could not at first distinguish who it might be, nothing but an arm and shoulder, cased in velveteen, met her view, but as their positions changed in conversation, she saw that it was Locksley, who had been the chief witness (not a vindictive one; he could not help himself) against her brother Richard, touching the murder of Hallijohn.

'What can be the matter with papa?' exclaimed Barbara. 'Locksley must have said something to anger him. He is coming in in the greatest passion, mamma: his face crimson, and his hands and arms working.'

'Oh dear, Barbara!' was all poor Mrs. Hare's reply. The justice's great gusts of passion frightened her.

In he came, closed the door, and stood in the middle of the room, looking alternately at Mrs. Hare and Barbara.

'What is this cursed report that's being whispered in the place?' quoth he, in a tone of suppressed rage, but not unmixed with awe.

'What report?' asked Mr. Carlyle, for the justice waited for an answer, and Mrs. Hare seemed unable to speak. Barbara took care to keep silence: she had some misgiving that the justice's words might be referring to herself, to the recent grievance.

'A report that he—*he*—has been here, disguised as a labourer! has dared to show himself in the place, where he'll come yet to the gibbet.'

Mrs. Hare's face turned as white as death. Mr. Carlyle rose, and dexterously contrived to stand before her, so that it should not be seen. Barbara silently locked her hands, one within the other, and turned to the window.

'Of whom do you speak?' asked Mr. Carlyle, in a matter-of-fact tone, as if he were putting the most matter-of-fact question. He knew too well; but he sought to temporize for the sake of Mrs. Hare.

'Of whom do I speak?' uttered the exasperated justice, nearly beside himself with passion: 'of whom should I speak, but the bastard Dick? Who else in West Lynne is likely to come to a felon's death?'

'Oh, Richard!' sobbed forth Mrs. Hare, as she sank back in her chair, 'be merciful! He is our own true son.'

'Never a true son of the Hares,' raved the justice. 'A true son of wickedness, and cowardice, and blight, and evil. If he has dared to show his face at West Lynne, I'll set the whole police of England upon his track, that he may be brought here as he ought, if he must come. When Locksley told me of it, just now, I raised my hand to knock him down, so infamously false did I deem the report. Do *you* know anything of his having been here?' continued the justice to his wife, in a pointed, resolute tone.

How Mrs. Hare would have extricated herself, or what she would have answered, cannot even be imagined, but Mr. Carlyle interposed.

'You are frightening Mrs. Hare, sir. Don't you see that the very report of such a thing is alarming her into illness? But—allow me to inquire what it may be that Locksley said.'

'I met him at the gate,' returned Justice Hare, turning his attention upon Mr. Carlyle. 'He was going by as I reached it. "Oh, justice," he began, "I am glad I met you. There's a nasty report in the place, that Richard has been seen here. I'd see what I could do towards hushing it up, sir, if I were you, for it may only serve to put the police in mind of bygone things, which it may be better they should forget." Carlyle, I went, as I tell you, to knock him down: I asked him how he could have the hardihood to repeat such slander to my face. He was on the high horse directly: said the parish spoke the slander, not he; and I got out of him what it was he had heard.'

'And what was it?' interrupted Mr. Carlyle, more eagerly than he generally spoke.

'Why, they say that the fellow showed himself here some time ago, a year or so, disguised as a farm labourer—confounded fools! Not but what he'd have been the fool, had he done it.'

'To be sure he would,' repeated Mr. Carlyle, 'and he is not fool enough for that, sir. Let West Lynne talk, Mr. Hare: but do not you put faith in a word of its gossip. I never do. Poor Richard, wherever he may be—'

'I won't have him pitied in my presence,' burst forth the justice. 'Poor Richard, indeed! Villain Richard, if you please.'

'I was about to observe that wherever he may be, whether in the back-woods of America, or digging for gold in California, or wandering about the United Kingdom, there is little fear that he will quit his place of safety, to dare the dangerous ground of West Lynne. Had I been you, sir, I should have laughed at Locksley, and his words.'

'Why does West Lynne invent such lies?'

'Ah, there's the rub. I dare say West Lynne could not tell why, if it were paid for doing it. But it seems to have been a lame story it has got up this time. If they must have concocted a report that Richard had been seen at West Lynne, why put it back to a year ago? why not have fixed it for to-day or yesterday? If I heard anything more, I would treat it with the silence and contempt it deserves, justice.'

Silence and contempt were not greatly in the justice's line; noise and explosion were more so. But he had a high opinion of the judgment of Mr. Carlyle; and, growling a sort of assent, he once more set forth to pay his evening visit.

'Oh, Archibald!' uttered Mrs. Hare, when her husband was half way down the path, 'what a mercy that you were here! I should inevitably have betrayed myself.'

Barbara turned round from the window. 'But what could have possessed Locksley to say what he did?' she exclaimed.

'I have no doubt Locksley spoke with a good motive,' said Mr. Carlyle. 'He is not unfriendly to Richard, and thought, probably, that by telling Mr. Hare of the report, he might get it stopped. The rumour has been mentioned to me.'

Barbara turned cold all over. 'How can it have come to light?' she breathed.

'I am at a loss to know,' said Mr. Carlyle. 'The person to mention it to me was Tom Herbert. He met me yesterday and said, 'What's this row about Dick Hare?" "What row?" I asked him. "Why, that Dick was at West Lynne some time back, disguised as a farm labourer."—Just what Locksley said to Mr. Hare. I laughed at Tom Herbert,' continued Mr. Carlyle; 'turned his report into ridicule, and made him turn it into ridicule also, before I had done with him.'

'Will it be the means of causing Richard's detection?' murmured Mrs. Hare between her dry lips.

'No, no,' warmly responded Mr. Carlyle. 'Had the report arisen immediately after he was really here, it might not have been so pleasant: but nearly two years have elapsed since the period. Be under no uneasiness, dear Mrs. Hare, for rely upon it there is no cause.'

'But how *could* it have come out, Archibald?' she urged. 'And at this distant period of time!'

'I assure you I am quite at a loss to imagine. Had anybody at West Lynne seen and recognized Richard, they would have spoken of it at the time. Do not let it trouble you: the rumour will die away.'

Mrs. Hare sighed deeply, and left the room to proceed to her chamber. Barbara and Mr. Carlyle were alone.

'Oh, that the real murderer could be discovered!' she aspirated, clasping her hands. 'To be subjected to these shocks of fear is dreadful. Mamma will not be herself for days to come.'

'I wish the right man could be found; but it seems as far off as ever,' remarked Mr. Carlyle.

Barbara sat ruminating. It seemed that she had something to say to Mr. Carlyle, but a feeling caused her to hesitate. When she did at length speak, it was in a low, timid voice.

'You remember the description Richard gave, that last night—of the person he had met—the true Thorn?'

'Yes.'

'Did it strike you then—has it ever occurred to you to think—that it accorded with—with some one?'

'In what way, Barbara?' he asked after a pause. 'It accorded with the description Richard always gave of the man Thorn.'

'Richard spoke of the peculiar movement of throwing off the hair from the forehead—in this way. Did that strike you as being familiar—in connection with the white hand and the diamond ring?'

'Many have a habit of pushing off their hair: I think I do it myself sometimes. Barbara, what do you mean? Have you a suspicion of any one?'

'Have you?' she returned, answering the question by asking another.

'I have not. Since Captain Thorn was disposed of, my suspicions have not pointed anywhere.'

This sealed Barbara's lips. She had hers; certain vague doubts, bringing wonder more than anything else. At times she had thought the same doubts might have occurred to Mr. Carlyle, she now found that they had not. The terrible domestic calamity which had happened to Mr. Carlyle the same night that Richard protested he had seen Thorn, had prevented Barbara discussing the matter with him then; and she had never done so since. Richard had not been further heard of, and the affair had remained in abeyance.

'I begin to despair of its ever being discovered,' she observed. 'What will become of poor Richard?'

'The discovery that Thorn was not the Thorn completely checkmated us,' said Mr. Carlyle.

'It would have done so, had Richard not seen the other.'

'I have had my doubts whether that was not, after all, a flight of Richard's imagination. It is so extraordinary that he should meet the man by moonlight, and that nothing should have been seen of him at any other time; before or after. Richard's mind was imbued with the thought and image of

Thorn, and fancy may have conjured up his appearance in some ordinary passer-by.'

'That it never did!' cried Barbara. 'I wish I was as sure of heaven, as that Richard saw Thorn that night. You believed it yourself at the time.'

'I did. His earnestness impressed me. But I had not had time to reflect upon the facts. There was no one at West Lynne then, neither has there been since, to whom Richard's description could apply, Captain Thorn excepted.'

'At West Lynne—no,' said Barbara.

'We can but wait, and hope that time may bring forth its own elucidation,' concluded Mr. Carlyle.

'Ah,' sighed Barbara, 'but it is weary waiting; weary, weary!'

'How is it you contrive to get under the paternal displeasure?' he resumed, in a gayer tone. She blushed vividly, and it was her only answer.

'The Major Thorn, alluded to by your papa, is our old friend, I presume?' Barbara inclined her head.

'He is a very pleasant man, Barbara. Many a young lady would be proud to have him.'

'Yes, he is a pleasant man,' quietly answered Barbara, but she spoke in a tone that did not invite further discussion.

Captain Thorn, in visiting the Herberts in time gone by, had been much struck with Barbara. Had his circumstances allowed, he would have solicited her to become his wife then. Recently, he had acquired some property by inheritance, and had also been promoted a step in his profession. The first use he made of his ease was to write both to Barbara and her father. Barbara declined his offer, as you have seen, and the justice would be quite sure not to let her hear the last of it for some time to come.

'You will do all you can to quell this rumour touching Richard,' she said to Mr. Carlyle.

'Depend upon that. The less Richard's name is heard in West Lynne, the better. It puzzles me to know how it can have arisen.'

There was a pause. Barbara broke it: but she did not look at Mr. Carlyle as she spoke. 'The other rumour: is it a correct one?'

'What other rumour?'

'That you are to marry Louisa Dobede.'

'It is not. I have no intention of marrying any one. Nay, I will say it more strongly: it is my intention not to marry any one; to remain as I am.'

Barbara lifted her eyes to his in the surprise of the moment.

'You look amazed, Barbara. No. She—who was my wife—lives.'

'What of that?' uttered Barbara, in simplicity.

He did not answer for a moment, and when he did, it was in a low tone, as he stood by the table at which Barbara sat, and looked down upon her.

'"Whosoever putteth away his wife, and marrieth another, committeth adultery."'

And before Barbara could answer—if, indeed, she had found any answer to make—or had recovered her surprise, he had taken his hat and was gone.

❧ XIV ❧

An Accident

To return for a short time to Lady Isabel. As the year advanced she grew stronger, and in the latter part of the summer made preparations for quitting Grenoble. Where she would fix her residence, or what she would do, she knew not. She was miserable and restless, and cared little what became of her. The remotest spot on earth, one unpenetrated by the steps of civilized man, appeared the most desirable to her. Where was she to find this?

She set out on her search—she, the child, and a young peasant woman whom she had engaged as *bonne*; for Susanne, having a lover at Grenoble, entirely declined to leave the place. All her luggage, except the things absolutely requisite, Lady Isabel had forwarded to Paris, there to be warehoused until she sent further directions. It was a lovely day when she quitted Grenoble. The train travelled safely until in the dusk of the evening they approached a place called Cammère, where Lady Isabel proposed to rest for a day or two. Railway accidents are less frequent in France than they are with us, but when they do occur they are wholesale catastrophes, the memory of which lasts for a lifetime. The train was within a short distance of the station when there came a sudden shock and crash as of the day of doom; and engine, carriages, and passengers lay in one confused mass at the foot of a steep embankment. The gathering darkness added to the awful confusion.

The carriage, in which Lady Isabel with her child and *bonne* travelled, lay beneath a superincumbent mass of ruins: they were amongst the last passengers to be extricated. The *bonne* and the poor baby were quite dead. Lady Isabel was alive and conscious, but so severely injured that the medical men who had been brought to the spot in all haste turned from her to give their attention to other sufferers whose case seemed less desperate—she heard them say that she would not survive amputation, and that nothing else could be done, that she must die whether there was an operation or not. The injuries lay in one leg, and the lower part of her face. She had not counted upon dying in this manner, and death in the guise of horrible suffering was not the abstract thing of release and escape which it had seemed, when she had wished for it as the end of all her wretchedness. She was unable to move, but the shock had deadened sensation; she was not yet in pain, and her mind was for a short interval preternaturally clear and lucid. A Sister of Charity approached the stretcher on which she had been laid, and offered her some water. Isabel drank eagerly.

'Is there aught else I can do?' asked the sister.

'My baby and its nurse were with me in the carriage—tell me, have they been found? is my child killed?' asked Isabel.

The sister turned to gain intelligence if she could, but the confusion and noise were so great that she could scarcely hope to ascertain anything with certainty. A poor little child quite dead, but not much disfigured, had been carried into the railway shed, and laid down not far from Lady Isabel. The sister took it tenderly up.

'Was this your child?' said she, turning to Lady Isabel. 'It is a little angel, and is beholding the face of its Father in heaven.'

It was the ill-starred child of Lady Isabel: she pressed its little face to her bosom, and her first feeling was a deep thankfulness that it had been so soon taken away from the evil to come. She believed she was to die also in the space of a few hours, or less; and the dull, apathetic indifference to all belonging to this life, which generally sets in with the approach of death, was stealing over her. She motioned to the sister to remove it, saying softly,

'It is thus I would have wished it to be.'

'Have you no message or instructions for your friends? If you will trust me I will fulfil your wishes. Whilst your mind is preserved clear, it will be well to settle your duties towards those you are leaving behind.' The sister had heard what the doctor said of Lady Isabel's condition.

'All who ever knew me will rejoice to hear that I am no more,' said Isabel. 'My death will be the only reparation I can offer, for the grief and shame my life has brought on all who had the evil fortune to belong to me. You understand I have been a great sinner.'

'Try to accept death as a just recompense for your sins—make in this last moment an act of faith and obedience, by uniting your own will with His who sends this suffering; it is then changed from the nature of punishment into a blessing. Our sorrows are the gifts of Almighty God, no less than our joys.'

'I will, I have taken up my cross,' said Lady Isabel faintly, for the pain of her injuries was beginning to make itself felt.

'Can I write to any one for you?' asked the sister, 'tell me now, whilst you can think of it.'

'Have you paper and writing things at hand? write then—direct the letter first, to the Earl of Mount—stay!' she interrupted, feeling how undesirable it was to make known her private affairs, even in that strange place. Besides, from the injury to her face, she could only speak with the greatest difficulty. 'Could I not write a line myself? I think I could, if you will hold the paper before me: my hands are not injured; my intellect is clear.'

The compassionate sister complied: and Lady Isabel contrived to scrawl a few words as she lay, first directing the letter to the earl's town house. They were to the effect that she was dying from the fatal injuries of the railway accident: that her baby was killed, and its nurse. She thanked Lord Mount Severn for all his goodness to her; she said she was glad to die, to deliver him and all who belonged to her from the disgrace and shame she had been to them. 'Go to Mr. Carlyle,' she continued; 'say that I humbly beg him to forgive me; that I also beg the forgiveness of his children when they shall be old enough to know the crime I have committed against them: tell him I repent, and have repented bitterly—there are no words to express that bitterness.' She had written so far, when the torture of pain, which had begun to make itself more and more felt, was becoming intolerable. Gathering her strength for a last effort, she wrote in characters, like those with which one on the rack might have signed his confession, 'Forgive; Isabel,' and whispered, 'Send it when I am dead; not before: and add a few words of confirmation.'

When at length the surgeons came up to Lady Isabel, to examine more minutely the injuries she had sustained, she was quite insensible, and they thought she was dead. They said so to the sister, who was then kneeling beside her, repeating the prayers appointed for the passing soul. She finished them and retired to a distance, other sufferers claiming her services. She did not return to Lady Isabel, whom she fully believed to be dead; and she despatched the letter, writing in it, as requested, some words of confirmation. The dead were buried, and a special mass was said for them. The survivors were sent to the hospital; all that could be done for them was done; neither skill nor kindness being wanted.

Lady Isabel recovered her consciousness, and found herself lying on a pallet in a ward in the hospital. It was long before she could recall what had happened, or understood that she had not died. The surgeons, on further inspection, had found life still lingering in her shattered frame. The injuries were terrible enough, but not of necessity fatal, though the prospect of recovery was faint. It would have been cruel to resort to an operation with such slender chances of success, and they tried other means, which to the honour and glory of their skill, promised to succeed. Lady Isabel was still fluctuating between life and death; but the tide began at length slowly to set in towards life. She remained three months in the hospital before she could be removed. The change that had passed over her in those three months was little less than death itself; no one could have recognized in the pale, thin, shattered, crippled invalid, her who had been known as Lady Isabel Vane.

The letter was duly delivered at the town house of Lord Mount Severn, as addressed. The countess was sojourning there for a few days: she had quitted it after the season, but some business, or pleasure, had called her again to town. Lord Vane was with her, but the earl was in Scotland. They were at breakfast, she and her son, when the letter was brought in: eightpence to pay.

Its strangely written address; its foreign aspect; its appearance, altogether, excited her curiosity: in her own mind she believed she had dropped upon a nice little conjugal mare's nest.

'I shall open this,' cried she.

'Why, it is addressed to papa!' exclaimed Lord Vane, who possessed all his father's notions of honour.

'But such an odd letter! It may require an immediate answer: or is some begging petition, perhaps. Go on with your breakfast.'

Lady Mount Severn opened the letter, and with some difficulty spelt through its contents. They shocked even her.

'How dreadful!' she uttered, in the impulse of the moment.

'What is dreadful?' asked Lord Vane, looking up from his breakfast.

'Lady Isabel—Isabel Vane—you have not forgotten her?'

'Forgotten her!' he echoed. 'Why, mamma, I must possess a funny memory to have forgotten her already!'

'She is dead. She has been killed in a railway accident in France.'

His large eyes, honest and true as they had been in childhood, filled, and his face flushed. He said nothing, for emotion was strong within him.

'But, shocking as it is, it is better for her,' went on the countess; 'for, poor creature! what could her future life have been?'

'Oh, don't say it!' impetuously broke out the young viscount. 'Killed in a railway accident, and for you to say that it is better for her!'

'So it is better,' said the countess. 'Don't go into heroics, William. You are quite old enough to know that she had brought misery upon herself, and disgrace upon all connected with her. No one could ever have taken notice of her again.'

'I would,' said the boy, stoutly.

Lady Mount Severn smiled derisively.

'I would. I never liked anybody in the world half so much as I liked Isabel.'

'That's past and gone. You could not have continued to like her, after the disgrace she wrought.'

'Somebody else wrought more of the disgrace than she did; and, had I been a man, I would have shot him dead,' flashed the viscount.

'You don't know anything about it.'

'Don't I,' he returned, not over dutifully. But Lady Mount Severn had not brought him up to be dutiful.

'May I read the letter, mamma?' he demanded, after a pause.

'If you can read it,' she replied, tossing it to him. 'She dictated it when she was dying.'

Lord Vane took the letter to a window, and stayed looking over it for some time; the countess ate an egg and a plate of ham meanwhile. Presently he came back with it folded, and laid it on the table.

'You will forward it to papa to-day?' he observed.

'I shall forward it to him. But there's no hurry; and I don't exactly know where your papa may be. I shall send the notice of her death to the papers; and am glad to do it: it is a blight removed from the family.'

'Mamma, I do think you are the unkindest woman that ever breathed!'

'I'll give you something to call me unkind for, if you don't mind,' retorted the countess, her colour rising. 'Dock you of your holiday, and pack you back to school to-day.'

A few mornings after this, Mr. Carlyle left East Lynne, and proceeded to his office as usual. Scarcely was he seated, when Mr. Dill entered, and Mr. Carlyle looked at him inquiringly, for it was not Mr. Carlyle's custom to be intruded upon by any person until he had opened his letters: then he would ring for Mr. Dill. The letters and the *Times* newspaper lay on his table before him. The old gentleman came up in a covert, timid sort of way, which made Mr. Carlyle look all the more.

'I beg your pardon, sir; will you let me ask if you have heard any particular news?'

'Yes, I have heard it,' replied Mr. Carlyle.

'Then, sir, I beg your pardon a thousand times over. It occurred to me that you probably had not, Mr. Archibald; and I thought I would have said a word to prepare you, before you came upon it suddenly in the paper.'

'To prepare me!' echoed Mr. Carlyle, as old Dill was turning away. 'Why, what has come to you, Dill? Are you afraid my nerves are growing delicate, or that I shall faint over the loss of a hundred pounds? At the very most, we shall not suffer above that extent.'

Old Dill turned back again. 'If I don't believe you are speaking of the failure of Kent and Green! It's not *that*, Mr. Archibald. They won't affect us much: and there'll be a dividend, report runs.'

'What is it, then?'

'Then you have not heard it, sir! I am glad that I'm in time. It might not have been well for you to have seen it without a word of preparation, Mr. Archibald.'

'If you have not gone demented, you will tell me what you mean, Dill, and leave me to my letters,' cried Mr. Carlyle, wondering excessively at his sober, matter-of-fact clerk's words and manner.

Old Dill laid his hand upon the *Times* newspaper. 'It's here, Mr. Archibald, in the column of the deaths: the first on the list. Please prepare yourself a little, before you look at it.'

He shuffled out quickly, and Mr. Carlyle as quickly unfolded the paper. It was as old Dill said, the first on the list of deaths.

'At Cammère, in France, on the 18th inst., Isabel Mary, only child of William, late Earl of Mount Severn.'

Clients called; Mr. Carlyle's bell did not ring; an hour or two passed, and old Dill protested that Mr. Carlyle was engaged, until he could protest no longer. He went in deprecatingly. Mr. Carlyle sat yet with the newspaper before him, and the letters unopened at his elbow.

'There's one or two who *will* come in, Mr. Archibald, who *will* see you: what am I to say?'

Mr. Carlyle stared at him for a moment, as if his wits had been in the next world. Then he swept the newspaper from before him, and was the calm, collected man of business again.

As the news of Lady Isabel's marriage had first come to the knowledge of Lord Mount Severn through the newspapers, so, singular to say, did the tidings of her death. The next post brought him the letter which his wife had tardily forwarded. But, unlike Lady Mount Severn, he did not take her death so entirely upon trust: he knew what mistakes are often made in these reports from a distance, and he deemed it incumbent on him to make inquiries. He wrote immediately to the authorities of the town (in the best French he could muster), asking for particulars, and whether she was really dead.

He received, in due course, a satisfactory answer; satisfactory in so far as that it set his doubts entirely at rest. He had inquired after her by her proper name and title, 'La Dame Isabelle Vane,' and as the authorities could find none of the survivors owning that name, they took it for granted she was dead. They wrote him word that the child and nurse whom he had mentioned were killed on the spot; two ladies, who had occupied the same compartment of the carriage, had since died, one of whom was no doubt the mother, the lady he inquired for. She was dead and buried, sufficient money having been found upon her person to defray the few necessary expenses. It will easily be comprehended that the lady of whom they spoke was one of those who had been in the same carriage as Lady Isabel, and who had died.

Thus, through no intention of Lady Isabel, news of her death went forth to Lord Mount Severn and to the world. *Her* first intimation that she was regarded as dead, was through a copy of that very day's *Times*, seen by Mr. Carlyle, seen by Lord Mount Severn. An English traveller, who had been amongst the sufferers, and lay in the hospital, received the English newspapers, and sometimes lent them her to read. She was not travelling under her own name; she left that behind her when she left Grenoble; she had rendered her own too notorious to risk the chance recognition of travellers; and the authorities did not suspect that the quiet, unobtrusive Madame Vine, slowly recovering at the hospital, was the Dame Isabelle Vane, respecting whom the grand English Comte wrote.

Lady Isabel understood it at once: that the despatching of her letter had been the foundation of the misapprehension: and she began to ask herself now, why she should undeceive Lord Mount Severn and the world. She longed, none knew with what intense longing, to be unknown, obscure, totally unrecognized by all: none can know it, till they have put a barrier between themselves and the world as she had done. She had no longer the child to support, she had only herself; and surely she could with ease earn enough for that: or she could starve: it mattered little which. No, there was no necessity for her continuing to accept the bounty of Lord Mount Severn, and she would let him and everybody else continue to believe she was dead, and be henceforth only Madame Vine. A resolution she adhered to.

Thus the unhappy Lady Isabel's career was looked upon as run. Lord Mount Severn forwarded her letter to Mr. Carlyle, with the confirmation of her death, which he had obtained from the French authorities. It was a nine days' wonder: 'That poor, erring Lady Isabel was dead'—people did not call her names in the very teeth of her fate—and then it was over.

It was over. Lady Isabel Vane was as one forgotten.

⚔ X V ⚔

An Unexpected Visitor at East Lynne

There went, sailing up the avenue to East Lynne, a lady one windy afternoon. If not a lady she was attired as one: a flounced dress, and a stylish looking shawl, and a white veil. A very pretty woman, tall and slender was she, and she minced as she walked, and coquetted with her head, and, altogether, contrived to show that she had quite as much vanity as brains. She went boldly up to the front entrance of the house, and boldly rang at it, drawing her white veil over her face as she did so.

One of the men-servants answered it, not Peter; and, seeing somebody very smart before him, bowed deferentially.

'Miss Hallijohn is residing here, I believe. Is she within?'

'Who, ma'am?'

'Miss Hallijohn; Miss Joyce Hallijohn,' somewhat sharply repeated the lady, as if impatient of any delay. 'I wish to see her.'

The man was rather taken aback. He had deemed it a visitor to the house, and was prepared to usher her to the drawing-room, at least; but it seemed it was only a visitor to Joyce. He showed her into a small parlour, and went upstairs to the nursery, where Joyce was sitting with Wilson—for there had been no change in the domestic department of East Lynne. Joyce remained as upper maid, partially superintending the servants, attending upon Lucy, and making Miss Carlyle's dresses as usual. Wilson was nurse still. Miss Carlyle had once or twice begun upon the point of extravagance of keeping both Wilson and Joyce; but Mr. Carlyle had wholly declined discussion upon the subject; and somehow Miss Carlyle did not find him bend to her will as he once had done.

'Mrs. Joyce, there's a lady asking for you,' said the man. 'I have shown her into the grey parlour.'

'A lady for me?' repeated Joyce. 'Who is it? Some one to see the children, perhaps?'

'It's for yourself, I think. She asked for Miss Hallijohn.'

Joyce looked at the man; but she put down her work and proceeded to the grey parlour. A pretty woman, vain and dashing, threw up her white veil at her entrance.

'Well, Joyce! How are you?'

Joyce always pale, turned paler still, as she gazed in blank consternation. Was it really *Afy* who stood before her?—Afy the erring.

Afy it was. And she stood there holding out her hand to Joyce with, what Wilson would have called, all the brass in the world. Joyce could not reconcile her mind to link her own with it.

'Excuse me, Afy, but I cannot take your hand. I cannot welcome you here. What could have induced you to come?'

'If you are going to be upon the high ropes, it seems I might as well have stayed away,' was Afy's reply, given in the pert but good-humoured manner she had ever used to Joyce. 'My hand won't damage yours. I am not poison.'

'You are looked upon in the neighbourhood as worse than poison, Afy,' returned Joyce, in a tone, not of anger, but of sorrow. 'Where's Richard Hare?'

Afy tossed her head. 'Where's who?' asked she.

'Richard Hare. My question was plain enough.'

'How should I know where he is? It's like your impudence to mention him to me. Why don't you ask me where old Nick is, and how he does? I'd rather own acquaintance with him than with Richard Hare, if I'd only my choice between the two.'

'Then you have left Richard Hare! How long since?'

'I have left—what do you say?' broke off Afy, whose lips were quivering ominously with suppressed passion. 'Perhaps you'll condescend to explain. I don't understand.'

'When you left here, Afy, did you not go after Richard Hare?—did you not join him?'

'I'll tell you what it is, Joyce,' flashed Afy, her face indignant and her voice passionate, 'I have put up with some things from you in my time, but human nature has its limits of endurance, and I won't bear *that*. I have never set eyes on Richard Hare since that night of horror. I wish I could: I'd help to hang him.'

Joyce paused. The belief that Afy was with him had been long and deeply imbued within her; it was the long-continued and firm conviction of all West Lynne: and a settled belief, such as that, is not easily shaken. Was Afy telling her the truth? She knew her propensity for making false statements when they served to excuse herself.

'Afy,' she said at length, 'let me understand you. When you left this place, was it not to share Richard Hare's flight? Have you not been living with him?'

'No,' burst forth Afy, with kindling eyes. 'Living with *him!* with our father's murderer! Shame upon you, Joyce Hallijohn! you must be precious wicked yourself to suppose it.'

'If I have judged you wrongly, Afy, I sincerely beg your pardon. Not only myself, but the whole of West Lynne believed you were with him; and the thought has caused me pain night and day.'

'What a cannibal-minded set you must all be, then!' was Afy's indignant rejoinder.

'Not one in the place but thought so, with the exception of Mr. Carlyle,' proceeded Joyce. 'He has said two or three times to me that he should not think you went to Richard Hare, or were living with him.'

'Mr. Carlyle has more sense than all the rest of West Lynne put together,' complacently observed Afy. 'Living with Richard Hare! why, I'd rather go and live with a scalped red Indian who goes about with his body tattooed in place of clothes, and keeps sixteen wives.'

'But, Afy, where did you go, then? Why did you leave at all?'

'Never mind why. It was not to be supposed that I could stop at home in the cottage with ghosts and dreams and all those sort of things, that attend a place where murder has been.'

'What have you been doing ever since? Where have you been?'

'Never mind, I say,' repeated Afy. 'West Lynne has not been so complimentary to me, it appears, that I need put myself out of my way to satisfy its curiosity. I was knocking about a bit at first, but I soon settled down as steady as Old Time; as steady as you.'

'Are you married?' inquired Joyce, noting the word 'settled.'

'Catch me marrying,' retorted Afy; 'I like my liberty too well. Not but what I might be induced to change my condition, if anything out of the way eligible occurred: it must be very eligible, though, to tempt me. I am what I suppose you call yourself—a lady's maid.'

'Indeed!' said Joyce, much relieved. 'And are you comfortable, Afy?—are you in a good service?'

'Middling for that. The pay's not amiss, but there's a great deal to do, and her ladyship's a Tartar. I had a good one with an old lady; a sort of companion I was to her, and stopped there till she died. What do you think? She made me go in to prayers with her, and read the Bible night and morning.'

'How very glad I am to hear this!' exclaimed Joyce. 'It must have been so good for you.'

'Very,' assented Afy; and Joyce failed to detect the irony of her tone. 'She'd used to read a chapter, and I'd used to read a chapter, and then we went to prayers. Edifying, wasn't it?'

'Delightfully so, Afy. I am sure you must have profited by it.'

'Law, yes: never doubt that. She left me thirty pounds when she died, over and above my salary. I used to like the Psalms best, because they were short and comforting.'

'So comforting!' echoed Joyce. 'Afy, I shall love you and be proud of you again, like I was when you first came home to us.'

Afy laughed, a ringing laugh. 'You and West Lynne always set me down for worse than I was. Though it poses me to imagine what on earth could have induced you to fancy I should go off with that Dick Hare,' she added, for she could not forget the grievance.

'Look at the circumstances,' argued Joyce. 'You both disappeared.'

'But not together!'

'Nearly together. There were only a few days intervening. And you had neither money nor friends.'

'You don't know what I had. But I would rather have died of want on my father's grave, than have shared his means,' continued Afy, growing passionate again. 'And you and the West Lynne idiots ought to have made sure of that.'

'If you had but dropped me a single line, Afy, it would have put a different aspect upon the whole affair. Your silence helped to misjudge you.'

'Misjudge me, indeed! Why, I never cared for Dick Hare. He was only half baked.'

'You encouraged him to the house.'

'Well—I don't deny it. He used to speak to me of marriage: and one would put up with a man not baked at all, to be made a real lady. Had I known he was to turn out what he did, I would have seen his coffin walk, before I'd ever have spoken to him. Where is he? Not hung, or I should have heard of it.'

'He has never been seen since that night, Afy.'

'Nor heard of?'

'Nor heard of. Most people think he is in Australia, or some other foreign land.'

'The best place for him; the more distance he puts between him and home, the better. If he ever does come back, I hope he'll get his deserts—which is a rope's end. I'd go to his hanging.'

'You are as bitter against him as Mr. Justice Hare. He would bring his son back to suffer, if he could.'

'A cross-grained old camel!' remarked Afy, in allusion to the qualities, social and amiable, of the revered justice. 'I don't defend Dick Hare, I hate him too much for that, but if his father had treated him differently, Dick might have been different. Well, let's talk of something else; the subject invariably gives me the shivers. Who is mistress here?'

'Miss Carlyle.'

'Oh. I might have guessed that. Is she as fierce as ever?'

'There is little alteration in her.'

'And there won't be on this side of the grave. I say, Joyce, I don't want to encounter her: she might set on at me, like she has done many a time in the old days. Little love was there lost between me and Corny Carlyle.'

'You need not fear meeting her. She is away: gone to Lynneborough for a week's visit.'

'That's good news for a rainy day! Then, who acts as mistress while she's absent?'

'I give the orders,' said Joyce. 'Master interferes very little.'

'Will he marry again?' went on Afy.

'How can I tell? There appears no probability of it at present. A few weeks or months ago, a rumour arose that he was to marry Miss Louisa Dobede; but it died away again.'

'Louisa Dobede! one of that ugly old baronet's daughters?'

'Yes. But Sir John Dobede is not ugly.'

'Not ugly! why he has a nose as long as a foundry chimney. Well, one would think Mr. Carlyle had had enough of marrying.'

'Lady Isabel is dead,' interrupted Joyce, hastily.

'So is Queen Anne. What is the good of telling me news that all the world knows?'

'I reminded you that she was dead that you might not speak against her,' said Joyce. 'Whatever may have been Lady Isabel's failings, they are buried in her grave.'

'Buried or not, their remembrance lasts,' cried Afy, 'and you may as well try to stop the sun's shining, as to stop folks giving their opinions. East Lynne must have been well rid of her—such a canker as that!'

Joyce put up her hand. 'Afy, be silent! You have no right so to speak of Lady Isabel: you know nothing of the facts.'

'I know all the facts by heart,' imperturbably rejoined Afy. 'You may take your oath they were conned over and over by us at Lady Mount Severn's?'

Joyce looked at her in surprise. 'What have you to do with Lady Mount Severn's?'

'Well, that's good. It's where I am in service.'

'At Lady Mount Severn's?'

'Why not! I have been there two years. It is not a great deal longer I shall stop, though; she has got too much vinegar in her for me. It happened just after I went there, and she had a cousin visiting her, a Miss Levison, and the two were for ever talking of it.'

'But not in your presence?'

'I heard,' significantly nodded Afy. 'Heard just as much as they had to tell.'

'You must have listened at keyholes.'

'Perhaps I did,' was Afy's cool response. 'I had a fancy to hear the particulars; and when I do make up my mind to know a thing, I don't let trifles stand in my way. Tell me about her, Joyce.'

Joyce shook her head. 'There's nothing much to tell. She was one of the sweetest ladies, one of the kindest mistresses—'

'Oh, I see,' interrupted Afy, with ineffable disdain. 'She was one of your angels.'

'Almost she was. Until that serpent came here to cross her path.'

'Manners! manners!' laughed Afy. 'It's not polite to call names.'

'I could call him names for ever,' warmly answered Joyce. 'And so I would if it could bring him punishment. It will come home to him: mark my words.'

'Lady Mount Severn throws all the blame on her.'

'It is more than Lord Mount Severn does,' angrily returned Joyce.

'I could have told you that. He casts some share of it to Lady Mount Severn. Sir Francis is her cousin, you know. Was she good-looking, Joyce?'

'Beautiful.'

'Better looking than I am?' cried vain Afy, glancing at herself in an opposite mirror.

'Oh, Afy! how absurd you are!'

'Many thanks. Because she was the Lady Isabel, and I am plain Afy Hallijohn, of course I can't be compared to her! Everybody thinks they may lance shafts at my back: but lady angels go wrong sometimes, you see; they are not universally immaculate. She must have been a queer angel, rather, to leave her children.'

'Afy, do you understand that this conversation is particularly disagreeable to me!' cried Joyce with spirit.

'It's a very disagreeable topic indeed, I should say,' equally replied Afy. 'She should not have acted so as to give rise to it. He soon tired of her, with all her beauty: he has tired—as it is said—of others. He is married now.'

'Yes,' indignantly spoke Joyce. 'and the wonder is, how any young lady, with a spark of delicacy or good feeling, could bring herself to marry so notorious a man.'

'Ladies don't dislike that sort of notoriety,' said Afy, laughing at Joyce's reproving face. 'That is, when the offenders are handsome, as he is.'

'You have seen him at Lady Mount Severn's?'

'Not I. I have seen him, but not there. Since the Carlyle affair, he dared not show his face within their doors: my lord would kick him out. What an awful thing that railway accident must have been!'

Joyce shuddered. 'Ay, it was an awful death.'

'And quite a judgment upon her, I should say,' went on Afy, probably seeing that the style of conversation aggravated Joyce.

Joyce would stand it no longer. 'Listen, Afy: I loved my mistress, and I love her memory still, in spite of what has taken place. If you are to speak against her, it must be in some other house, for it shall not be in Mr. Carlyle's, where she was once so honoured.'

'Have it your own way,' indifferently rejoined Afy. 'She's gone to kingdom come, so it's not worth while disputing over it. Is Mr. Carlyle at home?'

'He will be home to dinner. I dare say you would like some tea: you shall come and take it with me and Wilson in the nursery.'

'I was thinking you might have the grace to offer me something,' cried Afy. 'I intend to stop till to-morrow in the neighbourhood: my lady gave me two days' holiday—for she was going to see her dreadful old grandmother, where she can't take a maid—and I thought I'd use it in coming to have a look at the old place again. Don't stare at me in that blank way, as if you feared I should ask the grand loan of sleeping here. I shall sleep at the Mount Severn Arms.'

'I was not glancing at such a thought, Afy. Come and take your bonnet off.'

'Is the nursery full of children?'

'There's only one child in it. Miss Lucy and Master William are with the governess.'

Wilson received Afy with lofty condescension, having Richard Hare in her thoughts. But Joyce explained that it was all a misapprehension—that her sister had not been near Richard Hare, but was as indignant against him as they were. Upon which Wilson grew cordial and chatty, rejoicing in the delightful recreation her tongue would enjoy that evening.

Afy's account of herself, as to past proceedings, was certainly not the most satisfactory in the world, but altogether, taking in the present, it was so vast an improvement upon Joyce's conclusions, that she had not felt so elated for many a day. When Mr. Carlyle returned home Joyce sought him, and acquainted him with what had happened; that Afy was come; was maid to Lady Mount Severn; and, above all, that she had never been with Richard Hare.

'Ah! you remember what I said, Joyce,' he remarked. 'That I did not believe Afy was with Richard Hare.'

'I have been telling Afy so, sir, and she says you have got more sense than all West Lynne put together.'

Mr. Carlyle laughed.

'A terrible way she was in, to be sure, when I informed her what people had believed,' continued Joyce. 'She nearly went into one of her old passions.'

'Does she seem steady, Joyce?'

'I think so, sir—steady for her. Before she took Lady Mount Severn's service, she was with an old lady, where she read her Bible and joined in prayers night and morning.'

'Afy at prayers!' exclaimed Mr. Carlyle, a smile crossing his lips. 'I hope they were genuine.'

'I was thinking, sir, that as she appears to have turned out so respectable, and is with Lady Mount Severn, you perhaps might see no objection to her sleeping here for to-night. It would be better than for her to go to an inn, as she talks of doing.'

'None at all,' replied Mr. Carlyle. 'Let her remain.'

As Joyce returned to the nursery, Afy and Wilson were in the full flowing tide of talk, trying whose tongue could go the fastest. An unlucky sentence of Afy's caught Joyce's ears.

'It's as true as you are there, Wilson. She bothered me all day long with her religion. I had used to pick out the shortest psalm I could find, and when she asked me why, I said I did it that I might remember them. There's one with two verses in it; I chose that as often as I dared. And then, down I had to go on my marrow-bones, and put up my hands! I had used to wish my mistress and her prayers somewhere.'

Joyce groaned in spirit, and thought of the words just spoken by Mr. Carlyle—he had hoped the prayers were genuine!

Later in the evening, after Mr. Carlyle's dinner, a message came that Afy was to go to him. Accordingly she proceeded to his presence.

'So, Afy, you have returned to let West Lynne know that you are alive. Sit down.'

'West Lynne may go a-walking in future, sir, for all the heed I shall take of it,' retorted Afy. 'A set of wicked-minded scandalmongers, to take and say I had gone off after Richard Hare!'

'You should not have gone off at all, Afy.'

'Well, sir, that was my business, and I chose to go. I could not stop in the cottage after that night's work.'

'There is a mystery attaching to that night's work, Afy,' observed Mr. Carlyle: 'a mystery that I cannot fathom. Perhaps you can help me out.'

'What mystery, sir?' returned Afy.

Mr. Carlyle leaned forward, his arms on the table; Afy had taken a chair at the other end of it. 'Who was it that committed the murder?' he demanded, in a grave and somewhat imperative tone.

Afy stared some moments before she replied, evidently astonished at the question. 'Who committed the murder, sir?' she uttered at length. 'Richard Hare committed it. Everybody knows that.'

'Did you see it done?'

'No,' replied Afy. 'If I had seen it, the fright and horror would have killed me. Richard Hare quarrelled with my father, and drew the gun upon him in his passion.'

'You assume this to have been the case, Afy, as others have assumed it. I do not think it was Richard Hare who killed your father.'

'Not Richard Hare!' exclaimed Afy, after a pause. 'Then who do you think did it, sir? I?'

'Nonsense, Afy.'

'I know he did it,' proceeded Afy. 'It is true that I did not see it done, but I know it, for all that. I *know* it, sir.'

'You cannot know it, Afy.'

'I do know it, sir; I would not assert it to you if I did not. If Richard Hare were here present before us, and swore till he was black in the face that it was not he, I could convict him.'

'By what means?'

'I had rather not say, sir. But you may believe me, for I am speaking truth.'

'There was another friend of yours present that evening, Afy. Lieutenant Thorn.'

Afy's face turned crimson: she was evidently confused. But Mr. Carlyle's speech and manner were authoritative, and she saw that it would be useless to attempt to trifle with him.

'I know he was, sir. A young chap, who used to ride over some evenings to see me. He had nothing to do with what occurred.'

'Where did he ride from?'

'He was stopping with some friends at Swainson. He was nobody, sir.'

'What was his name?' questioned Mr. Carlyle.

'Thorn,' said Afy.

'I mean his real name. Thorn was an assumed one.'

'Oh, dear no,' returned Afy. 'Thorn was his name.'

Mr. Carlyle paused and looked at her.

'Afy, I have reason to believe that Thorn was only an assumed name. Now, I have a motive for wishing to know his real one, and you would very much oblige me by confiding it to me. What was it?'

'I don't know that he had any other name, sir; I am sure he had no other,' persisted Afy. 'He was Lieutenant Thorn then, and he was Captain Thorn afterwards.'

'You have seen him since?'

'Once in a way we have met.'

'Where is he now?'

'Now! Oh my goodness, I don't know anything about him now!' said Afy. 'I have not heard of him or seen him for a long while. I think I heard something about his going to India with his regiment.'

'What regiment is he in?'

'I'm sure I don't know about that,' said Afy. 'Is not one regiment the same as another: they are all in the army, aren't they, sir?'

'Afy, I must find this Captain Thorn. Do you know anything of his family?'

Afy shook her head. 'I don't think he had any. I never head him mention so much as a brother or a sister.'

'And you persist in saying his name was Thorn!'

'I persist in it because it was his name. I am positive it was his name.'

'Afy, shall I tell you why I want to find him? I believe that it was he who murdered your father: not Richard Hare.'

Afy's mouth and eyes gradually opened, and her face turned hot and cold alternately. Then passion mastered her, and she burst forth.

'It's a lie! I beg your pardon, sir, but whoever told you that, told you a lie. Thorn had no more to do with it, than I had: I'll swear it.'

'I tell you, I believe Thorn to have been the man. You were not present: you cannot know who actually did it.'

'Yes, I can, and do know,' said Afy, bursting into tears of hysterical passion. 'Thorn was with me when it happened, so it could not have been Thorn. It was that wicked Richard Hare. Sir! have I not said that I'll swear it?'

'Thorn was with you!—at the moment of the murder?' repeated Mr. Carlyle.

'Yes, he was,' shrieked Afy, nearly beside herself with emotion. 'Whoever has been trying to put it off Richard Hare, and on to him, is a wicked, false-hearted wretch. It was Richard Hare and nobody else, and I hope he'll be hung for it yet.'

'You are telling me the truth, Afy?' gravely spoke Mr. Carlyle.

'Truth!' echoed Afy, flinging up her hands. 'Would I tell a lie over my poor father's death? If Thorn had done it, would I screen him, or shuffle it off to Richard Hare? No, no.'

Mr. Carlyle felt uncertain and bewildered. That Afy was sincere in what she said was but too apparent. He spoke again, but Afy had risen from her chair to leave.

'Locksley was in the wood that evening: Otway Bethel was in it. Could either of them have been the culprit?'

'No, sir,' firmly retorted Afy; 'the culprit was Richard Hare; and I'd say it with my latest breath. I'd say it because I know it—though I don't choose to say how I know it; time enough when he gets taken.'

She quitted the room, leaving Mr. Carlyle in a state of puzzled bewilderment. Was he to believe Afy? or was he to believe the bygone assertion of Richard Hare?

❧ X V I ❧

A Night Invasion of East Lynne

In one of the comfortable sitting-rooms of East Lynne sat Mr. Carlyle and his sister one inclement January night. The contrast within and without was great. The warm, blazing fire, the handsome carpet on which it flickered, the exceedingly comfortable arrangement of the furniture of the room altogether, and the light of the chandelier which fell on all, presented a picture of home peace, though it may not have deserved the name of luxury. Without, heavy flakes of snow were falling thickly, flakes as large and nearly as heavy as a crown piece, rendering the atmosphere so dense and obscure, that a man could not see a yard before him. Mr. Carlyle had driven home in the pony-carriage, and the snow had so settled upon him, even in that short journey, that Lucy, who happened to see him as he entered the hall, screamed out laughingly that her papa had turned into a white man. It was now later in the evening; the children were in bed, the governess was in her own sitting-room—it was not often that Miss Carlyle invited her to theirs in an evening—and the house was quiet. Mr. Carlyle was deep in the pages of one of the monthly periodicals; and Miss Carlyle sat on the other side of the fire, grumbling, and grunting, and sniffing, and choking.

Miss Carlyle was one of your strong-minded ladies, who never condescend to be ill. Of course, had she been attacked with scarlet fever, or paralysis, or St. Vitus's dance, she must have given in to the enemy; but trifling ailments, such as headache, influenza, sore-throat, which other people get, passed her by. Imagine, therefore, her exasperation at finding her head stuffed up, her chest sore, and her voice going: in short, at having, for once in her life, caught a cold like ordinary mortals.

'It was that ale,' she groaned.

'Ale!' echoed Mr. Carlyle, lifting his eyes from his book.

'Yes, the ale,' she tartly proceeded. 'Dear me, Archibald, you need not stare as if I had said it was the moon gave it me.'

'But how could ale give it you? Unless you drank a great draught of it cold, when you were in a perspiration.'

Miss Carlyle lifted her hands in pitying contempt for his ignorance.

'You'll be a baby in common sense to the end of your life, Archibald. When do I drink great draughts of ale? Pray, the last two barrels that we have had in tap, has there not been, throughout, a complaint that the taps leaked?'

'Well?' said he.

'Well, I knew that the fault lay in the putting in the taps in the first instance; servants are such incapables; so, when Peter came to me after breakfast this morning, and said there had better be another barrel of ale tapped, for that the one in hand was stooped yesterday, "Very well," said I, "I'll come and see to it myself!" And down I went, out of these warm rooms, and the cellar struck like an ice-house, and I stopped in it for twenty minutes, good.'

'Does it take all that time to tap a barrel of ale?'

'No, it doesn't take it when things are in order, but it does when you have to bother over the taps, rejecting one, rejecting another,' responded Miss Carlyle, in a tone of exasperation. 'And a pretty state that cellar was in! not a thing in place. I had the cook down, and a sharp dressing I gave her: if her hams had been turned for three days, I'll eat them, raw as they are! That's how I must have caught this cold, stopping down there.'

Mr. Carlyle made no observation; had he told her that there was no need whatever for her interference, that Peter was perfectly competent to his duties, she would only have flown at him. He became absorbed in his book again, while Miss Carlyle fretted and grunted, and drew her chair into the fire and pushed it back again, and made violent starts with her hands and feet: in short, performed all the antics of a middle-aged gentlewoman suffering under an attack of fidgets.

'What's the time, I wonder?' she exclaimed by-and-by.

Mr. Carlyle looked at his watch. 'It is just nine, Cornelia.'

'Then I think I shall go to bed. I'll have a basin of arrowroot or gruel, or some slop of that sort, after I'm in it: I'm sure I have been free enough all my life from requiring such sick dishes!'

'Do so,' said Mr. Carlyle. 'It may do you good.'

'There's one thing excellent for a cold in the head, I know. It's to double your flannel petticoat crossways, or any other large piece of flannel you may conveniently have at hand, and put it on over your nightcap: I'll try it.'

'I would,' said Mr. Carlyle, smothering an irreverent laugh.

She sat on five minutes longer, and then left, wishing Mr. Carlyle good night. He resumed his reading. But another page or two concluded the article; upon which Mr. Carlyle threw the book on the table, rose, and stretched himself, as if tired of sitting.

He stirred the fire into a brighter blaze, and stood on the hearth-rug. 'I wonder if it snows still?' he exclaimed to himself.

Proceeding to the window, one of those opening to the ground, he drew aside the half of the warm crimson curtain. It all looked dull and dark outside; Mr. Carlyle could see little what the weather was, and he opened the window and stepped half out.

The snow was falling faster and thicker than ever. Not at that did Mr. Carlyle start with surprise, if not with a more unpleasant sensation; but, at feeling a man's hand touch his, and finding a man's face nearly in contact with his own.

'Let me come in, Mr. Carlyle, for the love of life! I see you are alone. I'm dead beat: and I don't know but I am dodged also.'

The tones struck familiarly on Mr. Carlyle's ear. He drew back mechanically; a thousand perplexing sensations overwhelmed him; and the man followed him into the room. A white man, as Lucy had called her father. Ay, for he had been hours and hours on foot in the snow: his hat, his clothes, his eyebrows, his large whiskers, all were white. 'Lock the door, sir,' were his first words. Need you be told that it was Richard Hare?

Mr. Carlyle fastened the window, drew the heavy curtain across it, and turned rapidly to lock the two doors; for there were two to the room, one of them leading into the adjoining one. Richard, meanwhile, took off his wet smock-frock—the old smock-frock of former memory—his hat, and his false black whiskers, wiping the snow from the latter with his hand.

'Richard,' uttered Mr. Carlyle, 'I am thunderstruck. I fear you have done wrong to come here.'

'I cut off from London at a moment's notice,' replied Richard, who was literally shivering with the cold. 'I'm dodged, Mr. Carlyle; I am indeed; the police are after me, set on by that wretch, Thorn.'

Mr. Carlyle turned to the sideboard and poured out a wine glass of brandy. 'Drink it, Richard: it will warm you.'

'I'd rather have it in some hot water, sir.'

'But how am I to get the hot water brought in? Drink this for now. Why, how you tremble!'

'Ah. A few hours outside in that cold snow is enough to make the strongest man tremble, sir. And it lies so deep in some places that you have to come along at a snail's pace. But I'll tell you about this business. A fortnight ago, I was at a cab-stand at the West-end, talking to a cab-driver, when some drops of rain came down. A gentleman and lady were passing at the time, but I had not paid any attention to them. "By Jove!" I heard him exclaim to her, "I think we are going to have pepper. We had better take a cab, my dear." With that, the man I was talking to swung open the door of his cab, and she got in—such a fair young girl! I turned to look at him, and you might just have knocked me down with astonishment. Mr. Carlyle, it was the man Thorn.'

'Indeed!'

'You thought I might be mistaken in him that moonlight night; but there was no mistaking him in broad daylight. I looked him full in the face, and he looked me. He turned as white as a cloth: perhaps I did; I don't know.'

'Was he well dressed?'

'Very. Oh, there's no mistaking his position. That he moves in the higher circles, there's no doubt. The cab drove away and I got up behind it. The driver thought boys were there, and turned his head and his whip, but I made him a sign. We didn't go much more than the length of a street. I was on the pavement before Thorn was, and looked at him again; and again he went white. I marked the house, thinking it was where he lived, and, and—'

'Why did you not give him into custody, Richard?'

Richard shook his head. 'And my proofs of his guilt, Mr. Carlyle? I could bring none against him: no positive ones. No, I must wait till I can get proofs, to do that. He would turn round upon me now, and swear my life away, to render his secure: perhaps testify that he saw me commit the murder. Well, I thought I'd ascertain for certain what his name was, and that night I went to the house and got into conversation with one of the servants, who was standing at the door. "Does Captain Thorn live here?" I asked him. "Mr. Westleby lives here," said he; "I don't know any Captain Thorn." Then that's his name, thought I to myself. "A youngish man, isn't he? very smart, with a pretty wife?" "I don't know what you call youngish," he laughed, "my master's turned sixty, and his wife's as old." That checked me. "Perhaps he has sons?" I asked. "Not any," the man answered; "there's nobody but their two selves." So, with that, I told him what I wanted—that a lady and gentleman had alighted there in a cab that day, and I wished to know his name. Well, Mr. Carlyle, I could get at nothing satisfactory; the fellow said a great many had called there that day, for his master was just up from a long illness, and people came to see him.'

'Is this all, Richard?'

'All! I wish it had been all. I kept looking about for him in all the best streets: I was half mad—'

'Do you not wonder, if he is in this position of life and resides in London, that you have never dropped upon him previously?' interrupted Mr. Carlyle.

'No, sir: and I'll tell you why. I have been afraid to show myself in those better parts of the town, fearing I might meet with some I used to know at home who would recognize me, so I have kept mostly in obscure places; stables, and such-like. I had gone up to the West-end this day on a matter of business.'

'Well, go on with your story.'

'In a week's time I came upon him again. It was at night. He was coming out of one of the theatres, and I went up and stood before him. "What do you want, fellow?" he asked. "I have seen you watching me before this." "I

want to know your name," I said, "that's enough for me at present." He flew
into a fierce passion, and swore that if he ever caught sight of me near him
again, he would hand me over into custody. "And, remember, men are not
given into custody for *watching* others," he significantly added. "I know
you, and if you have any regard for yourself, you'll keep out of my way." He
got into a private carriage as he spoke, and it drove away. I could see that it
had a great coat-of-arms upon it.'

'When do you say this happened?'

'A week ago. Well, I could not rest; I was half mad, I say, and I went about
still, trying if I could not discover his name and who he was. I did come upon
him once: but he was walking quickly, arm-in-arm with—another gentleman. Again I saw him standing at the entrance to Tattersall's, talking to the
same gentleman; and his face turned savage—I believe with fear as much as
anger—when he saw me. He seemed to hesitate, and then—as if he acted in
a passion—suddenly beckoned a policeman, pointed me out, and said something to him in a fast tone. That frightened me, and I slipped away. Two
hours later, when I was in quite a different part of the town, in turning my
head, I saw the same policeman following me. I bolted under the horses of a
passing vehicle, cut into some turnings and passages, through into another
street, and got up beside a cabman who was on his box, driving a fare past. I
reached my lodgings in safety, as I thought; but, happening to glance into the
street, there I saw the man again, standing opposite, and reconnoitring the
house. I had gone home hungry, but this took all my hunger away from me. I
opened the box where I kept my disguise, put it on, and got out by a back
way. I have been pretty nearly ever since on my feet coming here; I only got a
lift now and then.'

'But, Richard, do you know that West Lynne is the very worst place you
could have flown to? It has come to light that you were here before, disguised
as a farm labourer.'

'Who the deuce betrayed that?' ejaculated Richard.

'I am unable to tell; I cannot even imagine. The rumour was rife in the
place, and it reached your father's ears. That rumour may make people's wits
sharper to know you in your disguise, than they otherwise might have been.'

'But what was I to do? I was forced to come here first, to get a little money.
I shall fix myself in some other big town, far away from London; Liverpool,
or Manchester perhaps; and see what employment I can get into, but I must
have something to live upon till I can get it. I don't possess a penny piece,'
drawing out his trousers-pockets for the inspection of Mr. Carlyle. 'The last
coppers I had, threepence, I spent in bread-and-cheese and half a pint of beer
at mid-day. I had been outside that window for more than an hour, sir.'

'Indeed!'

'As I neared West Lynne, I began to think what I should do. It was of no
use trying to catch Barbara's attention on such a night as this; I had no

money to pay for a lodging; so I turned off here, hoping I might, by good luck, drop upon you. There was a little partition in this window curtain; it had not been drawn close; and through it I could see you and Miss Carlyle. I saw her leave the room; I saw you come to the window and open it, and then I spoke. Mr. Carlyle,' he added, after a pause, 'is this sort of life to go on with me for ever?'

'I am deeply sorry for you, Richard,' was the sympathizing answer. 'I wish I could remedy it.'

Before another word was spoken, the room door was tried, and then gently knocked at. Mr. Carlyle placed his hand on Richard, who was looking scared out of his wits.

'Be still; be at ease, Richard: no one shall come in. It is only Peter.'

Not Peter's voice, however, but Joyce's was heard, in response to Mr. Carlyle's demand of who was there.

'Miss Carlyle has left her handkerchief downstairs, sir, and has sent me for it.'

'You cannot come in; I am busy,' was the answer, delivered in a clear and most decisive tone.

'Who was it?' quivered Richard, as Joyce was heard going away.

'It was Joyce.'

'What, is she here still? Has anything ever been heard of Afy, sir?'

'Afy was here herself two or three months ago.'

'Was she?' said Richard, beguiled for an instant from the thought of his own danger. 'What is she doing?'

'She is in service as a lady's-maid. Richard, I questioned Afy about Thorn. She protested solemnly to me that it was not Thorn who committed the deed; that it could not have been he, for Thorn was with her at the moment of its being done.'

'It's not true,' said Richard. 'It was Thorn.'

'Richard, you cannot tell: you did not *see* it done.'

'I know that no man could have rushed out in that frantic manner, with those signs of guilt and fear about him, unless he had been engaged in a bad deed,' was Richard Hare's answer. 'It could have been no one else.'

'Afy declares he was with her,' repeated Mr. Carlyle.

'Look here, sir: you are a sharp man, and folks say I am not, but I can see things, and draw my reasonings as well as they can, perhaps. If Thorn were not Hallijohn's murderer, why should he be persecuting me?—what would he care about me? And why should his face turn livid, as it has done, each time he has seen my eyes upon him? Whether he committed the murder or whether he didn't, he must know that I did not, because he came upon me, waiting, as he was tearing from the cottage.'

Dick's reasoning was not bad.

'Another thing,' he resumed. 'Afy swore at the inquest that she was *alone* when the deed was done: that she was alone in the wood at the back of the cottage, and knew nothing about it till afterwards. How could she have sworn she was alone, if Thorn was with her?'

The fact had entirely escaped Mr. Carlyle's memory in his conversation with Afy, or he would not have failed to point out the discrepancy, and to inquire how she could reconcile it. Yet her assertion to him had been most positive and solemn. There were difficulties in the matter which he could not reconcile.

'Now that I have overgot my passion for Afy, I can see her faults, Mr. Carlyle. She'd no more stick at an untruth than she'd stick—'

A most awful thundering at the room door: loud enough to bring the very house down. No officers of justice, searching for a fugitive, ever made a louder. Richard Hare, his face turned to chalk, his eyes starting, and his own light hair bristling up with horror, struggled into his wet smock-frock after a fashion, the tails up about his ears, and the sleeves hanging, forced on his hat and its false whiskers, looked round in a bewildered manner for some cupboard or mouse-hole into which he might creep, and, seeing none, rushed to the fireplace and placed his foot on the fender. That he purposed an attempt at chimney climbing was evident, though how the fire would have agreed with his pantaloons, not to speak of what they contained, poor Dick appeared completely to ignore. Mr. Carlyle drew him back, keeping his calm, powerful hand upon his shoulder, while certain sounds in an angry voice were jerked through the keyhole.

'Richard, be a man; put aside this weakness, this fear. Have I not told you that harm shall not come near you in my house?'

'It may be that officer man from London; he may have brought half-a-dozen more with him,' gasped the unhappy Richard. 'I said they might have dodged me all the way here.'

'Nonsense. Sit down, and be at rest. It is only Cornelia: and she will be as anxious to shield you from danger as I can be.'

'Is it?' cried the relieved Richard. 'Can't you make her keep out?' he continued, his teeth still chattering.

'No, that I cannot; if she has a mind to come in,' was the candid answer. 'You remember what she was, Richard: she is not altered.'

Knowing that to speak on this side the door to his sister, when she was in one of her resolute moods, would be of no manner of use, Mr. Carlyle opened the door, dexterously swung himself through it, and shut it after him. There she stood; in a towering passion, too.

But, just a word of interlude, as to what brought her there. Miss Carlyle had gone up to bed, taking her cold with her, ordered her gruel, and forthwith proceeded to attire herself for the night, beginning with her head. Her day-cap off, and her night-cap on, of the remarkable form of which the reader had once the opportunity of taking the pattern of, she next considered about the flannel. Finding a piece convenient, some three yards square, she contrived to muffle that over all: but the process was long and difficult, her skill not accustomed to it, and the flannel perverse. The result was such that I only wish her picture could have been taken, and placed in the British Museum. A conical pyramid rose on the crown of her head, and a couple of small flannel corners flapped over her forehead; the sides resembled nothing but a judge's wig.

Now, during this ceremony—previous to the settling on of the flannel ornament, or she could not have heard—it had struck Miss Carlyle that certain sounds, as of talking, proceeded from the room beneath, which she had just quitted. She possessed a remarkably keen sense of hearing: though, indeed, none of her faculties lacked the quality of keenness. The servants, Joyce and Peter excepted, would not be convinced but that she must 'listen': but, in that, they did her injustice. At first she believed her brother must be reading aloud to himself; but she soon decided otherwise. 'Who on earth has he got in there with him?' said Miss Carlyle aloud.

The head-dress arranged she rang her bell. Joyce answered it.

'Who is it that is with your master?'

'Nobody, ma'am.'

'But I say there is. I can hear him talking.'

'I don't think anybody can be with him,' persisted Joyce. 'And the walls of this house are too well built, ma'am, for sounds from the downstairs rooms to penetrate here.'

'That's all you know about it,' cried Miss Carlyle. 'When talking goes on in that room, there's a certain sound given out which does penetrate here, and which my ears have grown accustomed to. Go and see who it is. I believe I left my handkerchief on the table: you can bring it up.'

Joyce departed, and Miss Carlyle proceeded to take off her things; her dress first, her silk petticoat next. She had arrived as far as the flannel petticoat when Joyce returned.

'Yes, ma'am, some one is talking with master. I could not go in, for the door was bolted, and master called out that he was busy.'

Food for Miss Carlyle. She, feeling sure that no visitor had come to the house, ran her thoughts rapidly over the members of the household, and came to the conclusion that it must be the governess, Miss Manning, who had dared to closet herself with Mr. Carlyle. This unlucky governess was pretty, and Miss Carlyle had been cautious to keep her and her prettiness very much out of her brother's sight: she knew the attraction he would present to her visions, or to those of any other unprovided-for governess. Oh yes; it was Miss Manning; she had stolen in, believing she, Miss Carlyle, was safe for the night; but she'd just unearth my lady. And what in the world could possess Archibald?—to lock the door!

Looking round for something warm to throw over her shoulders, and catching up an article that looked as much like a green baize table-cover as anything else, and throwing it on, down stalked Miss Carlyle. And in this trim Mr. Carlyle beheld her when he came out.

'Who have you got in that room?' she curtly asked.

'It is some one on business,' was his prompt reply. 'Cornelia, you cannot go in.'

She very nearly laughed. 'Not go in!'

'Indeed it is much better that you should not. Pray go back. You will make your cold worse, standing here.'

'Now I want to know whether you are not ashamed of yourself?' she deliberately pursued. 'You! a married man, with children in your house! I'd rather have believed anything downright wicked of myself, than of you, Archibald.'

Mr. Carlyle stared considerably.

'Come; I'll have her out. And out of this house she tramps to-morrow morning. A couple of audacious ones, to be in there with the door locked, the moment you thought you had got rid of me! Stand aside, I say, Archibald: I *will* enter.'

Mr. Carlyle never felt more inclined to laugh. And to Miss Carlyle's exceeding discomposure, she, at this juncture, saw the governess emerge from the grey parlour, glance at the hall clock, and retire again.

'Why! she's there!' she uttered. 'I thought she was with you.'

'Miss Manning locked in with me! Is that the mare's nest, Cornelia? I think your cold must have obscured your reason.'

'Well, I shall go in all the same. I tell you, Archibald, that I will see who is there.'

'If you persist in going in, you must go. But allow me to warn you that you will find tragedy in that room, not comedy. There is no woman in it; but there is a man; a man who came in through the window, like a hunted stag; a man upon whom a ban is set, and who fears the police are upon his track. Can you guess his name?'

It was Miss Carlyle's turn to stare now. She opened her dry lips to speak, but they closed again.

'It is Richard Hare, your kinsman. There's not a roof in the wide world open to him this bitter night.'

She said nothing. A long pause of dismay, and then she motioned to have the door opened.

'You will not show yourself in—in that guise?'

'Not show myself in this guise to Richard Hare?—whom I have whipped— when he was a child—ten times a day! stand on ceremony with *him*! I dare say he looks no better than I do. But it's nothing short of madness, Archibald, for him to come here.'

He left her to enter, telling her to lock the door as soon as she got inside, and went into the adjoining room, which, by another door, opened to the one Richard was in. There he rang the bell. It was answered by a footman.

'Send Peter to me.'

'Lay supper here, Peter, for two,' began Mr. Carlyle, when the old servant appeared. 'A person is with me on business. What have you in the house?'

'There's the spiced beef, sir: and some home-made raised pork-pies.'

'That will do,' said Mr. Carlyle. 'Put a jug of ale on the table, and everything likely to be wanted. And then the household can go to bed: we may be late, and the things can be removed in the morning. Oh—and, Peter,—none of you must come near the rooms, this or the next, under any pretence whatever, unless I ring, for I shall be too busy to be disturbed.'

'Very well, sir. Shall I serve the ham also?'

'The ham?'

'I beg pardon, sir; I guessed it might be Mr. Dill, and he is so fond of our hams.'

'Ah, you were always a shrewd guesser, Peter,' smiled his master. 'He is fond of ham, I know: yes, you may put it on the table. Don't forget the small kettle.'

The consequence of which little finesse on Mr. Carlyle's part was, that Peter announced in the kitchen that Mr. Dill had arrived, and supper was to be served for two. 'But what a night for the old gentleman to have trudged through on foot!' ejaculated he.

'And what a trudge he'll have of it back again, for it'll be worse then!' chimed in one of the maids.

When Mr. Carlyle got back to the other room, his sister and Richard Hare had scarcely finished staring at each other. Richard had no doubt seen many a fancifully-attired lady in the class amidst whom he had recently lived, but he could scarcely have had the luck to meet one who beat Miss Carlyle. Sure, two such guys never stood face to face! She: black shoes; black stockings; a flannel petticoat that reached to the calf; the nondescript shawl, which, to crown its other virtues, was finished off with jagged fringe; and the unsightly head-dress that was like nothing on earth! He: fustian clothes underneath, somewhat short of buttons; the smock frock still on, tails up and sleeves down; the battered hat and the bushy whiskers; with the trembling hands and the scared white face of terror! I have been at many a carnival abroad, but I assure you I never saw in the maskers a couple equal to the spectacle those two would have presented, borne along in a triumphal carnival car.

'Please lock the door, Miss Cornelia,' began poor shivering Dick, when he had feasted his eyes.

'The door's locked,' snapped she. 'But what on earth brought you here, Richard? You must be worse than mad.'

'The Bow-street officers were after me in London,' he meekly responded, unconsciously using a term which had been familiar to his boyish years. 'I had to cut away without a thing belonging to me; without so much as a clean shirt.'

'They must be polite officers not to have been after you before,' was the consolatory remark of Miss Carlyle. 'Are you going to dance a hornpipe through the streets of West Lynne to-morrow, and show yourself openly?'

'Not if I can help it,' replied Richard.

'You might just as well do that, if you come to West Lynne at all, for you can't be here now without being found out. There was a bother about you having been here before: I should like to know how it got abroad.'

'The life I lead is dreadful,' cried Richard. 'I might make up my mind to the toil, though that's hard, after being reared a gentleman; but to be in exile, banned, disgraced, afraid to show my face in broad daylight amidst my fellow-men, in dread every hour that the sword may fall! I would almost as soon be dead, as continue to live it.'

'Well, you have got nobody to grumble at: you brought it upon yourself,' philosophically returned Miss Carlyle, as she opened the door to admit her brother. 'You would go hunting after that brazen hussy, Afy, you know, in defiance of all that could be said to you.'

'That would not have brought it upon me,' said Richard. 'It was through that fiend's having killed Hallijohn: that was what brought the ban upon me.'

'It's a most extraordinary thing, if anybody else *did* kill him, that the facts can't be brought to light,' retorted Miss Carlyle. 'Here you tell a cock-and-bull story of some man having done it—some Thorn; but nobody ever saw or heard of him: at the time or since. It looks like a made-up story, Mr. Dick, to whiten yourself.'

'Made up!' panted Richard, in agitation, for it seemed cruel to him, especially in his present frame of mind, to have a doubt cast upon his tale. 'It is Thorn who is setting the officers upon me. I have seen him three or four times within the last fortnight.'

'And why did you not turn the tables, and set the officers upon him?' demanded Miss Carlyle.

'Because it would lead to no good. Where's the proof, save my bare word, that he committed the murder?'

Miss Carlyle rubbed her nose. 'Dick Hare,' said she.

'Well?'

'You know you always were the greatest natural that ever was let loose out of leading-strings.'

'I know; I was always told so.'

'And it's what you always will be. If I were accused of committing a crime, which I knew another had committed, and not myself, should I be such an idiot as not to give that other into custody, if I got the chance? If you were not in such a cold, shivery, shaky state, I would treat you to a bit of my mind: you may rely upon that.'

'He was in league with Afy at that period,' pursued Richard; 'a deceitful, bad man; and he carries it in his countenance. And he must be in league with her still, if she asserts that he was in her company at the moment the murder was committed. Mr. Carlyle says she does; that she told him so the other day when she was here. He never was; and it was he, and no other, who did the murder.'

'Yes,' burst forth Miss Carlyle, for the topic was sure to agitate her, 'that Jezebel of Brass did presume to come here! She chose her time well: and may thank her lucky stars I was not at home. Archibald—he's a fool, too; quite as bad as you are, Dick Hare, in some things—actually suffered her to lodge here for two days! A vain, ill-conducted hussy, given to nothing but finery and folly!'

'Afy said that she knew nothing of Thorn's movements now, Richard, and had not for some time,' interposed Mr. Carlyle, allowing his sister's compliment to pass in silence. 'She heard a rumour, she thought, that he had gone abroad with his regiment.'

'So much the better for her, if it is true that she knows nothing of him,' was Richard's comment. 'I can answer for it that he is not abroad, but in England.'

'And where are you going to lodge to-night?' abruptly spoke Miss Carlyle, confronting Richard.

'I don't know,' was the broken-spirited answer sighed forth. 'If I lie myself down in a snow-drift and am found frozen in the morning, it won't be of much moment.'

'Was that what you thought of doing?' returned Miss Carlyle.

'No,' he mildly said. 'What I had thought of doing was to ask Mr. Carlyle for the loan of a few shillings, and then I can get a bed. I know a place where I shall be in safety, two or three miles from this.'

'Richard, I would not turn a dog out, to go two or three miles, on such a night,' impulsively uttered Mr. Carlyle. 'You must stop here.'

'Indeed I don't see how he is to get up to a bedroom; or how a room is to be made ready for him, for the matter of that, without betraying his presence to the servants,' snapped Miss Carlyle. And poor Richard Hare laid his aching head upon his hands.

But now, Miss Carlyle's manner was more in fault than her heart. Will it be believed that, before speaking the above ungracious words, before Mr. Carlyle had touched upon the subject, she had been casting about in her busy mind for the best plan of sleeping Richard—how it could be accomplished.

'One thing is certain,' she resumed. 'That it will be impossible for you to sleep here without its being known to Joyce. And I suppose you and Joyce are upon the friendly terms of drawn daggers, for she believes you were the murderer of her father.'

'Let me disabuse her,' interrupted Richard, his pale lips working as he started up. 'Allow me to see her and convince her. Mr. Carlyle, why did you not tell Joyce better.'

'There's that small room at the back of mine,' said Miss Carlyle, returning to the practical part of the subject. 'He might sleep there. But Joyce must be taken into confidence.'

'Joyce had better come in,' said Mr. Carlyle. 'I will say a word to her first.'

He unlocked the door and quitted the room, Miss Carlyle as jealously locking it again; called to Joyce, and beckoned her into the adjoining apartment. He knew that Joyce's belief of the guilt of Richard Hare was confirmed and strong: but he must uproot that belief, if Richard was to be lodged in his house that night.

'Joyce,' he began, 'you remember how thoroughly imbued with the persuasion you were, that Afy went off after Richard Hare, and was living with him. I several times expressed my doubts upon the point: the fact was, I had positive information that she was not with him, and never had been, though I considered it expedient to keep my information to myself. You are convinced now that she was not with him?'

'Of course I am, sir.'

'Well, you see, Joyce, that my opinion would have been worth listening to. Now I am going to try to shake your belief upon another point, and if I assure you that I have equally good grounds for doing so, you will believe me.'

'I am quite certain, sir, that you would state nothing but what is true; and I know that your judgment is sound,' was Joyce's answer.

'Then I must tell you that I do not believe it was Richard Hare who murdered your father.'

'*Sir!*' uttered Joyce, amazed out of her senses.

'I believe Richard Hare to be as innocent of the murder as you or I,' he deliberately repeated. 'I have held grounds for this opinion, Joyce, for many years.'

'Then, sir, who did do it?'

'Afy's other lover. That dandy fellow, Thorn, as I truly believe.'

'And you say you have grounds, sir?' Joyce asked, after a pause.

'Good grounds: and I tell you I have been in possession of them for years. I should be glad for you to think as I do.'

'But, sir,—if Richard Hare was innocent, why did he run away, and keep away?'

'Ah, why indeed! it is that which has done the mischief. His own weak cowardice was in fault; he feared to come back; and he felt that he could not remove the odium of circumstances. Joyce, I should like you to see him, and hear his story.'

'There is not much chance of that, sir. I dare say he will never venture here again.'

'He is here now.'

Joyce looked up, considerably startled.

'Here, in this house,' repeated Mr. Carlyle. 'He has taken shelter in it, and for the few hours that he will remain, we must extend our hospitality and protection to him, concealing him in the best manner we can. I thought it well that this confidence should be reposed in you, Joyce. Come now, and see him.'

Considering that it was a subdued interview—the voices subdued, I mean —it was a confused one. Richard talking vehemently, Joyce asking question after question, Miss Carlyle's tongue going as fast as theirs. The only silent one was Mr. Carlyle. Joyce could not refuse to believe protestations so solemn, and her suspicion veered round upon Captain Thorn.

'And now about the bed,' interjected Miss Carlyle, impatiently. 'Where's he to sleep, Joyce? The only safe room, that I know of, will be the one through mine.'

'He can't sleep there, ma'am. Don't you know that the key of the door was lost last week, and we cannot open it.'

'So much the better. He'll be all the safer.'

'But how is he to get in?'

'To get in? Why, through my room, of course. Does not mine open to it, stupid?'

'Oh, well, ma'am, if you would like him to go through yours, that's different.'

'Why shouldn't he go through? Do you suppose I mind young Dick Hare? Not I, indeed,' she irascibly continued. 'I only wish he was young enough for me to flog him as I used to, that's all: he deserves it as much as anybody ever did, playing the fool as he has done, in all ways. I shall be in bed with curtains drawn, and his passing through won't harm me, and my lying there won't harm him. Stand on ceremony with Dick Hare! what next, I wonder?'

This point being settled, Joyce went to put sheets upon the bed, and Miss Carlyle returned to her own. Mr. Carlyle meanwhile took Richard in to supper, and fed him plentifully, and made him comfortable. Under the influence of the good cheer, the good fire, and the hot glass of brandy-and-water, which wound up the entertainment, Richard fell asleep in his chair. Not five minutes had he slept, however, when he started up, wild and haggard, beating off, as it were, some imaginary assailant.

'It was not I!' he uttered fearfully and passionately. 'It is of no use to take me, for it was not I. It was another; he who—'

'Richard, Richard!' soothingly said Mr. Carlyle.

Richard cast his bewildered eyes on the supper-table, the fire, on Mr. Carlyle, all reassuring objects to look upon. 'I declare, sir, I dreamt that they had grabbed me. What stupid things dreams are!'

At this moment there came a gentle knock at the door, and Mr. Carlyle opened it. It was Joyce.

'The room is ready, sir,' she whispered, 'and all the household are in bed.'

'Then now is your time, Richard. Good night.'

He stole upstairs after Joyce, who piloted him through the room of Miss Carlyle. Nothing could be seen of that lady, though something might be heard: one, given to truth more than politeness, might have called it snoring. Joyce showed Richard his chamber, gave him the candle, and closed the door upon him.

Poor hunted Richard! good night to you!

❧ X V I I ❧

Barbara's Heart at Rest

Morning dawned. The same dull weather, the same heavy fall of snow. Miss Carlyle took her breakfast in bed, an indulgence she had not favoured for ever so many years. Richard Hare rose, but remained in his chamber, and Joyce carried his breakfast in to him.

Mr. Carlyle entered whilst he was taking it. 'How did you sleep, Richard?'

'I slept well. I was so dead tired. What am I to do next, Mr. Carlyle? The sooner I get away from this the better. I can't feel safe.'

'You must not think of it before evening. I am aware that you cannot remain here, save for a few temporary hours, as it would inevitably become known to the servants. You say you think of going to Liverpool or Manchester?'

'To any large town: they are all alike to me; but one, pursued as I am, is safer in a large place than a small one.'

'I am inclined to think that this man, Thorn, only made a show of threatening you, Richard. If he be really the guilty party, his policy must be to keep all in quietness. The very worst thing that could happen for him, would be your arrest.'

'Then why molest me? Why send an officer to dodge me?'

'He did not like your molesting him, and he thought he would frighten you. After that day, you would probably have seen no more of the officer. You may depend upon one thing, Richard: had the policeman's object been to take you, he would have done so: he would not have contented himself with following you about from place to place. Besides, when a detective officer is employed to watch a party, he takes care not to allow himself to be seen: now this man showed himself to you more than once.'

'Yes, there's a good deal in that,' observed Richard. 'For, to one in his class of life, the bare suspicion of such a crime, brought against him, would crush him for ever in the eyes of his compeers.'

'It is difficult to me, Richard, to believe that he is in the class of life you speak of,' observed Mr. Carlyle.

'There's no doubt about it; there's none indeed. But that I did not much like to mention the name, for it can't be a pleasant name to you, I should have said last night who I have seen him walking with,' continued simple-hearted Richard.

Mr. Carlyle looked inquiringly. 'Say on, Richard.'

'I have seen him, sir, with Sir Francis Levison: twice. Once he was talking to him at the door of the betting-rooms, and once they were walking arm-in-arm. They are apparently upon intimate terms.'

At this moment, a loud, flustering, angry voice was heard calling from the stairs, and Richard leaped up as if he had been shot. His door—not the one leading to the room of Miss Carlyle—opened upon the corridor, and the voice sounded close, just as if its owner were coming in with a bound. It was the voice of Mr. Justice Hare.

'Carlyle, where are you? Here's a pretty thing happened. Come down.'

Mr. Carlyle for once in his life lost his calm equanimity, and sprang to the door, to keep it against invasion, as eagerly as Richard could have done. He forgot that Joyce had said the door was safely locked and the key mislaid. As to Richard, he rushed on his hat and his black whiskers, and hesitated between under the bed and inside the wardrobe.

'Don't agitate yourself, Richard,' whispered Mr. Carlyle: 'there is no real danger. I will go and keep him safely.'

But when Mr. Carlyle got through his sister's bed-room, he found that lady had taken the initiative, and was leaning over the balustrades, having been arrested in the process of dressing. Her clothes were on, but her night-cap was not off: little cared she, however, who saw her night-cap.

'What on earth brings you up in this weather?' began she in a tone of exasperation.

'I want to see Carlyle. Nice news I have had!'

'What about? Anything concerning Anne, or her family?'

'Anne be bothered!' replied the justice, who was certainly, from some cause, in a furious temper. 'It concerns that precious rascal, whom I am forced to call son. I am told he is here.'

Down the stairs leaped Mr. Carlyle, four at a time, wound his arm within Mr. Hare's, and led him to a sitting-room.

'Good morning, justice. You had courage to venture up through the snow! What is the matter? you seem excited.'

'Excited!' raved the justice, dancing about the room, first on one leg, then on the other, like a cat on hot bricks; 'so would you be excited, if your life were worried out, as mine is, over a wicked scamp of a son. Why can't folks trouble their heads about their own business, and let my affairs alone? A pity but what he were hanged, and the thing done with!'

'But what has happened?' questioned Mr. Carlyle.

'Why, this has happened,' retorted the justice, throwing a letter on the table. 'The post brought me this, just now—and pleasant information it gives!'

Mr. Carlyle took up the note and read it. It purported to be from 'a friend' to Justice Hare, informing that gentleman that his 'criminal son' was likely to have arrived at West Lynne, or would arrive in the course of a day or so: and it recommended Mr. Hare to speed his departure from it, lest he should be 'pounced upon.'

'This letter is anonymous!' exclaimed Mr. Carlyle.

'Of course it is,' stamped the justice.

'The only notice I should ever take of an anonymous letter would be to put it in the fire,' cried Mr. Carlyle, his lip curling with scorn.

'But who has written it?' danced Justice Hare. 'And *is* Dick at West Lynne?—that's the question!'

'Now, is it likely that he would come to West Lynne?' remonstrated Mr. Carlyle. 'Justice, will you pardon me if I venture to give you my candid opinion?'

'The fool at West Lynne: running into the very jaws of death. By Jupiter! if I can drop upon him, I'll retain him in custody, and make out a warrant for his committal! I'll have this everlasting bother over.'

'I was going to give you my opinion,' quietly put in Mr. Carlyle. 'I fear, justice, you bring these annoyances upon yourself.'

'Bring them upon myself!' ranted the indignant justice. 'I? Did I murder Hallijohn? Did I murder Hallijohn? did I fly away from the law? Am I in hiding, Beelzebub knows where? Do I take starts, right down into my native parish disguised as a labourer, on purpose to worry my own father? Do I write anonymous letters? Bring them upon myself, do I? That cobs all, Carlyle.'

'You will not hear me out. It is known that you are much exasperated against Richard—'

'And if your son serves you the same when he is grown up, sha'nt you be exasperated, pray?' fired Justice Hare.

'Do hear me. It is known that you are much exasperated, and that any allusion to him excites and annoys you. Now, my opinion is, justice, that some busybody is raising these reports, and writing these letters on purpose to annoy you. It may be somebody at West Lynne, very near us, for all we know.'

'That's all rubbish,' peevishly responded the justice, after a pause. 'It's not likely. Who'd do it?'

'It is very likely: but you may be sure they will not give us a clue as to the "who." I should put that letter in the fire, and think no more about it. That's the only way to serve them. A pretty laugh they have had in their sleeve, if it is anybody near, at seeing you wade up here through the snow this morning! They would know you were bringing the letter to consult me.'

The justice—in spite of his obstinacy, he was somewhat easily persuaded to different views of things, especially by Mr. Carlyle—let fall his coat-tails, which had been gathered in his arms, as he stood with his back to the fire, and brought both his hands upon the table with a force enough to break it. 'If I thought that,' he spluttered, 'if I could think it, I'd have the whole parish of West Lynne before me to-day, and commit them for trial.'

'It's a pity but what you could,' said Mr. Carlyle.

'Well, it may be, or it may not be, that that villain is coming here,' he resumed. 'I shall call in at the police-station, and tell them to keep a sharp look-out.'

'You will do nothing of the sort, justice,' exclaimed Mr. Carlyle almost in agitation. 'Richard is not likely to make his appearance at West Lynne; but, if he did, would you, his own father, turn the flood upon him? Not a man living, but would cry shame upon you. Yes, Mr. Hare, they would: if other people shrink from telling you the truth, I do not. You have boasted that you would deliver Richard up, if he ever threw himself in your path; and your unnatural harshness has been commented upon in no measured terms: it has, I give you my word. But of course nobody believed that you would really *do* it. You might take leave of your friends if you did, for you would find none willing to own you for one afterwards.'

'I took an oath I'd do it,' said the justice.

'You did not take an oath to go open-mouthed to the police-station, upon the receipt of any despicable anonymous letter, or any foolish report, and say, "I have news that my son will be here to-day: look after him." Nonsense, justice! let the police look out for themselves; but don't *you* set them on.'

The justice growled, whether in assent or dissent did not appear, and Mr. Carlyle resumed.

'Have you shown this letter to Mrs. Hare? or mentioned it to her?'

'Not I. I didn't give myself time. I had gone down to the front gate, to see how deep the snow lay in the road, when the postman came up; so I read it as I stood there. I went in for my coat and umbrella to come off to you, and Mrs. Hare wanted to know where I was going to in such a hurry; but I did not satisfy her.'

'I am truly glad to hear it,' said Mr. Carlyle. 'Such information, as this, could not fail to have a dangerous effect upon Mrs. Hare. Do not suffer a hint of it to escape you, justice: consider how much anxiety she has already suffered.'

'It's partly her own fault. Why can't she drive the ill-doing boy from her mind?'

'If she could,' said Mr. Carlyle, 'she would be acting against human nature. There is one phase of the question which you may possibly not have glanced at, justice. You speak of delivering your son up to the law: has it ever struck you that you would be delivering up at the same time your wife's life?'

'Stuff!' said the justice.

'You would find it no "stuff." So sure as Richard is brought to trial, whether through your means or through any other, so sure will it kill your wife.'

Mr. Hare took up the letter, which had laid open on the table, folded it, and put it in its envelope. 'I suppose you don't know the writing?' he asked of Mr. Carlyle.

'I never saw it before, that I remember. Are you returning home?'

'No, I shall go on to Beauchamp's and show him this, and hear what he says. It's not much farther.'

'Tell him not to speak of it, then. Beauchamp's safe, for his sympathies are with Richard—oh yes, they are, justice: ask him the question plainly if you like, and he will confess to it. I can tell you more sympathy goes with Richard than is acknowledged to you. But I would not show the letter to any one but Beauchamp,' added Mr. Carlyle: 'neither would I speak of it.'

'Who can have written it?' repeated the justice. 'It bears, you see, the London post-mark.'

'It is too wide a speculation to enter upon. And no satisfactory conclusion could come of it.'

Justice Hare departed. Mr. Carlyle watched him down the avenue, striding under his umbrella, and then went up to Richard. Miss Carlyle was sitting with the latter then.

'I thought I should have died,' spoke poor Dick. 'I declare, Mr. Carlyle, my very blood seemed turned to water, and I thought I should have died with fright. Is he gone away, all safe?'

'He is gone, and it is all safe.'

'And what did he want? What was it he had heard of me?'

Mr. Carlyle gave a brief explanation, and Richard immediately set down the letter as the work of Thorn. 'Will it be possible for me to see my mother this time?' he demanded of Mr. Carlyle.

'I think it would be highly injudicious to let your mother know that you are here, or have been here,' was the answer of Mr. Carlyle. 'She would naturally be inquiring into particulars, and when she came to hear that you were pursued, she would never have another minute's peace. You must forego the pleasure of seeing her this time, Richard.'

'And Barbara?'

'Barbara might come and stay the day with you. Only—'

'Only what, sir?' cried Richard, for Mr. Carlyle had hesitated.

'I was thinking what a wretched morning it is for her to come out in.'

'She would go through an avalanche, she'd wade through mountains of snow, to see me,' cried Richard eagerly, 'and be delighted to do it.'

'She always was a little fool,' put in Miss Carlyle, jerking some stitches out of her knitting.

'I know she would,' observed Mr. Carlyle, in answer to Richard. 'We will try and get her here.'

'She can arrange about the money I am to have, just as well as my mother could, you know, sir.'

'Yes. For Barbara is in receipt of money of her own now, and I know she would wish for nothing better than to apply some of it to you. Cornelia, as an excuse for getting her here, I must say to Mrs. Hare that you are ill, and wish Barbara to come for the day and bear you company. Shall I?'

'Say I am dead, if you like,' responded Miss Corny, who was in one of her cross moods.

Mr. Carlyle ordered the pony-carriage, and drove forth with John. He drew in at the Grove. Barbara and Mrs. Hare were seated together, and looked surprised at the early visit.

'Did you want Mr. Hare, Archibald? He is out. He went while the breakfast was on the table, apparently in a desperate hurry.'

'I don't want Mr. Hare. I want Barbara. I have come to carry her off.'

'To carry off Barbara!' echoed Mrs. Hare.

'Cornelia is not well: she has caught a violent cold, and wishes Barbara to spend the day with her.'

'Oh, Mr. Carlyle, I cannot leave mamma to-day. She is not well herself, and she would be so dull without me.'

'Neither can I spare her, Archibald. It is not a day for Barbara to go out.'

How could he get to say a word to Barbara alone? Whilst he deliberated, talking on all the while to Mrs. Hare, a servant arrived at the sitting-room door.

'The fishmonger's boy is come up, ma'am. His master has sent him to say that he fears there'll be no fish in to-day in anything like time. The trains cannot get up, with this weather.'

Mrs. Hare rose from her seat, to hold a conference at the door with her maid; and Mr. Carlyle seized his opportunity.

'Barbara,' he whispered, 'make no opposition. You *must* come. What I really want you for is connected with Richard.'

She looked up at him, a startled glance, and the crimson flew to her face. Mrs. Hare returned to her seat. 'Oh, such a day!' she shivered. 'I am sure Cornelia cannot expect Barbara.'

'But Cornelia does. And there is my pony-carriage waiting to take her before I go to the office. Not a flake of snow can come near her, Mrs. Hare. The large warm apron will be up, and an umbrella will shield her bonnet and face. Get your things on, Barbara.'

'Mamma, if you would not very much mind being left, I should like to go,' said Barbara, with almost trembling eagerness.

'But you would be sure to take cold, child.'

'Oh dear no. I can wrap up well.'

'And I will see that she comes home all right this evening,' added Mr. Carlyle.

In a few minutes they were seated in the pony-carriage. Barbara's tongue was burning to ask questions, but John sat behind them, and would have overheard. When they arrived at East Lynne, Mr. Carlyle gave her his arm up the steps, and took her into the breakfast-room.

'Will you prepare yourself for a surprise, Barbara?'

Suspense—fear—had turned her very pale. 'Something has happened to Richard!' she uttered.

'Nothing that need agitate you. He is here.'

'Here! Where?'

'Here. Under this roof. He slept here last night.'

'Oh, Archibald!'

'Only fancy, Barbara! I opened the window at nine last night, to look at the weather, and in burst Richard. We could not let him go out again in the snow, so he slept here, in that room next Cornelia's.'

'Does she know of it?'

'Of course. And Joyce also: we were obliged to tell Joyce. Imagine Richard's fear. Your father came this morning, calling up the stairs after me, saying he heard Richard was here. He meant at West Lynne. I thought Richard would have gone out of his mind with fright.'

A few more explanations, and Mr. Carlyle took Barbara into the room, Miss Carlyle and her knitting still keeping Richard company. In fact, that was to be the general sitting-room of the day, and a hot lunch, Richard's dinner, would be served in Miss Carlyle's chamber at one o'clock, Joyce only admitted to wait on them.

'And now I must go,' said Mr. Carlyle, after chatting a few minutes. 'The office is waiting for me, and my poor ponies are in the snow.'

'But you'll be sure to be home early, Mr. Carlyle!' said Richard. 'I dare not stop here: I must be off not a moment later than six or seven o'clock.'

'I will be home, Richard.'

Anxiously did Richard and Barbara consult that day, Miss Carlyle of course putting in her word. Over and over again did Barbara ask the particulars of the slight interviews Richard had had with Thorn; over and over again did she openly speculate upon what his name really was. 'If you could but discover some one whom he knows, and inquire it!' she exclaimed.

'I have seen him with one person, but I can't inquire of him. They are too thick together, he and Thorn, and are birds of a feather also, I suspect. Great swells, both.'

'Oh, Richard, don't use those expressions. They are unsuited to a gentleman.'

Richard laughed bitterly. 'A gentleman!'

'Who is it you have seen Thorn with?' inquired Barbara.

'Sir Francis Levison,' replied Richard, glancing at Miss Carlyle, who drew in her lips ominously.

'With whom?' uttered Barbara, betraying complete astonishment.

'Do you know Sir Francis Levison?'

'Oh yes, I know *him*. Nearly the only man about town that I do know.'

Barbara seemed lost in a puzzled reverie, and it was some time before she roused herself from it.

'Are they at all alike?' she asked.

'Very much so, I suspect. Both bad men.'

'But I meant in person.'

'Not in the least. Except that they are both tall.'

Again Barbara sank into thought. Richard's words had surprised her. She was aroused from it by hearing a child's voice in the next room. She ran into it, and Miss Carlyle immediately fastened the intervening door.

It was little Archibald Carlyle. Joyce had come in with the tray to lay the luncheon, and before she could lock the door, Archibald ran in after her. Barbara lifted him in her arms to carry him back to the nursery.

'Oh, you heavy boy!' she exclaimed.

Archie laughed. 'Wilson says that,' he lisped, 'if ever she has to carry me.'

'I have brought you a truant, Wilson,' cried Barbara.

'Oh, is it you, Miss Barbara? How are you, Miss? Naughty boy!—yes; he ran away without my noticing him—he can open the door now.'

'You must be so kind as to keep him strictly in, for to-day,' continued Barbara, authoritatively. 'Miss Carlyle is not well, and cannot be subjected to the annoyance of his running into her room.'

Evening came, and the time of Richard's departure. It was again snowing heavily, though it had ceased in the middle of the day. Money for the present had been given to him; arrangements had been discussed. Mr. Carlyle insisted upon Richard's sending him his address, as soon as he should own one to send, and Richard faithfully promised. He was in very low spirits, almost as low as Barbara, who could not conceal her tears: they dropped in silence on her pretty silk dress. He was smuggled down the stairs, a large cloak of Miss Carlyle's enveloping him, into the room he had entered by storm on the previous night. Mr. Carlyle held the window open.

'Good-bye, Barbara dear. If ever you should be able to tell my mother of this day, say that my chief sorrow was, not to see her.'

'Oh, Richard!' she sobbed forth, broken-hearted, 'good-bye. May God be with you and bless you!'

'Farewell, Richard!' said Miss Carlyle: 'don't you be fool enough to get into any more scrapes.'

Last of all, he wrung the hand of Mr. Carlyle. The latter went outside with him for an instant, and their leavetaking was alone.

Barbara returned to the chamber he had quitted. She felt that she must indulge in a few moment's sobbing: Joyce was there, but Barbara was sobbing when she entered it.

'It *is* hard for him, Miss Barbara; if he is really innocent?'

Barbara turned her streaming eyes upon her. '*If!* Joyce do you doubt that he is innocent?'

'I quite believe him to be so now, Miss. Nobody could so solemnly assert what was not true. The thing at present will be to find that Captain Thorn.'

'Joyce!' exclaimed Barbara in excitement, seizing hold of Joyce's hands, 'I thought I had found him; I believed, in my own mind, that I knew who he was. I don't mind telling you, though I have never before spoken of it: and with one thing or other this night I feel just as if I should die; as if I must speak. I thought it was Sir Francis Levison.'

Joyce stared with all her eyes. 'Miss Barbara!'

'I did. I have thought it ever since the night that Lady Isabel went away. My poor brother was at West Lynne then; he had come for a few hours, and he met the man, Thorn, walking in Bean-lane. He was in evening dress, and Richard described a peculiar motion of his, the throwing off his hair from his brow: he said his white hand and his diamond ring glittered in the moonlight. The white hand, the ring, the motion—for he was always doing it—all reminded me of Captain Levison, and from that hour until to-day I did believe him to be the man Richard saw. To-day Richard tells me that he knows Sir Francis Levison, and that he and Thorn are intimate. What I think now is, that this Thorn must have paid a flying visit to the neighbourhood that night, to assist Captain Levison in the wicked work he had on hand.'

'How strange it all sounds!' uttered Joyce.

'And I never could tell my suspicions to Mr. Carlyle! I did not like to mention Francis Levison's name to him.'

Barbara returned downstairs. 'I must be going home,' she said to Mr. Carlyle. 'It is half-past seven, and mamma will be uneasy.'

'Whenever you like, Barbara.'

'But can I not walk? I am so sorry to take out your ponies again, and in this storm.'

Mr. Carlyle laughed. 'Which would feel the storm worse, you or the ponies?'

But when Barbara got outside, she saw that it was not the pony-carriage, but the chariot that was in waiting for her. She turned inquiringly to Mr. Carlyle.

'Did you think I should allow you to go home in an open carriage to-night, Barbara?'

'Are you coming also?'

'I suppose I had better,' he smiled. 'To see that you and the carriage do not come to harm.'

Barbara withdrew to her corner of the chariot, and cried silently. Very, very deeply did she mourn the unhappy situation, the privations, of her brother: and she knew that he was one to feel them deeply: he could not battle with the world's hardships so bravely as many could have done. Mr. Carlyle only detected her emotion as they were nearing the Grove. He leaned forward, took her hand, and held it between his.

'Don't grieve, Barbara. Bright days may be in store for Richard yet.' The carriage stopped.

'You may go back,' he said to the servants when he alighted. 'I shall walk home.'

'Oh,' exclaimed Barbara, 'I do think you intend to spend the evening with us! Mamma will be so glad.'

Her voice showed that she was glad also. Mr. Carlyle drew her hand within his arm as they walked up the path.

But Barbara had reckoned without her host. Mrs. Hare was in bed, consequently could not be pleased at the visit of Mr. Carlyle. The justice had gone out, and she, feeling tired and not well, thought she would retire to rest. Barbara stole into her room, but found her asleep; so that it fell to Barbara to entertain Mr. Carlyle.

They stood together before the large pier-glass in front of the blazing fire. Barbara was thinking over the events of the day. What Mr. Carlyle was thinking of was best known to himself: his eyes, covered with their drooping eyelids, were cast upon Barbara. There was a long silence: at length Barbara seemed to feel that his gaze was on her, and she looked up at him.

'Will you marry me, Barbara?'

The words were spoken in the quietest, most matter-of-fact tone, just as if he had said, Shall I give you a chair, Barbara. But oh! the change that passed

over her countenance! the sudden light of joy; the scarlet flush of emotion
and of happiness. Then it all faded down to paleness and sadness.

She shook her head in the negative. 'But you are very kind to ask me,' she
added in words.

'What is the impediment, Barbara?'

Another rush of colour as before, and a deep silence. Mr. Carlyle put his
arm round her, and bent his face on a level with hers.

'Whisper it to me, Barbara.'

She burst into a flood of tears.

'Is it because I once married another?'

'No, no. It is the remembrance of that night—you cannot have forgotten
it, and it is stamped on my brain in letters of fire. I never thought so to betray
myself. But for what passed that night, you would not have asked me now.'

'Barbara!'

She glanced up at him; the tone was so painful.

'Do you know that I *love* you? that there is none other in the world whom
I would care to marry, but you? Nay, Barbara, when happiness is within our
reach, let us not throw it away upon a chimera.'

She cried more softly, leaning upon his arm. 'Happiness? Would it be happiness for you?'

'Great and deep happiness,' he whispered.

She read truth in his countenance, and a sweet smile illumined her sunny
features. Mr. Carlyle read its signs.

'You love me as much as ever, Barbara!'

'Far more; far more,' was the murmured answer, and Mr. Carlyle held her
closer, and drew her face fondly to his. Barbara's heart was at length at rest;
and she had been content to remain where she was for ever.

And Richard? Had he got clear off? Richard was stealing along the road,
plunging into the snow by the hedge, because it was more sheltered there
than in the beaten path, when his umbrella came in contact with another
umbrella. Miss Carlyle had furnished it to him; not to protect his battered
hat, but to protect his face from being seen by the passers-by. The umbrella
he encountered was an aristocratic silk one, with an ivory handle: Dick's was
a democratic cotton, with hardly any handle at all; and the respective owners
had been bearing on, heads down and umbrellas out, till they, the umbrellas,
met smash, right underneath a gas-lamp. Aside went each umbrella, and the
antagonists stared at each other.

'How dared you, fellow? Can't you see where you are going to?'

Dick thought he should have dropped. He would have given all the money
his pockets held, if the friendly earth had but opened and swallowed him in.
For he, now peering into his face, was his own father.

Uttering an exclamation of dismay, which broke from him involuntarily,
Richard sped away with the swiftness of an arrow. Did Justice Hare recog-

nize the tones? It cannot be said. He saw a rough, strange-looking man with bushy black whiskers, who was evidently scared at the sight of him. That was nothing; for the justice, being a justice and a strict one, was regarded with considerable awe in the parish, by those of Dick's apparent calibre. Nevertheless, he stood still and gazed in the direction, until all sound of Richard's footsteps had died away in the distance.

❦ XVIII ❦

Frozen to Death in the Snow

Tears were streaming down the face of Mrs. Hare. It was a bright morning after the snow-storm, so bright that the sky was blue and the sun was shining, but the snow lay deeply upon the ground. Mrs. Hare sat in her chair, enjoying the brightness, and Mr. Carlyle stood near her. The tears were of joy and of grief mingled: of grief at hearing that she should at last have to part with Barbara; of joy that she was going to one so entirely worthy of her as Mr. Carlyle.

'Archibald, she has had a happy home here: you will render yours as much so?'

'To the very utmost of my power.'

'You will be ever kind to her, ever cherish her?'

'With my whole heart and strength. Dear Mrs. Hare, I thought you knew me too well to doubt me.'

'Doubt you! I do not doubt you: I trust you implicitly, Archibald. Had the whole world laid themselves at Barbara's feet, I should have prayed that she might choose you.'

A smile flitted over Mr. Carlyle's lips. *He* knew it was what Barbara would have done.

'But, Archibald, what about Cornelia?' resumed Mrs. Hare. 'I would not for a moment interfere in your affairs, or in the arrangements you and Barbara may agree upon: but I cannot help thinking that married people are better alone.'

'Cornelia will quit East Lynne,' said Mr. Carlyle. 'I have not spoken to her yet, but I shall do so now. I have long made up my mind to that; that if ever I married again, I and my wife would live alone. It is said she interfered too much with my former wife: had I suspected it, Cornelia should not have remained in the house a day. Rest assured that Barbara shall not be subjected to the chance.'

'How did *you* come over her?' demanded the justice, who had already given his gratified consent, and who now entered in his dressing-gown and morning wig. 'Others have tried it on, and Barbara would not listen to any of them.'

'I suppose I must have cast a spell upon her,' answered Mr. Carlyle, breaking into a smile.

'Here she is. Barbara,' cried the unceremonious justice, 'what is it that you see in Carlyle more than anybody else?'

Barbara's scarlet cheeks answered for her. 'Papa,' she said, 'Otway Bethel is at the door, asking to speak to you. Jaspar says he won't come in.'

'Then I'm sure I am not going out to him in the cold. Here, Mr. Otway, what are you afraid of? Come in.'

Otway Bethel made his appearance in his usual sporting costume. But he did not seem altogether at his ease in the presence of Mrs. Hare and Barbara.

'The colonel wished me to see you, justice, to ask if you had any objection to the meeting being put off from one o'clock till two,' cried he, after nodding to Mr. Carlyle. 'He has got a friend coming to see him unexpectedly, who will leave again by the two o'clock train.'

'I don't care which it is,' answered Mr. Hare. 'Two o'clock will do as well as one for me.'

'That's all right, then, and I'll drop in upon Herbert and Pinner, and acquaint them. Have you heard of the dead man being found?'

'What dead man?' cried Justice Hare.

'Some chap who must have missed his way last night: or who perhaps laid himself down overcome with fatigue. He was found this morning, frozen to death. I have seen him: he is lying in that hollow, just out of the road, as you turn down to Hallijohn's old cottage. I saw a lot of folks making for the place, so I went too.'

'Who is he?' inquired Justice Hare.

'A stranger, I think; I didn't recognize his face. He is in a smock-frock; a young man with a profusion of dark whiskers.'

'By George, but I shouldn't wonder but it's the fellow who last night nearly broke my umbrella!' ejaculated the justice. 'He wore a smock-frock, and looked young, and his whiskers were fierce enough for an Irishman's. I thought the fellow a little cracked. He was coming blundering along, his umbrella before him, seeing nothing, and he ran right against me. I blew him up naturally; but no sooner had he looked at me, than he uttered an exclamation of dismay, and made off like a shot. I thought it curious. Perhaps it was the man you speak of, Mr. Otway?'

'I shouldn't wonder, sir.'

Mr. Carlyle glanced at Barbara. She had turned deadly white. He saw what was passing in her mind. Could it be the ill-fated Richard? As Mr. Carlyle crossed the room to the door, he contrived to whisper a word to her in passing.

'I will go and see, and bring you back the news. Bear up, my darling.'

'Are you departing, Archibald?' said Mrs. Hare.

'I am going to have a look at this man that Bethel talks of. Curious as any school-girl you see, yet.'

He walked very quietly down the garden, and Barbara watched him from the gate. *How* should she bear the sickening suspense until he returned? Something seemed to tell her fears that it was Richard. Otway Bethel departed; and the justice, exchanging his wig and gown for a sprucer wig and coat, followed next: he, too, must have a look at the deceased. In a small place like West Lynne, every little event causes a stir and excites curiosity: what would not be noticed in a large town, is there magnified into a wonder that all folks run after.

Mr. Carlyle was the first back. Barbara went to the porch, and waited; had it been to save her life, she could not have gone to meet him: the suspense was fearful.

But, as he neared her, he smiled and nodded gaily, as if he would say, Fear not. Barbara's heart acquired a grain of courage from it; but still it throbbed painfully.

'We were falsely alarmed, Barbara,' he whispered. 'It is a complete stranger; some poor man who did not know the road. He is not in the least like Richard, and his whiskers are red.'

For the moment she thought she should have fainted, so great was the relief.

'But, Archibald, could it have been Richard, think you, who ran against papa—as he spoke of?'

'There is little doubt it was. The cry of dismay, when he recognized Justice Hare, and his speeding off, would betray that it was Richard.'

'And papa did not know him! What a merciful escape!'

'Is the poor man quite dead, Archibald?' inquired Mrs. Hare, when he reached the sitting-room.

'Quite so. He seems to have been dead some hours.'

'Did you recognize him?'

'Not at all. He is a stranger.'

Miss Carlyle's cold was better that evening; in fact, she seemed quite herself again, and Mr. Carlyle introduced the subject of his marriage. It was after dinner that he began upon it.

'Cornelia, when I married Lady Isabel Vane, you reproached me severely with having kept you in the dark—'

'If you had not kept me in the dark, but consulted me, as any other Christian would, the course of events might have been wholly changed and the wretchedness and disgrace, that fell on this house, been spared to it,' fiercely interrupted Miss Carlyle.

'We will leave the past,' he said, 'and consider the future. I was about to remark, that I do not intend to fall under your displeasure for the like offence. I believe you have never wholly forgiven it.'

'And never shall,' cried she impetuously. 'I did not deserve the slight.'

'Therefore, almost as soon as I know it myself, I acquaint you. I am about to marry a second time, Cornelia.'

Miss Carlyle started up. Her spectacles dropped off her nose, and a knitting-box, which she happened to have on her knee, clattered to the ground.

'What did you say?' she uttered, aghast.

'I am about to marry.'

'You!'

'I. Is there anything so very astonishing in it?'

'For the love of common sense don't go and make such a fool of yourself! You have done it once: was not that enough for you, but you must run your head into the noose again?'

'Now, Cornelia, can you wonder, that I do not speak to you of such things, when you meet them in this way? You treat me just as you did when I was a child. It is very foolish.'

'When folks act childishly, they must be treated as children. I always thought you were mad when you married before, but I shall think you doubly mad now.'

'Because you have preferred to remain single and solitary yourself, is it any reason why you should condemn me to do the same? You are happy alone; I should be happier with a wife.'

'That she may go and disgrace you, as the last one did!' intemperately spoke Miss Carlyle, caring not a rush what she said in her storm of anger. Mr. Carlyle's brow flushed; but he controlled his temper.

'No,' he calmly replied. 'I am not afraid of that, in the one I have now chosen.'

Miss Corny gathered her knitting together; he had picked up her box. Her hands trembled, and the lines of her face were working. It was a blow to her as keen as the other had been.

'Pray who is it that you have chosen?' she jerked forth. 'The whole neighbourhood has been after you.'

'Let it be who it will, Cornelia, you will be sure to grumble. Were I to say that it was a royal princess, or a peasant's daughter, you would equally see grounds for finding fault.'

'Of course I should. I know who it is—that stuck-up Louisa Dobede.'

'No, it is not. I never had the slightest intention of choosing Louisa Dobede;

nor she of choosing me. I am marrying to please myself; and, for a wife, Louisa Dobede would not please me.'

'As you did before,' sarcastically put in Miss Corny.

'Yes; as I did before.'

'Well, can't you open your mouth, and say who it is?' was the exasperated rejoinder.

'It is Barbara Hare.'

'Who?' shrieked Miss Carlyle.

'You are not deaf, Cornelia.'

'Well, you *are* an idiot!' she exclaimed, lifting up her hands and eyes.

'Thank you,' he said, but without any signs of irritation.

'And so you are; *you are*, Archibald. To suffer that girl who has been angling after you so long, to catch you at last.'

'She has not angled after me: had she done so, she would probably never have been Mrs. Carlyle. Whatever passing fancy she may have entertained for me in earlier days, she has shown no symptoms of it of late years: and I am quite certain that she had no more thought or idea, that I should choose her for my second wife, than you that I should choose you. Others have angled after me too palpably, but Barbara has not.'

'She is a little conceited minx; as vain as she is high.'

'What else have you to urge against her?'

'I would have married a girl without a slur—if I must have married,' aggravatingly returned Miss Corny.

'Slur?'

'Slur, yes! Dear me, is it an honour—to possess a brother such as Richard?'

'That is no slur upon Barbara. And the time may come when it will be taken off Richard.'

Miss Corny sniffed. 'Pigs may fly; but I never saw them try at it.'

'The next consideration, Cornelia, is about your residence. You will go back, I presume, to your own home.'

Miss Corny did not believe her own ears. 'Go back to mine own home!' she exclaimed. 'I shall do nothing of the sort. I shall stop at East Lynne. What's to hinder me?'

Mr. Carlyle shook his head. 'It cannot be,' he said, in a low, decisive tone.

'Who says so?' she sharply asked.

'I do. Have you forgotten that night—when *she* went away—the words spoken by Joyce? Cornelia, whether they were true or false, I will not subject another to the chance.'

She did not answer. Her lips only parted and closed again. Somehow Miss Carlyle could not bear to be reminded of that revelation of Joyce's: it subdued even her.

'I cast no reflection upon you,' hastily continued Mr. Carlyle. 'You have been mistress of a house for many years, and you naturally look to be so; it is right you should. But two mistresses in a house do not answer, Cornelia: they never did and they never will.'

'Why did you not give me so much of your sentiments when I first came to East Lynne?' she burst forth. 'I hate hypocrisy.'

'They were not my sentiments then: I possessed none. I was ignorant upon the subject, as I was upon others. Experience has come to me since.'

'You will not find a better mistress of a house than I have made you,' she said resentfully.

'I do not look for it. The tenants leave your house in March, do they not?'

'Yes, they do,' snapped Miss Corny. 'But as we are on the subject of details, of ways and means, allow me to tell you that if you did what is right *you* would move into that house of mine, and I will go to a smaller—as you seem to think I shall poison Barbara if I remained with her. East Lynne is a vast deal too fine and too grand for you.'

'I do not consider it so. I shall not quit East Lynne.'

'Are you aware that, in leaving your house, I take my income with me, Mr. Archibald?'

'Most certainly. Your income is yours, and you will require it for your own purposes. I have neither right to it, nor wish for it.'

'The withdrawal will make a pretty hole in your income, I can tell you that. Take care that you and East Lynne don't go bankrupt together.'

Mr. Carlyle laughed. 'I will take care of that, Cornelia. If I were not fully justified in living at East Lynne, I should not do so. With all my extravagance—as you are pleased to term it—I am putting by plenty of money, and you know it.'

'You might put by more, were your expenses less,' rebuked Miss Carlyle.

'I have no fancy to live as a hermit, or a miser.'

'No; nor as a man of common sense. To think that you should sacrifice yourself again!' she wailed in a tone of lamentation. 'And to Barbara Hare! an extravagant, vain, upstart little reptile.'

Mr. Carlyle took the compliments to Barbara with composure. It was of no use doing otherwise. Miss Corny was not likely to regard her with more graciousness since it was Barbara's coming there that turned herself out of East Lynne.

At this moment the summons of a visitor was heard. Even that excited the ire of Miss Carlyle. 'I wonder who's come bothering to-night?' she uttered.

Peter entered. 'It is Major Thorn, sir. I have shown him into the drawing-room.'

Mr. Carlyle was surprised. He proceeded to the drawing-room, and Miss Carlyle rang for Joyce. Strange to say, she had no thought of rebelling against the decree. An innate consciousness had long been hers that, should Mr. Carlyle marry again, her sojourn in the house would terminate. East Lynne was

Mr. Carlyle's: she had learnt that he could be firm upon occasions, and the tone of his voice had told that this was one of them.

'Joyce,' began she, after her own unceremonious fashion, 'your master is going to make a simpleton of himself a second time, so I shall leave him and East Lynne to it. Will you go with me, and be my upper maid again?'

'What, ma'am?' exclaimed Joyce in bewilderment: 'what did you say master was going to do?'

'To make a simpleton of himself,' irascibly repeated Miss Carlyle. 'He is going to tie himself up again with a wife; that's what he's going to do. Now, do you stop here, or will you go with me?'

'I would go with you, ma'am, but—but for one thing.'

'What's that?'

'The promise I gave to Lady Isabel. She exacted it from me when she thought she was about to die—a promise that I would remain with her children. She did not leave them by death after all: but it comes to the same thing.'

'Not exactly,' sarcastically spoke Miss Carlyle. 'But there's another side of the question, Joyce, which you may not have looked at. When there shall be another mistress at East Lynne, will you be permitted to remain here?'

Joyce considered: she could not see her way altogether clear. 'Allow me to give you my answer a little later,' she said to Miss Carlyle.

'Such a journey!' Major Thorn was saying, meanwhile, to Mr. Carlyle. 'It is my general luck to get ill weather when I travel. Rain and hail, thunder and heat, nothing bad comes amiss, when I am out. The snow lay on the rails, I don't know how thick: at one station we were detained two hours.'

'Are you proposing to make any stay at West Lynne?'

'Off again to-morrow. My leave, this time, is to be spent at my mother's. I may bestow a week of it, or so, on West Lynne, but am not sure. I must be back in Ireland in a month. Such a horrid bog-hole we are quartered in just now! The truth is, Carlyle, a lady has brought me here!'

'Indeed!'

'I am in love with Barbara Hare. The little jade has said No to me by letter; but, as Herbert says, there's nothing like urging your suit in person. And I have come to do so.'

Mr. Carlyle took an instant's counsel with himself, and decided that it would be a good thing to tell the major the state of the case: far more kind than to subject him to another rejection from Barbara, and to suffer the facts to reach him by common report.

'Will you shoot me, major, if I venture to tell you—that any second application to Barbara would be futile.'

'She is not appropriated, is she?' hurriedly cried Major Thorn. 'She's not married?'

'She's not married. She is going to be.'

'Oh! That's just like my unlucky fate. And who is the happy man?'

'You must promise not to call me out, if I disclose his name.'

'Carlyle! It is not yourself?'

'You have said it.'

There was a brief silence. It was Mr. Carlyle who broke it.

'It need not make us the less good friends, Thorn. Do not allow it to do so.'

The major put out his hand, and grasped Mr. Carlyle's. 'No, by Jove, it shan't! It's all fate. And if she must go beside me, I'd rather see her yours than any other man's upon earth. Were you engaged when I asked Barbara to be my wife, some months ago?'

'No. We have been engaged but very recently.'

'Did Barbara betray to you that I asked her?' proceeded Major Thorn, a shade of mortification rising to his face.

'Certainly not: you do not know Barbara, if you fancy she could be guilty of it. The justice managed to let it out to me during an explosion of wrath.'

'Wrath because I asked for his daughter?'

'Wrath against Barbara, for refusing. Not particularly at her refusing you,' added Mr. Carlyle, correcting himself; 'but she was in the habit of refusing all who asked her, and thereby fell under displeasure.'

'Did she refuse you?'

'No,' smiled Mr. Carlyle, 'she accepted me.'

'Ah, well; it's all fate, I say. But she is an uncommon nice girl, and I wish it had been my luck to get her.'

'To go from one subject to another,' resumed Mr. Carlyle, 'there is a question I have long thought to put to you, Thorn, if we ever met again. Which year was it that you were staying at Swainson?'

Major Thorn mentioned it. It was the year of Hallijohn's murder.

'As I thought—in fact, knew,' said Mr. Carlyle. 'Did you, while you were stopping there, ever come across a namesake of yours, one Thorn?'

'I believe I did. But I don't know the man of my own knowledge, and I saw him but once only. I don't think he was living at Swainson. I never observed him in the town.'

'Where did you meet with him?'

'At a roadside beer-shop, about two miles from Swainson. I was riding one day, when a fearful storm came on, and I took shelter there. Scarcely had I entered, when another horseman rode up, and he likewise took shelter: a tall, dandified man, aristocratic and exclusive. When he departed—for he quitted first, the storm being over—I asked the people who he was. They said they did not know, though they often saw him ride by: but a man who was in there, drinking, said he was a Captain Thorn. The same man, by the way, volunteered the information that he came from a distance, somewhere near West Lynne: I remember that.'

'That Captain Thorn did?'

'No; that he himself did. He appeared to know nothing of Captain Thorn, beyond the name.'

It seemed to be ever so! Scraps of information, but nothing tangible, nothing to lay hold of, or to know the man by. Would it be thus always?

'Should you recognize him again, were you to see him?' resumed Mr. Carlyle, awaking from his reverie.

'I think I should. There was something peculiar in his countenance, and I remember it well yet.'

'Were you by chance to meet him, and discover his real name—for I have reason to believe that Thorn, the one he went by then, was an assumed one—will you oblige me by letting me know it?'

'With all the pleasure in life,' replied the major. 'The chances are against it, though, confined as I am to that confounded sister country. Other regiments get the luck of being quartered in the metropolis, or near it: ours doesn't.'

When Major Thorn had departed, and Mr. Carlyle was about to return to the room where he had left his sister, he was interrupted by Joyce.

'Sir,' she began, 'Miss Carlyle tells me that there is going to be a change at East Lynne.'

The words took Mr. Carlyle by surprise. 'Miss Carlyle has been in a hurry to tell you!' he remarked, a certain haughty displeasure in his tone.

'She did not speak for the sake of telling me, sir, but I fancy she was thinking about her own plans. She inquired whether I would go with her when she left, or whether I meant to remain at East Lynne. I could not answer her, sir, until I had spoken to you.'

'Well?' said Mr. Carlyle.

'I gave a promise, sir, to—to—my late lady, that I would remain with her children so long as I was permitted: she asked it of me when she was ill; when she thought she was going to die. What I would inquire of you, sir, is, whether the changes will make any difference in my staying?'

'No,' he decisively replied. 'I also, Joyce, wish you to remain with the children.'

'It is well, sir,' Joyce answered; and her face looked bright as she quitted the room.

❧ XIX ❧

Mr. Dill in an Embroidered Shirt-Front

It was a lovely morning in June, and all West Lynne was astir. West Lynne generally was astir in the morning, but not in the bustling manner that might be observed now. People were abroad in numbers, pressing down to St. Jude's church, for it was the day of Mr. Carlyle's marriage to Barbara Hare.

Miss Carlyle made herself into a sort of martyr. She would not go near it: fine weddings in fine churches did not suit her, she said; they could tie themselves up together fast enough without her presence. She had invited the little Carlyles and their governess and Joyce to spend the day with her; and she persisted in regarding the children as martyrs too, in being obliged to submit to the advent of a second mother. She was back in her old house again, next door to the office, settled there for life now, with her servants. Peter had mortally offended her, in electing to remain at East Lynne.

Mr. Dill committed himself terribly on the wedding morning, and lucky was he to escape a shaking, like the one he had received on Mr. Carlyle's first marriage. About ten o'clock he made his appearance at Miss Carlyle's: he was a man of the old school, possessing old-fashioned notions, and he had deemed that to step in, to congratulate her on the auspicious day, would be only good manners.

Miss Carlyle was seated in her dining-room, her hands folded before her. It was rare indeed that *she* was caught doing nothing. She turned her eyes on Mr. Dill as he entered.

'Why, what on earth has taken you?' began she, before he could speak. 'You are decked out like a young buck.'

'I am going to the wedding, Miss Cornelia. Did you not know it? Mrs. Hare was so kind as to invite me to the breakfast, and Mr. Archibald insists upon my going to church. I am not too fine, am I?'

Poor old Dill's 'finery' consisted of a white waistcoat with gold buttons, and an embroidered shirt-front. Miss Corny was pleased to regard it with sarcastic wrath.

'Fine!' echoed she, 'I don't know what *you* call it. I would not make myself such a spectacle for untold gold. You'll have all the ragamuffins in the street forming a tail after you, thinking you are the bridegroom. A man of your years to deck yourself out in a worked shirt! I would have had some rosettes on my coat tails, while I was about it.'

'My coat's quite plain, Miss Cornelia!' he meekly remonstrated.

'Plain! what would you have it?' snapped Miss Corny. 'Perhaps you covet a wreath of embroidery round it, gold leaves and scarlet flowers, with a swansdown collar? It would only be in keeping with that shirt and waistcoat.

I might as well go and order a white tarlatan dress, looped up with sweet peas, and stream through the town in that guise. It would be just as consistent.'

'People like to dress a little out of the common at a wedding, Miss Cornelia: it's only respectful when they are invited guests.'

'I don't say people should go to a wedding in a hop-sack. But there's a medium. Pray do you know your age?'

'I am turned sixty, Miss Corny.'

'You just are. And do you consider it decent for an old man, turned sixty, to be decorated off, as you are now? I don't; and so I tell you my mind. Why, you'll be the laughing-stock of the parish! Take care the boys don't tie a tin kettle to you!'

Mr. Dill thought he would leave the subject. His own impression was, that he was *not* too fine, and that the parish would not regard him as being so: still, he had a great reverence for Miss Corny's judgment, and was not altogether easy. He had had his white gloves in his hand when he entered, but he surreptitiously smuggled them into his pocket, lest they might offend. He passed to the subject which had brought him thither.

'What I came in for, was, to offer you my congratulations on this auspicious day, Miss Cornelia. I hope Mr. Archibald and his wife, and you, ma'am—'

'There! you need not trouble yourself to go on,' interrupted Miss Corny, hotly arresting him. 'We want condolence here to-day, rather than the other thing. I'm sure I'd nearly as soon see Archibald go to his hanging.'

'Oh, Miss Corny!'

'I would; and you need not stare at me as if you were throttled. What business has he to go and fetter himself with a wife again? one would have thought he had had enough with the other. It is as I have always said: there's a soft place in Archibald's brain.'

Old Dill knew there was no 'soft place' in the brain of Mr. Carlyle, but he deemed it might be as well not to say so, in Miss Corny's present humour. 'Marriage is a happy state, as I have heard, ma'am, and honourable; and I am sure Mr. Archibald—'

'Very happy! very honourable!' fiercely cried Miss Carlyle, sarcasm in her tone. 'His last marriage brought him all that, did it not?'

'That's past and done with, Miss Corny, and none of us need recall it. It brought him some happy years before that happened. I hope he will find in his present wife a recompense for what's gone: he could not have chosen a prettier or nicer young lady than Miss Barbara: and I am glad to my very heart that he has got her.'

'Couldn't he!' jerked Miss Carlyle.

'No, ma'am, he could not. Were I young, and wanting a wife, there's not one in all West Lynne I would so soon look out for as Miss Barbara. Not that she'd have me; and I was not speaking in that sense, Miss Corny.'

'It's to be hoped you were not,' retorted Miss Corny. 'She is an idle, insolent, vain fagot, caring for nothing but her own doll's face and for Archibald.'

'Ah, well, ma'am, never mind that: pretty young girls know they are pretty, and you can't take their vanity from them. She'll be a good and loving wife to him; I know she will; it is in her nature; she won't serve him as—as—that other poor unfortunate did.'

'If I feared she was one to bring shame to him as that other did, I'd go into the church this hour and forbid the marriage; and if that didn't do, I'd— I'd—smother her!' shrieked Miss Carlyle. 'Look at that piece of impudence.'

The last sentence was uttered in a different tone, and concerned somebody in the street. Miss Carlyle hopped off her chair and strode to the window. Mr. Dill's eyes turned in the like direction.

In a gay summer's dress, fine and sparkling, with a coquettish little bonnet, trimmed with pink, shaded by one of those nondescript articles at present called veils, which article was made of white spotted net, with a pink ruche round it, sailed Afy Hallijohn, conceited and foolish and good-looking as ever. Catching sight of Mr. Dill, she made him a flourishing and gracious bow. The courteous old gentleman returned it, and was pounced upon by Miss Corny's tongue for his pains.

'Whatever possessed you to do that?'

'Well, Miss Corny, she spoke to me. You saw her.'

'I saw her! yes, I did see her, the brazen bell-wether! And she saw me, and spoke to you in her insolence. And you must answer her, in spite of my presence, instead of shaking your fist and giving her a reproving frown. You want a little sharp talking to, yourself.'

'But, Miss Corny, it's always best to let bygones be bygones,' he pleaded. 'She was flighty and foolish, and all that, was Afy; but now that it's proved she did not go with Richard Hare, as was suspected, and is at present living creditably, why should she not be noticed?'

'If the very deuce himself stood there with his horns and tail, you would find excuses to make for him,' fired Miss Corny. 'You are as bad as Archibald! Notice Afy Hallijohn! when she dresses and flirts, and minces, as you saw her but now! What creditable servant would flaunt about in such a dress and bonnet as that?—with that flimsy gauze thing over her face! It's as disreputable as your shirt-front.'

Mr. Dill coughed humbly, not wishing to renew the point of the shirt-front. 'She is not exactly a servant, Miss Corny, she's a lady's-maid; and ladies'-maids dress outrageously fine. I had a great respect for her father, ma'am: never a better clerk came into our office.'

'Perhaps you'll tell me you have a respect for her! The world's being turned upside down, I think. Formerly, mistresses kept their servants to work; now, it seems they keep them for play. She's going to St. Jude's, you may be sure of it, to stare at this fine wedding, instead of being at home in a cotton gown and white apron, making beds. Mrs. Latimer must be a droll mistress, to give her her liberty in this way. What's that fly for?' sharply added Miss Corny, as one drew up to the office door.

'Fly,' said Mr. Dill, stretching forward his bald head. 'It must be the one I ordered. Then I'll wish you good day, Miss Corny.'

'Fly for you!' cried Miss Corny. 'Have you got the gout, that you could not walk to St. Jude's on foot?'

'I am not going to church yet, I am going on to the Grove, Miss Corny. I thought it would look more proper to have a fly, ma'am; more respectful.'

'Not a doubt but you need it, in that trim,' retorted she. 'Why didn't you put on pumps, and silk stockings, with pink clocks?'

He was glad to bow himself out. But he thought he would do it with a pleasant remark, to show her he bore her no ill-will. 'Just look at the crowds pouring down, Miss Corny: the church will be as full as it can cram.'

'I dare say it will,' retorted she. 'One fool makes many.'

'I fear Miss Cornelia does not like this marriage, any more than she did the last,' quoth Mr. Dill to himself, as he stepped into his fly. 'Such a sensible woman as she is in other things, to be so bitter against Mr. Archibald because he marries! It's not like her. I wonder,' he added, his thoughts changing, 'whether I do look foolish in this shirt? I'm sure I never thought of decking myself out to appear young—as Miss Corny said: I only wished to testify respect to Mr. Archibald and Miss Barbara: nothing else would have made me give five-and-twenty shillings for it. Perhaps it's not etiquette—or whatever they call it—to wear them in a morning? Miss Corny ought to know; and there must certainly be something wrong about it, by the way it put her up. Well, it can't be helped now; it must go; there's no time to return home to change it.'

St. Jude's church was crowded: all the world and his wife had flocked to see it. Those who could not get in took up their station in the churchyard and in the road. Tombstones were little respected that day, for irreverent feet stood upon them: five-and-twenty boys at least were mounted on the railings round Lord Mount Severn's grave, holding on, one to another. Was the bridal party never coming? Eleven o'clock, and no signs of it. The mob outside grew impatient; the well-dressed mob inside grew impatient too; some of them had been there for two hours. Hark! a sound of carriages! Yes, it was coming now; and the beadle and the pew-opener cleared the space before the altar rails, which had been invaded, and, until now, the invasion winked at.

Well, it was a goodly show. Ladies and gentlemen as smart as fine feathers could make them. Mr. Carlyle was one of the first to enter the church, self-possessed and calm, every inch a gentleman. Oh! but he was noble to look upon: though when was he ever otherwise? Mr. and Mrs. Clitheroe were there, Anne Hare that was: a surprise for some of the gazers, who had not known they were expected to the wedding. Gentle, delicate Mrs. Hare walked

up the church leaning on the arm of Sir John Dobede, a paler look than usual
on her sweet, sad face. 'She's thinking of her wretched, ill-doing son,' quoth
the gossips, one to another. But who comes in now, with an air as if the
whole church belonged to him? An imposing, pompous man, stern and grim,
in a new flaxen wig, and a white rose in his button-hole. It is Mr. Justice
Hare, and he leads in one, whom folks jump upon seats to get a look at.

Very lovely was Barbara, in her soft white silk robes, and her floating veil.
Her cheeks, now blushing rosy red, now pale as the veil that shaded them,
betrayed how intense was her emotion. The bridesmaids came after her with
jaunty steps, vain in their important office: Louisa Dobede, Augusta and
Kate Herbert, and Mary Pinner.

Mr. Carlyle was already in his place at the altar; and as Barbara neared
him, he advanced, took her hand, and placed her on his left. I don't think
that it was quite usual; but he had been married before, and ought to know.
The clerk directed the rest where to stand, and, after some little delay, the
service proceeded.

In spite of her emotion—and that it was great, scarcely to be repressed,
none could doubt—Barbara made the responses bravely. Be you very sure
that a woman who *loves* him to whom she is being united must experience
this emotion. 'Wilt thou have this man to thy wedded husband, to live together after God's ordinance in the holy state of matrimony?' spoke the Reverend Mr. Little. 'Wilt thou obey him, and serve him, love, honour, and keep
him in sickness and in health; and, forsaking all others, keep thee only unto
him, as long as ye both shall live?'

'I will.' Clearly, firmly, impressively was the answer given. It was as if Barbara had in her thoughts one, who had not 'kept only unto him,' and would
proclaim her own resolution never so to betray him, God helping her.

The ceremony was very soon over; and Barbara, the magic ring upon her
finger, and her arm within Mr. Carlyle's, was led out to his chariot, now
hers: had he not just endowed her with his worldly goods?

The crowd shouted and hurrahed as they caught a sight of her lovely face,
but the carriage was soon clear of the crowd, who concentrated their curiosity upon the other carriages that were to follow it. The company were
speeding back to the Grove, to breakfast. Mr. Carlyle, breaking the silence, suddenly turned to his bride and spoke, his tone impassioned, almost
unto pain.

'Barbara, *you* will keep your vows to me?'

She raised her shy blue eyes, so full of love, to his: earnest feeling had
brought the tears to them.

'Always: in the spirit and in the letter: until death shall claim me. So help
me Heaven!'

PART THE THIRD

✥ I ✥

Stalkenberg

More than a year had gone on.

The German watering-places were crowded that early autumn. They generally are crowded at that season, now that the English flock abroad in shoals, like the swallows quitting our cold country, to return again some time. France has been pretty well used up, so now we fall upon Germany. Stalkenberg was that year particularly full, for its size: you might have put it in a nut-shell: and it derived its importance, name, and most else belonging to it, from its lord of the soil, the Baron von Stalkenberg. A stalwart old man was the baron, with grizzly hair, a grizzly beard, and manners as loutish as those of the boars he hunted. He had four sons as stalwart as himself, and who promised to be in time as grizzled. They were all styled the Counts von Stalkenberg, being distinguished by their Christian names; all save the eldest son, and he was generally called the young baron. Two of them were away; soldiers; and two, the eldest and the youngest, lived with their father, in the tumble-down castle of Stalkenberg, situated about a mile from the village to which it gave its name. The young Baron von Stalkenberg was at liberty to marry! the three Counts von Stalkenberg were not—unless they could pick up a wife with enough money to keep herself and her husband. In this creed they had been brought up: it was a perfectly understood creed, and not rebelled against.

Stalkenberg differed in no wise from the other baths of its class in the Vaterland. It had its linden-trees, its fair scenery, its Kursaal, its balls, its concerts, its tables d'hôte, its gaming tables, where one everlasting sentence dins the visitor's ear—and one to which he will do well to be deaf—'Faites votre jeu, messieurs! faites votre jeu,' its promenades, and its waters. The last were advertised—and some accorded their belief—to cure every malady known or imagined, from apoplexy down to an attack of love-fever, provided you only took enough of them.

The young Baron von Stalkenberg (who was only styled young in contradistinction to his father, being in his forty-first year) was famous for a handsome person, and for his passionate love of the chase: he was the deadly enemy of wild boars and wolves. The Count Otto von Stalkenberg (eleven years his brother's junior) was famous for nothing but his fiercely-ringed moustache, a habit of eating, and an undue addiction to draughts of Marco-brunner. Somewhat meagre fare, so report ran, was the fashion in the castle of Stalkenberg; neither the old baron nor his heir cared for luxury; therefore Count Otto was sure to be seen at the table d'hôte, as often as anybody would invite him. And that was nearly every day: for the Count von Stalken-berg was a high-sounding title, and his baronial father, proprietor of all Stalkenberg, lorded it in the baronial castle close by; all of which appeared very grand and great; and that is bowed down to with an idol's worship.

Stopping at the Ludwig Bad, the chief hotel in the place, was a family of the name of Crosby. It consisted of Mr. and Mrs. Crosby, an only daughter, her governess, and two or three servants. What Mr. Crosby had done to England, or England to him, I can't say: but he never went near his native country. For years and years he had lived abroad: not in any settled place of residence: they would travel about, and remain a year or two in one place, a year or two in another, as the whim suited them. A respectable, portly man, of quiet and gentleman-like manners, looking as little like one who need be afraid of the laws of his own land as can be. Neither is it said, or insinuated, that he was afraid of them: a gentleman who knew him, had asserted, many years before, when it was once questioned, that Crosby was as free to go home and establish himself in a mansion in Piccadilly as the best of them. But he had lost fearfully by some roguish scheme, like the South Sea bubble, and could not live in the style he once had done, and therefore preferred to remain abroad. Mrs. Crosby was a pleasant, chatty woman, given to take as much gaiety as she could get, and Helena Crosby was a remarkably fine-grown girl of seventeen. You might have given her some years more, had you been guessing her age, for she was no child, either in appearance or manners, and never had been. She was an heiress, too: an uncle had left her twenty thousand pounds; and, at her mother's death, she would have ten thousand more. The Count Otto von Stalkenberg heard of the thirty thousand pounds, and turned his fierce moustache and his eyes on Miss Helena.

'Tirty tousand pound and von handsome girls!' cogitated he, for he prided himself upon his English. 'It is just what I have been seeking after.'

He found the rumour, touching her fortune, to be correct, and from that time was seldom apart from the Crosbys. They were as pleased to have his society as he was to be in theirs, for was he not the Count von Stalken-berg?—and the other visitors at Stalkenberg, looking on with envy, would have given their ears to have been honoured with a like intimacy. Whether Mr. Crosby cared so much for the distinction as did madame and mademoi-selle, must remain a question; he was civil to him, and made him welcome; and Mrs. Crosby, in all things relating to society, was the grey mare.

One day there thundered down in a vehicle the old Baron von Stalkenberg. The like of this conveyance, for its shape and its silver ornaments, had never been seen since the days of Adam. It had been the pride of the baron's forefathers, but was rarely disturbed in its repose now. Some jägers in green and silver attended it, and it drew up at the door of the Ludwig Bad, the whole of whose inmates thereupon flocked to the windows to feast their eyes. The old chief had come to pay a visit of ceremony to the Crosbys; and the host of the Ludwig Bad, as he appeared himself to marshal his chieftain to their saloon, bowed his body low with every step; 'Room there, room there, for the mighty Baron von Stalkenberg!'

The mighty baron had come to invite them to a feast at his castle—where no feast had ever been made so grand before as this would be; and Otto had *carte blanche* to engage other distinguished sojourners at Stalkenberg; English, French, and natives who had been civil to him. Mr. Crosby's head was turned.

And now, I ask you, knowing as you do our national notions, was it not enough to turn it? You will not, then, be surprised to hear that when, some days subsequent to the feast, the Count Otto von Stalkenberg laid his proposals at Helena's feet, they were not rejected.

'But she is so young,' remonstrated Mr. Crosby to his wife. 'If they would only wait a couple of years, I would say nothing against it.'

'And get the count snapped up meanwhile. No, no, Mr. Crosby. Counts von Stalkenberg are not secured every day.'

'If he has a title and ancestry, Helena has money.'

'Then they are pretty equally balanced,' returned Mrs. Crosby. 'I never thought of looking for such a match for her: the Countess von Stalkenberg; only listen to the sound!'

'I wish he would cut off those frightful moustaches,' grumbled Mr. Crosby.

'Now don't worry about minor details: Helena thinks they are divine. The worst is about the governess.'

'What about her?'

'Why, I engaged her, for certain, up to Christmas, and of course I must pay her; unless I can get her another place. I'll try.'

'Ah! Helena would be much better with her, than getting married. I don't like girls to marry so young,' lamented Mr. Crosby. 'I don't know what the English here will say to it!'

'If you don't let out her age, nobody need know it,' cried his wife. 'Helena looks a woman, not a child. As to the English, they are going mad that the luck has not fallen upon them.'

Mr. Crosby's objections seemed to be met in every way, so he relapsed into silence. He knew it was of no use carrying on the war.

Helena Crosby, meanwhile, had rushed into her governess's room. 'Madame! madame! only think! I am going to be married!'

Madame lifted her pale, sad face: a very sad and pale face was hers. 'Indeed!' she gently replied.

'And my studies are to be over from to-day. Mamma says so.'

'You are over young to marry, Helena.'

'Now, don't bring up that, madame. It is just what papa is harping upon,' returned Miss Helena.

'Is it to Count Otto?' asked the governess. And it may be remarked that her English accent was perfect, although the young lady addressed her as 'Madame.'

'Count Otto, of course. As if I would marry anybody else!'

Look at the governess, reader, and see whether you know her. You will say no. But you do, for it is Lady Isabel Vane. But how strangely she is altered! Yes; the railway accident did that for her; and what the accident left undone, grief and remorse accomplished. She limps slightly as she walks, and stoops, which takes from her former height. A scar extends from her chin above her mouth, completely changing the character of the lower part of her face; some of her teeth are missing, so that she speaks with a lisp, and the sober bands of her grey hair—it is nearly silver—are confined under a large and close cap. She herself tries to make the change greater, that the chance of being recognized may be at an end, for which reason she wears disfiguring green spectacles, or, as they are called, preservers, going round the eyes, and a broad band of grey velvet coming down low upon her forehead. Her dress, too, is equally disfiguring. Never is she seen in one that fits her person, but in those frightful 'loose jackets' which must surely have been invented by some-body envious of a pretty shape. As to her bonnet, it would put to shame those masquerade things tilted on to the back of the head, for it actually shaded her face; and she was never seen out of doors without a thick veil. She was pretty easy upon the score of being recognized now: for Mrs. Ducie and her daughters had been sojourning at Stalkenberg, and they did not know her in the least. Who could know her? What resemblance was there between that grey, broken-down woman, with her disfiguring marks, and the once lovely Lady Isabel, with her bright colour, her beauty, her dark flowing curls, and her agile figure? Mr. Carlyle himself would not have known her. But she was good-looking still, in spite of it all, gentle, and interesting; and people wondered to see that grey hair on one yet young.

She had been with the Crosbys nearly two years. After her recovery from the railway accident, she removed to a quiet town in its vicinity, where they were living, and she became daily governess to Helena. The Crosbys were given to understand that she was English, but the widow of a Frenchman— she was obliged to offer some plausible account. There were no references; but she so won upon their esteem as the daily governess, that they soon took her into the house: had Lady Isabel surmised that they would be travelling to so conspicuous a spot as an English-frequented German watering-place, she might have hesitated to accept the engagement. However, it had been of ser-vice to her; the meeting with Mrs. Ducie proving that she was altered beyond chance of recognition. She could go anywhere now.

But now, about the state of her mind? I do not know how to describe the vain yearning, the inward fever, the restless longing for what might not be. Longing for what? For her children. Let a mother, be she a duchess, or be she an apple-woman at a standing, be separated for a while from her little children: let *her* answer how she yearns for them. She may be away on a tour of pleasure: for a few weeks, the longing to see their little faces again, to hear their prattling tongues, to feel their soft kisses, is kept under; and there may be frequent messages, 'The children's dear love to mamma': but as the weeks lengthen out, the desire to see them again becomes almost irrepressible. What must it have been, then, for Lady Isabel, who had endured this longing for years? Talk of the *mal du pays*, which is said to attack the Swiss when exiled from their country, that is as nothing compared to the heart-sickness which clung to Lady Isabel. She had passionately loved her children: she had been anxious for their welfare in all ways; and, not the least that she had to endure now, was the thought that she had abandoned them to be trained by strangers. Would they be trained to goodness, to morality, to religion? Careless as she herself had once been upon these points, she had learnt better now. Would Isabel grow up to indifference, to—perhaps do as she had done? Lady Isabel flung her hands before her eyes, and groaned in anguish.

Of late, the longing had become intense. It was indeed a very fever; and a fever of the worst kind, for it attacked both the mind and body. Her pale lips were constantly parched; her throat had that malady in it, which those who have suffered from some hideous burden, know only too well. She had never heard a syllable of or from East Lynne since that visit of Lord Mount Severn's to Grenoble, nearly three years ago. An English newspaper never came in her way. Mr. Crosby sometimes had them, but they were not sent up to the governess; and, as Lady Isabel would say to herself, what should there be about East Lynne in a newspaper? She might have asked Mrs. Ducie for news, but she did not dare: what excuse could *she*, Madame Vine, make, for wishing tidings of East Lynne? For all she knew, Mr. Carlyle and the children might be dead and buried. Oh! that she could see her children but for a day, an hour? that she might press one kiss upon their lips! Could she live without it? News, however, she was soon to have.

It happened that Mrs. Latimer, a lady living at West Lynne, betook herself about that time to Stalkenberg; and, with her, three parts maid, and one part companion, went Afy Hallijohn. Not that Afy was admitted to the society of Mrs. Latimer, to sit with her or dine with her, nothing of that; but she did enjoy more privileges than most ladies'-maids; and Afy, who was never backward at setting off her own consequence, gave out that she was 'companion.' Mrs. Latimer was an easy woman, fond of Afy; and Afy had made her own tale good to her, respecting the ill-natured reports at the time of the murder, so that Mrs. Latimer looked upon her as one to be compassionated.

Mrs. Latimer and Mrs. Crosby, whose apartments in the hotel adjoined, struck up a violent friendship the one for the other. Ere the former had been a week at the Ludwig, they had sworn something like eternal sisterhood—as both had probably done for others fifty times before.

On the evening of the day Helena Crosby communicated her future prospects to Lady Isabel, the latter strolled out in the twilight and took her seat on a bench in an unfrequented part of the gardens, where she was fond of sitting. Now it came to pass that Afy, some few minutes afterwards, found herself in the same walk—and a very dull one too, she was thinking.

'Who's that?' quoth Afy to herself, her eyes falling upon Lady Isabel. 'Oh, it's that governess of the Crosbys. She may be known a mile off, by her grandmother's bonnet. I'll go and have a chat with her.'

Accordingly Afy, who was never troubled with bashfulness, went up and seated herself beside Lady Isabel. 'Good evening, Madame Vine,' cried she.

'Good evening,' replied Lady Isabel, courteously, not having the least idea of whom Afy might be.

'You don't know me, I fancy,' pursued Afy, so gathering from Lady Isabel's looks. 'I am companion to Mrs. Latimer; and she is spending the evening with Mrs. Crosby. Precious dull, this Stalkenberg!'

'Do you think so?'

'It is for me. I can't speak German or French, and the upper attendants of families here can't, most of them, speak English. I'm sure I go about like an owl, able to do nothing but stare. I was sick enough to come here, but I'd rather be back at West Lynne, quiet as it is.'

Lady Isabel had not been encouraging her companion, either by words or manner, but the last sentence caused her heart to bound within her. Control herself as she would, she could not quite hide her feverish interest.

'Do you come from West Lynne?'

'Yes. Horrid place! Mrs. Latimer took a house there soon after I went to live with her. I'd rather she had taken it at Botany Bay.'

'Why do you not like it?'

'Because I don't,' was Afy's satisfactory answer.

'Do you know East Lynne?' resumed Lady Isabel, her heart beating and her brain whirling, as she deliberated how she could put all the questions she wished to ask.

'I ought to know it,' returned Afy. 'My own sister, Miss Hallijohn, is head maid there. Why? Do you know it, Madame Vine?'

Lady Isabel hesitated: she was deliberating upon her answer. 'Some years ago, I was staying in the neighbourhood for a little time,' she said. 'I should like to hear of the Carlyles again: they were a nice family.'

Afy tossed her head. 'Ah! but there have been changes since that. I dare say you knew them in the time of Lady Isabel?'

Another pause. 'Lady Isabel? Yes. She was Mr. Carlyle's wife.'

'And a nice wife she made him!' ironically rejoined Afy. 'You must have heard of it, Madame Vine, unless you have lived in a wood. She eloped: abandoned him and her children.'

'Are the children living?'

'Yes, poor things. But the one's on its road to consumption—if ever I saw consumption yet. Joyce—that's my sister—is in a flaring temper with me when I say it. She thinks it will get strong again.'

Lady Isabel passed her handkerchief across her moist brow. 'Which of the children is it?' she faintly asked. 'Isabel?'

'Isabel!' retorted Afy. 'Who's Isabel?'

'The eldest child, I mean; Miss Isabel Carlyle.'

'There's no Isabel. There's Lucy. She's the only daughter.'

'When—when—I knew them, there was only one daughter; the other two were boys: I remember quite well that she was called Isabel.'

'Stay,' said Afy; 'now you speak of it, what was it that I heard? It was Wilson told me, I recollect—she's the nurse. Why, the very night that his wife went away, Mr. Carlyle gave orders that the child in future should be called Lucy; her second name. No wonder,' added Afy, violently indignant, 'that he could no longer endure the sound of her mother's, or suffer the child to bear it.'

'No wonder,' murmured Lady Isabel. 'Which child is it that is ill?'

'It's William, the eldest boy. He is not to say ill, but he is as thin as a herring, with an unnaturally bright look on his cheeks, and a glaze upon his eyes. Joyce says his cheeks are no brighter than his mother's used to be, but I know better. Folks in health don't have those brilliant colours.'

'Did you ever see Lady Isabel?' she asked, in a low tone.

'Not I,' returned Afy; 'I should have thought it demeaning. One does not care to be brought into contact with that sort of misdoing lot, you know, Madame Vine.'

'There was another one, a little boy; Archibald, I think his name was. Is he well?'

'Oh, the troublesome youngster! he is as sturdy as a Turk. No fear of his going into a consumption. He is the very image of Mr. Carlyle, is that child. I say, though, madame,' continued Afy, changing the subject unceremoniously, 'if you were stopping at West Lynne, perhaps you heard some wicked mischief-making stories concerning me?'

'I believe I did hear your name mentioned. I cannot charge my memory now with the particulars.'

'My father was murdered—you must have heard of that?'

'Yes, I recollect so far.'

'He was murdered by a chap called Richard Hare, who decamped instanter. Perhaps you know the Hares also? Well, directly after the funeral I left West Lynne; I could not bear the place; and I stopped away. And what do you suppose they said of me?—that I had gone after Richard Hare! Not that I knew they were saying it, or I should pretty soon have been back and given them the length of my tongue. But now, I just ask you, as a lady, Madame Vine, whether a more infamous accusation was ever pitched upon?'

'And had you not gone after him?'

'No: that I swear,' passionately returned Afy. 'Make myself a companion of my father's murderer! If Mr. Calcraft the hangman finished off a few of those West Lynne scandalmongers, it might be a warning to the others. I said so to Mr. Carlyle.'

'To Mr. Carlyle,' repeated Lady Isabel, hardly conscious that she did repeat it.

'He laughed, I remember, and said that would not stop the scandal. The only one who did not misjudge me was himself: he did not believe that I was with Richard Hare: but he was ever noble-judging, was Mr. Carlyle.'

'I suppose you were in a situation?'

Afy coughed. 'To be sure. More than one. I lived as companion with an old lady who so valued me that she left me a handsome legacy in her will. I lived two years with the Countess Mount Severn.'

'With the Countess of Mount Severn!' echoed Lady Isabel, surprised into the remark. "Why, she—she—was related to Mr. Carlyle's wife. At least, Lord Mount Severn was.'

'Of course: everybody knows that. I was living there at the time the business happened. Didn't the countess pull Lady Isabel to pieces! She and Miss Levison used to sit, cant, cant, all day over it. Oh, I assure you I know all about it. Have you got the headache, that you are leaning on your hand?'

'Headache and heartache both,' she might have answered. Miss Afy resumed.

'So after the flattering compliment West Lynne had paid me, you may judge I was in no hurry to go back to it, Madame Vine. And if I had not found that Mrs. Latimer's promised to be an excellent place, I should have left it, rather than be marshalled there. But I have lived it down: I should like to hear any of them fibbing against me now. Do you know that blessed Miss Corny?'

'I have seen her.'

'She shakes her head and makes eyes at me still. But so she would at an angel: a cross-grained old cockatoo!'

'Is she still at East Lynne?'

'Not she, indeed. There would be drawn battles between her and Mrs. Carlyle, if she were.'

A dart, as of an ice-bolt, seemed to arrest the blood in Lady Isabel's veins. 'Mrs. Carlyle?' she faltered. 'Who is Mrs. Carlyle?'

'Mr. Carlyle's wife. Who should she be?'

The rushing blood leaped on now, fast and fiery. 'I did not know he had married again.'

'He has been married now—getting on for fifteen months: a twelve-month last June. I went to the church to see them married. Wasn't there a cram! She looked beautiful that day.'

Lady Isabel laid her hand upon her beating heart. But for that delectable 'loose jacket,' Afy might have detected her bosom's rise and fall. She steadied her voice sufficiently to speak.

'Did he marry Barbara Hare?'

'You may take your oath of that,' said Afy. 'If folks tell true, there were love scenes between them before he ever thought of Lady Isabel. I had that from Wilson, and she ought to know, for she lived at the Hares'. Another thing is said—only you must just believe one word of West Lynne talk, and disbelieve ten: that if Lady Isabel had not died, Mr. Carlyle never would have married again: he had scruples. Half-a-dozen were given to him by report: Louisa Dobede for one, and Mary Pinner for another. Such nonsense! folks might have made sure it would be Barbara Hare. There's a baby now.'

'Is there?' was the faint answer.

'A beautiful boy, three or four months old. Mrs. Carlyle is not a little proud of him. She worships her husband.'

'Is she kind to the first children?'

'For all I know. I don't think she has much to do with them. Archibald is in the nursery, and the other two are mostly with the governess.'

'There is a governess?'

'Nearly the first thing that Mr. Carlyle did, after his wife's moonlight flitting, was to seek a governess, and she has been there ever since. She is going to leave now: to be married, Joyce told me.'

'Are you much at East Lynne?'

Afy shook her head. 'I am not going much, I can tell you, where I am looked down upon. Mrs. Carlyle does not favour me. She knew that her brother Richard would have given his head to marry me, and she resents it. No such great catch, I'm sure, that Dick Hare, even if he had gone on right,' continued Afy, somewhat after the example of the fox, looking at the unattainable grapes. 'He had no brains to speak of; and what he had were the colour of a peacock's tail—green. Ah me! the changes that take place in this world! But for that Lady Isabel's mad folly in quitting him, and leaving the field open, Miss Barbara would never have had the chance of being Mrs. Carlyle.'

Lady Isabel groaned in spirit.

'There is one person who never will hear a word breathed against her, and that's Joyce,' went on Afy. 'She was as fond of Lady Isabel, nearly, as Mr. Carlyle was.'

'Was he so fond of her?'

'He worshipped the very ground she trod upon. Ay, up to the hour of her departure; Joyce says she knows he did; and that's how she repaid him. But it's sure to be the way in this world: let a man, or woman, make an idol of another, and see if they don't get served out. The night that Mr. Carlyle brought his new wife home, Joyce, who was attending on her, went into the dressing-room, leaving Mrs. Carlyle in the bed-chamber. "Joyce," she called out. "My lady?" answered Joyce—proving who was filling up her thoughts. I don't know how Mrs. Carlyle liked it. Joyce said she felt as mad as could be with herself.'

'I wonder,' cried Lady Isabel, in a low tone, 'how the tidings of her death were received at East Lynne?'

'I don't know anything about that. They held it as a jubilee, I should say, and set all the bells in the town to ring, and feasted the men upon legs of mutton and onion sauce afterwards. *I* should, I know. A brute animal deaf and dumb clings to its offspring: but *she* abandoned hers. Are you going in, Madame Vine?'

'I must go in now. Good evening to you.'

She had sat till she could sit no longer; her very heart-strings were wrung. And she might not rise up in defence of herself. Defence? Did she not deserve more, ten thousand times more reproach than had met her ears now? This girl did not say of her half what the world must say.

To bed at the usual time, but not to sleep. What she had heard only increased her vain, insensate longing. A stepmother at East Lynne, and one of her children gliding on to death! Oh! to be with them! to see them once again! To purchase that boon, she would willingly forfeit all the rest of her existence.

Her frame was fevered; the bed was fevered; and she rose and paced the room. This state of mind would inevitably bring on bodily illness, possibly an attack of the brain. She dreaded that; for there was no telling what she might reveal in her delirium. Her temples were throbbing, her heart was beating; and she once more threw herself upon the bed, and pressed the pillow down upon her forehead. There is no doubt that the news of Mr. Carlyle's marriage helped greatly the excitement. She did not pray to die; but she did wish that death might come to her.

What would have been the ending it is impossible to say, but a strange turn in affairs came: one of those wonderful coincidences which are sometimes, but not often, to be met with. Mrs. Crosby appeared in Madame Vine's room after breakfast, and gave her an account of Helena's projected marriage. She then apologized (the real object of her visit) for dispensing so summarily with madame's services, but she had reason to hope that she could introduce her to another situation. Would madame have any objection to take one in England? Madame was upon the point of replying that she did not choose to enter one in England, when Mrs. Crosby stopped her, saying she would call in Mrs. Latimer, who could tell her about it better than she could.

Mrs. Latimer came in, all eagerness and volubility. 'Ah, my dear madame,' she exclaimed, 'you would be fortunate indeed if you were to get into this family. They are the nicest people; he so liked and respected; she so pretty and engaging. A most desirable situation. You will be treated as a lady, and have all things comfortable. There is only one pupil, a girl; one of the little boys, I believe, goes in for an hour or two, but that is not much; and the salary is seventy guineas. The Carlyles are friends of mine; they live at a beautiful place, East Lynne.'

The Carlyles! East Lynne! Go governess there? Lady Isabel's breath was taken away.

'They are parting with their governess,' continued Mrs. Latimer, 'and when I was there a day or two before I started on my tour to Germany, Mrs. Carlyle said to me, "I suppose you could not pick us up a desirable governess for Lucy: one who is mistress of French and German." She spoke in a half-joking tone, but I feel sure that were I to write word that I *had* found one, it would give her pleasure. Now, Mrs. Crosby tells me your French is quite that of a native, Madame Vine; that you read and speak German well, and that your musical abilities are excellent. I think you would be just the one to suit; and I have no doubt I could get you the situation. What do you say?'

What could she say? Her brain was in a whirl.

'I am anxious to find you one if I can,' put in Mrs. Crosby. 'We have been very much pleased with you, and I should like you to be desirably placed. As Mrs. Latimer is so kind as to interest herself, it appears to me an opportunity that should not be missed.'

'Shall I write to Mrs. Carlyle?' rejoined Mrs. Latimer.

Lady Isabel roused herself, and so far cleared her intellects as to under-stand and answer the question. 'Perhaps you will kindly give me until to-morrow morning to consider of it? I had not intended to take a situation in England.'

She had a battle with herself that day. Now resolving to go, and risk it; now shrinking from the attempt. At one moment it seemed to her that Pro-vidence must have placed this opportunity in her way that she might see her children, in her desperate longing; at another, a voice appeared to whisper that it was a wily, dangerous temptation flung across her path, one which it was her duty to resist and flee from. Then came another phase of the pic-ture—how could she bear to see Mr. Carlyle the husband of another?—to live in the same house with them, to witness his attentions, possibly his ca-resses? It might be difficult; but she could force and school her heart to en-durance: had she not resolved in her first bitter repentance, to *take up her cross* daily, and bear it? No; her own feelings, let them be wrung as they would, should not prove the obstacle.

Evening came, and she had not decided. She passed another night of pain, of restlessness, of longing for her children: this intense longing appeared to be overmastering all her powers of mind and body. The temptation at length proved too strong: the project, having been placed before her covetous eyes, could not be relinquished, and she finally resolved *to go*. 'What is it that should keep me away?' she argued. 'The dread of discovery? Well, if that comes, it must: they could not hang me, or kill me. Deeper humiliation than ever would be my portion, when they drive me from East Lynne with abhorrence and ignominy, as a soldier is drummed out of his regiment; but I could bear that, as I must bear the rest, and I can shrink under some hedge and lay myself down to die. Humiliation for me! no; I will not put that in comparison with seeing and being with my children.'

Mrs. Latimer wrote to Mrs. Carlyle. She had met with a governess: one desirable in every way, who could not fail to suit her views precisely. She was a Madame Vine, English by birth, but the widow of a Frenchman: a Protestant, a thorough gentlewoman, an efficient linguist and musician, and competent to her duties in all ways. Mrs. Crosby, with whom she had lived two years, regarded her as a treasure, and would not have parted with her but for Helena's marriage with a German nobleman. 'You must not mind her appearance,' went on the letter. 'She is the oddest-looking person: wears spectacles, caps, enormous bonnets, and has a great scar on her mouth and chin; and though she can't be more than thirty, her hair is grey: she is also slightly lame. But understand you, she is a *gentlewoman* with it all; and looks one.'

When this description reached East Lynne, Barbara laughed as she read it aloud to Mr. Carlyle. He laughed also.

'It is well governesses are not chosen according to their looks,' he said, 'or I fear Madame Vine would stand but a poor chance.'

They resolved to engage her. And word went back to that effect.

A strangely wild tumult filled Lady Isabel's bosom. She first of all hunted her luggage over, her desk, everything belonging to her, lest any scrap of paper, any mark on linen might be there, which could give a clue to her former self. The bulk of her luggage remained at Paris, warehoused, where it had been sent ere she quitted Grenoble. She next saw to her wardrobe, making it still more unlike anything she had formerly worn: her caps, save that they were simple, and fitted closely to the face, nearly rivalled those of Miss Carlyle. She had been striving for two years to change the character of her handwriting, and had so far succeeded that none would now take it for Lady Isabel Vane's. But her hand shook when she wrote to Mrs. Carlyle—who had written to her. She—*she* writing to Mr. Carlyle's wife! and in the capacity of a subordinate! How would she like to live with her as a subordinate?— a servant, it may be said—where she had once reigned, the idolised lady? She must bear that; as she must bear all else. Hot tears came into her eyes, with a gush, as they fell on the signature 'Barbara Carlyle.'

All ready, she sat down and waited the signal of departure: but that was not to be yet. It was finally arranged that she should travel to England and to

West Lynne with Mrs. Latimer, and that lady would not return until October. Lady Isabel could only fold her hands and strive for patience.

But the day came at last; and Mrs. Latimer, Lady Isabel, and Afy quitted Stalkenberg. Mrs. Latimer would only travel slowly, and the impatient, fevered woman thought the journey would never end.

'You have been informed, I think, of the position of these unhappy children to whom you are going,' Mrs. Latimer said one day. 'You must not speak to them of their mother. She left them.'

'Yes.'

'It is never well to speak to children of a mother who has disgraced them. Mr. Carlyle would not like it. And I dare say they are taught to forget her, to regard Mrs. Carlyle as their only mother.'

Her aching heart had to assent to all.

It was a foggy afternoon, grey with the coming twilight, when they arrived at West Lynne. Mrs. Latimer, believing the governess was a novice in England, kindly put her into a fly, and told the driver his destination. 'Au revoir, madame,' she said. 'and good luck to you!'

Once more she was rolling along the familiar road. She saw Justice Hare's house, she saw other marks which she knew well. And once more she saw *East Lynne*, the dear old house, for the fly had turned into the avenue. Lights were moving in the windows, it looked gay and cheerful, a contrast to her. Her heart was sick with expectation, her throat was beating; and as the man thundered up with all the force of his one horse, and halted at the steps, her sight momentarily left her. Would Mr. Carlyle come to the fly to hand her out? She wished she had never undertaken the project, now, in the depth of her fear and agitation. The hall door was flung open, and there gushed forth a blaze of light.

❦ 11 ❦

Change and Change

The hall doors of East Lynne were thrown open, and a flood of golden light streamed out upon the steps.

Two men-servants stood there. One remained in the hall, the other advanced to the chaise. He assisted Lady Isabel to alight, and then busied himself with the luggage. As she ascended to the hall she recognised old Peter: strange, indeed, did it seem, not to say, 'How are you, Peter?' but to meet him as a stranger. For a moment she was at a loss for words: what should she say, or ask, coming to her own home? Her manner was embarrassed, her voice low.

'Is Mrs. Carlyle within?'

'Yes, ma'am.'

At that moment, Joyce came forward to receive her. 'It is Madame Vine, I believe?' she respectfully said. 'Please to step this way, madame.'

But Lady Isabel lingered in the hall, ostensibly to see that her boxes came in right: Stephen was bringing them up then: in reality to gather a short respite, for Joyce might be about to usher her into the presence of Mr. and Mrs. Carlyle.

Joyce, however, did nothing of the sort. She merely conducted her to the grey parlour: a fire was burning in the grate, looking cheerful on the autumn night.

'This is your sitting-room, madame. What will you please to take? I will order it to be brought in, while I show you your bed-chamber.'

'A cup of tea,' answered Lady Isabel.

'Tea, and some cold meat with it,' suggested Joyce. But Lady Isabel interrupted her.

'Nothing but tea; and a little cold toast.'

Joyce rang the bell, ordered the refreshment to be made ready, and then preceded Lady Isabel upstairs. On she followed, her heart palpitating: past the rooms that used to be hers, along the corridor, towards the second staircase. The doors of her old bed and dressing-rooms stood open, and she glanced in with a yearning look. No, never more, never more could they be hers: she had put them from her by her own free act and deed. Not less comfortable did they look now, than in former days: but they had passed into another's occupancy. The fire threw its blaze on the furniture: there were the little ornaments on the large dressing table, as they used to be in *her* time, and the cut glass of the crystal essence bottles was glittering in the fire-light. On the sofa lay a shawl and a book, and on the bed a silk dress, as if thrown there after being taken off. No: these rooms were not for her now: and she followed Joyce up the other staircase. The bed-room to which she was shown was commodious and well furnished: it was the one Miss Carlyle had occupied when she, Isabel, had been taken, a bride, to East Lynne, though that lady had subsequently quitted it for one on the lower floor. Joyce put down the waxlight she carried, and looked round.

'Would you like a fire lighted here, madame, for to-night? Perhaps it will feel welcome, after travelling.'

'Oh no, thank you,' was the answer.

Stephen, with somebody to help him, was bringing up the luggage. Joyce directed him where to place it, telling him to uncord the boxes. That done, the man left the room, and Joyce turned to Lady Isabel, who had stood like a statue, never so much as attempting to remove her bonnet.

'Can I do anything for you, madame?' she asked.

Lady Isabel declined. In these, her first moments of arrival, she was dreading detection: how was it possible that she should not?—and feared Joyce's keen eyes more perhaps than she feared any others. She was only wishing that the girl would go down.

'Should you want any one, please to ring, and Hannah will come up,' said Joyce, preparing to retire. 'She is the maid who waits upon the grey parlour, and will do anything you like up here.'

Joyce had quitted the room, and Lady Isabel had got her bonnet off, when the door opened again. She hastily thrust it on—somewhat after the fashion of Richard Hare's rushing on his hat and his false whiskers. It was Joyce.

'Do you think you shall find your way down alone, madame?'

'Yes, I can do that,' she answered. Find her way!—in that house.

Lady Isabel slowly took her things off. Where was the use of lingering?— she *must* meet their eyes sooner or later. Though, in truth, there was little, if any, fear of her detection, so effectually was she disguised, by nature's altering hand, or by art's. It was with the utmost difficulty she kept tranquil: had the tears once burst forth, they would have gone on to hysterics, without the possibility of control. The coming home again to East Lynne! Oh, it was indeed a time of agitation; terrible, painful agitation; and none can wonder at it. Shall I tell you of what she did? Yes, I will. She knelt down by the bed, and prayed for courage to go through the task she had undertaken, prayed for self-control: even she, the sinful, who had quitted that house under circumstances so notorious. But I am not sure that this mode of return to it was an expedition precisely calculated to call down a blessing.

There was no excuse for lingering longer, and she descended, the waxlight in her hand. Everything was ready in the grey parlour; the tea-tray on the table, the small urn hissing away, the tea-caddy in proximity to it. A silver rack of dry toast, butter, and a hot muffin covered with a small silver cover. The things were to her sight as old faces; the rack, the small cover, the butter-dish, the tea-service; she remembered them all. Not the urn; a copper one: she had no recollection of that. It had possibly been bought for the use of the governess, when a governess came into use at East Lynne. If she had reflected on the matter, she might have known, by the signs observable in the short period she had been in the house, that governesses at East Lynne were regarded as gentlewomen; treated well and liberally. Yes; for East Lynne owned Mr. Carlyle for its master.

She made the tea, and sat down with what appetite she might. Her brain, her thoughts, all in a chaos together. She wondered whether Mr. and Mrs. Carlyle were at dinner: she wondered in what part of the house were the children. She heard bells ring now and then; she heard servants cross and recross the hall. Her meal over, she rang her own.

A neat-looking, good-tempered maid answered it. Hannah; who—as Joyce had informed her—waited upon the grey parlour, and was at her, the governess's, especial command. She took away the things, and then Lady Isabel sat on alone. For how long she scarcely knew, when a sound caused her heart to beat as if it would burst its bounds, and she started from her chair like one who has received an electric shock.

It was nothing to be startled at—for ordinary people; it was but the sound of children's voices. *Her* children! were they being brought in to her? She pressed her hand upon her heaving bosom.

No: they were but traversing the hall, and the voices faded away up the wide staircase. Perhaps they had been in to dessert, as in the old times, and were now going up to bed. She looked at her new watch: half-past seven.

Her *new* watch. The old one had been changed away for it. All her trinkets had been likewise parted with, sold, or changed away, lest they should be recognized at East Lynne. Nothing whatever had she kept, except her mother's miniature and the small golden cross, set with its seven emeralds. Have you forgotten that cross? Francis Levison accidentally broke it for her the first time they ever met. If she had looked upon the breaking of that cross, which her mother had enjoined her to set such store by, as an evil omen, at the time of the accident, how awfully had the subsequent events seemed to bear her fancy out! These two articles, the miniature and the cross, she could not bring her mind to part with. She had sealed them up, and placed them in the remotest spot of her dressing-case, away from all chance of public view. Peter entered.

'My mistress says, ma'am, she would be glad to see you, if you are not too tired. Will you please to walk into the drawing-room?'

A mist swam before her eyes. Was she about to enter the presence of Mr. Carlyle?—had the moment really come? She moved to the door, which Peter held open. She turned her head from the man, for she could feel how ashy white were her face and lips.

'Is Mrs. Carlyle alone?' she asked, in a subdued voice. The most indirect way she could put the question, as to whether Mr. Carlyle was there.

'Quite alone, ma'am. My master is dining out to-day. Madame Vine, I think?' he added, waiting to announce her, as, the hall traversed, he laid his hand on the drawing-room door.

'Madame Vine,' she said, correcting him. For Peter had spoken the name, Vine, broadly, according to our English habitude; she set him right, and pronounced it à la mode française.

'Madame Veen, ma'am,' quoted Peter to his mistress, as he ushered in Lady Isabel.

The old familiar drawing-room; its large, handsome proportions, its well-arranged furniture, its bright chandelier! It all came back to her with a heart-sickness. No longer *her* drawing-room, that she should take pride in it: she had flung it away from her when she flung away the rest.

Seated under the blaze of the chandelier was Barbara. Not a day older did she look than when Lady Isabel had first seen her at the churchyard gates, when she had inquired of her husband who was that pretty girl. 'Barbara Hare,' he had answered. Ay. She was Barbara Hare, then, but now she was Barbara Carlyle: and she, she, who had been Isabel Carlyle, was Isabel Vane again! Oh woe! woe!

Inexpressibly more beautiful looked Barbara than Lady Isabel had ever seen her—or else she fancied it. Her evening dress was of pale sky blue—no other colour suited Barbara so well, and there was no other she was so fond of—and on her fair neck was a gold chain, and on her arms were gold bracelets. Her pretty features were attractive as ever, her cheeks were flushed; her blue eyes sparkled, and her light hair was rich and abundant. A contrast, her hair, to that of the worn woman opposite to her.

Barbara came forward, her hand stretched out with a kindly greeting. 'I hope you are not very much tired after your journey?'

Lady Isabel murmured something: she did not know what: and pushed the chair set for her as much as possible into the shade.

'You are not ill—are you?' asked Barbara, noting the intensely pale face—as much as could be seen of it for the cap and spectacles.

'Not ill,' was the low answer: 'only a little fatigued.'

'Would you prefer that I should speak with you in the morning? You would like, possibly, to retire to bed at once.'

But this Lady Isabel declined. Better get the first interview over by candle-light than by daylight.

'You looked so very pale. I feared you might be ill.'

'I am generally pale; sometimes remarkably so: but my health is good.'

'Mrs. Latimer wrote us word that you would be quite sure to suit us,' freely said Barbara. 'I hope you will; and I hope you may find your residence here agreeable. Have you lived much in England?'

'In the early portion of my life.'

'And you have lost your husband and children? Stay. I beg your pardon if I am making a mistake: I think Mrs. Latimer did mention children.'

'I have lost them,' was the faint, quiet response.

'Oh, but it must be terrible grief when children die!' exclaimed Barbara, clasping her hands in emotion. 'I would not lose my baby for the world; I *could* not part with him.'

'Terrible grief, and hard to bear,' outwardly assented Lady Isabel. But, in her heart she was thinking that death was not the worst kind of parting. There was another, far more dreadful. Mrs. Carlyle began to speak of the children about to be placed under her charge.

'You are no doubt aware that they are not mine! Mrs. Latimer would tell you. They are the children of Mr. Carlyle's first wife.'

'And Mr. Carlyle's,' interrupted Lady Isabel. What in the world made her say that? She wondered, herself, the moment the words were out of her mouth. A scarlet streak flushed her cheeks, and she remembered that there must be no speaking upon impulse at East Lynne.

'Mr. Carlyle's, of course,' said Barbara, believing Madame Vine had but asked the question. 'Their position—the girl in particular—is a sad one, for their mother left them. Oh, it was a shocking business.'

'She is dead, I hear,' said Lady Isabel, hoping to turn the immediate point of conversation. Mrs. Carlyle, however, continued, as though she had not heard her.

'Mr. Carlyle married Lady Isabel Vane, the late Lord Mount Severn's daughter. She was attractive and beautiful, but I do not fancy she cared very much for her husband. However that may have been, she ran away from him.'

'It was very sad,' observed Lady Isabel, feeling that she was expected to say something. Besides, she had her *rôle* to play.

'Sad? It was wicked, it was infamous,' returned Mrs. Carlyle, giving way to some excitement. 'Of all men living, of all husbands, Mr. Carlyle least deserved such a requital. You will say so when you come to know him. And the affair altogether was a mystery: for it never was observed or suspected, by any one, that Lady Isabel entertained a liking for another. She eloped with Francis Levison—Sir Francis, he is now. He had been staying at East Lynne, but no one detected any undue intimacy between them, not even Mr. Carlyle. To him, as to others, her conduct must always remain a mystery.'

Madame Vine appeared to be occupied with her spectacles, setting them straight. Barbara continued.

'Of course the disgrace is reflected on the children, and always will be; the shame of having a divorced mother—'

'Is she not dead?' interrupted Lady Isabel.

'She is dead. Oh yes. But they will not be the less pointed at, the girl especially, as I say. They allude to their mother now and then, in conversation, Wilson tells me: but I would recommend you, Madame Vine, not to encourage them in that. They had better forget her.'

'Mr. Carlyle would naturally wish them to do so.'

'Most certainly. There is little doubt that Mr. Carlyle would blot out all recollection of her, were it possible. But unfortunately she was the children's mother, and for that there is no help. I trust you will be able to instil principles into the little girl which will keep her from a like fate.'

'I will try,' answered Lady Isabel, with more fervour than she had yet spoken. 'Are the children much with you, may I inquire?'

'No. I never was fond of being troubled with children. When my own grow up into childhood, I shall deem the nursery and the schoolroom the

best places for them. I hold an opinion, Madame Vine, that too many moth-
ers pursue a mistaken system in the management of their family. There are
some, we know, who, lost in the pleasures of the world, in frivolity, wholly
neglect them: of those I do not speak; nothing can be more thoughtless,
more reprehensible; but there are others who err on the opposite side. They
are never happy but when with their children; they must be in the nursery;
or, the children in the drawing-room. They wash them, dress them, feed
them; rendering themselves slaves, and the nurse's office a sinecure. The children are noisy, troublesome, cross; all children will be so; and the mother's
temper gets soured, and she gives slaps where, when they were babies, she
gave kisses. She has no leisure, no spirits for any higher training: and as they
grow old she loses her authority. One who is wearied, tired out with her children, cross when they play or make a little extra noise, which jars on her
unstrung nerves, who says, "You shan't do this; you shall be still," and that
perpetually, is sure to be rebelled against at last: it cannot be otherwise. Have
you never observed this?'

'I have.'

'The discipline of that house soon becomes broken. The children run wild;
the husband is sick of it, and seeks peace and solace elsewhere. I could mention instances in this neighbourhood,' continued Mrs. Carlyle, 'where things
are managed precisely as I have described, even in our own class of life. I
consider it a most mistaken and pernicious system.'

'It undoubtedly is,' answered Lady Isabel, feeling a sort of thankfulness,
poor thing, that the system had not been hers—when she had a home and
children.

'Now, what I trust I shall never give up to another, will be the *training* of
my children,' pursued Barbara. 'Let the offices, properly pertaining to a
nurse, be performed by the nurse—of course taking care that she is thoroughly to be depended on. Let her have the *trouble* of the children, their
noise, their romping; in short, let the nursery be her place and the children's
place. But I hope I shall never fail to gather my children round me daily, at
stated and convenient periods, for higher purposes: to instil into them Christian and moral duties; to strive to teach them how best to fulfil the obliga-
tions of life. *This* is a mother's task—as I understand the question; let her do
this work well, and the nurse can attend to the rest. A child should never
hear aught from its mother's lips but persuasive gentleness; and this becomes
impossible, if she is very much with her children.'

Lady Isabel silently assented. Mrs. Carlyle's views were correct.

'When I first came to East Lynne, I found Miss Manning, the governess,
was doing everything necessary for Mr. Carlyle's children in the way of the
training that I speak of,' resumed Barbara. 'She had them with her for a short
period every morning, even the little one: I saw that it was all right, therefore
did not interfere. Since she left—it is nearly a month now—I have taken

them myself. We were sorry to part with Miss Manning; she suited very well. But she has been long engaged to an officer in the navy, and now they are to be married. You will have the entire charge of the little girl: she will be your companion out of school hours: did you understand that?'

'I am quite ready and willing to undertake it,' said Lady Isabel, her heart fluttering. 'Are the children well? Do they enjoy good health?'

'Quite so. They had the measles in the spring, and the illness left a cough upon William, the eldest boy. Mr. Wainwright says he will outgrow it.'

'He has it still, then?'

'At night and morning. They went last week to spend the day with Miss Carlyle, and were a little late in returning home. It was foggy, and the boy coughed dreadfully after he came in. Mr. Carlyle was so concerned, that he left the dinner-table and went up to the nursery: he gave Joyce strict orders that the child should never again be out in the evening air, so long as the cough was upon him. We had never heard him cough like that.'

'Do you fear consumption?' asked Lady Isabel in a low tone.

'I do not fear that, or any other incurable disease for them,' answered Barbara. 'I think, with Mr. Wainwright, that time will remove the cough. The children come of a healthy stock on their father's side; and I have no reason to think they do not on their mother's. She died young, you will say. Ay, but she did not die of disease; her death was the result of accident. How many children had you?' pursued Mrs. Carlyle, somewhat abruptly.

At least, the question fell with abruptness upon the ear of Lady Isabel, for she was not prepared for it. What should she answer? In her perplexity she stammered forth the actual truth.

'Three. And—and a baby. That died. Died an infant, I mean.'

'To lose four dear children!' uttered Barbara, with sympathising pity. 'What did they die of?'

A hesitating pause. 'Some of one thing, some of another,' was the answer, given in almost an inaudible tone.

'Did they die before your husband? Otherwise the grief must have been worse to bear.'

'The—baby—died after him,' stammered Lady Isabel, as she wiped the drops from her pale forehead.

Barbara detected her emotion, and felt sorry to have made the inquiries: she judged it was caused by the recollection of her children.

'Mrs. Latimer wrote us word you were of gentle birth and breeding,' she resumed, presently. 'I am sure you will excuse my asking these particular questions,' Barbara added, in a tone of apology, 'but this is our first interview; our preliminary interview, it may in a measure be called, for we could not say much by letter.'

'I was born and reared a gentlewoman,' answered Lady Isabel.

'Yes, I am sure of it: there is no mistaking the tone of a gentlewoman,' said Barbara. 'How sad it is when pecuniary reverses fall upon us! I dare say you never thought to go out as governess.'

A half smile positively crossed her lips. She, think to go out as a governess!—the Earl of Mount Severn's only child! 'Oh no, never,' she said, in reply.

'Your husband, I fear, could not leave you well off. Mrs. Latimer said something to that effect.'

'When I lost him I lost all,' was the answer. And Mrs. Carlyle was struck with the wailing pain betrayed in the tone. At that moment a maid entered.

'Nurse says the baby is undressed, and quite ready for you, ma'am,' she said, addressing her mistress.

Mrs. Carlyle rose, but hesitated as she was moving away.

'I will have the baby here to-night,' she said to the girl. 'Tell nurse to put a shawl round him and bring him down. It is the hour for my baby's supper,' she smiled, turning to Lady Isabel. 'I may as well have him here for once, as Mr. Carlyle is out. Sometimes I am out myself, and then he has to be fed.'

'You do not stay in-doors for the baby, then?'

'Certainly not. If I and Mr. Carlyle have to be out in the evening baby gives way. I should never give up my husband for my baby; never, dearly as I love him.'

The nurse came in. Wilson. She unfolded a shawl, and placed the baby on Mrs. Carlyle's lap. A proud, fine, fair young baby, who reared his head and opened wide his great blue eyes, and beat his arms at the lights of the chandelier, as no baby of nearly six months old ever did yet. So thought Barbara. He was in his clean white night-gown and night-cap, with their pretty crimped frills and border; altogether a pleasant sight to look upon. *She* had once sat in that very chair, with a baby as fair upon her knee: but all that was past and gone. She leaned her hot head upon her hand, and a rebellious sigh of envy went forth from her aching heart.

Wilson, the curious, was devouring her with her eyes; Wilson was thinking she never saw such a mortal fright as the new governess. Them blue spectacles capped everything, she decided: and what made her tie up her throat, in that fashion, for? As well wear a man's collar and stock, at once! If her teaching was no better than her looks, Miss Lucy might as well go to the parish charity school!

'Shall I wait, ma'am?' demurely asked Wilson, her investigations being concluded.

'No,' said Mrs. Carlyle. 'I will ring.'

Baby was exceedingly busy, taking his supper. And of course, according to all baby precedent, he ought to have gone off into a sound sleep over it. But the supper concluded, the gentleman seemed to have no more sleep in his eyes than he had before he began. He sat up, crowed at the lights, stretched out his hands for them, and set his mother at defiance, absolutely refusing to be hushed up.

'Do you wish to keep awake all night, you rebel?' cried Barbara, fondly looking on him.

A loud crow by way of answer. Perhaps it was intended to intimate that he did. She clasped him to her with a sudden gesture of rapture, a sound of love, and devoured his pretty face with kisses. Then she took him in her arms, putting him to sit upright, and approached Madame Vine.

'Did you ever see a more lovely child?'

'A fine baby indeed,' she constrained herself to answer: and she could have fancied it was her own little Archibald over again when he was a baby. 'But he is not much like you.'

'He is the very image of my darling husband. When you see Mr. Carlyle—' Barbara stopped, and bent her ear, as if listening.

'Mr. Carlyle is probably a handsome man?' said poor Lady Isabel, believing that the pause was made to give her opportunity of putting in an observation.

'He is handsome; but that is the least good about him. He is the most noble man! revered, respected by every one, I may say, loved. The only one who could not appreciate him was his wife. How ever she could leave him,—how she could even look at another after calling Mr. Carlyle husband, will always be a marvel to those who know him.'

A bitter groan—and it nearly escaped her lips.

'That certainly is the pony carriage,' cried Barbara, bending her ear again. 'If so, how very early Mr. Carlyle is home! Yes, I am sure it is the sound of the wheels.'

How Lady Isabel sat, she scarcely knew: how she concealed her trepidation she never would know. A pause; an entrance to the hall; Barbara, baby in arms, advanced to the drawing-room door, and a tall form entered. Once more Lady Isabel was in the presence of her sometime husband.

He did not perceive that any one was present, and he bent his head and fondly kissed his wife. Isabel's jealous eyes were turned upon them. She saw Barbara's passionate, lingering kiss in return, she heard her fervent whispered greeting. 'My darling!' and she watched him turn to press the same fond kisses on the rosy, open lips of his child. Isabel flung her hands over her face. Had she bargained for this? It was part of the cross she had undertaken to carry, and she *must* bear it.

Mr. Carlyle came forward and saw her. He looked somewhat surprised. 'Madame Vine,' said Barbara; and he held out his hand and welcomed her in the same cordial, pleasant manner that his wife had done. She put her shaking hand in his: there was no help for it: little thought Mr. Carlyle that that

hand had been tenderly clasped in his a thousand times; that it was the one
pledged to him at the altar at Castle Marling.

She sat down on her chair again, unable to stand, feeling as though every
drop of blood within her had left her body. It had certainly left her face. Mr.
Carlyle made a few civil inquiries as to her journey, but she did not dare to
raise her eyes to him, as she breathed forth the answers.

'You are at home soon, Archibald,' Barbara exclaimed. 'I did not expect
you so early. I did not think you could get away. I know what the justices'
annual dinner at the Buck's Head is; they always make it late.'

'As they will to-night,' laughed Mr. Carlyle. 'I watched my opportunity,
and got away when the pipes were brought in: I had determined to do so, if
possible. Dill—who means to stick it out with the best of them—has his tale
ready when they miss me. "Suddenly called away: important business; could
not be helped."'

Barbara laughed also. 'Was papa there?'

'Of course. He took the table's head. What would the dinner be without
the chairman of the bench, Barbara?'

'Nothing at all, in papa's opinion,' merrily said Barbara. 'Did you ask him
how mamma was?'

'I asked him,' said Mr. Carlyle. And there he stopped.

'Well?' cried Barbara. 'What did he say?'

'"Full of nervous fidgets," was the answer he made me,' returned Mr. Carlyle, with an arch look at his wife. 'It was all I could get out of him.'

'That is just like papa. Archibald, do you know what I have been thinking
to-day?'

'A great many foolish things, I dare say,' he answered: but his tone was a
fond one: all too palpably so for one ear.

'No, but listen. You know papa is going to London with Squire Pinner, to
see those new agricultural implements—or whatever it is. They are sure to be
away three days. Don't you think so?'

'And three to the back of it,' said Mr. Carlyle, with a wicked smile upon
his lips. 'When old gentlemen get plunged into the attractions of London,
there's no answering for their getting out of them in a hurry, country justices
especially. Well, Barbara?'

'I was thinking if we could but persuade mamma to come to us for the
time he is away. It would be a delightful little change for her; a break in her
monotonous life.'

'I wish you could,' warmly spoke Mr. Carlyle. 'Her life, since you left, is a
monotonous one; though, in her gentle patience, she will not say so. It is a
happy thought, Barbara, and I only hope it may be carried out. Mrs. Carlyle's mother is an invalid, and lonely, for she has no child at home with her
now,' he added, in a spirit of politeness, addressing himself to Madame Vine.

She simply bowed her head: she did not trust herself to speak. Mr. Carlyle scanned her face attentively, as she sat, her head bent downwards. She did not appear inclined to be sociable, and he turned to the baby, who was wider awake than ever.

'Young sir, I should like to know what brings you up, and here, at this hour?'

'You may well ask,' said Barbara. 'I had him brought down, as you were not here, thinking he would be asleep directly. And only look at him! no more sleep in his eyes than in mine.'

She would have hushed him to her as he spoke, but the young gentleman stoutly repudiated it. He set up a half cry, and struggled his arms and head free again, crowing the next moment most impudently. Mr. Carlyle took him.

'It is of no use, Barbara, he is beyond your coaxing this evening,' And he tossed the child in his arms, held him up to the chandelier, made him bob at the baby in the pier-glass, until the rebel was in an ecstasy of delight. Finally he smothered his face with kisses, as Barbara had done. Barbara rang the bell.

Oh! can you imagine what it was, for Lady Isabel? So had he tossed, so had he kissed her children, she standing by, the fond, proud, happy mother, as Barbara was standing now. Mr. Carlyle came up to her.

'Are you fond of these little troubles, Madame Vine? This one is a fine fellow, they say.'

'Very fine. What is his name?' she replied, by way of saying something.

'Arthur.'

'Arthur Archibald,' put in Barbara to Madame Vine. 'I was vexed that his name could not be entirely Archibald, but that was already monopolised. Is that you, Wilson? I don't know what you'll do with him, but he looks as if he would not be asleep by twelve o'clock.'

Wilson satisfied her curiosity by taking another prolonged stare at Madame Vine, received the baby from Mr. Carlyle, and departed with him.

Madame Vine rose. Would they excuse her? she asked, in a low tone: she was tired, and would be glad to retire to rest.

Of course. And would she ring for anything she might wish in the way of refreshment. Barbara shook hands with her in her friendly way; and Mr. Carlyle crossed the room to open the door for her, and bowed her out with a courtly smile.

She went up to her chamber at once. To rest? Well, what think you? She strove to say to her lacerated and remorseful heart, that the cross—far heavier though it was proving than anything she had imagined or pictured—was only what she had brought upon herself, and *must* bear. Very true: but none of us would like such a cross to be upon our shoulders.

'Is she not droll looking?' cried Barbara, when she was alone with Mr.

Carlyle. 'I can't think why she wears those blue spectacles: it cannot be for her sight, and they are very disfiguring.'

'She puts me in mind of—of—' began Mr. Carlyle, in a dreamy tone.

'Of whom?'

'Her face, I mean,' he said, still dreaming.

'So little can be seen of it,' returned Mrs. Carlyle. 'Of whom does she put you in mind?'

'I don't know, nobody in particular,' returned he, rousing himself. 'Let us have tea in, Barbara.'

⚔ III ⚔

The Yearning of a Breaking Heart

At her bedroom door, the next morning, stood Lady Isabel, listening whether the coast was clear, ere she descended to the grey parlour, for she had a shrinking dread of encountering Mr. Carlyle. When he was glancing narrowly at her face the previous evening, she had felt the gaze, and it impressed upon her a dread of his recognition. Not only that: he was the husband of another: therefore it was not expedient that she should see too much of him, for he was far dearer to her heart than he had ever been.

Almost at the same moment, there burst out of a remote room, the nursery, an upright, fair, noble boy of some five years old, who began careering along the corridor, astride upon a hearth-broom. She did not need to be told that it was her boy, Archibald; his likeness to Mr. Carlyle would have proclaimed it, even if her heart had not. In an impulse of unrestrainable tenderness, she seized the child as he was galloping past her, and carried him into her room, broom and all.

'You must let me make acquaintance with you,' said she to him, by way of excuse. 'I love little boys.'

Love! Down she sat upon a low chair, the child held upon her lap, kissing him passionately, and the tears raining from her eyes. She could not have helped the tears, had it been to save her life; she could as little have helped the kisses. Lifting her eyes, there stood Wilson, who had entered without ceremony. A sick feeling came over Lady Isabel: she felt as if she had betrayed herself. All that could be done now, was to make the best of it; to offer some lame excuse. What possessed her, thus to forget herself?

'He put me in remembrance of my own children,' she said to Wilson, gulping down her emotion, and hiding her tears in the best manner she could;

whilst the astonished Archibald, now released, stood with his finger in his mouth and stared at her spectacles, his great blue eyes opened to their utmost width. 'When we have lost children of our own, we are apt to love fondly all we come near.'

Wilson, who stared only in a less degree than Archie, for she deemed the new governess had gone suddenly mad, gave some voluble assent, and turned her attention upon Archie.

'You naughty young monkey, how dare you rush out in that way with Sarah's hearth-broom? I'll tell you what it is, sir; you are getting too owdacious and rumbustical for the nursery; I shall speak to your mamma about it.'

She seized hold of the child and shook him. Lady Isabel started forward, her hands up, her voice one of painful entreaty.

'Oh, don't, don't beat him! I cannot see him beaten.'

'Beaten!' echoed Wilson; 'if he got a good beating it would be all the better for him; but it's what he never does get. A little shake, or a tap, is all I must give; and it's not half enough. You wouldn't believe the sturdy impudence of that boy, madame; he runs riot, he does. The other two never gave a quarter of the trouble. Come along, you figure! I'll have a bolt put at the top of the nursery door!—And if I did, he'd be for climbing up the door-post to get at it.'

The last sentence Wilson delivered to the governess, as she jerked Archie out of the room, along the passage and into the nursery. Lady Isabel sat down with a wrung heart, a chafed spirit. Her own child! and she might not say to the servant, you shall not beat him!

She descended to the grey parlour. The two elder children, and breakfast, were waiting: Joyce quitted the room when she entered it.

A graceful girl of eight years old, a fragile boy a year younger, both bearing her own once lovely features, her once bright and delicate complexion, her large, soft, brown eyes. How utterly her heart yearned to them! but there must be no scene like there had just been above. Nevertheless, she stooped and kissed them both; one kiss each of impassioned fervour. Lucy was naturally silent, William somewhat talkative.

'You are our new governess,' said he.

'Yes. We must be good friends.'

'Why not?' said the boy. 'We were good friends with Miss Manning. I am to go into Latin soon, as soon as my cough's gone. Do you know Latin?'

'No. Not to teach it,' she said, studiously avoiding all endearing epithets.

'Papa said you would be almost sure not to know Latin, for that ladies rarely did. He said he should send up Mr. Kane to teach me.'

'Mr. Kane?' repeated Lady Isabel, the name striking upon her memory. 'Mr. Kane the music-master?'

'How did you know he was a music-master?' cried shrewd William. And Lady Isabel felt the red blood flush to her face at the unlucky admission she had made. It flushed deeper at her own falsehood, as she muttered some evasive words about hearing of him from Mrs. Latimer.

'Yes, he is a music-master; but he does not get much money by it, and he teaches the classics as well. He has come up to teach us music since Miss Manning left: mamma said that we ought not to lose our lessons.'

Mamma! How the word, applied to Barbara, grated on her ear. 'Whom does he teach?' she asked.

'Us two,' replied William, pointing to his sister and himself.

'Do you always take bread-and-milk for breakfast?' she inquired, perceiving that to be what they were eating.

'We get tired of it sometimes, and then we have milk-and-water and bread-and-butter, or honey: and then we take to bread-and-milk again. It's Aunt Cornelia who thinks we should eat bread-and-milk for breakfast: she says papa never had anything else when he was a boy.'

Lucy looked up. 'Papa would give me an egg when I breakfasted with him,' cried she, 'and Aunt Cornelia said it was not good for me, but papa gave it me all the same. I always had breakfast with him then.'

'And why do you not now?' asked Lady Isabel.

'I don't know. I have not since mamma came.'

The word 'stepmother' rose up rebelliously in the heart of Lady Isabel. Was Mrs. Carlyle putting away the children from their father?

Breakfast over, she gathered them to her, asking them various questions; about their studies, their hours of recreation, the daily routine of their lives.

'This is not the school-room, you know,' cried William, when she made some inquiry as to their books.

'No?'

'The school-room is upstairs. This is for our meals, and for you in an evening.'

The voice of Mr. Carlyle was heard at this juncture in the hall, and Lucy was springing towards the sound. Lady Isabel, fearful lest he might enter, if the child showed herself, stopped her with a hurried hand.

'Stay here, Isabel.'

'Her name's Lucy,' said William, looking quickly up. 'Why do you call her Isabel?'

'I thought—thought I had heard her called Isabel,' stammered the unfortunate lady, feeling quite confused with the errors she was committing.

'My name is Isabel Lucy,' said the child, 'but I don't know who could have told you, for I am never called Isabel. I have not been, since—since—Shall I tell you? Since mamma went away,' she concluded, dropping her voice. 'Mamma that was, you know.'

'Did she go?' cried Lady Isabel, full of emotion, and possessing a very faint idea of what she was saying.

'She was kidnapped,' whispered Lucy.

'Kidnapped!' was the surprised answer.

'Yes; or she would not have gone. There was a wicked man on a visit to papa, and he stole her. Wilson said she knew he was a kidnapper, before he took mamma. Papa said I was never to be called Isabel again, but Lucy. Isabel was mamma's name.'

'How do you know your papa said it?' dreamily returned Lady Isabel.

'I heard him. He said it to Joyce, and Joyce told the servants. I put only Lucy to my copies. I did put Isabel Lucy, but papa saw it one day, and he drew his pencil through Isabel, and told me to show it to Miss Manning. After that, Miss Manning let me put nothing but Lucy. I asked her why, and she told me papa preferred the name, and that I was not to ask questions.'

She could not well stop the child, but every word was rending her heart.

'Lady Isabel was our very own mamma,' pursued Lucy. 'This mamma is not.'

'Do you love this one as you did the other?' breathed Lady Isabel.

'Oh, I loved mamma! I loved mamma!' uttered Lucy, clasping her hands. 'But it's all over. Wilson said we must not love her any longer, and Aunt Cornelia said it. Wilson said, if she had loved us, she would not have gone away from us.'

'Wilson said so?' resentfully spoke Lady Isabel.

'She said she need not have let that man kidnap her. I am afraid he beat her: for she died. I lie in my bed at night, and wonder whether he did beat her, and what made her die. It was after she died that our new mamma came home. Papa said she was come to be our mamma in place of Lady Isabel, and we were to love her dearly.'

'*Do* you love her?' almost passionately asked Lady Isabel.

Lucy shook her head. 'Not as I loved mamma.'

Joyce entered to show the way to the school-room, and they followed her up-stairs. As Lady Isabel stood at the window, she saw Mr. Carlyle depart on foot, on his way to the office. Barbara was with him, hanging fondly on his arm, about to accompany him to the park gates. So had *she* fondly hung, so had *she* accompanied him, in the days gone for ever.

Barbara came into the school-room in the course of the morning, and entered upon the subject of their studies, the differently allotted hours, some to play, some to work. She spoke in a courteous but most decided tone, showing that she was the unmistakable mistress of the house and children, and meant to be. Never had Lady Isabel felt her position more keenly; never had it so galled and fretted her spirit: but she bowed in meek obedience. A hundred times that day did she yearn to hold the children to her heart, and a hundred times she had to repress the longing.

Before tea, when the beams of the sun were slanting across the western horizon, she went out with the two children. They took the field path, leading parallel with the high-road, the hedge only dividing them; the path that Captain Levison used to take when he went to pry into the movements of Mr. Carlyle. To the excessive dismay of Lady Isabel, whom should they come upon, but Mr. and Mrs. Carlyle: they were walking home from West Lynne together, and had chosen the field way.

A confused greeting: it was confused to the senses of Lady Isabel: and then they were all returning together. Mr. and Mrs. Carlyle in advance: she and the children behind.

She slackened her pace. She strove to put all possible distance between herself and them. It did not avail her. Coming to a stile, Mr. Carlyle helped his wife over it, and then waited. The children were soon on the other side: little need of help for them: but he remained, in his courtesy, to assist the governess.

'I thank you,' she panted, as she came up. 'I do not require help.'

Words that fell idly on his ear. He stood waiting for her, and she had no resource but to mount the stile: an awkward stile: she remembered it of old. Not more awkward, however, than she herself was at that moment. Before her was Mr. Carlyle's outstretched hand, and she could do no less than put the tips of her fingers into it: but, in her trepidation she got her feet entangled in her petticoats; and, in attempting to jump, would have fallen, had not Mr. Carlyle caught her in his arms.

'You are not hurt, I trust!' he exclaimed, in his kindly manner.

'I beg your pardon, sir; my foot caught. Oh no, I am not hurt. Thank you.'

He walked forward and took his wife upon his arm, who had turned to wait for him. Lady Isabel lingered behind, striving to still her beating heart.

They were at tea in the grey parlour, she and the two children, when William was seized with a fit of coughing. It was long and violent. Lady Isabel left her seat: she had drawn him to her, and was hanging over him with unguarded tenderness, when, happening to lift her eyes, they fell upon Mr. Carlyle. He had been descending the stairs, on his way from his dressing-room, heard the cough, and came in. Had Lady Isabel been killing the boy, she could not have dropped him more suddenly.

'You possess a natural love for children, I perceive,' he said, looking at her with his sweet smile.

She did not know what she answered: some confused, murmured words. If Mr. Carlyle made sense of them, he was clever. Into the darkest corner of the room retreated she.

'What is the matter?' interrupted Mrs. Carlyle, looking in. She also had been descending, and was in her dinner dress. Mr. Carlyle had the boy on his own knee then.

'William's cough is troublesome. I don't like it, Barbara. I shall have Wainwright up again.'

'It's nothing,' said Barbara. 'He was at his tea: perhaps a crumb went the wrong way. Dinner is waiting, Archibald.'

Mr. Carlyle put the boy down, but stood for a minute looking at him. The cough over, he was pale and exhausted, all his brilliant colour gone: it was too brilliant, as Afy had said. Mrs. Carlyle entwined her arm within her husband's, but turned her head to speak as they were walking away.

'You will come into the drawing-room by-and-by with Miss Lucy, Madame Vine. We wish to hear you play.'

Miss Lucy! And it was spoken in the light of a command. Well? Barbara was Mrs. Carlyle, and she was—what she was. Once more she drew to her her first-born son, and laid her aching forehead upon him.

'Do you cough at night, my darling child?'

'Not much,' he answered. 'Joyce puts me some jam by the bedside, and if I have a fit of coughing, I eat that. It's black currant.'

'He means jelly,' interposed Lucy, her mouth full of bread-and-butter. 'It is black currant jelly.'

'Yes, jelly,' said William. 'It's all the same.'

'Does any one sleep in your room?' she inquired of him.

'No. I have a room to myself.'

She fell into deep thought, wondering whether they would let a little bed be put in her room for him, wondering whether she might dare to ask it. Who could watch over him and attend to him as she would? In this one day's intercourse with William, she had become aware that he was possessed of that precocious intellect which too frequently attends weakness of body. He had the sense of a boy of fourteen, instead of one of seven: his conversation betrayed it. 'Knowing,' 'understands more than's good for a child,' say old wives, as they look and listen, coupling their remark with another, 'he'll never live.'

'Should you like to sleep in my room?' asked Lady Isabel.

'I don't know. Why should I sleep in your room?'

'I could attend to you; could give you jelly, or anything else you might require, if you were to cough in the night. I would love you, I would be tender with you as your own mamma could have been.'

'Mamma did not love us,' cried he. 'Had she loved us she would not have left us.'

'She did love us,' exclaimed Lucy, somewhat fiercely. 'Joyce says she did, and I remember it. It wasn't her fault that she was kidnapped.'

'You be quiet, Lucy: girls know nothing about things. Mamma—'

'Child, child,' interposed Lady Isabel, the scalding tears filling her eyes, 'your mamma did love you: loved you dearly: loved you, as she could never love anything again.'

'You can't tell that, Madame Vine,' persisted William, disposed to be resolute. 'You were not here; you did not know mamma.'

'I am sure she must have loved you,' was all Madame Vine dared to answer. 'I have been here but a day, and I have learnt to love you. I love you already, very, very much.'

She pressed her lips to his hot cheek as she spoke, and the rebellious tears would not be restrained, but fell on it also.

'Why do you cry?' asked William.

'I once,' she answered, in a low tone, 'lost a dear little boy like you, and I am so glad to have you to replace him: I have had nothing to love since.'

'What was his name?' cried curious William.

'William.' But the word was scarcely out of her lips before she thought how foolish she was to say it.

'William Vine,' cogitated the boy. 'Did he speak French or English? His papa was French, was he not?'

'He spoke English. But you have not finished your tea,' she added, finding the questions were becoming close.

It was Barbara's custom, when they were at home, to leave Mr. Carlyle at the dessert-table and to go up for a few minutes to her baby, before entering the drawing-room. As she was descending on this evening, she saw Lucy, who was peeping out of the grey parlour.

'May we come in now, mamma?'

'Yes. Ask Madame Vine to bring in some music.'

Madame Vine, delaying as long as she dared, arrived at the drawing-room door at an inopportune moment, for Mr. Carlyle was just coming from the dining-room. She paused when she saw him: her first impulse was to retreat; but he looked round and appeared to wait for her. Lucy had already gone in.

'Madame Vine,' he began, his hand upon the door-handle, and his tone suppressed, 'have you had much experience in the ailments of children?'

She was about to answer 'No.' For her own children, so long as she had been with them, were remarkably healthy. But she remembered that she was supposed to have lost four by death, and must speak accordingly.

'Not a very great deal, sir. Somewhat, of course.'

'Does it strike you that this is an ugly cough of William's?'

'I think that he wants care; that he should be continually watched, especially at night. I was wishing that he might be allowed to sleep in my room,' she added, some strong impulse prompting her to prefer this request to Mr. Carlyle, trembling inwardly and outwardly, as she did so. 'His bed could be readily moved in, and I would attend to him, sir, as—as—I would attend more cautiously than any servant could be likely to do.'

'By no means,' warmly responded Mr. Carlyle. 'We would not think of giving you the trouble. He is not ill, to require night nursing: and, if he were, our servants are to be depended on.'

'I am so fond of children,' she ventured to plead. 'I have already taken a great liking for this one, and would wish to make his health my care by night and by day. It would be a pleasure to me.'

'You are truly kind. But I am sure Mrs. Carlyle would not hear of it: it would be taxing you unreasonably.'

His tone was one of decision, and he opened the door for her to pass in.

What she most dreaded, of all, was her singing. The lisp was not perceptible when she sang, and she feared her voice, her tones, might be recognized. She was determined not to attempt any song that she had ever sung in that house, and to give her voice but half its full compass. She remembered how ardently her husband had admired her singing in the days gone by. Barbara sang to him now.

For that evening there was a respite. Not many minutes had elapsed after her entrance, when one of the servants appeared, showing in Justice Hare, his march pompous as ever, his wig in elaborate order. No singing when he was present, for the sweetest melody was lost upon him. Barbara and Mr. Carlyle both rose to greet him.

'Oh, papa; what a wonder to see you in an evening! I am very glad. Come to the easy-chair. Madame Vine,' added Barbara, as the justice was passing that lady to get to an easy-chair.

'Hope you are well, madmoselle. Nong parley Frongsey, me,' said the justice, with an air that seemed to say, 'And thank goodness that I don't.'

Madame Vine could not suppress a smile. 'There is no necessity, sir. I am not French, but English.'

'Beg pardon,' said the Justice. 'But I heard there was a French madam coming here: and I'm sure you look like French,' he added, staring at her blue spectacles and her disfiguring dress. 'I shouldn't have taken you for English, if you had not told me; but I'm glad to hear it. No good ever comes of a French governess in one's house. Keep 'em at arm's length, say I.'

'Do you think not?' returned Lady Isabel.

'I know it,' bluntly replied the justice. 'When our girls were young, Anne and Barbara, my wife must needs have a French maid for 'em: after that, she must have a French governess. I was dubious about it. "She'll turn us all papists," said I, "and require frogs to be served up for her dinner." But Mrs. Hare represented that the girls must learn French, like other folks, and I let one come. Two years and some months she stopped, and—'

'And what, sir?'

'Well, it's not just drawing-room talk. I had a brother staying with us most of the time, a post-captain in the navy. On the sick-list he was invalided for three years. And we found them out. From nearly the first day that French madmoselle put her foot inside our door, up to the day I cleared her out of it, a nice game they had been carrying on. It gave Mrs. Hare a sickener for French jesuits of governesses, and I told her she was just served right. When I heard that Mrs. Carlyle had engaged a madmoselle for these children at East Lynne, I said she wanted her ears boxed.'

'But, papa, I told you then that Madame Vine was English, not French.'

The justice growled some answer, and continued his narrative to Madame Vine.

'I gave it my brother right and left; in fact, the quarrel, we had then, may be said to have lasted his life, for he never forgave me. He returned to service, and got his flag early. But he died close upon it, and left all his money to Barbara. Like a donkey, as he was.'

'The effects of the quarrel, you see, papa,' laughingly said Barbara; the justice thought, saucily.

'You are in Carlyle's hands now, and not in mine, or I'd tell you what I think of that speech, ma'am,' was the grim retort to Barbara, as the justice once more turned to Madame Vine.

'You must have seen some of the pranks of these French madmoselles, these governesses?'

'Not very much. I have not been brought into contact with them. I am English, as I tell you.'

'And a good thing for you, ma'am, I should say,' returned the justice, in his abrupt bluntness. 'But the mistake was natural, you must see. Being called by a French title, and living in France, or some of those outlandish places over the water, one could but take you for French. If I set up my quarters in France, and called myself Mosseer, I'd forgive the very dickens himself if he mistook me for a French frog.'

Lucy clapped her hands, and laughed in merriment.

'You may laugh, Miss Lucy: but I can tell you, you'd have been changed into a frog, or something worse, if they had turned you over to a French madmoselle. If your poor mother hadn't had a French madmoselle of a governess in the first years of her life, she'd never have—have—'

'Have—what?' said Lucy, who was staring with all her might at Justice Hare.

'Done as she did. There! It's out. Barbara, what's this nonsense that you have been putting into your mamma's head?'

'I don't know what you mean, papa. I and Archibald want her to be with us while you are in London: if you allude to that.'

'And are determined to have her, justice,' put in Mr. Carlyle. 'Even though we should have to make a night assault on the Grove, and carry her off by storm.'

'The Grove, yes,' growled Justice Hare. 'Much either Barbara or you care what becomes of that. A pretty high life below stairs there would be, with the master and mistress both away! You young ones have no more consideration than so many calves.'

'Oh, papa, how can you fancy such things?' uttered Barbara. 'The Grove would be just as safe and quiet without you and mamma, as with you. The servants are all steady, and have been with us a long while.'

'If you want your mamma here for more than a day, why can't you get her to come when I am at home?'

'Because she will not leave you; you know that, papa. If you are at home, she will be there too. I am sure there never was a pattern wife like mamma: if Archibald finds me only half such a one, in years to come, he may think himself lucky.'

The above remark was accompanied by a glance at Mr. Carlyle, meant to express saucy independence: but her deep love shone out in spite of herself. Mr. Carlyle lifted his drooping eyelids, and smiled as he nodded to her.

'Papa, you always have your own way, but you must allow us to have ours for once. Mamma wishes to come to us: she gave quite a glad start when I proposed it to-day: and you must be kind enough not to oppose it. The house and servants will go on swimmingly; I'll answer for it.'

'Rather too swimmingly,' cried Justice Hare.

'She *requires* a change, sir,' said Mr. Carlyle. 'Think what your wife's inward life is.'

'Fretting after that vagabond! Whose fault is it? Why does she do it?'

'She has been a good and loving wife to you, sir.'

'I didn't say she hadn't.'

'Then encourage her to take this little holiday. The change of coming here for a few days will do her good; Barbara's society will do her good: remember how fond Mrs. Hare is of her.'

'A vast deal fonder than Barbara deserves,' retorted the justice. 'She's as perky as she can be now she thinks she's beyond my correction.'

'She's not beyond mine,' said Mr. Carlyle, quite gravely. 'I assure you, justice, I keep her in order.'

'*I* know,' cried the justice, his tone rather rough. 'You'd kill her with indulgence, before you'd keep her in order. That's you, Carlyle.'

The justice thought he could relish a glass of ale, and some was brought in. During the slight stir occasioned by this, Lady Isabel slipped round to Mrs. Carlyle. 'Might she retire? She believed she was not wanted,' and Mrs. Carlyle graciously acceded to the request.

An evening to herself in the grey parlour. A terrible evening; one made up of remorse, grief, rebellion, and bitter repentance: repentance of the wretched past, rebellion at existing things. Between nine and ten she dragged herself upstairs, purposing to retire to rest.

As she was about to enter her chamber, Sarah, Wilson's assistant in the nursery, was passing, and a sudden thought occurred to Lady Isabel. 'In which room does Master Carlyle sleep?' she asked. 'Is it on this floor?'

The girl pointed to a door near. 'In there, ma'am.'

Lady Isabel watched her downstairs, and then entered the room softly. A little white bed, and William's beautiful face lying on it. His cheeks were flushed, his hands were thrown out, as if with inward fever; but he was sleeping quietly. By the bedside stood a saucer, some currant jelly in it, and a teaspoon; there was also a glass of water.

She glided down upon her knees and let her face rest on the bolster beside him, her breath in contact with his. Her eyes were wet; but that she might wake him, she would have taken the sleeper on to her bosom, and caressed him there. Death for him? She could hardly think it.

'My gracious heart alive! Seeing a light here, if I didn't think the room was on fire. It did give me a turn.'

The speaker was Wilson, who had discerned the light, in passing the door. Lady Isabel sprang up as though she had been shot. She feared the detection of Wilson and Joyce more than she feared that of Mrs. Carlyle.

'I am looking at Master William,' she said, as calmly as she could speak. 'Mr. Carlyle appears somewhat uneasy respecting his cough. He has a flushed, delicate look.'

'It is nothing,' returned Wilson. 'It's just the look that his mother had. The first time I saw her, nothing would convince me but what she had got paint on.'

'Good night,' was all the reply made by Lady Isabel, as she retreated to her own room.

'Good night, madame,' replied Wilson, returning towards the nursery. 'I'll be blest if I know what to think of that French governess!' she mentally continued. 'I hope it may turn out that she's not deranged, that's all.'

❧ I V ❧

Then You'll Remember Me

In a soft grey damask dress, not unlike the colour of the walls from which the room took its name, a cap of Honiton lace shading her delicate features, sat Mrs. Hare. The justice was in London with Squire Pinner, and Barbara had gone to the Grove, and brought her mamma away in triumph. It was evening now, and kind Mrs. Hare was paying a visit to the grey parlour. Miss Carlyle had been dining there, and Lady Isabel, under plea of a violent headache, had begged to decline the invitation to take tea in the drawing-room, for she feared the sharp eyes of Miss Carlyle. Barbara, upon leaving the dessert-table, went to the nursery as usual to her baby, and Mrs. Hare took the opportunity to go and sit a few minutes with the governess; she feared that governess must be very lonely. Miss Carlyle, scorning usage and ceremony, had remained in the dining-room with Mr. Carlyle, a lecture for him, upon some defalcation or other, most probably in store. Lady Isabel was alone. Lucy had gone to keep a birthday in the neighbourhood, and William was in the nursery. Mrs. Hare found her in a sad attitude, her two hands pressed upon her temples. She had not yet made acquaintance with her beyond a formal introduction.

'I am sorry to hear you are not well this evening,' she gently said.

'Thank you. My head aches much'—which was no false plea.

'I fear you must feel your solitude irksome. It is dull for you to be here all alone.'

'I am so used to solitude.'

Mrs. Hare sat down, and gazed with sympathy at the young, though somewhat strange-looking woman before her; she detected the signs of mental suffering on her face. 'You have seen sorrow,' she uttered, bending forward and speaking with the utmost sweetness.

'Oh, great sorrow,' burst from Lady Isabel, for her wretched fate was very palpable to her mind that evening, and the tone of sympathy rendered it nearly irrepressible.

'My daughter tells me that you have lost your children, that you have lost your fortune and position. Indeed, I feel for you. I wish I could comfort you!'

This did not decrease her anguish. She completely lost all self-control, and a gush of tears fell from her eyes. 'Don't pity me! don't pity me, dear Mrs. Hare: indeed, it only makes endurance harder. Some of us,' she added, looking up with a sickly smile, 'are born to sorrow.'

'We are all born to it,' cried Mrs. Hare. 'I, in truth, have cause to say so. Oh, you know not what my portion has been—the terrible weight of grief that I have to bear. For many years, I can truly say that I have not known one completely happy moment.'

'All have not to bear this killing sorrow,' said Lady Isabel.

'Rely upon it, sorrow of some nature comes sooner or later to all. In the brightest lot on earth dark days must mix. Not that there is a doubt but that it falls unequally. Some, as you observe, seem born to it, for it clings to them all their days: others are more favoured. As we reckon favour: perhaps this great amount of trouble is no more than is necessary to take us to heaven. You know the saying; "Adversity hardens the heart, or it opens it to Paradise." It may be, that our hearts are so hard, that the long-continued life's trouble is requisite to soften them. My dear,' Mrs. Hare added, in a lower tone, while the tears glistened on her pale cheeks, 'there will be a blessed rest for the weary, when this toilsome life is ended: let us find comfort in that thought.'

'Ay! ay!' murmured Lady Isabel. 'It is all that is left to me.'

'You are young to have acquired so much experience of sorrow.'

'We cannot estimate sorrow by years. We may live a whole lifetime of it in a single hour. But we generally bring ill fate upon ourselves,' she continued, in a desperation of remorse: 'as our conduct is, so will our happiness or misery be.'

'Not always,' sighed Mrs. Hare. 'Sorrow, I grant you, comes all too frequently from ill-doing: but the worst is, that the consequences of this wrong doing fall upon the innocent as well as upon the guilty. A husband's errors will involve his innocent wife; the sins of the parents will fall upon their children; children will break the hearts of their parents. I can truly say—speaking in all humble submission—that I am unconscious of having deserved the great sorrow which came upon me; that no act of mine invited it; but, though it has nearly killed me, I entertain no doubt that it is lined with mercy, if I could only bring my weak rebellious heart to look for it. You, I feel sure, have been equally undeserving.'

Mrs. Hare did not mark the flush of shame, the drooping of the eyelids.

'You have lost your little ones,' Mrs. Hare resumed. 'This is grief; great grief, I would not underrate it; but believe me it is as *nothing* compared to the awful fate of finding your children grow up and become that which makes you wish they had died in their infancy. There are times when I am tempted to regret that *all* my treasures are not in the next world: that they have not gone before me. Yes; sorrow is the lot of all.'

'Surely not of all,' dissented Lady Isabel. 'There are some bright lots on earth.'

'There is not a lot, but must bear its appointed share,' returned Mrs. Hare. 'Bright as it may appear, ay, and as it may continue to be for years, depend upon it some darkness must overshadow it earlier or later.'

'Mr. and Mrs. Carlyle—what sorrow can there be in store for them?' asked Lady Isabel, her voice ringing with a strange sound: which Mrs. Hare noted, though she understood it not.

'Mrs. Carlyle's lot is bright,' she said, a sweet smile illumining her features. 'She loves her husband with an impassioned love; and he is worthy of it. A happy fate indeed is hers; but she must not expect to be exempted from sorrow. Mr. Carlyle has had his share of it,' concluded Mrs. Hare.

'Ah!'

'You have doubtless been made acquainted with his history. His first wife left him; left her home and her children. He bore it bravely before the world; but I know that it wrung his very heart strings. She was his heart's early idol.'

'She! Not Barbara?'

The moment the word 'Barbara' had escaped her lips, Lady Isabel re-collected herself. She was only Madame Vine, the governess: what would Mrs. Hare think of her familiarity?

Mrs. Hare did not appear to have noticed it: she was absorbed in the subject. 'Barbara?' she uttered: 'certainly not. Had his first love been given to Barbara, he would have chosen her then. It was given to Lady Isabel.'

'It is given to his wife now.'

Mrs. Hare nearly laughed. 'Of course it is: would you wish it to be buried in the grave with the dead?—and with one who was false to him? But, my dear, she was the sweetest woman, that unfortunate Lady Isabel. I loved her then, and I cannot help loving her still. Others blamed her, but I pitied. They were well matched: he, so good and noble; she, so lovely and endearing.'

'And she left him; threw him to the winds, with all his nobility and love!' exclaimed that poor governess, with a gesture of the hands, that looked very like despair.

'Yes. It will not do to talk of: it is a miserable subject. How she could abandon such a husband, such children, was a marvel to many; but to none more than it was to me and my daughter. The false step—though I feel almost afraid to speak out the thought, lest it may appear to savour of triumph—while it must have secured her own wretchedness, led to the happiness of my child; for it is pretty certain Barbara would never have loved another as she loves Mr. Carlyle.'

'You think it did secure wretchedness to her?' cried Lady Isabel, her tone one of bitter mockery, more than anything else.

Mrs. Hare was surprised at the question. 'No woman ever took that step yet, without its entailing on her the direst wretchedness,' she replied. 'It cannot be otherwise. And Lady Isabel was of a nature to feel remorse, to meet it half way. Refined, modest, with every feeling of an English gentlewoman, she was the very last one would have expected to act so. It was as if she had gone away in a dream, not knowing what she was doing: I have thought so many a time. That terrible mental wretchedness and remorse did overtake her, I know.'

'How did you know it? Did you hear it?' exclaimed Lady Isabel, her tone all too eager, had Mrs. Hare been suspicious. 'Did *he* proclaim that—Francis Levison? Did you hear it from him?'

Mrs. Hare, gentle Mrs. Hare, drew herself up, for the words grated on her feelings and on her pride. Another moment, and she was mild and kind again, for she reflected that that poor sorrowful governess must have spoken without thought.

'I know not what Sir Francis Levison may have chosen to proclaim,' she said, 'but you may be sure he would not be allowed opportunity to proclaim anything to me, or to any other friend of Mr. Carlyle's: nay, I should say, nor to any one good and honourable. I heard it from Lord Mount Severn.'

'From Lord Mount Severn!' repeated Lady Isabel. And she opened her lips to say something more, but closed them again.

'He was here on a visit in the summer; he stayed a fortnight. Lady Isabel was the daughter of the late earl—perhaps you may not have known that. He—Lord Mount Severn—told me, in confidence, that he had sought out Lady Isabel when the man, Levison, left her: he found her sick, poor, broken-hearted, and in some remote French town, utterly borne down with remorse and repentance.'

'Could it be otherwise?' sharply asked Lady Isabel.

'My dear, I have said it could not. The very thought of her deserted children would entail it, if nothing else did. There was a baby born abroad,' added Mrs. Hare, dropping her voice, 'an infant in its cradle then, Lord Mount Severn said: but that child, we know, could only bring pain and shame.'

'True,' issued from her trembling lips.

'Next, came her death: and I cannot but think it was sent to her in mercy. I trust she was prepared for it, and had made her peace with God. When all else is taken from us, we turn to Him: I hope she had learned to find the Refuge.'

'How did Mr. Carlyle receive the news of her death?' murmured Lady Isabel, a question which had been often in her thoughts.

'I cannot tell: he made no outward sign, either of satisfaction or grief. It was too delicate a subject for any one to enter upon with him, and most assuredly, he did not enter upon it himself. After he was engaged to my child, he told me that he should never have married during Lady Isabel's life.'

'From—from—the remains of affection?'

'I should think not. I inferred it to be from conscientious scruples. All his affection is given to his present wife. There is no doubt that he loves her with a true, a fervent, a lasting love: though there perhaps was more romantic sentiment in the early passion felt for Lady Isabel. Poor thing! she gave up a sincere heart, a happy home.'

Ay, poor thing! She had very nearly wailed forth her vain despair.

'I wonder whether the drawing-room is tenanted yet,' smiled Mrs. Hare, breaking a pause which had ensued. 'If so, I suppose they will be expecting me there.'

'I will ascertain for you,' said Lady Isabel, speaking in the impulse of the moment: for she was craving an instant to herself, even though it were but in the hall.

She quitted the grey parlour and approached the drawing-room. Not a sound came from it; and believing it was empty, she opened the door and looked cautiously in.

Quite empty. The fire blazed, the chandelier was lighted, but nobody was enjoying the warmth or the light. From the inner room, however, came the sound of the piano, and the tones of Mr. Carlyle's voice. She recognized the chords of the music: they were those of the accompaniment to the song he had so loved when she sang it to him. Who was about to sing it to him now?

Lady Isabel stole across the drawing-room to the other door, which was ajar. Barbara was seated at the piano, and Mr. Carlyle stood by her, his arm on her chair, and bending his face on a level with hers, possibly to look at the music. So, once had stolen, so, once had peeped the unhappy Barbara, to hear this self-same song. *She* had been his wife then; she had received his kisses when it was over. Their positions were reversed.

Barbara began. Her voice had not the brilliant power of Lady Isabel's, but it was a sweet and pleasant voice to listen to.

> 'When other lips and other hearts
>   Their tales of love shall tell,
> In language whose excess imparts
>   The power they feel so well.
> There may, perhaps, in such a scene
>   Some recollection be,
> Of days that have as happy been—
>   And you'll remember me.'

Days that had as happy been! Ay. *Did* he remember her? Did a thought of her, his first and best love, flit across him, as the words fell on his ear? Did a past vision of the time when she sat there and sang it to him, arouse his heart to even a momentary recollection?

Terribly, indeed, were their positions reversed; most terribly was she feeling. And by whose act and will had the change been wrought? Barbara was now the honoured and cherished wife, East Lynne's mistress. And what was she? Not even the welcomed guest of an hour, as Barbara had then been: but an interloper, a criminal woman who had thrust herself into the house; her act, in doing so, not justifiable, her position a most false one. Was it right, even if she should succeed in remaining undiscovered, that she and Barbara should dwell in the same habitation, Mr. Carlyle being in it? Did she deem it to be right? No, she did not: but one act of ill-doing entails more. These thoughts were passing through her mind as she stood there, listening to the song; stood there as one turned to stone, her throbbing temples pressed against the door's pillar.

The song was over, and Barbara turned to her husband, a whole world of love in her bright blue eyes. He laid his hand upon her head; Lady Isabel saw that, but she would not wait to see the caress that most probably followed it. She turned and crossed the room again, her hands clasped tightly on her bosom, her breath catching itself in hysterical sobs. Miss Carlyle was entering from the hall. They had not yet met, and Lady Isabel swept meekly past her with a hurried curtsey. Miss Carlyle spoke, but she dared not answer: to wait, would have been to betray herself.

Sunday came, and that was the worst of all. In the old East Lynne pew at St. Jude's, so conspicuous to the congregation, sat she, as in former times: no excuse dared she, the governess, make, to remain away. It was the first time she had entered an English Protestant church since she had last sat in it, there, with Mr. Carlyle. That fact alone, with all the terrible remembrances it brought in its train, was sufficient to overwhelm her with emotion. She sat at the upper end now, with Lucy; Barbara occupied the place that had been hers, by the side of Mr. Carlyle. Barbara there, in her own right, his wife: she, severed from him for ever and for ever!

She scarcely raised her head: she tightened her thick veil over her face; she kept her spectacles bent towards the ground. Lucy thought she must be crying: she had never seen any one so still at church before. Lucy was mistaken: tears come not to solace the bitter anguish of hopeless, self-condemning remorse. How she sat out the service, she could not tell: she could not tell how she should sit out other services, as the Sundays came round. The congregation did not forget to stare at her: what an extraordinary looking governess Mrs. Carlyle had picked up!

They went out when it was over. Mr. and Mrs. Carlyle in advance; she, humbly following them, with Lucy. She glanced aside at the tomb in the churchyard's corner, where mouldered the remains of her father; and a yearning cry went forth from the very depth of her soul. 'Oh, that I were laid there with him! Why did I come back again to East Lynne?'

Why, truly? But she had never thought that her cross would be so sharp as this.

🐦 V 🐦

An M.P. for West Lynne

As this is not a history of the British constitution, it is not necessary to relate how or why West Lynne got into hot water with the House of Commons. The House threatened to disenfranchise it, and West Lynne, under the fear, went in mourning for its sins. The threat was not carried out; but one of the sitting members was unseated with ignominy, and sent to the right about. Being considerably humiliated thereby, and in disgust with West Lynne, he retired accordingly, and a fresh writ was issued. West Lynne then returned the Honourable Mr. Attley, a county nobleman's son, but he died in the very midst of his first session, and another writ had to be issued.

Of course the consideration now was, who should be the next candidate. All the notables within ten miles were discussed, not excepting the bench of justices. Mr. Justice Hare? No; he was too uncompromising; would study his own will, but not that of West Lynne. Squire Pinner? He never made a speech in his life, and had not an idea beyond turnips and farming stock. Colonel Bethel? He had no money to spend upon an election. Sir John Dobede? He was too old. 'By a good twenty years,' laughed Sir John himself. 'But here we stand, like a pack of noodles, conning over the incapables, and passing by the right one,' continued Sir John. 'There's only one man amongst us fit to be our member.'

'Who's that?' cried the meeting.

'Archibald Carlyle.'

A pause of consternation; consternation at their collective forgetfulness; and then a murmur of approbation, approaching to a shout, filled the room. Archibald Carlyle. It should be no other.

'If we can get him,' cried Sir John. 'He may decline, you know.'

All agreed that the best thing was to act promptly. A deputation, half the length of the street—its whole length, if you include the tagrag and bobtail that attended behind—set off, on the spur of the moment, to the office of Mr. Carlyle. They found that gentleman about to leave it for the evening, to return home to dinner. For, in the discussion of the all important topic, the meeting had suffered time to run on to a late hour; those gentlemen who dined at a somewhat earlier one, had for once in their lives patiently allowed their dinners and their stomachs to wait—which is saying a great deal for the patience of a justice.

Mr. Carlyle was taken by surprise. 'Make me your member?' cried he merrily. 'How do you know I should not sell you all?'

'We'll trust you, Carlyle. Too happy to do it.'

'I am not sure that I could spare the time,' deliberated Mr. Carlyle.

'Now, Carlyle, you must remember that you avowed to me, no longer ago than last Christmas, your intention of going into parliament some time,' struck in Mr. Justice Herbert. 'You can't deny it.'

'Some time!—yes,' replied Mr. Carlyle. 'But I did not say when. I have no thoughts of it yet awhile.'

'You must allow us to put you in nomination, you must indeed, Mr. Carlyle. There's nobody else fit for it. As good send a pig to the House, as some of us.'

'An extremely flattering reason for proposing to shift the honour upon me,' laughed Mr. Carlyle.

'Well, you know what we mean, Carlyle. There's not a man in the whole county so suitable as you, search it through: you must know there is not.'

'I don't know anything of the sort,' returned Mr. Carlyle.

'At any rate, we are determined to have you. When you walk into West Lynne to-morrow, you'll see the walls alive with placards, "Carlyle for ever!"'

'Suppose you allow me until to-morrow to consider of it, and defer the garnishing of the walls a day later,' said Mr. Carlyle, a serious tone peeping out in the midst of his jocularity.

'You do not fear the expense?'

It was but a glance he returned in answer. As soon as the question had been put—it was stupid old Pinner who propounded it—they had felt how foolish it was. And indeed the cost would be a mere nothing, were there no opposition.

'Come, decide now, Carlyle. Give us your promise.'

'If I decide now, it will be in the negative,' replied Mr. Carlyle. 'It is a question that demands consideration. Give me till to-morrow for that, and it is possible that I may accede to your request.'

This was the best that could be made of him: the deputation backed out, and, as nothing more could be done, departed to their several dinner tables. Mr. Dill, who had been present, remained rubbing his hands with satisfaction, and casting admiring glances at Mr. Carlyle.

'What's the matter, Dill?' asked the latter. 'You look as though you were pleased at this movement, and assumed that I should accept it.'

'And so you will, Mr. Archibald. And as to looking pleased, there's not a man, woman, or child in West Lynne who won't be glad.'

'Don't make too sure, Dill.'

'Of what, sir?—of your becoming our member, or of the people looking pleased?'

'Of either,' laughed Mr. Carlyle.

He quitted the office to walk home, revolving the proposition as he did so. That he had long thought of some time entering parliament, was certain; though no definite period of the 'when' had fixed itself in his mind. He did not see why he should confine his days entirely to toil, to the work of its calling. Pecuniary considerations did not require it, for his realised property, combined with the fortune brought by Barbara, was quite sufficient to meet expenses, according to their present style of living. Not that he had the least intention of giving up his business: it was honourable (as he conducted it) and lucrative; and he really liked it: he would not have been condemned to lead an idle life for the world. But there was no necessity for his being always at it. Mr. Dill made as good a principal as he did, and—if length of service and experience might be counted—a better one. He could safely be left to manage, during the time it would be necessary for Mr. Carlyle to be in London. He would rather represent West Lynne than any other spot on the face of the earth, no matter what might be that other's importance; and as West Lynne was now in want of a member, perhaps his opportunity had come. That he would make a good and efficient public servant, he believed; his talents were superior, his oratory was persuasive, and he had the gift of a true and honest spirit. That he would have the interest of West Lynne at heart, was certain, and he knew that he should serve his constituents to the very best of his power and ability. They knew it also.

Before Mr. Carlyle had reached East Lynne, he had decided that it should be.

It was a fine spring evening, for the months had gone on. The lilac was in bloom, the hedges and trees were clothed in their early green, all things seemed full of promise. Even Mr. Carlyle's heart was rejoicing in the prospect opened to it: he was sure he should like a public life. But, in the sanguine moments of realisation or of hope, some dark shade will step in to mar the brightness.

Barbara stood at the drawing-room window watching for him. Not in her was the dark shade. Her dress was a marvel of vanity and prettiness, and she had chosen to place on her fair hair a dainty head-dress of lace. As if her hair required such adornment! She waltzed up to Mr. Carlyle when he entered, and saucily held up her face, the light of love dancing in her bright blue eyes.

'What do you want?' he provokingly asked, putting his hands behind him, and letting her stand there.

'Oh, well—if you won't say good evening to me! I have a great mind to say you should not kiss me for a week, Archibald.'

He laughed. 'Who would be most punished by that?' whispered he.

Barbara pouted her pretty lips, and the tears positively came to her eyes. 'Which is as much as to say it would be no punishment to you. Archibald! *don't* you care for me?'

He threw his arms round her and clasped her to his heart, taking plenty of kisses then. 'You know whether I care or not,' he fondly whispered.

But now, will you believe that that unfortunate Lady Isabel had been a witness to this? Well? it was only what his greeting to her had once been. Her pale face flushed scarlet, and she glided out of the room again as softly as she had entered it. They had not seen her. Mr. Carlyle drew his wife to the window, and stood there, his arm round her waist.

'Barbara, what should you say to living in London for a few months out of the twelve?'

'London? I am very happy where I am. Why should you ask me that? You are not going to live in London?'

'I am not sure of that. I think I am for a portion of the year. I have had an offer made me this afternoon, Barbara.'

She looked at him, wondering what he meant; wondering whether he was serious. An offer to him? What sort of an offer? Of what nature could it be?

He smiled at her perplexity. 'Should you like to see M.P. attached to my name? West Lynne wants me to become its member.'

A pause to take in the news; a sudden rush of colour; and then she gleefully clasped her hands round his arm, her eyes sparkling with pleasure.

'Oh, Archibald, how glad I am! I knew you were appreciated; and you will be appreciated more and more. This is right: it was not well for *you* to remain for life a private individual, a country lawyer.'

'I am perfectly contented with my lot, Barbara,' he said seriously, 'I am too busy to be otherwise.'

'I know that were you but a labouring man, toiling daily for the bread you eat, you would be contented, feeling that you were fulfilling your appointed duty to the utmost; but, Archibald, could you not still be a busy man at West Lynne, although you should become its representative?'

'If I could not, I would not accept the honour, Barbara. For some few months of the year I must of necessity be in town, but Dill is an efficient substitute; and I can run down for a week or so, between times. Part of Saturday, Sunday, and part of Monday I can always pass here, if I please. Of course, these changes have their drawbacks, as well as their advantages.'

'Where would be the drawbacks in this?' she interrupted.

'Well,' smiled Mr. Carlyle, 'in the first place, I suppose you could not always be with me.'

Her hands fell; her colour faded. 'Oh, Archibald!'

'If I do become their member, I must go up to town as soon as elected: and I don't think it will do for my little wife to be quitting her home to travel about just now.'

Barbara's face wore a very blank look. She could not dissent from Mr. Carlyle's reasoning.

'And you must remain in London to the end of the session, while I am here! Separated! Archibald,' she passionately added, while the tears gushed into her eyes, 'I could not *live* without you.'

'Then what is to be done? Must I decline it?'

'Decline it! Oh, of course not. I know: we are looking on the dark side of things. I can go very well with you for a month, perhaps two.'

'You think so?'

'I am sure so. And, mind! you must not encourage mamma to talk me out of it. Archibald,' she continued, resting her head upon his breast, her sweet face turned up beseechingly to his, 'you would rather have me with you, would you not?'

He bent his own down upon it. 'What do you think about it, my darling?'

Once more, an inopportune moment for her to enter—Lady Isabel. Barbara heard her this time, and sprang away from her husband. Mr. Carlyle turned round at the movement, and saw Madame Vine. She came forward; her lips ashy, her voice subdued.

She had now been six months at East Lynne, and had hitherto escaped detection. Time and familiarity render us accustomed to most things, to danger amongst the rest; and she had almost ceased to fear recognition. She and the children were upon the best terms: she had greatly endeared herself to them, and they loved her: perhaps nature was asserting her own hidden claims.

What of William? William had been better through the winter, but with the first blush of spring he had begun to fade again. He was constantly weary, had frequent pain in his side, and his appetite failed. Mr. Wainwright attended him daily now. In the day he looked tolerably well, for the exceeding beauty and brightness of his complexion disarmed suspicion; but towards evening, so soon as twilight came on, his illness showed itself outwardly. His face would be of a pallid whiteness, he could scarcely speak for weakness, and his favourite resting-place was the hearth-rug in the grey parlour. There he would lie down at full length, a cushion under his head, and his eyes closed.

'My child,' Madame Vine would say to him, 'you would be better on the sofa.'

'No. I like this.'

'But, if I draw it quite close to the fire for you? Try it, William.'

He did, one or two evenings: and then the old place was resumed, and he would not quit it. He was lying there as usual on this evening when Hannah came in with the tea-things. She gazed down for a minute or two at the boy, whom she supposed to be sleeping, so still and full of repose did he look, and then turned to Madame Vine.

'Poor child! he's one that's going fast on to his grave.'

The words utterly startled her. Daily familiarity with illness sometimes renders us partially blind to its worst features, and thus it had been with Lady Isabel. Upon her arrival at East Lynne, she had been, if not alarmed, much concerned at the appearance of William: the winter improvement had dispelled that concern; while the spring change had come on so gradually that her fears had not taken alarm. She judged him to be a delicate boy, one who required care.

'Hannah!' she uttered, in a tone of reproof, to the servant.

'Why, ma'am, I wonder that you can't see it yourself!' returned Hannah. 'It's plain, poor lad, that he has no mother, or there would have been an outcry over him long ago. Of course, Mrs. Carlyle can't be expected to have the feelings of one for him: and as to old Wainwright, he's as blind as any bat.'

She took the reproach to herself, and it smote upon her heart: had *she* been blind: she, his mother?

'There is nothing particular the matter with him, Hannah. He is only weakly.' But she spoke these words in braving defiance of her thoughts; anxious, if we may so say it, to deceive herself: even as she gave expression to them, her pulses were going pit-a-pat with the fear, the next to certainty, that there was worse the matter with him.

'Are you asleep, William?' she softly said, bending down towards him.

No reply. No movement in answer.

'He might not have been asleep, Hannah. You should be more cautious in your remarks.'

'Anybody may see that he's asleep, ma'am, lying so still as that. Of course I wouldn't say anything in his hearing.'

'Why do you fancy him to be in a critical state?'

'It is not fancy,' returned Hannah. 'I have had some experience in fading children.'

Lucy entered at this juncture, and nothing more was said. When Hannah quitted the room, Lady Isabel gazed down at William, as if she would have devoured him, a yearning, famished sort of expression upon her features. He was white as death. The blue veins were conspicuous in his face, and his nostrils were slightly working with every breath he drew, as will be the case with the sickly. From passive security she had jumped to the other extreme, for Hannah's words had roused every fear within her.

'Madame Vine, why are you looking like that at William?' asked Lucy, who was watching.

'Hannah thinks he is ill,' she mechanically answered. Her reflections were buried five fathoms deep, and she was debating whether she ought not on that very instant to make known these new fears to Mr. Carlyle. To *Mr.* Carlyle, you observe: her jealous heart would not recognize the right of Mrs. Carlyle over her children—although she had to submit to its exercise.

She quitted the parlour. She had heard Mr. Carlyle come in. Crossing the hall, she tapped softly at the drawing-room door, and then as softly entered. It was the moment of Mr. Carlyle's fond greeting to his wife. They stood together, heedless of her.

Gliding out again, she paced the hall, her hands pressed upon her beating heart. How *dared* that heart rise up in sharp rebellion at these witnessed tokens of love? Was Barbara not his wife? Had she not a legal claim to all his tenderness? Who was she, that she should resent them in her sick jealousy? What, though they had once been hers, hers only; had she not signed and sealed her own forfeit of them, and so made room for Barbara?

Back to the grey parlour, there she stood, her elbow on the mantelpiece, her eyes hidden by her hand. Thus she remained for some minutes, and Lucy thought how sad she looked.

But Lucy felt hungry, and was casting longing glances towards the tea-table. She wondered how long her governess meant to keep it waiting. 'Madame Vine,' cried she, presently, 'don't you know that tea is ready?'

This caused Madame Vine to raise her eyes. They fell upon the pale boy at her feet. She made no immediate answer, only placed her hand on Lucy's shoulder.

'Oh, Lucy dear, I—I have many sorrows to bear.'

'The tea will warm you, and there's some nice jam,' was Miss Lucy's offered consolation.

'Their greeting, tender as it may be, is surely over by this time,' thought Lady Isabel, an expression something like mockery curving her lips. 'I will venture again.'

Only to see him with his wife's face on his breast, and his own lips bent upon it. But they had heard her this time, and she had to advance, in spite of her spirit of misery and her whitened features.

'Would you be so good, sir, as to come and look at William?' she asked, in a low tone, of Mr. Carlyle.

'Certainly.'

'What for?' interjected Barbara.

'He looks so very ill. I do not like his looks. I fear he is worse than we have thought.'

They went to the grey parlour, all three of them. Mr. Carlyle was there first, and had taken a long, silent look at William before the others entered.

'What is he doing on the floor?' exclaimed Barbara, in her astonishment. 'He should not lie on the floor, Madame Vine.'

'He lies down there at the dusk hour, and I cannot get him up again. I try to persuade him to the sofa, but it is of no use.'

'The floor will not hurt him,' said Mr. Carlyle. *This* was the dark shade: his boy's failing health.

William opened his eyes. 'Who's that? Papa?'

'Don't you feel well, William?'

'Oh yes, I'm very well, but I am tired.'

'Why do you lie down here?'

'I like lying here. Papa, that pretty white rabbit of mine is dead.'

'Indeed. Suppose you get up and tell me all about it.'

'I don't know about it myself yet,' said William, slowly rising. 'Blair told Lucy when she was out just now; I did not go: I was tired. He said—'

'What has tired you?' interrupted Mr. Carlyle, taking the boy's hand.

'Oh, nothing. I am always tired!'

'Do you tell Mr. Wainwright that you are tired?'

'No. Why should I tell him? I wish he would not order me to take that nasty medicine, that cod-liver oil.'

'But it is to make you strong, my boy.'

'It makes me sick. I always feel sick after it, papa. Madame Vine says I ought to have cream. That would be nice.'

'Cream?' repeated Mr. Carlyle, turning his eyes on Madame Vine.

'I have known cream to do a vast deal of good in a case like William's,' she observed. 'I believe that no better medicine can be given; that it has, in fact, no substitute.'

'It can be tried,' said Mr. Carlyle.

'Pray give your orders, Madame Vine, for anything you think may be beneficial to him,' added Mrs. Carlyle. 'You have had more experience with children than I. Joyce—'

'What does Wainwright say?' interrupted Mr. Carlyle, speaking to his wife, his tone low.

'I do not always see him when he comes, Archibald. Madame Vine does, I believe.'

'Oh dear!' cried Lucy, 'can't we have tea? I want some bread-and-jam.'

Mr. Carlyle turned round, smiled, and nodded at her. 'Patience is good for little girls, Miss Lucy. Would you like some bread-and-jam, my boy?'

William shook his head. 'I can't eat jam. I am only thirsty.'

Mr. Carlyle cast a long and intent look at him, and then left the room. Lady Isabel followed him, her thoughts full of her ailing child.

'Do you think him very ill, sir?' she whispered.

'I think he looks so. What does Mr. Wainwright say?'

'He says nothing to me. I have not inquired his true opinion. Until to-night it did not occur to me that there was danger.'

'Does he look so much worse to-night?'

'Not any worse than usual. Latterly he has looked just like this in an evening. It was a remark of Hannah's that aroused my alarm: she thinks he is on the road to death. What can we do to save him?'

She clasped her hands as she spoke, in the intensity of her emotion: she almost forgot, as they stood there together, talking of the welfare of the child, their child, that he was no longer her husband. Almost; not quite; utterly impossible would it be for her wholly to forget the dreadful present. Neither he nor the child could belong to her again in this world.

A strange rising of the throat in her wild despair, a meek curtsey as she turned from him, his last words ringing in her ears. 'I shall call in further advice for him, Madame Vine.'

William was clinging round Mrs. Carlyle in a coaxing attitude, when she re-entered the grey parlour. 'I know what I could eat, mamma, if you would let me have it,' cried he, in answer to her remonstrance that he must eat something.

'What could you eat?'

'Some cheese.'

'Cheese! Cheese with tea!' laughed Mrs. Carlyle.

'For the last week or two he has fancied strange things—the effect of a diseased appetite,' exclaimed Madame Vine. 'But if I allow them to be brought in, he barely tastes them.'

'I am sure, mamma, I could eat some cheese now,' said William.

'You may have it,' answered Mrs. Carlyle.

As she turned to leave the room the impatient knock and ring of a visitor was heard. Barbara wondered who could be arriving at that, their dinner hour. Sailing majestically into the hall, her lips compressed, her aspect threatening, came Miss Carlyle.

Now it turned out that Miss Corny had been standing at her own window, grimly eyeing the ill-doings of the street, from the fine housemaid opposite, who was enjoying a flirtation with the baker, to the ragged urchins pitch-poling in the gutter and the dust: and there she caught sight of the string— justices and others, who came out of the office of Mr. Carlyle. So many of them were they, that Miss Corny involuntarily thought of a conjuror flinging flowers out of a hat: the faster they come, the more it seems there are to come. 'What on earth's up?' cried Miss Corny, pressing her nose flat against the pane, that she might see the better.

They filed off, some one way, some another. Miss Carlyle's curiosity was keener than her appetite, for she remained at the window, although just in-formed that her dinner was served. Presently Mr. Carlyle appeared, and she knocked on the window with her knuckles. He did not hear it; he had turned off at a quick pace towards his home. Miss Corny's temper rose.

The clerks came out next, one after another; and the last was Mr. Dill. He was less hurried than Mr. Carlyle had been, and heard Miss Corny's signal.

'What, in the name of wonder, did all those people want at the office?' began she, when Mr. Dill had entered in obedience to it.

'That was the deputation, Miss Cornelia.'

'What deputation?'

'The deputation to Mr. Archibald. They want him to become their new member.'

'Member of what?' cried she, not guessing at the actual meaning.

'Of parliament, Miss Corny; to replace Mr. Attley. The gentlemen came to solicit him to be put in nomination.'

'Solicit a donkey!' irascibly uttered Miss Corny, for the tidings did not meet her approbation. 'Did Archibald turn them out again?'

'He gave them no direct answer, ma'am. He will consider of it between now and to-morrow morning.'

'*Consider* of it?' shrieked she. 'Why, he'd never, never be such a flat as to comply! He go into Parliament! What next?'

'Why should he not, Miss Corny? I'm sure I should be proud to see him there.'

Miss Corny gave a sniff. 'You are proud of things more odd than even, John Dill. Remember that fine shirt-front! What has become of it? Is it laid up in lavender?'

'Not exactly in lavender, Miss Corny. It lies in the drawer; for I have never liked to put it on since, after what you said.'

'Why don't you sell it at half price, and buy a couple of good useful shirts with the money?' returned she, tartly. 'Better that, than keep the foppish thing as a witness of your folly. Perhaps *he'll* be buying embroidered fronts next, if he goes into that idle, do-nothing House of Commons. I'd rather enter myself for six months at the treadmill.'

'Oh, Miss Corny! I don't think you have well considered it. It's a great honour, and worthy of him: he will be elevated above us all: and he deserves to be.'

'Elevate him on to a weathercock,' raged Miss Corny. 'There! you may go. I have heard quite enough.'

Brushing past the old gentleman, leaving him to depart, or not, as he might please, Miss Carlyle strode upstairs, flung on her shawl and bonnet, and strode down again. Her servant looked considerably surprised, and addressed her as she crossed the hall.

'Your dinner, ma'am?' he ventured to say.

'What's my dinner to you?' returned Miss Corny, in her wrath. 'You have had yours.'

Away she strode. And thus it happened that she was at East Lynne almost as soon as Mr. Carlyle.

'Where's Archibald?' began she, without ceremony, the moment she saw Barbara.

'He is here. Is anything the matter?'

Mr. Carlyle, hearing the voice, came out, and she pounced upon him with her tongue.

'What's this about your becoming the new member for West Lynne?'

'West Lynne wishes it,' said Mr. Carlyle. 'Sit down, Cornelia.'

'Sit down yourself,' retorted she, keeping on her feet. 'I want my questions answered. *Of course* you will decline.'

'On the contrary, I have made up my mind to accept.'

Miss Corny untied the strings of her bonnet and flung them behind her. 'Have you counted the cost?' was asked, and there was something quite sepulchral in her solemn tone.

'I have given it consideration, Cornelia: both as regards money and time. The expense will not be worth naming, should there be no opposition. And if there is—'

'Ay!' groaned Miss Corny. 'If there is?'

'Well? I am not without some few hundreds to spare for the plaything,' he said, turning upon her the good-humoured light of his fine countenance.

Miss Carlyle emitted some dismal moans. 'That ever I should have lived to see this day! To hear money talked of as though it were dirt. And what's to become of your business?' she sharply added. 'Is that to run to rack and ruin, while you are kicking your heels in that wicked London, under plea of being at the House, night after night?'

'Cornelia,' he gravely said, 'were I dead, Dill could carry on the business just as well as it is being carried on now. I might go into a foreign country for seven years, and come back to find the business as flourishing as ever, for Dill could keep it together. And even were the business to drop off—though I tell you it will not do so—I am independent of it.'

Miss Carlyle faced tartly round upon Barbara. 'Have you been setting him on to this?'

'I think he had made up his mind before he spoke to me. But' added Barbara, in her truth, 'I urged him to accept it.'

'Oh! you did! Nicely moped and miserable you'll be here, if he goes to London for months upon the stretch! You did not think of that, perhaps.'

'But he would not leave me here,' said Barbara, her eyelashes becoming wet at the thought, as she unconsciously moved to her husband's side. 'He would take me with him.'

Miss Carlyle made a pause, and looked at them alternately.

'Is that decided?' she asked.

'Of course it is,' laughed Mr. Carlyle, willing to joke the subject and his sister into good humour. 'Would you wish to separate man and wife, Cornelia?'

She made no reply. She rapidly tied her bonnet-strings, the ribbon trembling ominously in her fingers.

'You are not going, Cornelia! You must stay dinner, now you are here. It is ready. And we will talk this further over afterwards.'

'This has been dinner enough for me for one day,' spoke she, putting on her gloves. 'That I should have lived to see my father's son throw up his business, and change himself into a lazy, stuck-up parliament man!'

'Do stay and dine with us, Cornelia! I think I can subdue your prejudices, if you will let me talk to you.'

'If you wanted to talk to me about it, why did you not come in when you left the office?' cried Miss Corny, in a greater amount of wrath than she had shown yet. And there is no doubt that, in his not having done so, lay one of the sore points.

'I did not think of it,' said Mr. Carlyle. 'I should have come in and told you of it to-morrow morning.'

'I dare say you would,' she ironically answered. 'Good evening to you both.' And in spite of their persuasions, she quitted the house, and went stalking down the avenue.

Two or three days more, and the address of Mr. Carlyle to the inhabitants of West Lynne appeared in the local papers, while the walls and posts, convenient, were embellished with various coloured placards: 'Vote for Carlyle.' 'Carlyle for ever!'

⚜ VI ⚜

Sir Francis Levison at Home

Wonders never cease. Surprises are the lot of man. But perhaps a greater surprise had never been experienced by those who knew him, than when it went forth to the world that Sir Francis Levison had converted himself from— from what he was, into a red-hot politician.

Had he been offered the post of prime minister? Or did his conscience smite him?—as was the case with a certain gallant captain, renowned in song. Neither the one nor the other. The simple fact was, that Sir Francis Levison was in a state of pecuniary embarrassment, and required something to prop him up: some snug sinecure; plenty to get and nothing to do.

'He, in pecuniary embarrassment!' cries the reader. 'How could that be?' No easier thing 'to be' in this world, if a man plunges into the amusements favoured by Francis Levison. When he came into his fortune, there was a weighty amount to pay for debts and damages, a far larger amount than he had believed. Not a farthing, beyond what was obliged to come to him by entail, did Sir Peter leave him; but, of that which remained, he was no sooner in possession than he began to squander right and left. His marriage intervened, but it did not stop him: on the contrary, it was an addition to the outlay: and, not contented with living as was suitable to his rank, he and his wife set up housekeeping in an outrageously costly manner. Added to this, he had, since his marriage, entered heart and soul into the pretty little pastimes of horse-racing, betting, and gambling. Cock-fighting he had always patronised.

The time went on: and things went on; till they could go on no longer, and Sir Francis woke up to his condition. Every shilling of available money was gone, every stiver of unsecured property was parted with; debts and duns had taken their place, and Francis Levison, the reigning baronet, was far more worried and embarrassed than ever had been Francis Levison, the obscure but half-expectant heir. He had fallen into the condition formerly described as being that of the late Lord Mount Severn. But, while the earl had contrived to weather out the storm for years, Francis Levison would not be able to weather it for as many months: and he knew it.

Patch himself up, he must. But how? He had tried the tables, but luck was against him; he made a desperate venture upon the turf, a grand coup, that would have set him on his legs for some time, but the venture turned out the wrong way, and Sir Francis was a defaulter. He began then to think there was nothing for it but to drop into some nice government nest, where, as I have told you, there would be plenty to get and nothing to do. Any place with much to do would not suit him, or he it: he was too empty-headed for work requiring talent—you may have remarked that a man given to Sir Francis Levison's favourite pursuits generally is.

He dropped into something good—or, that promised to be good: nothing less than the secretaryship to Lord Headthelot, who swayed the ministers of the Upper House. But that he was a connection of Lord Headthelot's, he never would have obtained it, and very dubiously the minister consented to try him. Of course, one condition was, that he should enter parliament the first opportunity, his vote to be at the disposal of the ministry: rather a shaky ministry, and supposed, by some, to be on its last legs. And this brings us to the present time.

In a handsome drawing-room in Eaton Square, one sunny afternoon, sat a lady, young and handsome. Her eyes were of a violet blue, her hair was auburn, her complexion delicate. But there was a stern look of anger, amounting to sullenness, on her well-formed features, and her pretty foot was beating the carpet in passionate impatience. It was Lady Levison.

The doings of the past had been coming home to her for some time now: past doings, be they good, or be they ill, are sure to come home, one day or another, and to bring their fruits with them. If you sow wheat it will come up wheat, gladdening you with its good: if you sow noxious weeds, noxious weeds spring forth, and you must do battle with them as you best can. It is the inevitable law of nature, and none can flee from it.

In the years past, many years past now, Francis Levison had lost his heart—or whatever the thing might be that, with him, did duty for one—to Blanche Challoner. He had despised her once to Lady Isabel—but that was done to suit his own purpose, for he had never, at any period, cared for Lady Isabel as he had cared for Blanche. He gained her affections in secret, and in secret they engaged themselves to each other. Blanche's sister, Lydia Challoner, two years older than herself, suspected it, and taxed Blanche with it. Blanche, true to her compact of keeping it a secret, denied it with many protestations. '*She* did not care for Captain Levison: rather disliked him in fact.' 'So much the better,' was Miss Challoner's reply; for she had no respect for Captain Levison, and deemed him an unlikely man to marry.

Years went on, and poor unhappy Blanche Challoner remained faithful to her love. In spite of what he was—and she could not blind her eyes to the fact that he was just the opposite of what he ought to be—her heart was true to him. She heard of his scrapes, she knew of his embarrassments, she bore with his neglect: but she loved on. Even the escapade with Lady Isabel Carlyle did not serve to extinguish her attachment, though it shook it for a time. Upon his return to London, after his accession to the title, their friendship was renewed: a cold, hollow, watery sort of friendship it had grown then on the gentleman's side, but Blanche never doubted that he would now marry her, impediments being removed.

He played fast and loose with her: professing attachment for her in secret, and visiting at the house: perhaps he feared an outbreak from her, an exposure that might be anything but pleasant, did he throw off all relations between them. Blanche summoned up her courage, and spoke to him, urging the marriage: she had not yet glanced at the fear that his intention of marrying her (had he ever possessed such) was over. Bad men are always cowards. Sir Francis shrank from an explanation; and, so far forgot honour, as to murmur some indistinct promise that the wedding should be speedy.

Lydia Challoner had married, and been left a well jointured widow. She was Mrs. Waring: and at her house resided Blanche; for the girls were orphans. Blanche was beginning to show symptoms of her nearly thirty years: not the years, but the long-continued disappointment, the heart-burnings, were telling upon her. Her hair was thin, her face was pinched, her form had lost its roundness. 'Marry *her*, indeed!' scoffed Sir Francis Levison to himself.

There came to Mrs. Waring's, upon a Christmas visit, a younger sister, Alice Challoner, a fair girl of twenty years. She resided generally with an aunt in the country. Far more beautiful was she, than Blanche had ever been: and Francis Levison, who had not seen her since she was a child, fell—as he would have called it—in love with her. Love! He became her shadow; he whispered sweet words in her ear; he turned her head giddy with its own vanity; and he offered her marriage. She accepted him, and preparations for the ceremony immediately began. Sir Francis urged speed, and Alice was nothing loth.

And what of Blanche? Blanche was stunned. A despairing stupor took possession of her; and when she awoke from it, desperation set in. She insisted upon an interview with Sir Francis; and evade it he could not, though he tried hard.

Will it be believed that he denied the past?—that he met with mocking suavity her indignant reminders of what had been between them. 'Love? marriage? Nonsense!' her fancy had been too much at work. Finally, he defied her to prove that he had regarded her with more than ordinary friendship, or had ever hinted at such a thing as a union.

She could not prove it. She had not so much as a scrap of paper, written on by him; she had not a single friend, or enemy, to come forward and testify that they had heard him breathe to her a word of love. He had been too wary for that. Moreover, there were her own solemn protestations to her sister Lydia, that there *was not* anything between her and Francis Levison: who would believe her if she veered round now, and avowed those protestations were false? No; she found that she was in a sinking ship, one there was no chance of saving.

But one chance she determined to try. An appeal to Alice. Blanche Challoner's eyes were suddenly and rudely opened to the badness of the man, and she was aware now how thoroughly unfit he was to become the husband of her sister. It struck her that only misery could result from the union, and that, if possible, Alice should be saved from entering upon it. Would she have married him herself then? Yes. But it was a different thing for that fair, fresh young Alice: *she* had not wasted her life's best years in waiting for him.

When the family had gone to rest and the house was quiet, Blanche Challoner proceeded to her sister's bedroom. Alice had not begun to undress: she was sitting in a comfortable chair before the fire, her feet on the fender, reading a love-letter from Sir Francis.

'Alice, I am come to tell you a story,' said she, quietly. 'Will you hear it?'

'In a minute. Stop a bit,' replied Alice. She finished the perusal of the letter, put it aside, and then spoke again. 'What did you say, Blanche? A story?'

Blanche nodded. 'Several years ago, there was a fair young girl, none too rich, in our station of life. A gentleman, who was none too rich either, sought and gained her love. He could not marry: he was not rich, I say. They loved on in secret, hoping for better times, she wearing out the years and her heart.

'Oh, Alice, I cannot describe to you how she loved him; how she has continued to love him up to this moment! Through evil report she clung to him tenaciously and tenderly as the vine clings to its trellis, for the world spoke ill of him.'

'Who was the young lady?' interrupted Alice. 'Is this a fable of romance, Blanche, or a real history?'

'A real history. I knew her. All those years; years and years I say; he kept leading her on to love, letting her think that his love was hers. In the course of time he succeeded to a fortune, and the bar to their marriage was over. He was abroad when he came into it, but returned home at once; their intercourse was renewed, and her fading heart woke up once more to life. Still, the marriage did not seem to come on; he said nothing of it; and she spoke to him. Very soon, now should it be, was his answer, and she continued to live on—in hope.'

'Go on, Blanche,' cried Alice, who had grown interested in the tale, never suspecting it could bear a personal interest.

'Yes, I will go on. Would you believe, Alice, that almost immediately after this last promise, he saw one whom he fancied he should like better, and asked her to be his wife, forsaking the one to whom he was bound by every tie of honour; repudiating all that had been between them, even his own words and promises!'

'How disgraceful! Were they married?'

'They are to be. Would you have such a man?'

'I!' returned Alice, quite indignant at the question. 'It is not likely that I would.'

'That man, Alice, is Sir Francis Levison.'

Alice Challoner gave a start, and her face became scarlet. 'How dare you say so, Blanche? It is not true. Who was the girl, pray? She must have traduced him.'

'She has not traduced him,' was the subdued answer. 'The girl was myself.'

An awkward pause. 'I know!' cried Alice, throwing back her head resentfully. 'He told me I might expect something of this: that you had fancied him in love with you, and were angry because he had chosen me.'

Blanche turned upon her with streaming eyes: she could no longer control her emotion. 'Alice, my sister, all the pride is gone out of me; all the reticence that woman loves to observe as to her wrongs and her inward feelings, I have broken through for you this night. As sure as that there is a heaven above us, I have told you but the truth. Until you came, I was engaged to Francis Levison.'

An unnatural scene ensued. Blanche, provoked at Alice's rejection of her words, told all the ill she knew, or had heard, of the man; she dwelt upon his conduct with regard to Lady Isabel Carlyle, his heartless after-treatment of that unhappy lady. Alice was passionate and fiery. She professed not to believe a word of her sister's wrongs, and, as to the other stories, they were no affairs of her, she said: what had she to do with his past life?

But Alice Challoner did believe: her sister's earnestness and distress, as she told the tale, carried conviction with them. She did not care very much for Sir Francis: he was not entwined round her heart, as he was round that of Blanche: but she was dazzled with the prospect of so good a settlement in life, and she would not give him up. If Blanche broke her heart—why, she must break it. But she need not have mixed taunts and jeers with her refusal to believe; she need not have *triumphed* openly over Blanche. Was it well done? As we sow, so, I tell you, we shall reap. She married Sir Francis Levison, leaving Blanche to her broken heart, or to any other calamity that might grow out of the injustice. And there sat Lady Levison now, her three years of marriage having served to turn her love for Sir Francis into contempt and hate.

A little boy, two years old, the only child of the marriage, was playing about the room. His mother took no notice of him; she was buried in all-absorbing thought; thought which caused her lips to contract and her brow to scowl. Sir Francis entered, his attitude lounging, his air listless. Lady Levison roused herself, but no pleasant manner or tone was hers, as she addressed him.

'I want some money,' she said.

'So do I,' he answered.

An impatient stamp of the foot, and a haughty toss. 'And I must have it. I *must*. I told you yesterday that I must. Do you suppose I can go on, without a sixpence of ready money, day after day?'

'Do you suppose it is of any use to put yourself in this fury?' retorted Sir Francis. 'A dozen times a week do you bother me for money, and a dozen times do I tell you I have got none. I have got none for myself. You may as well ask that baby for money, as ask me.'

'I wish he had never been born!' passionately said Lady Levison. 'Unless he had had a different father.'

That the last sentence, and the bitter scorn of its tone would have provoked a reprisal from Sir Francis, his flashing countenance betrayed. But at that moment, a servant entered the room.

'I beg your pardon, sir. That man, Brown, forced his way into the hall, and—'

'I can't see him, I won't see him,' interrupted Sir Francis, backing to the farthest corner of the room, in what looked very like abject terror, as if he had completely lost his presence of mind. Lady Levison's lips curled.

'We got rid of him, sir, after a dreadful deal of trouble, but while the door was open in the dispute, Mr. Meredith entered. He has gone on into the library, sir, and he vows he won't stir till he sees you, whether you are sick or well.'

A moment's pause, a half muttered oath, and then Sir Francis quitted the room. The servant retired, and Lady Levison caught up her child.

'Oh, Franky, dear,' she wailed forth, burying her face in his warm neck, 'I would leave him for good and all, if I dared: but I fear he might keep you.'

Now, the secret was, that for the last three days Sir Francis Levison had been desperately ill, obliged to keep his bed, and could see nobody: his life depending upon quiet. Such was the report, or something equivalent to it, which had gone into Lord Headthelot (or, rather to the official office, for that renowned chief was, himself, out of town): it had also been delivered to all callers at Sir Francis Levison's house. The real truth being, that Sir Francis was as well in health as you or I, but from something which had transpired, touching one of his numerous debts, did not dare to show. That morning the matter had been arranged; patched up for a time.

'My stars, Levison!' began Mr. Meredith, who was a whipper-in of the ministry, 'what a row there is about you! Why, you look as well as ever you were!'

'A great deal better to-day,' coughed Sir Francis.

'To think that you should have chosen the present moment for skulking! Here have I been, dancing attendance at your door, day after day, in a state of incipient fever, enough to put me into a real one, and could neither get admitted nor a letter taken up. I should have blown the house up to-day and got in amidst the flying débris. By the way, are you and my lady *two* just now?'

'Two?' growled Sir Francis.

'She was stepping into her carriage yesterday when they turned me from the door, and I made inquiry of her. Her ladyship's answer was, that she knew nothing either of Sir Francis, or his illness.'

'Her ladyship is subject to flights of temper,' chafed Sir Francis. 'What desperate need have you of me, just now? Headthelot's away, and there's nothing doing.'

'Nothing doing up here; a deal too much doing somewhere else. Attley's seat is in the market.'

'Well?'

'And you ought to have been down there about it three or four days ago. Of course you must step into it.'

'Of course I shan't,' returned Sir Francis. 'To represent West Lynne will not suit me.'

'Not suit you! West Lynne! Why, of all places, it is the most suitable. It's close to your own property.'

'If you call ten miles close. I shall not put up for West Lynne, Meredith.'

'Headthelot came up this morning,' said Mr. Meredith.

The information somewhat aroused Sir Francis. 'Headthelot! What brings him back?'

'You. I tell you, Levison, there's a hot row. Headthelot expected you would be at West Lynne days past, and he has come up in an awful rage. Every additional vote we can count in the house is worth its weight in gold: and you, as he says, are allowing West Lynne to slip through your fingers! You must start for it at once, Levison.'

'No.'

'Then you lose your post. Thornton goes in for West Lynne, and takes your place with Headthelot.'

'Did Headthelot send you here to say this?' asked Sir Francis.

'He did. And he means it, mind; that's more. I never saw a man more thoroughly in earnest.'

Sir Francis mused. Had the alternative been given him, he would have preferred to represent a certain warm place underground, rather than West Lynne. But, to quit Headthelot, and the snug post he anticipated, would be ruin irretrievable: nothing short of outlawry, or the Queen's prison. It was awfully necessary to get his threatened person into parliament, and he began to turn over in his mind whether he *could* bring himself to make further acquaintance with West Lynne. 'The thing must have blown over for good by this time,' was the result of his cogitations, unconsciously speaking aloud.

'I can understand your reluctance to appear at West Lynne,' cried Mr. Meredith; 'the scene, unless I mistake, of that notorious affair of yours. But private feelings must give way to public interests; and the best thing you can do is to *start*. Headthelot is angry enough as it is. He says, had you been down at first, as you ought to have been, you would have slipped in without opposition: but now there will be a contest.'

Sir Francis looked up sharply. 'A contest? Who is going to stand the funds?'

'Pshaw! As if we should let funds be any barrier! Have you heard who is in the field?'

'No,' was the apathetic answer.

'Carlyle.'

'Carlyle!' shouted Sir Francis. 'Oh, by George! I can't stand against him.'

'Well, there's the alternative. If you can't, Thornton will.'

'I should run no chance. West Lynne would not elect me if he is a candidate. I'm not sure, indeed, that West Lynne would have me in any case.'

'Nonsense! you know our interest there. Government put in Attley, and it can put in you. Yes or no, Levison.'

'Yes,' replied Sir Francis.

An hour's time, and Sir Francis Levison went forth. On his way to be conveyed to West Lynne? Not yet. He turned his steps to Scotland-yard. In considerably less than another hour, the following telegram, marked 'Secret,' went down from the head office to the superintendent of police at West Lynne.

'Is Otway Bethel at West Lynne? If not, where is he? and when will he be returning to it?'

It elicited a prompt answer.

'Otway Bethel is not at West Lynne. Supposed to be in Norway. Movements uncertain.'

Lady Levison heard of the scheme that was in the wind. When Sir Francis went to tell her (as a matter of the merest courtesy) that he was about to go into the country for some days, she turned upon him fiercely.

'If you have any sense of shame in you, you would shoot yourself, rather than go where you are going, to do what you are about to do.'

That ill feeling had come to an extreme pitch between her and her husband, and that he had been long giving her ample cause of resentment, you may be sure: otherwise she could not have so spoken. He bent his dark looks upon her.

'I know the errand you are bent upon. You are going forth to enter yourself in opposition to Mr. Carlyle. You must possess a front of brass, a recollection seared to shame, or you could not do it. Any one, but you, would sink into the earth with humiliation, at sight of a man so injured.'

'Hold your tongue,' said Sir Francis.

'I held it for months and months; held it because you were my husband; though I was nearly mad. I shall never hold it again. Night and morning one prayer goes up from me—that I may find a way of being legally separated from you. I *will* find it.'

'You had better have left me to Blanche,' sneered Sir Francis. 'The taking me was a dead robbery on her, you know. You knew it then.'

She sat, beating her foot on the carpet, really striving to calm down her irritability. 'Allow me to recommend you to pause and consider, ere you enter upon this insult to Mr. Carlyle,' she resumed.

'What is Carlyle to you? You don't know him.'

'I know him by reputation: know him to be a noble, honourable man, beloved by his friends, respected by all. If ever two men presented a contrast, it is you and he. Ask your uncle's widow what the world thinks of Mr. Carlyle.'

'Had another been my adversary, I should not have cared to stand the contest,' maliciously returned Sir Francis. 'The thought that it is he who is my opponent, spurs me on. I'll oppose and crush him.'

'Take care that you do not get crushed yourself,' retorted Alice Levison. 'Luck does not *always* attend the bad.'

'I'll take my chance,' sneered Sir Francis.

⚔ VII ⚔

A *Mishap to the Blue Spectacles*

Mr. Carlyle and Barbara were seated at breakfast, when, somewhat to their surprise, Mr. Dill was shown in. Following close upon his heels came Justice Hare; and close upon *his* heels came Squire Pinner; while, bringing up the rear, was Colonel Bethel. All the four had come up separately, not together, and all four were out of breath, as if it had been a race which should arrive soonest.

Quite impossible was it for Mr. Carlyle at first to understand the news they brought. All were talking at once, in the utmost excitement: and the fury of Justice Hare, alone, was sufficient to produce temporary deafness. Mr. Carlyle caught a word of the case presently.

'A second man? Opposition? Well, let him come on,' he good-humouredly cried. 'We shall have the satisfaction of ascertaining who wins in the end.'

'But you have not heard who it is, Mr. Archibald,' cried old Dill. 'It—'

'Stand a contest with *him!*' raved Justice Hare.

'He—'

'The fellow wants hanging,' interjected Colonel Bethel.

'Couldn't he be ducked?' suggested Squire Pinner.

Now all these sentences were ranted out together, and their respective utterers were fain to stop till the noise subsided a little. Barbara could only look from one to the other in astonishment.

'Who is this formidable opponent?' asked Mr. Carlyle.

There was a pause. Not one of them but had the delicacy to shrink from naming that man to Mr. Carlyle. The information came at last from old Dill, who dropped his voice while he spoke it.

'Mr. Archibald, the candidate who has come forward is that man, Levison.'

A scarlet flush dyed the brow of Mr. Carlyle. Barbara bent down her face, but her eyes flashed with anger.

'Benjamin went through the town early this morning, exercising his horses,' stuttered Justice Hare. 'He came back, telling me that the walls were placarded with "Levison for ever!" "Vote for Sir Francis Levison!" I nearly knocked him down. "It's true, master," says he, "as I'm a living sinner. And some folks I spoke to told me that he came down last evening." There was news for a respectable man to hear before breakfast!'

'He got here by the last train,' said Mr. Dill, 'and has put up at the Buck's Head. The printers must have sat up all night to get the placards ready. He has got an agent, or something of the sort, with him, and some other chap, said to be a member of the government.'

'Boasting that the field is theirs at the onset, and that the canvass will be a matter of mere form!' added Colonel Bethel, bringing down his cane violently. 'He is mad to offer himself as a candidate here.'

'It's done purposely to insult Mr. Carlyle,' said the meek voice of Squire Pinner.

'To insult us all, you mean, squire,' retorted Colonel Bethel. 'I don't think he will go off quite so glibly as he has come.'

'Of course, Carlyle, you'll go in for it now, neck and crop,' cried Justice Hare.

Mr. Carlyle was silent.

'You won't let the beast frighten you from the contest!' uttered Colonel Bethel, in a loud tone.

'There's a meeting at the Buck's Head at ten,' said Mr. Carlyle, not replying to the immediate question. 'I will be with you there.'

'Did you say he was at the Buck's Head?' asked Squire Pinner. 'I had not heard that.'

'That he was,' corrected Mr. Dill. 'I expect he is ousted by this time. I asked the landlord what he thought of himself, for taking in such a character, and what he supposed the justices would say to him. He vowed with tears in his eyes that the fellow should not be there another hour, and that he never should have entered the house had he known who he was.'

A little more conversation, and the visitors filed off. Mr. Carlyle sat down calmly to finish his breakfast. Barbara approached him.

'Archibald, you will not suffer this man's insolent doings to deter you from your plans? You will not withdraw?' she whispered.

'I think not, Barbara. He has thrust himself offensively upon me in this measure: I believe my better plan will be to take no more heed of him, than I should of the dirt under my feet.'

'Right, right,' she answered, a proud flush deepening the rose on her cheeks.

Mr. Carlyle was soon walking into West Lynne. There were the placards, sure enough, side by side with his own: bearing the name of that wicked coward, who had done him the greatest injury one man can do another. Verily he must possess a face of brass to venture there; as his wife had said, and Mr. Carlyle was thinking.

'Archibald? have you heard the disgraceful news?'

The speaker was Miss Carlyle, who had come down upon her brother like a ship with all its sails set. Her cheeks wore a flush, her eyes glistened, her tall form was drawn up to its most haughty height.

'I have heard it, Cornelia. And, had I not, the walls would have enlightened me.'

'Is he out of his mind?'

'Out of his reckoning, I fancy,' replied Mr. Carlyle.

'You will carry on the contest now,' she continued, her countenance flushing. 'I was averse to it before, but I now withdraw all my objection: you will be no brother of mine, if you yield the field to him.'

'I do not intend to yield it.'

'Good. You bear on upon your course; and let him crawl on upon his. Take no more heed of him than if he were a viper. Archibald, you must canvass now.'

'No,' said Mr. Carlyle, 'I shall be elected without canvass. You'll see, Cornelia.'

'There will be plenty canvassing for you, if you don't condescend to take the trouble, my indifferent brother. I will give a thousand pounds myself for ale, to the electors.'

'Take care,' laughed Mr. Carlyle. 'Keep your thousand pounds in your pocket, Cornelia. *I* have no mind to be unseated, on the plea of "bribery and corruption." Here's Sir John Dobede galloping in, with a face as red as the sun in a fog.'

'Well it may be. He has heard the news. I can tell you, Archibald, West Lynne is in a state of excitement, that has not been its lot for many a day.'

Miss Carlyle was right. Excitement and indignation had taken possession of West Lynne. How the people rallied round Mr. Carlyle! Town and country were alike up in arms. But government interest was rife at West Lynne, and, whatever the private and public feeling might be, collectively or individually, many votes would be recorded for Sir Francis Levison.

Barbara had accompanied her husband that morning to the park gates. In returning, she met Madame Vine and the two children. William seemed quite well; he always did in the morning.

'Mamma,' exclaimed Lucy, 'how warm you look! You have such a colour.'

'I am angry,' replied Barbara; smiling at her own answer.

'Why are you angry?'

'Because a man has come forward to oppose your papa. A second candidate.'

'Has he not a right?' asked William. 'Papa said the field was open.'

'Open to all the world but to him who has dared to enter it,' replied Barbara, her indignation getting ahead of her discretion. 'He is a base, contemptible man, one whom all good people scorn and shun. And he has had the face to thrust himself here in opposition to your papa.'

'What is his name, mamma?'

Barbara recollected herself then. But if the children did not hear the name from her they soon would from other quarters.

'It is Sir Francis Levison.'

Was it a sound of pain, or of terror, or of surprise, that burst from the governess? It sounded like a combination of all. Barbara turned to her; but she was leaning down her head then, coughing, her handkerchief to her face, which had changed to a deadly pallor.

'Are you in pain?' gently demanded Barbara.

'Pain! Oh no, thank you. Some—some dust must have got into my mouth, and caused the cough.'

Mrs. Carlyle said no more. But she wondered: for the words shook as she spoke them, almost as much as did her ashy lips.

'Can she know Francis Levison?' thought Barbara. 'Was it the mention of his name that has so agitated her?'

Strangely absent was Madame Vine at the lesson that day.

One of the first to become cognisant of the affair was Lord Mount Severn. He was at his club one evening in London, poring over an evening paper, when the names 'Carlyle,' 'West Lynne,' caught his view. Knowing that Mr. Carlyle had been named as the probable member, and heartily wishing he might become such, the earl naturally read the paragraph.

He read it, and read it again; he rubbed his eyes, he rubbed his glasses; he pinched himself to see whether he were awake or dreaming. For—believe what that newspaper asserted—that Sir Francis Levison had entered the lists in opposition to Mr. Carlyle, and was at West Lynne, busily canvassing—he could not.

'Do you know anything of this infamous assertion?' he inquired of an intimate friend—'infamous, whether it be true or false.'

'It is true. I heard of it an hour ago. Plenty of cheek that Levison must have.'

'*Cheek!*' repeated the dismayed earl, feeling as if every part of him, body and mind, were outraged by the news, 'don't speak of it in that way. The hound deserves to be gibbeted.'

He threw aside the paper, quitted the club, returned home for a carpet-bag, and went shrieking and whistling down to West Lynne, taking his son with him. Or, if he did not whistle and shriek, the engine did. Fully determined was the Earl of Mount Severn to show *his* opinion of the affair.

On these fine spring mornings, their breakfast over, Lady Isabel was in the habit of going into the grounds with the children. They were on the lawn before the house, when two gentlemen came walking up the avenue; or, rather, one gentleman and a handsome young stripling growing into another. Lady Isabel thought she should have dropped, for she stood face to face with Lord Mount Severn. The earl stopped to salute the children; and he raised his hat to the strange lady.

'It is my governess, Madame Vine,' said Lucy.

A silent curtsey from Madame Vine. She turned away her head and gasped for breath.

'Is your papa at home, Lucy?' cried the earl.

'Yes. I think he is at breakfast. I'm so glad you are come!'

Lord Mount Severn walked on, holding William by the hand, who had eagerly offered to 'take him' to papa. Lord Vane bent over Lucy to kiss her. A little while, a very few more years, and my young lady would not hold up her rosy lips so boldly.

'You have grown a dearer girl than ever, Lucy. Have you forgotten our compact?'

'No,' laughed she.

'And you will not forget it?'

'Never,' said the child, shaking her head. 'You shall see if I do.'

'Lucy is to be my wife,' cried he, turning to Madame Vine. 'It is a bargain, and we have both promised. I mean to wait for her till she is old enough. I like her better than anybody else in the world.'

'And I like him,' said Miss Lucy. 'And it's all true.'

Lucy was a child; it may almost be said an infant; and the viscount was not of an age to render such avowed previsions important: nevertheless the words thrilled through the veins of the hearer. She spoke, she thought, not as Madame Vine would have spoken and thought, but as the unhappy mother, the ill-fated Lady Isabel.

'You must not say these things to Lucy. It could never be.'

Lord Vane laughed. 'Why?' asked he.

'Your father and mother would not approve.'

'My father would. I know he would. He likes Lucy. As to my mother—oh, well, she can't expect to be master and mistress too. You be off for a minute, Lucy: I want to say something to Madame Vine. Has Carlyle shot that fellow?' he continued, as Lucy sprang away. 'My father is so stiff, especially when he's put up, that he would not sully his lips with the name, when we arrived, or make a single inquiry, neither would he let me, and I walked up here with my tongue burning.'

She would have responded, What fellow? but she suspected too well, and the words died away on her unwilling lips.

'That brute, Levison. If Carlyle riddled his body with shots for this move, and then kicked him till he died, he'd only get his deserts; and the world would applaud. *He* oppose Carlyle! I wish I had been a man a few years ago: he'd have got a shot through his heart then. I say,' dropping his voice, 'did you know Lady Isabel?'

'Yes—no—yes.' She was at a loss what to say: almost as unconscious what she did say.

'She was Lucy's mother, you know: and I loved her. I think that's why I love Lucy, for she is the very image of her. Where did you know her. Here?'

'I knew her by hearsay,' murmured Lady Isabel, arousing to recollection.

'O—hearsay! *Has* Carlyle shot the beast, or is he on his legs yet? By Jove! to think that he should sneak himself up in this way at West Lynne!'

'You must apply elsewhere for information,' she gasped. 'I know nothing of these things.'

She turned away with a beating heart, took Lucy's hand and departed. Lord Vane set off on a run towards the house, his heels flying behind him.

And now the contest began in earnest—that is, the canvass. Sir Francis Levison, his agent, and the friend from town, who, as it turned out, instead of being some great gun of the government, was a private chum of the baronet's, by name Drake, sneaked about the town like dogs with their tails burnt, for they were entirely alive to the odour in which they were held; their only attendants being a few young gentlemen and ladies in rags, who commonly brought up the rear. The other party presented a stately crowd: county gentry, magistrates, Lord Mount Severn. Sometimes Mr. Carlyle would be with them, arm-in-arm with the latter. If the contesting groups come within view of each other, and were likely to meet, the brave Sir Francis would disappear down an entry; behind a hedge; anywhere: with all his 'face of brass,' he could not meet Mr. Carlyle and that condemning jury around him.

One afternoon it pleased Mrs. Carlyle to summon Lucy and the governess to accompany her into West Lynne. She was going shopping. Lady Isabel had a dread and horror of appearing there, whilst that man was in the town, but she could not help herself. There was no pleading illness, for she was quite well; there must be no saying 'I will not go,' for she was only a dependent. They set off, and had walked as far as Mrs. Hare's gate, when Miss Carlyle turned out of it.

'Your mamma is not well, Barbara.'

'Is she not?' cried Barbara, with quick concern. 'I must go in and see her.'

'She has had one of those ridiculous dreams again,' pursued Miss Carlyle, ignoring the presence of the governess and Lucy. 'I was sure of it by her very look when I got in; shivering and shaking, and glancing fearfully around, as if she feared a dozen spectres were about to burst out of the walls. So I taxed her with it, and she could make no denial. Richard is in some jeopardy, she protests; or will be. And there she is, shaking still, although I told her that people who put faith in dreams were only fit for a lunatic asylum.'

Barbara looked distressed. She did not believe in dreams, any more than did Miss Carlyle: but she could not forget how strangely peril to Richard *had* supervened upon some of those dreams. 'I will go in now and see mamma,' she said. 'If you are returning home, Cornelia, Madame Vine can walk with you, and wait for me there.'

'Let me go in with you, mamma,' pleaded Lucy.

Barbara mechanically took the child's hand. The gate closed on them, and Miss Carlyle and Lady Isabel proceeded in the direction of the town. But not far had they gone when, in turning a corner, the wind which was high, flew away with the veil of Lady Isabel; and, in raising her hands in trepidation to save it before it was finally gone, she contrived to knock off her blue spectacles. They fell to the ground and were broken.

'However did you manage that?' uttered Miss Carlyle.

How indeed? She bent her face on the ground, looking at the damage. What should she do? The veil was over the hedge, the spectacles were broken: how could she dare to show her unshaded face? That face was rosy just then, as in former days, the eyes were bright, and Miss Carlyle caught their expression, and stared in very amazement.

'Good heavens above!' she muttered, 'what an extraordinary likeness!' and Lady Isabel's heart turned faint and sick within her.

Well it might. And, to make matters worse, bearing down right upon them, but a few paces distant, came Sir Francis Levison.

Would *he* recognize her?

❧ VIII ❧

A Treat in a Green Pond

Standing in the high wind at the turning of the road, were Miss Carlyle and Lady Isabel Vane. The latter, confused and perplexed, was picking up the remnant of her damaged spectacles: the former, little less perplexed, gazed at the face which struck her as being so familiar. Her attention, however, was called off to the apparition of Sir Francis Levison.

He was close upon them, Mr. Drake and the other comrade being with him, and some tag-rag in attendance, as usual. It was the first time he and Miss Carlyle had met, face to face. She bent her condemning brow, haughty in its bitter scorn, full upon him. Sir Francis, when he arrived opposite, raised his hat to her. Whether it was done in courtesy, in confused unconsciousness, or in mockery, cannot be told: Miss Carlyle assumed it to have been the latter; and her lips, in their anger, grew almost as pale as those of the unhappy woman who was cowering behind her.

'Did you intend that insult for me, Francis Levison?'

'As you please to take it,' returned he, calling up insolence to his aid.

'*You* dare to lift off your hat to me? Have you forgotten that I am Miss Carlyle?'

'It would be difficult for *you* to be forgotten, once seen.'

Now this answer *was* given in mockery; and his tone and manner were most insolent. The two gentlemen looked on in discomfort, wondering what it meant; Lady Isabel hid her face as best she could, terrified to death lest his eyes should fall upon her; while the spectators who had collected listened with interest, especially some farm labourers of Squire Pinner's.

'You contemptible worm!' ejaculated Miss Carlyle. 'Do you think you can outrage me with impunity, as you are outraging West Lynne? Out upon you for a bold, bad man!'

Now Miss Corny, in so speaking, had certainly no thought of present and immediate punishment for the gentleman: but it appeared that the mob around had. The motion was commenced by those stout-shouldered labourers. Whether excited thereto by the words of Miss Carlyle—who, whatever may have been her faults of manner, had the respect of the neighbourhood, and was looked up to only in a less degree than her brother; whether Squire Pinner, their master, had let drop in their hearing a word of the ducking he had hinted at when at East Lynne; or whether their own feelings alone spurred them on, was best known to the men themselves. Certain it is, that the ominous sound of 'Duck him,' was breathed forth by a voice, and it was caught up and echoed around.

'Duck him! Duck him! The pond be close at hand. Let's give him a taste of his deservings! What do he, the scum, turn himself up at West Lynne for, bearding Mr. Carlyle? What have he done with Lady Isabel? *Him* put up for us others at West Lynne! West Lynne don't want him: it have got a better man: it won't have a villain. Now, lads!'

His face turned white, and he trembled in his shoes: worthless men are frequently cowards. Lady Isabel trembled in hers: and, well she might, hearing that one illusion. They set upon him, twenty pairs of hands at least, strong, rough, determined hands; not to speak of the tag-rag's help, who went in with cuffs and kicks, and pokes, and taunts, and cheers, and a demoniac dance.

They dragged him through a gap in the hedge, a gap that no baby could have got through in a cool moment, but we most of us know the difference between coolness and excitement. The hedge was extensively damaged, but Justice Hare, to whom it belonged, would forgive that. Mr. Drake and the lawyer—for the other was a lawyer—were utterly powerless to stop the catastrophe. 'If they didn't mind their own business and keep theirselves clear, they'd get served the same,' was the promise held out in reply to their remonstrances; and the lawyer, who was short and fat, and could not have knocked a man down had it been to save his life, backed out of the mêlée, and contented himself with issuing forth confused threatenings of the terrors of the law. Miss Carlyle stood her ground majestically, and looked on with a grim countenance. Had she interfered for his protection, she could not have been heard, and it is by no means certain that she had any wish to interfere.

On, to the brink of the pond: a green, dank, dark, slimy, sour, stinking pond. His coat tails were gone by this time, and sundry rents and damages appeared in—in another useful garment. One pulled him, another pushed him, a third shook him by the collar, half-a-dozen buffeted him, and all abused him.

'In with him, boys!'

'Mercy! mercy!' shrieked the victim, his knees bending, and his teeth chattering, 'a little mercy, for the love of Heaven!'

'Heaven! Much he knows of Heaven!'

A souse, a splash, a wild cry, a gurgle, and Sir Francis Levison was floundering in the water, its green poison, not to mention its adders and toads and frogs, going down his throat by bucketfuls. A hoarse derisive laugh, and a hip, hip, hurrah! broke from the actors; while the juvenile tag-rag, in wild delight, joined hands around the pool, and danced the demon's dance, like so many red Indians. They had never had such a play acted for them before.

Out of the pea-soup before he was quite dead, quite senseless. Of all drowned rats he looked the worst, as he stood there with his white rueful face, his shivery limbs, and his dilapidated garments, shaking the wet off him. The labourers, their duty done, walked coolly away; the tag-rag withdrew to a safe distance, waiting for what might come next; and Miss Carlyle moved away also. Not more shivery was that wretched man than Lady Isabel, as she walked by her side. A sorry figure to cut, that, for her once chosen cavalier. What did she think of his beauty now? I know what she thought of her past folly.

Miss Carlyle did not speak a word. She sailed on, with her head up, though it was turned occasionally to look at the face of Madame Vine, at the deep, distressing blush which this gaze called into her cheeks. 'It's very odd,' thought Miss Corny. 'The likeness, especially in the eyes, is—Where are you going, madame?'

They were passing a spectacle shop, and Madame Vine had halted at the door, one foot on its step. 'I must leave my glasses to be mended, if you please.'

Miss Carlyle followed her in. She pointed out what she wanted done to the old glasses, and said she would buy a pair of new, to wear while the job was about. The man had no blue ones, no green; plenty of white. One ugly old pair of green things he had, with tortoise-shell rims, left by some stranger, ages and ages ago, to be mended, and never called for again. This very pair of ugly old green things was chosen by Lady Isabel. She put them on there and then, Miss Carlyle's eyes searching her face inquisitively all the time.

'Why do you wear glasses?' began Miss Corny, abruptly, as soon as they were within the doors of her own house.

Another deep flush, and an imperceptible hesitation. 'My eyes are not strong.'

'They look as strong as eyes can look. But, why wear coloured glasses? White ones would answer every purpose, I should suppose.'

'I am accustomed to coloured ones. I should not like white ones now.'

Miss Corny paused. 'What is your Christian name, madame?' began she again.

'Jane,' replied madame, popping out an unflinching story, in her alarm.

'Here! here! what's up? What's this?'

There was a crowd in the street, and rather a noisy one. Miss Corny flew to the window, Lady Isabel in her wake. Two crowds, it may almost be said; for, from the opposite way, the scarlet-and-purple party—as Mr. Carlyle's was called, in allusion to his colours—came in view. Quite a collection of gentlemen; Mr. Carlyle and Lord Mount Severn heading them.

What could it mean, the mob they were encountering? The yellow party doubtless, but in a disreputable condition. Who or what *was* that object in advance of it, supported between Drake and the lawyer, and looking like a drowned rat! Hair hanging, legs tottering, cheeks shaking, and clothes in tatters! While the mob, behind, had swollen to the length of the street, and was keeping up a perpetual fire of derisive shouts, groans, and hisses. The scarlet-and-purples halted in consternation, and Lord Mount Severn, whose sight was not as good as it had been twenty years back, stuck his pendant eyeglasses astride on the bridge of his nose.

Sir Francis Levison? Could it be? Yes, it actually was! What on earth had put him into that state? Mr. Carlyle's lip curled: he continued his way, and drew the peer with him.

'What the deuce is a-gate now?' called out the followers of Mr. Carlyle. 'That's Levison! Has he been in a railway smash, and got drenched by the engine?'

'He have been *ducked!*' grinned the yellows, in answer. 'They have been and ducked him in the rush pool, on Mr. Justice Hare's land. Go it, my pippin! keep up on your legs.'

The last sentence was pitched at the sufferer. 'Who did it?' asked the purples, striving to keep their countenances.

'Squire Pinner's men led it on, they did. Hooray!'

'Hooray!' echoed Squire Pinner himself, as he heard it, pushing forward to the front, with a great crimson-and-purple star in his coat, and totally forgetting his good manners. 'That is glorious news. My labourers? I'll give 'em a crown apiece for drink to-night, dashed if I don't.'

The soaked and miserable man increased his speed as much as his cold and trembling legs would allow him; he would have borne on without legs at all, rather than remain under the enemy's gaze. The enemy loftily continued their way, their heads in the air, and scorning further notice; all save young Lord Vane. He hovered round the ranks of the unwashed, and looked vastly inclined to enter upon an Indian jig, on his own account. 'What a thundering ass I was, to try it on at West Lynne!' was the enraged comment of the sufferer.

Miss Carlyle laid her hand upon the shrinking arm of her pale companion. 'You see him; my brother Archibald?'

'I see him,' faltered Lady Isabel.

'And you see *him*, that pitiful outcast, who is too contemptible to live? Look at the two, and contrast them. Look well.'

'Yes;' was the gasping answer.

'The woman who called that noble man husband, quitted him for the other! Did she come to repentance, think you?'

You may wonder that the submerged gentleman should be *walking* through the streets, on his way to his quarters, the Raven Inn—for he had been ejected from the Buck's Head—but he could not help himself. As he was dripping and swearing on the brink of the pond, wondering how he should get to the Raven, an empty fly drove past, and Mr. Drake immediately stopped it. But when the driver saw the passenger was Sir Francis Levison, he refused the job. His fly was just fresh lined with red velvet, and he warn't a-going to have it spoilt, he called out, as he whipped his horse and drove away, leaving the three in wrathful despair. Sir Francis wanted another conveyance procured: his friends urged that if he waited for that, he might catch his death, and that the shortest way would be to hasten to the inn on foot. He objected. But his jaws were chattering, his limbs were quaking, so they seized him between them, and made off. But they never bargained for the meeting with Mr. Carlyle and his party; Francis Levison would have stopped in the pond, of his own accord, head downwards, rather than face *them*.

Miss Carlyle went that day to dine at East Lynne, walking back with Mrs. Carlyle, Madame Vine, and Lucy. Lord Vane found them out and returned at the same time: of course East Lynne was the head-quarters of himself and father. He was in the seventh heaven, and had been, ever since the encounter with the yellows. 'You'd have gone into laughing convulsions, Lucy, had you seen the drowned cur. I'd give all my tin for six months to come, to have a photograph of him as he looked then!' Lucy laughed in glee: she was unconscious, poor child, how deeply the 'drowned cur' had injured her.

When Miss Carlyle was in her dressing-room taking her things off—the room where once had slept Richard Hare—she rang for Joyce. Those two rooms were still kept for Miss Carlyle—for she sometimes visited them for a few days—they were called 'Miss Carlyle's rooms.'

'A fine row we have had in the town, Joyce, this afternoon!'

'I have heard of it, ma'am. Serve him right, if they had let him drown! Bill White, Squire Pinner's ploughman, called in here and told us the news. He'd have burst with it if he hadn't, I expect: I never saw a chap so excited. Peter cried.'

'Cried!' echoed Miss Carlyle.

'Well, ma'am, you know he was very fond of Lady Isabel, was Peter, and somehow his feelings overcame him. He said he had not heard anything to please him so much for many a day; and with that he burst out crying, and gave Bill White half-a-crown out of his pocket. Bill White said it was he who held one leg when they soused him in. Afy saw it—if you'll excuse my mentioning her name to you, ma'am, for I know you don't think well of her; and when she got in here she fell into hysterics.'

'How did she see it?' snapped Miss Carlyle, her equanimity upset by the sound of the name. 'I didn't see her; and I was present.'

'She was coming here with a message from Mrs. Latimer to the governess: news that Mrs. Latimer had received from Germany, from some German count's young wife. Afy said she took the field way, and had just got to the stile, near the pond, when the uproar began.'

'What did she go into hysterics for?' again snapped Miss Carlyle.

'It upset her so, she said,' returned Joyce.

'It wouldn't have done her harm, had they ducked her too,' was the angry response.

Joyce was silent. To contradict Miss Corny brought triumph to nobody. And she was conscious, in her inmost heart, that Afy merited a little wholesome correction; not perhaps to the extent of a ducking.

'Joyce,' resumed Miss Carlyle, abruptly changing the subject, 'of whom does the governess put you in mind?'

'Ma'am?' repeated Joyce, in some surprise as it appeared. 'The governess? Do you mean Madame Vine?'

'Do I mean you? or do I mean me? Are we governesses?' irascibly cried Miss Corny. 'Who should I mean, but Madame Vine?'

She turned herself round from the looking-glass, gazed full in Joyce's face, waiting for the answer. Joyce lowered her voice as she gave it.

'There are times when she puts me in mind of my late lady, both in her face and manner. But I have never said so, ma'am: for you know Lady Isabel's name must be an interdicted one in this house.'

'Have you seen her without her glasses?'

'No: never,' said Joyce.

'I did, to-day,' returned Miss Carlyle. 'And I can tell you, Joyce, that I was confounded at the likeness. It is an extraordinary likeness. One would think it was the ghost of Lady Isabel Vane, come into the world again.'

'Oh, ma'am, please don't joke! it's not a topic for it,' cried Joyce, her tone an imploring one.

'Joke? When do you know me to joke?' returned Miss Carlyle. But she said no more. 'What is this that I hear, about William's being worse?' she resumed, after a pause.

'I don't think he's much worse, ma'am. Weak and poorly he seems, there's no denying it, especially towards night-time: but I never will believe that he is going in a bad way, as some of them want to make out.'

'If I am to believe what I hear, he is in a bad way,' said Miss Corny.

'Ma'am, who told you?'

'The governess; this afternoon. She spoke of it as being quite a case of despair—and her tone was as despairing as her words.'

'I know she thinks he is very ill. She has talked about him to me several times in the past few days.'

'I should not be surprised if he did drop off,' concluded Miss Corny, with equanimity. 'He is his mother again all over, so far as constitution goes: and I'm sure she never was good for much.'

That evening after dinner, Miss Carlyle and Lord Mount Severn sat side by side on the same sofa, coffee cups in hand. Sir John Dobede and one or two more gentlemen were of the party. Young Vane, Lucy, and Mrs. Carlyle were laughing together; and there was considerable noise and talking in the room. Under cover of it, Miss Carlyle turned to the earl.

'Was it a positively ascertained fact that Lady Isabel died?'

The earl stared with all his might: he thought it the strangest question that ever was asked him. 'I scarcely understand you, Miss Carlyle. Died? Certainly she died.'

'When the result of the accident was communicated to you, you made inquiry, yourself, into its truth, its details, I believe?'

'It was my duty to do so. There was no one else to undertake it.'

'Did you ascertain positively, beyond all doubt, that she did die?'

'Of a surety I did. She died in the course of the same night. She was terribly injured.'

A pause. Miss Carlyle was ruminating. But she returned to the charge, as if difficult to be convinced.

'You deem that there could be no possibility of an error? You are sure that she is dead?'

'I am as sure that she is dead as that we are living,' decisively replied the earl; and he spoke but according to his belief. 'Wherefore should you be inquiring this?'

'A thought came over me—only to-day—to wonder whether she was really dead.'

'Had any error occurred at the time, any false report of her death, I should soon have found it out by her drawing the annuity I settled upon her. It has never been drawn since. Besides, she would have written to me, as was agreed upon. No, poor thing! she is gone, beyond all doubt, and has taken her sins with her.'

Convincing proofs. And Miss Carlyle lent her ear to them.

The following morning, Lord Vane, Lucy, and William were running races on the lawn, the viscount having joined Madame Vine's breakfast-table without the ceremony of asking. William's racing, indeed, was more pretence than work, he and his breath were so soon tired; and Lord Vane gave Lucy 'half,' and beat her then, the forfeit if she lost, being five kisses. Lucy told him one was enough, but he battled it out, and got five. Lady Isabel had made prisoner of Archibald, and was holding him on her knee in the grey parlour, clasped to her in the impassioned manner that few, save a mother, can clasp a child, when Mr. Carlyle entered.

'Do you admit intruders here, Madame Vine?' cried he, with his sweet smile and his attractive manner.

She let the boy slip to the ground, and rose; her face burning, her heart throbbing. Archie immediately ran off to his elders on the grass.

'Keep your seat, pray,' said Mr. Carlyle, taking one opposite to her and admiring no doubt her tortoise-shell spectacles. 'How does William seem? for that is what I have come to ask you.'

She laid her hand upon her bosom, striving to make it still; she essayed to control her voice to calmness. Alone with him! 'There was no difference,' she murmured; and then she took courage, and spoke more openly.

'I understood you to say the other night, sir, that he should have further advice.'

'Ay. I intended to take him over to Lynneborough to Dr. Martin, and the drive would have done him good; but I have been so much engaged there has been no time to think of it. Neither do I know when I shall be at liberty.'

'Let me take him, sir,' she cried, yearningly. 'Indeed, I think no time should be lost. We could go by train. What objection have you?' she quickly added. 'Surely you can trust him with me!'

Mr. Carlyle smiled. 'I can trust him and you too,' cried he, 'and I think the plan would be a good one, if you do not mind the trouble.'

Mind the trouble! when her boy's life was at stake. 'Let us go to-day, sir,' she said, with feverish impatience.

'I will ascertain whether Mrs. Carlyle wants the pony carriage,' said he. 'It will be better to go in that than boxed up in the railway train.'

Her heart rose rebelliously as he quitted the room. Were Mrs. Carlyle's capricious 'wants' to be studied before her child's life? A moment's battle, and she clasped her hands meekly on her knee: was that the spirit in which she had promised to take up her daily cross? She had put the same question to herself many times lately.

Mr. Carlyle returned. 'The pony carriage will be at your service, Madame Vine. John will drive you to the Royal, the hotel I used in Lynneborough, and Dr. Martin lives within a few doors of it. Order any refreshment you please at the hotel: it will be put down to my account. Perhaps you had better dine there: it may not be well for William to wait.'

'Very well, sir. Thank you. What time can we start?'

'Any time you like. Ten o'clock? Will that suit?'

'O, quite well, sir. Thank you very much.'

'Thank me for what?' laughed Mr. Carlyle: 'for giving you a troublesome journey? Let me see—the doctor's fee will be a guinea,' he said, taking out his purse.

'Oh, that is nothing,' she hastily interrupted. 'I will pay for him myself: I would rather.'

Mr. Carlyle looked surprised. He said nothing; simply laid down the sovereign and shilling on the table. Madame Vine blushed vividly: how could she, the governess, so have forgotten herself?

Poor, unhappy Lady Isabel! A recollection flashed over her of that morning, years ago, when Lord Mount Severn had handed out to her some gold, three sovereigns; and of the hundred-pound note so generously left in her hands afterwards by another. *Then* she was his chosen love: ay, she was; though it had not been declared. *Now?*—A pang, as of death, shot through her bitter heart.

'You can remind Dr. Martin that the child's constitution is precisely what his mother's was,' continued Mr. Carlyle, a tinge lighting his face. 'It may be a guide to his treatment. He said, himself, it was, when he attended him for an illness a year or two ago.'

'Yes, sir.'

He crossed the hall on his entrance to the breakfast-room. She tore upstairs to her chamber, and sank down in an agony of tears and despair. Oh! to love him as she did now! to yearn after his affection with this passionate, jealous longing, and to know that they were separated for ever and for ever; that she was worse to him than nothing!

Softly, my lady! This is not bearing your cross.

⚔ I X ⚔

Appearance of a Russian Bear at West Lynne

Mr. Carlyle harangued the populace from the balcony of the Buck's Head, a substantial old house, renowned in the days of posting, now past and gone. Its balcony was an old-fashioned, roomy balcony, painted green, where there was plenty of space for his friends to congregate. He was a persuasive orator, winning his way to ears and hearts: but, had he spoken with plums in his mouth, and a stammer on his tongue, and a break-down at every sentence, the uproarious applause and shouts would have been equally rife. Mr. Carlyle was intensely popular in West Lynne, setting aside the candidateship and his oratory; and West Lynne made common cause against Sir Francis Levison.

Sir Francis Levison harangued the mob from the Raven, but in a more ignoble manner. For the Raven possessed no balcony, and he was fain to let himself down, with a stride and a jump, from the first-floor window to the top of the bow-window of the parlour, and stand there. The Raven, though a comfortable, old established, and respectable inn, could boast only of casements for its upper windows, and they are not convenient to deliver speeches from. He was wont, therefore, to take his stand on the ledge of the bow-window, and that was not altogether convenient either, for it was but narrow, and he hardly dared move an arm or a leg, for fear of pitching over, on to the upturned faces. Mr. Drake let himself down also, to support him on one side, and, the first day, the lawyer supported him on the other. For the first day only: for that worthy, being not so high as Sir Francis Levison's or Mr. Drake's shoulder, and about five times their breadth, had those two been rolled into one, experienced a slight difficulty in getting back again. It was accomplished at last, Sir Francis pulling him up, and Mr. Drake hoisting him from behind, just as a ladder was being brought to the rescue, amidst shouts of laughter. The stout man wiped the perspiration from his face when he was landed in safety, and recorded a mental vow never to descend from a window again. After that, the candidate and his friend shared the shelf between them. The lawyer's name was Rubiny, ill-naturedly supposed to be a corruption of Reuben.

They stood there one afternoon, the eloquence of Sir Francis in full play (but he was a shocking speaker), and the crowd laughing, hissing, groaning, and applauding, blocking up the road. Sir Francis could not complain of one thing—that he got no audience. For it was the pleasure of West Lynne extensively to support him in that respect: a few to cheer, a great many to jeer and hiss. Remarkably dense was the mob on this afternoon, for Mr. Carlyle had just concluded his address from the Buck's Head, and the crowd who had been listening to him, came rushing up to swell the ranks of the other crowd. They were elbowing and pushing and treading on each other's heels, when an open barouche drove suddenly up, to scatter them. Its horses wore scarlet and purple rosettes; and one lady, a very pretty one, sat inside it. Mrs. Carlyle.

But the crowd could not be so easily scattered: it was too thick: the carriage could advance but at a snail's pace, and now and then came to a standstill. Sir Francis Levison's speech came to a stand-still also, till the confusion should subside. He did not bow to Barbara: he remembered the result of his having done so to Miss Carlyle: and the little interlude of the pond had washed most of his impudence out of him. He remained at his post, not looking at Barbara, not looking at anything in particular, but waiting till the interruption should have passed.

Barbara, under cover of her dainty lace parasol, turned her eyes upon him. At that very moment he raised his right hand, slightly shook his head back, and tossed his hair off his brow. His hand, ungloved, was white and delicate as a lady's, and his rich diamond ring gleamed in the sun. The pink flush on Barbara's cheek deepened to a crimson damask, and her brow contracted as with a remembrance of pain.

'The very action Richard described! the action he was always using at East Lynne! I believe from my heart that man is Thorn: Richard was labouring under some mistake, when he said he knew Sir Francis Levison.'

She let her hands fall upon her knee as she spoke, heedless of the candidate, heedless of the crowd, heedless of all, save her own troubled thoughts. A hundred respectful salutations were uttered, she answered them mechanically; a shout was raised, 'Long live Carlyle! Carlyle for ever!' Barbara bowed her pretty head on either side, and the carriage at length got on.

The parting of the crowd brought Mr. Dill (who had come to listen for once to the speech of the second man) and Mr. Ebenezer James close to each other. Mr. Ebenezer James was one who for the last twelve or fifteen years had been trying his hand at many trades, and had not come out particularly well at any. A rolling stone gathers no moss. First, he had been clerk to Mr. Carlyle; next he had been seduced into joining the corps of the Theatre Royal at Lynneborough; then he turned auctioneer; then traveller in the oil and colour line; then a parson, the urgent pastor of some sect; then omnibus driver; then collector of the water-rate; and now he was clerk again; not in Mr. Carlyle's office, but in that of Ball and Treadman, other solicitors of West Lynne. A good-humoured, good-natured, idle chap was Mr. Ebenezer James, and that was the worst that could be urged against him, save that he was sometimes out at pocket and out at elbows. His father was a respectable man, had made money in trade; but he had married a second wife, had a second family, and his eldest son did not come in for much of the paternal money; though he did for a large share of the paternal anger.

'Well, Ebenezer, and how goes the world with you?' cried Mr. Dill, by way of salutation.

'Jogging on. It never gets to a trot.'

'Didn't I see you turning into your father's house yesterday?'

'I pretty soon turned out of it again. I'm like the monkey when I venture there—get more kicks than halfpence. Hush, old gentleman! we interrupt the eloquence.'

Of course 'the eloquence' applied to Sir Francis Levison, and they set themselves to listen, Mr. Dill with a serious face, Mr. Ebenezer with a grinning one. But, soon, a jostle and movement carried them to the outside of the crowd, out of sight of the speaker, though not entirely out of hearing. By these means they had a view of the street, and discerned something advancing towards them, which they took for a Russian bear on its hind legs.

'I'll—be—blest,' uttered Mr. Ebenezer James, after a prolonged pause of staring consternation, 'if I don't believe it's Bethel!'

'Bethel!' repeated old Dill, gazing at the approaching figure. 'What has he been doing to himself?'

Mr. Otway Bethel it was, just arrived from foreign parts in his travelling costume. Something shaggy, terminating all over with tails. A shaggy cap surmounted his head, and the hair on his face would have set up Mr. Justice Hare in wigs for his life. A wild object he looked, and Mr. Dill rather backed as he drew near, as if fearing he were a real animal which might bite him.

'What's your name?' cried he.

'It used to be Bethel,' replied the wild man, holding out his hand to Mr. Dill. 'So you are in the world, James, and kicking yet!'

'And hope to kick in it for some time to come,' replied Mr. James. 'Where did you hail from last? A settlement at the North Pole?'

'Didn't get quite so far. What's the row here?'

'When did you arrive, Mr. Otway?' inquired old Dill.

'Now. Four o'clock train. I say, what's up?'

'An election; that's all,' said Mr. Ebenezer. 'Attley went and kicked the bucket.'

'I don't ask about the election; I heard all that at the railway station,' returned Otway Bethel, impatiently. 'What's *this?*' waving his hand at the crowd.

'One of the candidates, wasting breath and words. Levison.'

'I say,' repeated Otway Bethel, looking at Mr. Dill, 'wasn't it rather— rather of the ratherest, for *him* to oppose Carlyle?'

'Infamous! contemptible!' was the old gentleman's excited answer. 'But he'll get his deserts yet, Mr. Otway; they have already begun. He was treated to a ducking yesterday in Justice Hare's green pond.'

'And he did look a miserable devil when he came out, trailing through the streets,' added Mr. Ebenezer, while Otway Bethel burst into a laugh. 'He was smothered into some hot blankets at the Raven, and a pint of burnt brandy put into him. He seems all right to-day.'

'Will he go in and win?'

'Chut! Win against Carlyle! He has not the ghost of a chance; and government—if it is the government who put him on it—must be a pack of fools: they can't know the influence of Carlyle. Bethel, is that style of costume the fashion where you come from?'

'For cold weather and slender pockets. I'll sell 'em to you now, James, at half price. Let's get a look at this Levison, though. I have never seen the fellow.'

Another interruption to the crowd, even as he spoke, caused by the railway van bringing up some luggage. They contrived, in the confusion, to push themselves to the front, not far from Sir Francis. Otway Bethel stared at him in unqualified amazement.

'Why—what brings *him* here? What is he doing?'

'Who?'

He pointed with his finger. 'The one with the white handkerchief in his hand.'

'That is Sir Francis.'

'No!' uttered Bethel, a whole world of astonished meaning in his tone. 'By Jove; *He* Sir Francis Levison?'

At that moment their eyes met, Francis Levison's and Otway Bethel's. Otway Bethel raised his shaggy cap in salutation, and Sir Francis appeared completely scared. Only for an instant did he lose his presence of mind. The next, his eye-glass was stuck in his eye, and turned on Mr. Bethel with a hard haughty stare; as much as to say, Who are you, fellow, that you should take such a liberty? But his cheeks and lips were growing as white as marble.

'Do you know Levison, Mr. Otway?' inquired old Dill.

'A little. Once.'

'When he was not Levison, but somebody else,' laughed Mr. Ebenezer James. 'Eh, Bethel?'

Bethel turned as reproving a stare on Mr. Ebenezer, as the baronet had just turned on him. 'What do you mean, pray? Mind your own business.'

A nod to old Dill, and he turned off and disappeared, taking no further notice of James. The old gentleman questioned the latter.

'What was that little bit of by-play, Mr. Ebenezer?'

'Nothing, much,' laughed Mr. Ebenezer. 'Only he,' nodding towards Sir Francis, 'was not always the great man that he is now.'

'Ah!'

'I have held my tongue about it, for it's no affair of mine, but I don't mind letting you into the secret. Would you believe that that grand baronet there, would-be member for West Lynne, used years ago, to dodge about Abbey Wood, mad after Afy Hallijohn? He didn't call himself Levison then.'

Mr. Dill felt as if a hundred pins and needles were pricking at his memory, for there rose up in it certain doubts and troubles, touching Richard Hare and one Thorn. He laid his eager hand upon the other's arm. 'Ebenezer James, what did he call himself?'

'Thorn. A dandy then, as he is now. He used to come galloping down the Swainson road at dusk, tie his horse in the wood, and monopolise Miss Afy.'

'How do you know this?'

'Because I have seen it, a dozen times. I was spoony after Afy myself in those days and went down there a good deal in an evening. If it hadn't been for him, and—perhaps that murdering villain, Dick Hare, Afy would have listened to me. Not that she cared for Dick; but, you see they were gentlemen. I am thankful to the stars, now, for my luck in escaping her. With her for a wife, I should have been in a pickle always: as it is, I do get out of it once in a way.'

'Did you know then that he was Francis Levison?'

'Not I. He called himself Thorn, I tell you. When he came down, to offer himself for a member and oppose Carlyle, I was thunderstruck; like Bethel was, a minute ago. Ho, ho, said I, so Thorn's defunct, and Levison has risen.'

'What had Otway Bethel to do with him?'

'Nothing—that I know of. Only Bethel was fond of the wood also—after other game than Afy, though—and must have seen Thorn often. You saw that he recognized him.'

'Thorn—Levison, I mean—did not appear to like the recognition,' said Mr. Dill.

'Who would, in his position?' laughed Ebenezer James. 'I don't like to be reminded of many a wild scrape of my past life, in my poor station; and what would it be for Levison, were it to come out that he once called himself Thorn, and came running after Miss Afy Hallijohn.'

'Why did he call himself Thorn? Why disguise his own name?'

'Not knowing, can't say. *Is* his name Levison? or is it Thorn?'

'Nonsense, Mr. Ebenezer.'

Mr. Dill, bursting with the strange news he had heard, endeavoured to force his way through the crowd, that he might communicate it to Mr. Carlyle. The crowd was, however, too dense for him, and he had to wait the opportunity of escape with what patience he might. When it came he made the best of his way to the office, and entered Mr. Carlyle's private room. That gentleman was seated at his desk, signing letters.

'Why, Dill, you are out of breath!'

'Well I may be! Mr. Archibald, I have been listening to the most extraordinary statement I have found out about Thorn. Who do you think he is?'

Mr. Carlyle laid down his pen and looked full in the old man's face: he had never seen him so excited.

'It's that man, Levison.'

'I do not understand you,' said Mr. Carlyle. He did not. It was Hebrew to him.

'The Levison of to-day, your opponent, is the Thorn who went after Afy Hallijohn. It is so, Mr. Archibald.'

'It cannot be!' slowly uttered Mr. Carlyle, thought upon thought working through his brain. 'Where did you hear this?'

Mr. Dill told his tale. Otway Bethel's recognition of him; Sir Francis Levison's scared paleness—for he had noticed that; Mr. Ebenezer's revelation.

'Bethel has denied to me more than once that he knew Thorn, or was aware of such a man being in existence,' observed Mr. Carlyle.

'He must have had a purpose in it,' returned Mr. Dill. 'They knew each other to-day. Levison recognized him for certain; although he carried it off with a high hand, pretending that he did not.'

'And it was not as Levison, but as Thorn, that Bethel recognized him.'

'There's little doubt of that. He did not mention the name Thorn; but he was evidently struck with astonishment at hearing that it was Levison. If they have not some secret between them, Mr. Archibald, I'll never believe my own eyes again.'

'Mrs. Hare's opinion is, that Bethel had to do with the murder,' said Mr. Carlyle, in a low tone.

'If the murder is their secret, rely upon it Bethel had,' was the answer. 'Mr. Archibald, it seems to me that now or never is the time to clear up Richard.'

'Ay. But how to set about it?' responded Mr. Carlyle.

Meanwhile, Barbara had proceeded home in her carriage, her brain as busy as Mr. Carlyle's, perhaps more troubled. Her springing lightly and hastily out, the moment it stopped, disdaining the footman's arm, her compressed lips and absent countenance, proved that her resolution was set upon some plan of action. William and Madame Vine met her in the hall.

'We have seen Dr. Martin, Mrs. Carlyle.'

'And, mamma, he says—'

'I cannot stay to hear now, William. I will see you later, madame.'

She ran upstairs to her dressing-room, Madame Vine following her with her reproachful eyes. 'Why should she care?' thought madame. 'He is not her child.'

Throwing her parasol on one chair, her gloves on another, Barbara sat down to her writing-table. 'I will write to him, I will have him here, if it be but for an hour!' she passionately exclaimed. 'This shall be, so far, cleared up. I am sure that it is that man. The very action Richard described! and there was the diamond ring! For better, for worse, I will send for him: but it will not be for worse if God is with us.'

She dashed off a letter, getting up, ere she had well begun it, to order her carriage round again: she would trust none but herself to put it in the post.

'My dear Mr. Smith,—We want you here. Something has arisen that it is necessary to see you upon. You can get here by Saturday. Be in *these* grounds, near the covered walk, that evening at dusk.

'Ever yours,

'B.'

And the letter was addressed to Mr. Smith, of some street in Liverpool, the address furnished by Richard. Very cautious, you see, was Barbara. She even put 'Mr. Smith' inside the letter.

'Now stop,' cried Barbara to herself, as she was folding it, 'I ought to send him a five-pound note, for he may not have the means to come. And I don't think I have one of that amount in the house.'

She looked in her secretaire. Not a single five-pound note. Out of the room she ran, meeting Joyce, who was coming along the corridor.

'Do you happen to have a five-pound note, Joyce?'

'No, ma'am. 'Not by me.'

'I dare say Madame Vine has. I paid her last week, and there were two five-pound notes amongst it.' And away went Barbara to the grey parlour.

'Could you lend me a five-pound note, Madame Vine? I have occasion to enclose one in a letter, and find I do not possess one.'

Madame Vine went to her room to get it. Barbara waited. She asked William what Dr. Martin said.

'He tried my chest with—oh, I forget what they call it; and he said I must be a brave boy and take my cod-liver oil well. And port wine, and everything I liked that was good. And he said he should be at West Lynne next Wednesday afternoon, and I am to be there, and he would call in and see me.'

'Where are you to meet him?'

'He said either at papa's office, or at Aunt Cornelia's, as we might decide. Madame fixed it for papa's office, for she thought he might like to see Dr. Martin. I say, mamma?'

'What?' asked Barbara.

'Madame Vine has been crying ever since. Why should she?'

'I'm sure I don't know. Crying?'

'Yes: but she wipes her eyes under her spectacles, and thinks I don't see her. I know I am very ill, but why should she cry for that?'

'Nonsense, William! Who told you you were very ill?'

'Nobody. I suppose I am,' he thoughtfully added. 'If Joyce or Lucy cried, now, there'd be more sense in it, for they have known me all my life.'

'You are so apt to fancy strange things! you are always doing it. It is not likely that madame would be crying because you were ill.'

Madame came in with the bank-note. Barbara thanked her, ran upstairs, and in another minute or two was in her carriage.

She was back again and dressing, when the gentlemen returned to dinner. Mr. Carlyle came upstairs. Barbara, like most persons who do things without reflection, having had time to cool down from her ardour, was doubting whether she had acted wisely in sending so precipitately for Richard. She carried her doubt and care to her husband: her sure refuge in perplexity.

'Archibald, I do fear I have done a foolish thing.'

He laughed. 'I fear we all do that at times, Barbara. What is it?'

He had seated himself in one of Barbara's favourite low chairs, and she stood before him, leaning on his shoulder, her face a little behind, so that he could not see it. In her delicacy, she would not look at him while she spoke what she was going to speak.

'It is something that I have had upon my mind for years. And I did not like to tell it to you.'

'For years!'

'You remember that night, years ago, when Richard was at the Grove in disguise? He—'

'Which night, Barbara? He came more than once.'

'The night—the night that Lady Isabel quitted East Lynne,' she answered, not knowing how better to bring it to his recollection: and she stole her hand lovingly into his as she said it. 'Richard came back after his departure, saying he had met Thorn in Bean-lane. He described the peculiar motion of his hand as he threw back his hair from his brow: he spoke of the white hand and the diamond ring, how it glittered in the moonlight. Do you remember?'

'I do.'

'The motion appeared perfectly familiar to me, for I had seen it repeatedly used by one then staying at East Lynne. I wondered you did not recognize it. From that night I had little doubt as to the identity of Thorn. I believed that he and Captain Levison were one.'

A pause. 'Why did you not tell me so, Barbara?'

'How could I speak of that man to you?—at that time? Afterwards, when Richard was here, that snowy winter's day, he asserted that he knew Sir Francis Levison: that he had seen him and Thorn together; and that put me off the scent. But, to-day, as I was passing the Raven in the carriage, going very slow on account of the crowd, he was perched out there, addressing the people, and I saw the very same action, the old action that I remember so well.'

Barbara paused. Mr. Carlyle did not interrupt her.

'I feel a conviction that they are the same: that Richard must have been under some unaccountable mistake, in saying he knew Francis Levison. Besides, who but he, in evening dress, would have been likely to go through Bean-lane that night. It leads to no houses: but one, who wished to avoid the high road, could get into it from these grounds, and so on to West Lynne. It was proved, you know, that he met—met the carriage coming from Mrs. Jeafferson's, and returned in it to East Lynne. He must have gone back directly on foot to West Lynne, to get the post-chaise, as was proved; and he would naturally go through Bean-lane. Forgive me, Archibald, for recalling these things to you, but I feel so sure that Levison and Thorn are one.'

'I know they are,' he quietly said.

Barbara, in her astonishment, drew back and stared him in the face. A face of severe dignity it was, just then.

'Oh, Archibald! Did you know it at that time?'

'I did not know it until this afternoon. I never suspected it.'

'I wonder you did not. I have wondered often.'

'So do I—now. Dill, Ebenezer James, and Otway Bethel—who came home to-day—were standing before the Raven, listening to his speech when Bethel recognized him. Not as Levison: he was infinitely astonished to find he was Levison. Levison, they say, was scared at the recognition, and changed colour. Bethel could give no explanation, and moved away, but James told Dill that Levison was the man Thorn, who used to be after Afy Hallijohn.'

'How did he know?' breathlessly asked Barbara.

'Because Mr. Ebenezer was after Afy himself, and repeatedly saw Thorn in the wood. Barbara, I believe now that it was Levison who killed Hallijohn: but I should like to know what Bethel had to do with it.'

Barbara clasped her hands. 'How strange it is!' she exclaimed, in some excitement. 'Mamma told me yesterday that she was convinced some discovery was impending relative to the murder. She had had the most distressing dream, she said, connected with Richard and Bethel and somebody else, whom she appeared to know in the dream, but could not recognize, or remember, when she awoke. She was very ill; she puts so much faith in these wretched dreams.'

'One would think you did also, Barbara, by your vehemence.'

'No, no; you know better. But it is strange—you must acknowledge that it is—that so sure as anything fresh happens, touching the subject of the murder, so sure is a troubled dream the forerunner of it. Mamma does not dream at other times. Bethel denied to you that he knew Thorn.'

'I know he did.'

'And now it turns out that he does know him; and he is always in mamma's dreams; none more prominent in them than Bethel. But, Archibald, I am not telling you—I have sent for Richard.'

'You have?'

'I felt sure that Levison was Thorn; I did not expect that others would recognize him, and I acted in the impulse of the moment and wrote to Richard, telling him to be here on Saturday evening. The letter is gone.'

'Well, we must shelter him as we best can.'

'Archibald, dear Archibald, what can be done to clear him?' she asked, the tears rising to her eyes.

'I cannot act against Levison.'

'Not act? not act for Richard?'

He bent his clear, truthful eyes upon her. 'My dearest, how can I?'

She looked a little rebellious, and the tears fell.

'You have not considered, Barbara. It would look like my own revenge?'

'Forgive me,' she softly whispered. 'You are always right. I did not think of it in that light. But what steps can be taken?'

'It is a case encompassed with difficulties,' mused Mr. Carlyle. 'Let us wait till Richard comes.'

'Do you happen to have a five-pound note in your pocket, Archibald? I had not one to send to him, and borrowed it from Madame Vine.'

He took out his pocket-book and gave her the money.

❧ X ❧

A Fading Child

In the grey parlour, in the dark twilight of the April evening, for it was getting on into the night, were William Carlyle and Lady Isabel. It had been a warm day, but the spring evenings were still chilly, and a fire burned in the grate. There was no blaze, the red embers were smouldering and half dead, but Madame Vine did not heed the fire. William lay on the sofa, and she sat by, looking at him. Her glasses were off, for the tears wetted them continually: and it was not the recognition of the children that she feared. He was tired with the drive to Lynneborough and back, and lay with his eyes shut; she thought asleep. Presently he opened them.

'How long will it be before I die?'

The words took her utterly by surprise, and her heart went round in a whirl. 'What do you mean, William? Who said anything about your dying?'

'Oh, I know. I know by the fuss there is over me. You heard what Hannah said the other night?'

'What? When?'

'When she brought in the tea, and I was lying on the rug. I was not asleep, though you thought I was. You told her she ought to be more cautious, for that I might not have been asleep.'

'I don't remember much about it,' said Lady Isabel, at her wits' end how to remove the impression Hannah's words must have created, had he indeed heard them. 'Hannah talks great nonsense sometimes.'

'She said I was going on fast to the grave.'

'Did she? Nobody attends to Hannah. She is only a foolish girl. We shall soon have you well, when the warm weather comes.'

'Madame Vine.'

'Well, my darling?'

'Where's the use of your trying to deceive me? Do you think I don't see that you are doing it? I am not a baby: you might if it were Archibald. What is it that's the matter with me?'

'Nothing. Only you are not strong. When you get strong again you will be as well as ever.'

William shook his head in disbelief. He was precisely that sort of child from whom it is next to impossible to disguise facts; quick, thoughtful, observant, and advanced beyond his years. Had no words been dropped in his hearing, he would have suspected the evil by the care evinced for him, but plenty of words had been dropped; hints, by which he had gathered suspicion; broad assertions, like Hannah's which had too fully supplied it; and the boy, in his inmost heart, knew as well that death was coming for him, as that death itself did.

'Then, if there's nothing the matter with me, why could not Dr. Martin speak to you before me to-day? Why did he send me into the other room while he told you what he thought? Ah, Madame Vine, I am as wise as you.'

'A wise little boy, but mistaken sometimes,' she said, from her aching heart.

'It's nothing to die, when God loves us. Lord Vane says so. He had a little brother who died.'

'A sickly child who was never likely to live; he had been pale and ailing from a baby,' said Lady Isabel.

'Why! did you know him?'

'I—I heard so,' she replied, turning off her thoughtless avowal in the best manner she could.

'Don't *you* know that I am going to die?'

'No.'

'Then why have you been grieving since we left Dr. Martin's? And why do you grieve at all for me? I am not your child.'

The words, the scene altogether, overcame her. She knelt down by the sofa, and her tears burst forth freely. 'There! you see,' cried William.

'Oh, William, I—I had a little boy of my own once, and when I look at you, I think of him, and that is why I cry.'

'I know. You have told us of him before. His name was William, too.'

She leaned over him, her breath mingling with his; she took his little hand in hers. 'William, do you know that those whom God loves best, He takes the first. Were you to die, you would go to heaven, leaving all the cares and sorrows of the world behind you. It would have been happier for many of us had we died in infancy.'

'Would it have been happier for you?'

'Yes,' she faintly said. 'I have had more than my share of sorrow. Sometimes I think that I cannot support it.'

'Is it not past then? Have you sorrow now?'

'I have it always. I shall have it till I die. Had I died a child, William, I should have escaped it. Oh! the world is full of it! full and full.'

'What sort of sorrow?'

'Pain, sickness, care, trouble, sin, remorse, weariness,' she wailed out. 'I cannot enumerate the half that the world brings upon us. When you are very, very tired, William, does it not seem a luxury, a sweet happiness, to lie down at night in your little bed, waiting for sleep?'

'Yes. And I am often tired: as tired as that.'

'Then, just so do we, who are tired out with the world's cares, long for the grave in which we shall lie down to rest. We *covet* it, William; long for it; almost pray for it: but you cannot understand that.'

'*We* don't lie in the grave, Madame Vine.'

'No, no, child. Our bodies lie there, to be raised again in beauty at the last day. We go into a blessed place of rest, where sorrow and pain cannot come. I wish—I wish,' she added with a bursting heart, 'that you and I were both there!'

'Who says the world is so sorrowful, Madame Vine? I think it is lovely, especially when the sun's shining on a hot day, and the butterflies come out. You should see East Lynne on a summer's morning, when you are running up and down the slopes, and the trees are waving overhead, and the sky's blue, and the roses and flowers are all out. You would not call it a sad world.'

'A pleasant world; one we might regret to leave, if we were not wearied by pain and care. But, what is this world, take it at its best, in comparison with that other world, heaven? I have heard of some people who are afraid of death: they fear they shall not go to it: but when God takes a little child there, it is because He loves him. It is a land, as Mrs. Barbauld says, where the roses are without thorns, where the flowers are not mixed with brambles—'

'I have seen the flowers,' interrupted William, rising in his earnestness. 'They are ten times brighter than our flowers are here.'

'Seen the flowers! The flowers we shall see in heaven!' she echoed.

'I have seen a picture of them. We went to Lynneborough to see Martin's pictures of the Last Judgment. I don't mean Dr. Martin,' said William, interrupting himself.

'I know.'

'There were three large pictures. One was called the "Plains of Heaven," and I liked that best; and so we all did. Oh, you should have seen it! Did you ever see them, Madame Vine?'

'No. I have heard of them.'

'There was a river, you know, and boats, beautiful gondolas they looked, taking the redeemed to the shores of heaven. They were shadowy figures in white robes, myriads and myriads of them, for they reached all up in the air to the holy city: it seemed to be in the clouds, coming down from God. The flowers grew on the banks of the river, pink and blue, and violet; all colours they were, but so bright and beautiful; brighter than our flowers are.'

'Who took you to see the pictures?'

'Papa. He took me and Lucy: and Mrs. Hare went with us, and Barbara—she was not our mamma then. But, madame'—dropping his voice—'what do you think Lucy asked papa?'

'What did she ask him?'

'She asked whether mamma was amongst that crowd in the white robes; whether she was gone up to heaven? Our mamma that was, you know: Lady Isabel. We were in front of the picture at the time, and lots of people heard what she said.'

Lady Isabel dropped her face upon her hands. 'What did your papa answer?' she breathed.

'I don't know. Nothing, I think: he was talking to Barbara. But it was very stupid of Lucy, because Wilson has told her over and over again that she must never talk of Lady Isabel to papa. Miss Manning has told her so too. When we got home and Wilson heard of it, she said Lucy deserved a good shaking.'

'Why must Lady Isabel not be talked of to him?' A moment after the question had left her lips she wondered what possessed her to give utterance to it.

'I'll tell you,' said William, in a whisper. 'She ran away from papa. Lucy talks nonsense about her having been kidnapped, but she knows nothing. I do; though they don't think it perhaps.'

'She may be among the redeemed some time, William, and you with her.'

He fell back on the sofa pillow with a weary sigh and lay in silence. Lady Isabel shaded her face and remained in silence also. Soon she was aroused from it: William was in a fit of loud, sobbing tears.

'Oh, I don't want to die! I don't want to die! Why should I go, and leave papa and Lucy?'

She hung over him; she clasped her arms around him; her tears, her sobs mingled with his. She whispered to him sweet and soothing words: she placed him so that he might sob out his grief upon her bosom: and in a little while the paroxysm had passed.

'Hark!' exclaimed William. 'What's that?'

A sound of talking and laughter in the hall. Mr. Carlyle, Lord Mount Severn, and his son were leaving the dining-room. They had some committee appointment that evening at West Lynne, and were departing to keep it. As the hall door closed upon them, Barbara came into the grey parlour. Up rose Madame Vine, hastily assumed her spectacles, and took her seat soberly upon a chair.

'All in the dark! And your fire going out!' exclaimed Barbara, as she hastened to stir the latter and send it into a blaze. 'Who is that on the sofa? William! you ought to be in bed.'

'Not yet, mamma. I don't want to go yet.'

'But it is quite time that you should,' she returned, ringing the bell. 'To sit up at night is not the way to make you strong.'

William was dismissed. And then she turned to Madame Vine and inquired what Dr. Martin had said.

'He said the lungs were undoubtedly affected; but, like all doctors, he would give no decisive opinion. I could see that he had formed one.'

Mrs. Carlyle looked at her. The firelight played upon her face, played especially upon the spectacles, and she moved her chair into the shade.

'Dr. Martin will see him again next week: he is coming to West Lynne. I am sure by the tone of his voice, by his evasive manner, that he anticipates the worst, although he would not say so in words.'

'I will take William into West Lynne myself,' said Barbara. 'The doctor will, of course, tell me. I came in to pay my debts,' she added, dismissing the subject of the child, and holding out a five-pound note.

Lady Isabel mechanically stretched out her hand for it.

'Whilst we are upon the money topic,' resumed Barbara, in a gay tone, 'will you allow me to intimate that both myself and Mr. Carlyle very much disapprove of your making presents to the children? I was calculating, at a rough guess, the cost of the toys and things you have bought for them, and I think it must amount to a very large portion of the salary you have received. Pray do not continue this, Madame Vine.'

'I have no one else to spend my money on: I love the children,' was madame's answer, somewhat sharply given, as if she were jealous of the interference between her and the children, and would resent it.

'Nay, you have yourself. And if you do not require much outlay, you have, I should suppose, a reserve fund to which to put your money. Be so kind as take the hint, madame; otherwise I shall be compelled more peremptorily to forbid your generosity. It is very good of you, very kind; but if you do not think of yourself, we must for you.'

'I will buy them less,' was the murmured answer. 'I must give them a little token of love now and then.'

'That you are welcome to do; a "little token," once in a way; but not the costly toys you have been purchasing. Have you ever had any acquaintance with Sir Francis Levison?' continued Mrs. Carlyle, passing with abruptness from one topic to another.

An inward shiver, a burning cheek, a heart-pang of wild remorse, and a faint answer. 'No.'

'I fancied, from your manner when I was speaking of him the other day, that you knew him, or had known him. No compliment, you will say, to assume an acquaintanceship with such a man. He is a stranger to you, then?'

Another faint reply. 'Yes.'

Barbara paused. 'Do you believe in fatality, Madame Vine?'

'Yes, I do,' was the steady answer.

'I don't:' and yet the very question proved that she did not wholly disbelieve it. 'No, I don't,' added Barbara, stoutly, as she approached the sofa vacated by William, and sat down upon it, thus bringing herself opposite and near to Madame Vine. 'Are you aware that it was Francis Levison who wrought the evil to this house?'

'The evil—' stammered Madame Vine.

'Yes, it was he,' she resumed, taking the hesitating answer for an admission that the governess knew nothing, or but little, of past events. 'It was he who took Lady Isabel from her home—though, perhaps, she was as willing to go, as he to take her: I do not know—'

'Oh no, no!' broke from the lips of unguarded Madame Vine. 'At least—I mean—I should think not,' she added, in confusion.

'We shall never know. And of what consequence is it? One thing is certain, *she went*: another thing, almost equally certain, is she did not go against her will. Did you ever hear the details?'

'N—o.' Her answer would have been Yes; but possibly the next question might have been, From whom did you hear them?

'He was staying at East Lynne. The man had been abroad: outlawed: dared not show his face in England, and Mr. Carlyle, in his generosity, invited him to East Lynne as a place of shelter where he would be safe from his creditors, while something was arranged. He was a connection of Lady Isabel's. And they repaid Mr. Carlyle, he and she, by quitting East Lynne together.'

'Why did Mr. Carlyle give that invitation?' The words were uttered in a spirit of remorseful wailing: Mrs. Carlyle believed they were a question put; and she rose up haughtily against it.

'Why did he give the invitation! Did I hear you aright, Madame Vine? Did Mr. Carlyle know he was a reprobate? And, if he had known it, was not Lady Isabel his wife? Could he dream of danger for her? If it pleased Mr. Carlyle to fill East Lynne with bad men to-morrow, what would that be to me?—to my safety; to my well-being; to my love and allegiance to my husband? What were you thinking of, madame?'

Thinking of! She leaned her troubled head upon her hand. Mrs. Carlyle resumed.

'Sitting alone in the drawing-room just now, and thinking matters over, it did seem to me very like people call a fatality. That man, I say, was the one who wrought the disgrace, the trouble, to Mr. Carlyle's family; and it is he, I have every reason now to believe, who brought equal disgrace and trouble upon mine. Did you know'—Mrs. Carlyle lowered her voice—'that I have a brother in exile—in shame?'

Lady Isabel did not dare to answer that she did know it. Who had there been, likely to inform her, the strange governess, of the tale of Richard Hare?

'So the world calls it—shame,' pursued Barbara, growing excited. 'And it is shame—but not as the world thinks it. The shame lies with another, who has thrust the suffering and shame upon Richard: and that other is Francis Levison. I will tell you the tale. It is worth the telling.'

She could only dispose herself to listen; but she wondered what Francis Levison had to do with Richard Hare.

'In the days long gone by, when I was little more than a child, Richard went after Afy Hallijohn. You have seen the cottage in the wood: she lived there with her father and Joyce. It was very foolish of him: but young men will be foolish. Many more went after her—or wanted to go after her. Among them, chief of them, more favoured even than Richard, was one called Thorn, by social position a gentleman. He was a stranger, and used to ride over in secret. A night of murder came; a dreadful murder: Hallijohn was shot down dead. Richard ran away; testimony was strong against him, and the coroners' jury brought in a verdict of "wilful murder against Richard Hare the younger." We never supposed but what he was guilty—of the act, mind you; not of the intention: even mamma, who so loved him, believed he had done it; but she believed it was the result of accident, not design. Oh, the trouble that has been the lot of my poor mamma!' cried Barbara, clasping her hands. 'And she had no one to sympathize with her, no one, no one! I, as I tell you, was little more than a child; and papa, who might have done it, took part against Richard. The sorrow went on for three or four years, and there was no mitigation. At the end of that period Richard came for a few hours to West Lynne, came in secret, and we learnt for the first time that he was *not* guilty. The man who did the deed was Thorn; Richard was not then present. The next question was, how to find Thorn. Nobody knew anything about him: who he was, what he was; where he came from, where he went to: and thus more years passed on. Another Thorn came to West Lynne; an officer in her Majesty's service; and his appearance tallied with the description that Richard had given. I assumed it to be the one: Mr. Carlyle assumed it; but, before anything could be done, or even thought of, Captain Thorn was gone again.'

Barbara paused to take breath. Madame Vine sat, listless enough. What was this tale to her?

'Again, years went on. The period came of Francis Levison's sojourn at East Lynne. Whilst he was there Captain Thorn arrived once more, on a visit to the Herberts. We then strove to find out points of his antecedents, Mr. Carlyle and I, and we became nearly convinced that he was the man. I had to come here often to see Mr. Carlyle, for mamma did not dare to stir in the affair, papa was so violent against Richard. Thus I often saw Francis Levison: but he was visible to no other visitor, being at East Lynne *en cachette*.

He intimated that he was afraid of encountering creditors: I now begin to doubt whether that was not a false plea; and I remember Mr. Carlyle said at the time, that he had no creditors in or near West Lynne.'

'Then, what was his motive for shunning society, for never going out?' interrupted Lady Isabel. Too well she remembered that bygone time: Francis Levison had told her that the fear of his creditors kept him so closely; though he had once said to her they were not in the immediate neighbourhood of East Lynne.

'He had a worse fear upon him than that of creditors,' returned Mrs. Carlyle. 'Singular to say, during this visit of Captain Thorn to the Herberts, we received an intimation from my brother that he was once more about to venture for a few hours to West Lynne. I brought the news to Mr. Carlyle; I had to see him and consult with him more frequently than ever: mamma was painfully restless and anxious, and Mr. Carlyle as eager as we were for the establishment of Richard's innocence, for Miss Carlyle and papa are related, consequently the disgrace may be said to reflect on the Carlyle name.'

Back went Lady Isabel's memory and her bitter repentance. She remembered how jealously she had attributed these meetings between Mr. Carlyle and Barbara to another source. Oh, why had she suffered her mind to be so falsely and fatally perverted?

'Richard came. It was hastily arranged that he should go privately to Mr. Carlyle's office, after the clerks had left for the night, be concealed there, have an opportunity given him of seeing Captain Thorn. There was no difficulty, for Mr. Carlyle was transacting some matter of business for the captain, and appointed him to be at the office at eight o'clock. A memorable night, that, to Mr. Carlyle, for it was the one of his wife's elopement.'

Lady Isabel looked up with a start.

'It was, indeed. She, Lady Isabel, and Mr. Carlyle were engaged to a dinner-party: and Mr. Carlyle had to give it up, otherwise he could not have served Richard. He is always considerate and kind, thinking of others' welfare; never of his own gratification. Oh, it was an anxious night! Papa was out. I waited at home with mamma, doing what I could to soothe her restless suspense: for there was hazard to Richard in his night walk through West Lynne to keep the appointment: and, when it was over, he was to come home for a short interview with mamma, who had not seen him for several years.'

Barbara stopped, lost in thought. Not a word spoke Madame Vine. She still wondered what this affair, touching Richard Hare and Captain Thorn, could have to do with Francis Levison.

'I watched from the window, and saw them come in at the garden gate, Mr. Carlyle and Richard—between nine and ten o'clock I think it must have been. The first words they said to me were, that it was not the Captain Thorn spoken of by Richard. I felt a shock of disappointment, which was wicked enough of me, but I had been so sure he was the man; and, to hear he was not, seemed to throw us further back than ever. Mr. Carlyle, on the contrary, was glad, for he had taken a liking for Captain Thorn. Well, Richard went in to mamma, and Mr. Carlyle was so kind as to accede to her request that he would remain and pace the garden with me. We were so afraid of papa's coming home: he was bitter against Richard, and would inevitably have delivered him up at once to justice. Had he come in, Mr. Carlyle was to keep him in the garden by the gate, whilst I ran in to give notice and conceal Richard in the hall. Richard lingered; papa did not come; and I cannot tell how long we paced there: it was a lovely moonlight night.'

That unhappy listener clasped her hands to pain. The matter-of-fact tone, the unconscious mention of commonplace trifles, proved that they had not been pacing about in disloyalty to her, or for their own gratification. *Why* had she not trusted her noble husband? why had she listened to that false man, as he pointed them out to her, walking there in the moonlight? Why had she given vent in the chariot to that burst of passionate tears, of angry reproach? why, oh why had she hastened to be revenged? But for seeing them together, she might not have done as she did.

'Richard came forth at last, and departed; to be again an exile. Mr. Carlyle also departed; and I remained at the gate, watching for papa. By-and-by Mr. Carlyle came back again: he had got nearly home when he remembered that he had left a parchment at our house. It seemed to be nothing but coming back, for, just after he had gone a second time, Richard returned in a state of excitement, stating that he had met Thorn—Thorn, the murderer, I mean—in Bean-lane. For a moment I doubted him, but not for long, and we ran after Mr. Carlyle. Richard described Thorn's appearance; his evening dress, his white hands, and his diamond ring; more particularly he described a peculiar motion of his hand as he threw back his hair. In that moment it flashed across me that Thorn must be Captain Levison; the description was exact. Many and many a time since, have I wondered that the thought did not strike Mr. Carlyle.'

Lady Isabel sat with her mouth open, as if she could not take in the sense of the words: and when it did become clear to her, she utterly rejected it.

'Francis Levison a murderer! Oh no. Bad man as he is, he is not that.'

'Wait,' said Mrs. Carlyle. 'I did not speak of this doubt—nay, this conviction—which had come to me: how could I mention to Mr. Carlyle the name of the man who did him that foul wrong?—and Richard has remained in exile, with the ban of guilt upon him. Today, as I passed through West Lynne in the carriage, Francis Levison was haranguing the people. I saw that very same action—the throwing back of the hair with his white hand: I saw the self-same diamond ring; and my conviction, that he was the man, became more firmly seated than ever.'

'It is impossible,' murmured Lady Isabel.

'Wait, I say,' said Barbara. 'When Mr. Carlyle came home this evening to dinner, I, for the first time, mentioned this to him. It was no news—the fact was out. This afternoon, during that same harangue, Francis Levison was recognized by two witnesses to be the man Thorn—the man who went after Afy Hallijohn. It is horrible.'

Lady Isabel sat, and looked at Mrs. Carlyle. Not yet did she believe it.

'Yes, it does appear to me as perfectly horrible,' continued Mrs. Carlyle. 'He murdered Hallijohn: he, that bad man; and my poor brother has suffered the odium. When Richard met him that night in Bean-lane, he was sneaking to West Lynne in search of the chaise that afterwards bore away him and his companion. Papa saw them drive away. Papa stayed out late, and, in returning home, a chaise and four tore past, just as he was coming in at the gate. If that miserable Lady Isabel had but known with whom she was flying! A murderer! In addition to his other achievements! It is a mercy for her that she is no longer alive. What would her feelings be?'

What were they then, as she sat there? A *murderer!* and she had—. In spite of her caution, of her strife for self-command, she turned of a deadly whiteness, and a low sharp cry of horror and despair burst from her lips.

Mrs. Carlyle was astonished. Why should her communication have produced this effect upon Madame Vine? A renewed suspicion, that she knew more of Francis Levison than she would acknowledge, stole over her.

'Madame Vine, what is he to you?' she asked, bending forward.

Madame Vine, doing fierce battle with herself, recovered her outward equanimity. 'I beg your pardon, Mrs. Carlyle,' she shivered: 'I am apt to picture things too vividly. It is, as you say, so very horrible.'

'Is he nothing to you? Do you know him?'

'He is nothing to me; less than nothing. As to knowing him—I saw him yesterday when they put him into the pond. A man like that! I should shudder to meet him.'

'Ay, indeed,' said Barbara, reassured. 'You will understand, Madame Vine, that this history has been given you in confidence. I look upon you as one of ourselves.'

There was no answer. Madame Vine sat on, with her white face. It wore altogether a ghastly look.

'It tells like a fable out of a romance,' resumed Mrs. Carlyle. 'Well for him if the romance be not ended with the gibbet. Fancy what it would be—for him, Sir Francis Levison, to be hanged for murder!'

'Barbara, my dearest!'

The voice was Mr. Carlyle's, and she flew off on the wings of love. It appeared that the gentlemen had not yet departed, and now thought they would take coffee first.

Flew off to her idolized husband, leaving her, who had once been the idolized, to her loneliness. She sank down on the sofa: she threw her arms up in her heart-sickness; she thought she should faint; she prayed to die. It *was* horrible, as Barbara had called it. For that man, with the red stain upon his hand and soul, she had flung away Archibald Carlyle.

If ever retribution came home to woman, it came home in that hour to Lady Isabel.

⚔ X I ⚔

Mr. Carlyle Invited to Some Pâté de Foie Gras

A sighing, moaning wind swept round the domains of East Lynne, bending the tall poplar-trees in the distance, swaying the oak and elms nearer, rustling the fine old chestnuts in the park: a melancholy, sweeping, fitful wind. The weather had changed, gathering clouds seemed to be threatening rain: so, at least, deemed one wayfarer, who was journeying on a solitary road, that Saturday night.

He was on foot. A man in the garb of a sailor, with black curling ringlets of hair, and black curling whiskers: a prodigious pair of whiskers, hiding his neck above his blue, turned collar, hiding partially his face. The glazed hat, brought low upon the brows, concealed it still more; and he wore a loose, rough pea-jacket, and wide rough trousers, hitched up with a belt. Bearing steadily on, he struck into Bean-lane, a by-way already mentioned in this history, and from thence, passing through a small, unfrequented gate, he found himself in the grounds of East Lynne.

'Let's see,' mused he, as he closed the gate behind him, and slipped its bolt. 'The covered walk? That must be near the acacia-trees. Then I must wind round to the right. I wonder if either of them will be there, waiting for me?'

Yes. Pacing the covered walk in her bonnet and mantle, as if taking an evening stroll—had any one encountered her, which was very unlikely, seeing that it was the most retired spot in the grounds—was Mrs. Carlyle.

'Oh, Richard! my poor brother!'

Locked in a yearning embrace, emotion overpowered both. Barbara sobbed like a child. A little while, and then he put her from him, to look at her.

'So, Barbara, you are a wife now!'

'Oh, the happiest wife! Richard, sometimes I ask myself what I have done, that God should have showered down blessings so great upon me. But for the sad trouble when I think of you, my life would be as one long summer's day. I have the sweetest baby; he is now nearly a year old—I shall have another soon, God willing. And Archibald—oh, I am so happy.'

She broke suddenly off with the name 'Archibald:' not even to Richard could she speak of her intense love for her husband.

'How is it at the Grove?' he asked.

'Quite well; quite as usual. Mamma has been in better health lately. She does not know of this visit, but—'

'I must see her,' interrupted Richard. 'I did not see her last time, you remember.'

'All in good time to talk of that. How are you getting on in Liverpool? What are you doing?'

'Don't inquire too closely, Barbara. I have no regular work, but I get a job at the docks, now and then, and rub on. It is seasonable help, that, which comes to me from you. Is it from you or Carlyle?'

Barbara laughed. 'How are we to distinguish? His money is mine now, and mine is his. We have not separate purses, Richard; we send it to you jointly.'

'Sometimes I have fancied it came from my mother.'

Barbara shook her head. 'We have never allowed mamma to know that you left London, or that we hold an address where we can write to you. It would not have done.'

'Why have you summoned me here, Barbara? What has turned up?'

'Thorn has—I think. You would know him again, Richard?'

'Know him!' passionately echoed Richard Hare.

'Were you aware that a contest for the membership is now going on at West Lynne?'

'I saw it in the newspapers. Carlyle against Sir Francis Levison. I say, Barbara, how could he think of coming here, to oppose Carlyle?'

'*I* don't know,' said Barbara. 'I wonder that he should come here for other reasons also. First of all, Richard, tell me how you came to know Sir Francis Levison. You said you knew him, and that you had seen him with Thorn.'

'So I do know him,' answered Richard. 'And I saw him with Thorn twice.'

'Know him by sight only, I presume. Let me hear how you came to know him.'

'He was pointed out to me. I saw Thorn walking arm-in-arm with a gentleman, and I showed him to the waterman at the cab-stand hard by. "Do you know that fellow?" I asked him, indicating Thorn, for I wanted to come at who he really is. "I don't know that one," the old chap answered, "but the one with him is Levison the baronet. They are often together; a couple of swells, both." And a couple of swells they looked.'

'And that was how you got to know Levison?'

'That was it,' said Richard Hare.

'Then, Richard, you and the watchman made a mistake between you. He pointed out the wrong, or you did not look at the right. Thorn is Sir Francis Levison.'

Richard stared at her with all his eyes. 'Nonsense, Barbara!'

'He is. I have suspected it ever since the night you saw him in Bean-lane. The action you described, of his pushing back his hair, his white hands, his sparkling diamond ring, could only apply to one person; Francis Levison. On Thursday I drove by the Raven when he was addressing the people, and I noticed the self-same action. In the impulse of the moment I wrote off for you, that you might come and set the doubt at rest. I need not have done so: for when Mr. Carlyle returned home that evening and I acquainted him with what I had done, he told me that Thorn and Francis Levison are one and the same. Otway Bethel recognized him that same afternoon; and so did Ebenezer James.'

'They would both know him,' cried Richard, eagerly. 'James, I am positive, would, for he was skulking down to Hallijohn's often then, and saw Thorn a dozen times. Otway Bethel must have seen him also—though he protested he had not.—Barbara!'

The name was uttered in affright, and Richard plunged amidst the trees, for somebody was in sight—a tall, dark form, advancing from the end of the walk. Barbara smiled; it was only Mr. Carlyle; and Richard emerged again.

'Fears still, Richard!' Mr. Carlyle exclaimed, as he shook Richard cordially by the hand. 'So! you have changed your travelling costume!'

'I couldn't venture here again in the old suit; it had been seen, you said,' returned Richard. 'I bought this rig-out yesterday, second-hand. Two pounds for the lot: I think they shaved me.'

'Ringlets and all?' laughed Mr. Carlyle.

'It's the old hair, oiled and curled,' cried Dick. 'The barber charged a shilling for doing it, and cut my hair into the bargain. I told him not to spare grease, for I liked the curls to shine: sailors always do. Mr. Carlyle, Barbara says that Levison and that brute Thorn have turned out to be the same.'

'They have, Richard; as it appears. Nevertheless, it may be as well for you to take a private view of Levison before anything is done—as you once did of the other Thorn. It would not do to make a stir, and then discover that there was a mistake—that he was not Thorn.'

'When can I see him?' asked Richard eagerly.

'It must be contrived, somehow. Were you to hang about the doors of the Raven—this evening—you'd be sure to get the opportunity, for he is always passing in and out. No one will know you; or think of you either: their heads are turned with the election.'

'I shall look odd to people's eyes. You don't see many sailors in West Lynne.'

'Not odd at all. We have a Russian bear here at present; and you'll be nobody, beside him.'

'A Russian bear!' repeated Richard, while Barbara laughed.

'Mr. Otway Bethel has returned in what is popularly supposed to be a bear's hide; hence the new name he is greeted with. Will it turn out, Richard, that he had anything to do with the murder?'

Richard shook his head. 'It was not possible, Mr. Carlyle: I have said so all along. But, about Levison? If I find him to be the man Thorn—what steps can then be taken?'

'That's the difficulty,' said Mr. Carlyle.

'Who will set it agoing? Who will move in it?'

'You must, Richard.'

'I?' uttered Richard Hare, in consternation. '*I* move in it?'

'You, yourself. Who else is there? I have been thinking it well over.'

'Will you not take it upon yourself, Mr. Carlyle?'

'No. Being Levison,' was the quiet answer.

'Curse him!' impetuously retorted Richard. 'But why should you scruple, Mr. Carlyle? Most men, wronged as you have been, would leap at the opportunity for revenge.'

'For the crime perpetrated upon Hallijohn, I would pursue him to the scaffold. For my own wrong, no. But the remaining negative has cost me something. Many a time, since this appearance of his at West Lynne, have I been obliged to exercise violent control upon myself, or I should have horsewhipped him within an ace of his life.'

'If you horsewhipped him to death he would only meet his deserts.'

'I leave him to a higher retribution: to One who says "Vengeance is mine." I believe him to be guilty of the murder: but if the lifting of my finger would send him to his disgraceful death, I would tie down my hand, rather than lift it. For I could not, in my own mind, separate the man from my injury. Though I might ostensibly pursue him as the destroyer of Hallijohn, to me he would appear ever as the destroyer of another; and the world, always charitable, would congratulate Mr. Carlyle upon gratifying his revenge. I stir in it not, Richard.'

'Couldn't Barbara?' cried Richard.

Barbara was standing with her arm entwined within her husband's, and Mr. Carlyle looked down at her as he answered.

'Barbara is my wife.' It was a sufficient answer.

'Then the thing's again at an end,' said Richard, gloomily, 'and I must give up the hope of ever being cleared.'

'By no means,' said Mr. Carlyle. 'The one who ought to act in this is your father, Richard: but we know he will not. Your mother cannot: she has neither health nor energy for it; and if she had a full supply of both, she would not dare to brave her husband and use them in the cause. My hands are tied: Barbara's equally so, as part of me. There only remains yourself.'

'And what can I do?' wailed poor Dick. 'If your hands are tied I am sure my whole body is; hands, and legs, and *neck*. It's in jeopardy, that is, every hour.'

'Your acting in this affair need not put it any the more in jeopardy. You must stay in the neighbourhood for a few days—'

'I dare not,' interposed Richard, in a fright. 'Stay in the neighbourhood for a few days! No; that I never may.'

'Listen, Richard. You must put away these timorous fears; or else you must make up your mind to remain under the ban for good: and, remember, your mother's happiness is at stake equally with yours—I could almost say her life. Do you suppose I would advise you for danger? You used to say there was some place, a mile or two from this, where you could sojourn in safety.'

'And so there is. But I always feel safer when I get away from it.'

'There your quarters must be, for two or three days, at any rate. I have turned matters over in my own mind, and will tell you what I think should be done, so far as the preliminary step goes.'

'Only the preliminary step! There must be a pretty many to follow it, sir, if it's to come to anything. Well, what is it?'

'Apply to Ball and Treadman; and get them to take it up.'

They were now slowly pacing the covered walk, Barbara on her husband's arm; Richard by the side of Mr. Carlyle. Dick stopped when he heard the last words.

'I don't understand you, Mr. Carlyle. You might as well advise me to go before the bench of magistrates at once. Ball and Treadman would walk me off there as soon as I showed myself.'

'Nothing of the sort, Richard. I do not tell you to go openly to their office, as another client would. What I would advise, is this: make a friend of Mr. Ball; he can be a good man and true, if he chooses: tell the whole story to him in a private place and interview, and ask him whether he will carry it through. If he is as fully impressed with the conviction that you are innocent and the other guilty, as the facts appear to warrant, he will undertake it. Treadman need know nothing of the affair at first; and when Ball puts things in motion he need not know where you are to be found.'

'I don't dislike Ball,' mused Richard; 'and if he would only give his word to be true, I know he would be. The difficulty will be, who is to get the promise from him?'

'I will,' said Mr. Carlyle. 'I will so far pave the way for you. That done, my interference is over.'

'How will he go about it, think you—if he does take it up?'

'That is his affair. I know how I should.'

'How, sir?'

'You cannot expect me to say, Richard. I might as well act for you.'

'I know. You'd go at it slap dash, and arrest Levison off-hand, on the charge.'

A smile parted Mr. Carlyle's lips, for Dick had just guessed it.

A thought flashed across Richard's mind; a thought which rose up on end even his false hair. 'Mr. Carlyle!' he uttered, in an accent of horror, 'if Ball should take it up that way, against Levison, he must apply to the bench for a warrant!'

'Well?' quietly returned Mr. Carlyle.

'And they'd send and clap me into prison! You know the warrant is always out against me.'

'You would never make a conjuror, Richard. I don't pretend to say, or guess, what Ball's proceedings may be. But, in applying to the bench for a warrant against Levison—should that form part of them—is there any necessity for him to bring you in?—to say, "Gentlemen, Richard Hare is within reach, ready to be taken?" Your fears run away with your common sense, Richard.'

'Ah, well; if you had lived with the cord round your neck this many a year, not knowing, any one hour, but it might get tied the next, you would lose your common sense too, at times,' humbly sighed poor Richard. 'What's to be my first move, sir?'

'Your first move, Richard, must be to go to this place of concealment, which you know of, and remain quiet there until Monday. On Monday, at dusk, be here again. Meanwhile, I will see Ball. By the way, though, before speaking to Ball, I must hear from yourself that Thorn and Levison are one.'

'I'll go down to the Raven at once,' eagerly cried Richard. 'I'll come back here, into this walk, as soon as I have obtained sight of him.' With the last words, he turned, and was speeding off, when Barbara caught him.

'You will be so tired, Richard!'

'Tired!' echoed Richard Hare. 'A hundred miles on foot would not tire me if Thorn was at the end of them, waiting to be identified. I may not be back for two or three hours, but I will come; and wait here till you come out to me.'

'You must be hungry and thirsty,' returned Barbara, the tears in her eyes. 'How I wish we dared have you in, and shelter you! But I can manage to bring some refreshment out here.'

'I don't require it, Barbara. I left the train at the station before West Lynne, and dropped into a roadside public-house, as I walked, and got a good supper. Let me go, dear; I am all in a fever.'

Richard departed, reached that part of West Lynne where the Raven was situated, and was so far favoured by fortune that he had not long to wait. Scarcely had he taken up his lounge outside, when two gentlemen came from it, arm-in-arm. Being the head-quarters of one of the candidates, the idlers of the place thought they could not do better than make it their head-quarters also, and the road and pavement were never free from loitering starers and gossipers. Richard Hare, his hat well over his eyes, and his black ringlets made the most of, only added one to the rest.

Two gentlemen came forth arm-in-arm. The loiterers raised a feeble shout of 'Levison for ever!' Richard did not join in the shout, but his pulses were beating and his heart leaped up within him. The one was Thorn; the other the gentleman he had seen with Thorn in London, pointed out to him—as he had believed—as Sir Francis Levison.

'Which of those two is Levison?' he inquired of a man, near whom he stood.

'Don't you know? Him with the hat off, bowing his thanks to us, is Levison.'

No need to inquire further. It was the Thorn of Richard's memory. His ungloved hand, raised to his hat, was white as ever: more sparkling than ever, as it flashed in the gas-light, was the diamond ring. By the hand and ring alone, Richard could have sworn to the man, had it been needful.

'Who is the other one?' he continued.

'Some gent as come down from London with him. His name's Drake. Be you yellow, sailor? or be you scarlet-and-purple?'

'I am neither. I am only a stranger, passing through the town.'

'On the tramp?'

'Tramp!—no.' And Richard moved away, to make the best of his progress to East Lynne, and report to Mr. Carlyle.

Now it happened, on that windy night, that Lady Isabel, her mind disordered, her brow fevered with its weight of care, stole out into the grounds, after the children had left her for the night; courting the boisterous gusts, courting any discomfort she might meet. As if they could, even for a moment, cool the fire within! To the solitude of this very covered walk bent she her steps; and, not long had she paced it, when she descried some man advancing, in the garb of a sailor. Not caring to be seen, she turned short off amidst the trees, intending to emerge again when he had passed. She wondered who he was, and what brought him there.

But he did not pass. He lingered in the walk, keeping her a prisoner. A minute more, and she saw him joined by Mrs. Carlyle. They met with a loving embrace.

Embrace a strange man! Mrs. Carlyle! All the blood in Lady Isabel's body rushed to her brain. Was she, his second wife, false to him?—more shamelessly false than even herself had been, inasmuch as she had the grace to quit him and East Lynne before, as the servant girls say when they change their sweethearts, 'taking up' with another. The positive conviction that such was the case seized firm hold upon her fancy: her thoughts were in a tumult, her mind was a chaos. Was there any small corner of rejoicing in her heart that it was so? And yet—what was it to her? It could not alter by one iota her own position: it could not restore to her the love she had forfeited.

Coupled lovingly together, they were now sauntering up the walk, the sailor's arm thrown round the waist of Mrs. Carlyle. 'Oh! the shameless woman!' Ay; she could be bitter enough upon graceless doings when enacted by another.

But, what was her astonishment when she saw Mr. Carlyle advance, and that it caused not the slightest change in their gracelessness, for the sailor's arm was not withdrawn. Two or three minutes they stood, the three, talking together in a group. Then, good nights were exchanged, the sailor left them, and Mr. Carlyle, his own arm lovingly pressed where the other's had been, withdrew with his wife. The truth—that it was Barbara's brother—flashed to the mind of Lady Isabel.

'Was I mad?' she cried, with a hollow laugh. '*She* false to him. No, no: that fate was reserved for me alone.'

She followed them to the house; she glanced in at the windows of the drawing-room. Lights and fire were in the room, but the curtains and windows were not closed for the night, for it was through those windows that Mr. Carlyle and his wife had passed in and out, on their visits to the covered walk. There they were, alone in their happiness, and she stopped to glance in upon it. Lord Mount Severn had departed for London, to be down again early in the week. The tea was on the table, but Barbara had not begun to make it. She sat on the sofa by the fire, her face, with its ever-loving gaze upon it, turned up to her husband's. He stood near, was talking with apparent earnestness, and looking down at Barbara. Another moment, and a smile crossed his lips, the same sweet smile so often bent upon *her* in the bygone days. Yes, they were together in their unclouded happiness; and she—she turned away towards her own lonely sitting-room, sick and faint at heart.

Ball and Treadman—as the brass plate on their office-doors intimated—were conveyancers and attorneys-at-law. Mr. Treadman, who attended chiefly to the conveyancing, lived at the office with his family; Mr. Ball, a bachelor, lived away; Lawyer Ball, West Lynne styled him. Not a young bachelor; midway, he may have been, between forty and fifty. A short, stout man, with a keen face and green eyes. He took up any practice that was brought to him, dirty odds and ends that Mr. Carlyle would not have touched with his toe: but, as that gentleman had remarked, he could be honest and true upon occasions, and there was no doubt that he would be so to Richard Hare. To his house, on Monday morning early, so as to catch him before he went out, proceeded Mr. Carlyle. A high respect for Mr. Carlyle had Lawyer Ball, as he had had for his father before him: many a good turn had the Carlyles done him, if only helping him and his partner to clients, whom they were too fastidious to take up. But the two, Mr. Carlyle and Lawyer Ball, did not rank alike, though their profession was the same: Lawyer Ball knew that they did not, and was content to feel humble. The one was a received gentleman: the other was a country attorney.

Lawyer Ball was at breakfast when Mr. Carlyle was shown in.

'Halloa, Carlyle! You are here betimes.'

'Sit still, don't disturb yourself. Don't ring: I have breakfasted.'

'The most delicious pâté de foie,' urged Lawyer Ball, who was a regular gourmand. 'I get 'em direct from Strasburg.'

Mr. Carlyle resisted the offered dainty with a smile. 'I have come on business,' said he: 'not to feast. Before I enter upon it, you will give me your word, Ball, that my communication shall be held sacred, in the event of your not consenting to pursue it further.'

'Certainly I will. What business is it? Some that offends the delicacy of the Carlyle office?' he added, with a laugh. 'A would-be client, whom you turn over to me, in your exclusiveness?'

'It is a client for whom I cannot act. But not from the motives you assume. It concerns that affair of Hallijohn's,' Mr. Carlyle continued, bending forward and somewhat dropping his voice. 'The murder.'

Lawyer Ball, who had just taken a delicious bonne bouche of the foie gras, bolted it whole in his surprise. 'Why, that was enacted ages and ages ago! it is past and done with,' he exclaimed.

'Not done with,' said Mr. Carlyle. 'Circumstances have come to light which tend to indicate that Richard Hare was innocent: that it was another who committed the murder.'

'In conjunction with him?' interrupted the attorney.

'No: alone. Richard Hare had nothing whatever to do with it. He was not present at the time.'

'Do you believe that?' asked Lawyer Ball.

'I have believed it for years.'

'Then who did commit that murder?'

'Richard accuses one of the name of Thorn. Several years back, I had a meeting with Richard Hare, and he disclosed certain facts to me which, if correct, could not fail to prove that he was innocent. Since that period this impression has been gradually confirmed, by little and by little, trifle upon trifle; and I would now stake my life upon his innocence. I should long ago have moved in the matter, hit or miss, could I have lighted upon Thorn, but he was not to be found, nor any clue to him, and we now know that this name Thorn was an assumed one.'

'Is he to be found?'

'He is found. He is at West Lynne. Mark you, I don't accuse him: I do not offer an opinion upon his guilt: I only state my belief in Richard's innocence:

it may have been another who did it, neither Richard nor Thorn. It was my firm intention to take Richard's cause up the instant I saw my way clearly in it: and now that that time has come, I am debarred from doing so.'

'What debars you?' asked Lawyer Ball.

'Hence I come to you,' continued Mr. Carlyle, disregarding the question. 'I come on the part of Richard Hare. I have seen him lately, and conversed with him. I gave him my reasons for not personally acting, advised him to apply to you, and promised to come here and open the matter. Will you see Richard, in good faith, and hear his story?—giving the understanding that he shall depart in secret and unmolested, as he came, if you do not decide to undertake the business.'

'I'll give it with all the pleasure in life,' freely returned the attorney. 'I am sure I don't want to harm poor Dick Hare. And if he can convince me of his innocence, I'll do my best to establish it.'

'Of his own tale you must be the judge. I do not wish to bias you. I have stated my belief in his innocence, but I repeat that I give no opinion, myself, as to who else may be guilty. Hear his account, and then take up the affair, or not, as you may think fit. He would not come to you without your previous promise to hold him harmless; to be his friend, in short, for the time being: when I bear this promise to him from you, my part is done.'

'I give it you in all honour, Carlyle. Tell Dick he has nothing to fear from me. Quite the contrary; for if I can befriend him I shall be glad to do it, and I won't spare trouble. What can possibly be your objection to act for him?'

'My objection applies not to Richard; I would willingly appear for him: but I will not take proceedings against the man he accuses. If that man is to be denounced and brought before justice, I will hold neither act nor part in it.'

The words aroused the curiosity of Lawyer Ball, and he began to turn over all persons, likely and unlikely, in his mind: never, according to usage, giving a suspicion to the right one. 'I cannot fathom you, Carlyle.'

'You will do that better, possibly, when Richard shall have made his disclosure.'

'It's—it's—never his own father that he accuses?—Justice Hare?'

'Your wits must be wool-gathering, Ball.'

'Well, so they must, to give utterance to so preposterous a notion,' acquiesced the attorney, pushing back his chair, and throwing his breakfast napkin on the carpet. 'But I don't know a soul you could object to go against, except the justice. What's anybody else in West Lynne, to you, in comparison with restoring Dick Hare to his fair fame? I give it up.'

'So do I, for the present,' said Mr. Carlyle, as he rose. 'And now, about the ways and means for your meeting this poor fellow. Where can you see him?'

'Is he at West Lynne?'

'No. But I can get a message conveyed to him, and he could come.'

'When?'

'To-night, if you liked.'

'Then let him come here, to this house. He will be perfectly safe.'

'So be it. My part is now over,' concluded Mr. Carlyle. And with a few more preliminary words, he departed. Lawyer Ball looked after him.

'It's a queer business. One would think Dick accuses some old flame of Carlyle's: some demoiselle or dame he daren't go against.'

❧ X I I ☙

An Application to the Bench

On Monday evening the interview between Lawyer Ball and Richard Hare took place. With some difficulty would the lawyer believe his tale: not as to its broad details; he saw that he might give credit to them: but as to the accusation against Sir Francis Levison. Richard persisted; mentioning every minute particular he could think of: his meeting him the night of the elopement in Bean-lane; his meetings with him again in London, and Sir Francis' evident fear of him; and the previous Saturday night's recognition at the door of the Raven; not forgetting to tell of the anonymous letter received by Justice Hare, the morning that Richard was in hiding at Mr. Carlyle's.

There was no doubt in the world it had been sent by Francis Levison to frighten Mr. Hare into despatching him out of West Lynne, had Richard taken refuge in his father's house. None had more cause to keep Dick from falling into the hands of justice than Francis Levison.

'I believe what you say, I believe all you say, Mr. Richard, touching Thorn,' debated the attorney, 'but it's next to impossible to take in so astounding a fact, as that he is Sir Francis Levison.'

'You can satisfy yourself of the fact from other lips than mine,' said Richard. 'Otway Bethel could testify to it if he would, though I doubt his willingness. But there's Ebenezer James.'

'What does he know about it?' asked the attorney, in surprise. 'Ebenezer James is in our office at present.'

'He saw Thorn often enough in those days, and has, I hear, recognized him as Levison. You had better inquire of him. Should you object to take cause against Levison?'

'Not a bit of it. Let me be assured that I am upon safe grounds, as to the identity of the man, and I'll proceed in it forthwith. Levison is an out-and-out scoundrel, *as* Levison, and deserves hanging. I will send for James at once, and hear what he says,' he concluded after a pause of consideration.

Richard Hare started wildly up. 'Not while I am here: he must not see me. For Heaven's sake, consider the peril to me, Mr. Ball!'

'Pooh! pooh!' laughed the attorney. 'Do you suppose I have but this one reception-room? We don't let cats into cages where canary-birds are kept.'

Ebenezer James returned with the messenger despatched after him. 'You'll be sure to find him at the singing saloon,' Mr. Ball had said: and there the gentleman was found.

'Is it any copying, sir, wanted to be done in a hurry?' cried James, as he came in.

'No,' replied the attorney. 'I wish a question or two answered; that's all. Did you ever know Sir Francis Levison to go by any name but his own?'

'Yes, sir, he has gone by the name of Thorn.'

A pause. 'When was this?'

'It was the autumn when Hallijohn was killed. Thorn used to be prowling about there in an evening: in the wood and at the cottage, I mean.'

'What did he prowl for?'

Ebenezer James laughed. 'For the same reason that several more did. I, for one. He was sweet upon Afy Hallijohn.'

'Where was he living at the time? I never remember him at West Lynne.'

'He was not at West Lynne, sir. On the contrary, he seemed to take precious good care that West Lynne and he kept separate. A splendid horse he rode, thoroughbred, and he used to come galloping into the wood at dusk, get over his chat with Miss Afy, mount, and gallop away again.'

'Where to? Where did he come from?'

'From somewhere near Swainson: a ten miles' ride, Afy used to say, he had. Now that he has appeared here in his own plumage, of course I can put two and two together, and not be at much fault for the exact spot.'

'And where's that?' asked the lawyer.

'Levison Park,' said Mr. Ebenezer. 'There's little doubt he was stopping at his uncle's; and you know that is close to Swainson.'

Lawyer Ball thought things were becoming clearer—or darker, whichever you may please to call it. He paused again, and then put a question impressively.

'James, have you any doubt whatever, or shadow of doubt, that Sir Francis Levison is the same man you knew as Thorn?'

'Sir, have I any doubt that you are Mr. Ball, or that I am Eb. James?' retorted Mr. Ebenezer. 'I am as certain of that man's identity as I am of yours.'

'Are you ready to swear to the fact in a court of justice?'

'Ready and willing; in any court in the world. To-morrow, if I am called upon.'

'Very well. You may go back to your singing club now. Keep a silent
tongue in your head.'

'All close, sir,' answered Mr. Ebenezer James.

Far into the middle of the night sat Lawyer Ball and Richard Hare, the
former chiefly occupied in taking notes of Richard's statement. 'It's half a
crotchet, this objection of Carlyle's to interfere with Levison!' said Richard,
suddenly, in the midst of some desultory conversation. 'Don't you think so,
Mr. Ball?'

The lawyer pursed up his lips. 'Um—a delicate point. Carlyle was always
fastidiously honourable. *I* should go at him, thunder and fury, in his place;
but I and Carlyle are different.'

The following day, Tuesday, Mr. Ball was much occupied in putting, to use
nearly Ebenezer James's words, that and that together. Later in the day, he
took a journey to Levison Park, ferretted out some information, and came
home again. In the evening of that same day, Richard departed for Liverpool; he was done with for the present; Mr. and Mrs. Carlyle being, as before, alone cognizant of his address.

Wednesday morning witnessed the return of the Earl of Mount Severn.
Lord Vane came also. The latter ought to have gone back to Eton, but he had
teased and prayed to be allowed to 'see the fun out,' meaning the election.
'And that devil's discomfiture when he finds himself beaten,' he surreptitiously added, behind his father's back, who was a great stickler for the
boy's always being 'gentlemanlike.' So the earl had yielded. They arrived, as
before, about breakfast-time, having travelled at night. Subsequently they
and Mr. Carlyle walked into West Lynne together.

West Lynne was alive and astir. The election was to come off that week,
and people made it their business to be in a bustle over it, collectively and
individually. Mr. Carlyle's committee sat at the Buck's Head, and the traffic
in and out was enough to wear the stones away. The bench of justices were
remarkably warm over it, neglecting the judicial business, and showing
themselves at the Buck's Head windows in purple-and-scarlet streamers.

'I will be with you in ten minutes,' said Mr. Carlyle, withdrawing his arm
from Lord Mount Severn's, as they approached his office, 'but I must go in
and read my letters.'

So the earl went on to the Buck's Head, and Lord Vane took a foot canter
down to the Raven, to reconnoitre it outside. He was uncommonly fond of
planting himself where Sir Francis Levison's eyes were sure to fall upon him;
which eyes were immediately dropped, while the young gentleman's would
be fixed in an audacious stare. Being Lord Vane—or, it may be more correct
to say, being the Earl of Mount Severn's son, and under control—he was
debarred from dancing and jeering after the yellow candidate, as the unwashed gentry of his own age indulged in, but his tongue and his feet itched
to do it.

Mr. Carlyle took his seat in his private room, opened his letters, sorted them, marked on the back of some what was to be the purport of their answers, and then called in Mr. Dill. Mr. Carlyle put the letters in his hand, gave some rapid instructions, and rose.

'You are in a hurry, Mr. Archibald.'

'They want me at the Buck's Head. Why?'

'A curious incident occurred to me last evening, sir. I overheard a dispute between Levison and Otway Bethel.'

'Indeed,' carelessly replied Mr. Carlyle, who was busy at the time, looking for something in the deep drawer of his desk.

'And what I heard would go far to hang Levison, if not Bethel. As sure as we are here, Mr. Archibald, they hold the secret of Hallijohn's murder. It appears that Levison—'

'Stop,' interposed Mr. Carlyle. 'I would prefer not to hear this. Levison may have murdered him, but it is no affair of mine: neither shall I make it such.'

Old Dill felt checkmated. 'Meanwhile, Richard Hare suffers, Mr. Archibald,' he observed in a remonstrating tone.

'I am aware he does.'

'Is it right that the innocent shall suffer for the guilty?'

'No. Very wrong. But the case is all too common.'

'If some one would take up Richard Hare's cause now, he might be proved innocent,' added the old man, with a wistful look at Mr. Carlyle.

'It is being taken up, Dill.'

A pause and a glad look. 'That's the best news I have had for many a day, sir. But my evidence will be necessary to the case. Levison—'

'I am not taking up the case. You must carry your news elsewhere. It is no affair of mine, I say.'

'Then who is taking it up?' echoed Mr. Dill, in astonishment.

'Ball. He has had a meeting with Richard, and is now acting for him.'

Mr. Dill's eyes sparkled. 'Is he going to prosecute, Mr. Archibald?'

'I tell you I know nothing. I will know nothing.'

'Ah well! I can understand. But I shall go on to their office at once, Mr. Archibald, and inform them of what I overheard,' said old Dill, in vehement decision.

'That is not my affair, either,' laughed Mr. Carlyle; 'it is yours. But remember—if you do go—it is Ball, not Treadman.'

Waiting only to give certain orders to the head clerk, Mr. Dill proceeded to the office of Ball and Treadman. A full hour was he closeted there with the senior partner.

Not until three o'clock that afternoon did the justices take their seats on the bench. Like renegade schoolboys, they had been playing truant, conjugating the verb *s'amuser*, instead of *travailler*, and now scuffled in to their duties at the tenth hour. It was scarcely to be called coming in, either, for there were but two of them, one slinking in after the other, with conscious faces of neglect: Justice Herbert and Squire Pinner.

Two important cases were disposed of, both arising out of the present rollicking state of West Lynne. Two ladies, one declaring for the purple-and-scarlet, the other for the yellow, had disputed in a public-house over the merits of the respective candidates, winding it up with a pewter-pot fight. The second case was that of a knot of boys, who had carried Sir Francis Levison (in straw) through the town, and then burnt him on a convenient grass-plot, to the exceeding terror of the grass-plot's owners, and destruction of certain linen of theirs, which, lying out there to dry, got burnt. The two ladies were condemned to a week's imprisonment; and the boys were ordered the treat of a private whipping.

Scarcely had the latter case been disposed of, and the boys removed, all howling, when Lawyer Ball bustled in and craved a secret hearing. His application was of the last importance, he premised, but, that the ends of justice might not be defeated, it was necessary that their worships should entertain it in private; he therefore craved the bench to accord it to him.

The bench consulted, looked wise, and—possibly possessing some latent curiosity themselves upon the point—graciously acceded. They adjourned to a private room, and it was half-past four before they came out of it. Very long faces, scared and grim, wore their worships, as if Lawyer Ball's communication had both perplexed and confounded them.

ᷓ XIII ᷓ

The World Turned Upside Down

'This is the afternoon we are to meet Dr. Martin at papa's office,' William Carlyle had exclaimed that same day at dinner. 'Do we walk in, Madame Vine?'

'I do not know, William. Mrs. Carlyle is going to take you.'

'No, she is not. You are to take me.'

A flush passed over Lady Isabel's face at the bare thought: though she did not believe it. *She* go to Mr. Carlyle's office! 'Mrs. Carlyle told me herself that she should take you,' was her reply.

'All I know is, that mamma said this morning you would take me in to West Lynne to-day,' persisted William.

The discussion was interrupted by the appearance of Mrs. Carlyle: interrupted and decided also. 'Madame Vine,' she said, 'you will be ready at three o'clock to go in with William.'

Lady Isabel's heart beat. 'I understood you to say that you should go with him yourself, madam.'

'I know I did. I intended to do so. But I heard this morning that some friends from a distance are coming this afternoon to call upon me. Therefore I shall not go out.'

How she, Lady Isabel wished that she dared say also, 'I shall not go out, either.' But that might not be. Well—she must go through with it, as she had to go through with the rest.

William rode his pony into West Lynne, the groom attending to take it back again. He was to walk home with Madame Vine; who walked both ways.

Mr. Carlyle was not in when they arrived at the office. The boy went boldly on to the private room, leaving Madame Vine to follow him. Mr. Dill came in.

'Well, Master William! Have you come here to give instructions in a lawsuit, or to file a bill in Chancery?' laughed he. 'Take a seat, pray, ma'am.'

'I have come here to wait for Dr. Martin. He's coming to see me. I say, Mr. Dill, where's papa gone?'

'How should I know?' said Mr. Dill, pleasantly. 'But now, what do you want with Dr. Martin? I am sure you must be getting better—with that rosy colour!'

'I wish I could get better!' responded the boy. 'It's so nasty, having that cod-liver oil to take! Mamma was coming in with me, but she can't now.'

'How is your mamma, Master William?'

'Oh, she's very well. What a shouting there was, down by the police station! It frightened my pony, and I had to hold him in, and give him a little taste of whip. They were kicking a yellow rosette about.'

'Ah! There'll be no peace till this election's over,' responded old Dill. 'I wish it was: and the fellow clear of the town.'

'Do you mean that Levison?' asked William, who of course took his tone of politics from those around him.

'Yes, I do. The extraordinary thing is,' he continued, speaking to himself and not to his auditors, 'what could have possessed the fool to venture here.'

A hot glow illumined the face of Lady Isabel. What possessed 'the fool' to do many things that he had done? A fool in the extreme sense of the term, he verily and indeed was.

'Of course he could not expect to stand against my papa!' oracularly spoke William.

'He'll never stand against any good man,' warmly returned old Dill. 'No: God would never suffer it.'

'Do you mean for the election?' quoth William.

'No, my dear. I was not thinking of elections just then.'

A clerk appeared, showing in a stranger: a client. The clerk might have deemed that Mr. Carlyle was in his room. Old Dill took the client out again, into his own little private sanctum; but not before the governess had been honoured with a curious stare. She was dressed, as she ever was, in black silk. Sometimes her dresses were rich, sometimes plain and quiet; but the material was invariably the same: black silk. As indoors, the make of the upper part was the same—the loose jacket. The one she wore to-day was a handsome robe with embossed flounces; a mantle to match. And there was the large straw bonnet, with its hiding veil. The old blue spectacles were home again, and on. Lady Isabel wished herself anywhere else: she did not like that strange eyes should look upon her.

Presently Mr. Carlyle appeared. He was talking to Mr. Dill, who followed him.

'Oh—are you here, Madame Vine? I left word that you were to go in to Miss Carlyle's. Did I not leave word, Dill?'

'Not with me, sir.'

'I forgot it then. I meant to do so. What is the time?' He looked at his watch. Ten minutes to four. 'Did the doctor say at what hour he should call?' Mr. Carlyle added to Madame Vine.

'Not precisely. I gathered that it would not be very early in the afternoon.'

They went into Miss Carlyle's, Lady Isabel and William. That lady was out. Not expected in till dinner-time, the man said. William took up a comfortable position on the sofa, and, remaining quiet, dropped asleep.

How slowly the minutes seemed to flit past! how still the house seemed to be! You may have noticed that yourselves, when waiting long for anything. Lady Isabel sat on, listening to the silence; mechanically watching the passers-by through the Venetian blinds; glancing at the child's white face— white now; wishing the physician would come. It struck half-past five.

'Here he is!' she thought. An entrance at the hall door; and now advancing footsteps. Not physician's footsteps. Her heart would not have fluttered at them.

'Dr. Martin is late,' observed Mr. Carlyle, as he came in. 'I fear your patience will be tired, Madame Vine.'

'It is of no consequence, sir,' she replied, in that indistinct, whispered tone, above which her voice was scarcely, if ever, raised.

'How pale he looks!' involuntarily exclaimed Carlyle, glancing from Madame Vine to the boy. 'And this inclination to sleep! Is it good, I wonder?'

'I thought that Mrs. Carlyle would come in with him,' said madame, at a loss for something to say.

'Mrs. Carlyle is expecting friends. And I do not know that she would have come, had she not been. She has not felt well the last day or two, and I could not allow her to be fatigued, in her present state of health.'

A sharp pang. The time had been when it was she—*she*—whom he would not allow fatigue to touch. Oh! to be his once more; his, with the past blotted out.

'Here he is!' exclaimed Mr. Carlyle with alacrity, as he went into the hall. She supposed he alluded to the physician; supposed he had seen him pass the window. Their entrance together woke up William.

'Well,' said the doctor, who was a little man with a bald head, 'and how fares it with my young patient? Bon jour, madame.'

'Bon jour, monsieur,' responded she. She wished everybody would address her in French, and take her for French: there seemed less chance of recognition. She would have to speak in good plain English, however, if she must carry on a conversation with the doctor. Beyond a familiar phrase or two, he was something like Justice Hare—Nong parley Fronsay, me!

'And how does the cod-liver oil get on?' asked the doctor of William, as he drew him to the light. 'It is nicer now than it used to be, eh?'

'No,' said William, 'it's nastier than ever.'

Dr. Martin looked at the boy: felt his pulse, his skin, listened to his breathing. 'There,' said he, presently, 'you may sit down again, and have your nap out.'

'I wish I might have something to drink: I am very thirsty. May I ring for some water, papa?'

'Go and find your aunt's maid, and ask her for some,' said Mr. Carlyle.

'Ask her for milk,' called out Dr. Martin. 'Not water.'

Away went William. Mr. Carlyle was leaning against the side of the window; Dr. Martin folded his arms before it: Lady Isabel stood near the latter. The broad, full light was cast upon all, but the thick veil hid Lady Isabel's face. It was not often she could be caught without that veil, for she seemed to wear her bonnet at all sorts of seasonable and unseasonable times.

'What is your opinion, doctor?' asked Mr. Carlyle.

'Well,' began the doctor, in a *very* professional tone, 'the boy is certainly delicate. But—'

'Stay, Dr. Martin,' was the interruption, spoken in a low impressive voice, 'you will deal candidly with me. I must know the truth, without disguise. Tell it me, freely.'

Dr. Martin paused. 'The truth is not always palatable, Mr. Carlyle.'

'True. But for that very reason, all the more necessary. Let me hear the worst. And the child has no mother, you know, to be shocked with it.'

'I fear that it will be the worst.'

'Death?'

'Ay. The seeds of consumption must have been inherent in him. They are showing themselves all too plainly.'

What Mr. Carlyle felt was not suffered to appear: his feelings were entirely under his own control. That he was tenderly and sincerely attached to his

children, there was no doubt. He remained quite still, his eyes shaded by
their drooping lids. A few minutes and he broke the silence.

'How can consumption have come to *him*? It is not in the family: on my
side, or—or on his mother's.'

'Pardon me,' said the doctor. 'The child's grandmother died of consumption; the Countess of Mount Severn.'

'They did not call it consumption,' said Mr. Carlyle.

'I don't care what they called it. It was consumption. Very slow and lingering; mild, too; I grant you that.'

'Is there *no* hope for the child?'

Dr. Martin looked at him. 'You bade me give you the truth.'

'Nothing else! nothing but the truth,' returned Mr. Carlyle, his tone one of
mingled pain and command.

'Then there is none: no hope whatever. The lungs are extensively diseased.'

'And how long—'

'That I cannot say,' interrupted the doctor, divining what the next question was to be. 'He may linger on for months; for a year, it may even be; or, a
very short period may see the termination. Don't worry him with any more
lessons and stuff of learning: he'll never want it.'

The doctor cast his eyes upon the governess as he spoke; the injunction
concerning her as much as did Mr. Carlyle. And the doctor started, for he
thought she was fainting; her face had become so ghastly white: he could see
it through her veil.

'You are ill, madame! you are ill! Trouve malade! don't you?'

She opened her lips to speak; her trembling lips, that would not obey her.
Dr. Martin, in his concern, pulled off the blue spectacles. She caught them
from him with one hand, sat down on the nearest chair, and hid her face
with the other.

Mr. Carlyle, scarcely understanding the scuffle, came forward. 'Are you ill,
Madame Vine?'

She was putting on her spectacles under her veil, her face whiter than ever.
'Pray do not interrupt your conversation to pay attention to me! I thank you;
I thank you both. I am subject to—slight spasms, and they made me look ill
for the moment. It has passed now.'

The doctor turned from her: Mr. Carlyle resumed his place by the window. 'What should be the treatment?' asked the latter.

'Almost anything you please—that the boy himself likes. Let him play, or
rest; ride or walk; eat and drink, or let it alone: it cannot make much
difference.'

'Doctor! You yield to it, as a last hope, very lightly.'

Dr. Martin shook his head. 'I speak as I *know*. You insisted on having my
true opinion.'

'A warmer climate?' suggested Mr. Carlyle, eagerly, the idea crossing his mind.

'It might prolong the end for a very little while: a few weeks, perhaps: avert it, it could not. And who could take him? You could not go; and he has no mother. No: I should not advise it.'

'I wish you would see Wainwright—with reference to William.'

'I have seen him. I met him this afternoon, by chance, and told him my opinion. How is Mrs. Carlyle?'

'Pretty well. She is not in robust health, you are aware, just now.'

Dr. Martin smiled. 'These things will happen. Mrs. Carlyle has a thoroughly good constitution: a far stronger one than—than—'

'Than what?' said Mr. Carlyle, wondering why he hesitated.

'You must grant me pardon. I may as well finish, now I have begun; but I was not thinking when I spoke. She is stronger than was Lady Isabel. I must be off to catch the six train.'

'You will come over from time to time to East Lynne, to see William.'

'If you wish it. It may be a satisfaction, perhaps. Bon jour, madame.'

Lady Isabel bowed to him as he left the room with Mr. Carlyle. 'How fond that French governess of yours is of the boy!' the doctor whispered, as they crossed the hall. 'I detected it when she brought him to Lynneborough. And you saw her just now! that emotion was all because I said he could not live. Good-bye.'

Mr. Carlyle grasped his hand. 'Doctor, I wish you could save him!' he passionately uttered.

'Ah, Carlyle! if we humble mites of human doctors could but keep those whom it is the Great Physician's good pleasure to take, how we should be run after! There's hidden mercy, remember, in the darkest cloud. Farewell, my friend.'

Mr. Carlyle returned to the room. He approached Lady Isabel, looking down upon her as she sat: not that he could see much of her face. 'These are grievous tidings. But you were more prepared for them, I fancy, than I was.'

She started suddenly up, approached the window, and looked out; as if she saw somebody passing whom she would gaze at. All of emotion was stirred up within her; her temples throbbed, her throat beat, her breath became hysterical. Could she bear thus to hold confidential converse with him, over the state of their child? She pulled off her gloves for coolness to her burning hands, she wiped the moisture from her pale forehead, she struggled for calmness. What excuse could she offer to Mr. Carlyle?

'I love the boy so very much, sir,' she said, half turning round. 'And the doctor's fiat, too plainly pronounced, has given me pain—pain to agitation.'

Again Mr. Carlyle approached her, following close up to where she stood. 'You are very kind, thus to feel an interest in my child.'

She did not answer.

'Do not acquaint Mrs. Carlyle,' he resumed. 'I would prefer to tell her myself. She must not be suddenly grieved or alarmed just now.'

'Why should she be either grieved or alarmed? She is not his mother.' Passionately, fiercely, resentfully, were the words spoken, as if she would cast contempt to Barbara. But recollection returned to her before they had all left her lips, and the concluding sentence was wonderfully toned down. Mr. Carlyle raised his eyelids, and the tones of his voice rang haughtily on her ear.

'You speak hastily, madame.'

The reproof ate into her heart, and she remembered who she was; remembered it with shame and humiliation. She, the governess! Mr. Carlyle must have deemed her worse than mad, so to speak of his wife. He was moving from her, when she suddenly turned to him, a yearning petition on her lips.

'It appeared—if I understood aright—that there might be a difficulty about William's going to a warmer climate, no one, suitable, being at hand to take him. Sir! let me do it. Confide him to my charge.'

'He is not to go. You heard what Dr. Martin said—that it could not materially prolong his life.'

'Only for a few weeks,' she said. 'But are not those of value?'

'That it *might*. Where would be the use? They would be weeks of isolation from his family. No, Madame Vine. If my boy is to leave me, I must have him with me to the last.'

William's head appeared, pushed in at the door to reconnoitre. 'He's gone, isn't he? I would not come back while he was here, for fear he should give me some cod-liver oil now.'

Mr. Carlyle sat down and lifted William on his knees, his forehead pressed lovingly against the boy's silky hair. 'My darling child, the cod-liver oil is to do you good, you know; to make you strong.'

'But I don't think it *does* make me strong, papa. Does Dr. Martin say I shall die?'

'Who told you anything about dying?'

'Oh—some of them talk of it.'

'We must see what we can do towards curing you, instead of letting you die,' responded Mr. Carlyle, almost at a loss what answer to make, and suppressing the emotion of his own aching heart. 'But, whether we live or die, we are in the hands of God: you know that, William, and whatever God wills is always for the best.'

'Yes, I know that, papa.'

Mr. Carlyle rose and lifted the boy towards Madame Vine. 'Take care of him, madame,' he said, and passed in to the hall.

'Here, papa, papa! I want you,' cried William, breaking from Madame Vine's hand and running after him. 'Let me walk home with you! Are you going to walk?'

How could he find in his heart to deny anything to the child, then? 'Very well,' he said. 'Stay here till I come for you.'

'We are going home with papa,' proclaimed William to Madame Vine.

Madame Vine did not relish the news. But there was no help for it. In a very short time Mr. Carlyle appeared, and they set off: he holding William's hand; Madame Vine walking alone, on the other side of the child.

'Where's William Vane, papa?' asked the boy.

'He has gone on with Lord Mount Severn.'

Scarcely had the words been spoken, when some one came bolting out of the post-office, and met them face to face: almost ran against them, in fact, creating some hindrance. The man looked confused, and slunk off into the gutter. And you will not wonder that he did, when you hear that it was Francis Levison. William, child-like, turned his head to gaze at the intruder.

'I would not be an ugly, bad man like him for the world,' quoth he, as he turned it back again. 'Would you, papa?'

Mr. Carlyle did not answer, and she cast an involuntary glance upon him from her white face. His was impassive: save that a curl of ineffable scorn was upon his lips.

At Mr. Justice Hare's gate they encountered that gentleman, who appeared to be standing there to give himself an airing. William caught sight of Mrs. Hare seated on the garden bench, outside the window, and ran to kiss her. All children loved Mrs. Hare. The justice was looking—not pale; that would not be a term half strong enough; but yellow. The curls of his best wig were limp, and all his pomposity appeared to have gone out of him.

'I say, Carlyle, what on earth is this?' cried he, in a tone that, for him, was wonderfully subdued and meek. 'I was not on the bench this afternoon, but Pinner has been telling me of—of an application that was made to them in private. It's not true, you know; it can't be; it's too far-fetched a tale. What do you know about it?'

'Nothing,' said Mr. Carlyle. 'I have been privy to no application.'

'It seems they want to make out now that Dick never murdered Hallijohn,' proceeded the justice, in a half whisper, glancing round as if to be sure that there were no eavesdroppers amidst the trees.

'Oh!' said Mr. Carlyle.

'But that Levison did. *Levison!*'

Mr. Carlyle made no reply, save by a gesture: his face more impassive than before. Not so another face beside him.

'But it *can't* be, you know. It can't, I say.'

'So far as Richard's innocence goes, of that I have long been convinced,' spoke Mr. Carlyle.

'And that Levison's guilty?' returned the justice, opening his eyes in puzzled wonderment.

'I give no opinion upon that point,' was the cold rejoinder.

'It's impossible, I say. Dick can't be innocent. You may as well tell me the world's turned upside down.'

'It is sometimes, I think. That Richard was not the guilty man will be proved yet, justice, in the broad face of day.'

'If—if—that other did do it, I should think you'd take the warrant out of the hands of the police, and capture him yourself.'

'I would not touch him with a pair of tongs,' spake Mr. Carlyle, his lip curling again. 'If the man goes to his punishment, he goes; but I do not help him on his road thither.'

'*Can* Dick be innocent?' mused the justice, returning to the thought which so troubled his mind. 'Then, why has he kept away? Why did he not come back and say so?'

'That you might deliver him up, justice? You know you took an oath to do it.'

The justice looked remarkably humble.

'Oh, but, Carlyle,' impulsively said he, the thought occurring to him, 'what an awful revenge this would have been for you on—somebody—had she lived. How her false step would have come home to her now!'

'False steps come home to most people,' responded Mr. Carlyle, as he took William by the hand, who then ran up. And, lifting his hat to Mrs. Hare in the distance, he walked on.

She, Lady Isabel, walked on too, by the side of the child, as before; walked on with a shivering frame, and a heart sick unto death. The justice looked after them, his mind preoccupied. He was in a maze of bewilderment. Richard innocent! Richard, whom he had striven to pursue to a shameful end! And that other the guilty one? The world *was* turning upside down.

❧ XIV ☙

Miss Carlyle in Full Dress. Afy Also

Merrily rose West Lynne on the Thursday morning; merrily rang out the bells, clashing and chiming. The street was alive with people; the windows were crowded with heads; something unusual was astir. It was the day of nomination of the two candidates, and everybody took the opportunity to make a holiday.

Ten o'clock was the time named; but, before that hour struck, West Lynne was crammed. The country people had come in, thick and threefold; rich and poor; people of note and people of none; voters and non-voters: all eager to mix themselves up with the day's proceedings. You see, the notorious fact of Sir Francis Levison's having come forward to oppose Mr. Carlyle, caused greater interest to attach to this election than is usual even in small country places—and that need not be. Barbara drove in to West Lynne, in her carriage; the two children with her, and the governess. The governess had wished to remain at home. Barbara would not hear of it; almost felt inclined to resent it as a slight: besides, if she took no interest in Mr. Carlyle, she must go to take care of Lucy: she, Barbara, would be too much occupied to look after children. So Madame Vine, perforce, stepped into the barouche and sat opposite to Mrs. Carlyle, her thick veil shading her features, and their pallor contrasting with the blue spectacles.

They alighted at the residence of Miss Carlyle. Quite a gathering was already there. Lady and Miss Dobede, the Herberts, Mrs. Hare, and many others; for the house was in a good spot for seeing the fun: and all people were eager to testify their respect for Mr. Carlyle. Miss Carlyle was in great grandeur; a brocaded dress, and a scarlet-and-purple bow in front of it, the size of a pumpkin. It was about the only occasion, in all Miss Carlyle's life, that she had deemed it necessary to attire herself magnificently. Barbara wore no bow, but she exhibited a splendid bouquet of scarlet-and-purple flowers. Mr. Carlyle had himself given it to her that morning.

Mr. Carlyle saw them all at the windows of the large upper drawing-room, and came in; he was then on his way to the Town-hall. Shaking hands, laughter, hearty and hasty good wishes; and he quitted the room again. Barbara stole after him for a sweeter farewell.

'God bless and prosper you, Archibald, my dearest!'

The business of the day began. Mr. Carlyle was proposed by Sir John Dobede, and seconded by Mr. Herbert. Lord Mount Severn, than whom not a busier man was there, would willingly have been proposer and seconder too, but he had no local influence in the place. Sir Francis Levison was proposed also by two gentlemen of standing. The show of hands was declared to be in favour of Mr. Carlyle. It was about twenty to one. Upon which the baronet's friends demanded a poll.

Then all was bustle, and scuffle, and confusion. Everybody tearing away to the hustings, which had been fixed in a convenient spot, the Town-hall not affording the accommodation necessary for a poll. Candidates, and proposers and seconders, and gentlemen, and officers, and mob, hustling and jostling each other. Mr. Carlyle was linked arm-in-arm with Sir John Dobede; Sir John's arm was within Lord Mount Severn's—but, as to order, it was impossible to observe any. To gain the place, they had to pass the house of Miss Carlyle. Young Vane, who was in the thick of the crowd—of course—cast his eyes up to its lined windows, took off his hat and waved it. 'Carlyle and honour for ever!' shouted out he.

The ladies laughed and nodded, and shook their handkerchiefs, and displayed their scarlet-and-purple colours. The crowd took up the shout, till the very air echoed with it. 'Carlyle and honour for ever!' Barbara's tears were falling; but she smiled through them at one pair of loving eyes which sought out hers.

'A galaxy of beauty!' whispered Mr. Drake, in the ear of Sir Francis. 'How the women rally round him! I tell you what, Levison: you and the government were stupid, to go on with the contest: and I said so, days ago. You have no more chance against Carlyle than that bit of straw in the air has against the wind. You ought to have withdrawn in time.'

'Like a coward!' angrily retorted Sir Francis. 'No. I'll go on with it to the last.'

'How lovely his wife is!' resumed Mr. Drake, his admiring eyes cast up at Barbara. 'I say, Levison, was the first one as charming?'

Sir Francis looked perfectly savage: the allusion did not please him. But, ere another word could be spoken, some one in the garb of a policeman, who had wound his way through the crowd, laid his hand on the baronet.

'Sir Francis Levison, you are my prisoner.'

Nothing worse than *debt* occurred at the moment to the mind of Sir Francis. But that was quite enough, and he turned purple with rage.

'Your hands off, vermin! How dare you?'

A quick movement, a slight click, a hustle from the wondering crowd more immediately around, and the handcuffs were on. Utter amazement alone prevented Mr. Drake from knocking down the policeman. A dozen vituperating tongues assailed him.

'I'm sorry to do it in this public place and manner,' said the officer, partly to Sir Francis, partly to the gentlemen around; 'but I couldn't come across him last night, do as I would. And the warrant has been in my hands since five o'clock yesterday afternoon. Sir Francis Levison, I arrest you for the wilful murder of George Hallijohn.'

The crowd fell back; the crowd was paralyzed with consternation; the word was passing from one extreme to the other, back, and across again, and the excitement grew high. The ladies, looking from Miss Carlyle's windows, saw what had happened, though they could not divine the cause. Some of them turned pale at the sight of the handcuffs, and Mary Pinner, an excitable girl, screamed.

Pale? What was their gentle paleness, compared with the frightfully livid hue that disfigured the features of Francis Levison? His agitation was pitiable to witness, his face a terror to look upon: once or twice he gasped, as if in an agony; and then his eyes happened to fall on Otway Bethel, who stood near. Shorn of its adornments—which might not be thought adornments on paper—the following was the sentence that burst involuntarily from his lips:

'You hound! It is you who have done this!'

'No! by—' Whether Mr. Otway Bethel was about to swear by Jupiter, or June, never was decided, the sentence being cut ignominiously short at the above two words. Another policeman, in the summary manner exercised towards Sir Francis, had clapped a pair of handcuffs upon *him*.

'Mr. Otway Bethel, I arrest you as an accomplice in the murder of George Hallijohn.'

You may be sure, the whole assembly was arrested too—figuratively; and stood with eager gaze and open ears. Colonel Bethel, quitting the scarlet-and-purple ranks, flashed into those of the yellows. He knew his nephew was graceless enough; but—to see him with a pair of handcuffs on!

'What does all this mean?' he authoritatively demanded of the officers.

'It's no fault of ours, colonel; we have but executed the warrant,' answered one of them. 'The magistrates issued it yesterday against these two gentlemen, on suspicion of their being concerned in the murder of Hallijohn.'

'In conjunction with Richard Hare?' cried the astounded colonel, gazing from one to the other, prisoners and officers, in scared bewilderment.

'It's alleged now, that Richard Hare didn't have nothing to do with it,' returned the man. 'It's said he is innocent. I'm sure *I* don't know.'

'I swear that *I* am innocent,' passionately uttered Otway Bethel.

'Well, sir, you have only got to prove it,' civilly rejoined the policeman.

Miss Carlyle and Lady Dobede leaned from the window; their curiosity too excited to remain silent longer. Mrs. Hare was standing by their side. 'What is the matter?' both asked of the upturned faces immediately beneath.

'Them two, the fine member, as wanted to be, and young Bethel, be arrested for murder,' spoke a man's clear voice in answer. 'The tale runs as they murdered Hallijohn, and then laid it on the shoulders of young Dick Hare, who didn't do it, after all.'

A faint wailing cry of startled pain, and Barbara flew to Mrs. Hare, from whom it proceeded. 'Oh, mamma, my dear mamma, take comfort! Do not suffer this to agitate you to illness. Richard is innocent, and it will surely be so proved. Archibald,' she added, beckoning to her husband, in her alarm, 'come, if you can, and say a word of assurance to mamma.'

It was impossible that Mr. Carlyle could hear the words: but he could see that his wife was agitated, and wanted him. 'I will be back with you in a few moments,' he said to his friends, as he began to elbow his way through the crowd: which made way, when they saw who the elbower was.

Into another room, away from the gay visitors, they got Mrs. Hare: and Mr. Carlyle locked the door to keep them out, unconsciously taking out the key. Only himself and his wife were with her, except Madame Vine, who had been despatched by somebody with a bottle of smelling salts. Barbara knelt at her mamma's feet; Mr. Carlyle leaned over her, her hands sympathizingly held in his. Madame Vine would have escaped, but the key was gone.

'Oh, Archibald, tell me the truth! *You* will not deceive me,' she gasped, in earnest entreaty, the cold dew gathering on her pale, gentle face. 'Is the time come to prove my boy's innocence?'

'It is.'

'Is it possible that it can be that false, bad man who is guilty?'

'From my soul I believe him to be,' replied Mr. Carlyle, glancing round to make sure that none could hear the assertion, save those present. 'But what I say to you and Barbara, I would not say to the world. Whatever be the man's guilt, I am not his Nemesis. Dear Mrs. Hare, take courage; take comfort: happier days are coming round.'

Mrs. Hare was weeping silently. Barbara rose, and laid her mamma's head lovingly upon her bosom.

'Take care of her, my darling,' Mr. Carlyle whispered to his wife. 'Don't leave her for a moment: and don't let that chattering crew in, from the next room. I beg your pardon, madame.'

His hand had touched Madame Vine's neck, in turning round; that is, had touched the jacket that encased it. He unlocked the door and regained the street: while Madame Vine sat down, with her beating and rebellious heart.

Amidst the shouts, the jeers, and the escort of the mob, Sir Francis Levison and Otway Bethel were lodged in the station-house, preparatory to their examination before the magistrates. Never, sure, was so mortifying an interruption known. So thought Sir Francis's party. And they deemed it well, after some consultation amongst themselves, to withdraw his name as a candidate for the membership. That he never had a shadow of chance from the first, most of them knew.

But there's an incident yet to tell of the election-day. You have seen Miss Carlyle in her glory, her brocaded silk, standing on end with richness, her displayed colours, her pride in her noble brother! But could she have divined who and what was right above her head, at an upper window, I know not what the consequences would have been.

No less than that 'brazen huzzy,' Afy Hallijohn! Smuggled in by Miss Carlyle's servants, there she was, in full dress too. A green-and-white-checked sarcenet, flounced up to the waist, over a crinoline extending from here to yonder; a fancy bonnet, worn on the plait of her hair behind, with a wreath and a veil; delicate white gloves, and a swinging handkerchief of lace, redolent of musk. It was well for Miss Corny's peace that she remained in ignorance of that daring act. There stood Afy bold as a sunflower exhibiting herself and her splendour to the admiring eyes of the mob below, gentle and simple.

'He is a handsome man, after all,' quoth she to Miss Carlyle's maids, when Sir Francis Levison arrived opposite the house.

'But such a horrid creature!' was the response. 'And to think that he should come here to oppose Mr. Archibald!'

'What's that?' cried Afy. 'What are they stopping for? There are some po-
licemen there! Oh,' shrieked Afy, 'if they haven't put handcuffs on him!
Whatever has he done? What can he have been up to?'

'Where? Who? What?' cried the servants bewildered with the crowd. 'Put
'ancuffs on which?'

'Sir Francis Levison. Hush! What is it they say?'

Listening; looking; turning from white to red, from red to white, Afy
stood. But she could make nothing of it: she could not divine the cause of the
commotion. The man's answer to Miss Carlyle and Lady Dobede, clear
though it was, did not quite reach her ears. 'What did he say?' she cried.

'Good Heavens!' cried one of the maids, whose hearing had been quicker
than Afy's. 'He says they are arrested for the wilful murder of Hal—of your
father, Miss Afy. Sir Francis Levison and Otway Bethel.'

'*What?*' shrieked Afy, her eyes starting.

'Levison was the man who did it, he says,' continued the servant, bending
her ear to listen. 'And young Richard Hare, he says, has been innocent all
along.'

Afy slowly gathered in the sense of the words; she gasped twice, as if her
breath had gone; and then, with a stagger and a shiver, fell heavily to the
ground. Afy Hallijohn was in a fainting fit.

☙ X V ❧

Mr. Jiffin

Afy Hallijohn, recovered from her fainting fit, had to be smuggled out of
Miss Carlyle's, as she had been smuggled in. She was of an elastic nature, and
the shock, or the surprise, or the heat—or whatever it might have been—
being over, Afy was herself again. She minced along, in all her vanity, on her
return to Mrs. Latimer's; her laced handkerchief flourishing from one hand,
and her flounces jauntily raised with the other, to the display of her worked
petticoat, and her kid boots, the heels a mile high. Let Afy alone for following the fashion, however preposterous it might be.

Not very far removed from the residence of Miss Carlyle was a shop, in the
cheese and ham and butter line. A very respectable shop, too, and kept by a
very respectable man. A young man of a mild countenance, who had purchased the good-will of the business; and came down from London to take
possession. His predecessor had amassed enough to retire, and people fore-

told that Mr. Jiffin would do the same. To say that Miss Carlyle dealt at the shop, will be sufficient to proclaim the good quality of the articles kept in it.

When Afy arrived opposite the shop, Mr. Jiffin was standing at the door; his shopman, inside, being at some urgent employment over the contents of a butter-cask. Afy stopped. Mr. Jiffin admired her uncommonly, and she, always ready for anything in that way, had already enjoyed several passing flirtations with him.

'Good day, Miss Hallijohn,' cried he, warmly, tucking up his white apron and pushing it round the back of his waist, in the best manner he could, as he held out his hand to her. For Afy had once hinted in terms of disparagement at that very apron.

'Oh—how are you, Jiffin?' cried Afy, loftily, pretending not to have seen him standing there. And she condescended to put the tips of her white gloves into the offered hand, as she coquetted with her handkerchief, her veil, and her ringlets. 'I thought you would have shut up your shop to-day, Mr. Jiffin, and taken holiday.'

'Business must be attended to,' responded Mr. Jiffin, quite lost in the contemplation of Afy's numerous attractions, unusually conspicuous as they were. 'Had I known that you were abroad, Miss Hallijohn, and enjoying holiday, perhaps I might have taken one, too, in the hope of coming across you somewhere or other.'

His words were bonâ fide as his admiration; Afy saw that. 'And he's as simple as a calf,' thought she.

'The greatest pleasure I have in life, Miss Hallijohn, is to see you go by the shop window,' continued Mr. Jiffin. 'I'm sure it's like as if the sun itself passed.'

'Dear me!' bridled Afy, with a simper, 'I don't know any good *that* can do you. You might have seen me go by, an hour or two ago—if you had possessed eyes. I was on my way to Miss Carlyle's,' she continued, with the air of one who proclaims the fact of a morning call upon a duchess.

'Where *could* my eyes have been?' ejaculated Mr. Jiffin, in an agony of regret. 'In some of them precious butter-tubs, I shouldn't wonder! We have had a bad lot in, Miss Hallijohn, and I am going to return them.'

'Oh,' said Afy, conspicuously resenting the remark. 'I don't know anything about that sort of thing. Butter-tubs are beneath me.'

'Of course, of course, Miss Hallijohn,' deprecated poor Jiffin. 'They are very profitable, though, to those who understand the trade.'

'What *is* all that shouting?' cried Afy, alluding to a tremendous noise in the distance, which had continued for some little time.

'It's the voters cheering Mr. Carlyle. I suppose you know that he's elected, Miss Hallijohn?'

'No, I don't.'

'The other was withdrawn by his friends, so they made a short work of it;

and Mr. Carlyle is our member. God bless him! there is not many like *him*.'

'Are all these customers? Dear me, you'll have enough to do to attend to them; your man can't do it all; so I won't stay talking any longer.'

With a gracious flourish of her flounces, and wave of the handkerchief, Afy sailed off. And Mr. Jiffin, when he could withdraw his fascinated eyes from following her, turned into his shop, to assist in serving four or five servant-girls, who had entered it.

'It wouldn't be such a bad catch, after all,' soliloquized Afy, as she and her crinoline swayed along. 'Of course I'd never put my nose inside the shop—unless it was to order things, like another customer. There is a private entrance, thank goodness! And they say he has got the room over the shop beautifully fitted up as a drawing-room, with a plate-glass chiffonier, and Brussels carpet, and rosewood chairs and sofa, and all the rest of it. The parlour, too, behind the shop, is comfortable, and I'd take care it was well furnished, if it isn't already. I'd make him buy a piano for the drawing-room: it looks stylish, even if one doesn't play upon it. And I'd keep two servants, cook and housemaid: 'tisn't I that would marry, to be waited upon by a black tinker of a maid-of-all-work. Jiffin is such a soft, he'd agree to anything. I'm sure he'd let me turn the house into a theatre, if I liked, so that I left him the shop free for his business. He is welcome to that: the shop shall be his department, and the rest of the house mine. What's the good of a husband, except to work for you? They are only a worry, looking at them in any other light. I wonder how many bedrooms there are? If there's none in the house of a good size, I'll have two rooms knocked into one. I never could sleep in a closet of a place. And I'll have a handsome bed with damask moreen hangings, one of those new Arabians, and a large mahogany wardrobe with wings, and a handsome glass and toilette, and a cheval-glass—besides the other necessary furniture. I'm not sure that I won't have a little iron bed put up for him, in a corner. Separate beds are quite the fashion now, amongst the nobility. I'll see. Yes; take it for all in all, it wouldn't be so bad a catch. The worst is the name. Jiffin. Joe Jiffin! How could I ever bear to be called Mrs. Joe Jiffin? Not but—Goodness me! what do you want?'

The interruption to Afy's aerial castle was caused by Mr. Ebenezer James. That gentleman, who had been walking with quick steps to overtake her, gave her flounces a twitch behind, to let her know somebody had come up.

'How are you, Afy? I was going after you to Mrs. Latimer's, not knowing but you had returned home. I saw you this morning at Miss Corny's windows.'

'Now, I don't want any of your sauce, Ebenezer James. Afy-ing me! The other day, when you were on with your nonsense, I said you should keep your distance. You told Mr. Jiffin that I was an old sweetheart of yours. I heard of it!'

'So you were,' laughed Mr. Ebenezer.

'I never was,' flashed Afy. 'I was the company of your betters in those days: and if there had been no betters in the case, I should have scorned *you*. Why, you have been a strolling player!'

'And what have you been?' returned Mr. Ebenezer, a quiet tone of meaning running through his good-humoured laughter.

Afy's cheeks flushed scarlet, and she raised her hand with a quick, menacing gesture. But that they were in the public street, Mr. Ebenezer might have found his ears boxed. Afy dropped her hand again, and made a dead stand-still.

'If you think any vile, false insinuations, that you may concoct, will injure me, you are mistaken, Ebenezer James. I am too much respected in the place. So don't you try it on.'

'Why, Afy, what has put you out? *I* don't want to injure you. Couldn't do it, if I tried, as you say,' he added, with another quiet laugh. 'I have been in too many scrapes myself, to let my tongue bring other folks into one.'

'There, that's enough. Just take yourself off. It's not over reputable to have you at one's side in public.'

'Well, I will relieve you of my company, if you'll let me deliver my commission. Though as to "reputable"—however, I won't put you out further. You are wanted at the justice-room at three o'clock this afternoon. And don't fail, please.'

'Wanted at the justice-room!' retorted Afy. 'I! What for?'

'And must not fail, as I say,' repeated Mr. Ebenezer. 'You saw Levison taken up; your old flame—'

Afy stamped her foot in indignant interruption. 'Take care what you say, Ebenezer James! Flame! He? I'll have you up for defamation of character.'

'Don't be a goose, Afy. It's of no use riding the high horse with me. You know where I saw you; and saw him. People here said you were with Dick Hare: I could have told them better: but I did not. It was no affair of mine, that I should proclaim it, neither is it now. Levison, *alias* Thorn, is taken up for your father's murder, and you are wanted to give evidence.'

A change came over Miss Afy. Her lofty looks changed to an aspect particularly cowed and humble, not to say of terror. 'I know nothing of the murder!' she stammered, striving to brave it out still, in words and tone. 'And I will not attend.'

'You must, Afy,' he answered, putting a piece of paper in her hand. 'There! that's your subpœna. Ball thought you would not come without one.'

'I will never give evidence against Levison,' she uttered, tearing the subpœna to pieces, and scattering them in the street. 'I swear I won't. There, for you! Will I help to hang an innocent man, when it was Dick Hare who was the guilty one? No! I'll walk myself off a hundred miles away first, and stop in hiding till it's over. I shan't forget this turn that you have chosen to play me, Ebenezer James.'

'*I* chosen! Why, do you suppose I have anything to do with it? Don't take up that notion, Afy. Mr. Ball put that subpœna in my hand, and told me to serve it. He might have given it to the other clerk, just as he gave it to me: it was all chance. If I could do you a good turn, I'd do it: not a bad one.'

Afy strode on at railway speed, waving him off. 'Mind you don't fail, Afy!' he said, as he prepared to return.

'Fail,' answered she, with flashing eyes. 'I shall fail giving evidence, if you mean that. They don't get me up to their justice-room. Neither by force nor stratagem.'

Ebenezer James looked after her as she tore along. 'What a spirit that Afy has got, when it's put up!' quoth he. 'She'll be off out of reach, unless she's stopped. She's a great simpleton! nothing particular need come out about her and Thorn: unless she lets it out herself in her tantrums. Here comes Ball, I declare! I must tell him.'

On went Afy, and gained Mrs. Latimer's. That lady, suffering from indisposition, was confined to the house. Afy, divesting herself of certain little odds and ends of her finery, made her way into Mrs. Latimer's presence.

'Oh, ma'am, such heart-rending news as I have had!' began she. 'A relation of mine is dying, and wants to see me. I ought to be away by the next train.'

'Dear me!' cried Mrs. Latimer, after a pause of dismay. 'But how can I do without you, Afy?'

'It's a dying request, ma'am,' pleaded Afy, covering her eyes with her handkerchief—not the lace one—as if in the depth of woe. 'Of course I wouldn't ask you, under any other circumstances, suffering as you are!'

'Where does your relation live?' asked Mrs. Latimer. 'How long shall you be away?'

Afy mentioned the first town that came uppermost, and 'hoped' she might be back to-morrow.

'What relation is it?' continued Mrs. Latimer. 'I thought you had no relatives; except Joyce, and your aunt, Mrs. Kane.'

'This is another aunt,' cried Afy, softly. 'I have never mentioned her, not being friends. Differences divided us. Of course that makes me all the more anxious to obey her request.'

An uncommon good hand at an impromptu tale was Afy. And Mrs. Latimer consented to her demand. Afy flew upstairs, attired herself once more, put up one or two things in a small leather bag, placed some money in her purse, and left the house.

Sauntering idly on the pavement on the sunny side of the street, was a policeman. He crossed over to Afy, with whom he had a slight acquaintance.

'Good-day, Miss Hallijohn. A fine day, is it not?'

'Fine enough,' returned Afy, provoked at being hindered. 'I can't talk to you now, for I am in a hurry.'

The faster she walked, the faster he walked, keeping at her side. Afy's pace increased to a run. His increased to a run too.

'Why are you in such haste?' asked he.

'Well, it's nothing to you. And I'm sure I don't want you to dance attendance upon me just now. There's a time for all things. I'll have some chatter with you another day.'

'One would think you were hurrying to catch a train.'

'So I am—if you must have your curiosity gratified. I am going out on a little pleasure excursion, Mr. Inquisitive.'

'For long?'

'U—m. Home to-morrow, perhaps. Is it true that Mr. Carlyle's elected?'

'Oh yes. Don't go up that way, please.'

'Not up this way?' repeated Afy. 'It's the nearest road to the station. It cuts off all that corner.'

The officer laid his hand upon her gently. Afy thought he was venturing it in sport—as if deeming her too charming to be parted with.

'What do you mean by your nonsense? I tell you I have not time for it now. Take your hand off me,' she added angrily—for the hand was clasping her closer.

'I am sorry to hurt a lady's feelings, especially yours, Miss: but I daren't take it off, and I daren't part with you. My instructions are to take you on at once to the witness-room. Your evidence is wanted this afternoon.'

If you ever saw a ghost more livid than ghosts in ordinary, you may picture to your mind the appearance of Afy Hallijohn just then. She did not faint, as she had done once before, that day, but she looked as if she should die. One sharp cry, instantly suppressed, for Afy did retain some presence of mind, and remembered that she was in the public road; one sharp tussle for liberty, and she resigned herself, perforce, to her fate.

'I have no evidence to give,' she said, in a calmer tone. 'I know nothing of the facts.'

'I'm sure *I* don't know anything of them,' returned the man. 'I don't know why you are wanted. When instructions are given us, miss, we can't ask what they mean. I was bid to watch that you didn't go off out of the town, and to bring you on to the witness-room, if you attempted it, and I have tried to do it as politely as possible.'

'You don't imagine I am going to walk through West Lynne with your hand upon me.'

'I'll take it off, Miss Hallijohn, if you'll give a promise not to bolt. You see, 'twould come to nothing, if you did; for I should be up with you in a couple of yards—besides it would be drawing folks' attention on you. You couldn't hope to outrun me, or to be a match for me in strength.'

'I will go quietly,' said Afy. 'Take it off.'

She kept her word. Afy was no simpleton, and knew that she *was* no match for him. She had fallen into the hands of the Philistines, and must make the best of it. So they walked through the street as if they were but taking a quiet stroll; he gallantly bearing the leather bag. Miss Carlyle's shocked eyes happened to fall upon them as they passed her window: she wondered where could be the eyes of the man's inspector.

Afy was lodged in the witness-room; a small room with a skylight at the top. She passed her time pretty agreeably, considering all things: partly in concocting a tale to tell to Mrs. Latimer; partly in deliberating how much she might admit before the justices, without compromising herself. But, in using the word 'compromising,' you must not suppose it refers to the murder. Afy was as innocent of that as you or I: she firmly believed in Levison's innocence, and in the guilt of Richard Hare. Still Afy was aware that her doings at that period would not shine out clearly in the full light of day, or in the gossip of West Lynne.

❧ X V I ☙

The Justice-Room

The magistrates took their seats on the bench. The bench would not hold them: all in the Commission of the Peace flocked in. Any other day, they would not have been at West Lynne. As to the room, the wonder was, how it ever got emptied again, so densely was it packed. Sir Francis Levison's friends were there in a body. They did not believe a word of the accusation: a scandalous affair, cried they, got up probably by some of the scarlet-and-purple party. Lord Mount Severn, who chose to be present, had a place assigned him on the bench; Lord Vane got the best place he could fight for amidst the crowd. Mr. Justice Hare sat as chairman, unusually stern, unbending, and grim. No favour would he show; but no unfairness: had it been to save his son from hanging, he would not adjudge guilt to Sir Francis Levison against his conscience. Colonel Bethel was likewise on the bench; stern also.

In that primitive place—primitive in what related to the justice-room and the justices—things were not conducted with the regularity of the law. The law there was often a dead letter. No very grave cases were decided there: they went to Lynneborough; a month at the treadmill, or a week's imprisonment, or a bout of whipping for juveniles, were pretty nearly the harshest sentences pronounced. In this examination, as in others, evidence was advanced that was inadmissible—at least that would have been inadmissible in a more orthodox court; hearsay testimony, and irregularities of that nature. Mr. Rubiny watched the case on behalf of Sir Francis Levison.

Mr. Ball opened the proceedings; giving the account which had been imparted to him by Richard Hare, but not mentioning Richard as his informant. He was questioned as to whence he obtained his information, but replied that it was not convenient at present to disclose the source. The stumbling-block to the magistrates appeared to be, the identifying Levison with Thorn. Ebenezer James came forward to prove it.

'What do you know of the prisoner, Sir Francis Levison?' questioned Justice Herbert.

'Not much,' responded Mr. Ebenezer. 'I used to know him as Captain Thorn.'

'*Captain* Thorn?'

'Afy Hallijohn called him captain; but I understood he was but a lieutenant.'

'From whom did you understand that?'

'From Afy. She was the only person I heard speak of him.'

'And you say you were in the habit of seeing him?—in the place mentioned, the Abbey Wood?'

'I saw him there repeatedly: also at Hallijohn's cottage.'

'Did you speak with him—as Thorn?'

'Two or three times. I addressed him as Thorn, and he answered to the name. I had no suspicion but what it was his name. Otway Bethel'—casting his eyes on Mr. Otway, who stood in his shaggy attire—'also knew him as Thorn; and so, I make no doubt, did Locksley, for he was always in the wood.'

'Anybody else?'

'Poor Hallijohn himself knew him as Thorn. He said to Afy one day, in my presence, that he would not have that confounded dandy, Thorn, coming there.'

'Were those the words he used?'

'They were. "That confounded dandy, Thorn." I remember Afy's reply: it was rather insolent. She said Thorn was as free to come there as anybody else; and she would not be found fault with, as though she was not fit to take care of herself.'

'That is nothing to the purpose. Were any others acquainted with Thorn?'

'I should imagine the elder sister, Joyce, was. And the one who knew him best of all, was young Richard Hare.'

Old Richard Hare, from his place on the bench, frowned menacingly at an imaginary Richard.

'What took Thorn into the wood so often?'

'He was courting Afy.'

'With an intention of marrying her?'

'Well—no,' cried Mr. Ebenezer, with a twist of the mouth; 'I should not suppose he entertained any intention of that sort. He used to come over from Swainson, or its neighbourhood; riding a splendid horse.'

'Whom did you suppose him to be?'

'I supposed him to be moving in the upper ranks of life. There was no doubt of it. His dress, his manners, his tone, all proclaimed it. He appeared to wish to shun observation, and evidently did not care to be seen. He rarely arrived until twilight.'

'Did you see him there on the night of Hallijohn's murder?'

'No. I was not there myself that evening, so could not have seen him.'

'Did a suspicion cross your mind at any time that he may have been guilty of the murder?'

'Never. Richard Hare was accused of it, and it never occurred to me to suppose that he had not done it.'

'Pray how many years is this ago?' sharply interrupted Mr. Rubiny, perceiving that the witness was done with.

'Let's see,' responded Mr. Ebenezer. 'I can't be sure as to a year, without reckoning up. A dozen, if not more.'

'And you mean to say that you can swear to Sir Francis Levison being that man—with all those years intervening?'

'I swear that he is the same man. I am as positive of his identity as I am of my own.'

'Without having seen him from that time to this!' derisively returned the lawyer. 'Nonsense, witness!'

'I did not say that,' returned Mr. Ebenezer.

The court pricked up its ears. 'Have you seen him between then and now?' asked one of them.

'Once.'

'Where, and when?'

'It was in London. About eighteen months after the period of the murder.'

'What communication had you with him?'

'None at all. I only saw him. Quite by chance.'

'And whom did you suppose him to be then? Thorn?—or Levison?'

'Thorn, certainly. I never dreamt of his being Levison, until he appeared here now to oppose Mr. Carlyle.'

A wild, savage curse shot through Sir Francis's heart as he heard the words. What demon *had* possessed him to venture his neck into the lion's den? There had been a strong, hidden power holding him back from it, independent of his dislike to face Mr. Carlyle: how could he have been so mad as to disregard it? How?

'You may have been mistaken, witness, as to the identity of the man you saw in London. It may not have been the Thorn you had known here.'

Mr. Ebenezer James smiled a peculiar smile. 'I was not mistaken,' he said, his tone sounding remarkably significant. 'I am upon my oath.'

'Call Aphrodite Hallijohn.'

The lady appeared, supported by her friend the policeman. And Mr. Ebenezer James was desired by Mr. Ball to leave the court while she gave her evidence. Doubtless he had his reasons.

'What is your name?'

'Afy,' replied she, looking daggers at everybody, and sedulously keeping her back turned upon Francis Levison and Otway Bethel.

'Your name in full, if you please. You were not christened "Afy?"'

'Aphrodite Hallijohn. You all know my name as well as I do. Where's the use of asking useless questions?'

'Swear the witness,' said Mr. Justice Hare. The first word he had uttered.

'I won't be sworn,' said Afy.

'You must be sworn,' said Mr. Justice Herbert.

'But I say I won't,' repeated Afy.

'Then we must commit you to prison for contempt of court.'

There was no mercy in his tone, and Afy turned white. Sir John Dobede interposed.

'Young woman, had *you* a hand in the murder of your father?'

'I!' returned Afy, struggling with passion, temper, and excitement. 'How dare you ask me so unnatural a question, sir? He was the kindest father!' she added, battling with her tears. 'I loved him dearly. I would have saved his life with mine.'

'And yet you refuse to give evidence that may assist in bringing his destroyer to justice!'

'No; I don't refuse on that score. I should like his destroyer to be hanged, and I'd go to see it. But who knows what other questions you may be asking me—about things that concern neither you nor anybody else? That's why I object.'

'We have only to deal with what bears upon the murder. The questions put to you will relate to that.'

Afy considered. 'Well, you may swear me, then,' she said. Little notion had she of the broad gauge those questions would run upon. And she was sworn accordingly. Very unwillingly yet. For Afy, who would have told lies by the bushel *unsworn*, did look upon an oath as a serious matter, and felt herself compelled to speak the truth when examined under it.

'How did you become acquainted with a gentleman you often saw in those days—Captain Thorn?'

'There!' uttered the dismayed Afy. 'You are beginning already. *He* had nothing to do with it. He did not do the murder.'

'You have sworn to answer the questions put,' was the uncompromising rejoinder. 'How did you become acquainted with Captain Thorn?'

'I met him at Swainson,' doggedly answered Afy. 'I went over there one day, just for a spree, and I met him at a pastrycook's.'

'And he fell in love with your pretty face?' said Lawyer Ball, taking up the examination.

In the incense to her vanity, Afy nearly forgot her scruples. 'Yes, he did,' she answered, casting a smile of general fascination round upon the court.

'And got out of you where you lived; and entered upon his courting; riding over nearly every evening to see you?'

'Well,' acknowledged Afy, 'there was no harm in it.'

'Oh, certainly not,' acquiesced the lawyer, in a pleasant, free tone, to put the witness at her ease. 'Rather good, I should say: I wish I had had the like luck. Did you know him at that time by the name of Levison?'

'No. He said he was Captain Thorn, and I thought he was.'

'Did you know where he lived?'

'No. He never said that. I thought he was stopping temporarily at Swainson.'

'And—dear me! what a sweet bonnet that is you have on!'

Afy—whose egregious vanity was her besetting sin, who possessed enough of it for any ten pretty women going—cast a glance out of the corners of her eyes at the admired bonnet, and became Mr. Ball's entirely.

'And how long was it, after your first meeting with him, before you discovered his real name?'

'Not for a long time. Several months.'

'Subsequent to the murder, I presume?'

'Oh yes.'

Mr. Ball's eyes gave a twinkle, and the unconscious Afy surreptitiously smoothed, with one finger, the glossy parting of her hair.

'Besides Captain Thorn, what gentlemen were in the wood, the night of the murder?'

'Richard Hare was there. Otway Bethel and Locksley also. Those were all I saw—until the crowd came.'

'Were Locksley and Mr. Otway Bethel martyrs to your charms—as the other two were?'

'No indeed,' was the witness's answer, with an indignant toss of the head. 'A couple of poaching fellows, like them! They had better have tried it on!'

'Which of the two, Hare or Thorn, was inside the cottage with you that evening?'

Afy came out of her vanity and hesitated. She was beginning to wonder where the questions would get to.

'You are upon your oath, witness,' thundered Mr. Justice Hare. 'If it was my—if it was Richard Hare who was with you, say so. But there must be no equivocation here.'

Afy was startled. 'It was Thorn,' she answered to Mr. Ball.

'And where was Richard Hare?'

'I don't know. He came down, but I sent him away: I would not admit him. I dare say he lingered in the wood.'

'Did he leave a gun with you?'

'Yes. It was one he had promised to lend my father. I put it down just inside the door: he told me it was loaded.'

'How long after this was it, before your father interrupted you?'

'He didn't interrupt us at all,' returned Afy. 'I never saw my father until I saw him dead.'

'Were you not in the cottage all the time?'

'No. We went out for a stroll at the back. Captain Thorn wished me good-bye there, and I stayed out.'

'Did you hear the gun go off?'

'I heard a shot, as I was sitting on the stump of a tree, and thinking. But I attached no importance to it, never supposing it was in the cottage.'

'What was it that Captain Thorn had to get from the cottage after he quitted you? What had he left there?'

Now this was a random shaft. Lawyer Ball, a keen man, who had well weighed all points in the tale imparted to him by Richard Hare, as well as other points, had made his own deductions, and spoke accordingly. Afy was taken in.

'He had left his hat there; nothing else. It was a warm evening, and he had gone out without it.'

'He told you, I believe, sufficient to convince you of the guilt of Richard Hare?' Another shaft thrown at random.

'I did not want convincing. I knew it without. Everybody else knew it.'

'To be sure,' equally returned Lawyer Ball. 'Did Captain Thorn *see* it done?—did he tell you that?'

'He had got his hat and was away down the wood some little distance, when he heard voices in dispute in the cottage, and recognized one of them to be that of my father. The shot followed close upon it, and he guessed some mischief had been done: though he did not suspect its extent.'

'Thorn told you this! When?'

'The same night; much later.'

'How came you to see him?'

Afy hesitated. But she was sternly told to answer the question.

'A boy came up to the cottage and called me out, and said a strange gentleman wanted to see me in the wood, and had given him sixpence to come for me. I went, and found Captain Thorn. He asked what the commotion was about, and I told him Richard Hare had killed my father. He said that now I spoke of him, he could recognize Richard Hare's as having been the other voice in the dispute.'

'What boy was that?—the one who came for you?'

'It was Mother Whiteman's little son.'

'And CaptainThorn then gave you this version of the tragedy?'

'It was the right version,' resentfully spoke Afy.

'How do you know that?'

'Oh, because I am sure it was. Who else would kill him but Richard Hare? It is a scandalous shame, you wanting to put it upon Thorn.'

'Look at the prisoner, Sir Francis Levison. Is it he whom you knew as Thorn?'

'Yes. But that does not make him guilty of the murder.'

'Of course it does not,' complacently assented Lawyer Ball. 'How long did you remain with Captain Thorn in London? Upon that little visit, you know.'

Afy stared like anybody moonstruck.

'When you quitted this place after the tragedy, it was to join Captain Thorn in London. How long, I ask, did you remain with him?' Entirely a random shaft, this.

'Who says I was with him? Who says I went after him?' flashed Afy, with scarlet cheeks.

'I do,' replied Lawyer Ball, taking note of her confusion. 'Come, it's over and done with; it's of no use to deny it now. We all go upon visits to friends sometimes.'

'I never heard anything so bold!' cried Afy. 'Where will you tell me I went next?'

'You are upon your oath, woman!' again interposed Justice Hare, and a trembling, as of agitation, might be detected in his voice, in spite of its ringing severity. 'Were you with the prisoner Levison, or were you with Richard Hare?'

'*I* with Richard Hare!' cried Afy, agitated in her turn, and shaking like an aspen-leaf, partly with discomfiture, partly with an unknown dread. 'How dare that cruel falsehood be brought up again to my face? I never saw Richard Hare after the night of the murder. I swear it. I swear that I have never seen him since. Visit *him!* I'd sooner visit Calcraft the hangman.'

There was truth in the words; in the tone. The chairman let fall the hand which had been raised to his face, holding on his eye-glasses; and a sort of self-condemning fear arose, confusing his brain. His son, proved innocent of one part, *might* be proved innocent of the other, and then—how would his own harsh conduct show out? West Lynne, in its charity, the justice, in his, had cast more odium to Richard with regard to his after-conduct touching this girl, than it had on the score of the murder.

'Come,' said Lawyer Ball, in a coaxing tone. 'let us be pleasant. Of course you were not with Richard Hare; West Lynne was always ill-natured; you were only on a visit to Captain Thorn, as—as any other young lady might be?'

Afy hung her head, cowed down to abject meekness.

'Answer the question,' came forth the chairman's voice again. '*Were* you with Thorn?'

'Yes.' Though the answer was feeble enough.

Mr. Ball coughed an insinuating cough. 'Did you remain with him—say, two or three years?'

'Not three.'

'A little over two, perhaps?'

'There was no harm in it,' shrieked Afy, with a catching sob of temper. 'If I chose to live in London, and he chose to make a morning call upon me now and then, as an old friend, what's that to anybody? Where was the harm, I ask?'

'Certainly—where was the harm? *I* am not insinuating any,' returned Lawyer Ball, with a wink of the eye furthest from the witness and the bench. 'And, during the time that—that he was making these little morning calls upon you, did you know him to be Levison?'

'Yes. I knew him to be Captain Levison then.'

'Did he ever tell you why he had assumed the name of Thorn?'

'Only for a whim, he said. The day he spoke to me in the pastrycook's shop at Swainson, something came over him, in the spur of the moment, not to give his right name, so he gave the first that came into his head. He never thought to retain it; or that other people would hear of him by it.'

'I dare say not,' said Lawyer Ball, drily. 'Well, Miss Afy, I believe that is all, for the present. I want Ebenezer James in again,' he whispered to an officer of the justice-room, as the witness retired.

Ebenezer James reappeared and took Afy's place. 'You informed their worships just now that you had met Thorn in London, some eighteen months subsequent to the murder,' began Lawyer Ball, launching another of his shafts. 'This must have been during Afy Hallijohn's sojourn with him. Did you also see *her?*'

Mr. Ebenezer opened his eyes. He knew nothing of the evidence just given by Afy, and wondered how on earth it had come out—that she had been with Thorn at all. He had never betrayed it. 'Afy?' stammered he.

'Yes, Afy,' sharply returned the lawyer. 'Their worships know that, when she left West Lynne, it was to join Thorn, not Richard Hare—though the latter has borne the credit of it. I ask you, did you see her? for she was then still connected with him.'

'Well—yes; I did,' replied Mr. Ebenezer, his own scruples removed, but wondering still how it had been discovered; unless Afy had—as he had half-prophesied she would—let it out in her 'tantrums.' 'In fact, it was Afy whom I first saw.'

'State the circumstances.'

'I was up Paddington way one afternoon, and saw a lady going into a house. It was Afy Hallijohn. She lived there, I found—had the drawing-room apartments. She invited me to stay tea with her, and I did.'

'Did you see Captain Levison there?'

'I saw Thorn—as I thought him to be. Afy told me I must be away by eight o'clock, for she was expecting a friend, who sometimes came to sit with her for an hour's chat. But, in talking over old times—not that I could tell her much about West Lynne, for I had left it almost as long as she had—the time slipped on, past the hour. When Afy found that out, she hurried me off, and I had barely got outside the gate when a cab drove up, and Thorn alighted from it, and let himself in with a latch-key. That is all I know.'

'When you knew that the scandal of Afy's absence rested on Richard Hare, why could you not have said this, and cleared him, on your return to West Lynne?'

'It was no affair of mine that I should make it public. Afy asked me not to say I had seen her, and I promised her I would not. As to Richard Hare—a little extra scandal on his back was nothing; while there remained on it the worse scandal of murder.'

'Stop a bit,' interposed Mr. Rubiny, as the witness was about to retire. 'You speak of the time being eight o'clock in the evening, sir. Was it dark?'

'Yes.'

'Then how could you be certain it was Thorn, who got out of the cab and entered?'

'I am quite certain. There was a gas-lamp right in the spot, and I saw him as well as I should have seen him in daylight. I knew his voice too: could have sworn to it anywhere: and I could almost have sworn to him by his splendid diamond ring. It flashed in the lamplight.'

'His voice! Did he speak to you?'

'No. But he spoke to the cabman. There was a half dispute between them. The man said Thorn had not paid him enough: that he had not allowed for the having kept him waiting twenty minutes on the road. Thorn swore at him a bit, and then flung him an extra shilling.'

The next witness was a man who had been groom to the late Sir Peter Levison. He testified that the prisoner, Francis Levison, had been on a visit to his master late in the summer and part of the autumn, the year that Hallijohn was killed. That he frequently rode out in the direction of West Lynne, especially towards evening, would be away three or four hours, and come home with the horse in a foam. Also that he picked up two letters at different times, which Mr. Levison had carelessly let fall from his pocket, and returned them to him. Both the notes were addressed 'Captain Thorn.' But they had not been through the post, for there was no further superscription on them; and the writing looked like a lady's. He remembered quite well hearing of the murder of Hallijohn, the witness added, in answer to a question; it made a great stir throughout the country. It was just at that same time that Mr. Levison concluded his visit and returned to London.'

'A *wonderful* memory!' Mr. Rubiny sarcastically remarked.

The witness, a quiet, respectable man, replied that he *had* a good memory: but the circumstances had impressed upon it particularly the fact that Mr. Levison's departure followed close upon the murder of Hallijohn.

'What circumstances?' demanded the bench.

'One day, when Sir Peter was round at the stables, gentlemen, he was urging his nephew to prolong his visit, and asked what sudden freak was taking him off. Mr. Levison replied that unexpected business called him to London. While they were talking, the coachman came up, all in a heat, telling that Hallijohn of West Lynne had been murdered by young Mr. Hare. I remember Sir Peter said he could not believe it; and that it must have been an accident, not murder.'

'Is this all?'

'There was more said. Mr. Levison, in a shame-faced sort of manner, asked his uncle, would he let him have five or ten pounds? Sir Peter seemed angry, and asked, what had he done with the fifty-pound note he had made him a present of, only the previous morning? Mr. Levison replied that he had sent that away in a letter to a brother officer, to whom he was in debt. Sir Peter refused to believe it, and said he was more likely to have squandered it upon some disgraceful folly. Mr. Levison denied that he had: but he looked confused: indeed, his manner altogether was confused that morning.'

'Did he get the five or ten pounds?'

'I don't know, gentlemen. I dare say he did, for my master was as persuadable as a woman, though he'd fly out a bit sometimes at first. Mr. Levison departed for London that same night.'

The last witness called was Mr. Dill. On the previous Tuesday evening, he had been returning home from spending an hour at Mr. Beauchamp's, when, in the field opposite to Mr. Justice Hare's, he suddenly heard a commotion. It arose from the meeting of Sir Francis Levison and Otway Bethel. The former appeared to have been enjoying a solitary moonlight ramble: and the latter to have encountered him unexpectedly. Words ensued. Bethel accused Sir Francis of 'shirking' him; Sir Francis answered angrily—that he knew nothing of him, and nothing he wanted to know.

'You were glad enough to know something of me the night of Hallijohn's murder,' retorted Bethel to this. 'Do you remember that I could hang you? One little word from me, and you would stand in Dick Hare's place.'

'You fool!' passionately cried Sir Francis. 'You could not hang me without putting your own head in the noose. Had you not your hush-money? Are you wanting to do me out of more?'

'A cursed paltry note of fifty pounds!' foamed Otway Bethel, 'which, many a time since, I have wished my fingers had been blown off before they touched. I never should have touched it, but that I was altogether over-whelmed with the moment's confusion. I have not been able to look Mrs. Hare in the face since—knowing I hold the secret that would save her son from the hangman.'

'And put yourself in his place,' sneered Sir Francis.

'No. Put you.'

'That's as it might be. But if I went to the hangman, you would go with me. There would be no excuse or escape for you. You know it.'

The warfare continued longer, but this was the cream of it. Mr. Dill heard the whole, and repeated it now to the magistrates. Mr. Rubiny protested that it was 'inadmissible;' 'hearsay evidence;' 'contrary to law:' but the bench oracularly put Mr. Rubiny down, and told him they did not require any stranger to come there and teach them their business.

Colonel Bethel had leaned forward at the conclusion of Mr. Dill's evidence, dismay on his face, agitation in his voice. 'Are you sure that you made no mistake?—that the other in this interview was Otway Bethel?'

Mr. Dill sadly shook his head. 'Am I one to swear to a wrong man, colonel? I wish I had not heard it—save that it may be the means of clearing Richard Hare.'

Sir Francis Levison had braved out the proceedings with a haughty, cavalier air, his delicate hands and his diamond ring remarkably conspicuous. Was that stone the real thing, or a false one substituted for the real? Hard up as he had long been for money, the suspicion might arise. A derisive smile crossed his features at parts of the evidence, as much as to say, You may convict me as to Mademoiselle Afy; but you cannot, as to the murder. When, however, Mr. Dill's testimony was given, what a change was there! His mood tamed down to what looked like abject fear.

'Of course your worships will take bail for Sir Francis,' said Mr. Rubiny, at the close of the proceedings.

Bail! The bench looked at one another.

'Your worships will not refuse it—a gentleman in Sir Francis Levison's position!'

The bench thought they had never had so insolent an application made to them. Bail for him—on this charge! No; not if the lord chancellor himself came down to offer it.

Mr. Otway Bethel, conscious, probably, that nobody would offer bail for him, not even the colonel, did not ask the bench to take it. So the two were fully committed to take their trial for the 'Wilful murder, otherwise the killing and slaying, of George Hallijohn.'

And that vain, ill-starred Afy? What of her? Well, Afy had again retired to the witness-room, after giving evidence, and there she remained till the close, agreeably occupied in mental debate. What would they make out from her admissions regarding her sojourn in London and the morning calls? How would that precious West Lynne construe it? She did not much care; she should brave it out, and assail them with towering indignation, did any dare to cast a stone at her.

Such was her final decision, arrived at just as the proceedings terminated. Afy was right glad to remain where she was till some of the bustle had gone.

'How has it ended?' asked she of Mr. Ball, who, being a bachelor, was ever regarded with much graciousness by Afy, for she kept her eyes open to contingencies; although Mr. Joe Jiffin was held as a reserve.

'They are both committed for wilful murder. Off to Lynneborough in an hour.'

Afy's choler rose. 'What a shame! To commit two innocent men upon such a charge!'

'I can tell you what, Miss Afy, the sooner you disabuse your mind of that prejudice the better. Levison has been as good as proved guilty to-day: but, if proof were wanting, he and Bethel have criminated each other. "When rogues fall out, honest men get their own." Not that I can quite fathom Bethel's share in the exploit: though I can pretty well guess at it. And, in proving themselves guilty, they have proved the innocence of Richard Hare.'

Afy's face was changing to whiteness; her confident air to one of dread; her vanity to humiliation.

'It—can't—be—true!' she gasped.

'It's true enough. The part you have hitherto ascribed to Thorn, was enacted by Richard Hare. He heard the shot from his place in the wood, and saw Thorn run, ghastly, trembling, horrified, from his wicked work. Believe me, it was Thorn who killed your father.'

Afy grew cold as she listened. That one awful moment, when conviction, that his words were true, forced itself upon her, was enough to sober her for a whole lifetime. *Thorn!* Her sight failed; her head reeled; her very heart turned to sickness. One struggling cry of pain; and for the second time that day, Afy Hallijohn fell forward in a fainting fit.

Shouts, hisses, execrations, yells! The prisoners were being brought forth to be conveyed to Lynneborough. A whole posse of constables was necessary to protect them against the outbreak of the mob, which outbreak was not directed against Otway Bethel, but against Sir Francis Levison. Cowering, like the guilty culprit that he was, he shivered, and hid his white face, wondering whether it would be a repetition of Justice Hare's green pond, or the tearing him asunder piece-meal; and cursing the earth because it did not open and let him in!

❧ XVII ☙

Fire

Miss Lucy was *en pénitence*. She had been guilty of some childish fault that day at Aunt Cornelia's, which, coming to the knowledge of Mrs. Carlyle after their return home, the young lady was ordered to the nursery for the rest of the day, to be regaled upon bread and water.

Barbara was in her pleasant dressing-room. There was to be a dinner party at East Lynne that evening, and she had just finished dressing. Very lovely she looked in her dinner-dress, with purple and scarlet flowers, just plucked from the conservatory, in her hair, and a bouquet of scarlet and purple flowers in her bosom. She glanced at her watch somewhat anxiously, for the gentlemen had not made their appearance. Half-past six! and they were to dine at seven.

Madame Vine tapped at the door. Her errand was to beg grace for Lucy, who had been promised half-an-hour in the drawing-room, when the ladies entered it from the dessert-table, and was now in an agony of grief at the disappointment. Would Mrs. Carlyle pardon her and allow her to be dressed?

'You are too lenient to that child, madame,' said Barbara. 'I don't think you ever would punish her at all. But when she commits faults, they must be corrected.'

'She is very sorry for her fault; she promises not to be rude again. She is crying as if she would cry her heart out.'

'Not for her ill-behaviour, but because she is afraid of missing the drawing-room to-night,' cried Barbara.

'Do pray restore her to favour,' pleaded madame.

'I shall see. Just look, Madame Vine! I broke this, a minute or two ago. Is it not a pity?'

Barbara held in her hand a beautiful toilet ornament, set in gold. One of the petals had come off.

Madame Vine examined it. 'I have some cement upstairs that would join it,' she exclaimed. 'I could do it in two minutes.'

'Oh, I wish you would,' was Barbara's delighted response. 'Do bring the cement here and join it now. Shall I bribe you?' she added, laughing. 'You make this all right, and then you shall bear back grace to Lucy—for I perceive that is what your heart is set upon.'

Madame Vine went, and returned with her cement. Barbara watched her, as she took the pieces in her hand, to see how the one must fit on to the other.

'This has been broken once before, Joyce tells me,' Barbara said. 'But it must have been imperceptibly joined, for I have looked in vain for the damage. Mr. Carlyle bought it for his first wife when they were in London after their marriage. She broke it. You will never do it, Madame Vine, if your hand shakes like that. What is the matter?'

A great deal was the matter. First, the ominous words had been upon her tongue. 'It was broken here, where the stem joins the flower:' but she recollected herself in time. Next, came up the past vision of the place and hour when the accident occurred. Her sleeve had swept it off the table; Mr. Carlyle was in the room, this very room, and he had soothed her sorrow, her almost childish sorrow, with kisses sweet. Ah me! poor thing! I think our hands would have shaken as hers did. The ornament and the kisses were Barbara's now.

'I ran quickly up the stairs and back again,' was the explanation she offered to Mrs. Carlyle for her shaking hands.

At that moment Mr. Carlyle and their guests were heard to return, and to ascent to their respective apartments, Lord Vane's gleeful voice echoing through the house. Mr. Carlyle came into his wife's dressing-room, and Madame Vine would have made a precipitate retreat.

'No, no,' said Barbara, 'finish it now you have begun. Mr. Carlyle will be going to his own room. Look at the misfortune I have had, Archibald! I have broken this.'

Mr. Carlyle glanced carelessly at the trinket, and at Madame Vine's white fingers. He crossed to the door of his dressing-room and opened it, then held out his hand in silence for Barbara to approach, and drew her in with him. Madame Vine went on with her work.

Presently Barbara returned: and approached the table, where stood Madame Vine, while she drew on her gloves. Her eyelashes were wet.

'I could not help shedding a few tears for joy,' said Barbara, perceiving that Madame Vine observed the signs. 'Mr. Carlyle has been telling me that my brother's innocence is now all but patent to the world. Lord Mount Severn was present at the proceedings, and says they have criminated each other. Papa sat in his place as chairman: I wonder that he liked to do so!'

Lower bent the head of Madame Vine over her employment. 'Has anything been proved against them?' she asked, in her usual soft tone, almost a whisper.

'There is not the least doubt of the guilt of Levison, but Otway Bethel's share in the affair is a puzzle yet,' replied Mrs. Carlyle. 'Both are committed for trial. Oh, that man, that man, how his sins come out!' she continued, in excitement.

Madame Vine glanced up through her spectacles.

'Would you believe,' continued Barbara, dropping her voice, 'that while West Lynne, and I fear we ourselves, gave that miserable Afy credit for having gone away with Richard, she was, all the time, with Levison? Ball the lawyer got her to confess to it to-day. I am unacquainted with the details: Mr. Carlyle would not give them to me. He said the bare fact was quite enough.'

Mr. Carlyle was right.

'Out it all seems to come, little by little! one wickedness after another!' resumed Barbara. 'I do not like Mr. Carlyle to hear it. Of course there is no help for it; but he must feel it terribly; as must Lord Mount Severn. She *was* his wife, you know, and the children are hers: and to think that she—I mean he must feel it *for her*,' went on Barbara after her sudden pause, and there was some hauteur in her tone, lest she should be misunderstood. 'Mr. Carlyle is one of the very few men, so entirely noble, whom the sort of disgrace, reflected from Lady Isabel's conduct, cannot touch.'

The carriage of the first guest. Barbara ran across the room and rattled at Mr. Carlyle's door. 'Archibald! do you hear?'

Back came the laughing answer. 'I shan't keep them long. But they may surely accord a few minutes' grace to a man who has just been converted into an M.P.'

Barbara descended into the drawing-room, leaving that unhappy lady to the cement and the broken pieces and to battle as she best could with her breaking heart. Nothing but stabs; nothing but stabs! Was her punishment ever to end? No. The step she had taken in coming back to East Lynne precluded that.

The guests arrived. All, save Mr. and Mrs. Hare. Barbara received a note from her mamma instead. The justice did not feel well enough to join them.

I should think he did not. If retribution came home sharply to Lady Isabel, it was coming home in some degree to him. Richard, his own unoffending son—unoffending in every sense of the term, until that escapade of falling in love with Afy—had been treated with unnatural harshness. West Lynne and the public would not fail to remember it—and the justice was remarkably alive to West Lynne and the public's opinion. The affection for Richard, which the justice had been pressing down and keeping under, and turning into all possible channels of hate, was now returning in unpleasant force. Unpleasant in so far that it did savage war with his conscience.

'I—I—might have hunted him to death, you know, Anne,' said the justice, sitting in his chair, and wiping his brows, and eating humble pie for perhaps the first time in his life.

'But it is over now, Richard dear,' said gentle loving Mrs. Hare, the happy tears coursing down her cheeks.

'But I *might*—had he made his appearance here. In fact I should.'

'Do not grieve, Richard; it will not recall the past. In a little time we may have him home again with us; and then we can both make it up to him.'

'And how are we to get him here? He may be dead. Who knows where he is? He may be dead, I say.'

'No, he is not. We shall get him when the time comes. Mr. Carlyle knows where he is; has known a long while, he told me to-day: even sees him sometimes. A true friend to us all, Richard, is Archibald Carlyle.'

'Ay. That jade, Barbara, is in luck. I shouldn't be surprised but what she knows too; if he does. A good girl, a good girl, though she puts up at times for saucy independence.'

Mrs. Hare could scarcely make her husband out, his tone and manner were so thoroughly changed from what she had ever known them.

'But I can't believe it's true yet, Anne. I can't indeed. If he is innocent, why couldn't he have been cleared before? It is so many years ago, you know! Do you think he is innocent?'

'Dear Richard, I know he is,' she answered, with a happy smile. 'I have been sure of it a long, long while. And so has Mr. Carlyle.'

'Well, that's something. Carlyle's judgment is. Is his room aired—and all that?'

'Whose room?' echoed Mrs. Hare.

'Poor Dick's.'

'My dear, you forget,' she returned, in wonderment. 'He cannot come home yet; not until after the assizes. The others must be proved guilty, and he innocent, before he can come home.'

'True, true,' said Mr. Justice Hare.

A pleasant party it was, at East Lynne; and twelve o'clock struck before the carriage of the last guest drove away. It might have been one to two hours after that, and the house was steeped in moonlight and quietness, everybody being a-bed and asleep, when a loud, alarming summons at the hall-bell echoed through the stillness.

The first to put her head out at a window was Wilson. 'Is it fire?' shrieked she, in the most excessive state of terror conceivable. Wilson had a natural dread of fire; some people possess this dread more than others; and had oftentime aroused the house to a commotion by declaring she smelt it. 'Is it fire?' shrieked Wilson.

'YES,' was shouted at the very top of a man's voice, who stepped from between the entrance pillars to answer.

Wilson waited for no more. Clutching at the baby with one hand—a fine young gentleman now of near twelve months old, promising fair to be as great a source of trouble to Wilson and the nursery as was his brother Archibald, whom he greatly resembled—and at Archie with the other, out she flew to the corridor, screeching 'Fire! fire! fire!' in every accent of horror. Into William's room, and dragging him out of bed; into Lucy's and dragging her; banging open the door of Madame Vine, and the shrieks, Fire! fire! fire! never ceasing; Wilson, with the four children, burst unceremoniously into the sleeping apartment of Mr. and Mrs. Carlyle. By this time the children, terrified out of their senses, not at Wilson's cry of alarm, but at the summary propelling downstairs, set up a shrieking too. Madame Vine, believing that half of the house at least was in flames, was the next to appear, throwing on a shawl she had caught up: and then came Joyce.

'Fire! fire! fire!' shouted Wilson; 'we're all a-being burnt up together.'

Poor Mrs. Carlyle, thus wildly roused from sleep, sprang out of bed and into the corridor in her night-dress. Everybody else was in a night-dress: when folks are flying for dear life, they don't stop to look for their dress-coats, and best blonde caps. Out came Mr. Carlyle, who had hastily assumed his pantaloons.

He cast a rapid glance down to the hall, and saw that the stairs were perfectly free for escape: therefore the hurry was not so violent. Every soul around him was shrieking in concert, making the confusion and din terrific. The bright moonlight streamed in at the corridor windows, but there was no other light.

'Where is the fire?' he exclaimed. 'I don't smell any. Who first gave the alarm?'

The bell answered him. The hall bell, which rang out ten times louder and longer than before. He opened one of the windows and leaned from it. 'Who's there?' Madame Vine caught up Archie.

'It's me, sir,' responded a voice, which he at once recognised to be that of one of Mr. Hare's men-servants. 'Master have been took in a fit, sir, and mistress sent me for you and Miss Barbara. You must please make haste, sir, if you want to see him alive.' Miss Barbara! It was more familiar to Jasper, in a moment of excitement, than the new name.

'You, Jasper! Is the house on fire? This house?'

'Well, I don't know, sir. I can hear a dreadful deal of screeching in it.'

Mr. Carlyle closed the window. He began to suspect that the danger lay in fear alone. 'Who told you there was fire?' he demanded of Wilson.

'That man ringing at the door,' sobbed Wilson. 'Thank goodness, I have saved the children.'

Mr. Carlyle felt somewhat exasperated at the mistake. His wife was trembling from head to foot; and he knew that she was not in a condition to be alarmed, necessarily or unnecessarily. She clung to him in terror, asking if they *could* escape.

'My darling, be calm! There is no fire. It is a stupid mistake. You may all go back to bed and sleep in peace,' he added to the rest. 'And the next time that you alarm the house in the night, Wilson, have the goodness to make yourself sure, first of all, that there's cause for it.'

Barbara, frightened still, bewildered and uncertain, escaped to the window, and threw it open. But Mr. Carlyle was nearly as quick as she: he caught her to him with one hand, and drew the window down with the other. To have these tidings told to her abruptly, would be worse than all. By this time, some of the servants had descended the other staircase, with a light (being in various stages of costume), and, hastening to open the hall-door, Jasper entered. The man had probably waited to help put out the 'fire.' Barbara caught sight of him ere Mr. Carlyle could prevent it, and grew sick with fear, believing some ill had happened to her mother.

Drawing her inside their chamber, he broke the news to her soothingly and tenderly, making light of it. She burst into tears. 'You are not deceiving me, Archibald? Papa is not dead?'

'Dead!' cheerily echoed Mr. Carlyle, in the same tone he might have used had Barbara wondered whether the justice was taking a night airing for pleasure in a balloon. 'Wilson has indeed frightened you, love. Dress yourself, and we will go and see him.'

At that moment, Barbara recollected William. Strange that she should be the first to do so; before Lady Isabel, before Mr.Carlyle. She ran out again to the corridor, where the boy stood shivering. 'He may have caught his death!' she uttered, snatching him up in her arms. 'Oh, Wilson! what have you done? His night-gown is damp and cold.'

Unfit as she was for the burden, she bore him to her own bed. Wilson was not at leisure to attend to reproaches just then. She was engaged in wordy war with Jasper, leaning over the balustrades to carry it on.

'I never told you there was a fire!' indignantly denied Jasper.

'You did. I opened the nursery window, and called out "Is it fire?" and you answered "Yes."'

'You called out "Is it Jasper?" What else should I say but, "Yes," to that? Fire! Where was the fire likely to be? In the park?'

'Wilson, take the children back to bed,' authoritatively said Mr. Carlyle, as he advanced to look down the hall. 'John, are you there? the close carriage instantly. Be quick. Madame Vine, pray don't continue to hold that heavy boy. Joyce, cannot you relieve madame?'

In crossing back to his room, Mr. Carlyle had brushed past madame, and noticed that she appeared to be shaking, as if with the weight of Archibald. In reality, she was still alarmed, not understanding yet the cause of the commotion. Joyce, who comprehended it as little, and had stood with her arms round Lucy, advanced to take Archibald; and Mr. Carlyle disappeared. Barbara had taken off her own night-dress then, and put it upon William in place of his own, had struck a light, and was busily dressing herself.

'Just feel his night-gown, Archibald! Wilson—'

A shrill cry of awful terror interrupted the words, and Mr. Carlyle made but one bound out again. Barbara followed: the least she thought, was, that Wilson had dropped the baby into the hall.

That was not the catastrophe. Wilson, with the baby and Lucy, had already disappeared up the staircase, and Madame Vine was disappearing. Archibald lay on the soft carpet of the corridor, where madame now stood; for Joyce, in the act of taking him, had let him slip to the ground, let him fall, from sheer terror. She held on by the balustrades, her face ghastly, her mouth open, her eyes fixed in horror; altogether an object to look upon. Archie gathered himself on to his sturdy legs, and stood staring.

'Why, Joyce! what is the matter with *you?*' cried Mr. Carlyle. 'You look as if you had seen a spectre.'

'Oh, master!' she wailed. 'I *have* seen one.'

'Are you all going deranged together?' retorted he, wondering what had come to the house. 'Seen a spectre? Joyce!'

Joyce fell on her knees, as if unable to support herself, and crossed her shaking hands upon her chest. Had she seen ten spectres, she could not have betrayed more dire distress. She was a sensible and faithful servant, one not given to flights of fancy, and Mr. Carlyle gazed at her in very amazement.

'Joyce, what is this?' he asked, bending down and speaking kindly.

'Oh! my dear master! Heaven have mercy upon us all!' was the inexplicable answer.

'Joyce, I ask you, what is this?'

She made no reply. She rose up shaking; and taking Archie's hand, slowly proceeded towards the upper stairs, low moans breaking from her, and the boy's naked feet pattering on the carpet.

'What can ail her?' whispered Barbara, following Joyce with her eyes. 'What did she mean, about a spectre?'

'She must have been reading a ghost-book,' said Mr. Carlyle. 'Wilson's folly has turned the house topsy-turvy. Make haste, Barbara.'

⚜ XVIII ⚜

Three Months Longer

Spring waned. Summer came, and would soon be waning too, for the hot days of July were now in. What had the months brought forth, since the election of Mr. Carlyle in April? Be you very sure they had not been without their events.

Mr. Justice Hare's illness had turned out to be a stroke of paralysis. People cannot act with unnatural harshness towards a child, and then discover they have been in the wrong, with impunity. Thus it proved with Justice Hare. He was recovering, but would never again be the man he had been. The fright, when Jasper had gone to tell of his illness at East Lynne, and was mistaken for fire, had done nobody any damage, save William and Joyce. William had caught a cold, which brought increased malady to the lungs; and Joyce seemed to have caught *fear*. She went about, more like one in a dream than awake, would be buried in a reverie for an hour at a time, and, if suddenly spoken to, would start and shiver.

Mr. Carlyle and his wife departed for London, immediately that Mr. Hare was pronounced out of danger; which was in about a week from the time of his seizure. William accompanied them: partly for the benefit of London advice, partly because Mr. Carlyle would not be parted from him. Joyce went, in attendance, with some of the other servants.

They found London ringing with the news of Sir Francis Levison's arrest. London could not understand it: and the most wild and improbable tales were in circulation. The season was at its height: the excitement in proportion; it was more than a nine days' wonder. On the very evening of their arrival, a lady, young and beautiful, was shown into the presence of Mr. and Mrs. Carlyle. She had declined to give her name, but there arose to Mr. Carlyle's memory, when he looked on her, one whom he had seen in earlier days, as a friend of his first wife: Blanche Challoner. It was not Blanche, however.

The stranger looked keenly at Mr. Carlyle. He was standing with his hat in his hand, on the point of going out. 'Will you pardon this intrusion?' she asked. 'I have come to you, as one human being, in need, comes to crave help of another. I am Lady Levison.'

Barbara's face flushed. Mr. Carlyle courteously invited the stranger to a chair, and remained standing himself. She sat for a moment, and then rose evidently in an excess of agitation.

'Yes, I am Lady Levison. Forced to call that man husband. That he has been a wicked man, I have long known; but now I hear he is a criminal. I hear it, I say, but I can get the truth from none. I went to Lord Mount Severn; he declined to give me particulars. I heard that Mr. Carlyle would be in town as to-day; and I resolved to come and ask them of him.'

She delivered the sentences in a jerking, abrupt tone, betraying her inward emotion. Mr. Carlyle made no immediate reply.

'You and I have both been deeply wronged by him, Mr. Carlyle. But I brought my wrong upon myself: you did not. My sister Blanche, whom he had cruelly treated—and, if I speak of it, I only speak of what is known to the world—warned me against him. Mrs. Levison, his grandmother, that ancient lady, who must now be bordering upon ninety, warned me also. The night before my wedding-day, she came on purpose to tell me that if I married Francis Levison I should rue it for life: there was yet time to retract, she said. Yes; there was time; but there was no *will*. I would not listen to either: I was led away by vanity, by folly, by something worse—the triumph over my own sister. Poor Blanche! And I have a child,' she continued, dropping her voice; 'a boy who inherits his father's name. Mr. Carlyle'—bending forward and clasping her hands, while her face looked like one carved from stone—'will they *condemn* him?'

'Nothing, as yet, is positively proved against him,' replied Mr. Carlyle, compassionately.

'If I could but get a divorce!' she cried passionately, apparently losing all self-control. 'I might have got one over and over again, since we married; but there would have been the *exposé* and the scandal. If I could but change my child's name; Tell me—does any chance of redress remain for me?'

There was none: and Mr. Carlyle did not attempt to speak of any. He said a few kind words of sympathy, and prepared to go out. She moved, and stood in his way.

'You will not leave until you have given me the particulars! I pray you, do not! I came trustingly to you, hoping to know them.'

'I have to keep an important engagement,' he answered; 'and, even if it were not so, I should decline to tell them to you: on my account, as well as on yours. Lay not discourtesy to my charge, Lady Levison: but if I were to speak of the man, even to you, his name would blister my lips.'

'In every word of hate, spoken by you, I should sympathize; every contemptuous expression of scorn, cast upon him from your heart, I would re-echo.'

Barbara was shocked. 'He is your husband after all,' she whispered.

'My husband!' burst out Lady Levison passionately. 'Yes, there is the wrong he has done me! Why—knowing what he was, and what he had done—why did he delude me into becoming his wife? You ought to feel pity for me, Mrs. Carlyle, and you do feel it, for you are a wife and a mother. How dare these bad men marry!' she cried incoherently. 'Were his other sins not hindrance enough, but with crime also on his conscience he must come with his bold face to woo me with lies! He has done me deep, irremediable wrong, and he has entailed upon his child an inheritance of shame which can never be thrown off.'

Barbara was half frightened at her vehemence: but Barbara might be thankful that she could not understand it. All Lady Levison's native gentleness, all her reticence of feeling, as a wife and a gentlewoman, had been goaded out of her. The process had been going on for some time, this last revelation was the crowning point, and Alice, Lady Levison, turned round upon the world in her helpless resentment, as vehemently as any poor charwoman might have done. There are certain wrongs which bring out human nature in the high and the low alike. 'Still, he is your husband,' was all Barbara could, with deprecation, again plead.

'He made himself my husband by deceit, and I will throw him off in the face of day,' returned Lady Levison. 'There is no moral obligation why I should not. He has worked ill and ruin, ill and ruin upon me and my child; and the world shall not think that I have borne my share in it. How was it you kept your hands off him, when he reappeared, to brave you, in West Lynne?' she added, in a changed tone, turning to Mr. Carlyle.

'I cannot tell. It was a marvel oftentimes to myself.'

He quitted the room as he spoke, adding a few kind-spoken words about leaving her with Mrs. Carlyle. When they were alone, Barbara yielded to Lady Levison's request, and gave her the outline of the dark tale. Its outline only: generously suppressing Afy's name beyond the evening of the fatal event. Lady Levison listened without interruption.

'Do you and Mr. Carlyle believe him to have been guilty?'

'Yes.'

'Was his first wife, Isabel Vane, mad?' she presently asked.

'Mad?' echoed Barbara, in surprise.

'When she quitted him for the other. It could have been nothing less than madness. I could understand a woman's flying from Francis Levison for love of Mr. Carlyle; but, now that I have seen your husband, I cannot understand the reverse.'

And, without another word, Alice Levison quitted the room as abruptly as she had entered it.

Barbara's stay in London was little more than three weeks, for it was necessary she should be safe at home again.

Mr. Carlyle, however, remained in town till the session was nearly over, though he made hurried visits down to East Lynne. In July, he returned home for good. There was another baby at East Lynne then, a lovely little lady— pretty as Barbara herself had been at a month old.

But William was rapidly fading away. The London physician had confirmed Dr. Martin's opinion; and it was evident to all that the end could not be long in coming.

Somebody else was fading—Lady Isabel. The cross had been too heavy, and she was sinking under its weight. Can you wonder at it? It might have been different had she yielded to its weight; striven to *bear* it in patience and in silence, after the manner she had carved out for herself. But she did not. She rebelled against it: and it was costing her her life. The hourly and daily excitement, arising from the false position in which she had placed herself by returning to East Lynne, calmed down with the departure of Mr. and Mrs. Carlyle for town. Then the reaction set in. The incessant irritation on the mind, the feelings, and the nerves was gone; but in its place had settled the no less dangerous apathy, the dull quiet of despair. It was the excitement which had kept her up: and, that over, she began to sink with alarming rapidity. There appeared to be no ostensible disease, but she was wasting away day by day, as her mother had done. Her fading was observed by none; and she still discharged her duties as Lucy's governess: though she snatched portions of her time to spend with William. Was she conscious of her own decay? Partially so: and, had anybody inquired what her malady was, would have answered, A broken heart.

An intensely hot day it was, under the July sun. Afy Hallijohn was sailing up the street in its beams, finer and vainer than ever. Afy had not shone out particularly clear in the eyes of West Lynne, after that examination. Besides the little episode, touching the London visit, Afy stood convicted, if not of perjury, of something very like it. It is true, that when the coroner's inquest on her father took place, she was not sworn to the truth of her evidence: and Richard Hare was mistaken in believing that she was. She had then asserted that nobody was at the cottage that night but Richard Hare, for she would not mention Thorn's name. Not that she had the remotest suspicion that he had anything to do with the tragedy; we must give her her due there: she did fully believe Richard Hare was guilty. Afy on that point but spoke as she believed. But when she was put upon her oath before the magistrates, she was compelled to convict herself of falsehood in other matters.

All this told badly at West Lynne, and Afy in public opinion became as graceless as ever. She stoutly stood up for herself: to listen to her you would have believed her a heroine immaculate; and some were convinced and espoused her cause. Not so Mrs. Latimer. Her faith was shaken. She discharged Afy, according her, however, the favour of a month's warning, which took off the chief stigma of the disgrace. Amongst her warmest advocates was Mr. Joe Jiffin. Somewhat dubious when the startling news came out, he suffered himself to be wholly talked over by Afy. She made her tale thoroughly good to him, and, in the ardour of the moment, Mr. Jiffin laid himself, his hand, and his cheesemongery at Afy's feet. Had a veritable saint come forth out of the world of spirits to testify against Afy, Mr. Jiffin would have turned a deaf ear from that time forth.

Who so proud now as Afy?—who so scornfully triumphant over West Lynne? She went into respectable lodgings, and began making her preparations, in the shape of fine bonnets and gowns. Handsome lodgings, and positively within sight of the windows of Miss Carlyle. Here Afy was the lady, and here Mr. Joe Jiffin was permitted the favour of an occasional evening visit, some female friend or other of Afy's being always present to play propriety. Indeed, you might have thought she had just emerged from a convent of nuns, so overscrupulous was she. 'Wretches!' ejaculted Mr. Jiffin, apostrophising West Lynne and its malicious gossipers, 'she's as particular and innocent as an angel.'

Afy was sailing up the street in the July sun. She surveyed the house of Mr. Joe Jiffin with satisfaction as she passed it, for it was being embellished outside and in, to receive her; while packages of new furniture were arriving by every train. She threw out hints, and the enraptured bridegroom elect acted upon them. He saw her from his shop, and came rushing out.

'They are getting on so well, Miss Afy! It will all be finished this week. The drawing-room paper is hung, and looks beautiful. The gold border is exquisite. Would you like to step upstairs with me and look at it?'

'Oh dear!' responded the shocked Afy. 'Go upstairs with you, Mr. Jiffin!

Has not West Lynne been ill-natured enough already? You don't understand these things.'

'I'm afraid I don't,' meekly responded the poor little man. 'I'm sure I beg your pardon, Miss Afy. I meant no offence.'

'I wish to *goodness*,' resumed Afy, with emphasis, 'you'd leave off those white badges of aprons!'

Mr. Jiffin coughed in perplexity. It was a sore and difficult point. 'I'd do almost anything you asked me, Miss Afy; you know I would: but only think how I should grease my—my—lower garments!'

Afy gave a shriek, and turned her modest cheeks the other way.

'Not to speak of my waistcoats,' went on Mr. Jiffin, all in dire confusion; 'but they'd come in for a touch of it. There's the work with the tubs of butter, and the cutting up of the bacon and hams, and the dirt off the cheeses, and the splashings from the pickled pork barrels: it's all greasy together. Besides the squashing of an egg now and then, which nobody can help. I assure you, Miss Afy, if I were to discard my aprons, I might put on a new pair of— articles—every week, and not be decent in front then.'

Afy groaned. Whether at the delicacy of the subject, or at the wholesale destruction hinted at, Mr. Jiffin did not know.

'You go to Lynneborough by the early train to-morrow, don't you, Miss Afy?' asked he, by way of changing the topic.

'Everybody knows that,' said Afy. 'A good many of us go. The trial comes on at nine, so of course it's necessary to be there early. Have you heard the rumour about Richard Hare?'

'No,' replied Mr. Jiffin. 'What rumour is it?'

'It is circulating through West Lynne. They say he is to be tried also.'

'Is he found?' cried Mr. Jiffin in surprise.

'I don't know anything about it, myself. It has been said lately that he was dead, you know. As to which is guilty, he or Levison, I don't think it much matters,' pursued Afy, with a lofty toss of the head, and a severe countenance. 'My opinion always was that they were a couple of bad ones, two I wouldn't have touched with a long pole.'

Afy sailed away, her crinoline sweeping each side of the wide pavement. If she purposed sporting that crinoline in the crowded assize court to-morrow, it would inevitably come to grief. A few steps farther, she encountered Mr. Carlyle.

'So, Afy, you are really going to be married at last?'

'Jiffin fancies so, sir. I am not sure yet but what I shall change my mind. Jiffin thinks there's nobody like me: if I could eat gold and silver, he'd provide it; and he's as fond as fond can be. But then, you know, sir, he's half soft.'

'Soft, as to you, perhaps,' laughed Mr. Carlyle. 'I consider him a very civil, respectable man, Afy.'

'And then, I never did think to marry a shopkeeper,' grumbled Afy. 'I looked a little higher than that. Only fancy, sir, having a husband who wears a white apron tied round him!'

'Terrible!' responded Mr. Carlyle, with a grave face.

'Not but what it will be a tolerable settlement,' rejoined Afy, veering round a point. 'He is having his house done up in style; and I shall keep two good servants, and do nothing myself but dress, and subscribe to the library. He makes plenty of money.'

'A very tolerable settlement, I should say,' returned Mr. Carlyle: and Afy's face fell before the glance of his eye, merry though it was. 'Take care you don't spend all his money for him, Afy.'

'I'll take care of that,' nodded Afy, significantly. 'Sir,' she somewhat abruptly added, 'what is it that's the matter with Joyce?'

'I do not know,' said Mr. Carlyle, becoming serious. 'There does appear to be something the matter with her, for she is much changed.'

'I never saw anybody so changed in my life,' exclaimed Afy. 'I told her, the other day, that she was just like one who had got some dreadful secret upon the mind.'

'It is really more like that than anything else,' observed Mr. Carlyle.

'But she's one of the close ones, is Joyce,' continued Afy. 'No fear that she'll give out a clue, if it does not suit her to do so. She told me, in answer, to mind my own business, and not to take absurd fancies in my head. How is the baby, sir? And Mrs. Carlyle?'

'All well. Good day, Afy.'

⚔ XIX ⚔

The Trial

Spacious courts were the assize courts at Lynneborough. And it was well they were so, otherwise more people had been disappointed, and numbers were, of hearing the noted trial of Sir Francis Levison for the murder of George Hallijohn.

The circumstances attending the case caused it to bear for the public an unparalleled interest. The rank of the accused, and his antecedents, more especially that particular local antecedent touching the Lady Isabel Carlyle; the verdict still out against Richard Hare; the length of time which had elapsed; the part played in it by Afy; the intense curiosity as to the part taken in it by Otway Bethel; the speculation as to what had been the exact details, and the doubt of a conviction; all contributed to fan the curiosity of the public. People came from far and near to be present. Friends of Mr. Carlyle, friends of the Hares, friends of the Challoner family, friends of the prisoner; besides the general public. Colonel Bethel, and Mr. Justice Hare, had conspicuous seats.

At a few minutes past nine the judge took his place on the bench. But not before a rumour had gone through the court; a rumour that seemed to shake it to its centre, and which people stretched out their necks to hear. Otway Bethel had turned Queen's evidence, and was to be admitted as witness for the crown.

Thin, haggard, pale, looked Francis Levison as he was placed in the dock. His incarceration had not in any way contributed to his personal advantages: and there was an ever-recurring expression of dread upon his countenance, not pleasant to look upon. He was dressed in black, and his diamond ring shone conspicuous still on his white hand, now whiter than ever. The most eminent counsel were engaged on both sides.

The testimony of the witnesses, already given, need not be recapitulated. The identification of the prisoner with the man Thorn was fully established. Ebenezer James proved that. Afy proved it: and also that he, Thorn, was at the cottage that night. Sir Peter Levison's groom was likewise re-examined. But still there wanted other testimony. Afy was made to re-assert that Thorn had to go to the cottage for his hat, after leaving her: but that proved nothing: and the conversation, or quarrel overheard by Mr. Dill, was not again put forward. If this was all the evidence, people opined that the case for the prosecution would break down.

'Call Richard Hare,' said the counsel for the prosecution.

Those present, who knew Mr. Justice Hare, looked up at him, wondering why he did not stir in answer to his name; wondering at the pallid hue which overspread his face. Not *he*, but another man came forward; a fair, placid young man, with blue eyes, fair hair, and a pleasant countenance. It was Richard Hare the younger. He had resumed his original position in life, so far as attire went, and in that, at least, was a gentleman again: in speech also. With his working dress, Richard had thrown off his working manners.

A strange hubbub arose in court. Richard Hare the exile! the reported dead! the man whose life was still in jeopardy! The spectators rose with one accord to get a better view; they stood on tiptoe; they pushed forth their necks; they strained their eyesight: and, amidst all the noisy hum, the groan, bursting from Justice Hare, was unnoticed. Whilst order was called for, and the judge threatened to clear the court, two officers moved quietly up and stood behind the witness. Richard Hare was in custody; though he might know it not. The witness was sworn.

'What is your name?'

'Richard Hare.'

'Son of Mr. Justice Hare, I believe; of the Grove, West Lynne?'

'His only son.'

'The same against whom a verdict of wilful murder is out?' interposed the judge.

'The same, my lord,' replied Richard Hare, who appeared, strange as it may seem, to have cast away all his old fearfulness.

'Then, witness, let me warn you that you are not obliged to answer any question that might tend to criminate yourself.'

'My lord,' answered Richard Hare, with some emotion, 'I wish to answer any and every question put to me. I have but one hope: that the full truth of all pertaining to that fatal evening may be made manifest this day.'

'Look round at the prisoner,' said the examining counsel. 'Do you know him?'

'I know him now as Sir Francis Levison. Up to April last, I believed his name to be Thorn.'

'State what occurred on the evening of the murder—so far as your knowledge goes.'

'I had an appointment that evening with Afy Hallijohn, and went down to their cottage to keep it—'

'A moment,' interrupted the counsel. 'Was your visit that evening made in secret?'

'Partially so. My father and mother were displeased at my intimacy with Afy Hallijohn: therefore I did not care that they should be cognisant of my visits there. I am ashamed to confess that I told my father a lie over it that very evening. He saw me leave the dinner-table to go out with my gun, and inquired where I was off to. I answered that I was going out with young Beauchamp.'

'When, in point of fact, you were not?'

'No. I took my gun, for I had promised to lend it to Hallijohn, while his own was being repaired. When I reached the cottage, Afy refused to admit me: she was busy, she said. I felt sure she had Thorn with her. She had, more than once before, refused to admit me when I had gone there by her own appointment; and I always found that Thorn's presence in the cottage was the obstacle.'

'I suppose you and Thorn were jealous of each other?'

'I was jealous of him: I freely admit it. I don't know whether he was of me.'

'May I inquire what was the nature of your friendship for Miss Afy Hallijohn?'

'I loved her with an honourable love: as I might have loved any young lady in my own station of life. I would not have married her in opposition to my father and mother: but I told Afy that if she was content to wait for me, until I was my own master, I would then make her my wife.'

'You had no views towards her of a different nature?'

'None. I cared for her too much for that. And I respected her father. Afy's mother had been a lady, too; although she had married Hallijohn, who was but clerk to Mr. Carlyle. No: I never had a thought of wrong towards Afy.'

'Now relate the occurrences of the evening.'

'Afy would not admit me, and we had a few words over it. But at length I went away; first giving her the gun and telling her it was loaded. She lodged it against the wall, just inside the door, and I went into the wood and waited, determined to see whether, or not, Thorn was with her, for she had denied that he was. Locksley saw me there, and asked why I was hiding. I did not answer; but I went farther off, quite out of view of the cottage. Some time afterwards, less than half-an-hour, I heard a shot in the direction of the cottage. Somebody was having a late shot at the partridges, I thought. Just then, I saw Otway Bethel emerge from the trees not far from me, and run towards the cottage. My lord,' added Richard Hare, looking at the judge, 'that was the shot that killed Hallijohn.'

'Could the shot,' asked the counsel, 'have been fired by Otway Bethel?'

'It could not. It was much farther off. Bethel disappeared: and, in another minute, there came one, flying down the path leading from the cottage. It was Thorn: in a state of intense terror. His face was livid, his eyes staring, and he panted and shook like one in the ague. Past me he tore, on down the path, and I afterwards heard the sound of his horse galloping away. It had been tied in the wood.'

'Did you follow him?'

'No. I wondered what had happened to put him in that state: but I made haste to the cottage, intending to reproach Afy with her duplicity. I leaped up the two steps, and fell over the prostrate body of Hallijohn. He was lying dead within the door. My gun, just discharged, was flung on the floor, its contents in Hallijohn's side.'

You might have heard a pin drop in court, so intense was the interest.

'There appeared to be no one in the cottage, upstairs or down. I called to Afy, but she did not answer. I caught up the gun, and was running from the cottage, when Locksley came out of the wood, and looked at me. I grew confused; fearful; and I threw the gun back again, and made off.'

'What were your motives for acting in that way?'

'A panic had come over me; and in that moment I must have lost the use of my reason, otherwise I never should have acted as I did. Thoughts, especially of fear, pass through our minds with astonishing swiftness, and I feared lest the crime should be fastened upon me. It was fear made me snatch up my gun, lest it should be found near the body; it was fear made me throw it back again when Locksley appeared in view; a fear, from which all judgment, all reason, had departed. But for my own conduct, the charge never would have been laid to me.'

'Go on.'

'In my flight, I came upon Bethel. I knew that if he had gone towards the cottage after the shot was fired, he must have encountered Thorn, flying from it. He denied that he had: he said he had only gone along the path for a few paces, and had then plunged into the wood again. I believed him; and departed.'

'Departed from West Lynne?'

'That night I did. It was a foolish, fatal step, the result of cowardice. I found the charge was laid to me, and I thought I would absent myself for a day or two, to see how things turned out. Next, came the inquest and the verdict against me; and I left for good.'

'This is the truth so far as you are cognisant of it?'

'I swear that it is the truth and the whole truth, so far as I am cognisant of it,' replied Richard Hare, with emotion. 'I could not assert it more solemnly, were I before God.'

He was subjected to a rigid cross-examination, but his testimony was not shaken in the least. Perhaps not one present but was impressed with its truth.

Afy Hallijohn was recalled, and questioned as to Richard's presence at her father's house that night. It tallied with the account given by Richard; but it had to be drawn from her.

'Why did you decline to receive Richard Hare into the cottage, after appointing him to come?'

'Because I chose,' returned Afy.

'Tell the jury why you chose.'

'Well—I had got a friend with me. It was Captain Thorn,' she added, feeling that she should only be questioned on the point, so might as well acknowledge it. 'I did not admit Richard Hare, for I fancied they might get up a quarrel if they were together.'

'For what purpose did Richard Hare bring down his gun? Do you know?'

'It was to lend to my father. My father's gun had something the matter with it, and was at the smith's. I had heard him the previous day ask Mr. Richard to lend him one of his, and Mr. Richard said he would bring one. As he did.'

'You lodged the gun against the wall. Safely?'

'Quite safely.'

'Was it touched by you after placing it there? Or by the prisoner?'

'I did not touch it. Neither did he, that I saw. It was the same gun which was afterwards found near my father, and had been discharged.'

The next witness called was Otway Bethel. He held share also in the curiosity of the public: but not in an equal degree with Afy: still less with Richard Hare. The substance of his testimony was as follows:—

'On the evening that Hallijohn was killed, I was in Abbey Wood, and I saw Richard Hare come down the path with a gun as if he had come from his own home.'

'Did Richard Hare see you?'

'No: he could not see me: I was right in the thicket. He went to the cottage door, and was about to enter, when Afy Hallijohn came hastily out of it, pulling the door to behind her, and holding it in her hand, as if afraid he would go in. Some colloquy ensued, but I was too far off to hear it, and then she took the gun from him and went in-doors. Some time after that, I saw Richard Hare amid the trees at a distance, farther off the cottage then, than I was, and apparently watching the path. I was wondering what he was up to, hiding there, when I heard a shot fired; close as it seemed, to the cottage, and—'

'Stop a bit, witness. Could that shot have been fired by Richard Hare?'

'It could not. He was a quarter of a mile, nearly, away from it. I was much nearer the cottage than he.'

'Go on.'

'I could not imagine what that shot meant, or who could have fired it. Not that I suspected mischief: and I knew that poachers did not congregate so near Hallijohn's cottage. I set off to reconnoitre, and as I turned the corner, which brought the house within my view, I saw Captain Thorn—as he was called—come leaping out of it. His face was white with terror, his breath was gone—in short, I never saw any living man betray so much agitation. I caught his arm as he would have passed me. "What have you been about?" I asked. "Was it you who fired?" He—'

'Stay. Why did you suspect him?'

'From his state of excitement; from the terror he was in. That some ill had happened, I felt sure—and so would you, had you seen him as I did. My arresting him increased his agitation: he tried to throw me off, but I am a strong man: and I suppose he thought it best to temporise. "Keep dark upon it, Bethel," he said, "I will make it worth your while. The thing was not premeditated: it was done in the heat of passion. What business had the fellow to abuse me? I have done no harm to the girl." As he thus spoke, he took out a pocket-book with the hand that was at liberty; I held the other—'

'As the prisoner thus spoke, you mean?'

'The prisoner. He took a bank-note from his pocket-book, and thrust it into my hands. It was a note for 50l. "What's done can't be undone, Bethel," he said, "and your saying that you saw me here can serve no good turn. Shall it be silence?" I took the note and answered that it should be silence. I had not the least idea that anybody was killed.'

'What did you suppose had happened, then?'

'I could not suppose; I could not think; it all passed in the haste and confusion of a moment, and no definite ideas occurred to me. Thorn flew on, down the path, and I stood looking at him. The next was, I heard footsteps, and I slipped within the trees. They were those of Richard Hare, who took the path to the cottage. Presently, he returned, little less agitated than Thorn had been. I had gone into an open space then, and he accosted me, asking if I had seen "that hound" fly from the cottage? "What hound?" I asked him. "That fine fellow, that Thorn, who comes after Afy," he answered, but I stoutly denied that I had seen any one. Richard Hare continued his way, and afterwards found that Hallijohn was killed.'

'And so, you took a bribe to conceal one of the foulest crimes that ever man committed, Mr. Otway Bethel?'

'I took the money: and am ashamed to confess to it. But it was done without reflection. I swear that had I known what crime it was intended to hush up, I never would have touched it. I was hard up for funds, and the amount tempted me. When I discovered what had really happened, and that Richard Hare was accused, I was thunderstruck at my own deed; many a hundred times since have I cursed the money; and the fate of Richard has been as a heavy weight upon my conscience.'

'You might have lifted the weight by confessing.'

'To what end? It was too late. Thorn had disappeared. I never heard of him, or saw him until he came to West Lynne, this last spring, as Sir Francis Levison, to oppose Mr. Carlyle. Richard Hare had also disappeared; had never been seen or heard of; and most people supposed he was dead. To what end, then, should I confess? Perhaps only to be suspected myself. Besides, I had taken the money upon a certain understanding, and it was only fair that I should keep to it.'

If Richard Hare was subjected to a severe cross-examination, a far more severe one awaited Otway Bethel. The judge spoke to him only once, his tone ringing with reproach.

'It appears, then, witness, that you have retained within you, all these years, the proofs of Richard Hare's innocence?'

'I can only acknowledge it with contrition, my lord.'

'What did you know of Thorn in those days?' asked the counsel.

'Nothing; save that he frequented the Abbey Wood, his object being Afy Hallijohn. I had never exchanged a word with him until this night; but I knew his name, Thorn—at least, the one he went by. And by his addressing me as Bethel, it appeared that he knew mine.'

The case for the prosecution closed. An able and ingenious speech was made for the defence, the learned counsel who offered it contending that there was still no proof of Sir Francis Levison having been the guilty man. Neither was there any proof that the catastrophe was not the result of pure accident. A loaded gun, standing against the wall in a small room, was not a safe weapon; and he called upon the jury not rashly to convict in the uncertainty, but to give the prisoner the benefit of the doubt. He should call no witnesses, he observed, not even as to character. Character! for Sir Francis Levison! The court burst into a grin, the only sober face in it being that of the judge.

The judge summed up. Certainly not in the prisoner's favour; but—to use the expression of some amongst the audience—dead against him. Otway Bethel came in for a side shaft or two from his lordship; Richard Hare for sympathy. The jury retired about four o'clock, and the judge quitted the bench.

A very short time were they absent. Scarcely a quarter of an hour. His lordship returned into court, and the prisoner was again placed in the dock. He was the hue of marble, and, in his nervous agitation, kept incessantly throwing back his hair from his forehead—the action so often spoken of. Silence was proclaimed.

'How say you, gentlemen of the jury? Guilty or not guilty?'

'GUILTY.' It was a silence to be felt: and the prisoner gasped once or twice convulsively. 'But,' added the foreman, 'we wish to recommend him to mercy.'

'On what grounds?' inquired the judge.

'Because, my lord, we believe that it was not a crime planned by the prisoner beforehand; but arose out of the bad passions of the moment, and was so committed.'

The judge paused: and drew something black from the receptacle of his pocket, buried deep in his robes.

'Prisoner at the bar! Have you anything to urge why the sentence of death should not be passed upon you?'

The prisoner clutched the front of the dock. He threw up his head as if shaking off the dread fear which had oppressed him, and the marble of his face changed to scarlet.

'Only this, my lord. The jury in giving their reason for recommending me to your lordship's mercy, have adopted the right view of the case, as it actually occurred. That the man's (Hallijohn's) life was taken by me, it will be useless for me to deny, in the face of the evidence given this day. But it was not taken in malice. When I quitted the girl, Afy, and went to the cottage for my hat, I no more contemplated injuring mortal man than I contemplate it at this moment. He was there; the father; and in the dispute that ensued, the catastrophe occurred. My lord, it was not wilful murder.'

The prisoner ceased. And the judge, the black cap upon his head, crossed his hands one upon the other.

'Prisoner at the bar. You have been convicted, by clear and undoubted evidence, of the crime of wilful murder. The jury have pronounced you guilty; and in their verdict I entirely coincide. That you took the life of that ill-fated and unoffending man, there is no doubt; you have, yourself, confessed it. It was a foul, a barbarous, a wicked act. I care not for what may have been the particular circumstances attending it: he may have provoked you by words, but no provocation of that nature could justify your drawing the gun upon him. Your counsel urged that you were a gentleman, a member of the British aristocracy, and therefore deserved consideration. I confess that I was very much surprised to hear such a doctrine fall from his lips. In my opinion your position in life makes your crime the worse: and I have always maintained that when a man possessed of advantages falls into sin, he deserves less consideration than does one who is poor, simple, and uneducated. Certain portions of the evidence given to-day (and I do not now allude to the actual crime) tell very greatly against you. You were pursuing the daughter of this man with no honourable purpose—and in this point your conduct contrasts badly with that of Richard Hare—equally a gentleman with yourself. In this pursuit you killed her father; and, not content with that, you still pursued the girl—and pursued her to ruin; basely deceiving her as to the actual facts, and laying the crime upon another. I cannot trust myself to speak further upon this point; nor is it necessary that I should: it is not to answer for that that you stand before me. Uncalled, unprepared, and by you unpitied, you hurried that unfortunate man into eternity; and you must now expiate the crime with your own life. The jury have recommended you to mercy: and the recommendation will be forwarded in due course to the proper quarter: but you must be aware how frequently this clause is appended to a verdict, and how very rarely it is attended to, just cause being wanting. I can but enjoin you, and I do so most earnestly, to pass the little time that probably remains to you on earth, in seeking repentance and forgiveness. You are best aware, yourself, what your past life has been: the world knows somewhat of it: but there is pardon above for the most guilty, when it is earnestly sought. It now only remains for me to pass upon you the dread sentence of the law. It is, that you, Francis Levison, be taken back to the place whence you came, and thence to the place of execution, and that you be there hanged by the neck until you are dead. And may the Lord God Almighty have mercy upon your immortal soul!'

'Amen!'

The court was cleared. The day's excitement was over, and the next case was inquired for. Not quite over yet, however, the excitement, and the audience crowded in again. For the next case proved to be the arraignment of Richard Hare the younger. A formal proceeding merely, in pursuance of the verdict of the coroner's inquest. No evidence was offered against him, and the judge ordered him to be discharged. Richard, poor, ill-used, baited Richard, was a free man again.

Then ensued the scene of all scenes. Half, at least, of those present were residents of, or from near West Lynne. They had known Richard Hare from infancy; they had admired the boy in his pretty childhood; they had liked him in his unoffending boyhood; but they had been none the less ready to cast their harsh stones at him, and to thunder down their denunciations when the time came. In proportion to their fierceness then, was their contrition now: Richard had been innocent all the while; they had been more guilty than he.

An English mob, gentle or simple, never gets up its excitement by halves. Whether its demonstration be of a laudatory or a condemnatory nature, the steam is sure to be put on to bursting point. With one universal shout, with one bound, they rallied round Richard: they congratulated him, they overwhelmed him with good wishes, they expressed with shame their repentance, they said that the future should atone for the past. Had he possessed a hundred hands, they would have been shaken off. And when Richard extricated himself, and turned, in his pleasant, forgiving, loving nature to his father, the stern old justice, forgetting his pride and his pomposity, burst into tears, and sobbed like a child, as he murmured something about he, also, needing forgiveness.

'Dear father,' cried Richard, his own eyes wet, 'it is forgiven and forgotten already. Think how happy we shall be again together! you and I, and my mother.'

The justice's hands, which had been wound round his son, relaxed their hold. They were twitching curiously; the face was twitching curiously; the body also began to twitch: and he fell upon the shoulder of Colonel Bethel, in a second stroke of paralysis.

⚜ X X ⚜

The Death Chamber

By the side of William Carlyle's dying bed knelt the Lady Isabel. The time was at hand, and the boy was quite reconciled to his fate. Merciful indeed is God to dying children! It is astonishing how very readily, where the right means are taken, they may be brought to look with pleasure, rather than fear, upon their unknown journey.

The brilliant, hectic type of disease had gone from his cheeks, his features were white and wasted, and his eyes large and bright. His silky brown hair was pushed off his temples, and his little hot hands were thrown outside the bed.

'It won't be so very long to wait, you know, will it, Madame Vine?'

'For what, darling?'

'Before they all come. Papa and mamma, and Lucy, and all of them.'

A jealous feeling shot across her wearied heart. Was *she* nothing to him? 'Do you not care that I should come to you, William?'

'Yes, I hope you will. But, do you think we shall know *everybody* in heaven? Or will it be only our own relations?'

'Oh, child! I think there will no relations, as you call them, up there. We can trust all that to God—however it may be.'

William lay looking upwards at the sky, apparently in thought. A dark blue, serene sky, from which shone the hot July sun. His bed had been moved near the window, for he liked to sit up in it and look at the landscape. The window was open now, and the butterflies and bees sported in the summer air.

'I wonder how it will be?' pondered he, aloud. 'There will be the beautiful city, with its gates of pearl, and its shining precious stones, and its streets of gold; and there will be the clear river, and the trees with their fruits and their healing leaves, and the lovely flowers: and there will be the harps, and music, and singing; and what else will there be?'

'Everything that is desirable and beautiful, William.'

Another pause. 'Madame Vine, will Jesus come for me, do you think, or will he send an angel?'

'Jesus has *promised* to come for his own redeemed; for those who love him and wait for him.'

'Yes, yes. And then I shall be happy for ever. It will be so pleasant to be there! never to be tired or ill again.'

'Pleasant? Ay! Oh, William! would that the time were come!' She was thinking of herself; her freedom; though the boy knew it not. She buried her face in her hands and continued speaking: William had to bend his ear to catch the faint whisper.

'"And there shall be no more death, neither sorrow, nor crying; neither shall there be any more pain: for the former things are passed away."'

'Madame Vine, do you think mamma will be there?' he presently asked. 'I mean mamma that was.'

'Ay. Ere long.'

'But how shall I know her? You see, I have nearly forgotten what she was like.'

She leaned over him, laying her forehed upon his wasted arm; she burst into a flood of impassioned tears. 'You will know her; never fear, William, she has not forgotten you.'

'But how can we be sure that she will be there?' debated William, after a pause of thought. 'You know'—sinking his voice, and speaking with hesitation—'she was not quite good. She was not good to papa or to us. Sometimes I think, suppose she did not grow good, and did not ask God to forgive her?'

'Oh, William,' sobbed the unhappy lady, 'her whole life, after she left you, was one long scene of repentance, of seeking forgiveness. Her repentance, her sorrow was greater than she could bear, and—'

'And what?' asked William, for there was a pause.

'Her heart broke in it; yearning after you and your father.'

'What makes you think it?'

'Child, I *know* it.'

William considered. Then—had he been strong enough—would have started up with energy: 'Madame Vine, you could only know that, by mamma's telling you! Did you ever see her? Did you know her abroad?'

Lady Isabel's thoughts were far away; up in the clouds, perhaps. She reflected not on the possible consequences of her answer: or she had never given it.

'Yes: I knew her abroad.'

'Oh!' said the boy. 'Why did you never tell us? What did she say? What was she like?'

'She said'—sobbing wildly—'that she was parted from her children here. But she should meet them in heaven and be with them for ever. William, darling! all the awful pain, and sadness, and guilt of this world will be washed out, and God will wipe our tears away.'

'What was her face like?' he questioned, softly.

'Like yours. Very much like Lucy's.'

'Was she pretty?'

A momentary pause. 'Yes.'

'Oh dear! I am ill! Hold me!' cried out William, as his head sank to one side, and great drops, as large as peas, broke forth upon his clammy face. It appeared to be one of the temporary faint attacks that had overpowered him at times lately, and Lady Isabel rang the bell hastily.

Wilson came in, in answer. Joyce was the usual attendant upon the sick room, but Mrs. Carlyle, with her infant, was passing the day at the Grove, unconscious of the critical state of William, and she had taken Joyce with her. It was the day following the trial. Mr. Justice Hare had been brought to West Lynne in his second attack, and Barbara had gone to see him, to console her mother, and to welcome Richard to his home again. If one carriage drove, that day, to the Grove, with cards and inquiries, fifty did; not to speak of the foot callers. 'It is all meant by way of attention to you, Richard,' said gentle Mrs. Hare, smiling through her loving tears at her restored son. Lucy and Archie were dining at Miss Carlyle's, and Sarah attended little Arthur; leaving Wilson free. She came in, in answer to Madame Vine's ring.

'Is he off in another faint?' unceremoniously cried she, hastening to the bed.

'I think so. Help me to raise him.'

William did not faint. No: the attack was quite different from those he was subject to. Instead of losing consciousness and power, as was customary, he shook as if he had the ague, and laid hold both of Madame Vine and Wilson, grasping them convulsively.

'Don't let me fall! don't let me fall!' he gasped.

'My dear, you cannot fall!' responded Madame Vine. 'You forget that you are on the bed.'

He clasped them yet, and trembled still, as from fear. 'Don't let me fall! don't let me fall!' was the incessant burden of his cry.

The paroxysm passed. They wiped his brow, and stood looking at him: Wilson with a pursed-up mouth, and a peculiar expression of face. She put a spoonful of restorative jelly between his lips, and he swallowed it, but shook his head when she would have given him another. Turning his face to the pillow, in a few minutes he was in a doze.

'What could it have been?' exclaimed Lady Isabel, in an under-tone to Wilson.

'*I* know,' was the oracular answer. 'I saw this same sort of attack once before, madame.'

'And what caused it?'

''Twasn't in a child, though,' went on Wilson. ''Twas in a grown-up person. But that's nothing: it comes for the same thing in all. I think he was taken for death.'

'Who?' uttered Lady Isabel, startled.

Wilson made no reply in words, but she pointed with her finger to the bed.

'Oh, Wilson! He is not so ill as that. Mr. Wainwright said this morning that he might last a week or two.'

Wilson composedly sat down in the easiest chair. She was not wont to put herself out of the way for the governess: and that governess was too much afraid of her in one sense, to let her know her place. 'As to Wainwright, he's nobody,' quoth she. 'And if he saw the child's breath going out before his face, and knew that the next moment would be his last, he'd vow to us all that he was good for twelve hours to come. You don't know Wainwright as I do, madame. He was our doctor at mother's; and he has attended in all the places I have lived in, since I went out to service. Five years I was head nurse at Squire Pinner's; going on for four I was lady's maid at Mrs. Hare's; I came here when Miss Lucy was a baby; and in all my places has he attended, like one's shadow. My Lady Isabel thought great guns of old Wainwright, I remember. It was more than I did.'

My Lady Isabel made no response to this. She took a seat, and watched William. His breathing was more laboured than usual.

'That idiot Sarah says to me to-day, says she, "Which of his two grand-papas will they bury him by—old Mr. Carlyle, or Lord Mount Severn?" "Don't be a calf!" I answered her. "D'ye think they'll stick him out in the corner with my lord?—he'll be put in the Carlyle vault, of course." It would have been different, you see, Madame Vine, if my lady had died at home, all proper, Mr. Carlyle's wife. They'd have buried her no doubt by her father, and the boy would have been laid with her. But she did not.'

No reply was made by Madame Vine; and a silence ensued. Nothing to be heard but that fleeting breath.

'I wonder how that beauty feels?' suddenly broke forth Wilson again, her tone one of scornful irony.

Lady Isabel, her eyes and her thoughts absorbed by William, positively thought Wilson's words must relate to him. She turned to her in surprise.

'That bright gem in the prison at Lynneborough,' explained Wilson. 'I hope he may have found himself pretty well since yesterday! I wonder how many trainfuls from West Lynne will go to his hanging?'

Her face turned crimson; her heart sick. She had not dared to inquire how the trial terminated. The subject altogether was too dreadful; and nobody had happened to mention it in her hearing.

'Is he condemned?' she asked, in a low tone.

'He is condemned; and good luck to him; and Mr. Otway Bethel's let loose again; and good luck to *him*. A nice pair they are! Nobody went from this house to hear the trial—it might not have been pleasant, you know, madame, to Mr. Carlyle—but people came in last night and told us all about it. Young Richard Hare chiefly convicted him. He is back again, and so nice-looking, they say, ten times more so than he was when quite a young man. You should have heard, they say, the cheerings and shouts which greeted Mr. Richard when his innocence came out: it pretty near rose off the roof of the court; and the judge didn't stop it.'

Wilson paused, but there was no answering comment. On she went again.

'When Mr. Carlyle brought the news home last evening, and broke it to his wife—telling her how Mr. Richard had been received with acclamations, she nearly fainted; for she's not strong yet. Mr. Carlyle called out to me to bring some water: I was in the next room with the baby: and there she was, the tears raining from her eyes, and he holding her to him. I always said there was a whole world of love between those two, though he did go and marry another. Mr. Carlyle ordered me to put the water down, and sent me away again. But I don't fancy he told her of old Hare's attack until this morning.'

Lady Isabel lifted her aching forehead. 'What attack?'

'Why madame, don't you know? I declare you box yourself up in the house, keeping from everybody, till you hear nothing. You might as well be living at the bottom of a coal-pit. Old Hare had another stroke in the court at Lynneborough; and that's why my mistress is gone to the Grove to-day.'

'Who says Richard Hare's come home, Wilson?'

The question, the weak, scarcely audible question, had come from the dying boy. Wilson threw up her hands, and made a bound to the bed. 'The like of that!' she uttered, aside to Madame Vine. 'One never knows when to take these sick ones. Master William, you hold your tongue and drop off to sleep again. Your papa will be home soon from Lynneborough, and you talk and get tired, he'll say it's my fault. Come, shut your eyes. Will you have a bit more jelly?'

William, making no reply to the offer of jelly, buried his face again on the pillow. But he was grievously restless. The nearly worn-out spirit was ebbing and flowing.

Mr. Carlyle was at Lynneborough. He always had much business there at assize time, in the Nisi Prius court. But, the previous day, he had not gone himself; Mr. Dill had been despatched to represent him.

Between seven and eight he returned home, and came into William's chamber. The boy brightened up at the well-known presence.

'Papa!'

Mr. Carlyle sat down on the bed and kissed him. The passing beams of the sun slanting from the horizon, shone into the room, and Mr. Carlyle could view well the dying face. The grey hue of death was certainly on it.

'Is he worse?' he exclaimed hastily to Madame Vine.

'He appears worse this evening, sir. More weak.'

'Papa,' panted William. 'is the trial over?'

'What trial, my boy?'

'Sir Francis Levison's.'

'It was over yesterday. Never trouble your head about him, my brave boy. He is not worth it.'

'But, I want to know. Will they hang him?'

'He is sentenced to it.'

'Did he kill Hallijohn?'

'Yes. Who has been talking to him upon the subject?' Mr. Carlyle continued to Madame Vine, marked displeasure in his tone.

'Wilson mentioned it, sir,' was the low answer.

'Oh, papa, what will he do? Will Jesus forgive *him*?'

'We must hope it.'

'Do you hope it, papa?'

'Yes. I wish that all the world may be forgiven, William: whatever may have been their sins. My child, how restless you seem!'

'I can't keep in one place. The bed gets wrong. Pull me up on the pillow, will you, Madame Vine?'

Mr. Carlyle gently lifted the boy himself. 'Madame Vine is an untiring nurse to you, William,' he observed, gratefully casting a glance towards her in the distance, where she had retreated, and was shaded by the window curtain.

William made no reply. He seemed to be trying to recall something. 'I forget; I forget!'

'Forget what?' asked Mr. Carlyle.

'It was something I wanted to ask you; or tell you. Isn't Lucy come home?'

'I suppose not.'

'Papa, I want Joyce.'

'I will send her home to you. I am going for your mamma after dinner.'

'For mamma?—oh, I remember now. Papa, how shall I know mamma in heaven? Not this mamma.'

Mr. Carlyle did not immediately reply. The question may have puzzled him. William continued hastily: possibly mistaking the motive of the silence.

'She *will* be in heaven, you know.'

'Yes, yes, child,' speaking hurriedly.

'Madame Vine knows she will. She saw her abroad: and mamma told her that—what was it, madame?'

Madame Vine grew sick with alarm. Mr. Carlyle turned his eyes upon her scarlet face—as much as he could get to see of it. She would have escaped from the room if she could.

'Mamma was more sorry than she could bear,' went on William, finding he was not helped. 'She wanted you, papa, and she wanted us, and her heart broke, and she died.'

A flush rose to Mr. Carlyle's brow. He turned inquiringly to Madame Vine.

'Oh, I *beg* your pardon, sir,' she murmured, with desperate energy, 'I ought not so to have spoken: I ought not to have interfered in your family affairs. I spoke only as I thought it must be, sir. The boy seemed troubled about his mother.'

Mr. Carlyle was at sea. 'Did you meet his mother abroad? I scarcely understand.'

She lifted her hand and covered her glowing face. 'No, sir.' Surely the recording angel blotted out the words! If ever a prayer for forgiveness went up from an aching heart, it must have gone up then, for the equivocation uttered over her child's death-bed!

Mr. Carlyle went towards her. 'Do you perceive the change in his countenance?' he whispered.

'Yes, sir, yes. He has looked like this since a strange fit of trembling that came on in the afternoon. Wilson thought he might be taken for death. I fear some four-and-twenty hours will end it.'

Mr. Carlyle rested his elbow on the window-frame, and his hand upon his brow, his drooping eyelids falling over his eyes. 'It is hard to lose him.'

'Oh, sir, he will be better off!' she wailed, choking down the sobs and the emotion, that arose threateningly. 'We *can* bear death; it is not the worst parting that the earth knows. He will be quit of this cruel world: sheltered in heaven. I wish we were all there!'

A servant came to say that Mr. Carlyle's dinner was served, and he proceeded to it with what appetite he had. When he returned to the sick-room, the daylight had faded, and a solitary candle was placed where its rays could not fall upon the child's face. Mr. Carlyle took the light in his hand to scan that face again. He was lying sideways on the pillow, his hollow breath echoing through the room. The light caused him to open his eyes.

'Don't papa, please. I like it dark.'

'Only for one moment, my precious boy.' And, not for more than a moment did Mr. Carlyle hold it. The blue, pinched, ghastly look was there yet. Death was certainly coming on quick.

At that moment Lucy and Archibald came in, on their return from their visit to Miss Carlyle. The dying boy looked up eagerly.

'Good-bye, Lucy,' he said, putting out his cold, damp hand.

'I am not going out,' replied Lucy. 'We have but just come home.'

'Good-bye, Lucy,' repeated he.

She laid hold of his little hand then, leaned over, and kissed him. 'Good-bye William: but indeed I am not going out anywhere.'

'I am,' said he. 'I am going to heaven. Where's Archie?'

Mr.Carlyle lifted Archie on to the bed. Lucy looked frightened. Archie surprised.

'Archie, good-bye; good-bye, dear. I am going to heaven: to that bright blue sky, you know. I shall see mamma there, and I'll tell her that you and Lucy are coming soon.'

Lucy, a sensitive child, broke into a loud storm of sobs: enough to disturb the equanimity of any sober sick-room. Wilson hastened in at the sound, and Mr. Carlyle sent the two children away, with soothing promises that they should see William in the morning, if he continued well enough.

Down on her knees, her face buried in the counterpane, a corner of it stuffed into her mouth that it might help to stifle her agony, knelt Lady Isabel. The moment's excitement was well nigh beyond her strength of endurance. Her own child; his child; they alone around its death-bed, and she might not ask or receive from him a word of comfort, of consolation!

Mr. Carlyle glanced at her as he caught her choking sobs; just as he would have glanced at any other attentive governess. Feeling her sympathy, doubtless; but nothing more; she was not heart and part with him and his departing boy. Lower and lower bent he over that boy, for his eyes were wet.

'Don't cry, papa,' whispered William, raising his feeble hand caressingly to his father's cheek. 'I am not afraid to go. Jesus is coming for me.'

'Afraid to go! Indeed I hope not, my gentle boy. You are going to God; to happiness. A few years—we know not how few—and we shall all come to you.'

'Yes, you will be sure to come: I know that. I shall tell mamma so. I dare say she is looking out for me now. Perhaps she is standing on the banks of the river, watching the boats.'

He had evidently got that picture of Martin's in his mind, the Plains of Heaven. Mr. Carlyle turned to the table. He saw some strawberry juice, pressed from the fresh fruit, and moistened with it the boy's fevered lips.

'Papa, I can't think how Jesus can be in all the boats! Perhaps they don't go quite at the same time? He must be, you know, because he comes to fetch us.'

'He will be in yours, darling,' was the whispered, fervent answer.

'Oh yes. He will take me all the way up to God, and say, "Here's a poor little boy come, and you must please to forgive him and let him go into Heaven, because I died for him!" Papa, did you know that mamma's heart broke?'

A caress was all the reply Mr. Carlyle returned. William's restlessness of body appeared to be extending to his mind. He would not be put off.

'Papa, did you know that mamma's heart broke?'

'William, I think it likely that your poor mamma's heart did break, ere death came. But let us talk of you; not of her. Are you in pain?'

'I can't breathe; I can't swallow. I wish Joyce was here.'

'She will not be long.'

The boy nestled himself in his father's arms, and in a few minutes appeared to be asleep. Mr. Carlyle, after a while, gently laid him on his pillow, watched him, and then turned to depart.

'Oh, papa, papa!' he cried out, in a tone of painful entreaty, opening wide his yearning eyes. 'say good-bye to me!'

Mr. Carlyle's tears fell upon the little upturned face, as he once more caught it to his breast.

'My darling, papa will soon be back. He is not going to leave you for more than an hour. He is going to bring mamma to see you.'

'And pretty little baby Anna?'

'And baby Anna, if you would like her to come in. I will not leave my darling boy for long: he need not fear. I shall not leave you again to-night, William, when once I am back.'

'Then put me down, and go, papa.'

A lingering embrace; a fond, lingering, tearful embrace, Mr. Carlyle holding him to his beating heart. Then he laid him comfortably on his pillow, gave him a teaspoonful of strawberry juice, and hastened away.

'Good-bye, papa,' came forth the little feeble cry.

It was not heard. Mr. Carlyle was gone. Gone from his living child—for ever. Up rose Lady Isabel, and flung her arms aloft in a storm of sobs.

'Oh, William, darling! in this dying moment let me be to you as your mother!'

Again he unclosed his weary eyelids. It is probable that he only partially understood.

'Papa's gone for her.'

'Not *her!* I—I—' Lady Isabel checked herelf, and fell sobbing on the bed.

No; not even at that last hour when the world was closing on him dared she say, I am your mother.

Wilson re-entered. 'He looks as if he were dropping off to sleep,' quoth she.

'Yes,' said Lady Isabel. 'You need not wait, Wilson. I will ring if he requires anything.'

Wilson, though withal not a bad-hearted woman, was not one to remain for pleasure, in a sick-room, if told she might leave it. Lady Isabel remained alone. She fell on her knees again, this time in prayer. In prayer for the departing spirit on its wing, and that God would mercifully vouchsafe herself a resting-place with it in heaven.

A review of the past then rose up before her. From the time of her first entering that house, the bride of Mr. Carlyle, to her present sojourn in it. The old scenes passed through her mind, like the changing pictures in a phantasmagoria. Why should they have come, there and then? She knew not.

William slept on silently: *she* thought of the past. The dreadful reflection, 'If I had not done as I did—how different would it have been now!' had been sounding its knell in her heart so often, that she had almost ceased to shudder at it. The very nails of her hands had, before now, entered the palms with the sharp pain it brought. Stealing over her more especially this night as she knelt there, her head lying on the counterpane, came the recollection of that first illness of hers. How she had lain, and, in her unfounded jealousy, imagined Barbara the house's mistress. She, dead; Barbara exalted to her place, Mr. Carlyle's wife, her child's stepmother! She recalled the day when, her mind excited by certain gossip of Wilson's—it was previously in a state of fever bordering on delirium—she had prayed her husband, in terror and anguish, not to marry Barbara. 'How could he marry her?' he had replied, in his soothing pity. 'She, Isabel, was his wife: who was Barbara? Nothing to them.' But it had all come to pass. *She* had brought it forth. Not Mr. Carlyle; not Barbara; she alone. Oh, the dreadful misery of the retrospect!

Lost in thought, in anguish past and present, in self-condemning repentance, the time passed on. Nearly an hour must have elapsed since Mr. Carlyle's departure, and William had not disturbed her. But—who was this, coming into the room? Joyce.

She hastily rose up, as Joyce, advancing with a quiet step, drew aside the clothes to look at William. 'Master says he has been wanting me,' she observed. 'Why—oh!'

It was a sharp, momentary cry, subdued as soon as uttered. Madame Vine sprang forward to Joyce's side, looking also. The pale young face lay calm in its utter stillness; the busy little heart had ceased to beat. Jesus Christ had indeed come, and taken the fleeting spirit.

Then she lost all self-control. She believed that she had reconciled herself to the child's death, that she could part with him without too great emotion.

But she had not anticipated it would be quite so soon; she had deemed that some hours more would at least be given him; and now the storm overwhelmed her. Crying, sobbing, calling, she flung herself upon him; she clasped him to her; she dashed off her disguising glasses; she laid her face upon his. Beseeching him to come back to her that she might say farewell; to her, his mother; her darling child, her lost William.

Joyce was terrified; terrified for consequences. With her full strength she pulled her from the boy, praying her to consider, to be still. 'Do not, do not, for the love of Heaven! *My lady! my lady!*'

It was the old familiar title that struck upon her ears and induced calmness. She stared at Joyce, and retreated backwards; after the manner of one receding from some hideous vision.

'My lady, let me take you into your room. Mr. Carlyle is come; he is but bringing up his wife. Only think if you should give way before him! Pray come away!'

'How did you know me?' she asked, in a hollow voice.

'My lady, it was that night when there was an alarm of fire. I went close up to you to take Master Archibald from your arms; and, as sure as I am now standing here, I believe that for the moment my senses left me. I thought I saw a spectre; the spectre of my dead lady. I forgot the present; I forgot that all were standing round me; that you, Madame Vine, were alive before me. Your face was not disguised then: the moonlight shone full upon it, and I knew it, after the first few moments of terror, to be, in dreadful truth, the *living* one of Lady Isabel. My lady, come away! we shall have Mr. Carlyle here.'

Poor thing! she sank upon her knees, in her humility, her dread. 'Oh, Joyce, have pity upon me! don't betray me! I will leave the house; indeed, I will. Don't betray me while I am in it!'

'My lady, you have nothing to fear from me. I have kept the secret buried within my breast since then. Last April! It has nearly been too much for me. By night and by day I have had no peace, dreading what might come out. Think of the awful confusion, the consequences, should it come to the knowledge of Mr. and Mrs. Carlyle. Indeed, my lady, you never ought to have come.'

'Joyce,' she said hollowly, lifting her haggard face. 'I could not keep away from my unhappy children. Is it no punishment to *me*, think you, the being here?' she added, vehemently. 'To see him—my husband—the husband of another? It is killing me.'

'Oh, my lady, come away! I hear him; I hear him!'

Partly coaxing, partly dragging her, Joyce took her into her own room, and left her there. Mr. Carlyle was at that moment at the door of the sick one. Joyce sprang forward. Her face, in her emotion and fear, was one of livid whiteness, and she shook as William had shaken, poor child, in the afternoon. It was only too apparent in the well-lighted corridor.

'Joyce!' he exclaimed in amazement, 'what ails you?'

'Sir! master!' she panted, 'be prepared. Master William—Master William—'

'Joyce! Not *dead?*'

'Alas, yes, sir!'

Mr. Carlyle strode into the chamber, but, ere he was well across it, turned back to slip the bolt of the door. On the pillow lay the white, thin face, at rest now.

'My boy! my boy! Oh, God!' he murmured, in bowed reverence, 'may'st Thou have received this child to his rest in Jesus! Even as, I trust, Thou hast already received his unhappy mother!'

❧ X X I ❧

Lord Vane Dating Forwards

To the funeral of William Carlyle came Lord Mount Severn and his son. Wilson had been right in her surmises as to the resting-place. The Carlyle vault was opened for him, and an order went forth to the sculptor, for an inscription to be added to their marble tablet in the church. 'William Vane Carlyle, eldest son of Archibald Carlyle, of East Lynne.' Amongst those who attended the funeral as mourners, went one more notable in the eyes of gazers than the rest; Richard Hare the younger.

Lady Isabel was ill. Ill in mind, and ominously ill in body. She kept her room; and Joyce attended on her. The household set down madame's illness to the fatigue of having attended upon Master William: it was not thought of seriously by anyone, especially as she declined to see a doctor. All her thoughts, now, were directed to the getting away from East Lynne, for it would never do to remain there to die; and she knew that death was on his way to her, and that no human power or skill, not all the faculty combined, could turn him back again. The excessive dread of detection was not upon her as it had been formerly; I mean, she did not dread the consequences so much, if detection came. In nearing the grave, all fears and hopes, of whatever nature, relating to this world, lose their force: and fears, or hopes, regarding the next world, take their place.

In returning to East Lynne, Lady Isabel had entered upon a daring act: and she found, in the working, that neither her strength nor spirit was equal to it. Presuming upon the extraordinary change which had taken place in her appearance, and which, with her own care, rendered detection next door to an impossibility, she had suffered it to blind her judgment, and lead her upon a course that could only end badly. Let people talk as they will, it is impossible to drive out human passions from the human heart. You may suppress them, deaden them, keep them in subjection, but you cannot root them out. The very best man that attains to the greatest holiness on earth has need constantly to strive and pray, if he would keep away evil from his thoughts, passions from his nature. His life must be spent in self-watchfulness; he must 'pray always,' at morning, at evening, at midday: and he cannot do it then. One of the greatest of our living divines, grey now with years and infirmities, said in a memorable sermon, preached in Worcester cathedral in the zenith of his fame and power, that the life, even of a good man, was made up of daily sinning and repenting. So it is. Human passions and tempers were brought with us into this world, and they can only quit us when we bid it farewell to enter upon immortality in the next.

When Lady Isabel was Mr. Carlyle's wife, she had never wholly loved him. The very utmost homage that esteem, admiration, affection, could give, was his; but that mysterious passion called by the name of love (and which, as I truly and heartily believe, cannot in its refined etherealism be known to many of us) had not been given to him. It was now. I told you some chapters back, that the world goes round by the rules of contrary—conter-rary, mind you, the children have it in their game—and we go round with it. We despise what we have, and covet that which we cannot get. From the very night she had come back to East Lynne, her love for Mr. Carlyle had burst forth with an intensity never before felt. It had been smouldering almost ever since she quitted him. 'Reprehensible!' groans a moralist. Very. Everybody knows that, as Afy would say. But her heart, you see, had *not* done with human passions: and they work ill, and conterariness (let the word stand, critic, if you please), and precisely everything they should not.

I shall get blame for it, I fear, if I attempt to defend her. But it was not exactly the same thing, as though she had suffered herself to fall in love with somebody else's husband. Nobody would defend *that*. We have not turned mormons yet, and the world does not walk upon its head. When Queen Eleanor handed the bowl of poison to Fair Rosamond, she challenged the execrations of posterity, and they have been liberally bestowed upon her from that hour to this. The queen gets all the blame, the lady all the sympathy. Putting the poison out of view, I think the judgment should be reversed. Had Lady Isabel fallen in love with—say—Mr. Crosby, she would have deserved a little judicious chastisement at Mr. Crosby's hands. Perhaps an hour or two spent in some agreeable pillory might have proved efficacious. But this was a

peculiar case. She, poor thing, almost regarded Mr. Carlyle as *her* husband.
The bent of her thoughts was only too much inclined to this. (That evil human heart again!) Many and many a time did she wake up from a reverie,
and strive to drive this mistaken view of things away from her, taking shame
to herself. Ten minutes afterwards, she would catch her brain revelling in the
same rebellious vision. Mr. Carlyle's love was not hers now; it was Barbara's:
Mr. Carlyle did not belong to her; he belonged to his wife. It was not only
that he was not hers; he was another's: you may, therefore, if you have the
pleasure of being experienced in this sort of thing, guess a little at what her
inward life was. Had there been no Barbara in the case, she might have lived
and borne it: as it was, it had killed her before her time—that and the remorse together.

There had been other things, too. The reappearance of Francis Levison at
West Lynne, in fresh contact, as may be said, with herself, had struck terror
to her heart; and the dark charge brought against him awfully augmented
her remorse. Then the sharp lances perpetually thrust upon her memory—
the Lady Isabel's memory—from all sides, were full of cruel stings, uninten-
tionally though they were hurled. And there was the hourly chance of discovery, and the never-ceasing battle with her conscience for being at East
Lynne at all. No wonder that the chords of life were snapping: the wonder
would have been had they remained whole.

'She brought it upon herself! she ought not to have come back to East
Lynne!' groans our moralist again. Don't I say so? Of course she ought not.
Neither ought she to have suffered her thoughts to stray in the manner they
did, towards Mr. Carlyle. She ought not; but she did. If we all did just what
we 'ought,' this lower world would be worth living in. You must just sit
down and abuse her, and so cool your anger. I agree with you that she ought
never to have come back; that it was an act little short of madness: but are
you quite sure that you would not have done the same, under the facility and
the temptation? And now you can abuse me for saying it, if it will afford you
any satisfaction.

She was nearer to death than she imagined. She knew—judging by her declining strength and her inner feelings—that it could not be far off; but she
did not deem it was coming so very soon. Her mother had died in a similar
way. Some said of consumption—Dr. Martin said so, you may remember;
some said of 'waste;' the earl, her husband, said of a broken heart—you
heard him say so to Mr. Carlyle in the first chapter of this history. The earl
was the one who might be supposed to know best. Whatever may have been
Lady Mount Severn's malady, she—to give you the phrase that was in people's mouths at the time—'went out like the snuff of a candle.' It was now
the turn of Lady Isabel. She had no decided disorder, yet Death had marked
her. She felt that it was so: and in the approach of Death she dreaded not, as

she had once done, the consequences that must ensue, did discovery come. Which brings us back to the point whence ensued this long digression. I dare say you are chafing at it, but it is not often I trouble you with one.

But she would not willingly let discovery come; neither had she the least intention of remaining at East Lynne to die. Where she should take refuge, was quite a secondary consideration: only let her get smoothly and plausibly away. Joyce, in her dread, was for ever urging it. Of course the preliminary step was, to arrange matters with Mrs. Carlyle, and in the afternoon of the day following the funeral, Lady Isabel proceeded to her dressing-room, and craved an interview.

Mr. Carlyle quitted the room as she entered it. Barbara, fatigued with a recent drive, was lying on the sofa.

'We shall be so sorry to lose you, Madame Vine! You are all we could wish for Lucy: and Mr. Carlyle feels truly grateful for your love and attention to his poor boy.'

'To leave will give me pain also,' Madame Vine answered, in a subdued tone. Pain? Ay. Mrs. Carlyle little guessed at its extent. All she cared for on earth, she should leave behind her at East Lynne.

'Indeed you must not leave,' resumed Barbara. 'It would be unjust to allow you to do so. You have made yourself ill, waiting upon poor William, and you must remain here and take holiday until you are cured. You will soon get well, if you will only suffer yourself to be properly waited on and taken care of.'

'You are very considerate. Pray do not think me insensible if I decline. I believe my strength is beyond getting up: that I shall never be able to teach again.'

'Oh, nonsense,' said Barbara, in her quick way. 'We are all given to fancy the worst when we are ill. I was feeling terribly weak, only a few minutes ago, and said something of the same sort to Archibald. He talked and soothed me out of it. I wish you had your dear husband living, Madame Vine, to support you and love you; as I have him.'

A tinge of scarlet streaked Madame Vine's pale face, and she laid her hand upon her beating heart.

'How could you think of leaving? We should be glad to help re-establish your health, in any case, but it is only fair to do it now. I felt sure, by the news brought to me when I was ill, that your attention upon William was overtaxing your strength.'

'It is not the attendance upon William that has brought me into this state,' was the quick answer. 'I *must* leave; I have well considered it over.'

'Would you like to go to the sea-side?' exclaimed Barbara, with sudden energy. 'I am going there on Monday next; Mr. Carlyle insists upon it that I try a little change. I had intended only to take my baby; but we can make different arrangements and take you and Lucy. It might do you good, Madame Vine.'

She shook her head. 'No: it would make me worse. All that I want is perfect quiet. I must beg you to understand that I shall leave. And I should be glad if you could allow the customary notice to be dispensed with, so that I may be at liberty to depart within a few days.'

'Look here, then,' said Barbara, after a pause of consideration; 'you remain at East Lynne until my return—which will be in a fortnight. Mr. Carlyle cannot stay with me, so I know I shall be tired in less time than that. He and his office are quite overwhelmed with business after his long sojourn in London. I did not care to go until August or September, when he will be at leisure, but he would not hear of it, and says we can go again then. I do not want you to remain to teach, you know, Madame Vine: I do not wish you to do a single thing. Lucy shall have holiday, and Mr. Kane can come up for her music. Only, I could not be content to leave her, unless under your surveillance: she is getting of an age now, not to be consigned to servants, not even to Joyce. Upon my return, if you still wish to leave, you shall then be at liberty to do so. What do you say?'

Madame Vine said 'Yes.' Said it eagerly. To have another fortnight with her children, Lucy and Archibald, was very like a reprieve, and she embraced it. Although she knew, as I have said, that grim death was on his way, she did not think he had drawn so near the end of his journey. Her thoughts went back to the time when *she* had been ordered to the sea-side after an illness. It had been a marvel if they had not. She remembered how her husband had urged the change upon her: how he had taken her, travelling carefully; how tenderly anxious he had been in the arrangements for her comfort, when settling her in the lodgings; how, when he came back again to see her, he had met her in his passionate fondness, thanking God for the visible improvement in her looks. That one injunction, which she had called him back to give him, as he was departing for the boat, was bitterly present to her now: 'Do not get making love to Barbara Hare.' All this care, and love, and tenderness, belonged now of right to Barbara; and were given to her.

Now Barbara, although she pressed Madame Vine to remain at East Lynne, and indeed would have been glad that she should do so, did not take her refusal to heart. Barbara could not fail to perceive that she was a thoroughly refined gentlewoman, far superior to the generality of governesses. That she was also truly fond of Lucy, and most anxious for her welfare in every way, Barbara also saw. For Lucy's sake, therefore, she would be grieved to part with Madame Vine, and would raise her salary to anything in reason, if she would but stay. But, on her own score, Barbara had as soon Madame Vine went, as not; for, in her heart of hearts, she had never liked her. She could not have told why. Was it instinct? Very probably. The birds of the air, the beasts of the field, the fishes of the sea, have their instincts; and man has his. Perhaps it was the unaccountable resemblance that Madame Vine bore to Lady Isabel. A strange likeness, Barbara often thought: but whether it lay in the face, the voice, or the manner, she could never decide. A suspicion of the truth did not cross her mind. How should it? And she never spoke of it: had the resemblance been to any one but Lady Isabel she would have talked of it freely. Or, it may have been that there was now and then a tone in Madame Vine's voice that grated on her ear: a wrung, impatient tone, wanting in respect, savouring of hauteur, which Barbara did not understand, and did not like. However it may have been, certain it is that Mrs. Carlyle would not shed tears after the governess. Only for Lucy's sake did she regret parting with her.

These different remembrances and reflections were separately passing through the minds of the two ladies, when Madame Vine at length rose from her chair to depart.

'Would you mind holding my baby for one minute?' cried Barbara.

Madame Vine quite started. 'The baby there!' she uttered. Barbara laughed.

'It is lying by my side, under the shawl, quiet, little sleeping thing.'

Madame Vine advanced and took the sleeping baby. How could she refuse? She had never had it in her arms before: had, in fact, scarcely seen it. One visit of ceremony she had paid Mrs. Carlyle, as in politeness bound, a day or two after the young lady's arrival, and had been shown a little face, nearly covered with lace, in a cradle.

'Thank you. I can get up now. I might have half smothered it, had I attempted before,' continued Barbara, still laughing. 'I have been here long enough, and am quite rested. Talking about smothering children, what accounts we have in the registrar-general's weekly returns of health. So many children "overlaid in bed;" so many children "suffocated in bed." One week there were nearly twenty, and often there are as many as eight and ten. Mr. Carlyle says he knows they are smothered on purpose.'

'Oh, Mrs. Carlyle!'

'I exclaimed, just as you do, when he said it, and laid my hand over his lips. He laughed and told me I did not know half the wickedness of the world. Thank you,' again repeated Mrs. Carlyle, taking her child from Lady Isabel. 'Is she not a pretty baby? Do you like the name: Anna?'

'It is a simple name,' replied Lady Isabel. 'And simple names are always the most attractive.'

'That is just what Archibald thinks. But he wanted this child to be Barbara. I would not have had it Barbara for the world. I remember his once saying, a long, long while ago, that he did not like elaborate names: they were mouthfuls; and he instanced mine, and his sister's, and his own. I recalled his words to him, and he said he may not have liked the name of Barbara then, but he loved it now. So we entered into a compromise; Miss Baby was named Anna Barbara, with an understanding that the first name was to be for use, and the last for the registers.'

'It is not christened,' said Lady Isabel.

'Only baptised. We should have had it christened before now, but for William's death. Not that we give christening dinners; but I waited for the trial at Lynneborough to be over, that my dear brother Richard might stand to the child.'

'Mr. Carlyle does not like christenings made into festivals,' Lady Isabel dreamily observed, her thoughts buried in the past.

'How did you know that?' exclaimed Barbara, opening her eyes. And poor Madame Vine, her pale face flushing, had to stammer forth some confused words that 'she had heard so somewhere.'

'It is quite true,' said Barbara. 'He has never given a christening dinner for any of his children. He cannot understand the analogy between a solemn religious rite, and the meeting together afterwards to eat and drink and make merry, according to the fashion of this world.'

As Lady Isabel quitted the room, young Vane was careering through the corridor, throwing his head in all directions, and calling out,

'Lucy! I want Lucy.'

'What do you want with her?' asked Madame Vine.

'*Il me'st impossible de vous le dire, madame,*' responded he. Being, for an Eton boy, wonderfully up in French, he was rather given to show it off, when he got the chance. He did not owe it to Eton: Lady Mount Severn had taken better care than that. Better care? What could she want? There was one whole real live French tutor—and he an Englishman—for the eight hundred boys. Very unreasonable for her ladyship to disparage that ample provision!

'Lucy cannot come to you just now. She is practising.'

'*Mais, il le faut. J'ai le droit de demander après elle. Elle m'appartient, vous comprenez, madame, cette demoiselle-là.*'

Madame could not forbear a smile. 'I wish you would speak English sense, instead of French nonsense.'

'Then the English sense is, that I want Lucy, and I must have her. I am going to take her for a drive in the pony-carriage if you must know. She said she would come, and John is getting it ready.'

'I could not possibly allow it,' said Madame Vine. 'You would be sure to upset her.'

'The idea!' he returned, indignantly. 'As if I should upset Lucy! Why, I am one of the great whips at Eton! I care for Lucy too much not to drive steadily. She is to be my wife, you know, *ma bonne dame.*'

At this juncture, two heads were pushed out from the library, close by: those of the earl and Mr. Carlyle. Barbara also, attracted by the talking, appeared at the door of her dressing-room.

'What's that about a wife?' asked my lord, of his son.

The blood mantled in the young gentleman's cheeks, as he turned round and saw who spoke. But he possessed all the fearlessness of an Eton boy, the honour of a right mind; and he disdained to equivocate.

'I intend Lucy Carlyle to be my wife, papa. I mean, in earnest,—when we shall both be grown up. If you will approve, and Mr. Carlyle will give her to me.'

The earl looked grave: Mr. Carlyle amused. 'Suppose,' said the latter, 'we adjourn the discussion to this day ten years?'

'But that Lucy is so very young, a child, I should reprove you seriously, sir,' said the earl. 'You have no right to bring Lucy's name into any such absurdity.'

'I mean it, papa: you'll all see. And I intend to keep out of scrapes—that is, of nasty dishonourable scrapes—on purpose that Mr. Carlyle shall find no excuse against me. I have made up my mind to be what he is—a man of honour. I am right glad you know about it, sir. And I shall let mamma know it, before long.'

The last sentence tickled the earl's fancy, and a grim smile passed over his lips. 'It will be war to the knife, if you do.'

'I know that,' laughed the viscount. 'But I am getting a better match for mamma in our battles than I used to be.'

Nobody saw fit to prolong the discussion. Barbara put her veto upon the drive in the pony-carriage, unless John sat behind to look after the driver, which Lord Vane's skill resented as an insult. Madame Vine, when the corridor became empty again, laid her hand upon the boy's arm, as he was moving away, and drew him to the window.

'In speaking, as you do, of Lucy Carlyle, do you forget the disgrace reflected on her through the conduct of her mother?'

'Her mother is not Lucy.'

'It may prove an impediment with Lord and Lady Mount Severn.'

'Not with his lordship. And I must do—as you heard me say—battle with my mother. Conciliatory battle, you understand, madame; bringing the enemy to reason.'

Madame Vine was agitated. She held her handkerchief to her mouth and the boy noticed how her hands trembled.

'I have learnt to love Lucy,' said she. 'It has appeared to me, in these few months' sojourn with her, that I have stood to her in the light of a mother. William Vane,' she solemnly added, keeping her hold upon him, 'I shall soon be where earthly distinctions are no more; where sin and sorrow are wiped away. Should Lucy Carlyle indeed become your wife in after years, never, never cast upon her, by so much as the lightest word of reproach, the sin of Lady Isabel.'

Lord Vane threw back his head, his honest eyes flashing in their indignant earnestness.

'What do you take me for?'

'It would be a cruel wrong upon Lucy. She does not deserve it. That unhappy lady's sin was all her own: let it die with her. Never speak to Lucy of her mother.'

The lad dashed his hand across his eyes, for they were filling. 'I shall. I shall speak to her often of her mother—that is, you know, after she's my wife. I shall tell how I loved Lady Isabel—that there's nobody I ever loved so much in the world, but Lucy herself. *I* cast a reproach to Lucy on the score of her mother!' he hotly added. 'It is through her mother that I love her. You don't understand, madame.'

'Cherish and love her for ever, should she become yours,' said Lady Isabel, wringing his hand. 'I ask this as one who is dying.'

'I will. I promise it. But I say, madame,' he continued, dropping his fervent tone, 'to what do you allude? Are you worse?'

Madame Vine did not answer. She glided away without speaking.

When she was sitting that evening by twilight in the grey parlour, cold and shivering, and wrapped up in a shawl, though it was hot summer weather, somebody knocked at the door.

'Come in,' cried she, apathetically.

It was Mr. Carlyle who entered. She rose up, her pulses quickening, her heart throbbing against her side. In her wild confusion, she was drawing forward a chair for him. He laid his hand upon it, and motioned her to her own.

'Mrs. Carlyle tells me that you have been speaking to her of leaving. That you find yourself too much out of health to continue with us.'

'Yes, sir,' she faintly replied, having a most imperfect notion of what she did say.

'What is it that you find to be the matter with you?'

'I—think—it is chiefly weakness,' she stammered.

Her face had grown as grey as the walls. A dusky, livid sort of hue, not unlike that which William's had worn the night of his death, and her voice sounded strangely hollow. The voice struck Mr. Carlyle, and awoke his fears.

'You cannot—you never can have caught William's complaint, in your close attendance on him!' he exclaimed, speaking in the impulse of the moment, as the idea flashed across him. 'I have heard of such things.'

'Caught it from him!' she rejoined, carried away also by impulse. 'It is more likely that he—'

She stopped herself just in time. '*Inherited it from me,*' had been the destined conclusion. In her alarm, she went off volubly, something to the effect that 'it was no wonder she was ill; illness was natural to her family.'

'At any rate, you have become ill at East Lynne, in attendance on my children,' rejoined Mr. Carlyle, decisively, when her voice died away; 'you must therefore allow me to insist that you permit East Lynne to do what it can towards renovating you. What is your objection to see a doctor?'

'A doctor could do me no good,' she faintly answered.

'Certainly not—so long as you will not consult one.'

'Indeed, sir, doctors could not cure me. Nor—as I believe—prolong my life.'

Mr. Carlyle paused. 'Do you believe yourself to be in danger?'

'Not in immediate danger, sir. Only in-so-far that I know I shall not live long.'

'And yet you will not see a doctor! Madame Vine, you must be aware that I could not permit such a thing to go on in my house. Dangerous illness and no advice!'

She could not say to him, 'My malady is on the mind; it is a breaking heart, and therefore no doctor of physic could serve me.' That would never do. She had sat with her hand across her face, between her spectacles, and her wrapped-up chin. Had Mr. Carlyle possessed the eyes of Argus, he could not have made anything of her features in the broad light of day. But *she* did not feel so sure of it. There was always an undefined terror of discovery when in his presence, and she wished the interview at an end.

'I will see Mr. Wainwright, if it will be any satisfaction to you, sir.'

'Madame Vine, I have intruded upon you here to say that you *must* see him. And, should he deem it necessary, Dr. Martin also.'

'Oh, sir,' she rejoined with a curious smile, 'Mr. Wainwright will be quite sufficient. There will be no need of another. I will write a note to him to-morrow.'

'Spare yourself the trouble. I am going into West Lynne, and will send him up. You will permit me to urge that you spare no pains or care—that you suffer my servants to spare no pains or care to re-establish your health. Mrs. Carlyle tells me that the question of your leaving remains in abeyance until her return—'

'Pardon me, sir. The understanding with Mrs. Carlyle was, that I should remain here until her return, and should then be at liberty at once to leave.'

'Exactly. That is what Mrs. Carlyle said. But I must express a hope that by that time you may be feeling so much better as to reconsider your decision, and continue with us. For my daughter's sake, Madame Vine, I trust it will be so.'

He rose as he spoke, and held out his hand. What could she do but rise also, drop hers from her face, and give it him in answer? He retained it, clasping it warmly.

'How shall I repay you; how thank you for your love to my poor lost boy?'

His earnest, tender eyes were on her double-spectacles; a sad smile mingled with the sweet expression of his lips, as he bent towards her—lips that had once been hers! A faint exclamation of despair; a vivid glow of hot crimson; and she caught up her new black silk apron, so deeply bordered with crape, in her disengaged hand, and flung it up to her face. He mistook the sound; mistook the action.

'Do not grieve for him. He is at rest. Thank you, thank you greatly for all your sympathy.'

Another wring of her hand, and Mr. Carlyle had quitted the room. She laid her head upon the table, and thought how merciful would be death when he should come.

❧ X X I I ☙

It Won't Do, Afy

Mr. Jiffin was in his glory. Mr. Jiffin's house was the same. Both were in apple-pie readiness to receive Miss Afy Hallijohn, who was, in a very short period indeed, to be converted into Mrs. Jiffin.

Mr. Jiffin had not seen Afy for some days: had never been able to come across her since the trial at Lynneborough. Every evening had he danced attendance at her lodgings, but could not get admitted. 'Not at home; not at home;' was the invariable answer, though Afy might be sunning herself at the window in his very sight. Mr. Jiffin, throwing off as he best could the temporary disappointment, was in an ecstasy of admiration, for he set it all down to Afy's retiring modesty on the approach of the nuptial day. 'And they could try to calumniate her!' he indignantly breathed.

But now, one afternoon, when Mr. Jiffin, and his shopman, and his shop, and his wares were all set out to the best advantage, and very tempting they looked as a whole, especially the spiced bacon, Mr. Jiffin, happening to cast his eyes to the opposite side of the street, beheld his beloved sailing by. She was got up in the fashion. A mauve silk dress with eighteen flounces, and about eighteen hundred steel buttons that glittered your sight away; a 'zouave' jacket, worked with gold; a black straw hat with no visible brim perched on the top of her skull, garnished in front with what court milliners are pleased to term a 'plume de coq,' but which, by its size and height, might have been taken for a 'coq' himself, while a white ostrich feather was carried round and did duty behind, and a spangled hair-net hung down to her waist. Gloriously grand was Afy that day; and if I had but a photographing machine at hand—or whatever may be the scientific name for the thing—you should certainly have been regaled with the sight of her. Joyce would have gone down in a fit, had she encountered her by any unhappy chance. Mr. Jiffin, dashing his apron anywhere, tore across.

'Oh, is it you?' said Afy, freezingly, when compelled to acknowledge him, but his offered hand she utterly repudiated. 'Really, Mr. Jiffin, I should feel obliged if you would not come out to me in this offensive and public manner.'

Mr. Jiffin grew cold. 'Offensive! Not come out!' gasped he. 'I do trust I have not been so unfortunate as to offend you, Miss Afy!'

'Well—you see,' said Afy, calling up all her impudence to say what she had made up her mind to say, 'I have been considering it well over, Jiffin, and I find that to carry out the marriage will not be for my—for our happiness. I intended to write and inform you this; but I shall be spared the trouble—as you *have* come out to me.'

The perspiration, cold as ice, began to pour off Mr. Jiffin in his agony and horror. You might have wrung every thread he had on. 'You—don't—mean—to—imply—that—you—give—me—up,—Miss Afy?' he jerked out, unevenly.

'Well; yes I do,' replied Afy . 'It's as good to be plain; and then there can be no misapprehension. I'll shake hands nów with you, Jiffin, for the last time: and I am very sorry that we both made such a mistake.'

Poor Jiffin looked at her. His gaze would have melted a heart of stone. 'Miss Afy, you *can't* mean it! You'd never, sure, crush a fellow in this manner, whose whole soul is yours; who trusted you entirely! There's not an earthly thing I would not do, to please you. You have been the—the light of my existence.'

'Of course,' returned Afy, with a lofty and indifferent air, as if to be the 'light of his existence' was only her due. 'But it's all done, and over. It is not at all a settlement that will suit me, you see, Jiffin. A butter and a bacon factor is very—so very—what I have not been accustomed to! And then, those aprons! I never could get reconciled to them.'

'I'll discard the aprons altogether,' cried he, in a fever. 'I'll get a second shopman, and buy a little gig, and do nothing but drive you out. I'll do anything if you will but have me still, Miss Afy. I have bought the ring, you know.'

'Your intentions are very kind,' was the distant answer. 'But it's a thing impossible: my mind is fully made up. So farewell for good, Jiffin: and I wish you better luck in your next venture.'

Afy, lifting her capacious dress, for the streets had just been watered, minced off. And Mr. Joe Jiffin, wiping his wet face as he gazed after her, insanely wished that he could be nailed up in one of his pickled pork barrels, and so be put out of his misery.

'That's done with, thank goodness!' soliloquized Afy. 'Have *him*, indeed! after what Richard Hare let out on the trial. As if I should now look after anybody less than Dick! I shall get him, too. Telling to the judge's face that he only wanted to make me his honourable wife. I always knew Dick Hare loved me above everything else on earth: and he does still, or he'd never have said what he did, in open court. It's better to be born lucky than rich. Won't West Lynne envy me! "Mrs. Richard Hare, of the Grove!" Old Hare is on his last legs, and then Dick comes into his own. Mrs. Hare must have her join-ture house elsewhere, for we shall want the Grove for ourselves. I wonder if Madame Barbara will condescend to recognize me? And that blessed Corny? I shall be a sort of cousin of Corny's then. I wonder how much Dick comes into?—three or four thousand a year. And to think that I had nearly escaped this by tying myself to that ape of a Jiffin! What sharks do get in our un-suspecting paths, in this world!'

On went Afy, through West Lynne till she arrived close to Mr. Justice Hare's. Then she paced slowly. It had been a frequent walk of hers since the trial. Luck favoured her to-day. As she was passing the gate, Richard Hare came up from the direction of East Lynne. It was the first time Afy had ob-tained speech of him.

'Good day, Mr. Richard. Why! you never were going to pass an old friend?'

'I have so many friends,' said Richard. 'I can scarcely spare time for them, individually.'

'But you might for me. Have you forgotten old days?' continued she, brid-ling and flirting, and altogether showing herself off to advantage.

'No, I have not,' replied Richard. 'And I am not likely to do so,' he point-edly added.

'Ah, I felt sure of that. My heart told me so. When you went off, that dreadful night, leaving me to anguish and suspense, I thought I should have died. I have never had, so to say, a happy moment until this, when I met you again.'

'Don't be a fool, Afy!' was Richard's gallant rejoinder, borrowing the favourite reproach of Miss Carlyle. 'I was young and green once: you don't suppose I have remained so. We will drop the past, if you please. How is Mr. Jiffin?'

'Oh, the wretch!' shrieked Afy. 'Is it possible you can have fallen into the popular scandal that I have anything to say to *him*? You know I'd never de-mean myself to it. That's West Lynne all over! nothing but inventions in it from week's end to week's end. A man who sells cheese! who cuts up bacon! Well, I am surprised at you, Mr. Richard!'

'I have been thinking what luck you were in, to get him,' said Richard, with composure. 'But it is your business; not mine.'

'Could *you* bear to see me stooping to him?' returned Afy, dropping her voice to the most insinuating whisper.

'Look you, Afy. What ridiculous folly you are nursing in your head, I don't trouble myself to guess: but, the sooner you get it out again, the better. I was an idiot once, I don't deny it: but you cured me of that; and cured me with a vengeance. You must pardon me for intimating that from henceforth we are strangers; in the street, as elsewhere. I have resumed my own standing again: which I perilled when I ran after you.'

Afy turned faint. 'How can you speak these cruel words?' gasped she.

'You have called them forth. I was told yesterday that Afy Hallijohn, dressed up to a caricature, was looking after me again. *It won't do, Afy.*'

'Oh-o-o-o-oh!' sobbed Afy, growing hysterical, 'and is this to be all my recompense for the years I have spent, pining after you? keeping single for your sake!'

'Recompense! Oh, if you want that, I'll get my mother to give Jiffin her custom.' And with a ringing laugh, which, though it had nothing of malice in it, showed Afy that he took her reproach for what it was worth, Richard turned in at his own gate.

It was a deadly blow to Afy's vanity. The worst it had ever recieved: and she took a few minutes to compose herself, and smooth her ruffled feathers. Then she turned and sailed back towards Mr. Jiffin's, her turban up in the skies and the plume de coq tossing, to the admiration of all beholders, especially of Miss Carlyle, who had the gratification of surveying her from her window. Arrived at Mr. Jiffin's, she was taken ill exactly opposite the door, and staggered into the shop in a most exhausted state.

Round the counter flew Mr. Jiffin, leaving the shopman, staring, behind it. What *was* the matter? What *could* he do for her?

'Faint—heat of the sun—walked too fast—allowed to sit down for five minutes!' gasped Afy, in disjointed sentences.

Mr. Jiffin tenderly conducted her through the shop—to his parlour. Afy cast half an eye round, saw how comfortable were its arrangements, and her symptoms of faintness increased. Gasps and hysterical sobs came forth together. Mr. Jiffin was as one upon spikes.

'She'd recover better there than in the public shop—if she'd only excuse his bringing her in, and consent to stop in it a few minutes. No harm could come to her, and West Lynne could never say it. He'd stand at the far end of the room, right away from her: he'd prop open the two doors and the window: he'd call in the maid—anything she thought right. Should he get her a glass of wine?'

Afy declined the wine by a gesture, and sat fanning herself, Mr. Jiffin looking on from a respectful distance. Gradually she grew composed; grew herself again. As she gained courage, Mr. Jiffin lost it, and he ventured upon some faint words of reproach, of remonstrance, touching her recent treatment of him.

Afy burst into a laugh. 'Did I not do it well?' she exclaimed. 'I thought I'd play off a joke upon you, so I came out this afternoon and did it.'

Mr. Jiffin clasped his hands. '*Was* it a joke?' he returned, trembling with agitation, uncertain whether he was in paradise or not. 'Are you still ready to let me call you mine?'

'Of course it was a joke,' said Afy. 'What a soft you must have been, Mr. Jiffin, not to see through it! When young ladies engage themselves to be married, you can't suppose they run back from it, close upon the wedding-day!'

'Oh, Miss Afy!' and the poor little man actually burst into delicious tears, as he caught hold of Afy's hand and kissed it.

'A great, green donkey!' thought Afy to herself, bending on him, however, the sweetest smile.

Mr. Jiffin is not the only green donkey in the world.

Richard Hare, meanwhile, had entered his mother's presence. She was sitting at the open window, the justice opposite to her, in an invalid chair, basking in the air and the sun. This last attack of the justice's had affected the mind more than the body. He was brought down to the sitting-room that day for the first time; but, of his mind, there was little hope. It was in a state of half imbecility: the most wonderful characteristic being, that all its self-will, its surliness had gone. Almost as a little child in tractability, was Justice Hare.

Richard came up to his mother, and kissed her. He had been to East Lynne. Mrs. Hare took his hand and fondly held it. The change in her was wonderful: she was a young and happy woman again.

'Barbara has decided to go to the sea-side, mother. Mr. Carlyle takes her on Monday.'

'I am glad, my dear. It will be sure to do her good. Richard'—bending over to her husband, but still retaining her son's hand—'Barbara has agreed to go the sea-side. It will set her up.'

'Ay, ay,' nodded the justice. 'set her up. Seaside? Can't we go?'

'Certainly, dear, if you wish it, when you shall be a little stronger.'

'Ay, ay,' nodded the justice again. It was his usual answer now. 'Stronger. Where's Barbara?'

'She goes on Monday, sir,' said Richard, likewise bending his head. 'Only for a fortnight. But they talk of going again later in the autumn.'

'Can't I go too?' repeated the justice, looking pleadingly in Richard's face.

'You shall, dear father. Who knows but a month or two's bracing will bring you quite round again? We might go all together, ourselves and the Carlyles. Anne comes to stay with us next week, you know, and we might go when her visit is over.'

'Ah, all go together. Anne coming?'

'Have you forgotten, dear Richard? She comes to stay a month with us, and Mr. Clitheroe and the children. I am so pleased she will find you better,' added Mrs. Hare, her gentle eyes filling. 'Mr. Wainwright says you may go out for a drive to-morrow.'

'And I'll be coachman,' laughed Richard. 'It will be the old times come round again. Do you remember, father, my breaking the pole, one moonlight night, and your not letting me drive for six months afterwards?'

The poor justice laughed in answer to Richard, laughed till the tears ran down his face, probably not knowing in the least what he was laughing at.

'Richard,' said Mrs. Hare to her son, almost in an apprehensive tone, her hand pressing his, nervously, 'was that not Afy Hallijohn I saw you speaking with at the gate?'

'Did you see her? What a spectacle she had made of herself! I wonder she is not ashamed to go through the streets in such a guise! Indeed, I wonder she shows herself at all.'

'Richard, you—you—will not be drawn in again?' were the next whispered words.

'Mother!' There was a sternness in his mild blue eyes as he cast them upon his mother. Those beautiful eyes! the very counterpart of Barbara's; both his and hers the counterpart of Mrs. Hare's. The look had been sufficient refutation without words.

'Mother mine, I am going to belong to you in future, and to nobody else. West Lynne is already busy for me, I understand, pleasantly carving out my destiny. One, marvels whether I shall lose myself again with Miss Afy; another, that I shall set on, off-hand, and court Louisa Dobede. They are all wrong: my place will be with my darling mother—at least, for several years to come.'

She clasped his hand to her bosom in her glad delight.

'We want happiness together, mother, to enable us to overget the past: for upon none did the blow fall as upon you and upon me. And happiness we shall find, in this our own home, living for each other, and striving to amuse my poor father.'

'Ay, ay,' complacently put in Justice Hare.

So it would be. Richard had returned to his home, had become, to all intents and purposes, its master: for the justice would never be in a state to hold sway again. He had reassumed his position: had regained the favour of West Lynne, which, always in extremes, was now wanting to kill him with kindness. A happy, happy home, from henceforth: and Mrs. Hare lifted up her full heart in thankfulness to God. Perhaps Richard's went up also.

One word touching that wretched prisoner in the condemned cell at Lynneborough. As you may have anticipated, the extreme sentence was not carried out. And—little favourite as Sir Francis is with you and me—we can but admit that justice did not demand that it should be. That he had wilfully killed Hallijohn, was certain; but the act was committed in a moment of wild rage: it had not been premeditated. The sentence was commuted to penal servitude for life. A far more disgraceful one in the estimation of Sir Francis: a far more unwelcome one in the eyes of his wife. It is of no use to mince the

truth. One little grain of comfort had penetrated to Lady Levison: the anticipation of the time when she and her ill-fated child should be alone, and
could hide themselves in some hidden nook of the wide world: *he,* and his
crime, and his end gone; forgotten. But it seems he was not to go, and be
forgotten: she and the boy must be tied to him still: and she was lost in horror and rebellion.

That man envied the dead Hallijohn, as he looked forth on the future. A
cheering prospect, truly! The gay Sir Francis Levison working in chains with
his gang! Where would his diamonds and his perfumed handkerchiefs and
his white hands be then? After a time he might get a ticket of leave. He
groaned in agony as the turnkey suggested it to him! A ticket of leave for
him! Oh, why did they not hang him? he wailed forth as he closed his eyes to
the dim light: to the light of the cell, you understand: he could not close
them to the light of the future. No; never again: it shone out all too plainly,
dazzling his brain as with a flame of living fire.

❧ XXIII ☙

Until Eternity

Barbara was at the sea-side; and Lady Isabel was in her bed, dying. You remember the old French saying, 'L'homme propose, et Dieu dispose.' An ex-
emplification of it was here.

She, Lady Isabel, had consented to remain at East Lynne during Mrs. Carlyle's absence, on purpose that she might be with her children. But the object
was frustrated; for Lucy and Archibald had been removed to Miss Carlyle's.
It was Mr. Carlyle's arrangement. He thought the governess ought to have
entire respite from all charge: and that poor governess dared not say, Let
them stay with me. Lady Isabel had also purposed to be safely away from
East Lynne before the time came for her to die: but that time had advanced
with giant strides, and the period for removal was past. She was going out as
her mother had done, rapidly, unexpectedly, 'like the snuff of a candle.' Wilson was in attendance on her mistress: Joyce remained at home.

Barbara had chosen a watering-place near, not thirty miles off, so that Mr.
Carlyle went there most evenings, returning to his office in the mornings.
Thus he saw little of East Lynne, paying it one or two flying visits only. From
the Saturday to the Wednesday in the second week he did not come home at
all; and it was in those few days that Lady Isabel had changed for the worse.
On the Wednesday he was expected home, to dinner and to sleep.

Joyce was in a state of frenzy—or next door to it. Lady Isabel was dying, and what would become of the ominous secret? A conviction, born of her fears, was on the girl's mind that, with death, the whole must become known: and, who was to foresee what blame might not be cast upon her, by her master and mistress, for not having disclosed it? She might be accused of having been an abettor in the plot from the first! Fifty times it was in Joyce's mind to send for Miss Carlyle, and tell her all.

The afternoon was fast waning, and the spirit of Lady Isabel seemed to be waning with it. Joyce was in the room, in attendance upon her. She had been in a fainting state all day, but felt better now. She was partially raised in bed by pillows, a white cashmere shawl over her shoulders, her night-cap off, to allow as much air as possible to come to her: and the windows stood open.

Footsteps sounded on the gravel, in the quiet stillness of the summer air. They penetrated even to her ear, for all her faculties were keen yet. Beloved footsteps: and a tinge of hectic rose to her cheeks. Joyce, who stood at the window, glanced out. It was Mr. Carlyle.

'Joyce!' came forth a cry from the bed, sharp and eager.

Joyce turned round. 'My lady?'

'I should die happier if I might see him.'

'See him!' uttered Joyce, doubting her own ears.

'My lady! See *him?* Mr. Carlyle?'

'What can it signify? I am already as one dead. Should I ask it, or wish it, think you, in rude life? The yearning has been upon me for days, Joyce: it is keeping death away.'

'It could not be, my lady,' was the decisive answer. 'It must not be. It is as a thing impossible.'

Lady Isabel burst into tears. 'I can't die for the trouble,' she wailed. 'You keep my children from me. They must not come, you say, lest I should betray myself. Now, you would keep my husband. Joyce, Joyce, let me see him!'

Her husband! Poor thing! Joyce was in a maze of distress, though not the less firm. Her eyes were wet with tears: but she believed she should be infringing her allegiance to her mistress, did she bring Mr. Carlyle to the presence of his former wife: altogether it might be productive of nothing but confusion.

A knock at the chamber door. Joyce called out, 'Come in.' The two maids, Hannah and Sarah, were alone in the habit of coming to the room, and neither of them had ever known Madame Vine as Lady Isabel. Sarah put in her head.

'Master wants you, Mrs. Joyce.'

'I'll come.'

'He is in the dining-room. I have just taken down Master Arthur to him.'

Mr. Carlyle had got 'Master Arthur' on his shoulder when Joyce entered.

Master Arthur was decidedly given to noise and rebellion, and was already, as Wilson expressed it, 'sturdy upon his pins.'

'How is Madame Vine, Joyce?'

Joyce scarcely knew how to answer. But she did not dare equivocate as to her precarious state. And, where the use, when a few hours would probably see the end of it?

'She is very ill indeed, sir.'

'Worse?'

'Sir, I fear she is dying.'

Mr. Carlyle, in his consternation, put down Arthur. 'Dying!'

'I hardly think she will last till morning, sir.'

'Why, what has killed her?' he uttered, in amazement.

Joyce did not answer. She looked pale and confused.

'Have you had Dr. Martin?'

'Oh no, sir. It would be of no use.'

'No use!' repeated Mr. Carlyle, in a sharp accent. 'Is that the way to treat dying people? Assume it is of no use to send for advice, and so, quietly let them die! If Madame Vine is as ill as you say, a telegraphic message must be sent off at once. I had better see her,' he said, moving to the door.

Joyce, in her perplexity, dared to place her back against it, preventing his egress. 'Oh, master!—I beg your pardon, but—but—it would not be right. Please, sir, do not think of going into her room!'

Mr. Carlyle thought Joyce was taken with a fit of prudery. 'Why can't I go in?' he asked.

'Mrs. Carlyle would not like it, sir,' stammered Joyce, her cheeks scarlet now.

Mr. Carlyle stared at her. 'Some of you take up odd ideas,' he cried. 'In Mrs. Carlyle's absence, it is necessary that some one should see her. Let a lady die in my house, and never see after her? You are out of your senses, Joyce. I shall go in after dinner; so prepare Madame Vine.'

The dinner was being brought in then. Joyce, feeling like one in a nervous attack, picked up Arthur and carried him to Sarah, in the nursery. What on earth was she to do?

Scarcely had Mr. Carlyle begun his dinner, when his sister entered. Some grievance had arisen between her and the tenants of certain houses of hers, and she was bringing the dispute to him. Before he would hear it, he begged her to go up to Madame Vine, telling her what Joyce had said of her state.

'Dying!' ejaculated Miss Corny, in disbelieving derision. 'That Joyce has been more like a simpleton, lately, than like herself. I can't think what has come to the woman.'

She took off her bonnet and mantle, and laid them on a chair, gave a twitch or two to her cap, as she surveyed it in the pier-glass, and went upstairs. Joyce answered her knock at the invalid's door: and Joyce, when she saw who it was, turned as white as any sheet.

'Oh ma'am! you must not come in!' she blundered out, in her confusion and fear, as she put herself right in the doorway.

'Who is to keep me out?' demanded Miss Carlyle, after a pause of surprise, her tone one of quiet power. 'Move away, girl. Joyce, I think your brain must be softening. What will you try at, next?'

Joyce was powerless, both in right and strength, and she knew it. She knew there was no help, that Miss Carlyle would, and must, enter. She stood aside, shivering, and passed out of the room as soon as Miss Carlyle was within it.

Ah! there could no longer be concealment now! There she was, her pale face lying against the pillow, free from its disguising trappings. The band of grey velvet, the spectacles, the wraps for the throat and chin, the huge cap, all were gone. It was the face of Lady Isabel: changed, certainly, very, very much; but still hers. The silvered hair fell on either side of her face, as the silky curls had once fallen; the sweet, sad eyes were the eyes of yore.

'Mercy be good to us!' uttered Miss Carlyle.

They remained gazing at each other, both panting with emotion: yes, even Miss Carlyle. Though a wild suspicion had once crossed her brain that Madame Vine might be Lady Isabel, it had died away again, from the sheer improbability of the thing, as much as from the convincing proofs offered by Lord Mount Severn. Not but what Miss Carlyle had borne in mind the suspicion, and had been fond of tracing the likeness in Madame Vine's face.

'How could you dare come back here?' she asked, her tone one of sad, soft wailing; not of reproach.

Lady Isabel humbly crossed her attenuated hands upon her chest. 'My children,' she whispered: 'how could I stay away from them? have pity, Miss Carlyle! Don't reproach me! I am on my way to God, to answer for all my sins and sorrows.'

'I do not reproach you,' said Miss Carlyle.

'I am so glad to go,' she continued to murmur, her eyes full of tears. 'Jesus did not come, you know, to save the good, like you: He came for the sake of us poor sinners. I tried to take up my cross, as He bade us, and bear it bravely for His sake; but its weight has killed me.'

The good, like you! Humbly, meekly, deferentially was it expressed, in all good faith and trust, as though Miss Corny were a sort of upper angel. Somehow the words grated on Miss Corny's ear; grated fiercely on her conscience. It came into her mind, then, as she stood there, that the harsh religion she had through life, professed, was not the religion that would best bring peace to her dying bed.

'Child,' said she, drawing near to and leaning over Lady Isabel, 'had *I* anything to do with sending you from East Lynne?'

Lady Isabel shook her head and cast down her gaze, as she whispered:

'You did not send me: you did not help to send me. I was not very happy with you, but that was not the cause of—of my going away. Forgive me, Miss Carlyle, forgive me!'

'Thank God!' inwardly breathed Miss Corny. 'Forgive *me*,' she said, aloud and in agitation, touching her hand. 'I could have made your home happier, and I wish I had done it. I have wished it ever since you left it.'

Lady Isabel drew the hands in hers. 'I want to see Archibald,' she whispered, going back, in thought, to the old time and the old name. 'I have prayed Joyce to bring him to me, and she will not. Only for a minute! just to hear him say he forgives me! What can it matter, now that I am as one lost to this world? I should die easier.'

Upon what impulse, or grounds, Miss Carlyle saw fit to accede to the request, cannot be told. Possibly she did not choose to refuse a death-bed prayer, possibly she reasoned, as did Lady Isabel—what could it matter? She went to the door. Joyce was in the corridor, leaning against the wall, her apron up to her eyes. Miss Carlyle beckoned to her.

'How long have you known of this?'

'Since that night in the spring, when there was an alarm of fire. I saw her then, with nothing on her face, and knew her; though, at the first moment, I thought it was her ghost. Ma'am, I have just gone about since, like a ghost myself, from the fear.'

'Go and request your master to come up to me.'

'Oh, ma'am! Will it be well to tell him?' remonstrated Joyce. 'Well that he should see her?'

'Go and request your master to come to me,' unequivocally repeated Miss Carlyle. 'Are you mistress, Joyce, or am I?'

Joyce went down, and brought Mr. Carlyle up from the dinner-table.

'Is Madame Vine worse, Cornelia? Will she see me?'

'She wishes to see you.'

Miss Carlyle opened the door as she spoke. He motioned to her to pass in first. 'No,' she said, 'you had better see her alone.'

He was going in, when Joyce caught his arm. 'Master! master! you ought to be prepared. Ma'am, won't you tell him?'

He looked at them, thinking they must be moon-struck, for their conduct seemed inexplicable. Both were in evident agitation; an emotion Miss Carlyle was not given to. Her face and lips were twitching, but she kept a studied silence. Mr. Carlyle knitted his brow, and went into the chamber. They shut him in.

He walked gently at once to the bed, in his straightforward manner. 'I am grieved, Madame Vine—'

The words faltered on his tongue. Did he think, as Joyce had once done, that it was a ghost he saw? Certain it is, that his face and lips turned the hue of death, and he backed a few steps from the bed: though he was as little given to show emotion as man can well be. The falling hair, the sweet, mournful eyes, the hectic which his presence brought to her cheeks, told too plainly of the Lady Isabel.

'Archibald!'

She put out her trembling hand. She caught him ere he had drawn quite beyond her reach. He looked at her, he looked round the room, as does one awaking from a dream.

'I could not die without your forgiveness,' she murmured, her eyes falling before him as she thought of her past sin. 'Do not turn from me! bear with me a little minute! Only say you forgive me, and I shall die in peace.'

'Isabel? Are you—are you—were you Madame Vine?' he cried, scarcely conscious of what he said.

'Oh, forgive, forgive me! I did not die. I got well from that accident, but it changed me dreadfully: nobody knew me, and I came here as Madame Vine. I could not stay away. Archibald, forgive me!'

His mind was in a whirl, his wits were scared away. The first clear thought that came thumping through his brain was, that he must be a man of two wives. She noticed his perplexed silence.

'I could not stay away from you and from my children. The longing for you was killing me,' she reiterated wildly, like one talking in a fever. 'I never knew a moment's peace after the mad act I was guilty of, in quitting you. Not an hour had I departed, when my repentance set in; and, even then, I would have retracted and come back, but I did not know how. See what it has done for me!' tossing up her grey hair, holding out her attenuated wrists. 'Oh, forgive, forgive me! My sin was great, but my punishment was greater. It has been as one long scene of mortal agony.'

'Why did you go?' asked Mr. Carlyle.

'Did you not know?'

'No. It has always been a mystery to me.'

'I went, out of love for you.'

A shade of disdain crossed his lips. Was she equivocating to him on her death-bed?

'Do not look in that way,' she panted. 'My strength is nearly gone; you must perceive that it is; and I do not, perhaps, express myself clearly. I loved you dearly, and I grew suspicious of you. I thought you were false and deceitful to me; that your love was all given to another; and, in my sore jealousy, I listened to the temptings of that bad man, who whispered to me of revenge. It was not so, was it?'

Mr. Carlyle had regained his calmness; outwardly, at any rate. He stood by the side of the bed, looking down upon her, his arms crossed upon his chest, and his noble form raised to its full height.

'Was it so?' she feverishly repeated.

'Can you ask it?—knowing me as you did then; as you must have known me since? I never was false to you in thought, in word, or in deed.'

'Oh, Archibald, I was mad, I was mad! I could not have done it in anything but madness. Surely you will forget and forgive!'

'I cannot forget. I have already forgiven.'

'Try and forget the dreadful time that has passed since that night!' she continued, the tears falling on her cheeks, as she held up to him one of her poor hot hands. 'Let your thoughts go back to the days when you first knew me; when I was here, Isabel Vane, a happy girl with my father. At times I have lost myself in a moment's happiness in thinking of it. Do you remember how you grew to love me, though you thought you might not tell it me?—and how gentle you were with me when papa died?—and the hundred pound note? Do you remember coming to Castle Marling, and my promising to be your wife?—and the first kiss you left upon my lips? And oh, Archibald! do you remember the loving days, after I was your wife?—how happy we were with each other?—do you remember when Lucy was born we thought I should have died; and your joy, your thankfulness that God restored me? Do you remember all this?'

Ay. He did remember it. He took that poor hand into his, retaining there its wasted fingers.

'Have you any reproach to cast to me?' he gently said, bending his head a little.

'Reproach to you! To you who must be almost without reproach in the sight of Heaven! you, who were ever loving to me, ever anxious for my welfare! When I think of what you were, and are, and how I requited you, I could sink into the earth with remorse and shame. My own sin I have surely expiated: I cannot expiate the shame I entailed upon you and upon our children.'

Never. He felt it as keenly now, as he had felt it then.

'Think what it has been for me!' she resumed; and he was obliged to bend his ear to catch her gradually weakening tones. 'To live in this house with your wife; to see your love for her; to watch the envied caresses that once were mine! I never loved you so passionately as I have done since I lost you. Think what it was to watch William's decaying strength; to be alone with you in his dying hour, and not be able to say, He is my child as well as yours! When he lay dead, and the news went forth to the household, it was *her* petty grief you soothed; not mine; mine, his mother's. God alone knows how I have lived through it all: it has been to me as the bitterness of death.'

'Why did you come back?' was the response of Mr. Carlyle.

'I have told you. I could not *live*, away from you and my children.'

'It was wrong. Wrong in all ways.'

'Wickedly wrong. You cannot think worse of it than I have done. But the consequences and the punishment would be mine alone, so long as I guarded against discovery. I never thought to stop here to die: but death seems to have come upon me with a leap, as it came to my mother.'

A pause of laboured breathing. Mr. Carlyle did not interrupt it.

'All wrong, all wrong,' she resumed: 'this interview, with you, amongst the rest. And yet—I hardly know: it cannot hurt the new ties you have formed, for I am as one dead now to this world, hovering on the brink of the next. But you *were* my husband, Archibald; and, the last few days, I have longed for your forgiveness with a fevered longing. Oh, that the past could be blotted out! that I could wake up and find it but a hideous dream; that I were here, as in the old days, in health and happiness, your ever-loving wife! Do *you* wish it?—that the dark past had never had place?'

She put the question in a sharp, eager tone, gazing up to him with an anxious gaze, as though the answer must be one of life or death.

'For your sake I wish it.' Calm enough were the words spoken; and her eyes fell again, and a deep sigh came forth.

'I am going to William. But Lucy and Archibald will be left. Oh, be ever kind to them! I pray you, visit not their mother's sin upon their heads! do not, in your love for your later children, lose your love for them!'

'Have you seen anything in my conduct that could give rise to fears of this?' he returned, reproach mingling in his sad tone. 'The children are dear to me as you once were.'

'As I once was. Ay! and as I might have been now.'

'Indeed you might,' he answered, with emotion.

'Archibald, I am on the very threshold of the next world. Will you not bless me—will you not say a word of love to me before I pass it? Let what I am be blotted for the moment from your memory: think of me, if you can, as the innocent, timid child, whom you made your wife. Only a word of love! my heart is breaking for it.'

He leaned over her, he pushed aside the hair from her brow with his gentle hand, his tears dropping on her face. 'You nearly broke mine when you left me, Isabel,' he whispered. 'May God bless you, and take you to His Rest in heaven! May He so deal with me, as I now fully and freely forgive you!'

Lower and lower bent he his head, until his breath nearly mingled with hers. But, suddenly, his face grew red with a scarlet flush, and he lifted it again. Did the form of one, then in a felon's cell at Lynneborough, thrust itself before him? or that of his absent and unconscious wife?

'To His Rest in heaven,' she murmured, in the hollow tones of the departing. 'Yes, yes: I know that God has forgiven me. Oh, what a struggle it has been! nothing but bad feelings; rebellion, and sorrow, and repining; for a long while after I came back here: but Jesus prayed for me and helped me; and you know how merciful He is to the weary and heavy-laden. We shall meet again, Archibald, and live together for ever and for ever. But for that great hope, I could hardly die. William said mamma would be on the banks of the river, looking out for him: but it is William who is looking for me.'

Mr. Carlyle released one of his hands; she had taken them both; and, with his own handkerchief, wiped the death-dew from her forehead.

'It is no sin to anticipate it, Archibald. For there will be no marrying or giving in marriage in heaven: Christ has said so. Though we do not know how it will be. My sin will be remembered no more there, and we shall be together with our children for ever and for ever. Keep a little corner in your heart for your poor lost Isabel.'

'Yes, yes,' he whispered.

'Are you leaving me?' she uttered, in a wild tone of pain.

'You are growing faint, I perceive. I must call assistance.'

'Farewell, then; farewell, until eternity,' she sighed, the tears raining from her eyes. 'It is death, I think; not faintness. Oh, but it is hard to part! Farewell, farewell, my once dear husband!'

She rose her head from the pillow, excitement giving her strength; she clung to his arm; she lifted her face, in its sad yearning. Mr. Carlyle laid her tenderly down again, and suffered his lips to rest upon hers.

'Until eternity,' he whispered.

She followed him with her eyes as he retreated, and watched him from the room; then turned her face to the wall. 'It is over. Only God now.'

Mr. Carlyle took an instant's counsel with himself, stopping at the head of the stairs to do it. Joyce, in obedience to a sign from him, had already gone into the sick chamber: his sister was standing at its door.

'Cornelia.'

She followed him down into the dining room.

'You will remain here to-night? With *her*.'

'Do you suppose I shouldn't?' crossly responded Miss Corny. 'Where are you off to now?'

'To the telegraph office, at present. To send for Lord Mount Severn.'

'What good can he do?'

'None. But I shall send for him.'

'Can't one of the servants go just as well as you? You have not finished your dinner: hardly begun it.'

He turned his eyes on the dinner-table, in a mechanical sort of way, his mind wholly pre-occupied, made some remark in answer, which Miss Corny did not catch, and went out.

On his return his sister met him in the hall, drew him inside the nearest room, and closed the door. Lady Isabel was dead. Had been dead about ten minutes.

'She never spoke after you left her, Archibald. There was a slight struggle at the last, a fighting for breath, otherwise she went off quite peacefully. I felt sure, when I first saw her this afternoon, that she could not last till midnight.'

❧ XXIV ❧

I. M. V.

Lord Mount Severn, wondering greatly what the urgent summons could mean, lost no time in obeying it, and was at East Lynne the following morning, early. Mr. Carlyle was in his carriage at the station; his close carriage; and, shut up in that, he made the communication to the earl as they drove to East Lynne.

The earl could with difficulty believe it. Never had he been so utterly astonished. At first he really could not understand the tale.

'Did she—did she—come back to your house to die?' he blundered. 'You never took her in? I don't comprehend.'

Mr. Carlyle explained farther. And the earl at length understood. But he could not recover his perplexed astonishment.

'What a mad act!—to come back here! Madame Vine! How on earth did she escape detection?'

'She did escape it,' said Mr. Carlyle. 'The strange likeness Madame Vine possessed to my first wife often struck me as being marvellous, but I never suspected the truth. It was a likeness, and not a likeness; for every part of her face and form was changed. Except her eyes: and those I never saw but through those disguising glasses.'

The earl wiped his hot face. The news had ruffled him in no measured degree. He felt angry with Isabel, dead though she was, and thankful that Mrs. Carlyle was away.

'Will you see her?' whispered Mr. Carlyle as they entered the house.

'Yes.'

They went up to the death-chamber, Mr. Carlyle procuring the key. Very peaceful she looked now, her pale features composed under her white cap and bands. Miss Carlyle and Joyce had done all that was necessary: nobody else had been suffered to approach her. Lord Mount Severn leaned over her, tracing the former looks of Isabel: and the likeness grew upon him in a wonderful degree.

'What did she die of?' he asked.

'She said, a broken heart.'

'Ah!' said the earl. 'The wonder is, that it did not break before. Poor thing! poor Isabel!' he added, touching her hand, 'how she marred her own happiness! Carlyle, I suppose this is your wedding-ring?'

Mr. Carlyle cast his eyes upon the ring. 'Very probably.'

'To think of her never having discarded it!' remarked the earl, releasing the cold hand. 'Well, I can hardly believe the tale now.'

He turned and quitted the room as he spoke. Mr. Carlyle looked steadfastly at the dead face for a minute or two, his fingers touching the forehead: but, what his thoughts or feelings may have been, none can tell. Then he replaced the sheet over the face, and followed the earl.

They descended in silence to the breakfast-room. Miss Carlyle was seated at the table waiting for them. 'Where *could* all your eyes have been?' exclaimed the earl to her, after a few sentences, referring to the event, had passed.

'Just where yours would have been,' retorted Miss Corny, with a touch of her old temper. 'You saw Madame Vine as well as we did.'

'But not continuously. Only two or three times in all. And I do not remember ever to have seen her without her bonnet and veil. That Carlyle should not have recognized her is almost beyond belief.'

'It *seems* so, to speak of it,' said Miss Corny; 'but facts are facts. She was young, gay, active, when she left here, upright as a dart, her dark hair drawn from her open brow and flowing on her neck, her cheeks like crimson paint, her face altogether beautiful. Madame Vine arrived here a pale, stooping woman, lame of one leg, *shorter* than Lady Isabel—and her figure stuffed out under those sacks of jackets. Not a bit, scarcely, of her forehead to be seen, for grey velvet, and grey bands of hair; her head smothered under a close cap, large blue double spectacles hiding the eyes and their sides, and the throat tied up; the chin partially. The mouth was entirely altered in its character, and that upward scar, always so conspicuous, made it almost ugly. Then she had lost some of her front teeth, you know, and she lisped when she spoke. Take her for all in all,' summed up Miss Carlyle, 'she looked no more like the Isabel who went away from here than I look like Adam. Just get your dearest friend damaged and disguised as she was, my lord, and see if you'd recognize him.'

The observation came home to Lord Mount Severn. A gentleman whom he knew well, had been so altered by a fearful accident, that little resemblance could be traced to his former self. In fact, his own family could not recognize him: and *he* used no artificial disguises. It was a case in point, and, reader! I assure you that it is a true one.

'It was the *disguise* that we ought to have suspected,' quietly observed Mr. Carlyle. 'The likeness was not sufficiently striking to cause suspicion.'

'But she turned the house from that scent as soon as she came into it,' struck in Miss Corny. 'Telling of the "neuralgic pains" that afflicted her head and face, rendering the guarding them from exposure necessary. Remember, Lord Mount Severn, that the Ducies had been with her in Germany, and had never suspected her. Remember also another thing: that, however great a likeness we may have detected, we could not and did not speak of it, one to another. Lady Isabel's name is never so much as whispered amongst us.'

'True; all true,' said the earl.

On the Friday, the following letter was despatched to Mrs. Carlyle:—

'MY DEAREST,

'I find I shall not be able to get to you on Saturday afternoon, as I promised, but will leave here by the late train that night. Mind you don't sit up for me. Lord Mount Severn is here for a few days: he sends his regards to you.

'And now, Barbara, prepare for news that will prove a shock. Madame Vine is dead. She grew rapidly worse, they tell me, after our departure, and died on Wednesday night. I am glad you were away.'

'Love from the children. Lucy and Archie are still at Cornelia's; Arthur wearing out Sarah's legs in the nursery.

'Ever yours, my dearest,
'ARCHIBALD CARLYLE.'

Of course, as Madame Vine, the governess, died at Mr. Carlyle's house, he could not in courtesy do less than follow her to the grave. So decided West Lynne, when they found which way the wind was going to blow. Lord Mount Severn followed also, to keep him company, being on a visit to him. And very polite indeed of his lordship to do it! Condescending also! West Lynne remembered another funeral at which those two had been the only mourners—that of the late earl. By some curious coincidence, the French governess was buried close to the earl's grave. As good there as anywhere else, quoth West Lynne: there happened to be a vacant spot of ground.

The funeral took place on the Saturday morning. A plain, respectacle funeral. A hearse and pair, and mourning coach and pair, with a chariot for the Reverend Mr. Little. No pall-bearers, or mutes, or anything of that show-off kind, and no plumes on the horses, only on the hearse. West Lynne looked on with approbation, and conjectured that the governess had left sufficient money to bury herself: but of course that was Mr. Carlyle's affair, not West Lynne's. Quiet enough lay she in her last resting-place.

They left her in it, the earl and Mr. Carlyle; and entered the mourning-coach to be conveyed back again to East Lynne.

'Just a little upright stone of white marble, two feet high by a foot and a half broad,' remarked the earl on their road, pursuing a topic they were speaking upon. 'With the initials, I. V. and the date of the year. Nothing more. What do you think?'

'I. M. V.,' corrected Mr. Carlyle. 'Yes.'

At that moment the bells of another church, not St. Jude's, broke out in a joyous peal, and the earl inclined his ear to listen.

'What can they be ringing for?' he cried.

They were ringing for a wedding. Afy Hallijohn, by the help of two clergymen and six bridesmaids (of whom you may be sure Joyce was *not* one), had just been converted into Mrs. Joe Jiffin. When Afy took a thing in her head, she somehow contrived to carry it through, and to bend even clergymen and bridesmaids to her will. Mr. Jiffin was blessed at last.

In the afternoon, the earl left East Lynne; and, somewhat later, Barbara arrived. Wilson scarcely gave her mistress time to step into the house before her, and she very nearly left the baby in the fly. Curiously anxious was Wilson to hear all particulars, as to what could have taken off that French governess. Mr. Carlyle was much surprised at their arrival.

'How could I stay away, Archibald, even until Monday, after the news you sent me?' said Barbara. 'What did she die of? It must have been awfully sudden.'

'I suppose so,' was his dreamy answer. He was debating a question with himself, one he had thought over a good deal since Wednesday night. Should he, or should he not, tell his wife? He would have preferred not to tell her: and, had the secret been confined to his own breast, he would decidedly not have done so. But it was known to three others: to Miss Carlyle, to Lord Mount Severn, and to Joyce. All trustworthy and of good intention: but it was impossible for Mr. Carlyle to make sure that not one of them would ever, through any chance unpremeditated word, let the secret come to the knowledge of Mrs. Carlyle. That would not do: if she must hear it at all, she must hear it from him, and at once. He took his course.

'Are you ill, Archibald?' she asked, noting his face. It wore a pale, worn look.

'I have something to tell you, Barbara,' he answered, drawing her hand into his as they stood together. They were in her dressing-room, where she was taking off her things. 'On Wednesday evening, when I got home to dinner, Joyce told me that she feared Madame Vine was dying: and I thought it right to see her.'

'Certainly,' returned Barbara. 'Quite right.'

'I went into her room, and I found that she was dying. But I found something else, Barbara. She was not Madame Vine.'

'Not Madame Vine!' echoed Barbara.

'It was my former wife, Isabel Vane.'

Barbara's face flushed crimson, and then grew white as marble; and she drew her hand from Mr. Carlyle's. He did not appear to notice the movement, but stood with his elbow on the mantelpiece while he talked, giving her a rapid summary of the interview; not its details.

'She could not stay away from her children,' he said, 'and came back as Madame Vine. What with the effects of the railway accident in France, and those spectacles she wore, and her style of dress, and her grey hair, she felt secure in not being recognized. I am astonished now that she was not discovered. Were such a thing related to me I should refuse credence to it.'

Barbara's heart felt faint with its utter sickness, and she turned her face from the view of her husband. Her first confused thoughts were as Mr. Carlyle's had been—that she had been living in his house with another wife. 'Did you suspect her?' she breathed in a low tone.

'Barbara! Had I suspected it, should I have allowed it to go on? She implored my forgiveness for the past, and for having returned here; and I forgave her fully. I went to West Lynne to telegraph to Mount Severn. She was dead when I came back. She said her heart was broken. Barbara, we cannot wonder at it.'

There was a pause. Mr. Carlyle began to perceive that his wife's face was hidden from him.

Still there was no reply. Mr. Carlyle took his arm from the mantelpiece, and moved so that he could see her countenance: a wan countenance then, telling of pain.

He laid his hand upon her shoulder and made her look at him. 'My dearest, what is this?'

'Oh, Archibald!' she uttered, clasping her hands together, all her pent-up feelings bursting forth, and the tears streaming from her eyes, 'has this taken your love from me?'

He took both her hands in one of his, he put the other round her waist, and held her there, before him, never speaking, only looking gravely into her face. Who could look at its sincere truthfulness, at the sweet expression of his lips, and doubt him? Not Barbara.

'I had thought my wife possessed entire trust in me.'

'Oh, I do, I do; you know I do. Forgive me, Archibald,' she softly whispered.

'I deemed it better to impart this to you. Barbara. My darling, I have told it you in love.'

She was leaning on his breast, sobbing gently, her repentant face turned towards him. He held her there in his strong protection, his enduring tenderness.

'My wife! my darling! now, and always.'

'It was a foolish feeling to cross my heart, Archibald. It is done with, and gone.'

'Never let it come back again, Barbara. Neither need her name be mentioned again between us. A barred name it has hitherto been: let it so continue.'

'Anything you will. My earnest wish is to please you; to be worthy of your esteem and love. Archibald,' she timidly added, her eyelids drooping, as she made the confession, while the colour rose in her fair face, 'there has been a feeling in my heart against your children, a sort of jealous feeling, can you understand, because they were hers; because she had once been your wife. I knew how wrong it was, and I have tried earnestly to subdue it. I have indeed, and I think it is nearly gone. I'—her voice sank lower—'constantly pray to be helped to do it; to love them and care for them as if they were my own. It will come with time.'

'Every good thing will come with time that we earnestly seek,' said Mr. Carlyle. 'Oh, Barbara, never forget—never forget that the only way to ensure peace in the end is, to strive always to be doing right, unselfishly, under God.'

THE END